LORE OLYMPUS

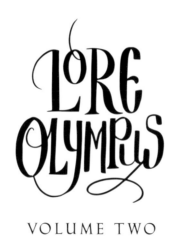

VOLUME TWO

VOLUME TWO

RACHEL SMYTHE

NEW YORK

Published in the United States by Del Rey, an imprint of Random House,
a division of Penguin Random House LLC, New York.

DEL REY and the HOUSE colophon are registered trademarks of Penguin Random House LLC.

Portions of this work originally appeared on Webtoons.com.

LIBRARY OF CONGRESS CATALOGING-IN-PUBLICATION DATA
Names: Smythe, Rachel (Comics artist), author, artist.
Title: Lore Olympus / Rachel Smythe.
Description: First edition. | New York : Del Rey, 2022
Identifiers: LCCN 2021008087 | Hardcover ISBN 9780593160305 (v. 2) |
Trade paperback ISBN 9780593356081 (v. 2)
Subjects: LCSH: Mythology, Greek—Comic books, strips, etc. | Graphic novels.
Classification: LCC PN6727.S54758 L67 2021 | DDC 741.5/973—dc23
LC record available at https://lccn.loc.gov/2021008087

Printed in China

Original WEBTOON editors: Bekah Caden, Annie LaHue
Rachel Smythe art assistants: Johana R. Ahumada, M. Rawlings, Court Rogers
WEBTOON translation: Anastasia Gkortsila
Penguin Random House team: Ted Allen, Erin Korenko, and Sarah Peed

randomhousebooks.com

2 4 6 8 9 7 5 3 1

First Edition

Book design by Edwin Vazquez

To Eunice Yooni Kim,
thank you for noticing me.

CONTENT WARNING
FROM RACHEL SMYTHE

Lore Olympus regularly deals with themes of physical and mental abuse, sexual trauma, and toxic relationships.

Some of the interactions in this volume may be distressing for some readers. Please exercise discretion, and seek out the support of others if you require it.

EPISODE 26

YOU CALLED

YOU ANSWERED

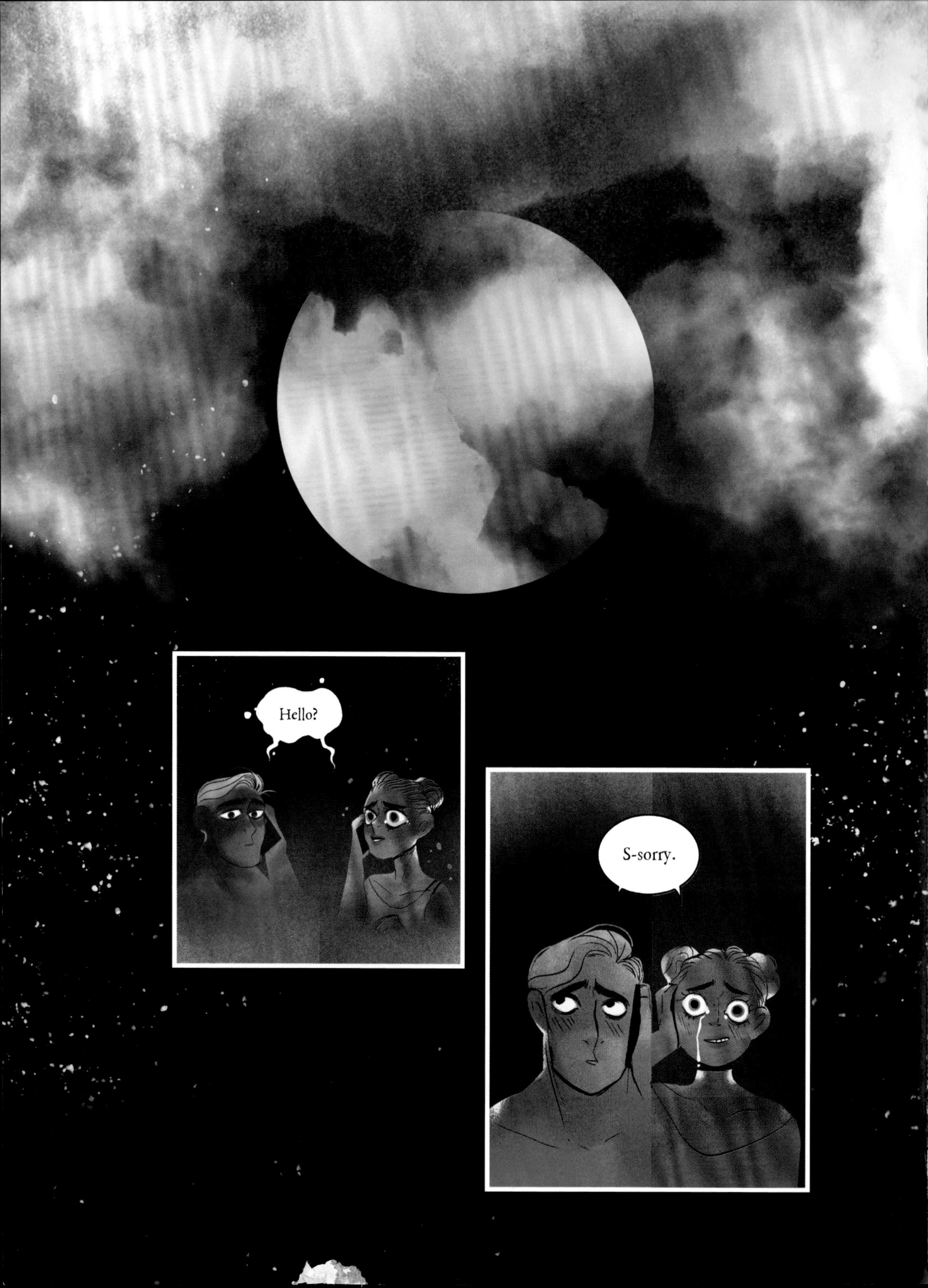
Hello?
S-sorry.

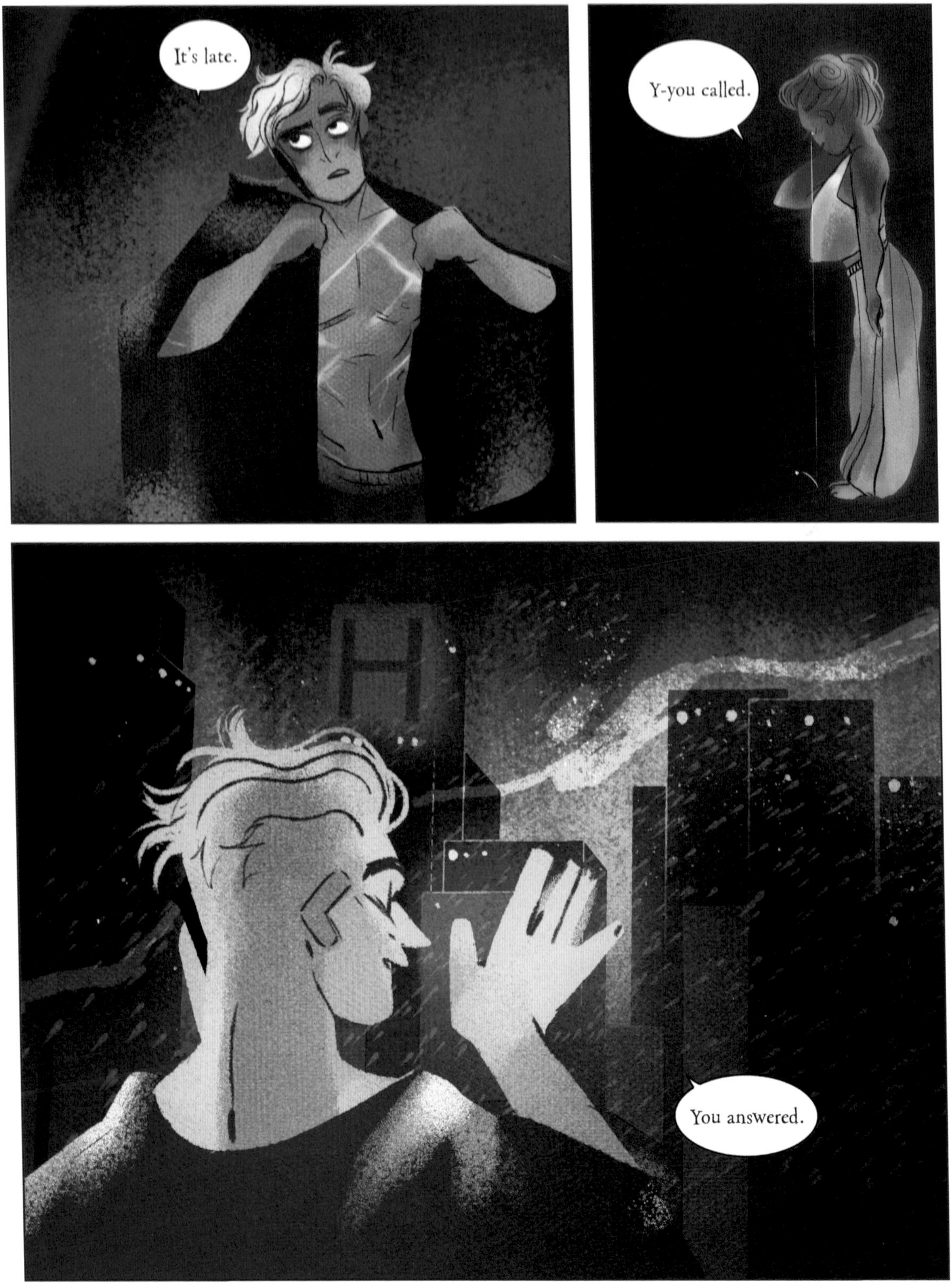
It's late.
Y-you called.
You answered.

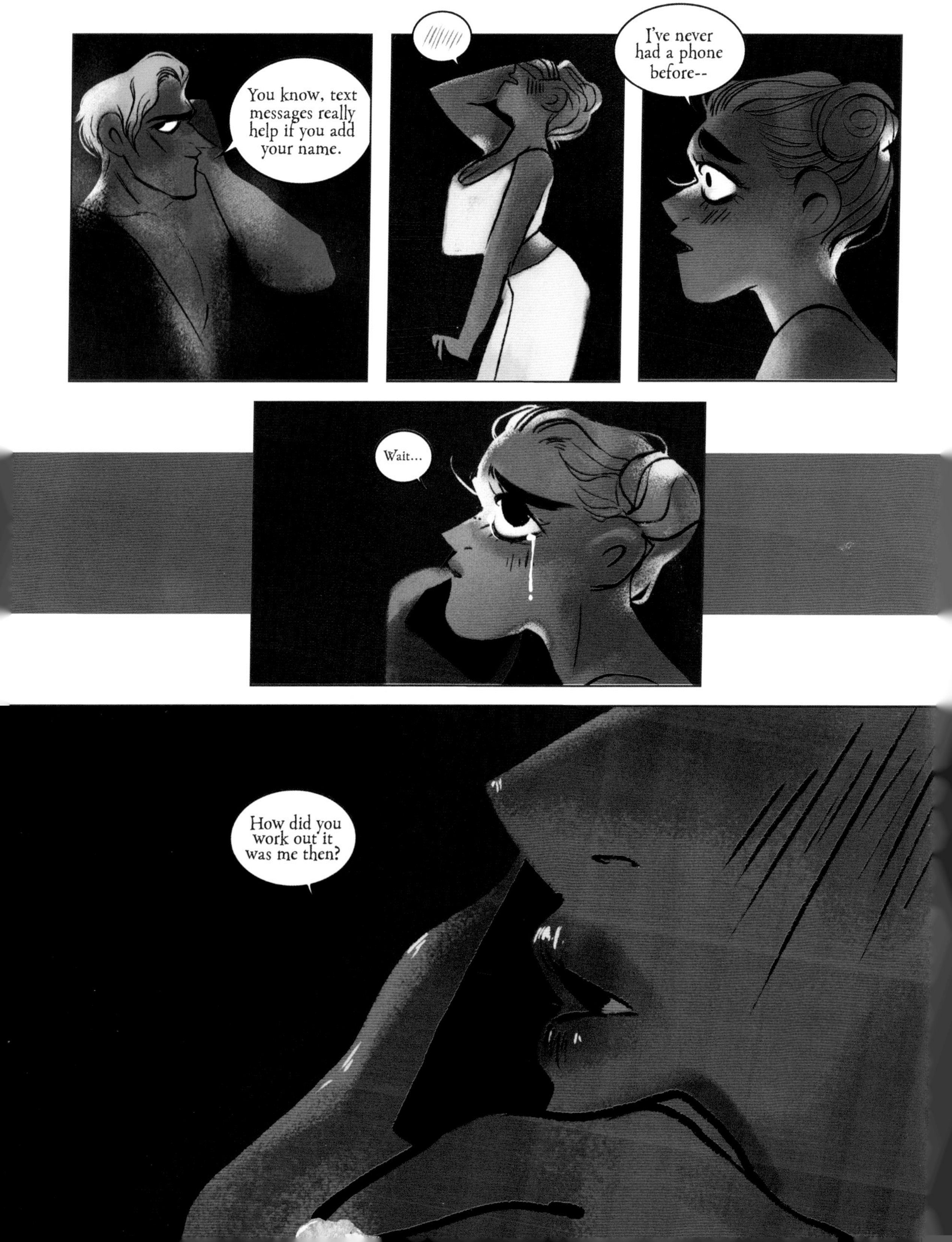
You know, text messages really help if you add your name.
//////
I've never had a phone before--
Wait...
How did you work out it was me then?

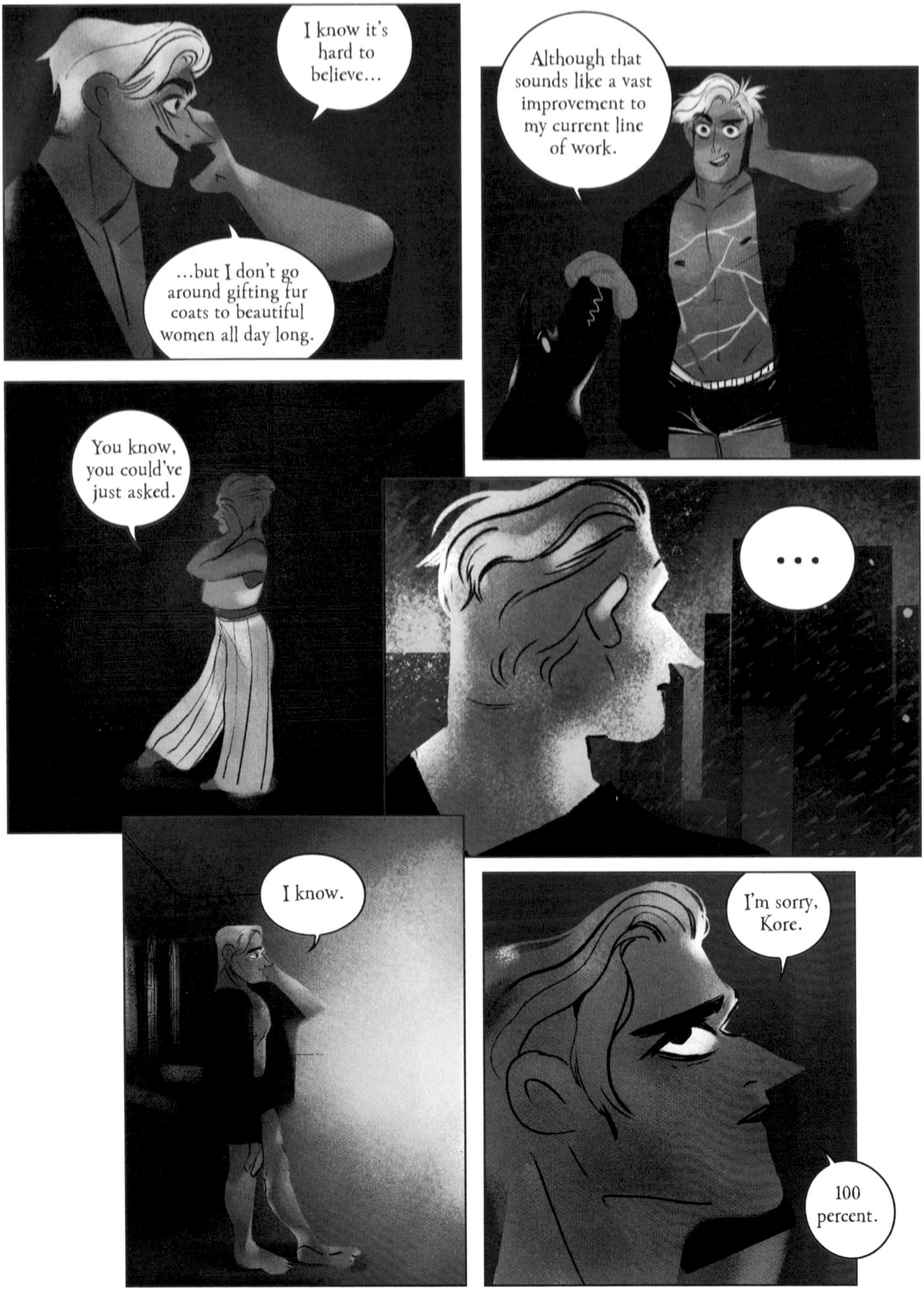
I know it's hard to believe...
...but I don't go around gifting fur coats to beautiful women all day long.
Although that sounds like a vast improvement to my current line of work.
You know, you could've just asked.
...
I know.
I'm sorry, Kore.
100 percent.

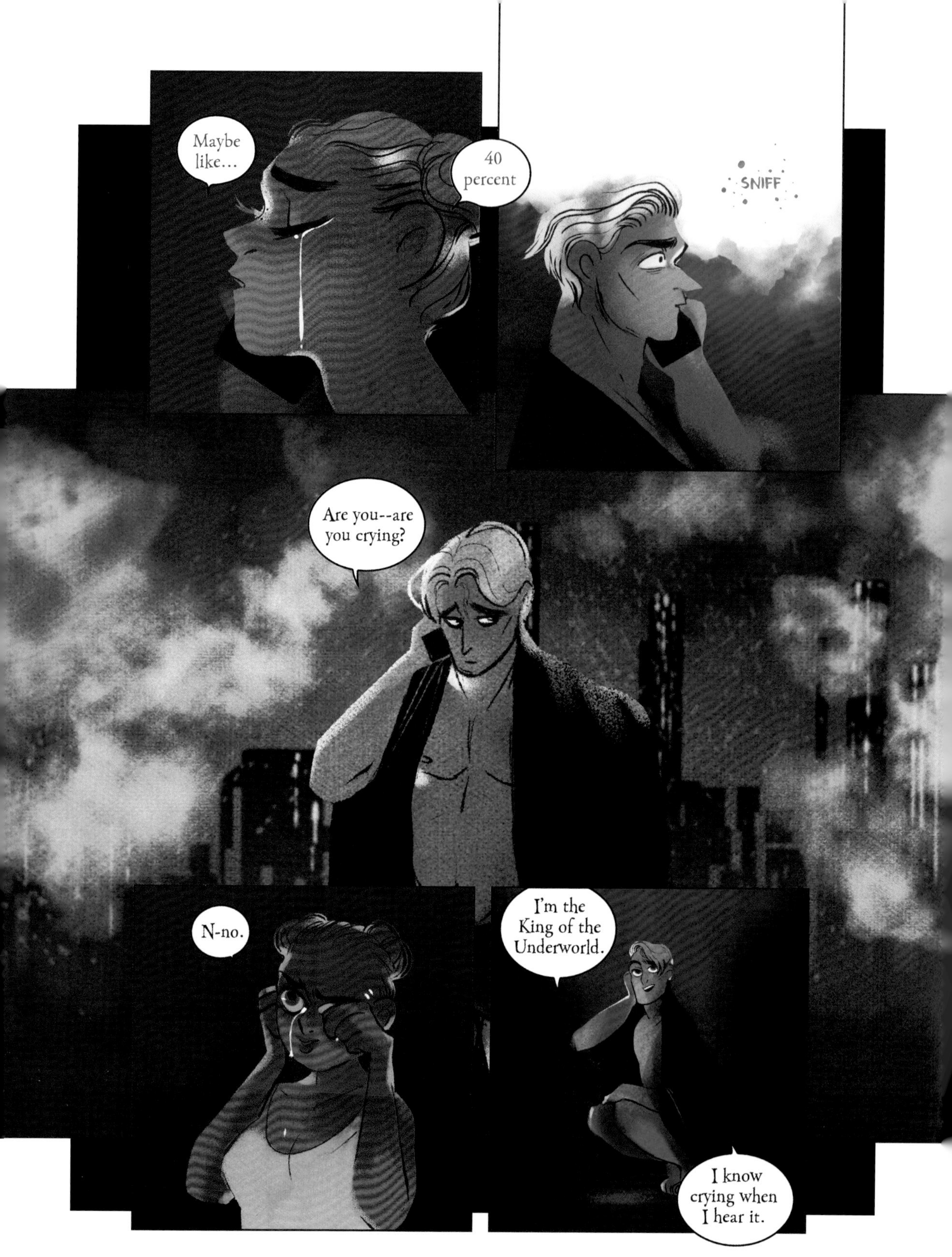
Maybe like...
40 percent
SNIFF
Are you--are you crying?
N-no.
I'm the King of the Underworld.
I know crying when I hear it.

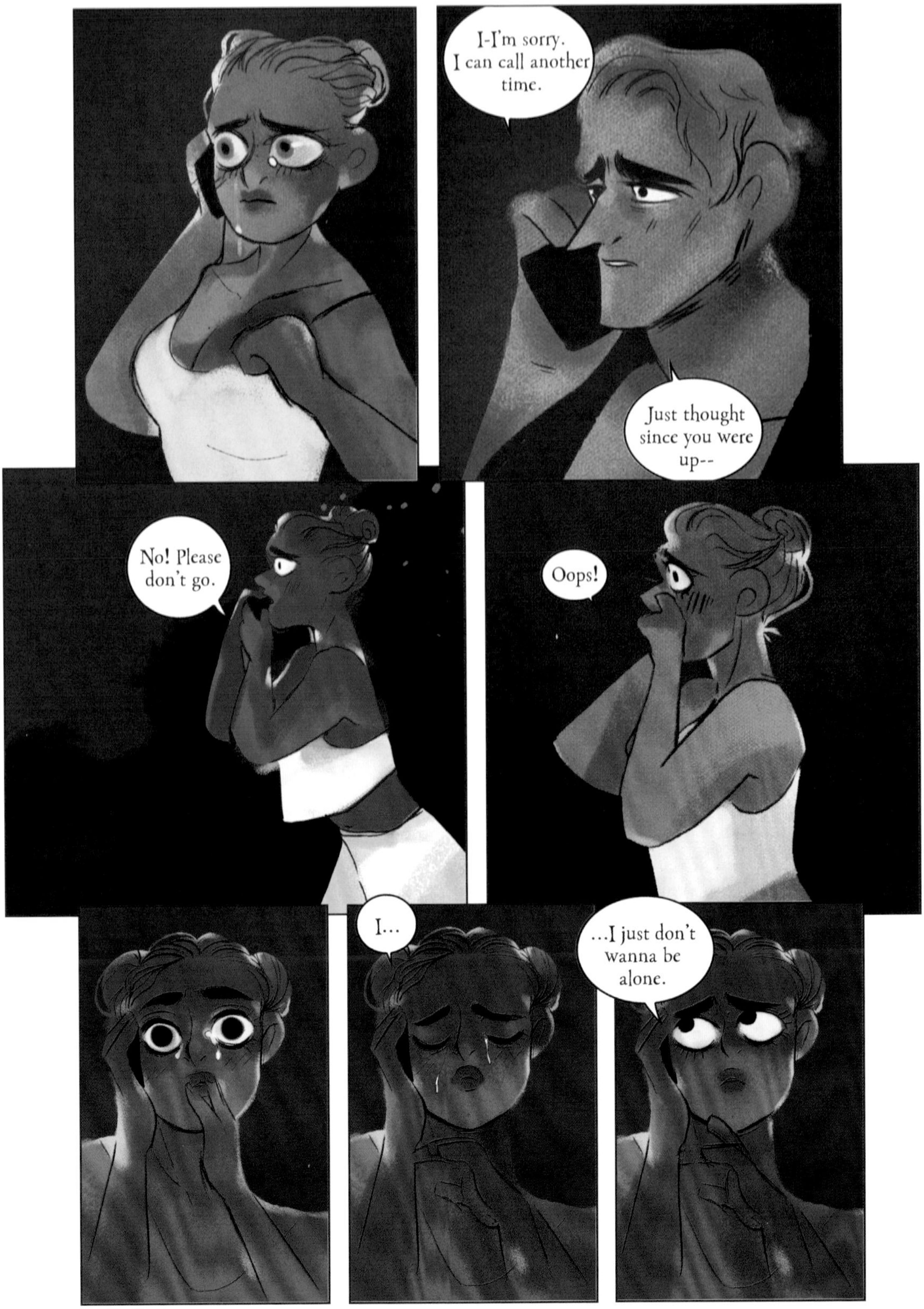
I-I'm sorry. I can call another time.
Just thought since you were up--
No! Please don't go.
Oops!
I...
...I just don't wanna be alone.

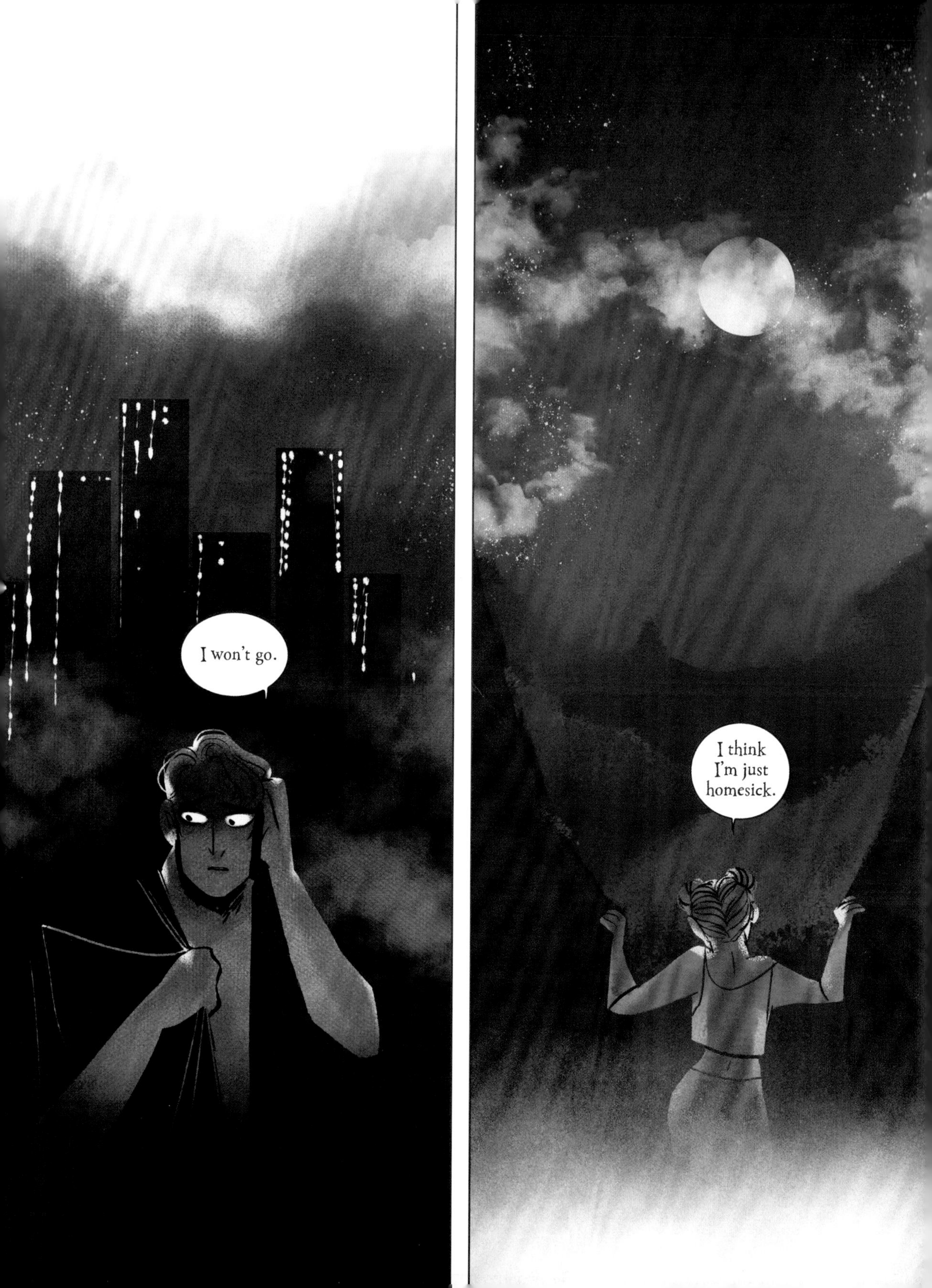
I won't go.
I think I'm just homesick.

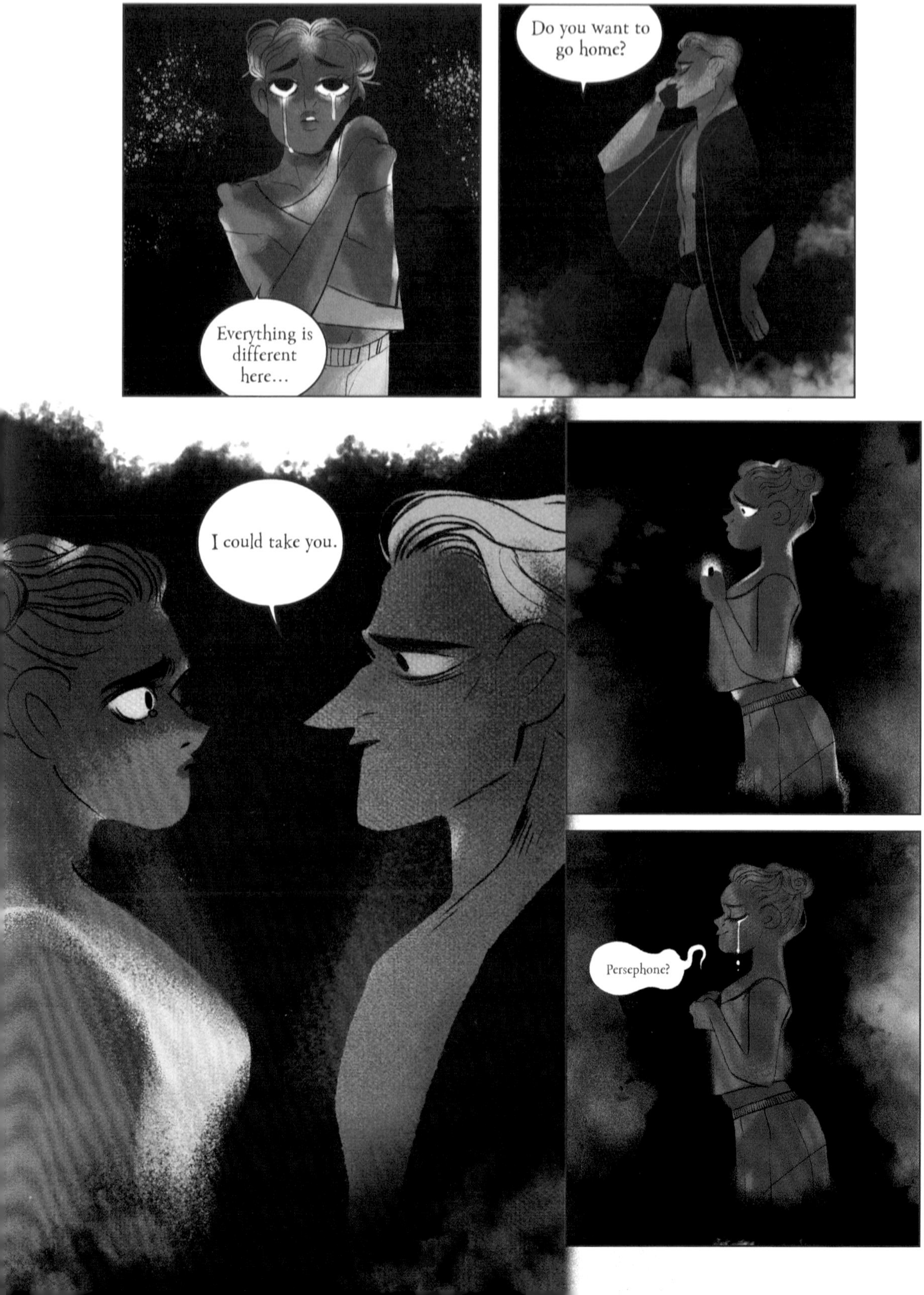
Everything is different here...
Do you want to go home?
I could take you.
Persephone?

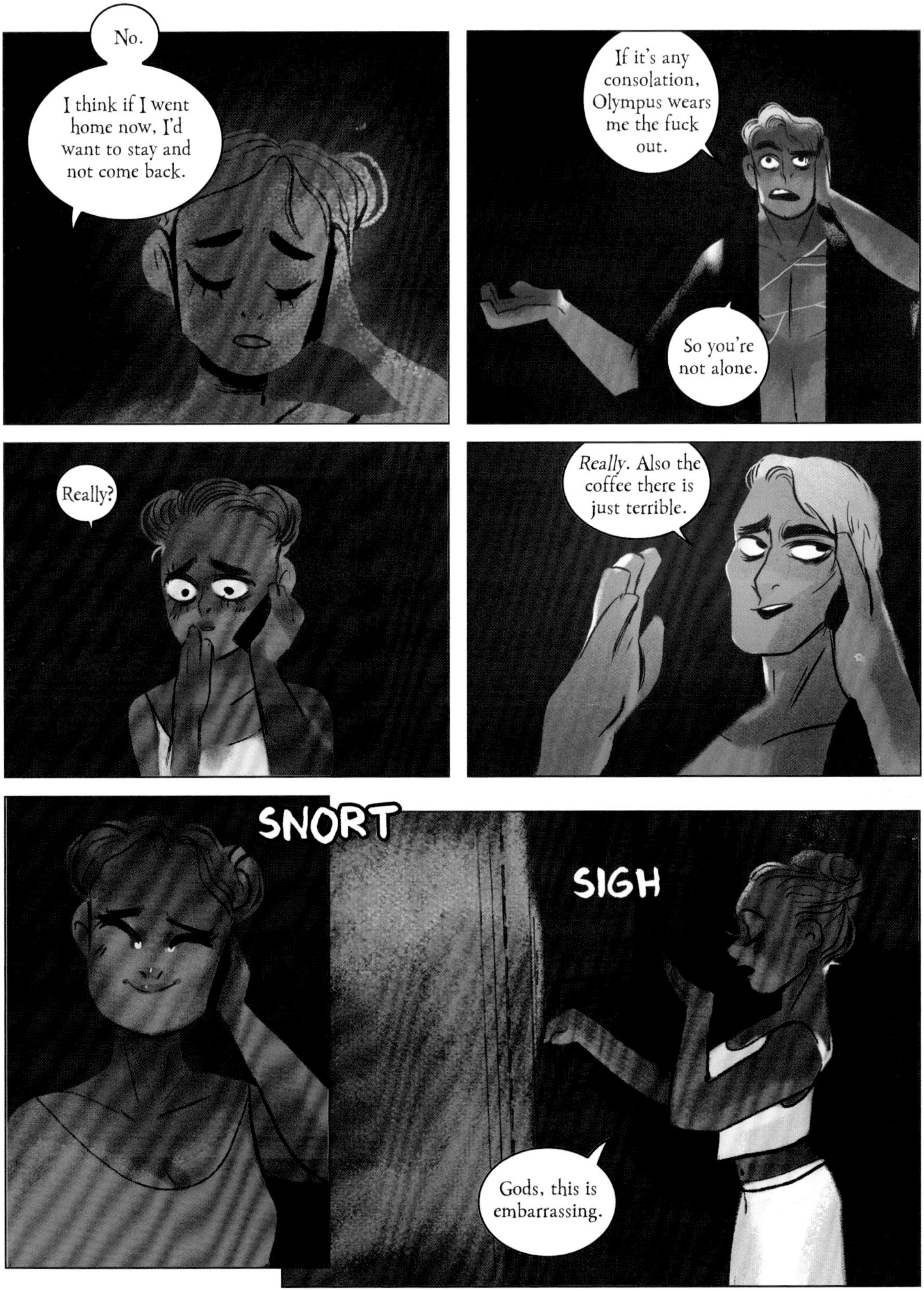
No.
I think if I went home now, I'd want to stay and not come back.
If it's any consolation, Olympus wears me the fuck out.
So you're not alone.
Really?
Really. Also the coffee there is just terrible.
SNORT
SIGH
Gods, this is embarrassing.

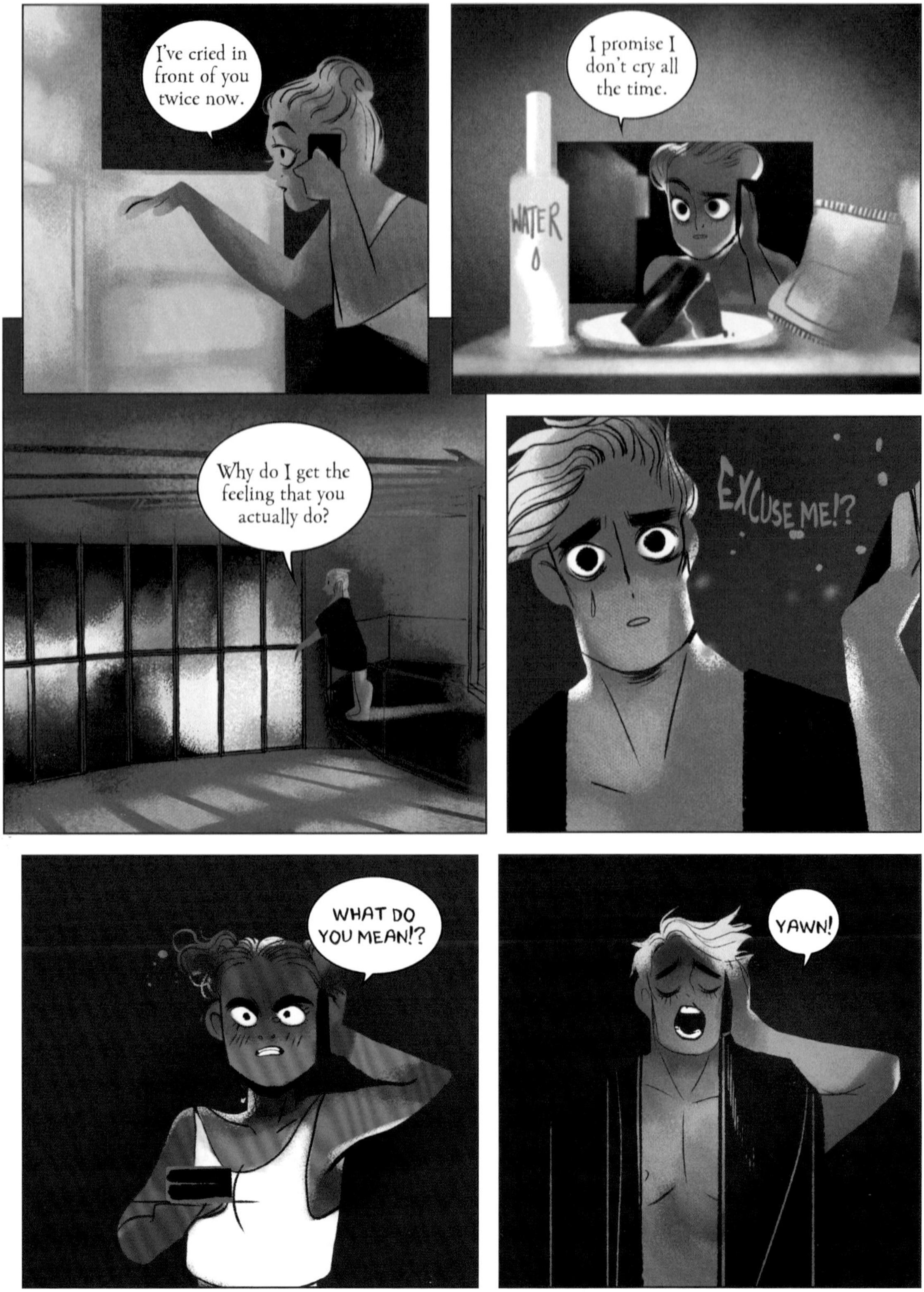

I've cried in front of you twice now.
I promise I don't cry all the time.
WATER
Why do I get the feeling that you actually do?
EXCUSE ME!?
WHAT DO YOU MEAN!?
YAWN!

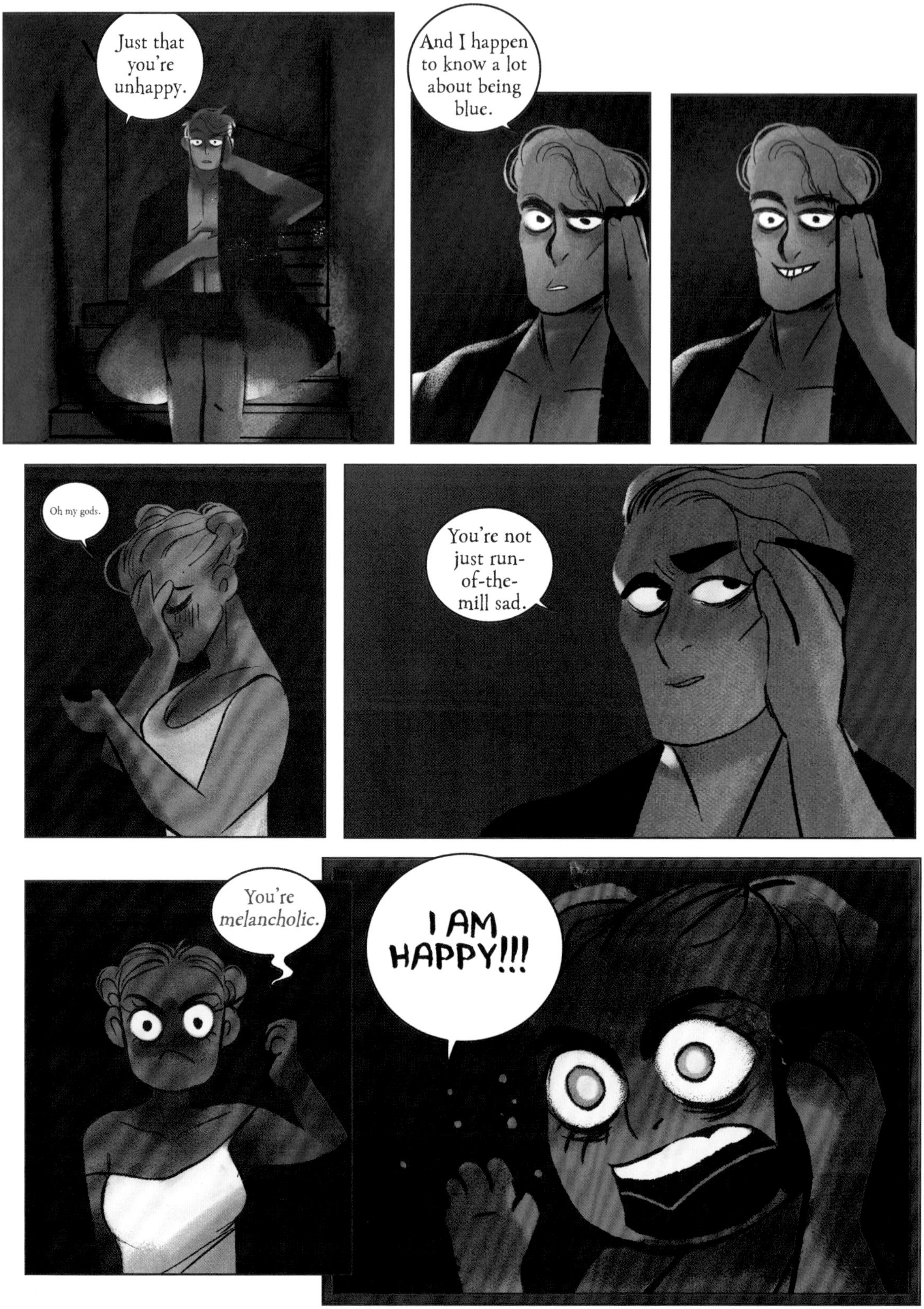
Just that you're unhappy.
And I happen to know a lot about being blue.
Oh my gods.
You're not just run-of-the-mill sad.
You're *melancholic*.
I AM HAPPY!!!

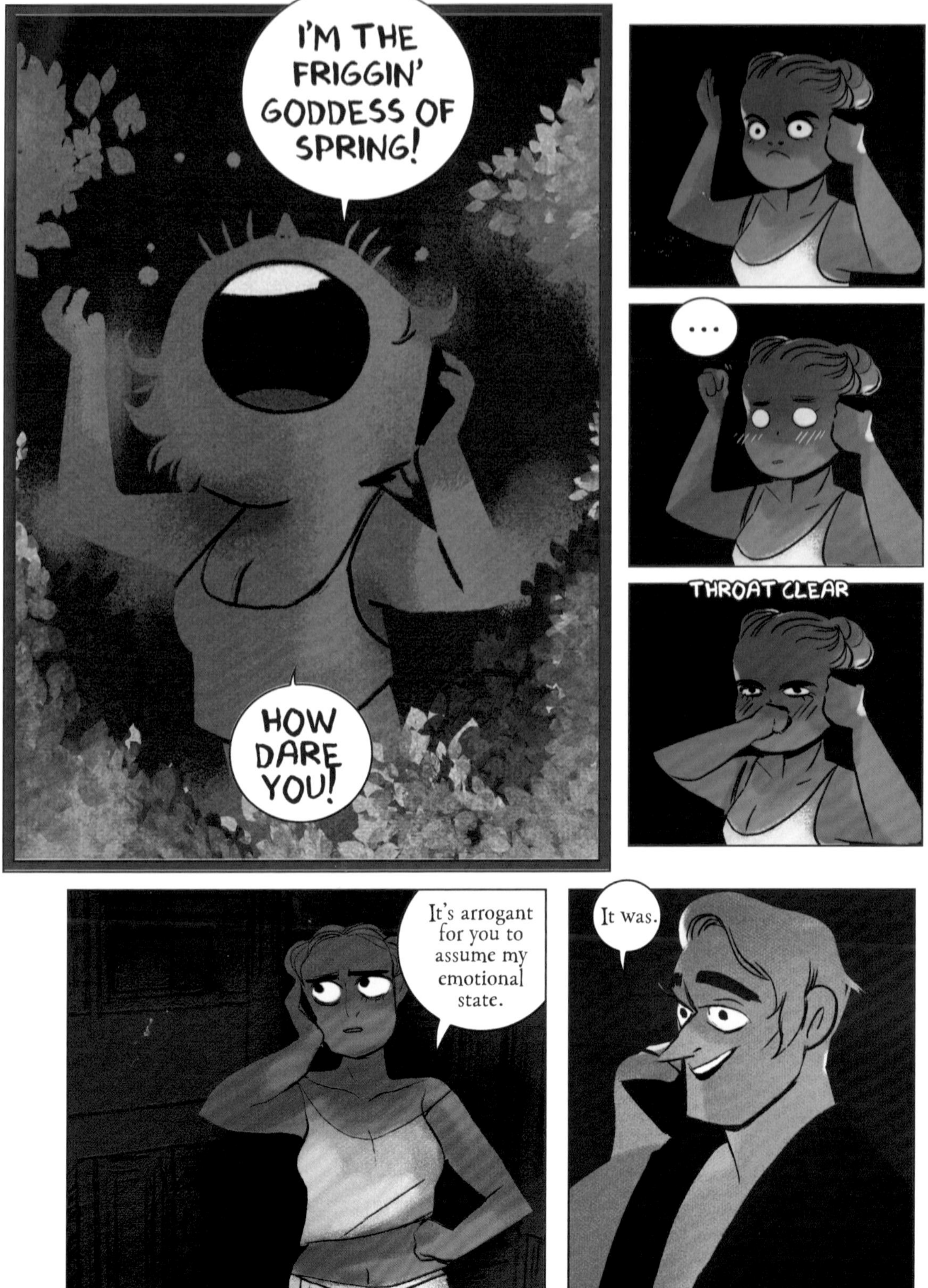
I'M THE FRIGGIN' GODDESS OF SPRING!
HOW DARE YOU!
...
THROAT CLEAR
It's arrogant for you to assume my emotional state.
It was.

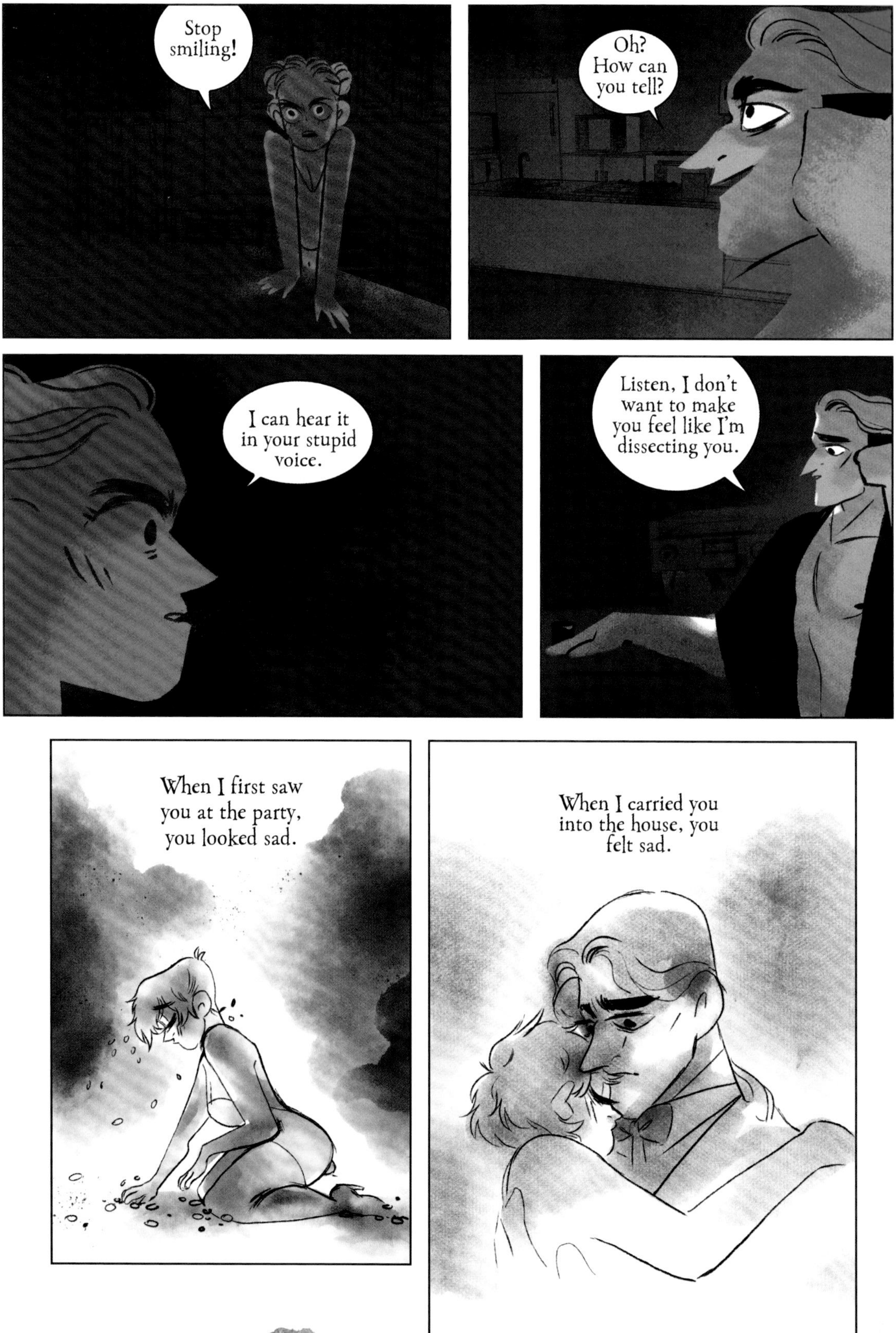
Stop smiling!
Oh? How can you tell?
I can hear it in your stupid voice.
Listen, I don't want to make you feel like I'm dissecting you.
When I first saw you at the party, you looked sad.
When I carried you into the house, you felt sad.

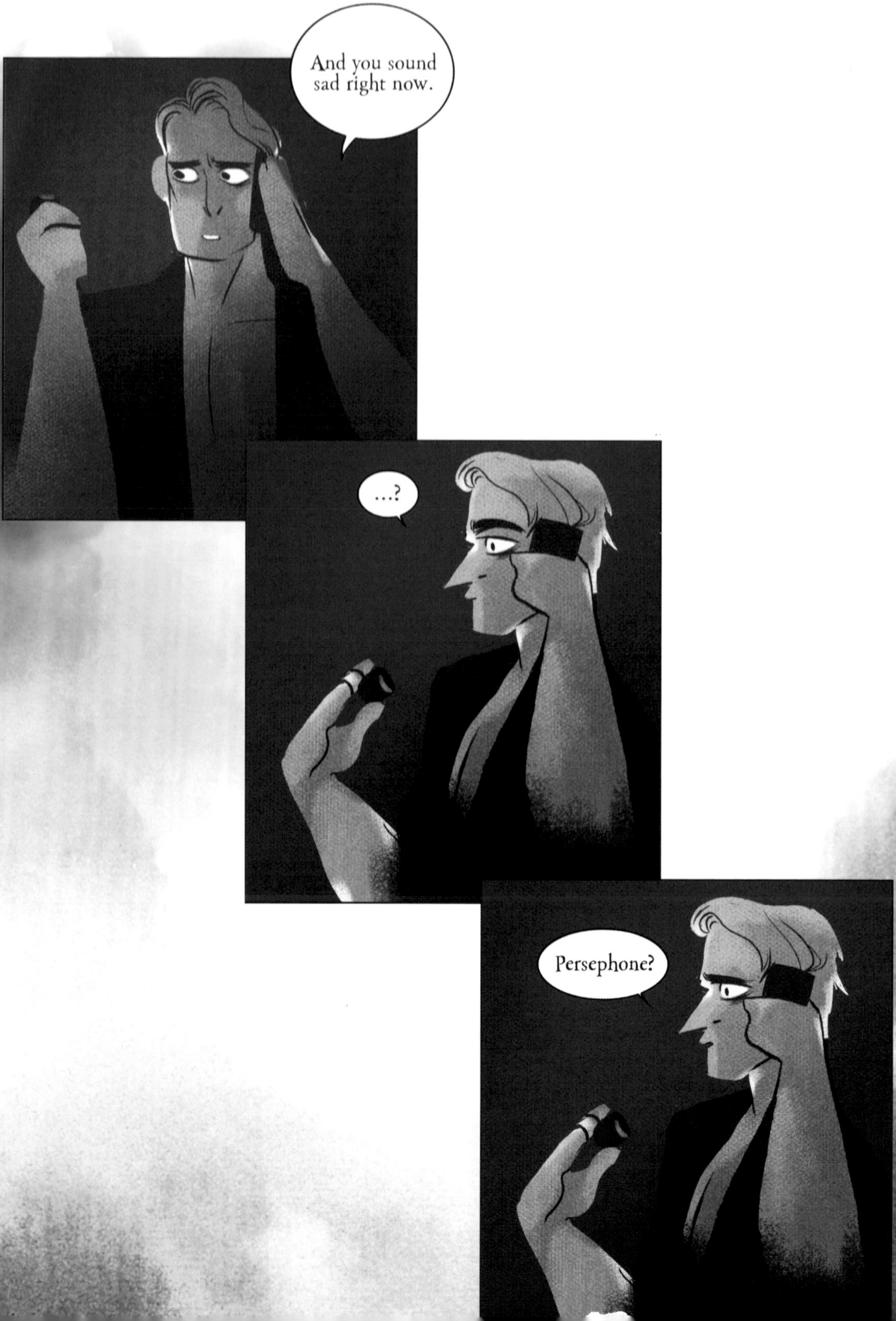

And you sound sad right now.
...?
Persephone?

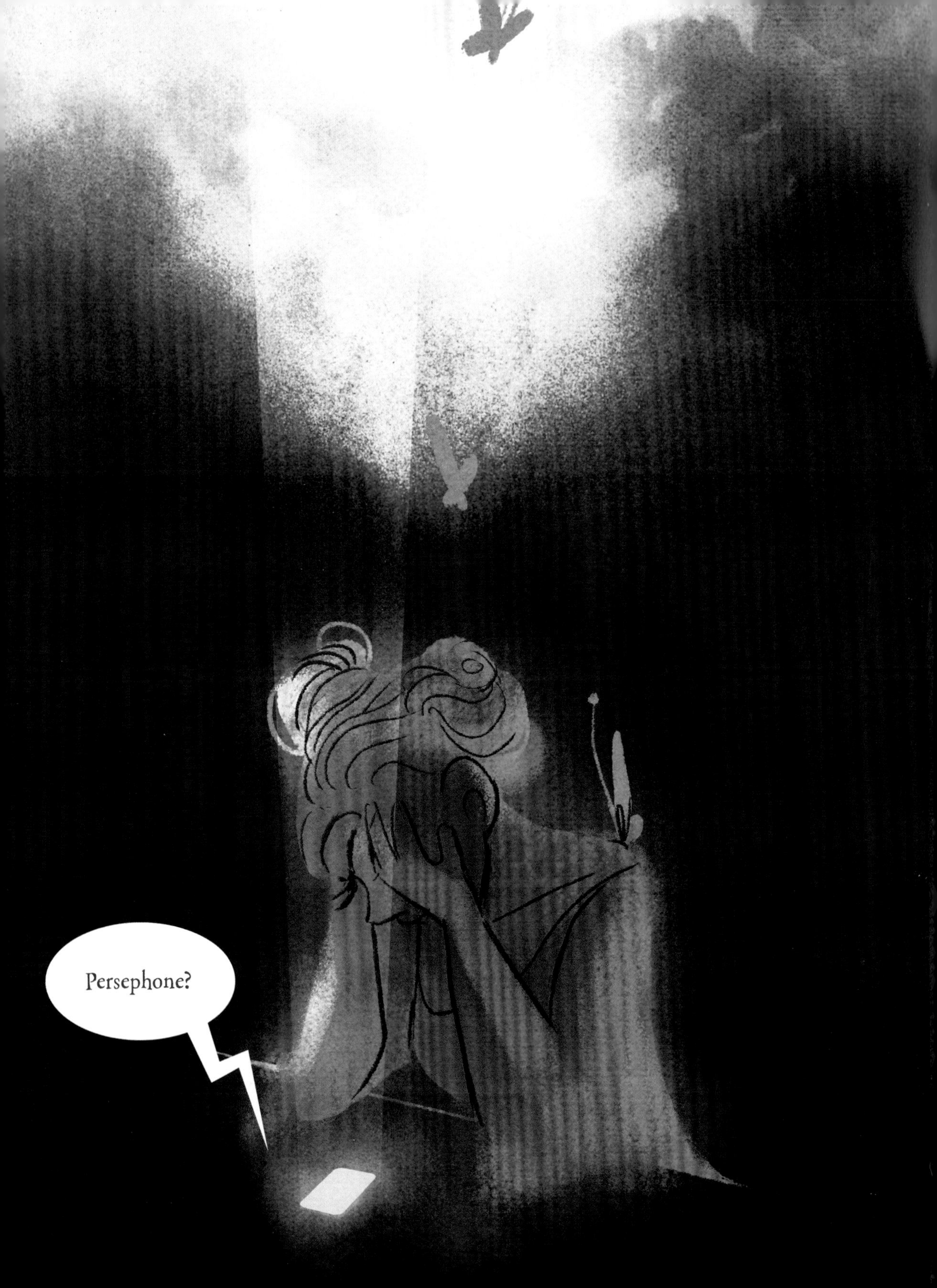
Persephone?

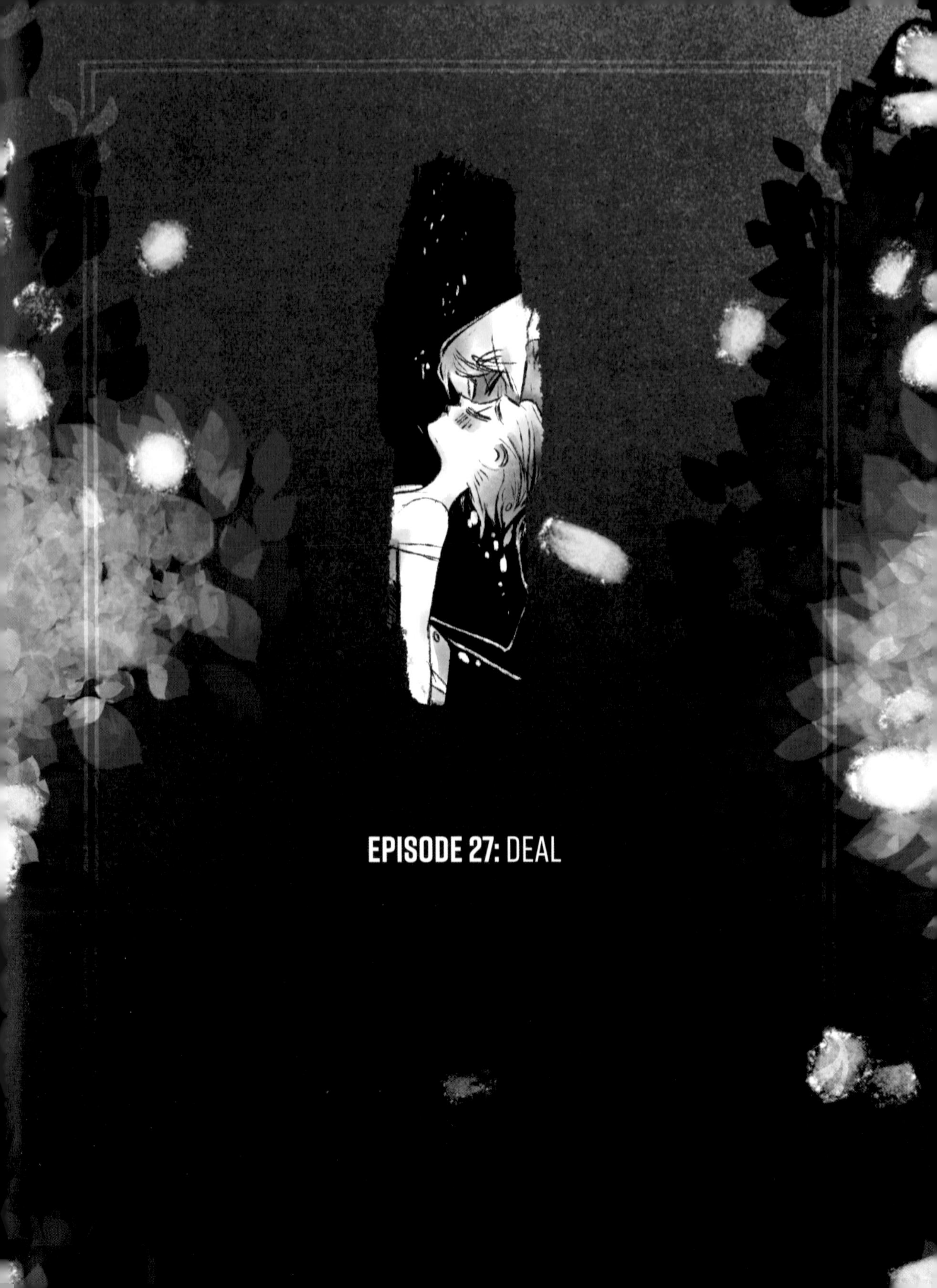

EPISODE 27: DEAL

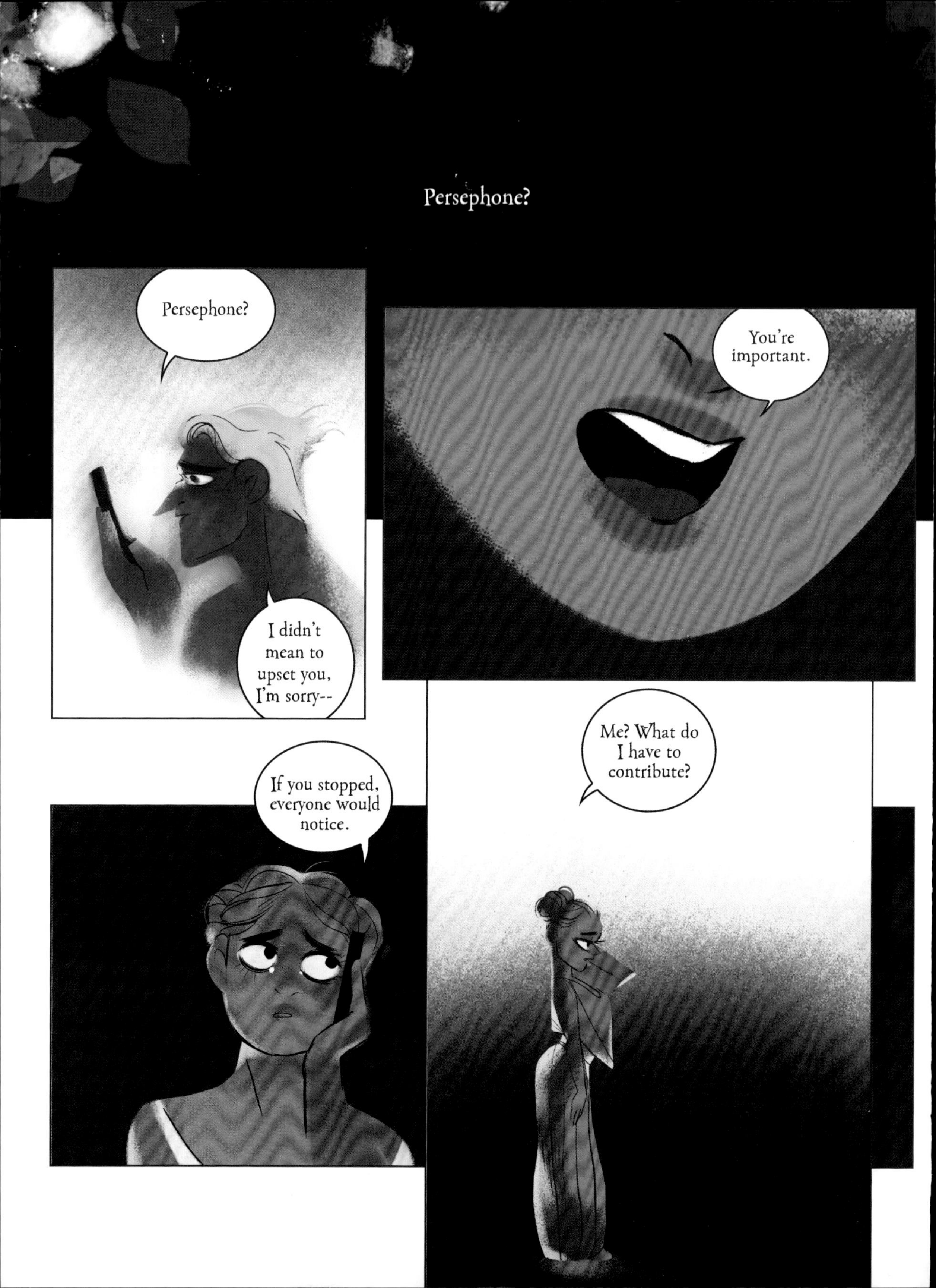
Persephone?
Persephone?
I didn't mean to upset you, I'm sorry--
You're important.
Me? What do I have to contribute?
If you stopped, everyone would notice.

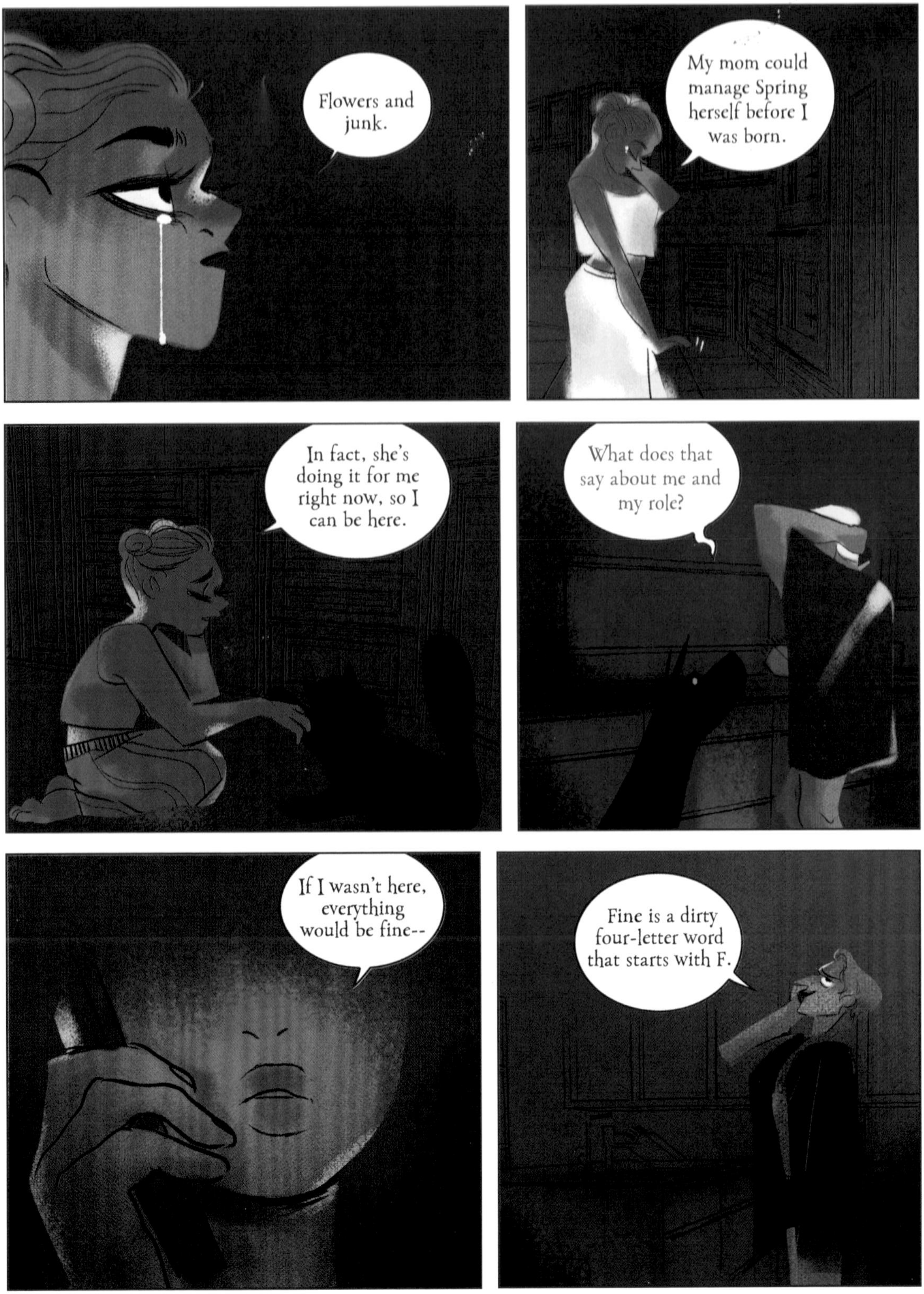
Flowers and junk.
My mom could manage Spring herself before I was born.
In fact, she's doing it for me right now, so I can be here.
What does that say about me and my role?
If I wasn't here, everything would be fine--
Fine is a dirty four-letter word that starts with F.

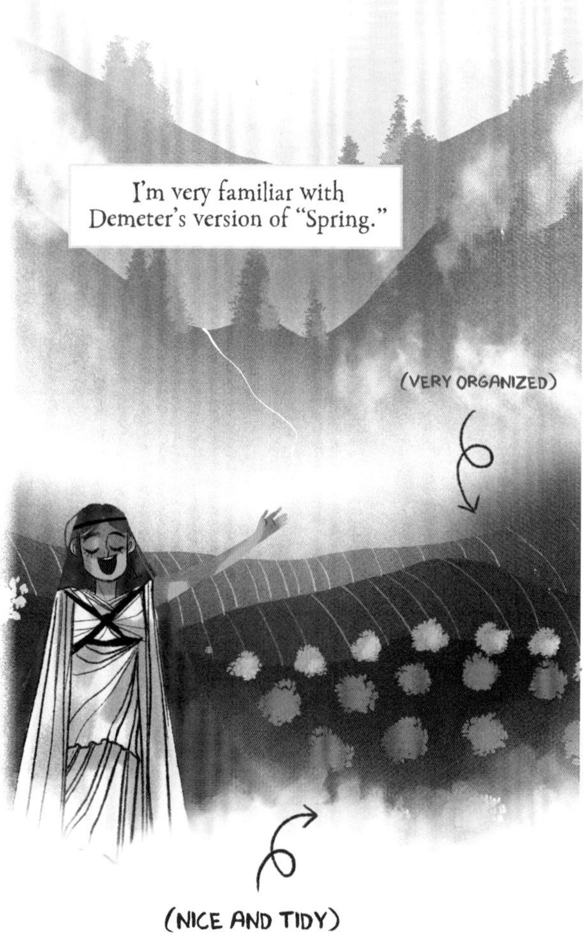
I'm very familiar with Demeter's version of "Spring."
(VERY ORGANIZED)
(NICE AND TIDY)

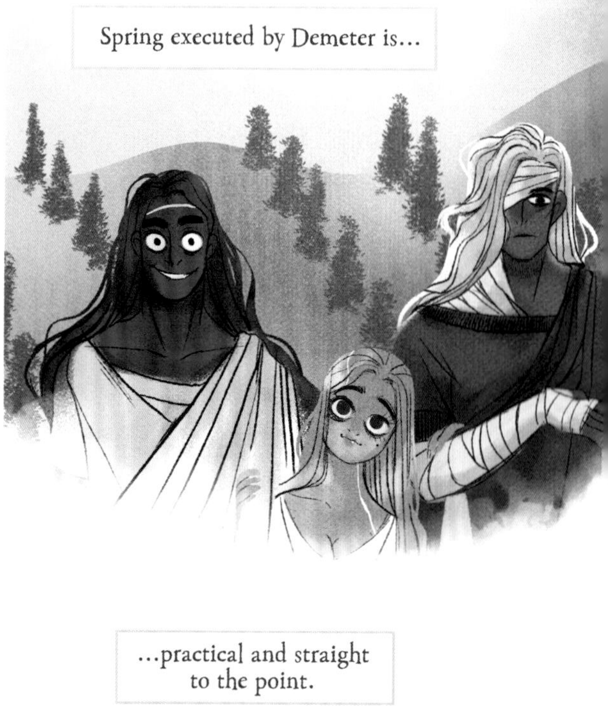
Spring executed by Demeter is...
...practical and straight to the point.

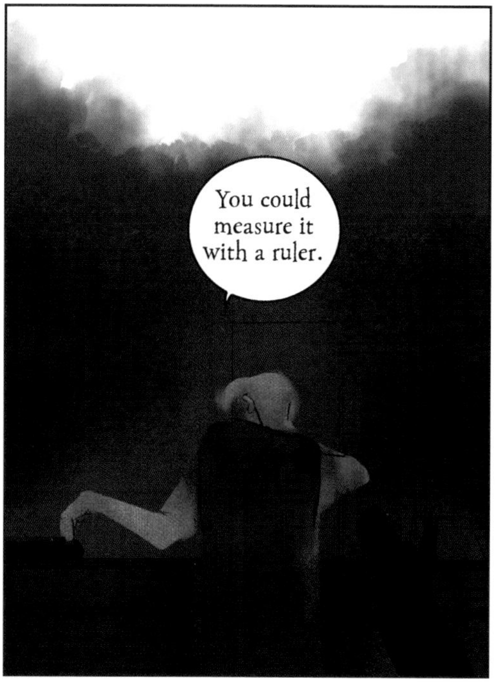
You could measure it with a ruler.

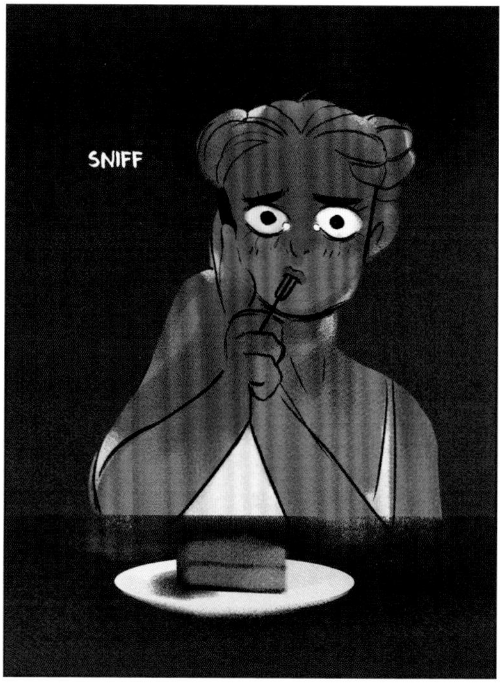
SNIFF

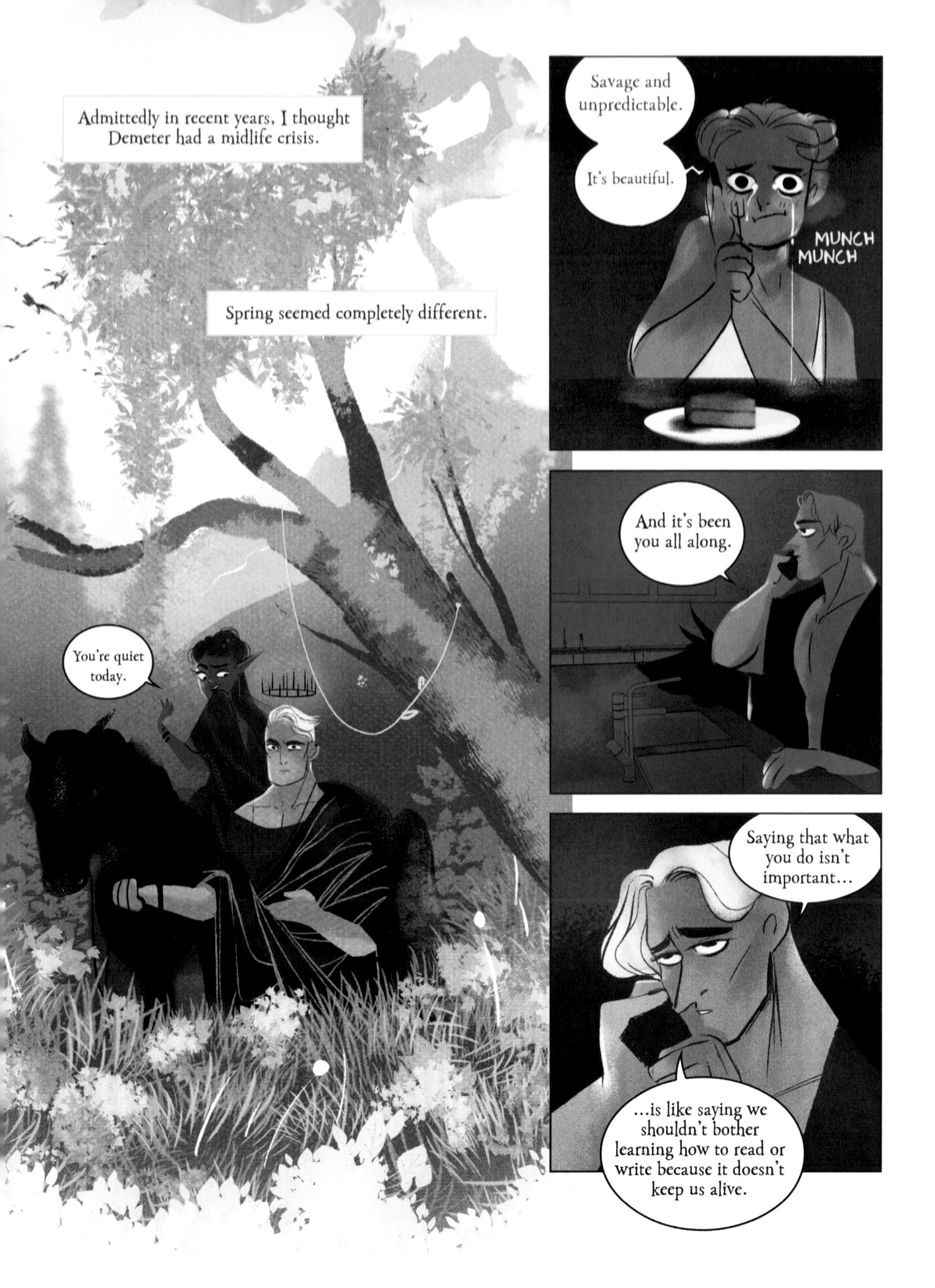
Admittedly in recent years, I thought Demeter had a midlife crisis.
Spring seemed completely different.
You're quiet today.
Savage and unpredictable.
It's beautiful.
MUNCH MUNCH
And it's been you all along.
Saying that what you do isn't important...
...is like saying we shouldn't bother learning how to read or write because it doesn't keep us alive.

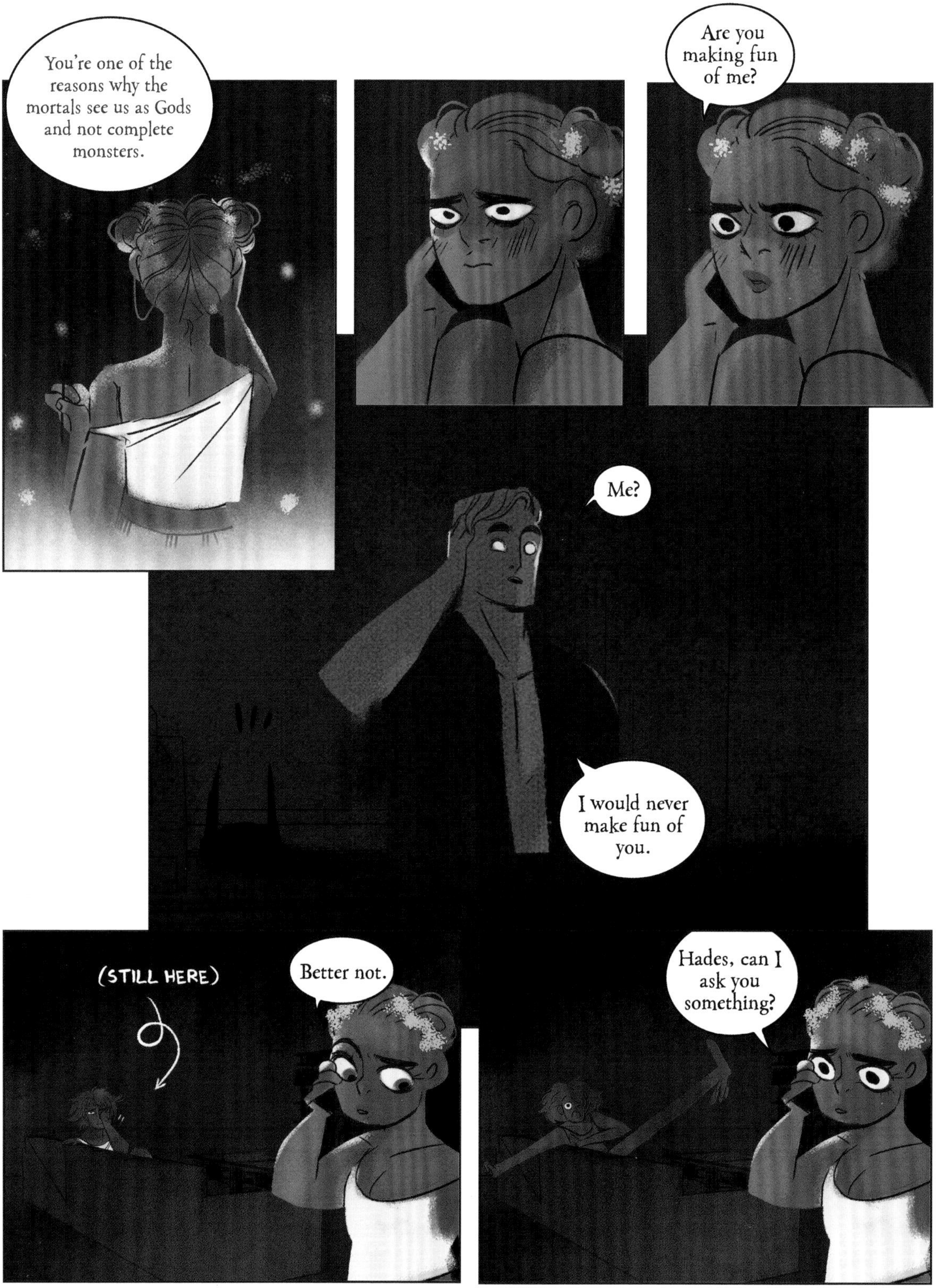
You're one of the reasons why the mortals see us as Gods and not complete monsters.
Are you making fun of me?
Me?
I would never make fun of you.
(STILL HERE)
Better not.
Hades, can I ask you something?

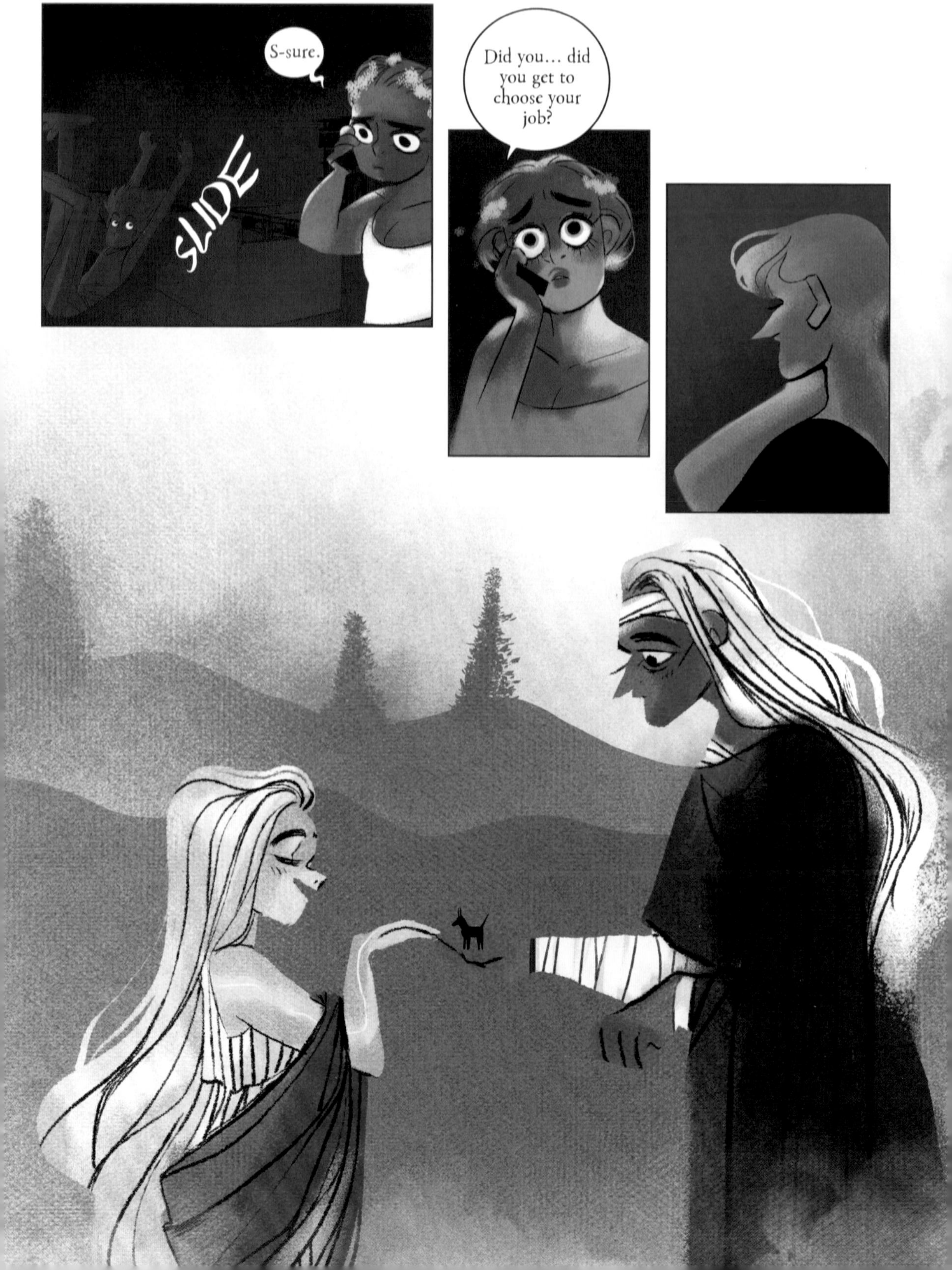
S-sure.
SLIDE
Did you… did you get to choose your job?

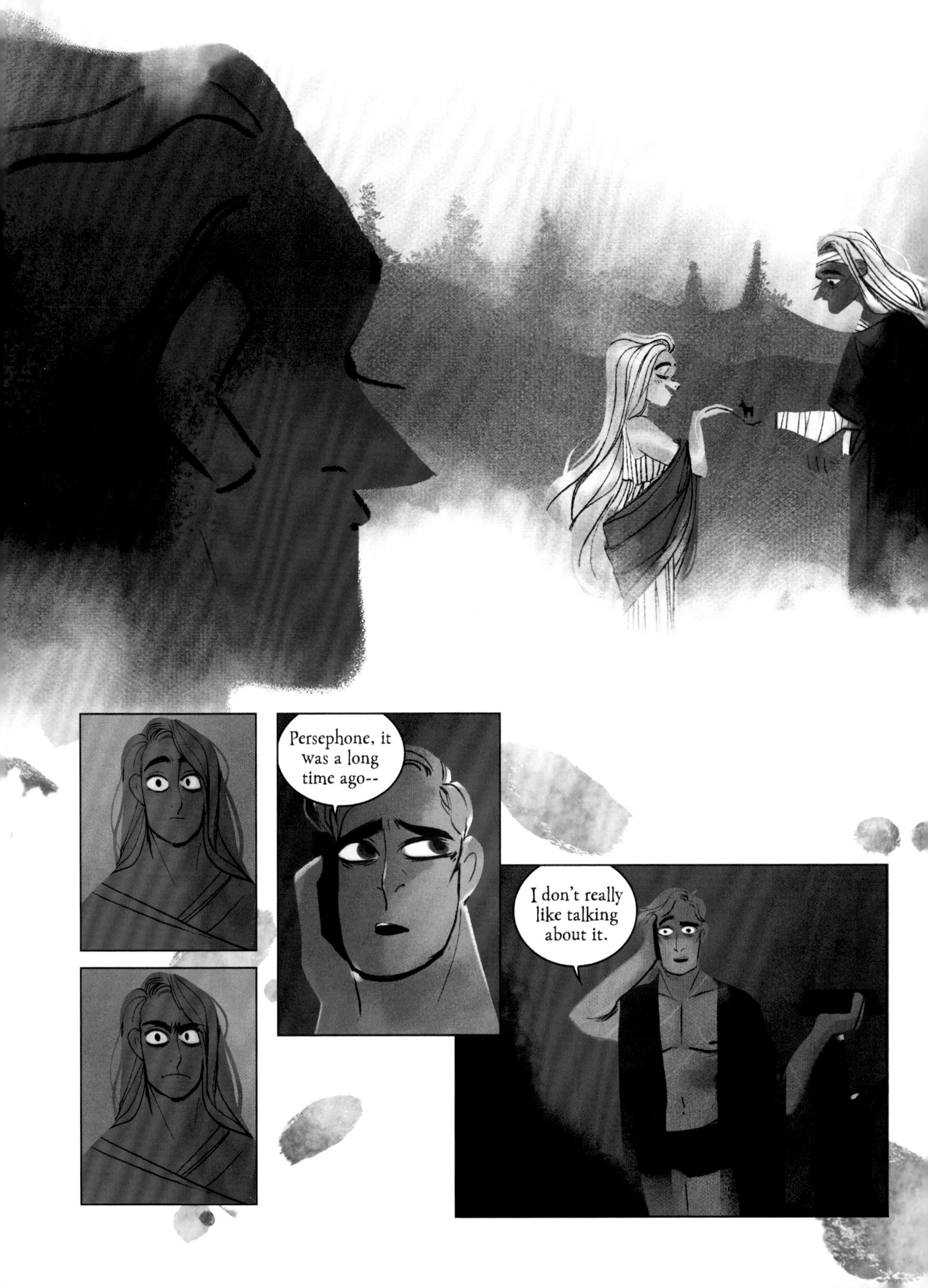
Persephone, it was a long time ago--
I don't really like talking about it.

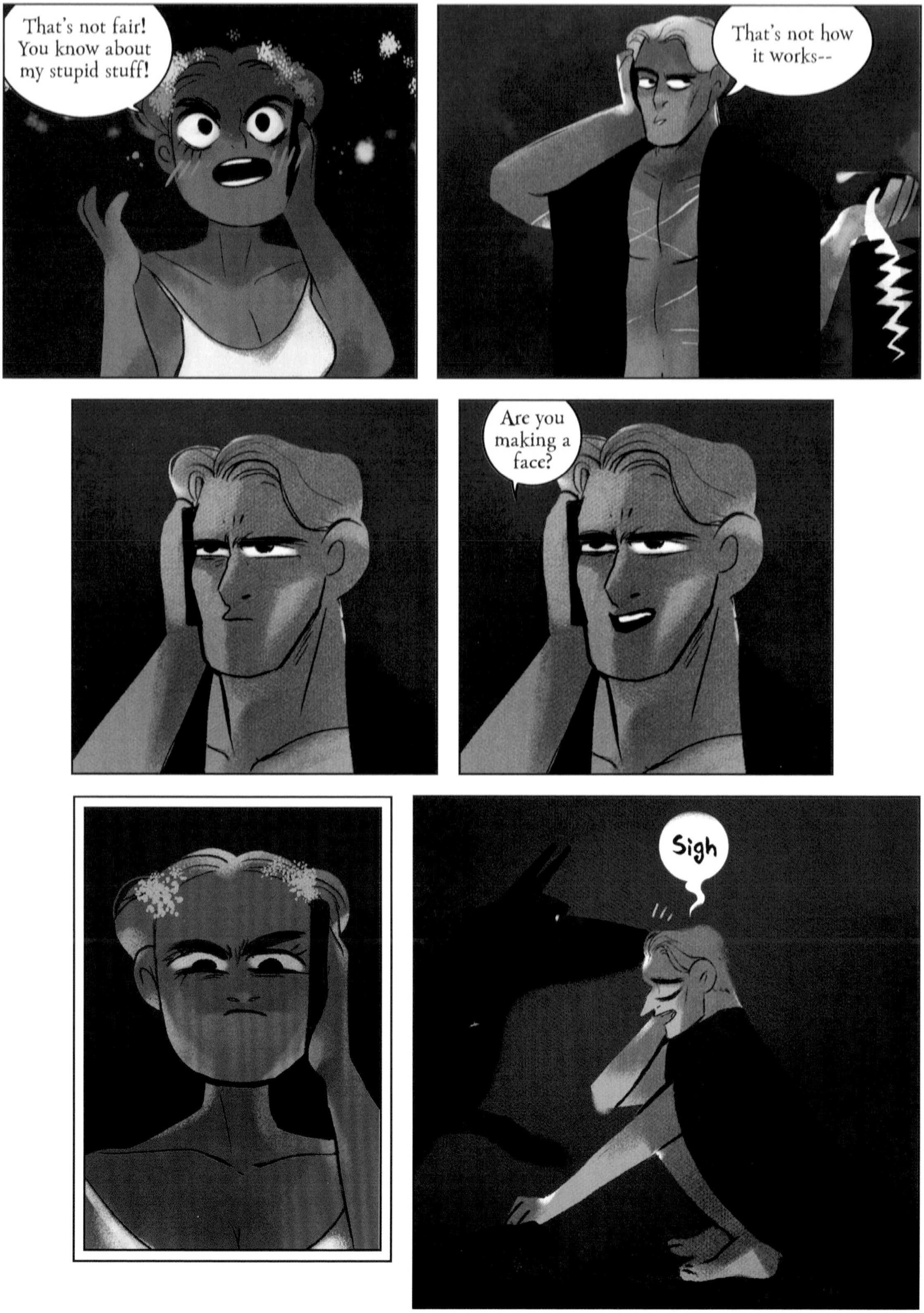
That's not fair! You know about my stupid stuff!
That's not how it works--
Are you making a face?
Sigh

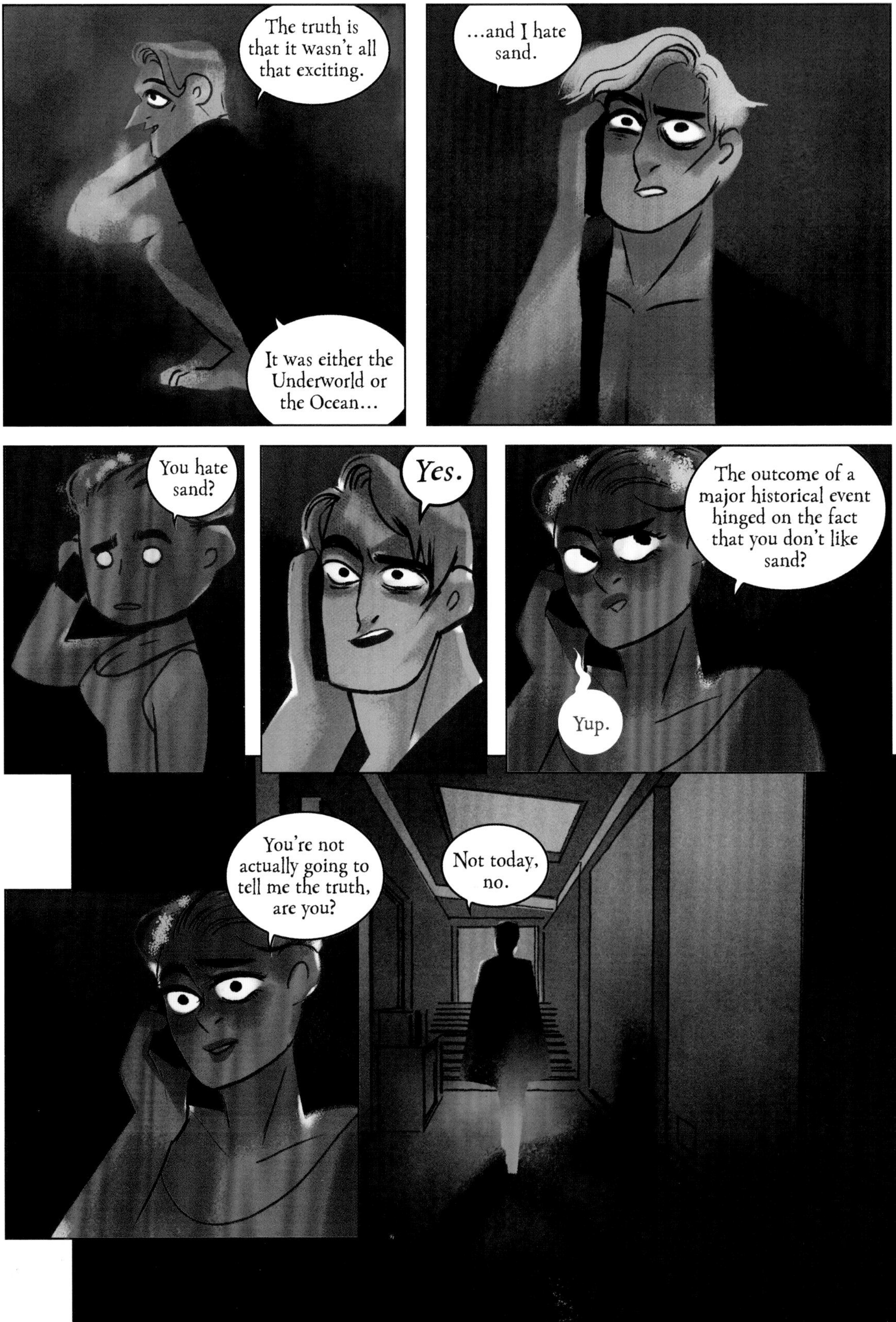
The truth is that it wasn't all that exciting.
It was either the Underworld or the Ocean...
...and I hate sand.
You hate sand?
Yes.
The outcome of a major historical event hinged on the fact that you don't like sand?
Yup.
You're not actually going to tell me the truth, are you?
Not today, no.

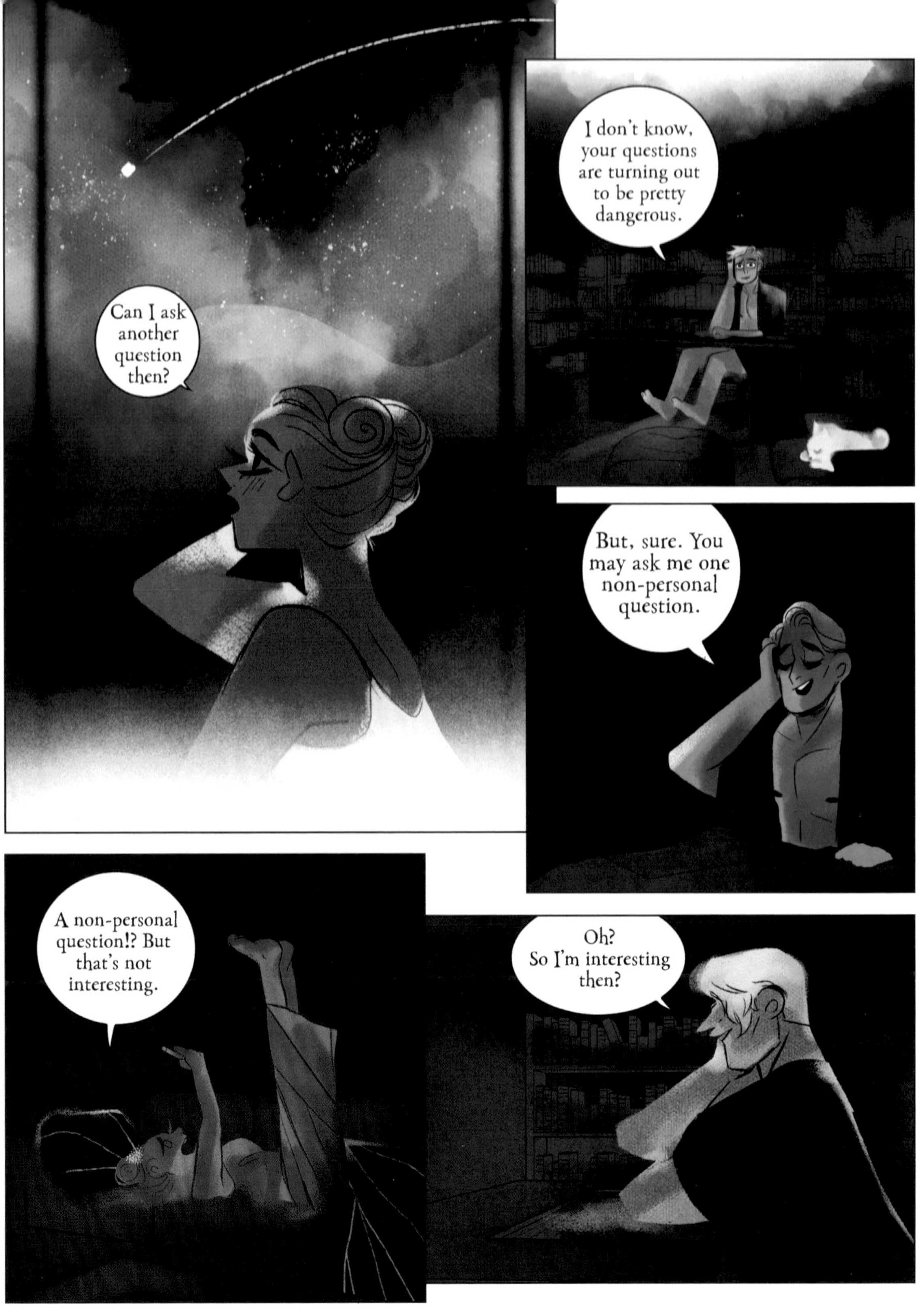
Can I ask another question then?
I don't know, your questions are turning out to be pretty dangerous.
But, sure. You may ask me one non-personal question.
A non-personal question!? But that's not interesting.
Oh? So I'm interesting then?

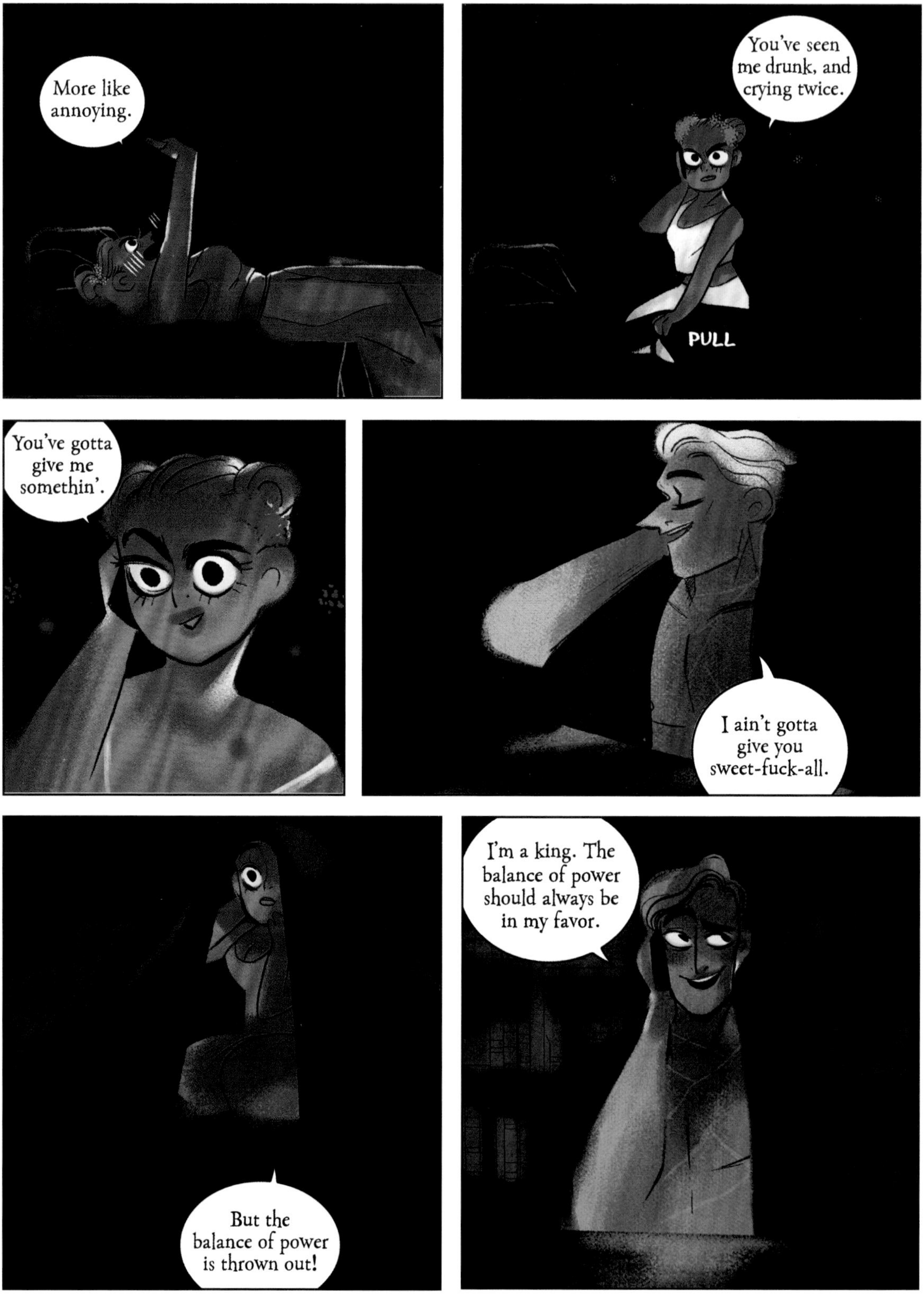
More like annoying.
You've seen me drunk, and crying twice.
PULL
You've gotta give me somethin'.
I ain't gotta give you sweet-fuck-all.
But the balance of power is thrown out!
I'm a king. The balance of power should always be in my favor.

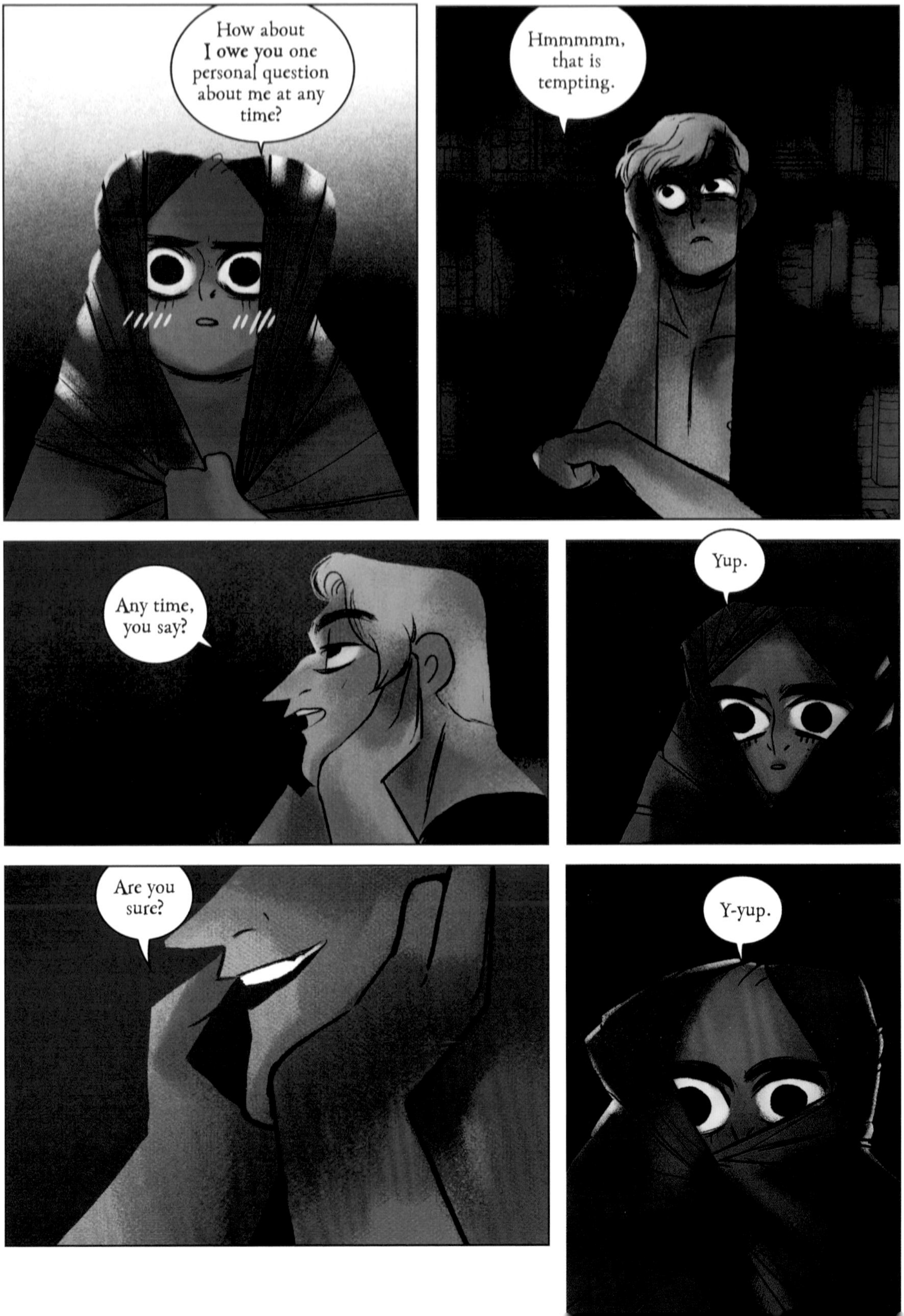
How about I owe you one personal question about me at any time?
Hmmmmm, that is tempting.
Any time, you say?
Yup.
Are you sure?
Y-yup.

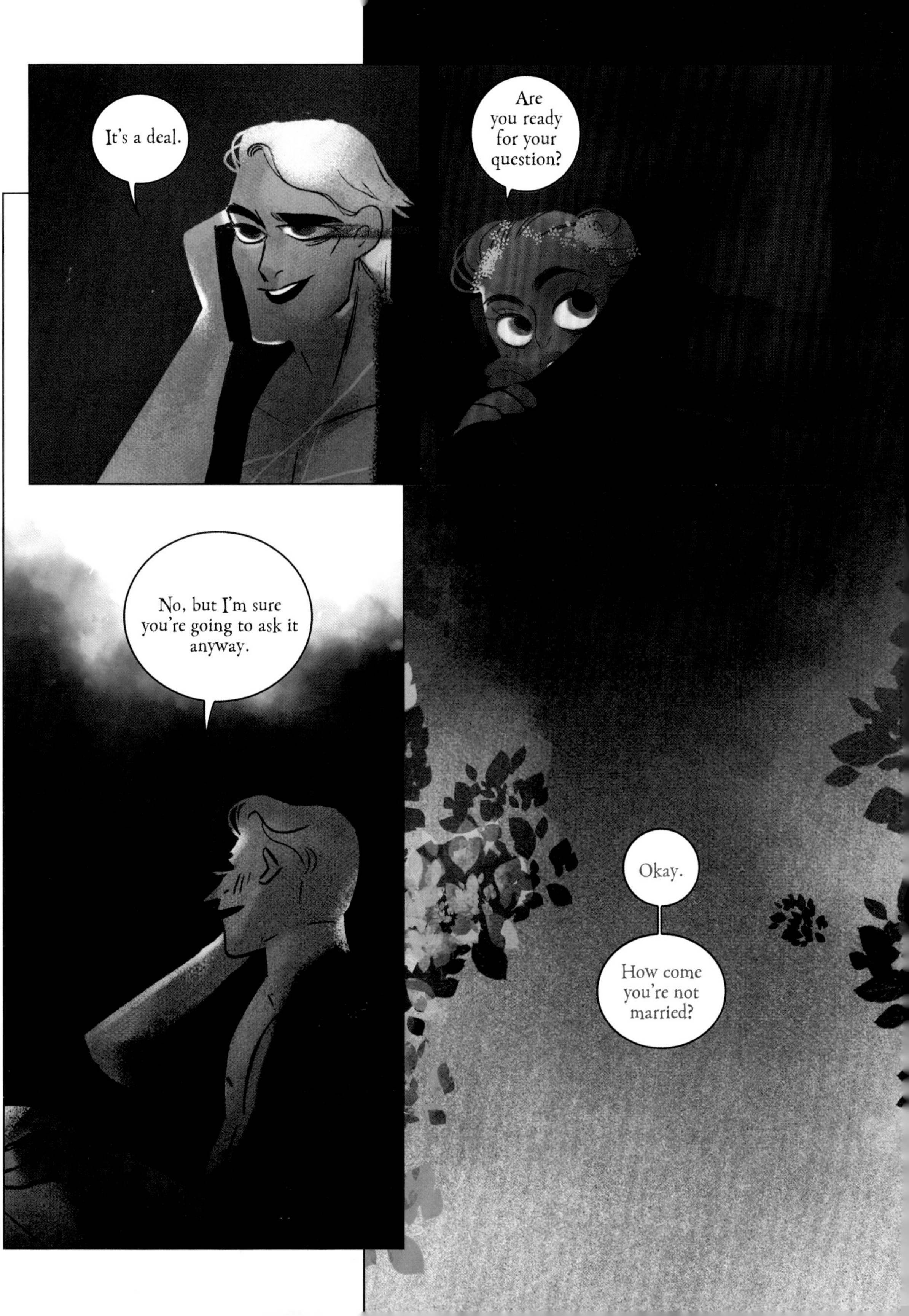
It's a deal.
Are you ready for your question?
No, but I'm sure you're going to ask it anyway.
Okay.
How come you're not married?

EPISODE 28: AWKWARD SILENCE

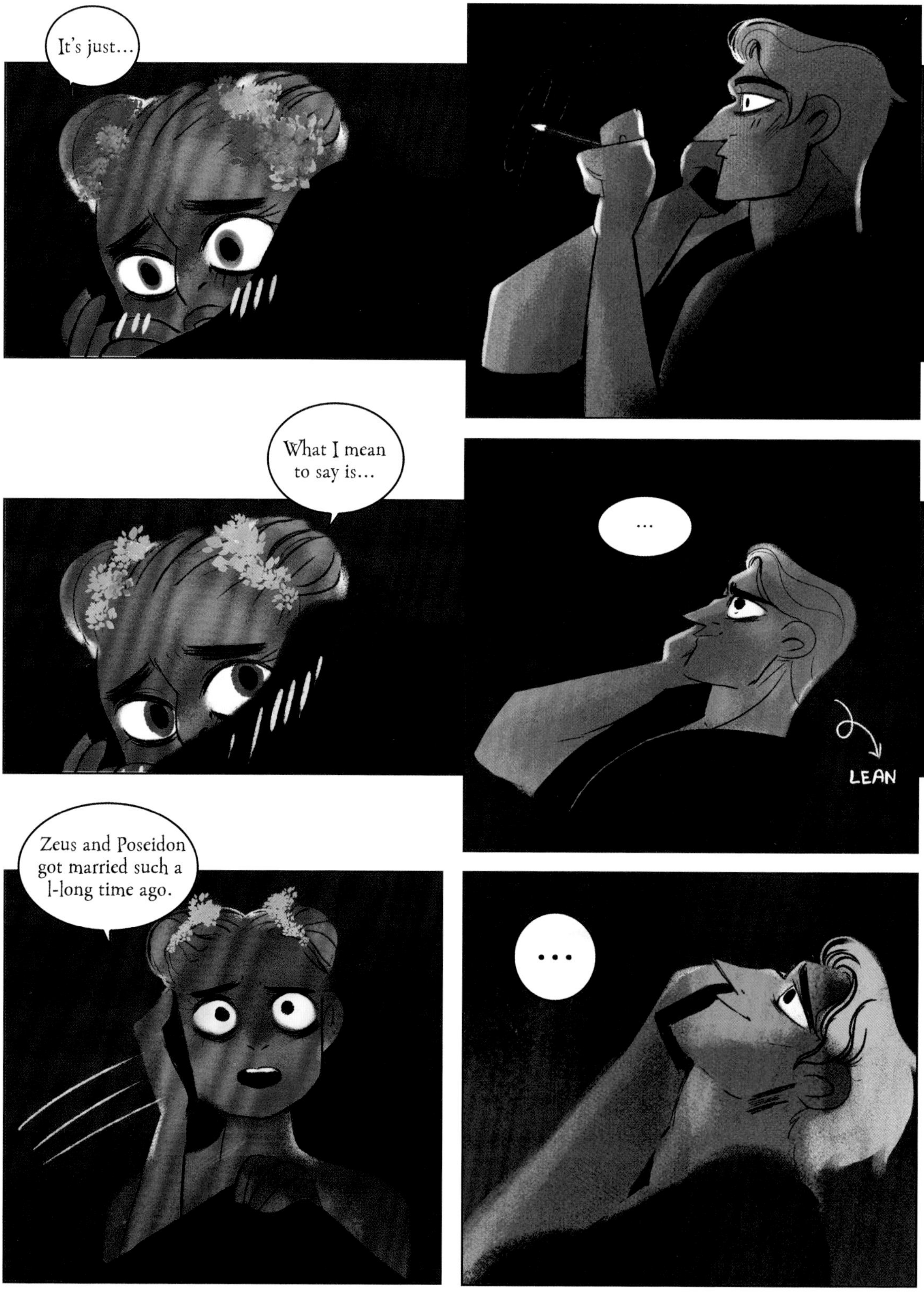
It's just...
What I mean to say is...
...
LEAN
Zeus and Poseidon got married such a l-long time ago.
...

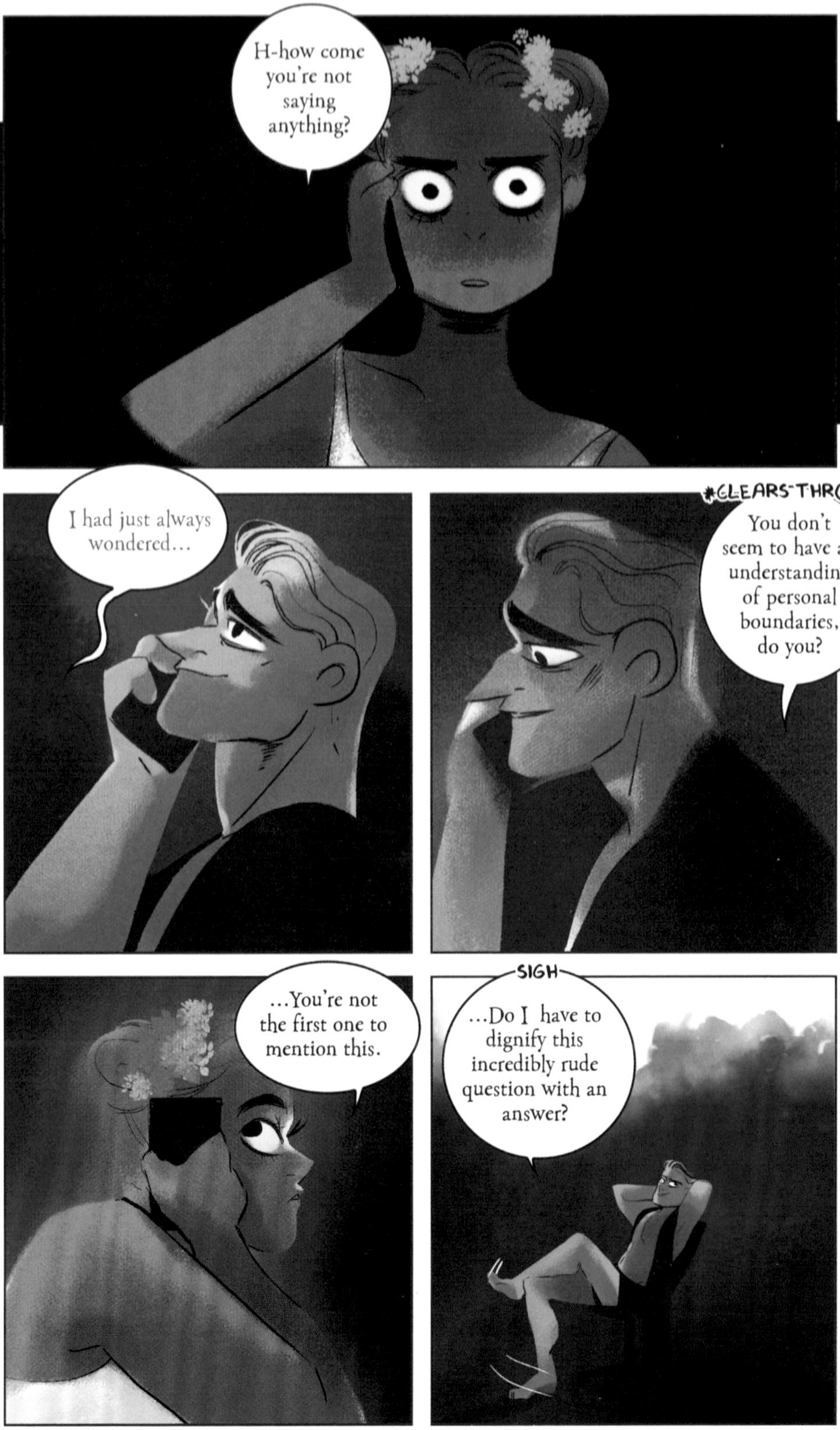
H-how come you're not saying anything?
I had just always wondered...
CLEARS THROAT
You don't seem to have an understanding of personal boundaries, do you?
...You're not the first one to mention this.
SIGH
...Do I have to dignify this incredibly rude question with an answer?

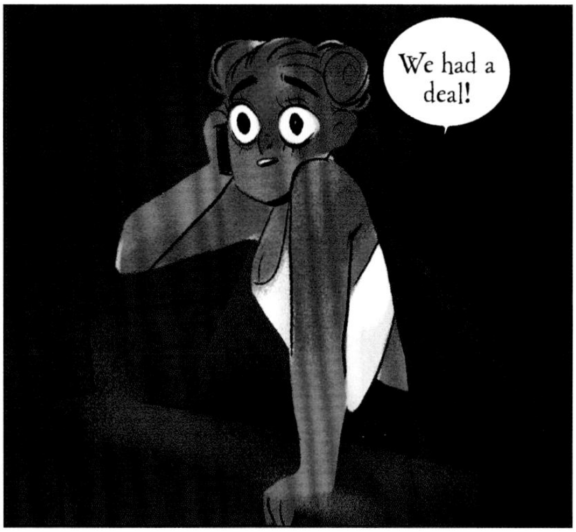
We had a deal!

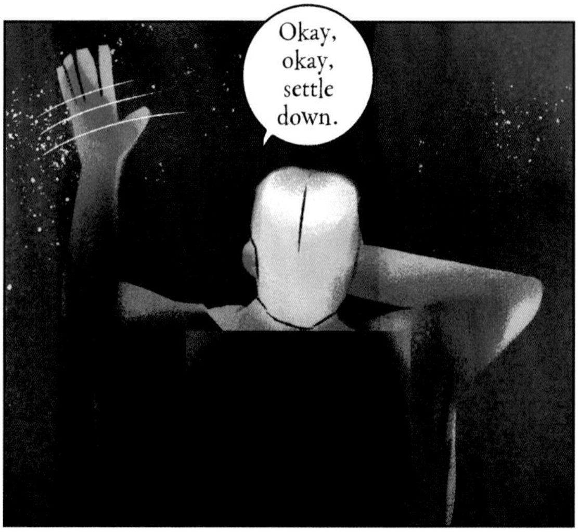
Okay, okay, settle down.

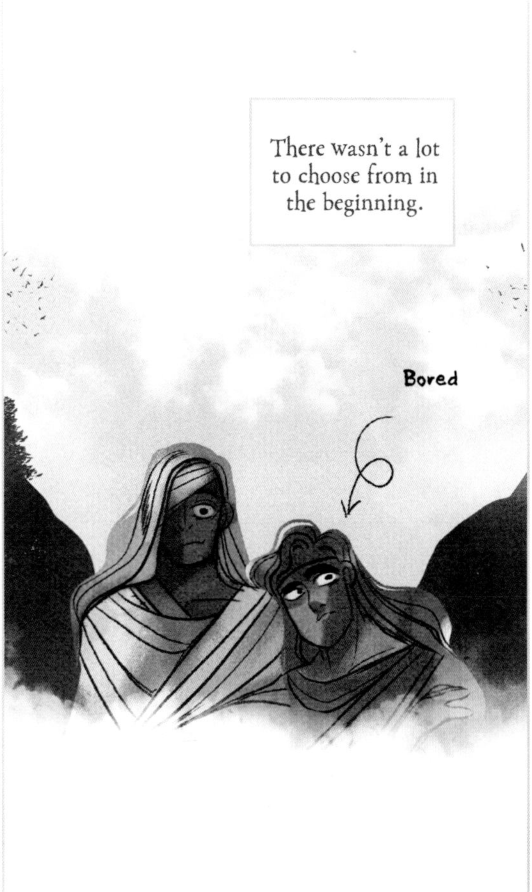
There wasn't a lot to choose from in the beginning.
Bored

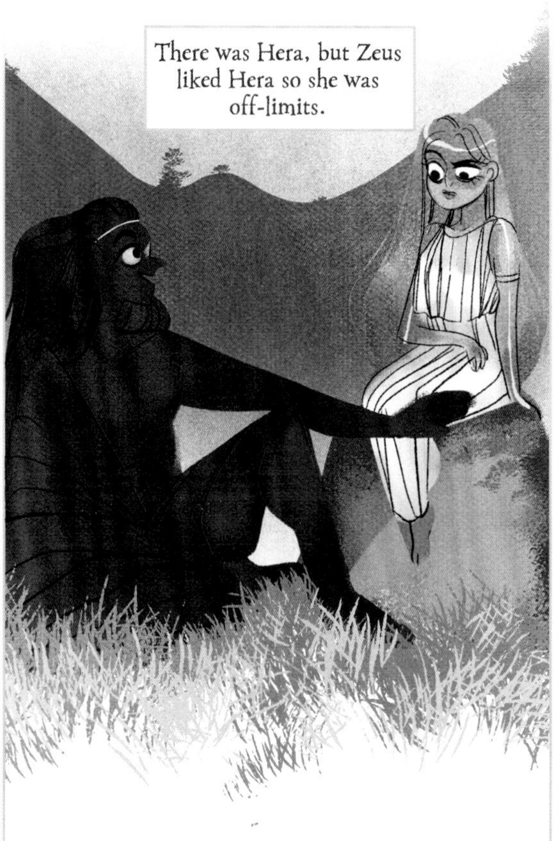
There was Hera, but Zeus liked Hera so she was off-limits.

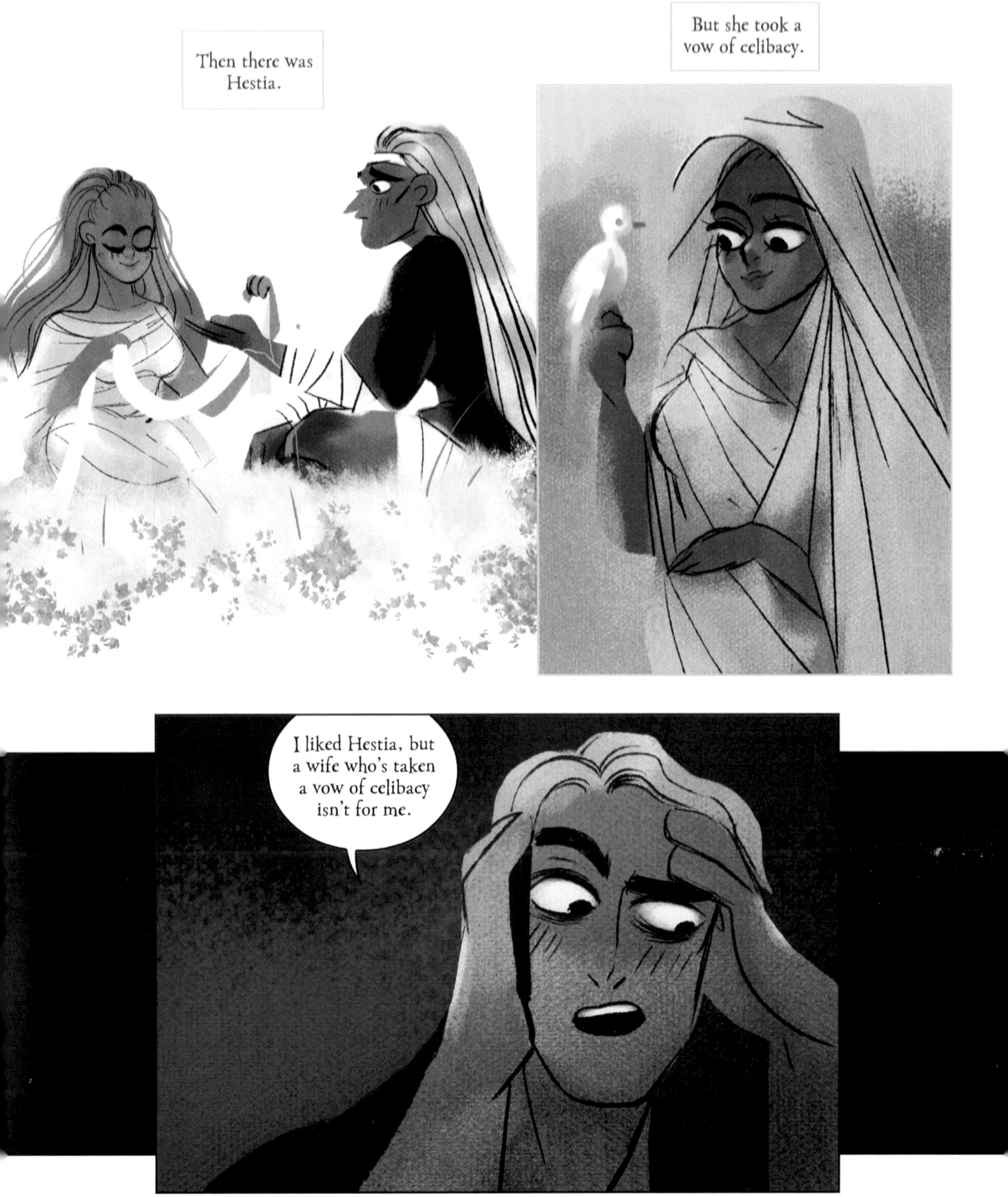
Then there was Hestia.
But she took a vow of celibacy.
I liked Hestia, but a wife who's taken a vow of celibacy isn't for me.

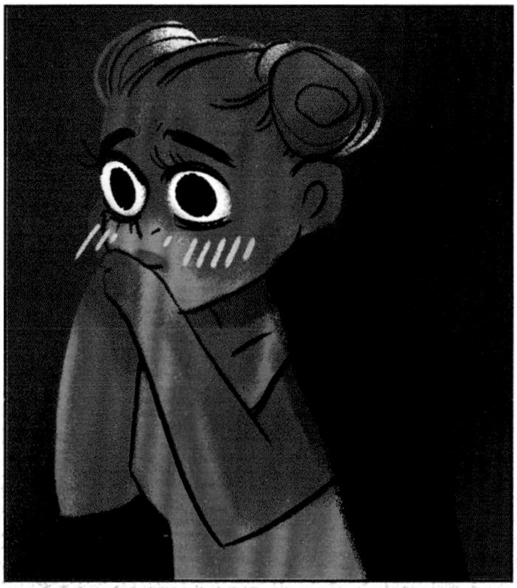

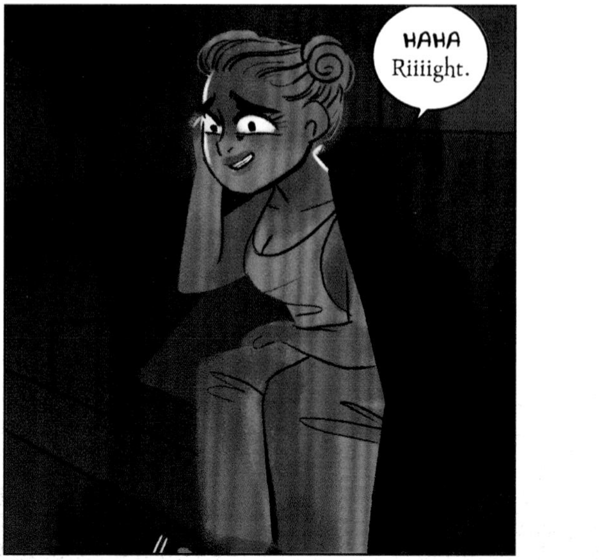
HAHA
Riiiight.

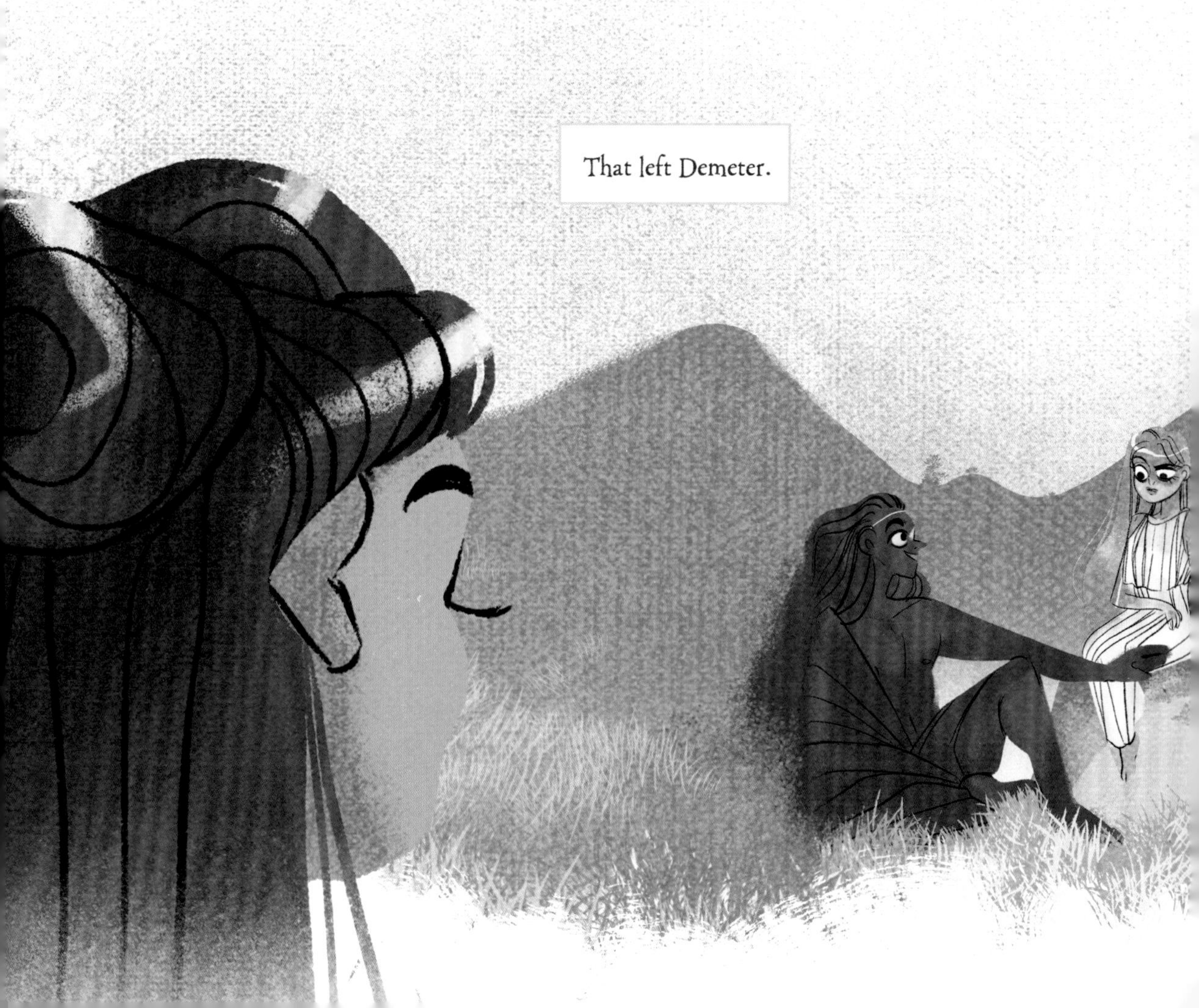
That left Demeter.

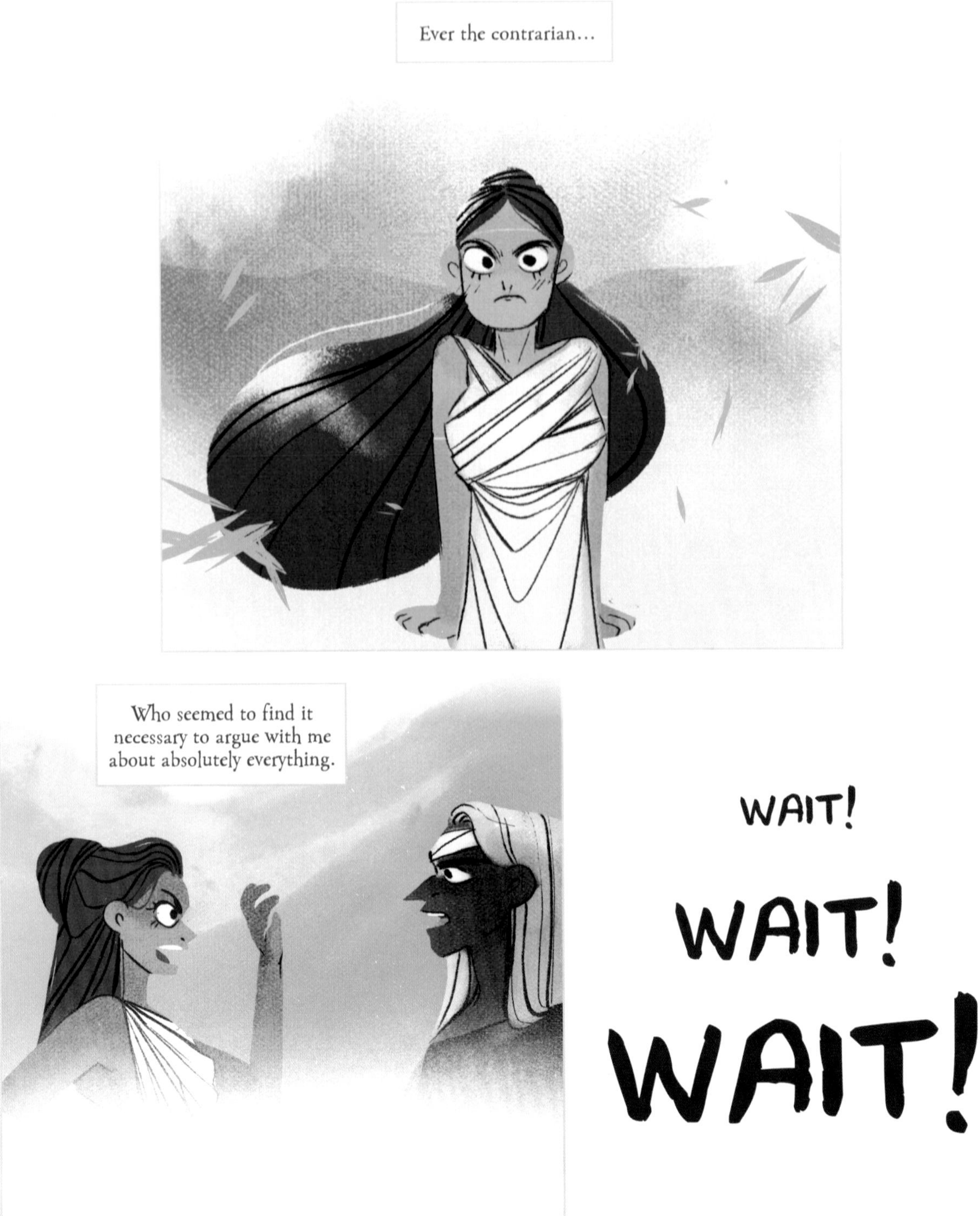
Ever the contrarian...
Who seemed to find it necessary to argue with me about absolutely everything.
WAIT!
WAIT!
WAIT!

Are you talking about my mom as a sexual prospect!?

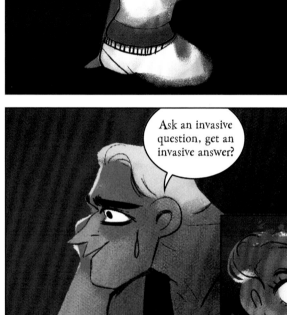

Ask an invasive question, get an invasive answer?

Should I stop?

NO!

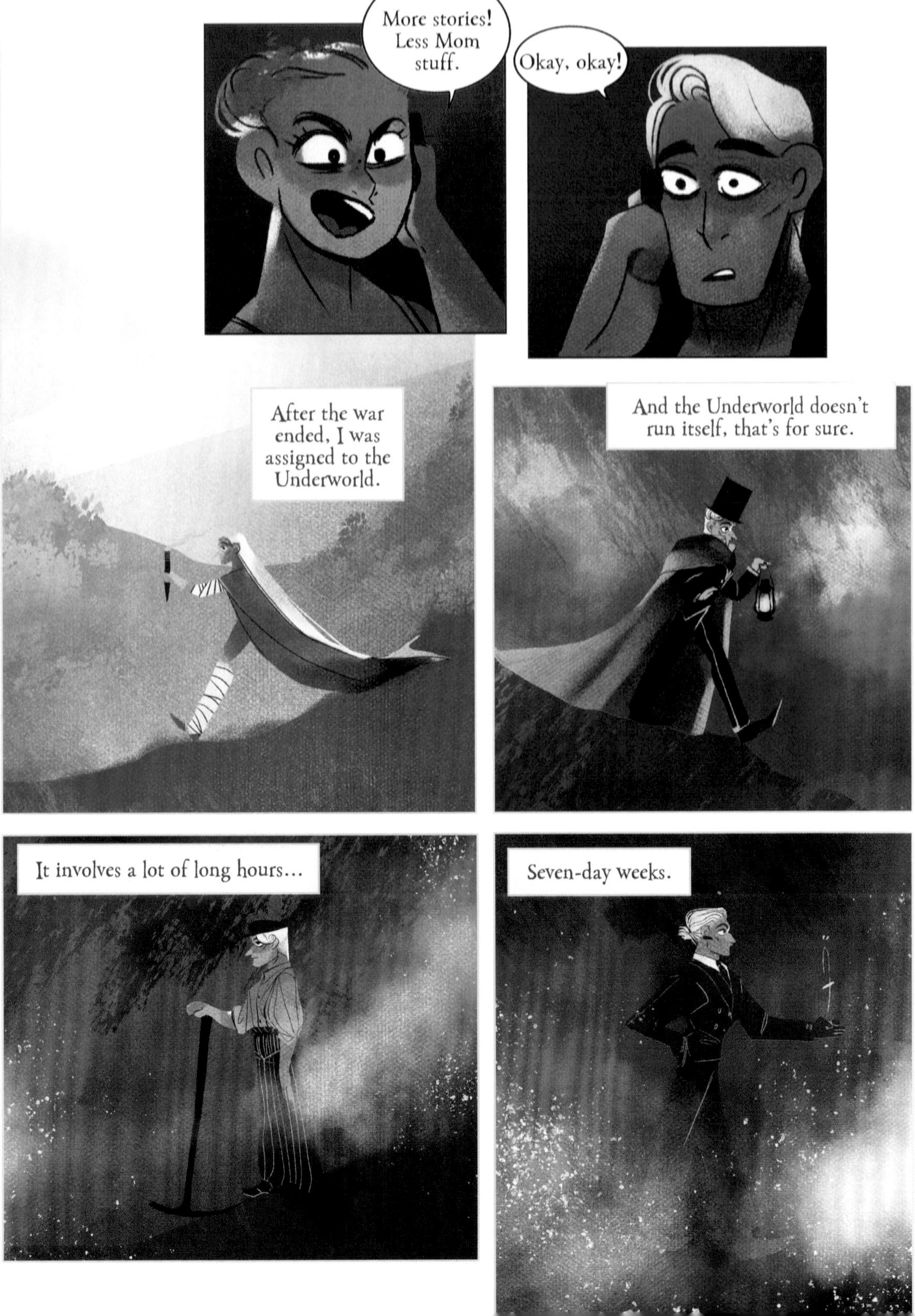
More stories! Less Mom stuff.
Okay, okay!
After the war ended, I was assigned to the Underworld.
And the Underworld doesn't run itself, that's for sure.
It involves a lot of long hours...
Seven-day weeks.

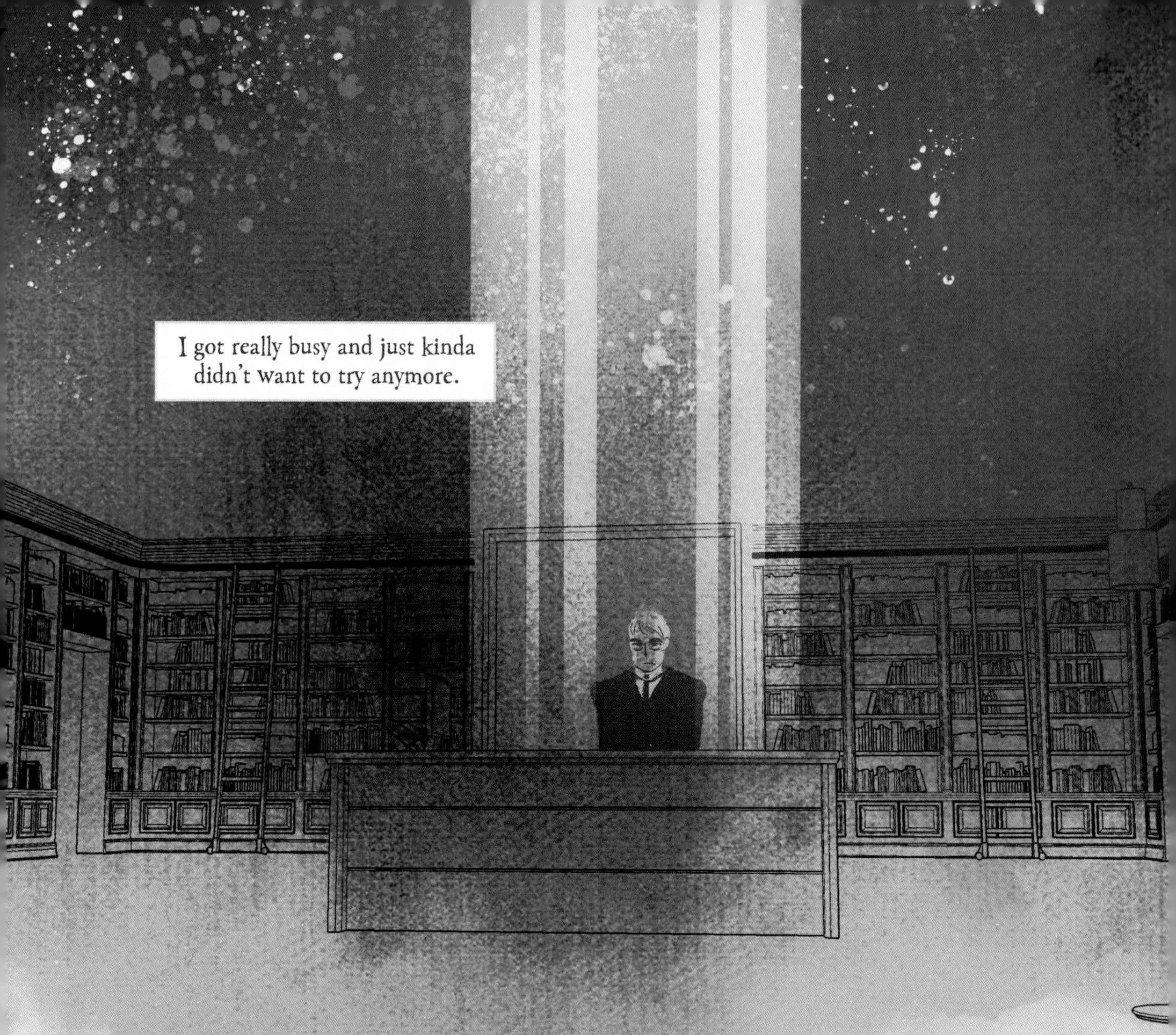
I got really busy and just kinda didn't want to try anymore.

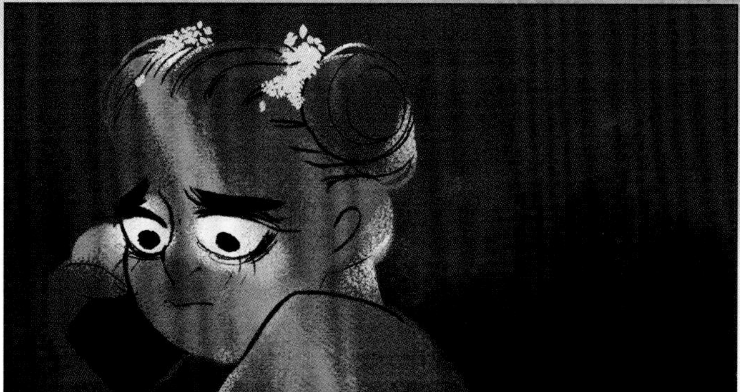

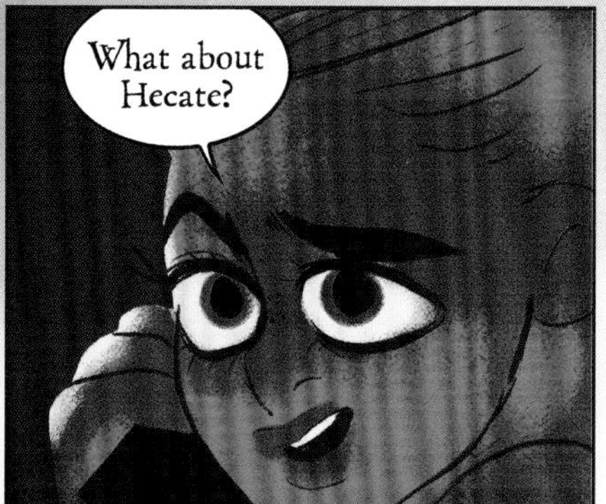
What about Hecate?
You work with her, right?

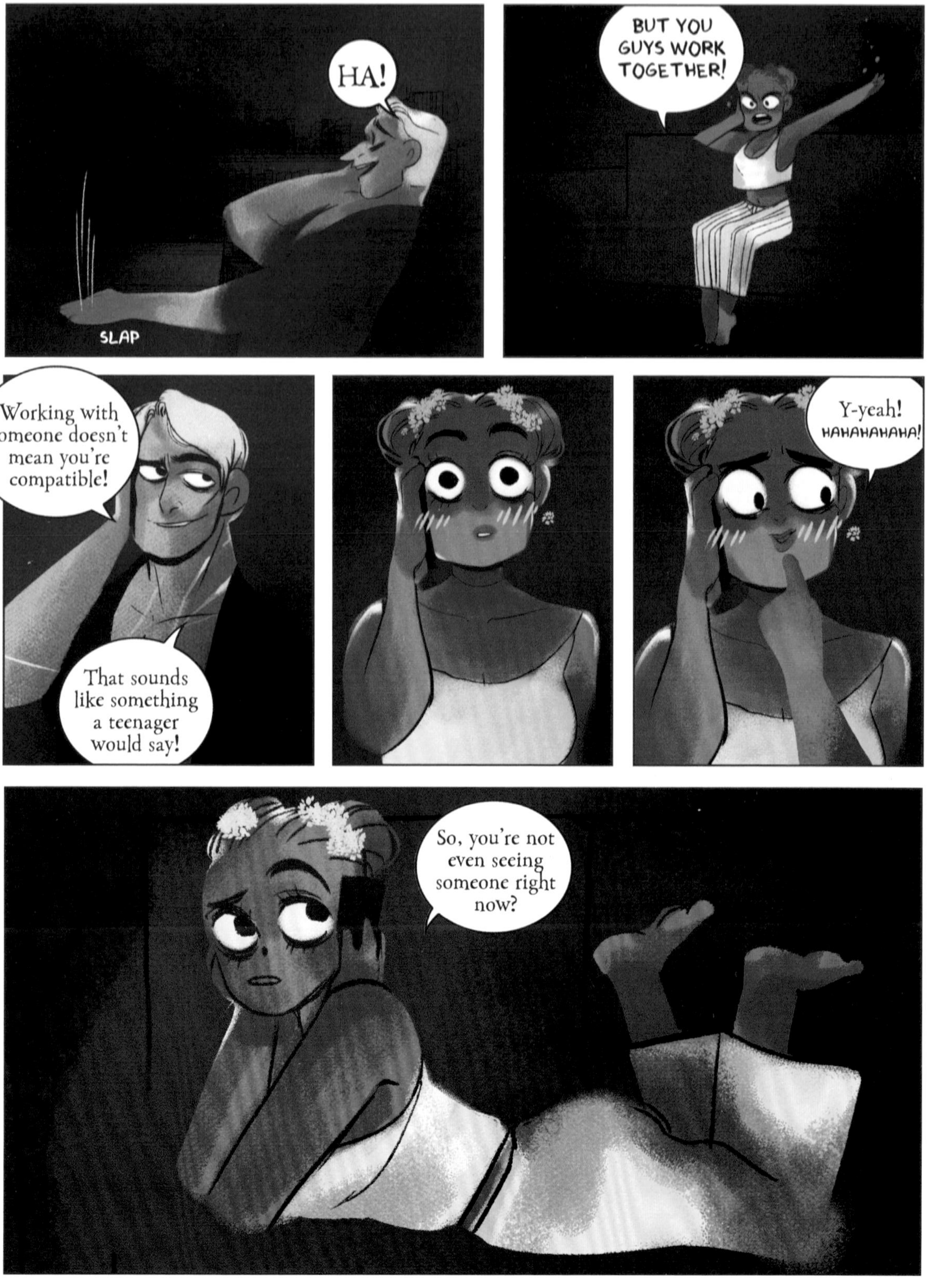
HA!
SLAP
BUT YOU GUYS WORK TOGETHER!
Working with someone doesn't mean you're compatible!
That sounds like something a teenager would say!
Y-yeah! HAHAHAHAHA!
So, you're not even seeing someone right now?

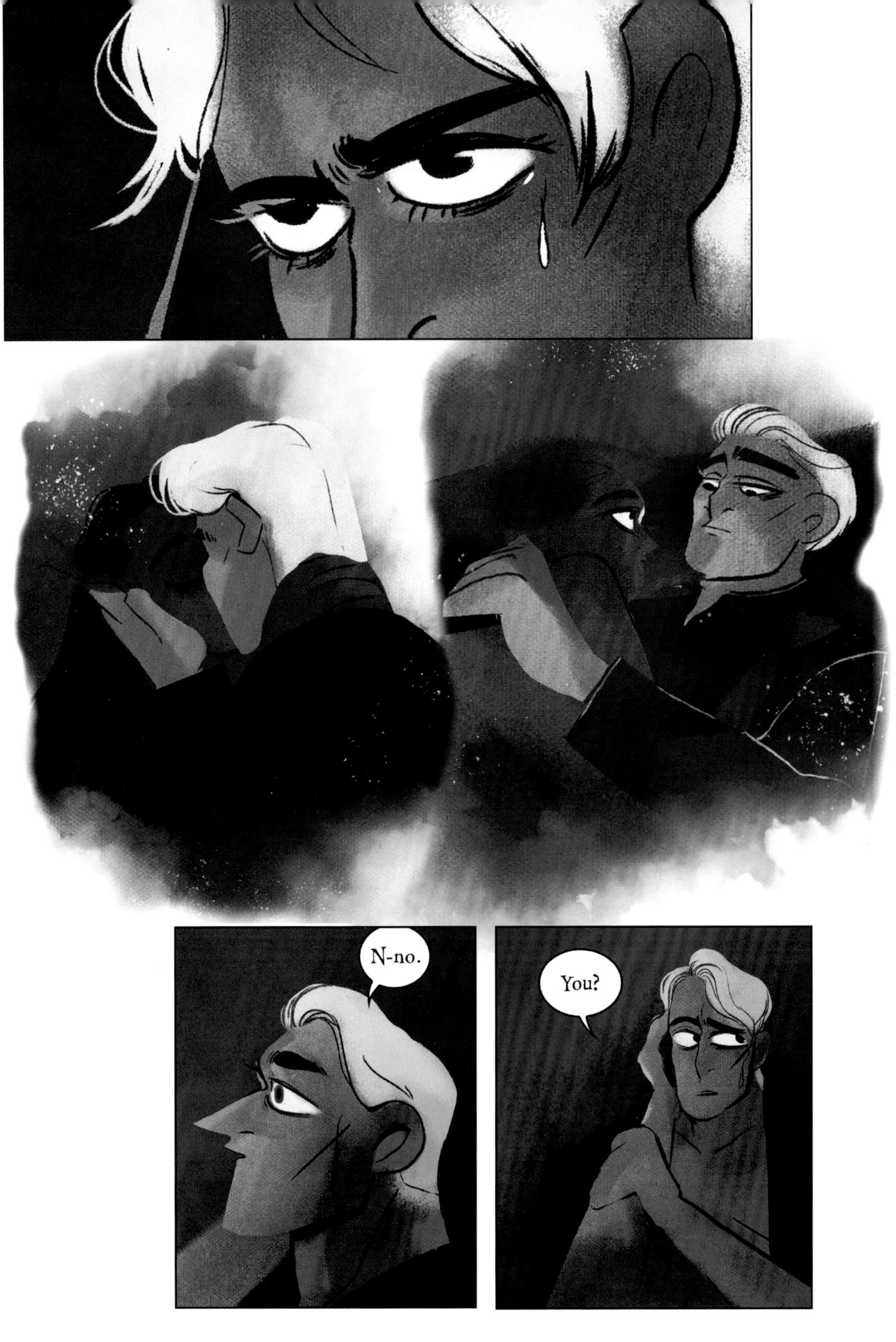
N-no.
You?

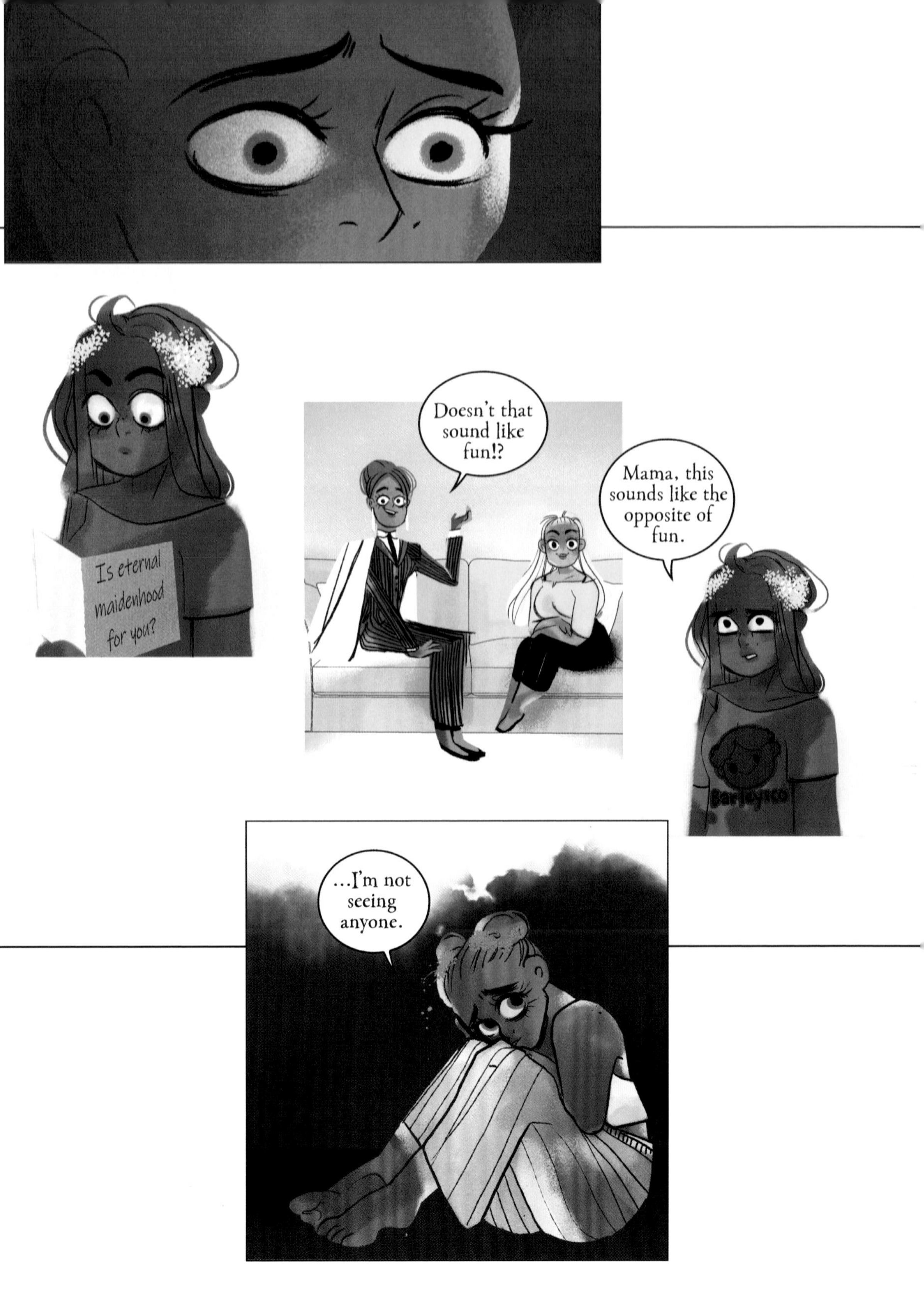
Is eternal maidenhood for you?
Doesn't that sound like fun!?
Mama, this sounds like the opposite of fun.
Barley&Co
...I'm not seeing anyone.

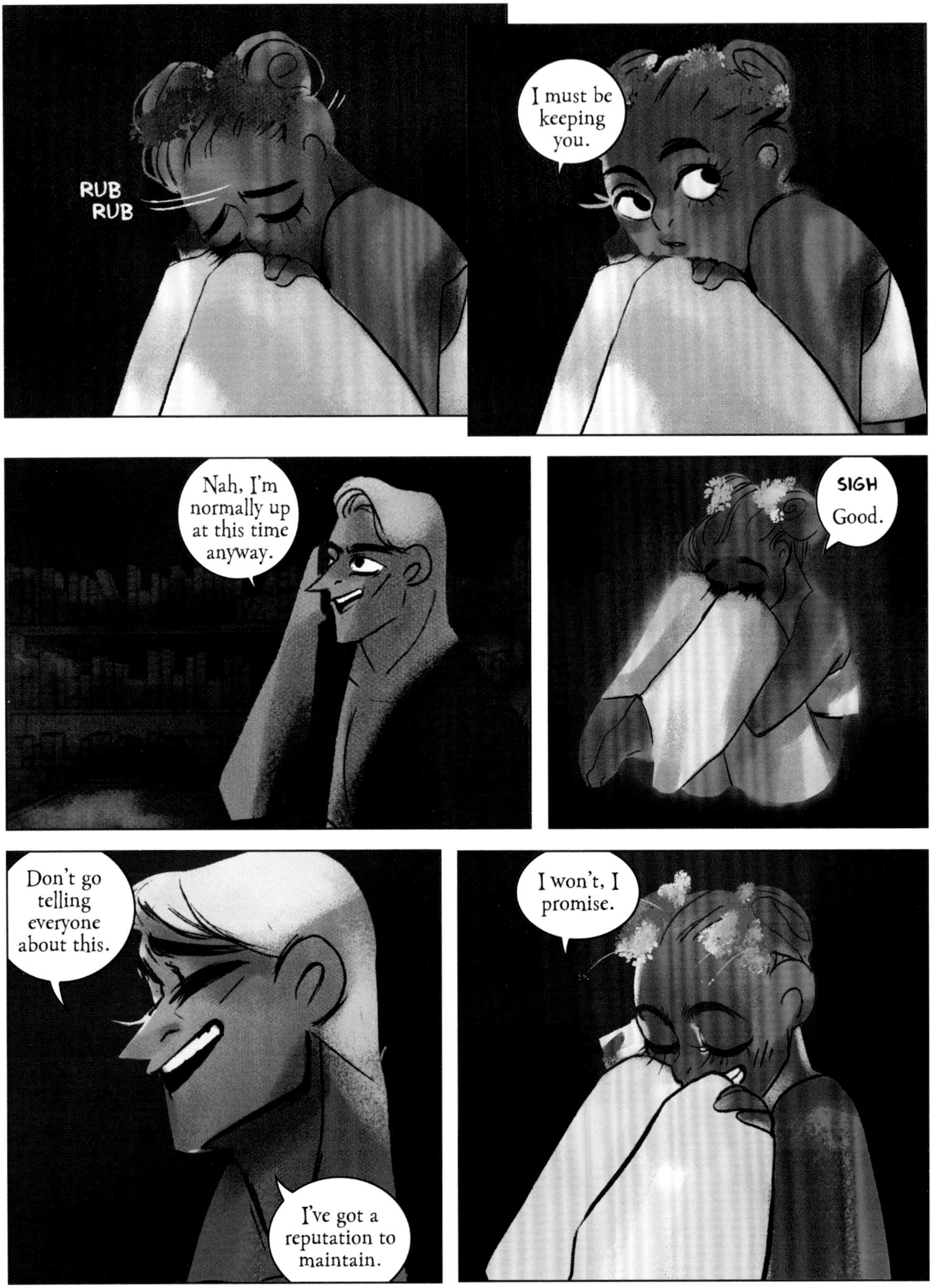
RUB RUB
I must be keeping you.
Nah, I'm normally up at this time anyway.
SIGH
Good.
Don't go telling everyone about this.
I've got a reputation to maintain.
I won't, I promise.

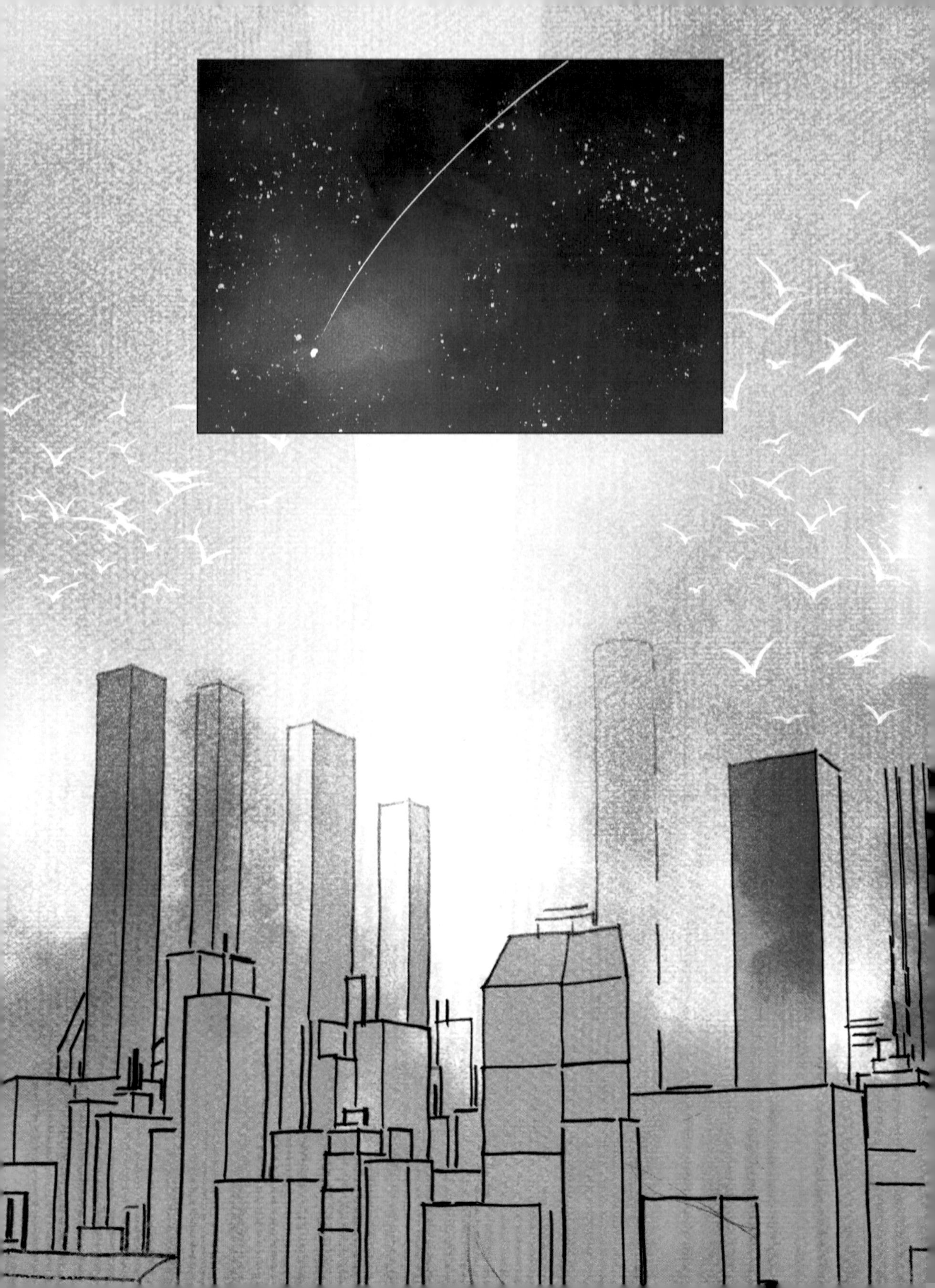

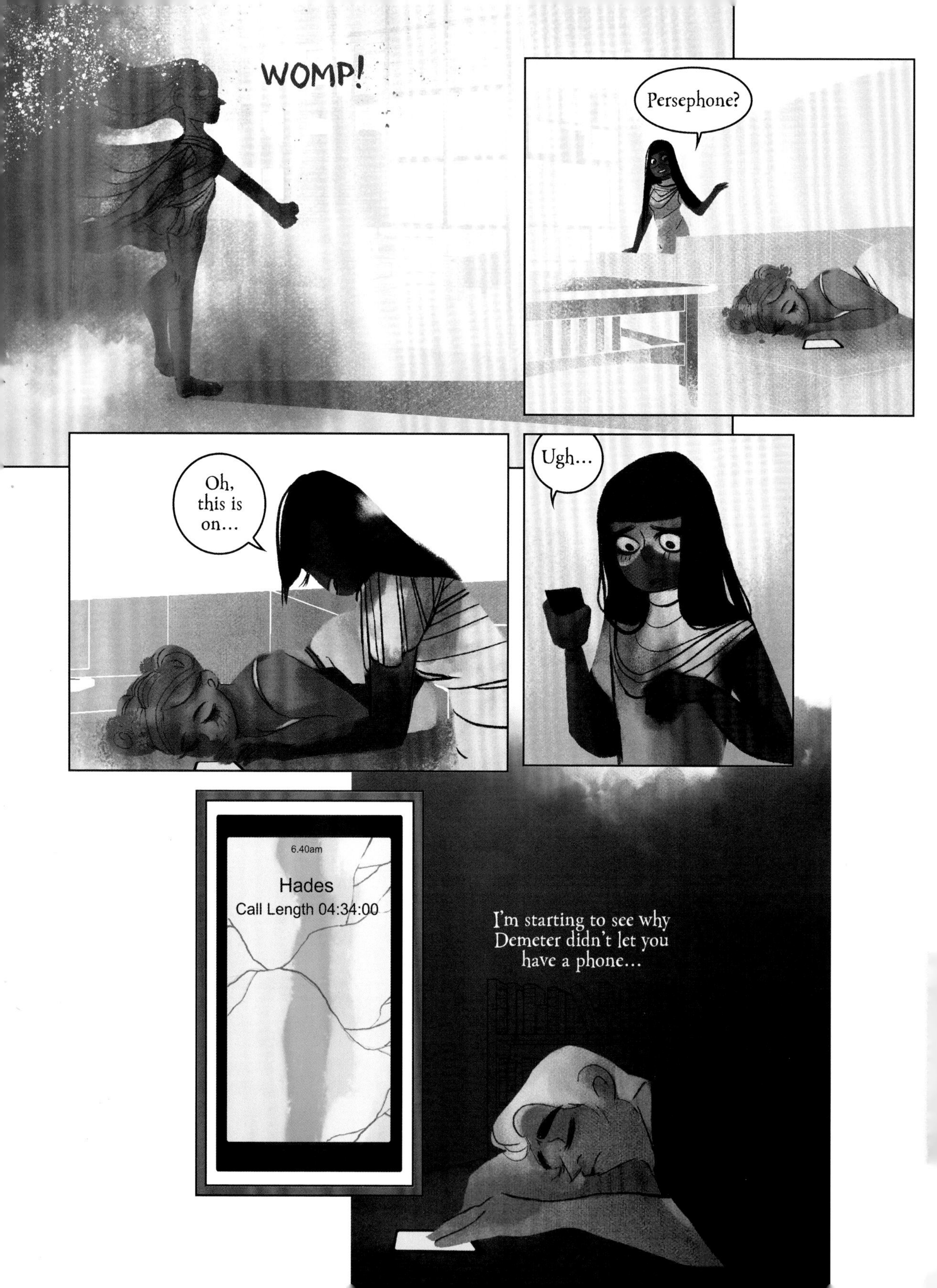
WOMP!
Persephone?
Oh, this is on...
Ugh...
6.40am
Hades
Call Length 04:34:00
I'm starting to see why Demeter didn't let you have a phone...

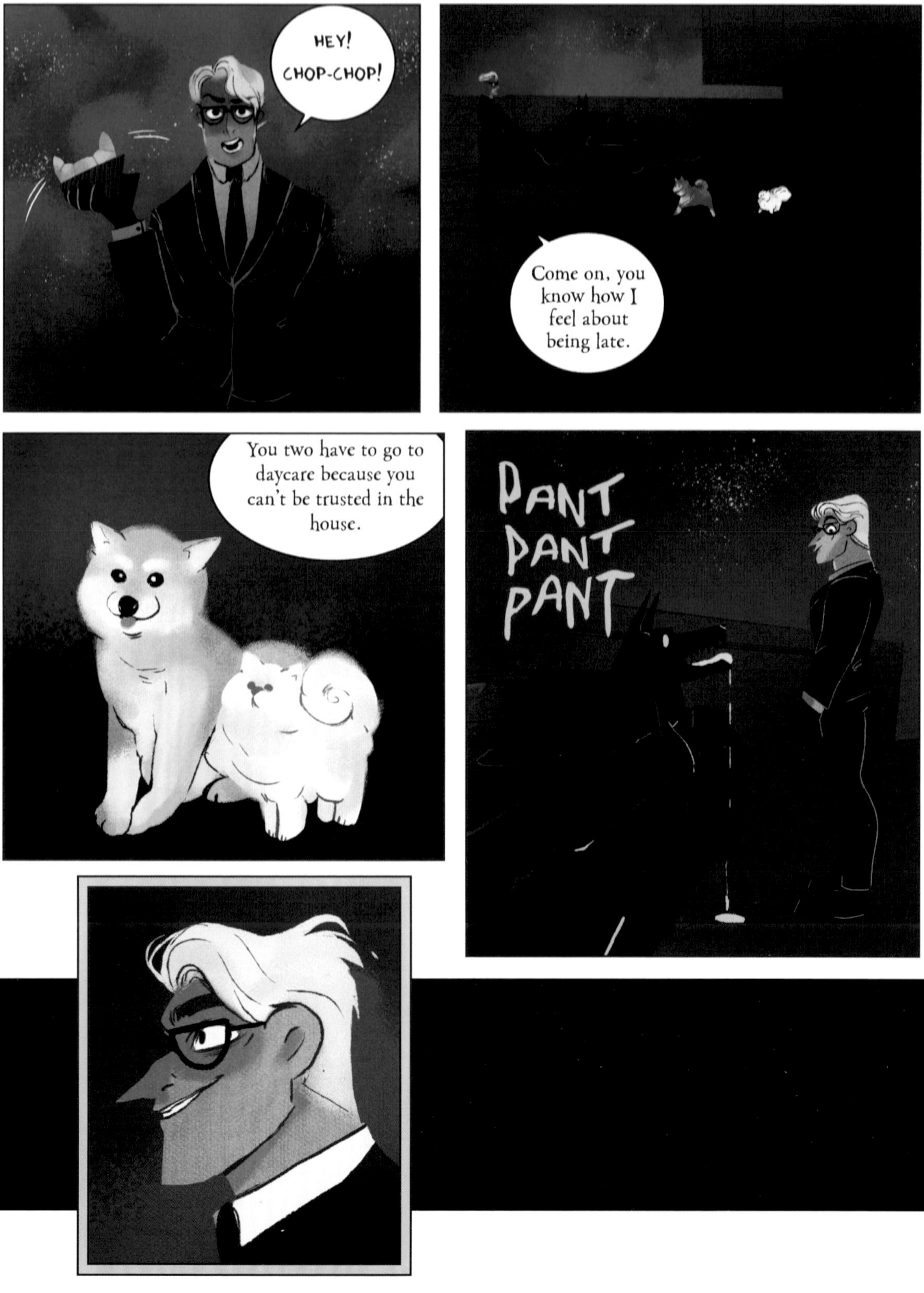
HEY! CHOP-CHOP!
Come on, you know how I feel about being late.
You two have to go to daycare because you can't be trusted in the house.
PANT PANT PANT

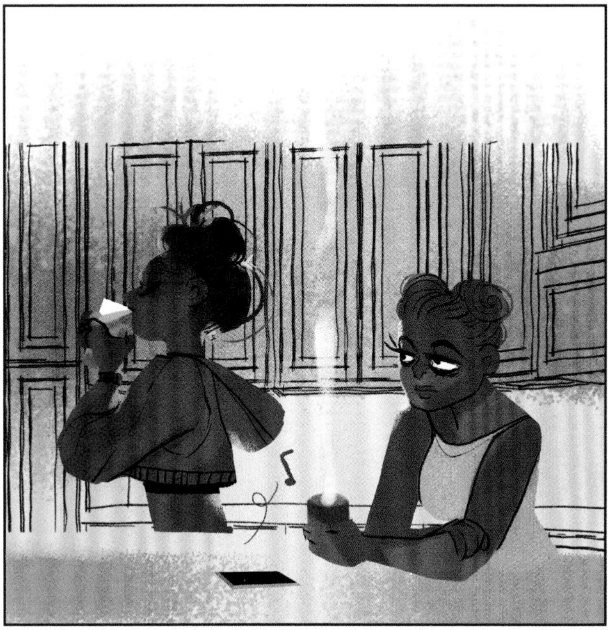

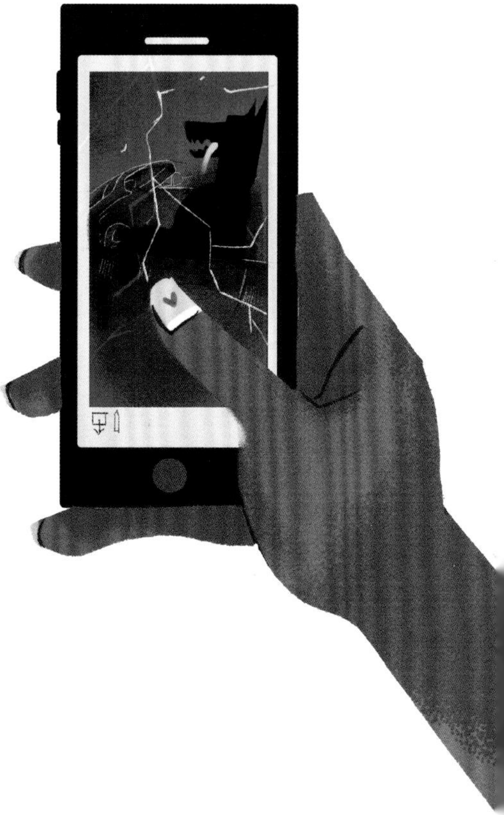

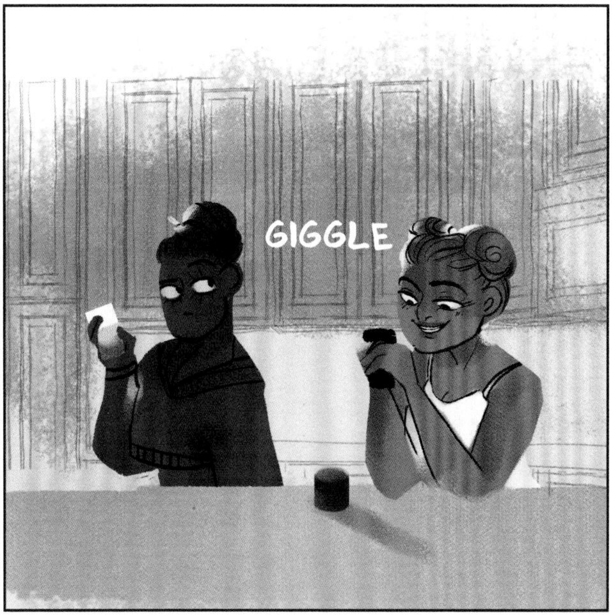
GIGGLE

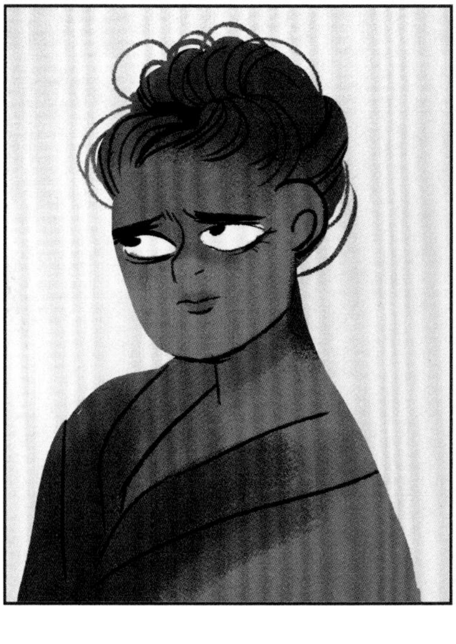

EPISODE 29: THUNDER

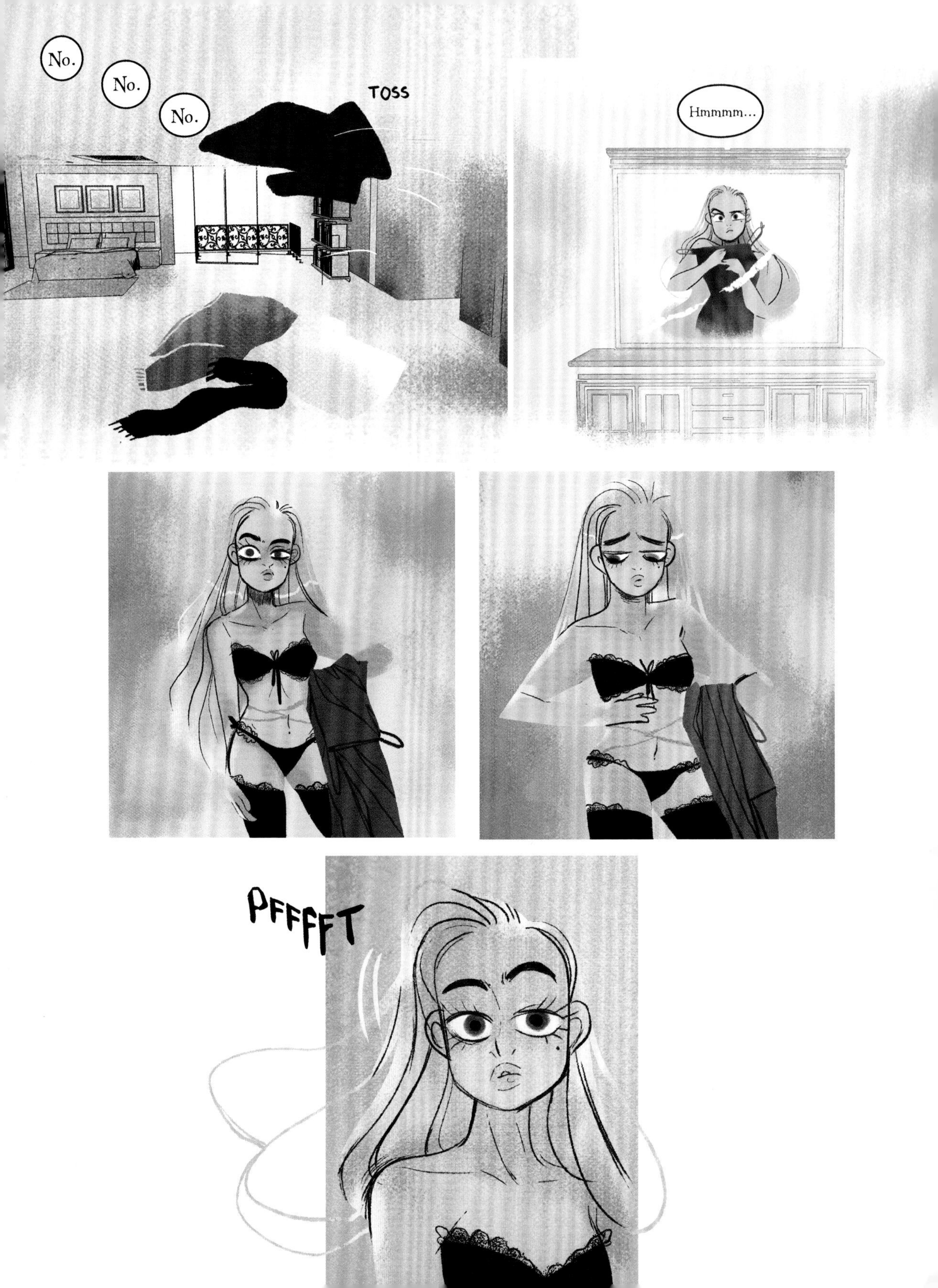
No.
No.
No.
TOSS
Hmmmm...
PFFFFT

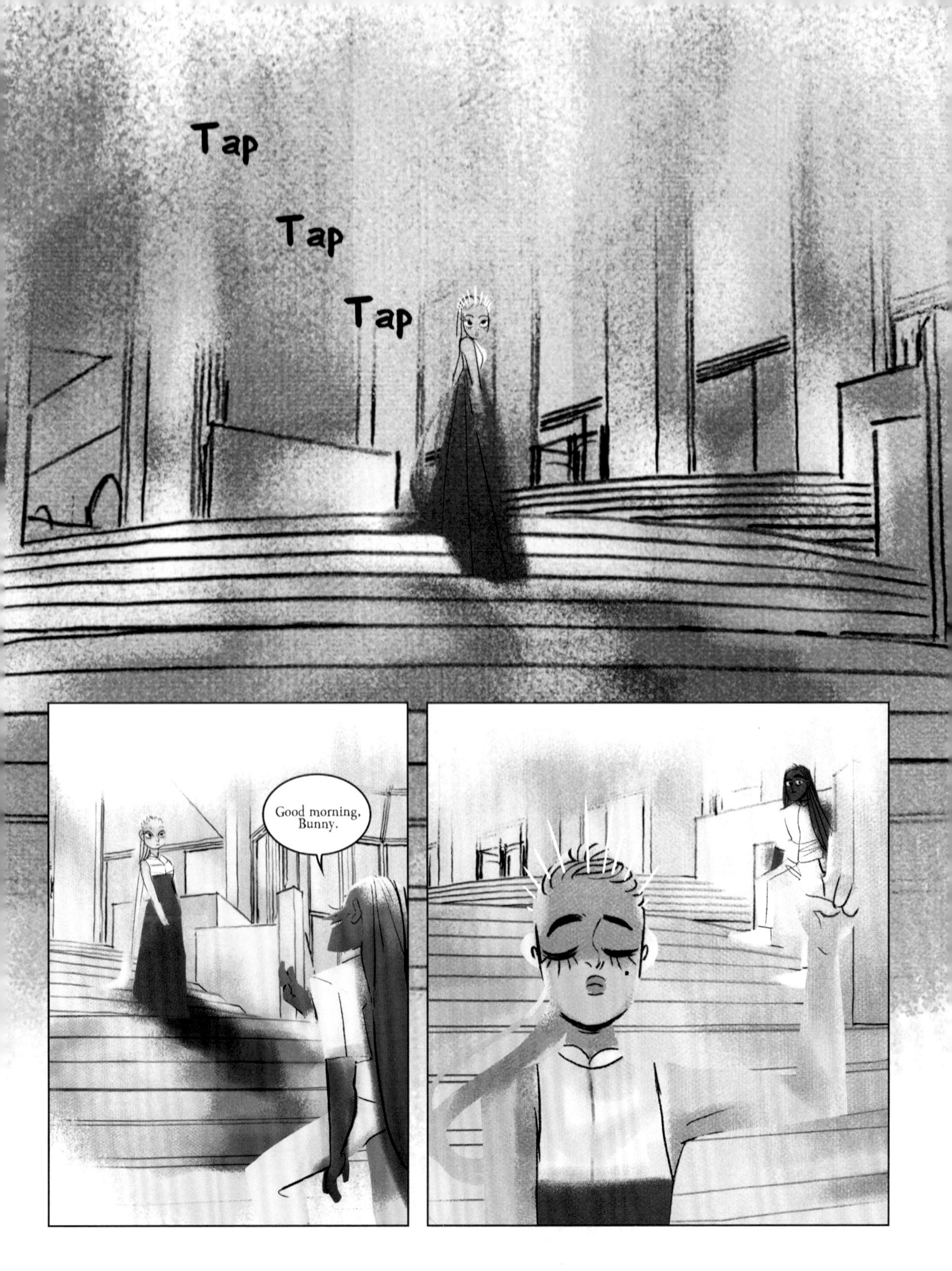
Tap
Tap
Tap
Good morning, Bunny.

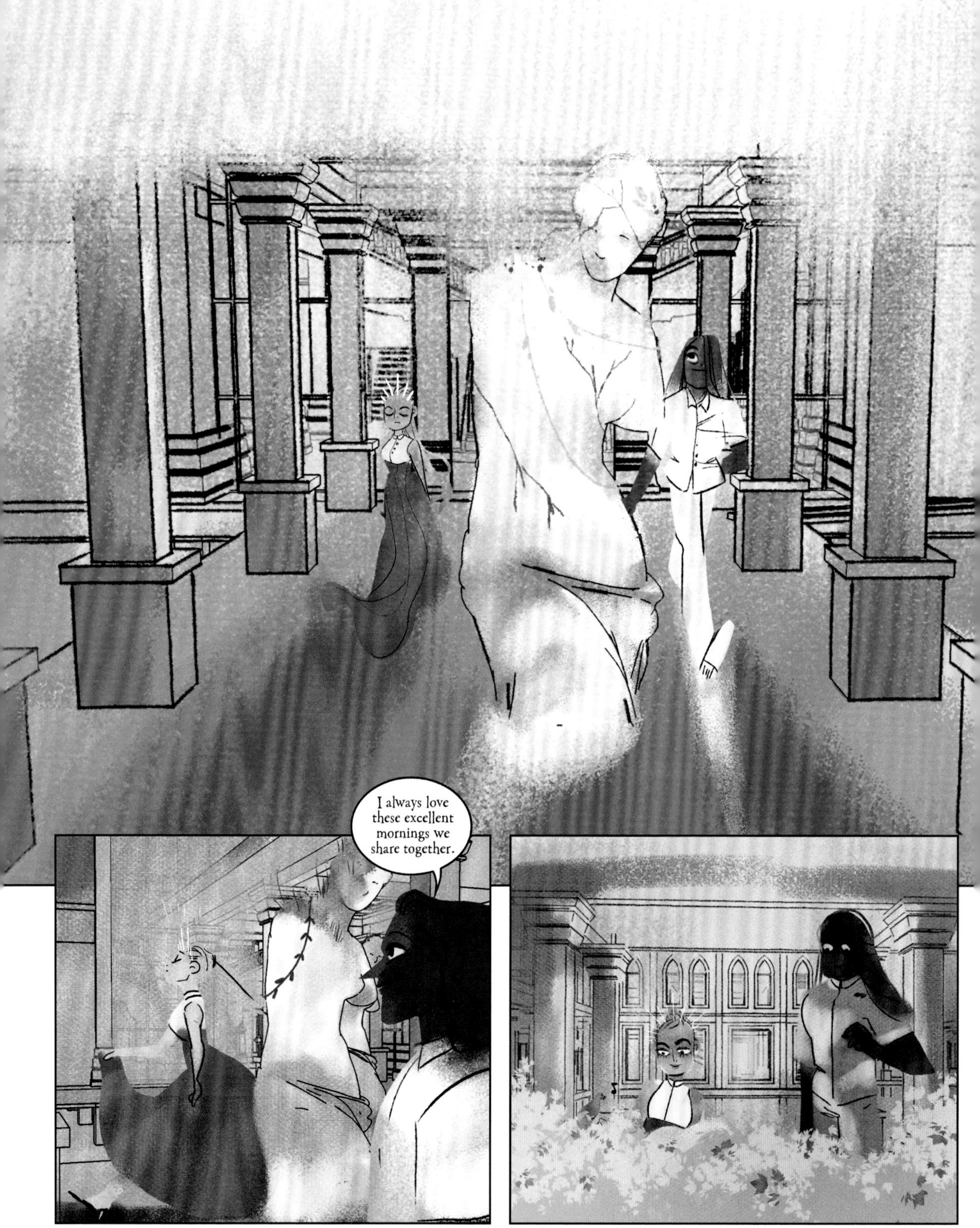
I always love these excellent mornings we share together.

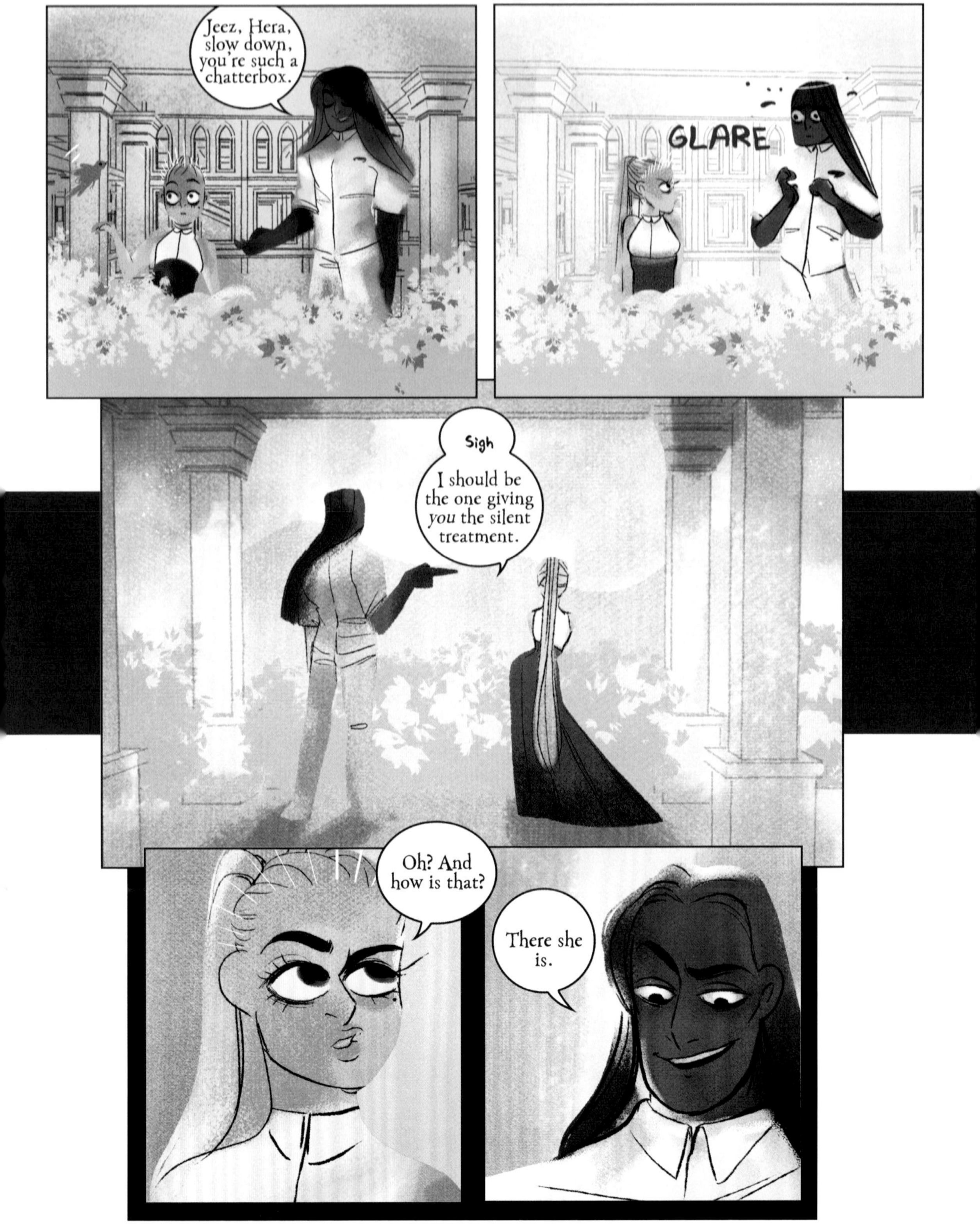
Jeez, Hera, slow down, you're such a chatterbox.
GLARE
Sigh
I should be the one giving *you* the silent treatment.
Oh? And how is that?
There she is.

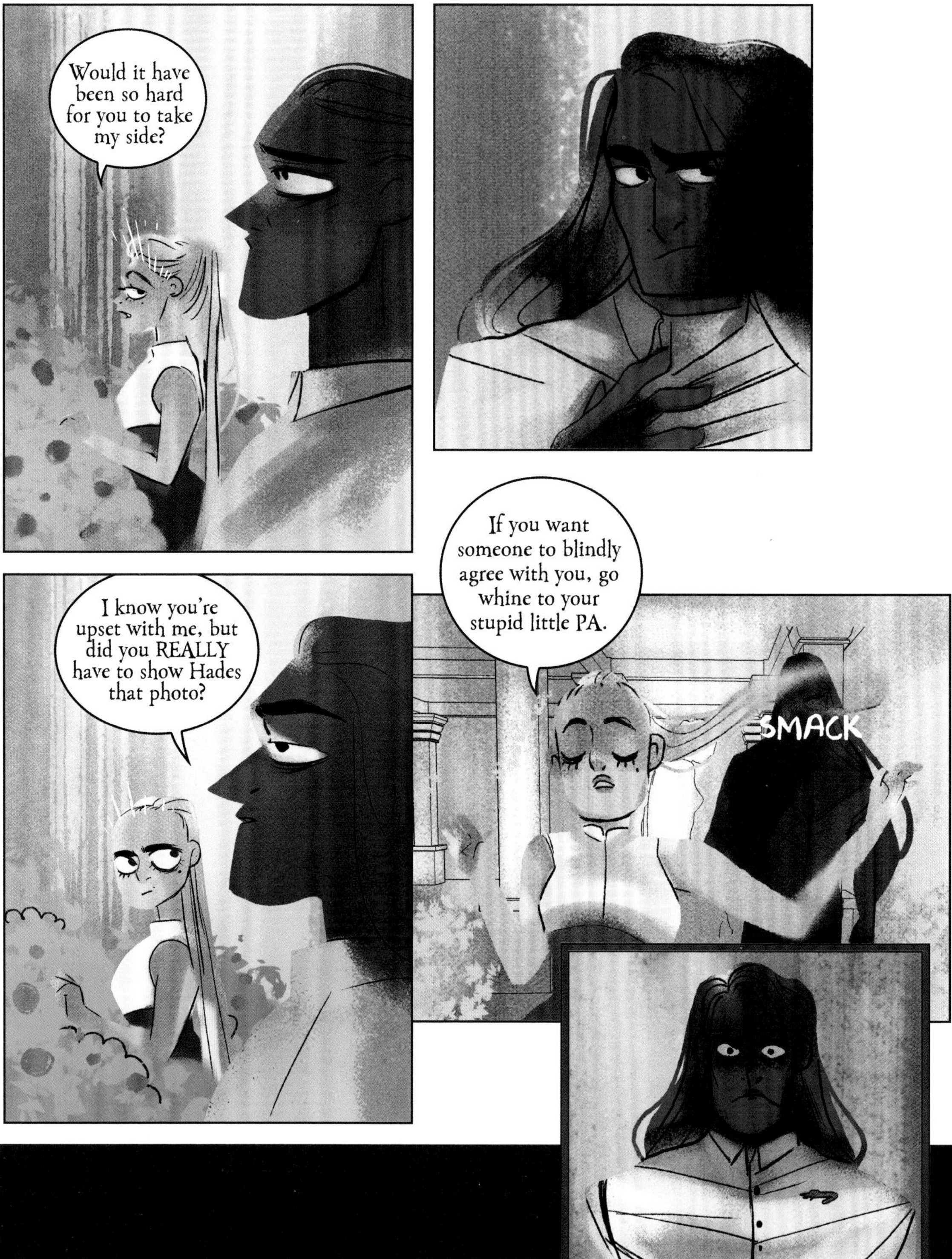
Would it have been so hard for you to take my side?
I know you're upset with me, but did you REALLY have to show Hades that photo?
If you want someone to blindly agree with you, go whine to your stupid little PA.
SMACK

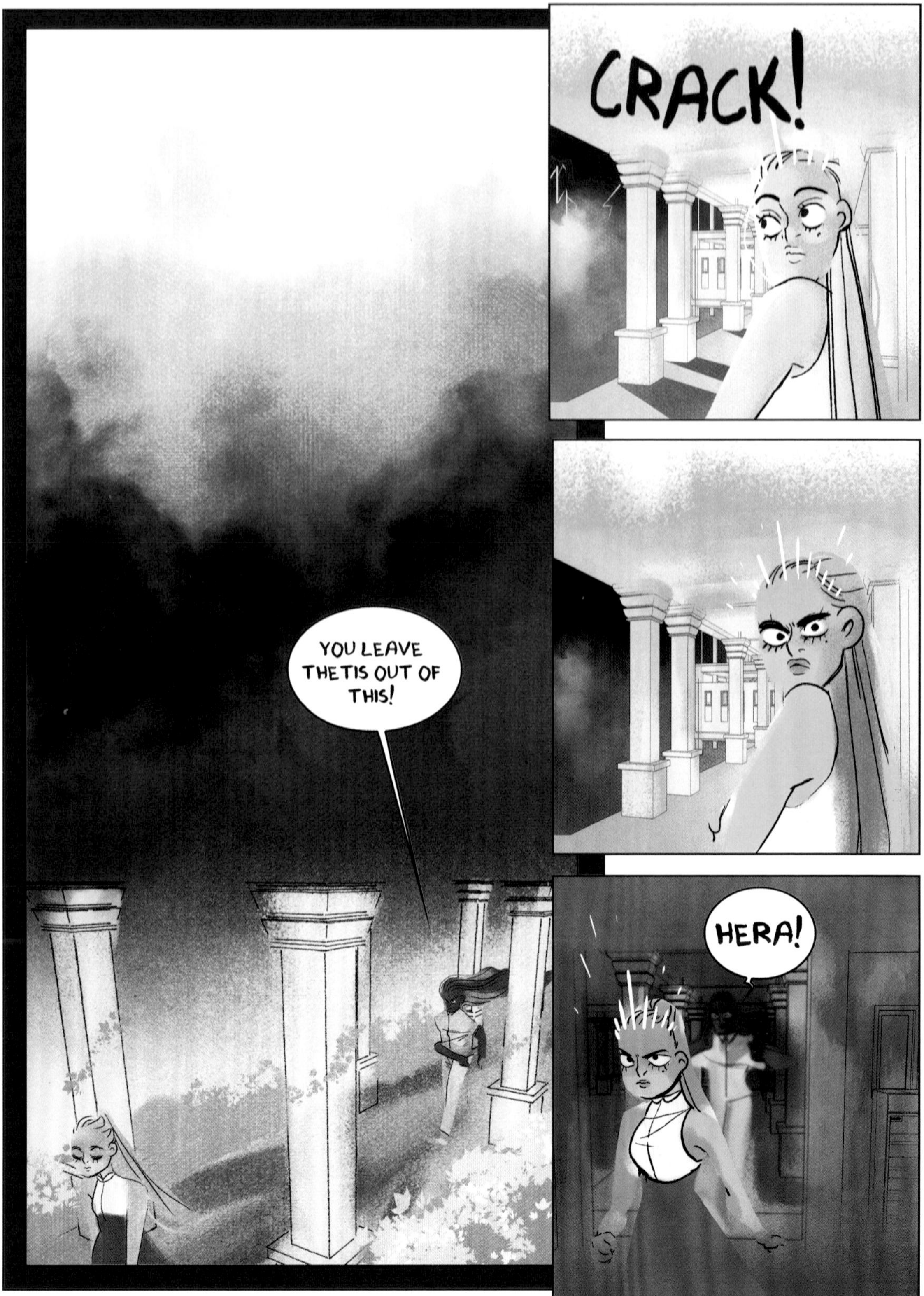
YOU LEAVE THETIS OUT OF THIS!
CRACK!
HERA!

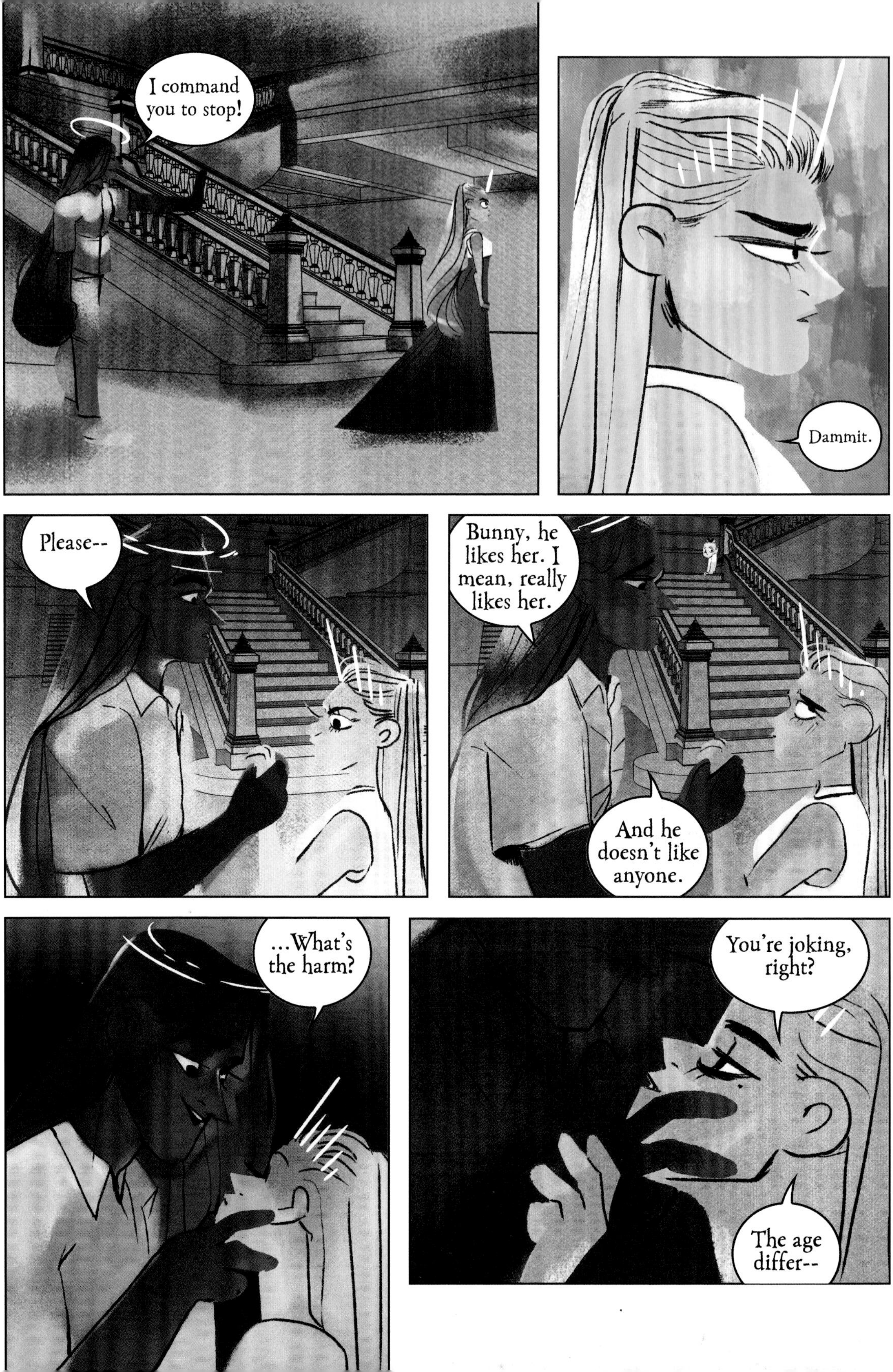
I command you to stop!
Dammit.
Please--
Bunny, he likes her. I mean, really likes her.
And he doesn't like anyone.
...What's the harm?
You're joking, right?
The age differ--

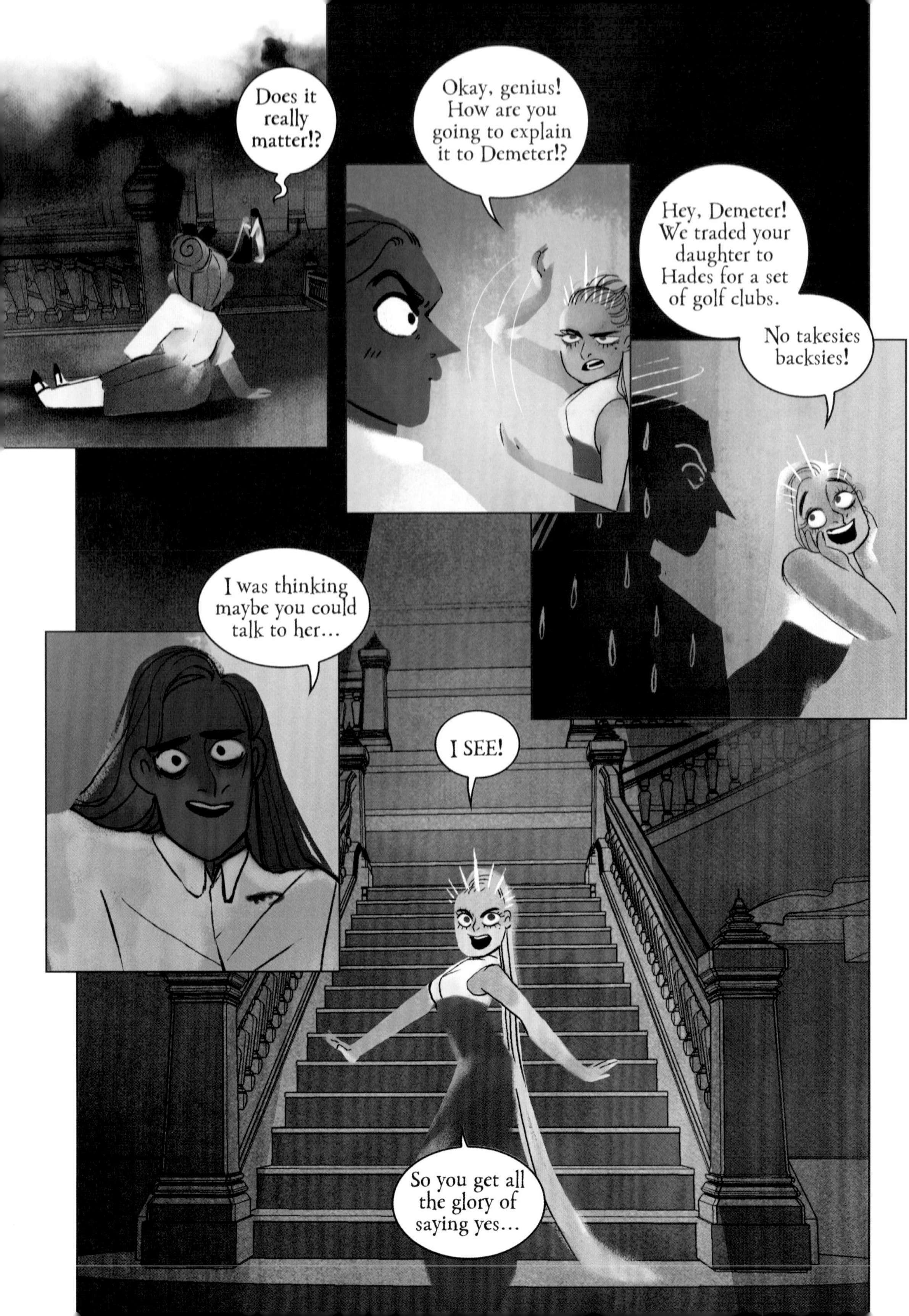
Does it really matter!?
Okay, genius! How are you going to explain it to Demeter!?
Hey, Demeter! We traded your daughter to Hades for a set of golf clubs.
No takesies backsies!
I was thinking maybe you could talk to her...
I SEE!
So you get all the glory of saying yes...

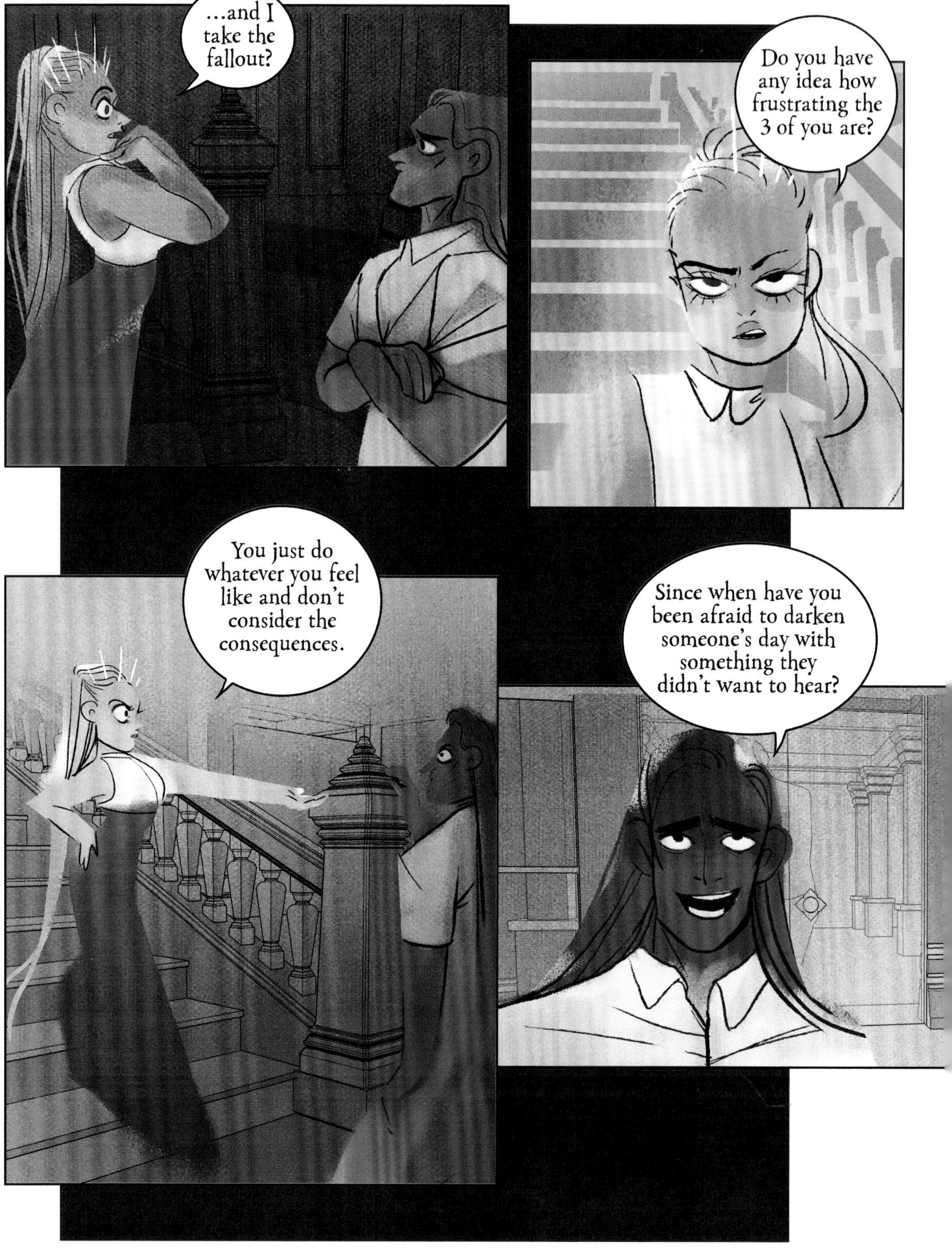
...and I take the fallout?
Do you have any idea how frustrating the 3 of you are?
You just do whatever you feel like and don't consider the consequences.
Since when have you been afraid to darken someone's day with something they didn't want to hear?

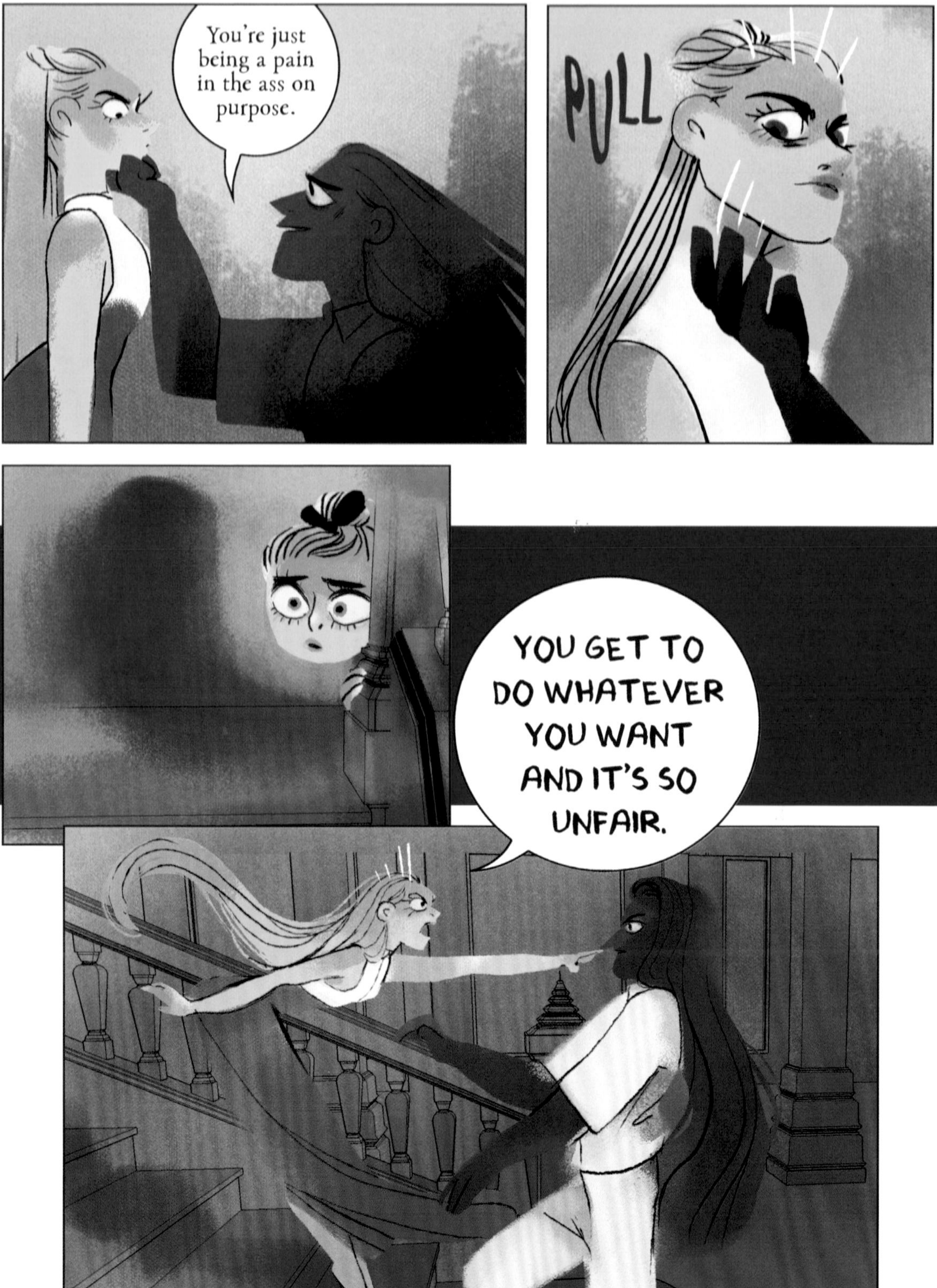
You're just being a pain in the ass on purpose.
PULL
YOU GET TO DO WHATEVER YOU WANT AND IT'S SO UNFAIR.

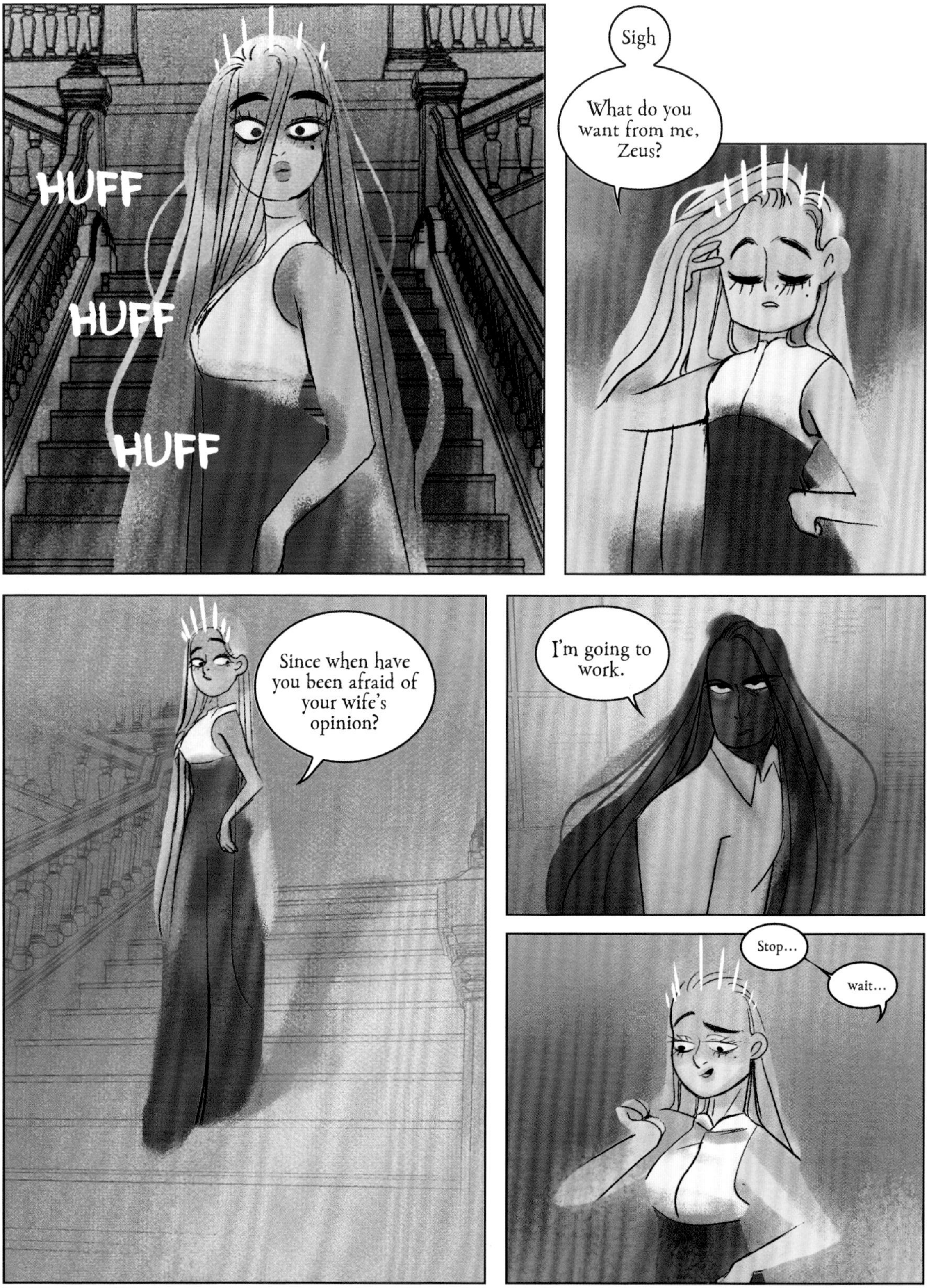
HUFF
HUFF
HUFF
Sigh
What do you want from me, Zeus?
Since when have you been afraid of your wife's opinion?
I'm going to work.
Stop...
wait...

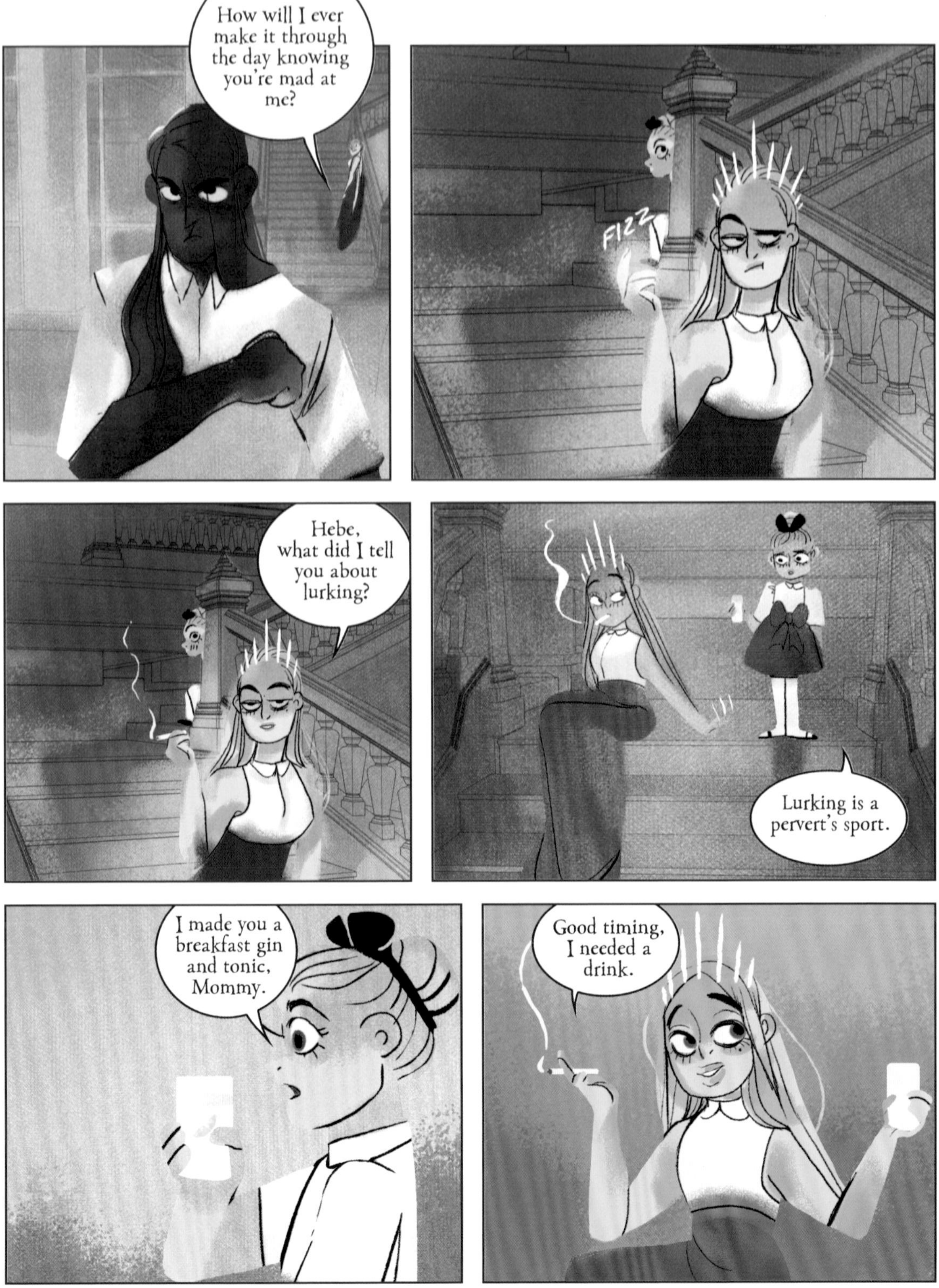
How will I ever make it through the day knowing you're mad at me?
FIZZ
Hebe, what did I tell you about lurking?
Lurking is a pervert's sport.
I made you a breakfast gin and tonic, Mommy.
Good timing, I needed a drink.

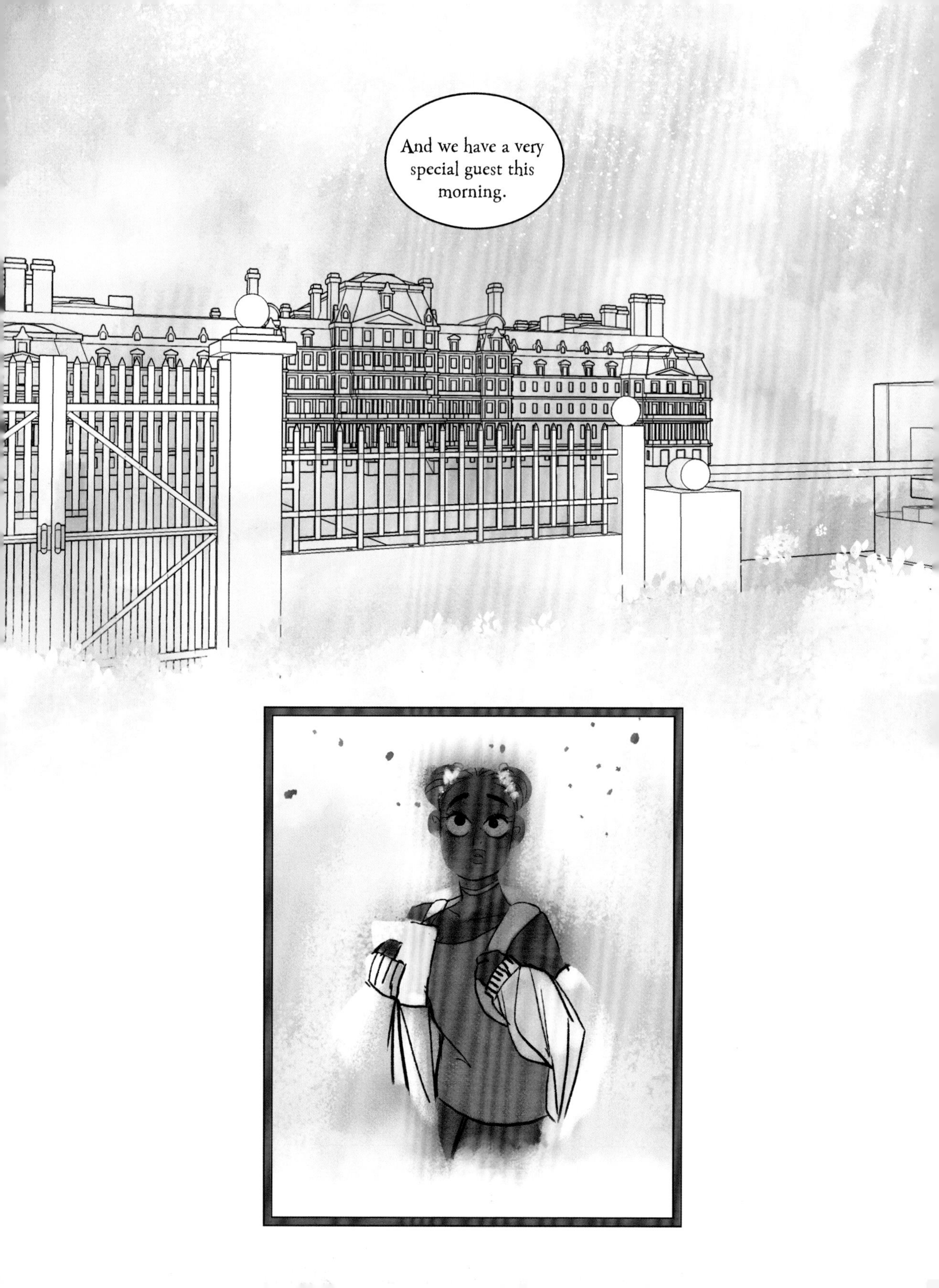
And we have a very special guest this morning.

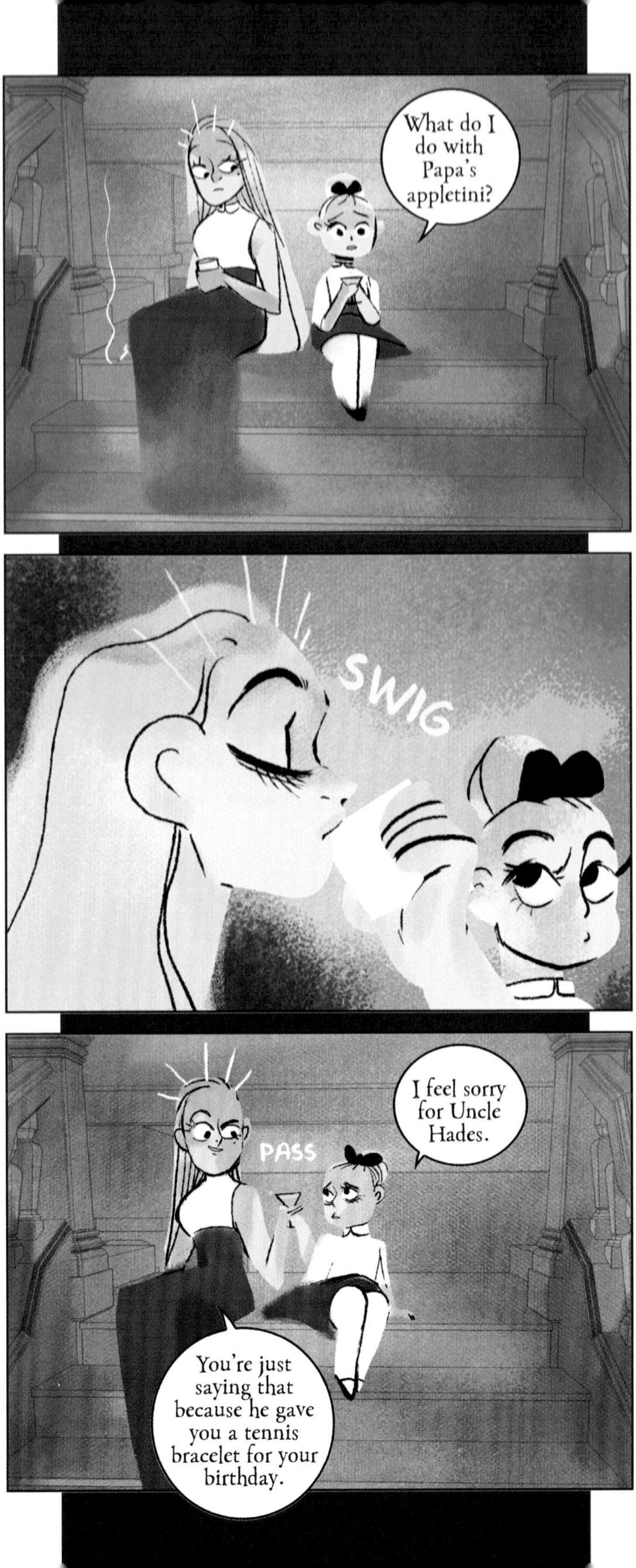

What do I do with Papa's appletini?
SWIG
I feel sorry for Uncle Hades.
PASS
You're just saying that because he gave you a tennis bracelet for your birthday.

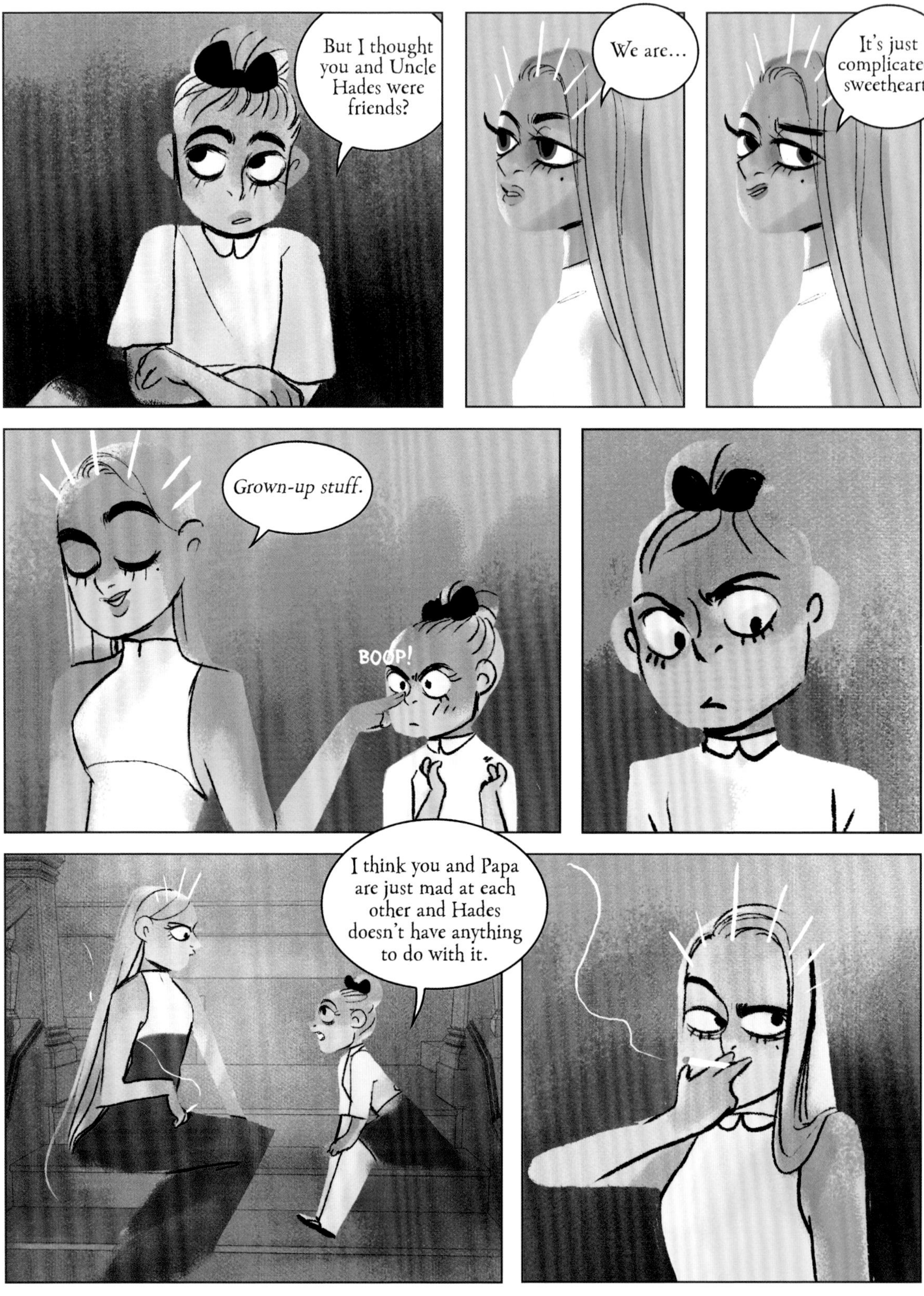
But I thought you and Uncle Hades were friends?
We are...
It's just complicated, sweetheart.
Grown-up stuff.
BOOP!
I think you and Papa are just mad at each other and Hades doesn't have anything to do with it.

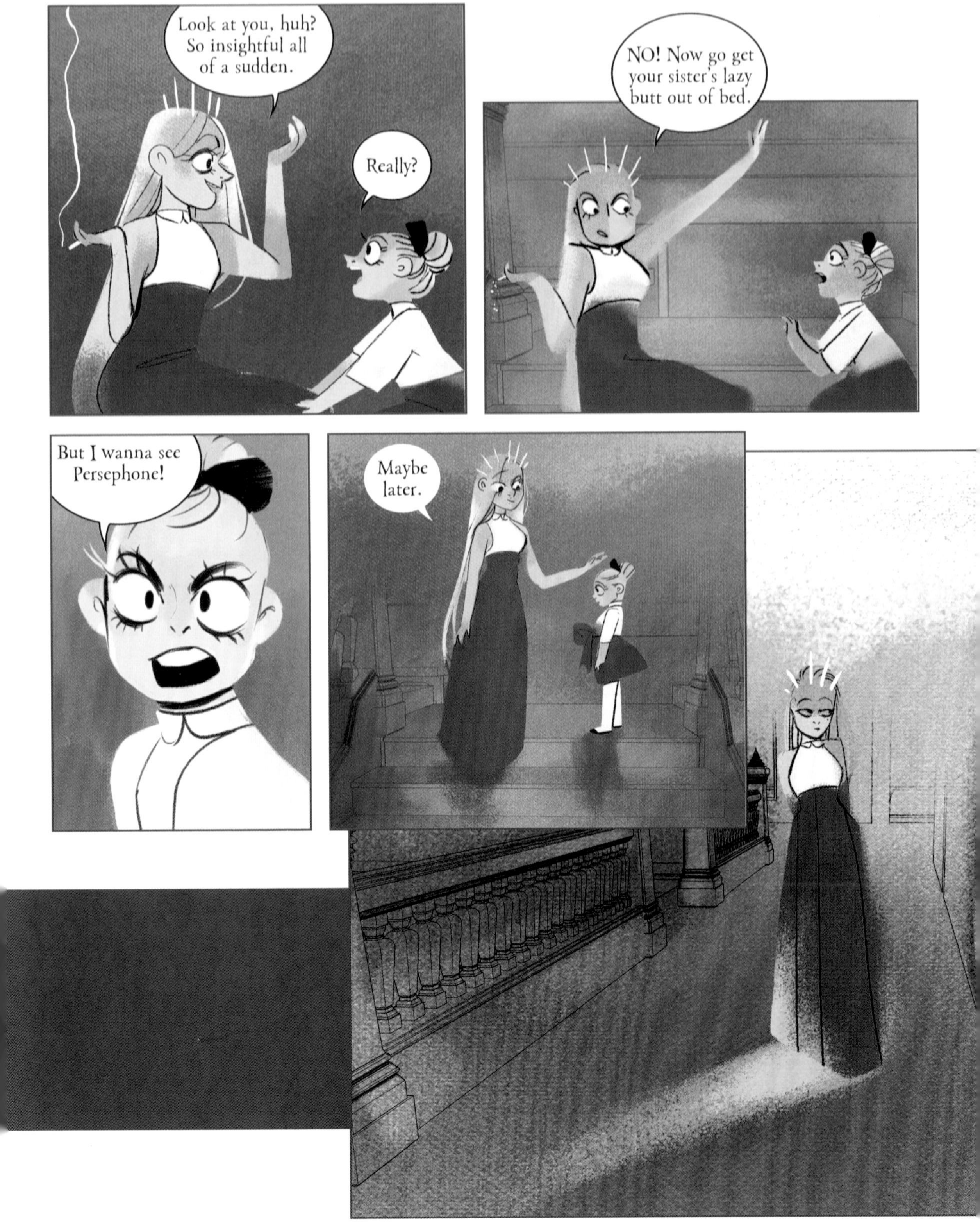
Look at you, huh? So insightful all of a sudden.
Really?
NO! Now go get your sister's lazy butt out of bed.
But I wanna see Persephone!
Maybe later.

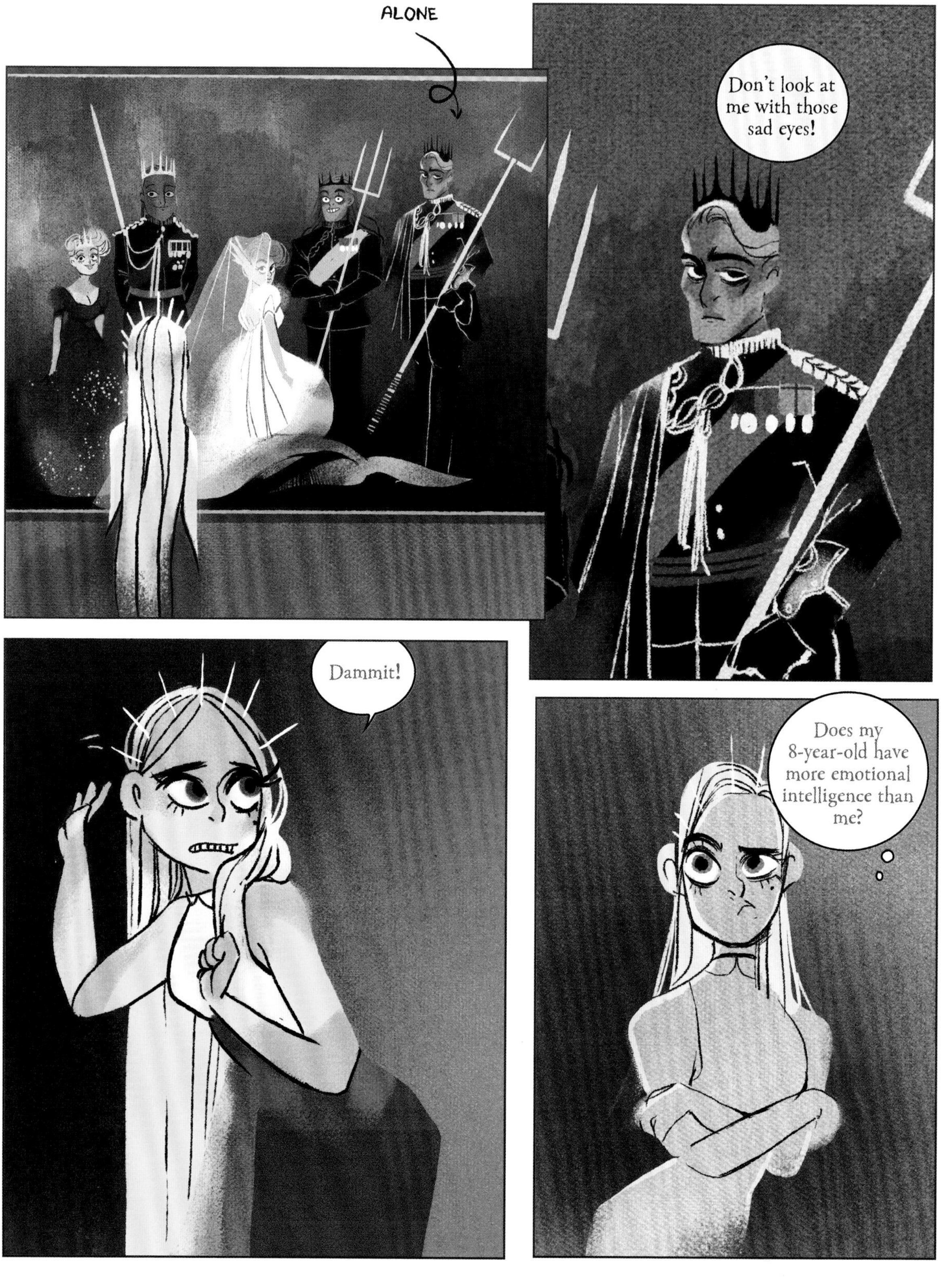
ALONE
Don't look at me with those sad eyes!
Dammit!
Does my 8-year-old have more emotional intelligence than me?

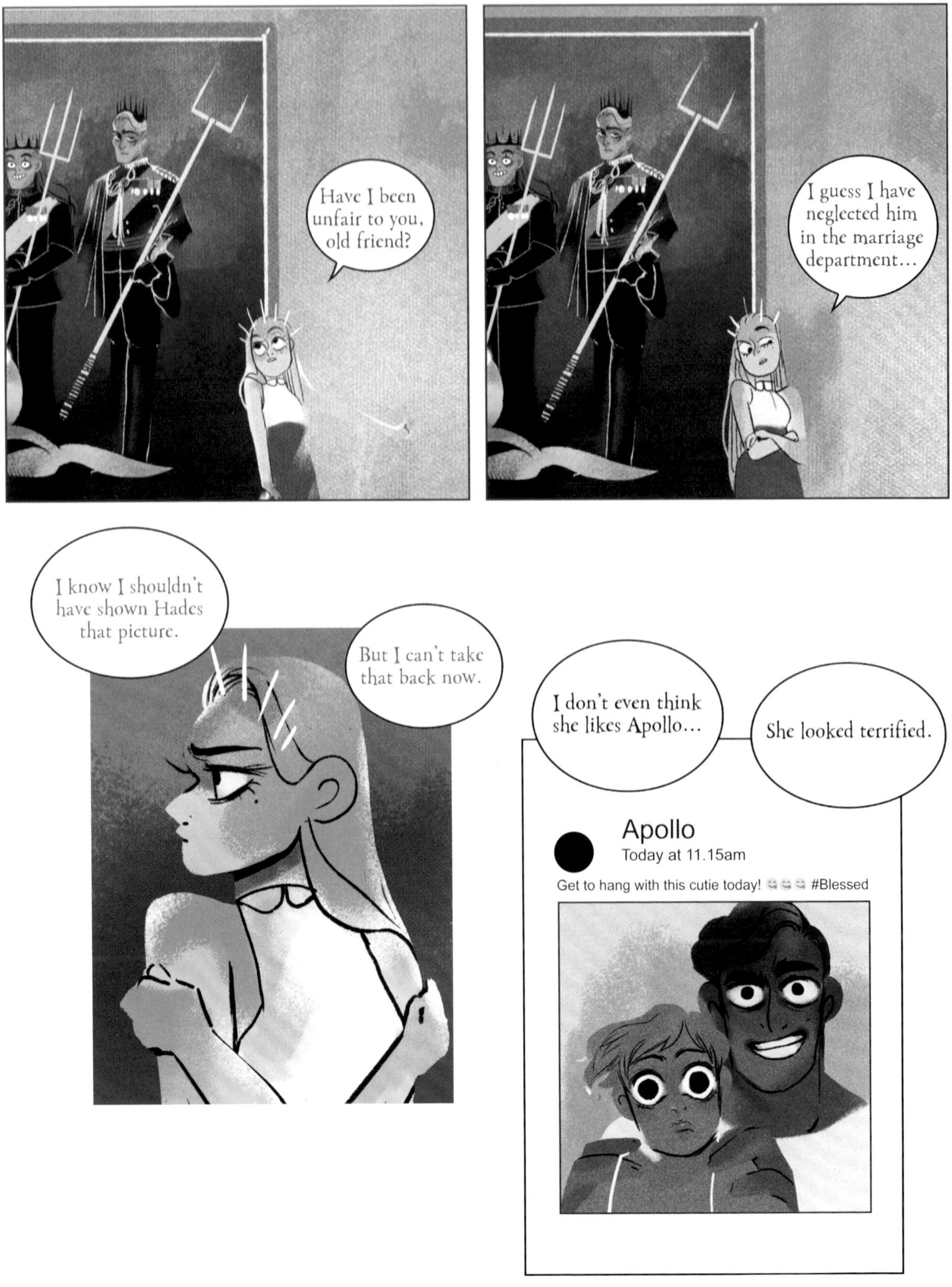

Have I been unfair to you, old friend?
I guess I have neglected him in the marriage department...
I know I shouldn't have shown Hades that picture.
But I can't take that back now.
I don't even think she likes Apollo...
She looked terrified.
Apollo
Today at 11.15am
Get to hang with this cutie today! #Blessed

SILENT PLOTTING

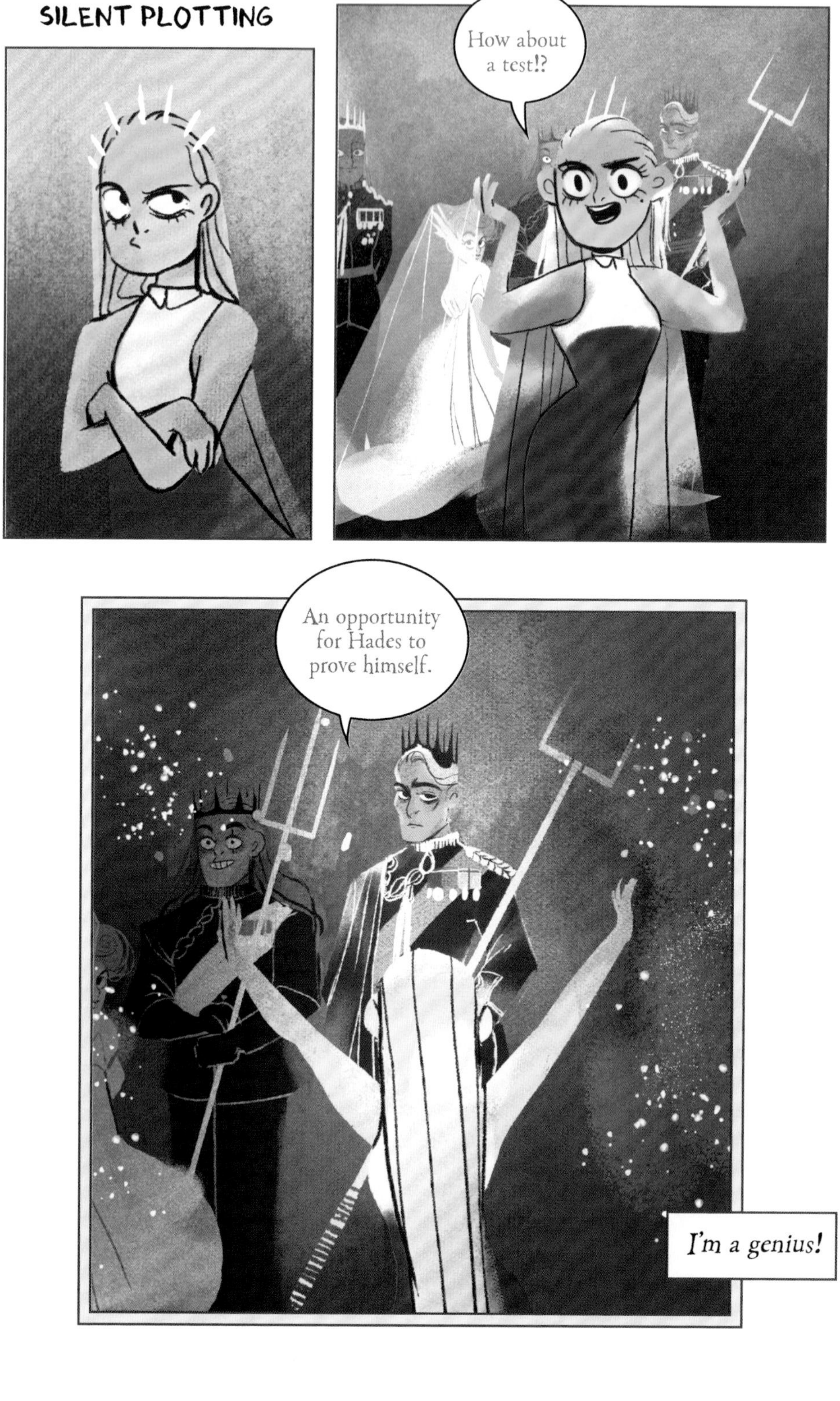
How about a test!?
An opportunity for Hades to prove himself.
I'm a genius!

EPISODE 30: HERA INTERFERES

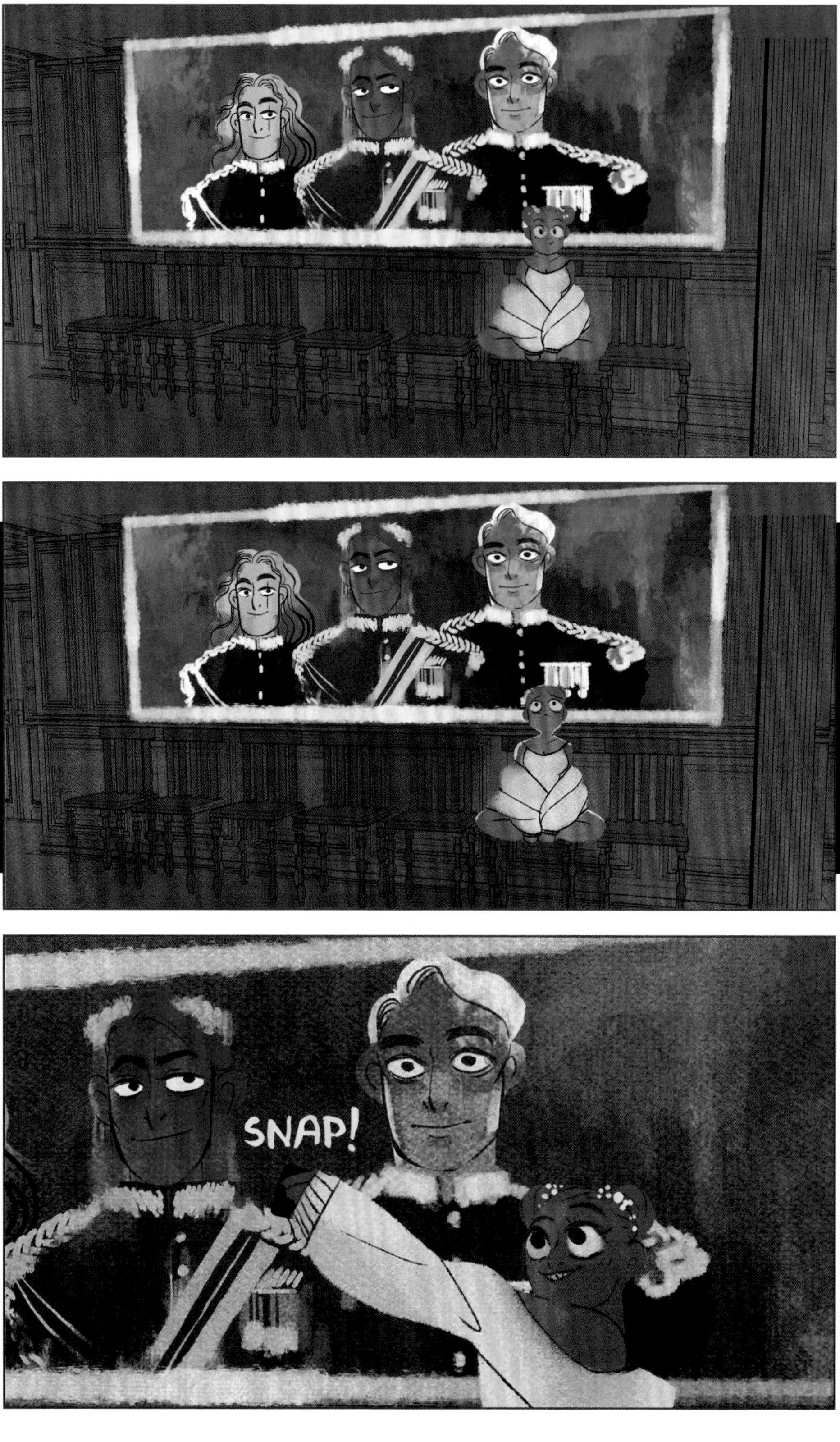
SNAP!

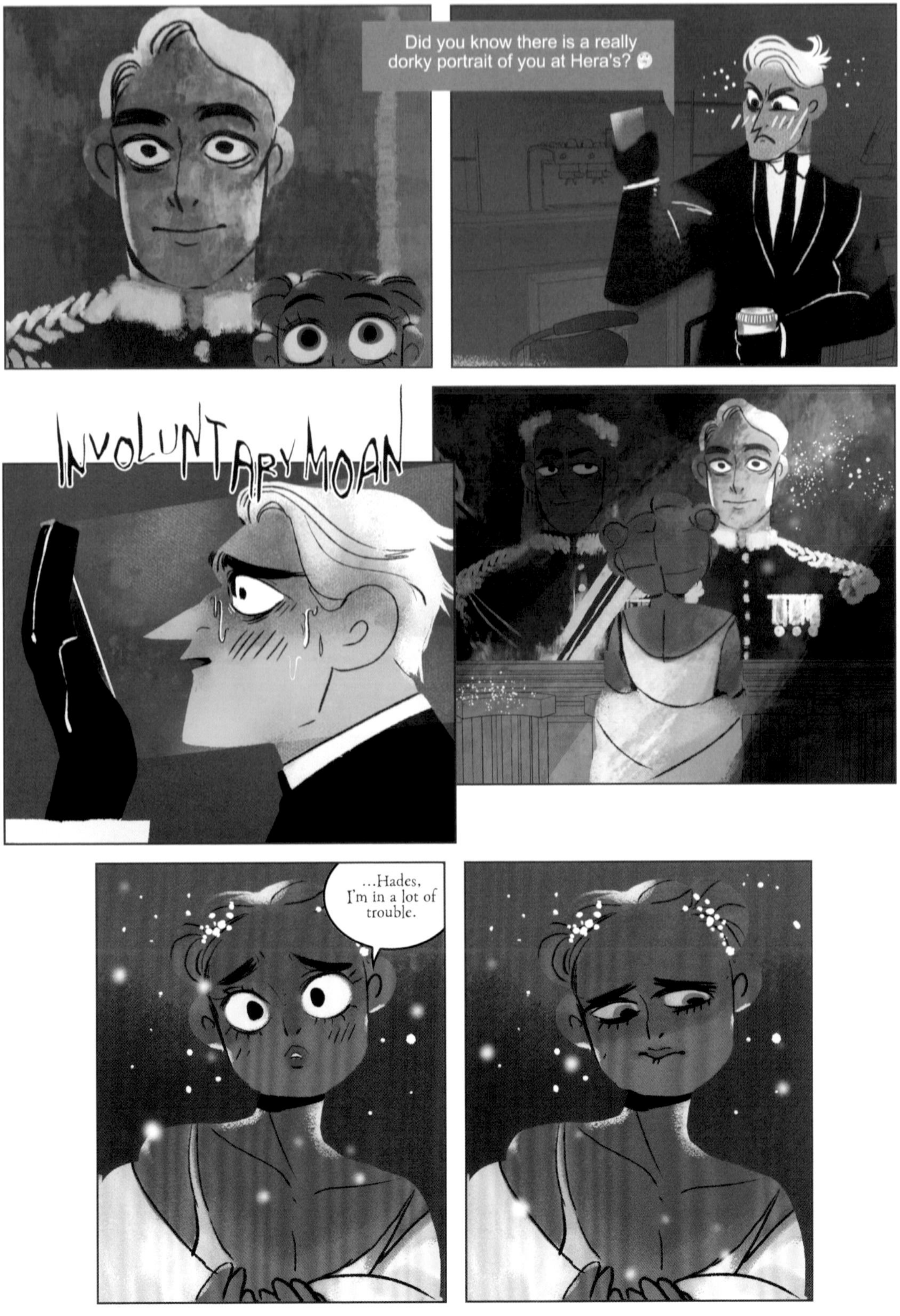
Did you know there is a really dorky portrait of you at Hera's?
INVOLUNTARY MOAN
...Hades, I'm in a lot of trouble.

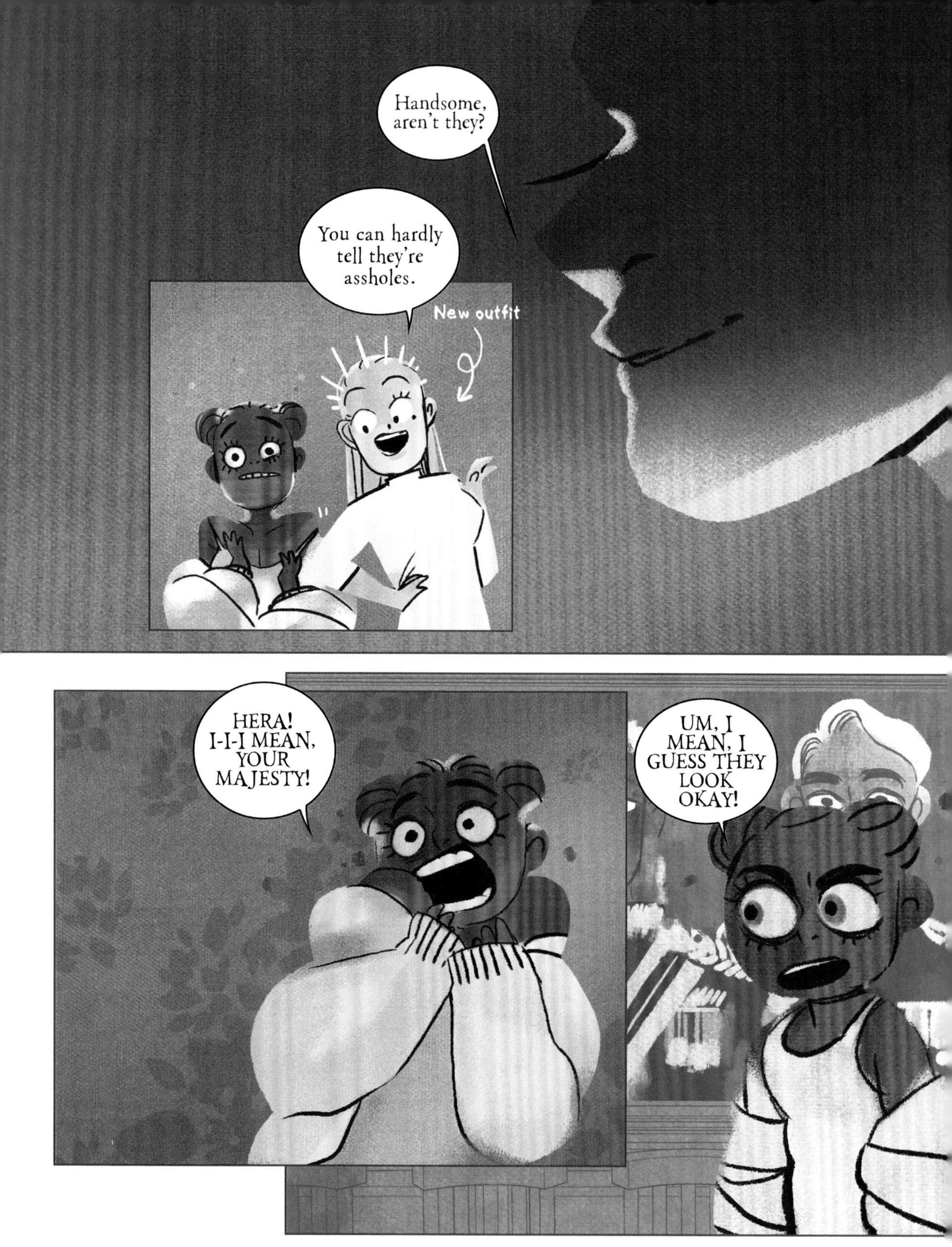

Handsome, aren't they?
You can hardly tell they're assholes.
New outfit
HERA! I-I-I MEAN, YOUR MAJESTY!
UM, I MEAN, I GUESS THEY LOOK OKAY!

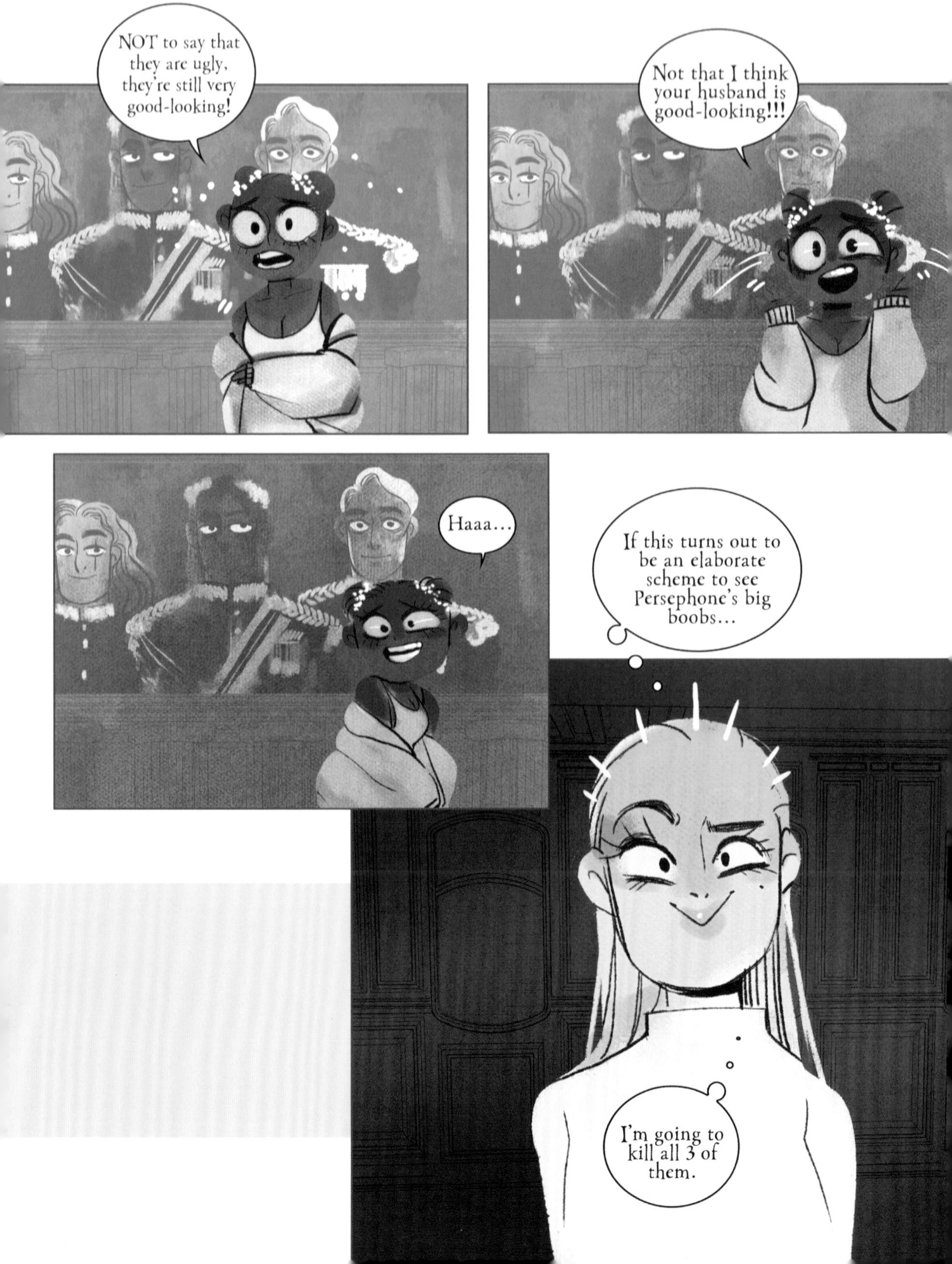
NOT to say that they are ugly, they're still very good-looking!
Not that I think your husband is good-looking!!!
Haaa...
If this turns out to be an elaborate scheme to see Persephone's big boobs...
I'm going to kill all 3 of them.

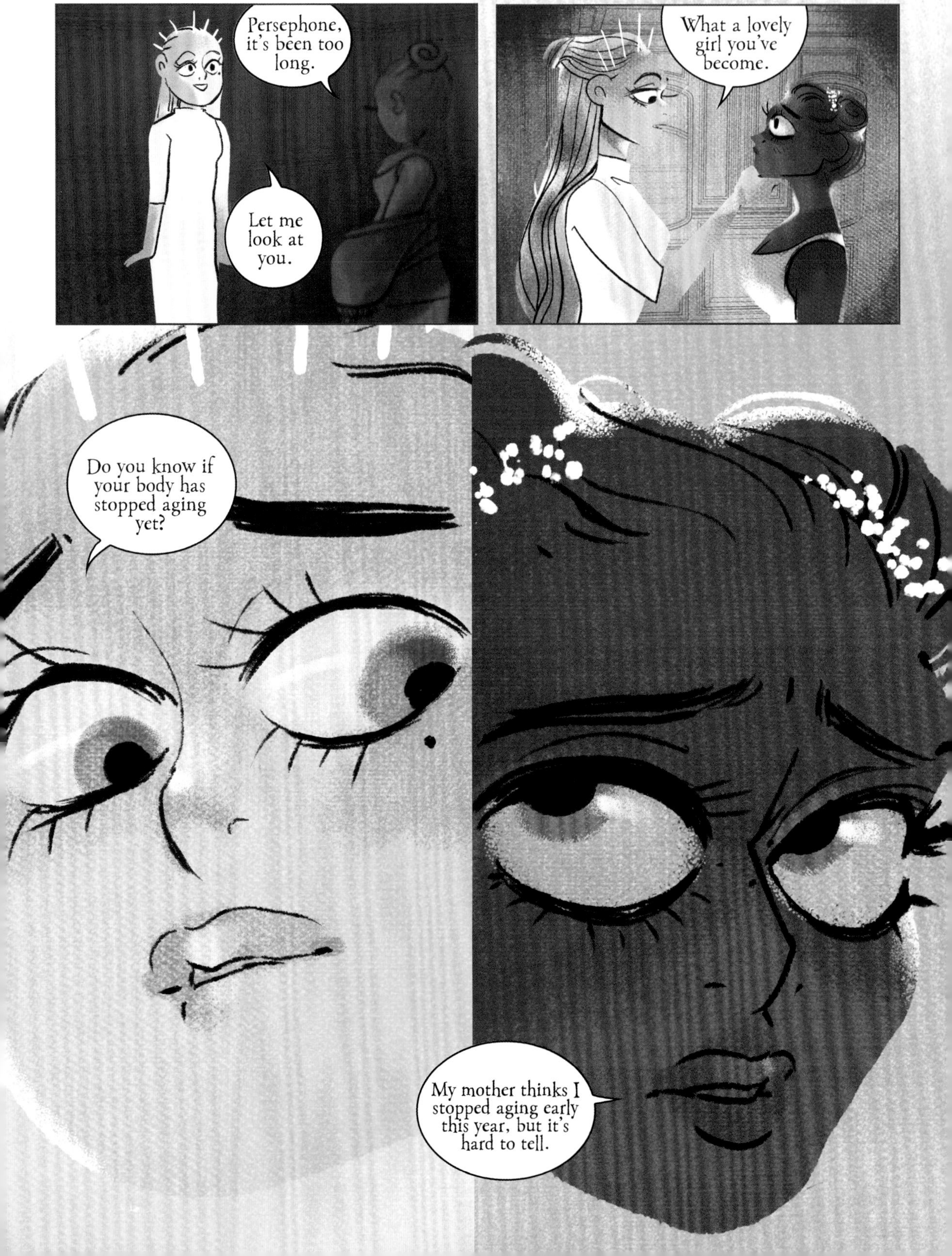
Persephone, it's been too long.
Let me look at you.
What a lovely girl you've become.
Do you know if your body has stopped aging yet?
My mother thinks I stopped aging early this year, but it's hard to tell.

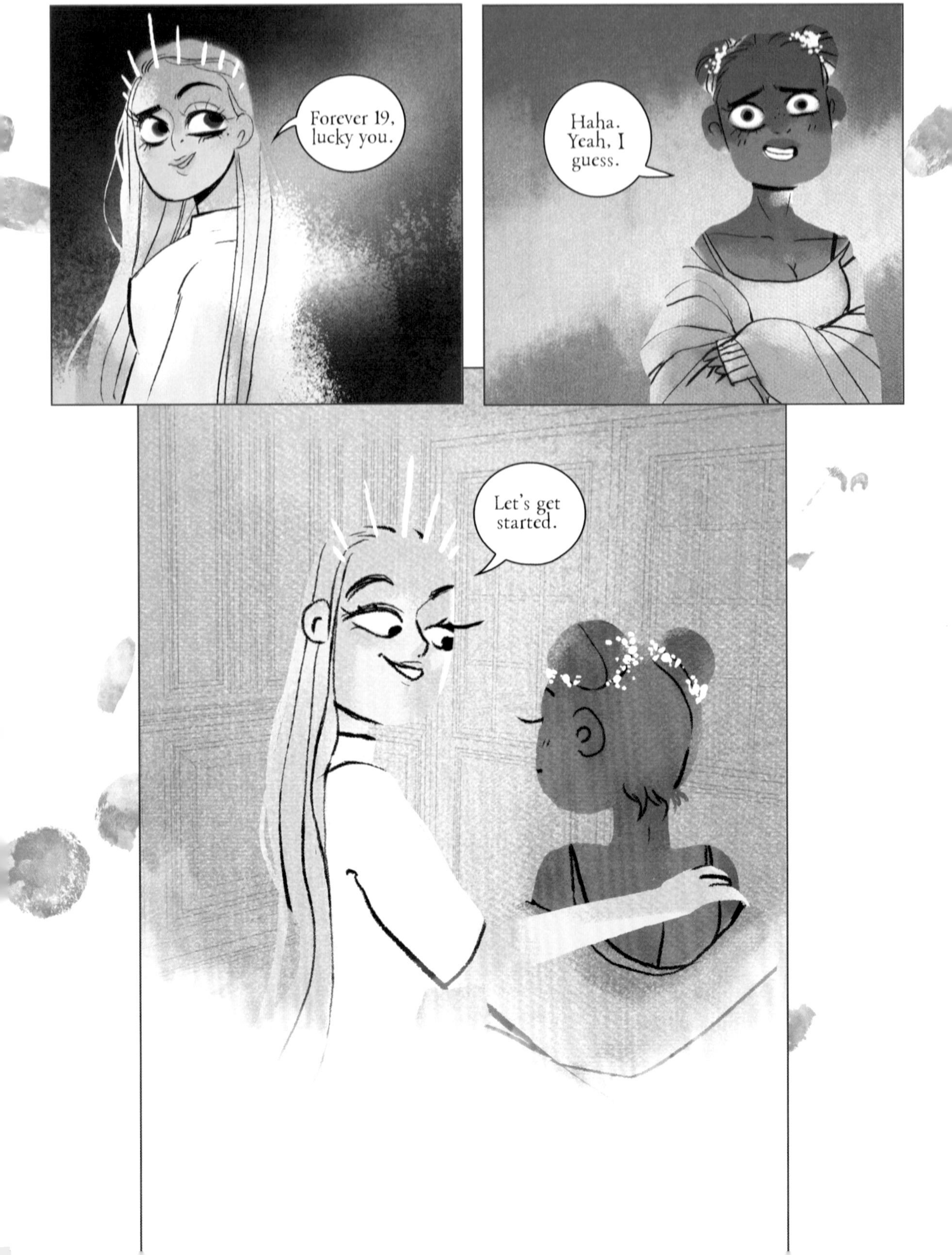
Forever 19, lucky you.
Haha. Yeah, I guess.
Let's get started.

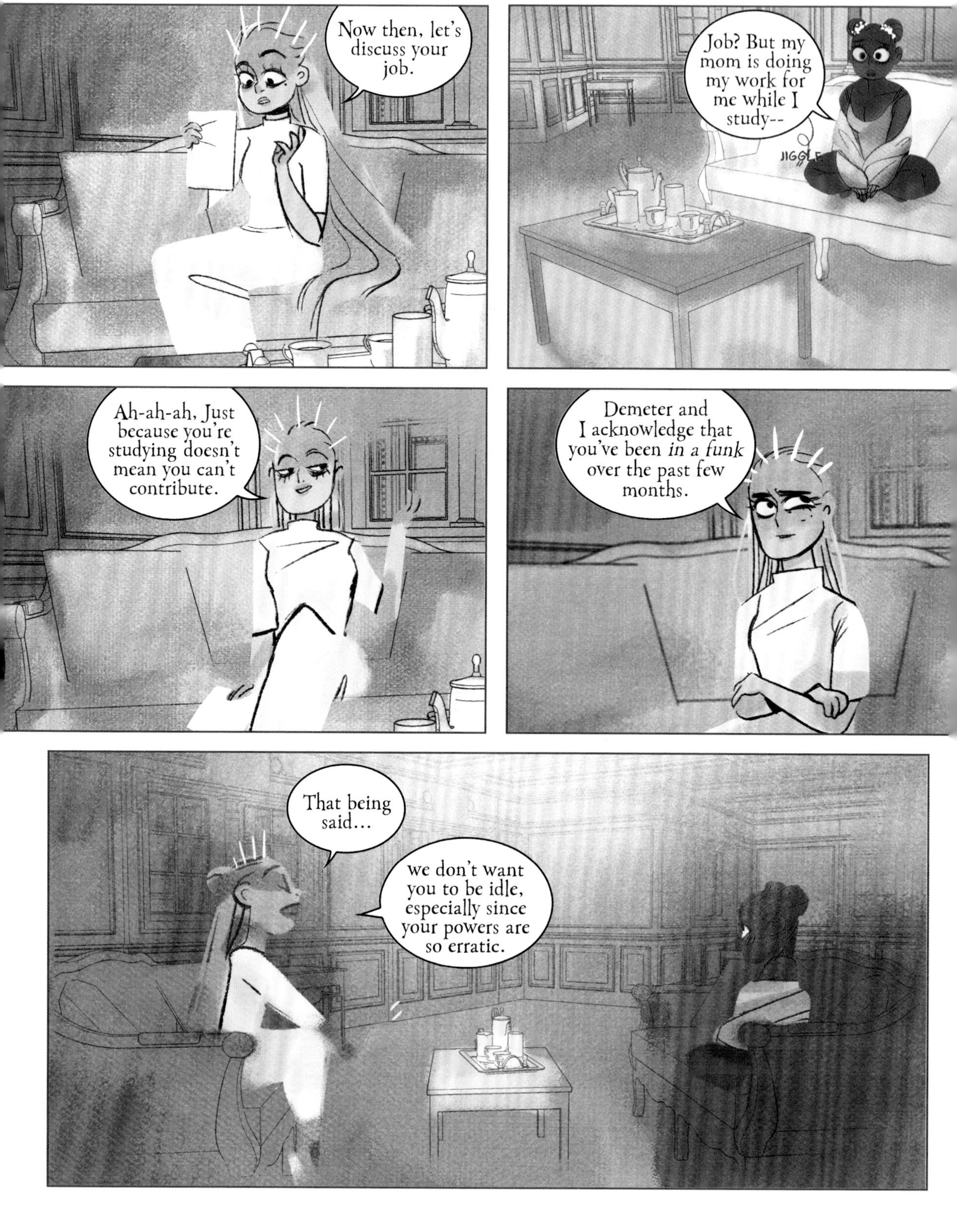
Now then, let's discuss your job.
Job? But my mom is doing my work for me while I study--
JIGGLE
Ah-ah-ah, Just because you're studying doesn't mean you can't contribute.
Demeter and I acknowledge that you've been *in a funk* over the past few months.
That being said...
we don't want you to be idle, especially since your powers are so erratic.

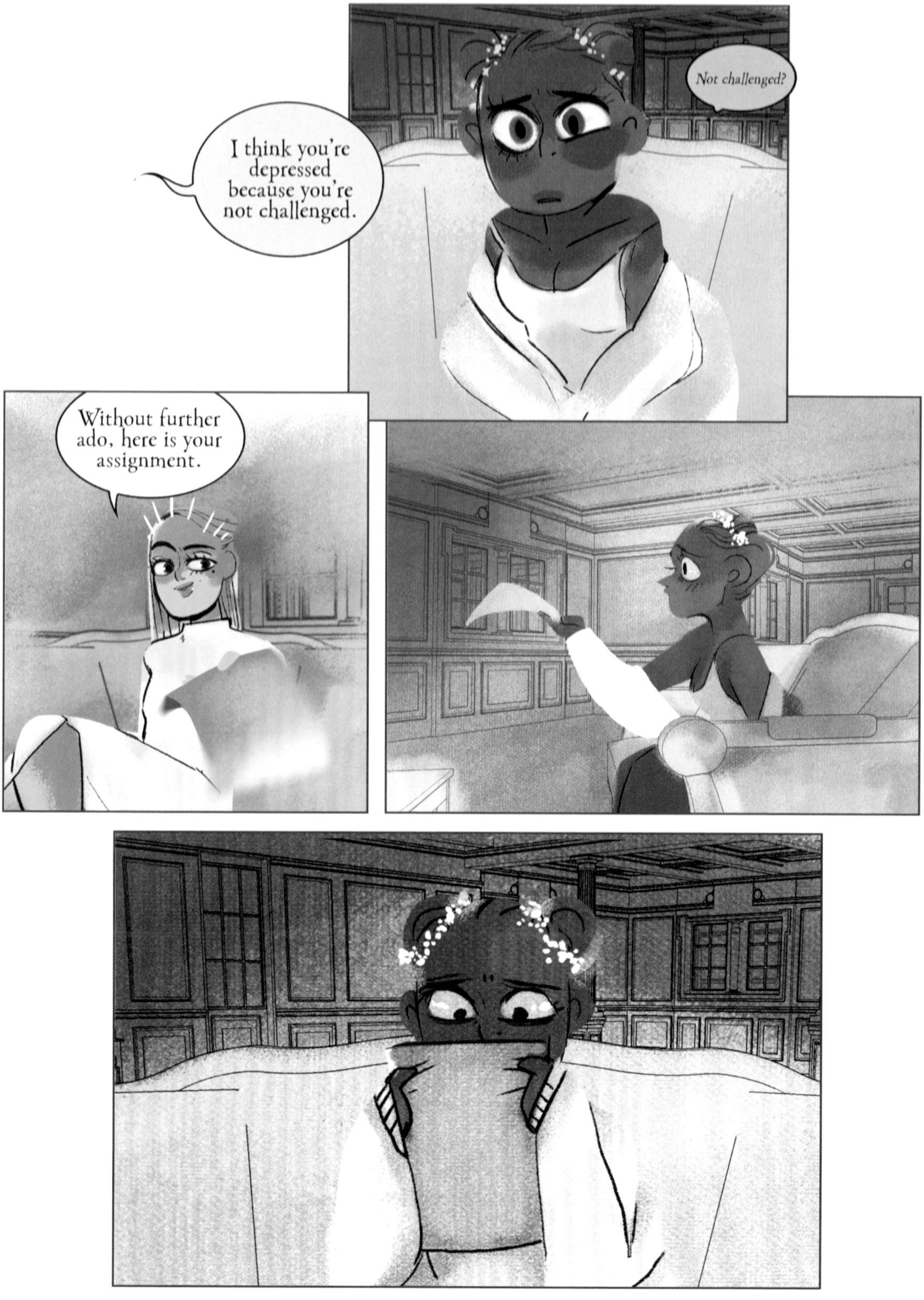
I think you're depressed because you're not challenged.
Not challenged?
Without further ado, here is your assignment.

WHAAAAATTTT!!!???

UNDERWORLD CORP

OLYMPUS TO UNDERWORLD INTERN EXCHANGE PROGRAM

APPLICANT: PERSEPHONE (KORE)

REPORT TO: HADES, GOD/KING OF THE DEAD/UNDERWORLD

LOCATION: UNDERWORLD CORP, TOWER I, LV 99

TIME: ASAP

INTERNSHIP ROLE DESCRIPTION : TO BE DISCUSSED

STATUS: APPROVED BY HERA, QUEEN OF THE GODS

[signature]

PLEASE ATTACH PHOTO ID

Embarrassing
old photo.

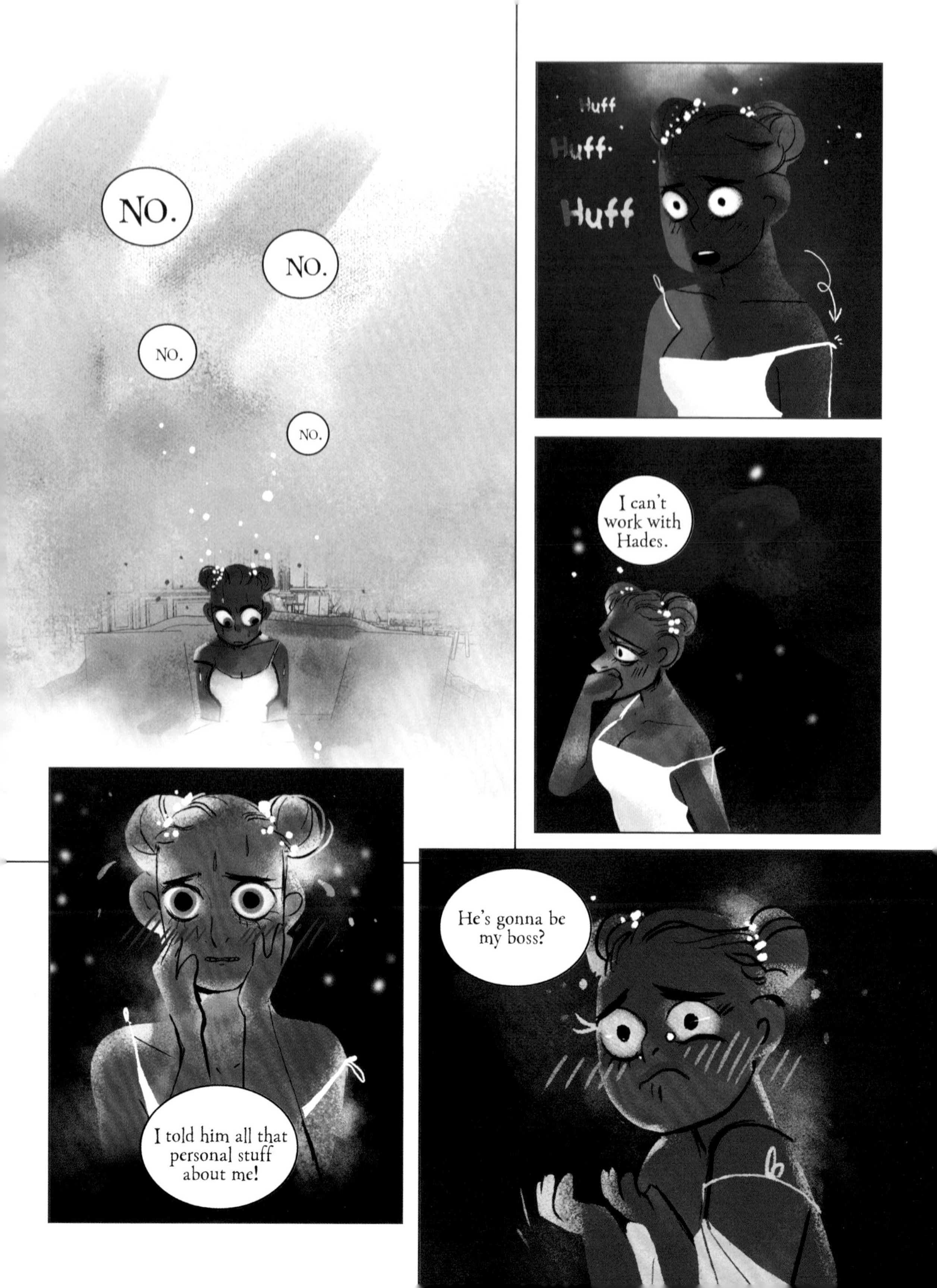
NO.
NO.
NO.
NO.
Huff
Huff
Huff
I can't work with Hades.
I told him all that personal stuff about me!
He's gonna be my boss?

He-- he can't be my boss.
TAP
TAP
TAP
He'll find out that I don't have any skills.
EP!
What if he thinks I'm incompetent?
He's going to realize what I am...
A dumb village girl.

EPISODE 31: A TREAT FOR BEING A FOOL

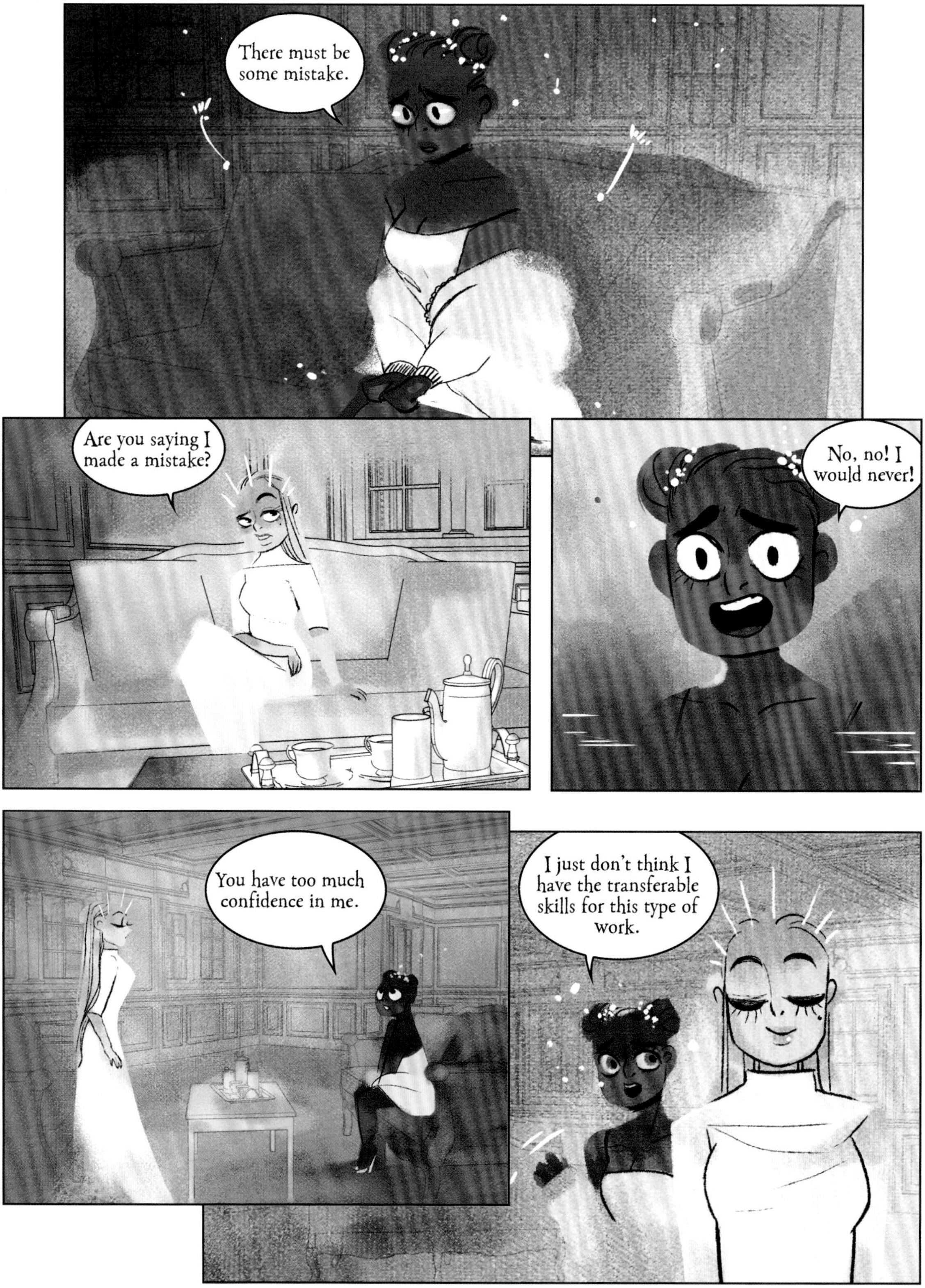
There must be some mistake.
Are you saying I made a mistake?
No, no! I would never!
You have too much confidence in me.
I just don't think I have the transferable skills for this type of work.

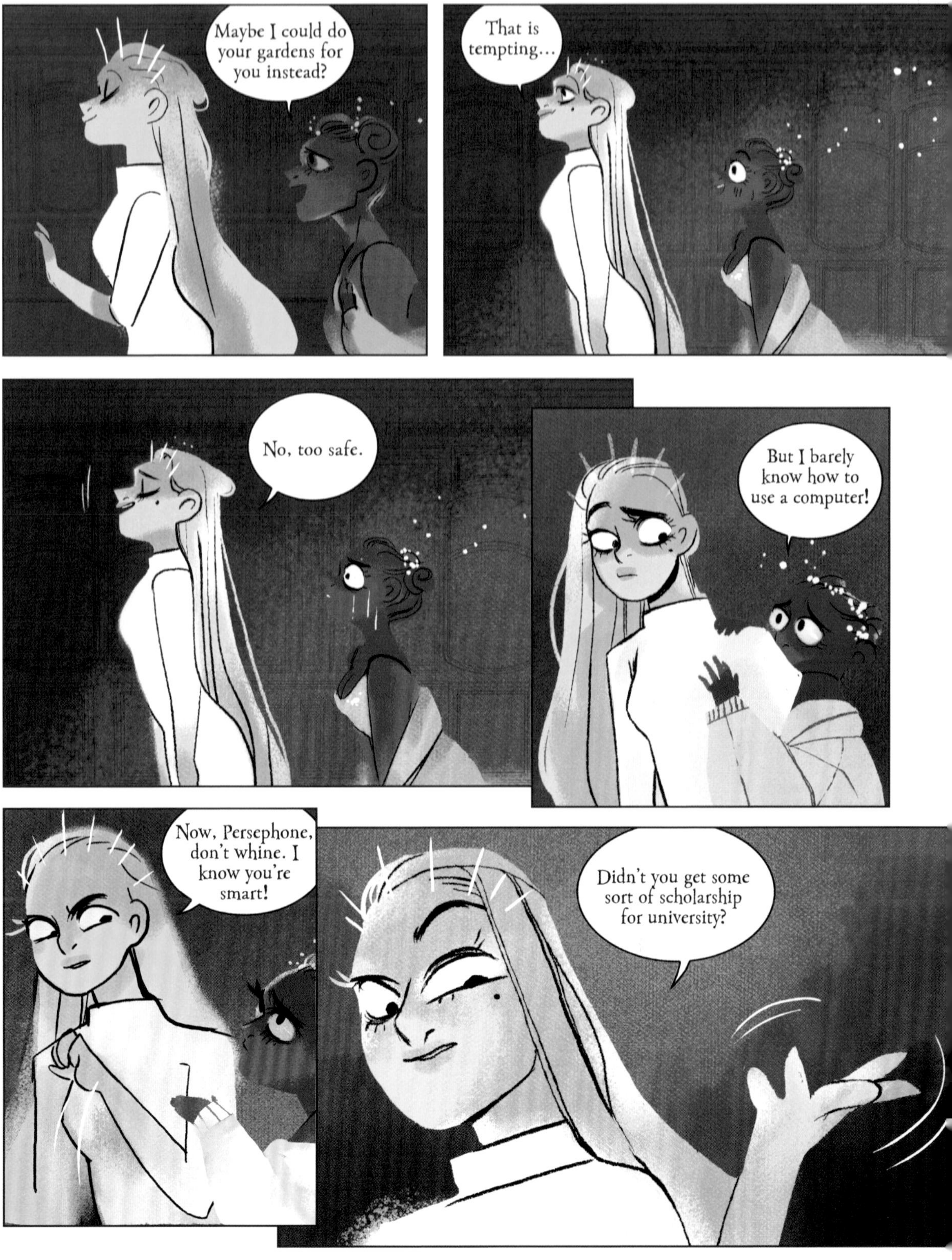
Maybe I could do your gardens for you instead?
That is tempting...
No, too safe.
But I barely know how to use a computer!
Now, Persephone, don't whine. I know you're smart!
Didn't you get some sort of scholarship for university?

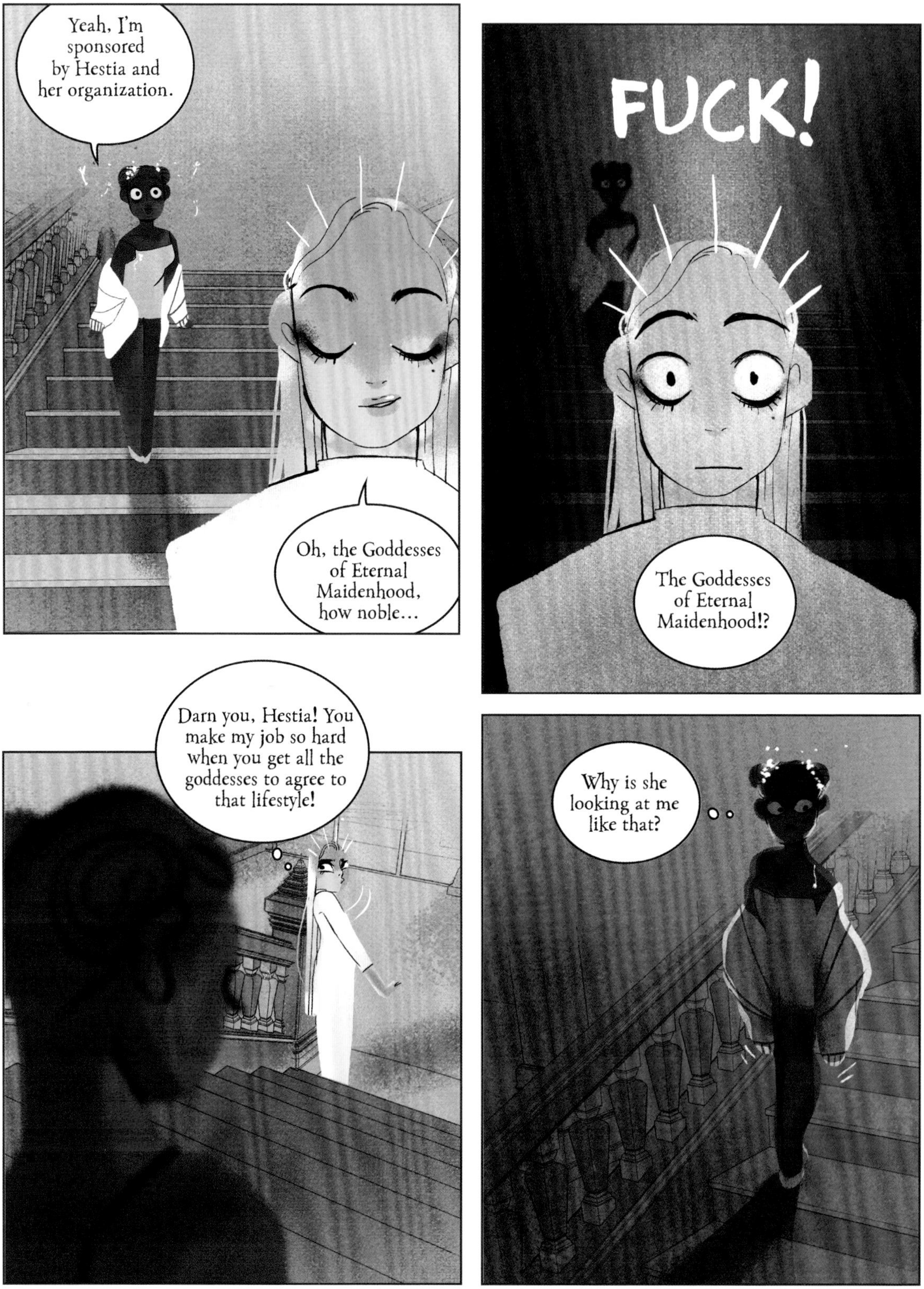
Yeah, I'm sponsored by Hestia and her organization.
Oh, the Goddesses of Eternal Maidenhood, how noble...
FUCK!
The Goddesses of Eternal Maidenhood!?
Darn you, Hestia! You make my job so hard when you get all the goddesses to agree to that lifestyle!
Why is she looking at me like that?

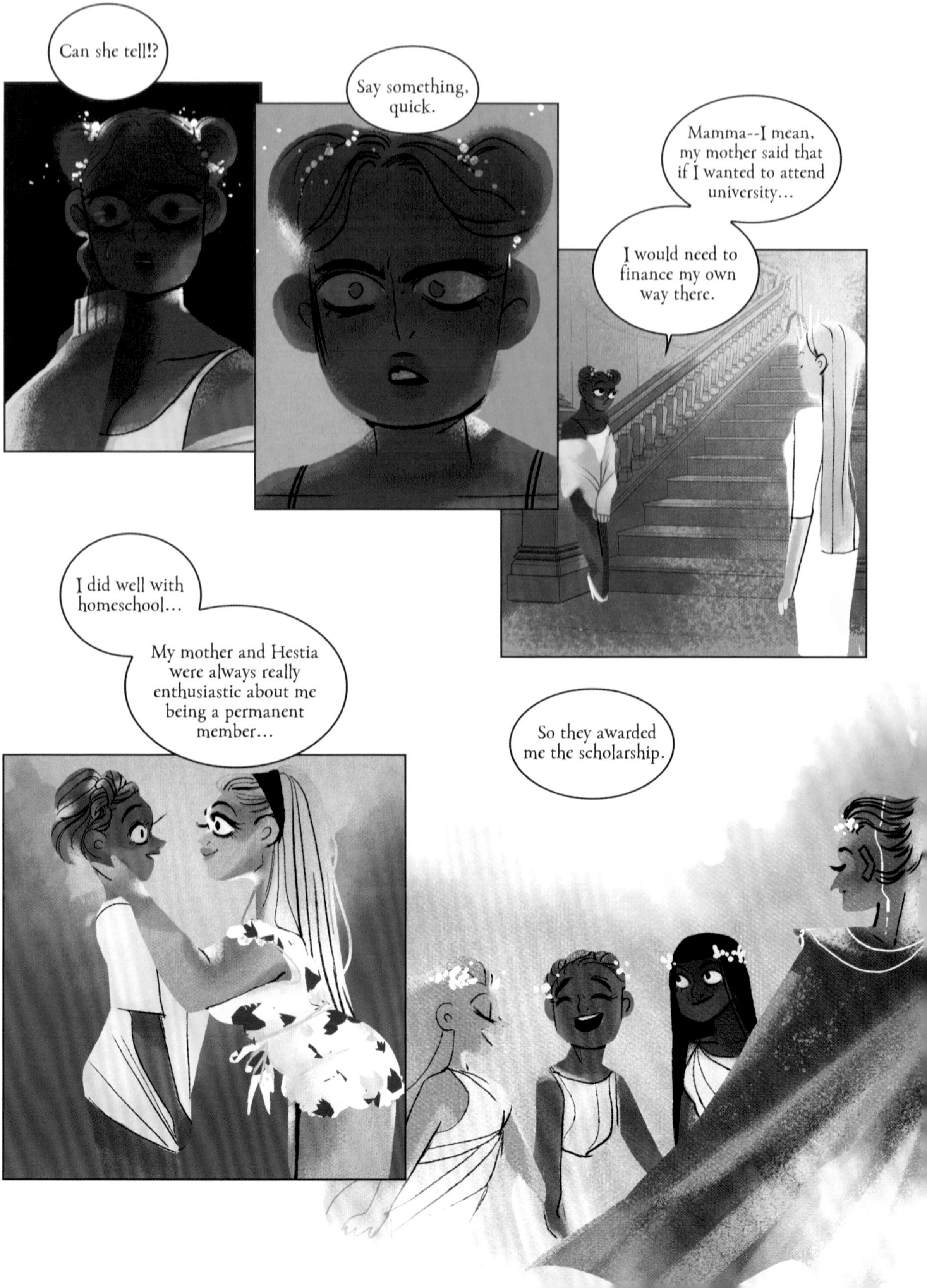
Can she tell!?
Say something, quick.
Mamma--I mean, my mother said that if I wanted to attend university...
I would need to finance my own way there.
I did well with homeschool...
My mother and Hestia were always really enthusiastic about me being a permanent member...
So they awarded me the scholarship.

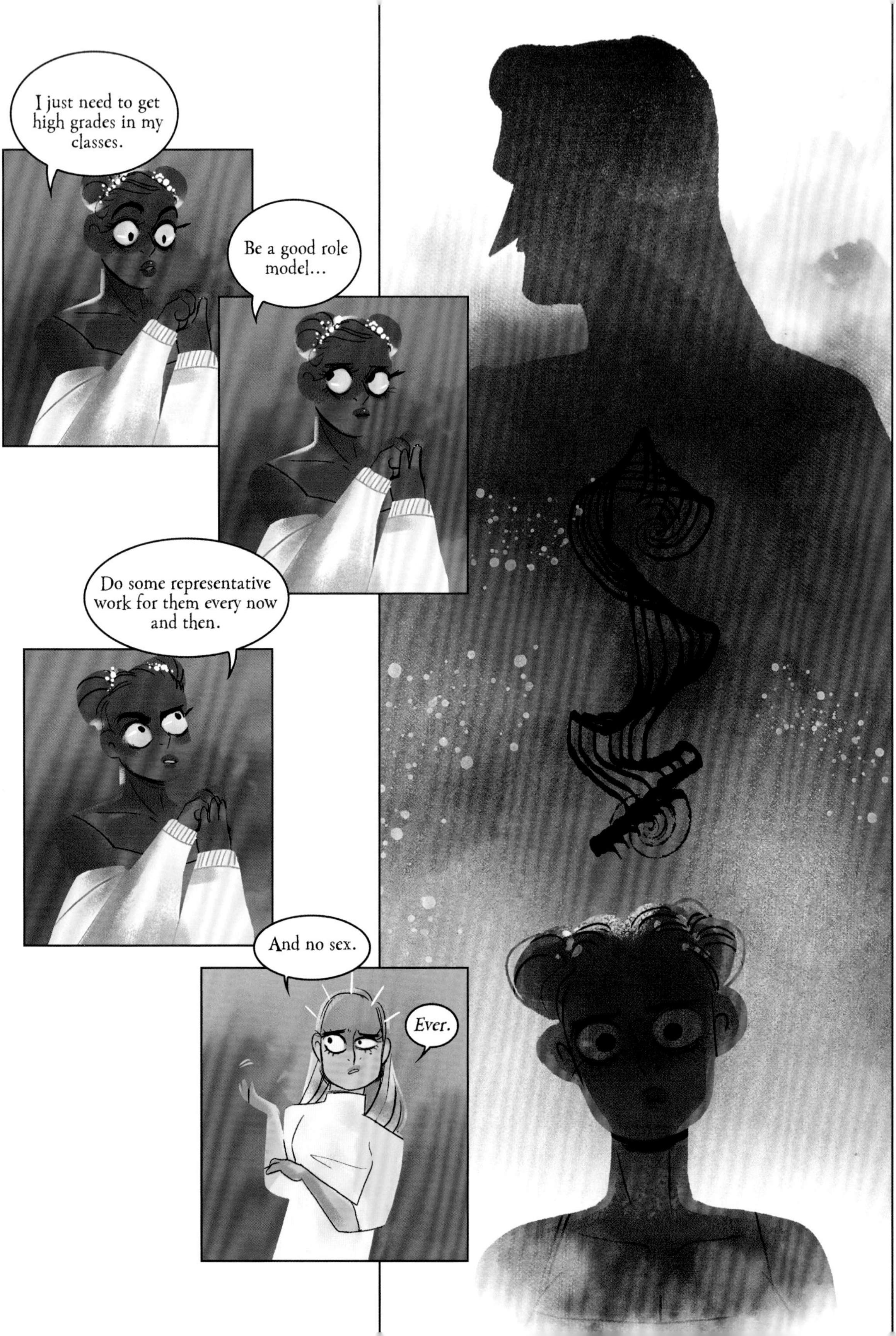

I just need to get high grades in my classes.
Be a good role model...
Do some representative work for them every now and then.
And no sex.
Ever.

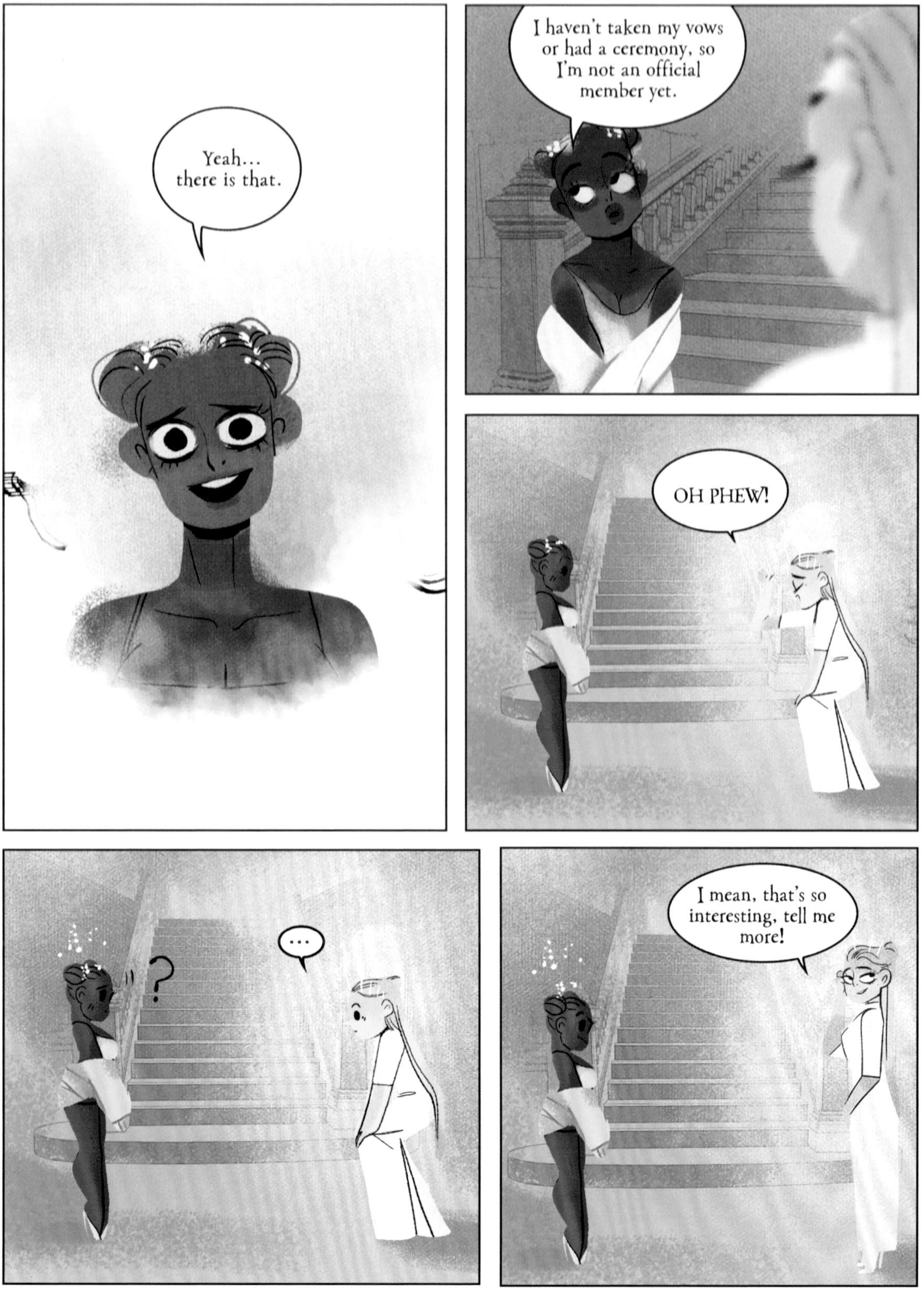
Yeah... there is that.
I haven't taken my vows or had a ceremony, so I'm not an official member yet.
OH PHEW!
...
I mean, that's so interesting, tell me more!

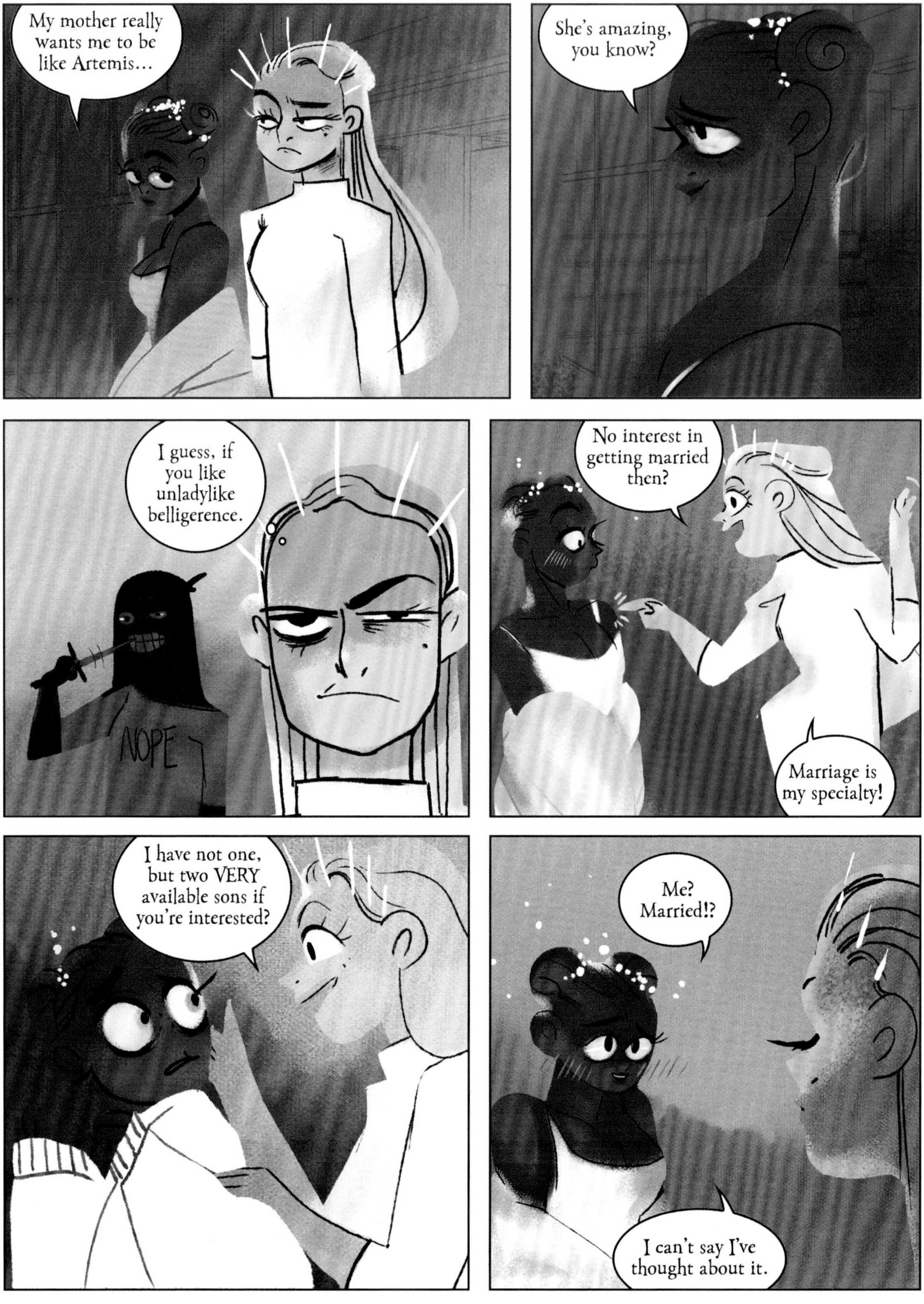
My mother really wants me to be like Artemis…
She's amazing, you know?
I guess, if you like unladylike belligerence.
NOPE
No interest in getting married then?
Marriage is my specialty!
I have not one, but two VERY available sons if you're interested?
Me? Married!?
I can't say I've thought about it.

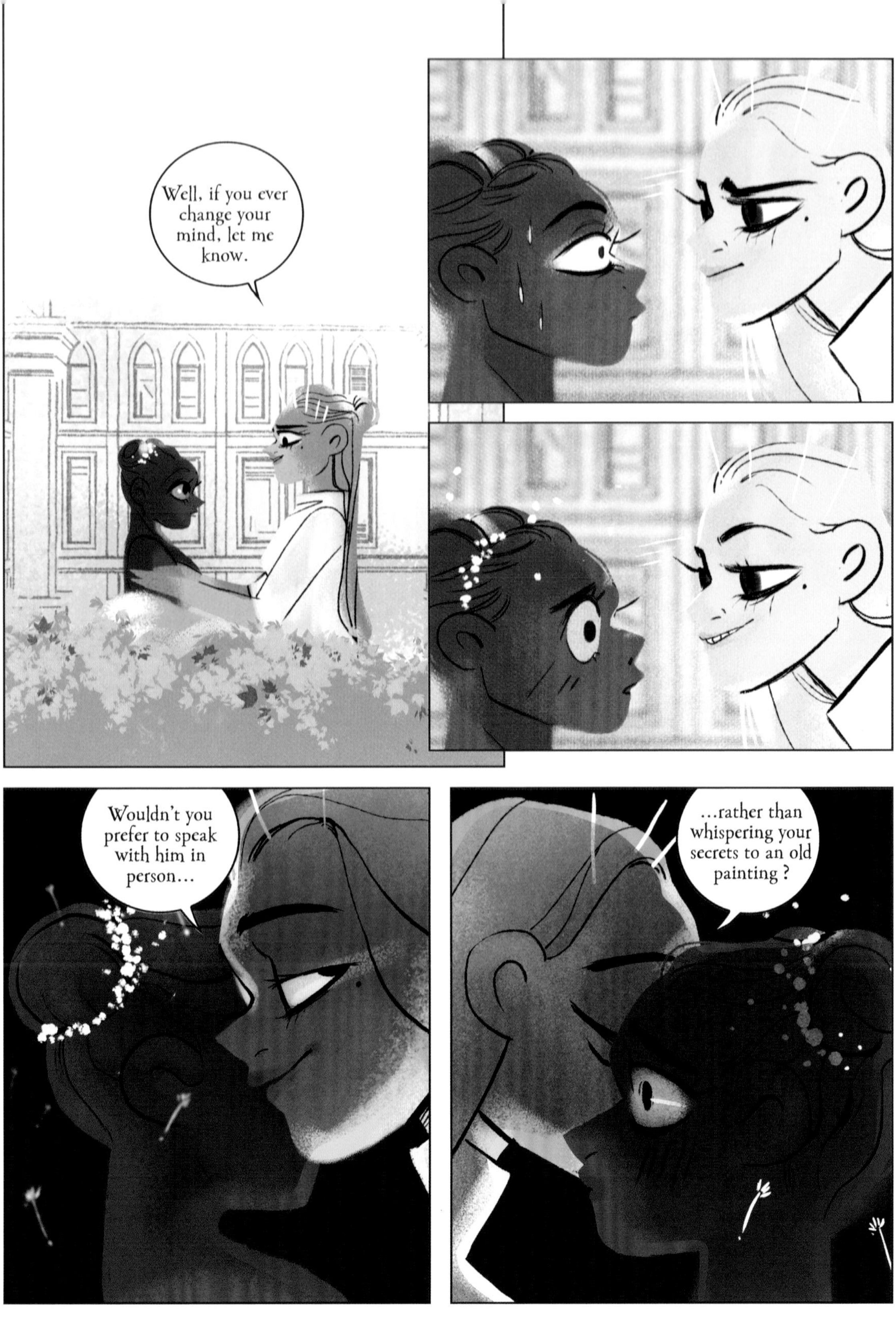
Well, if you ever change your mind, let me know.
Wouldn't you prefer to speak with him in person...
...rather than whispering your secrets to an old painting ?

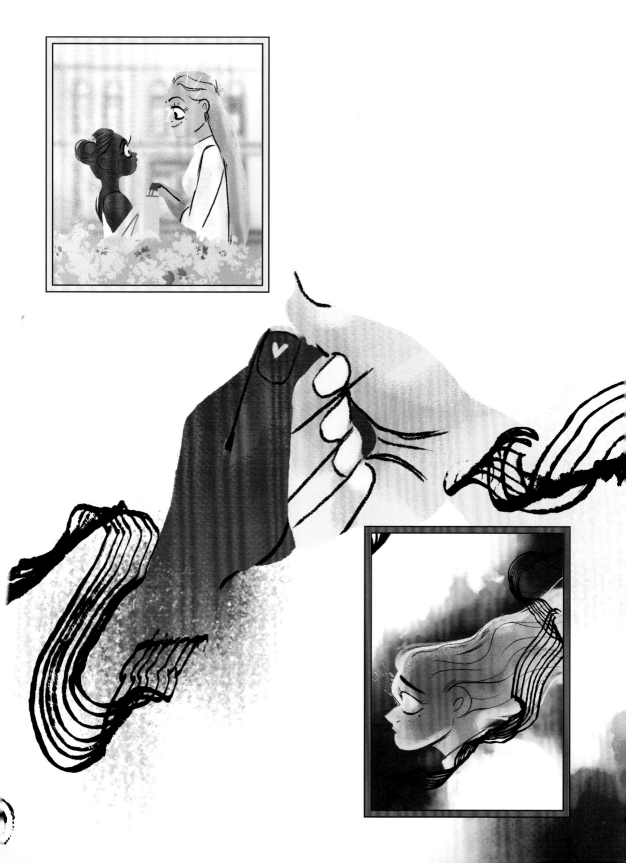

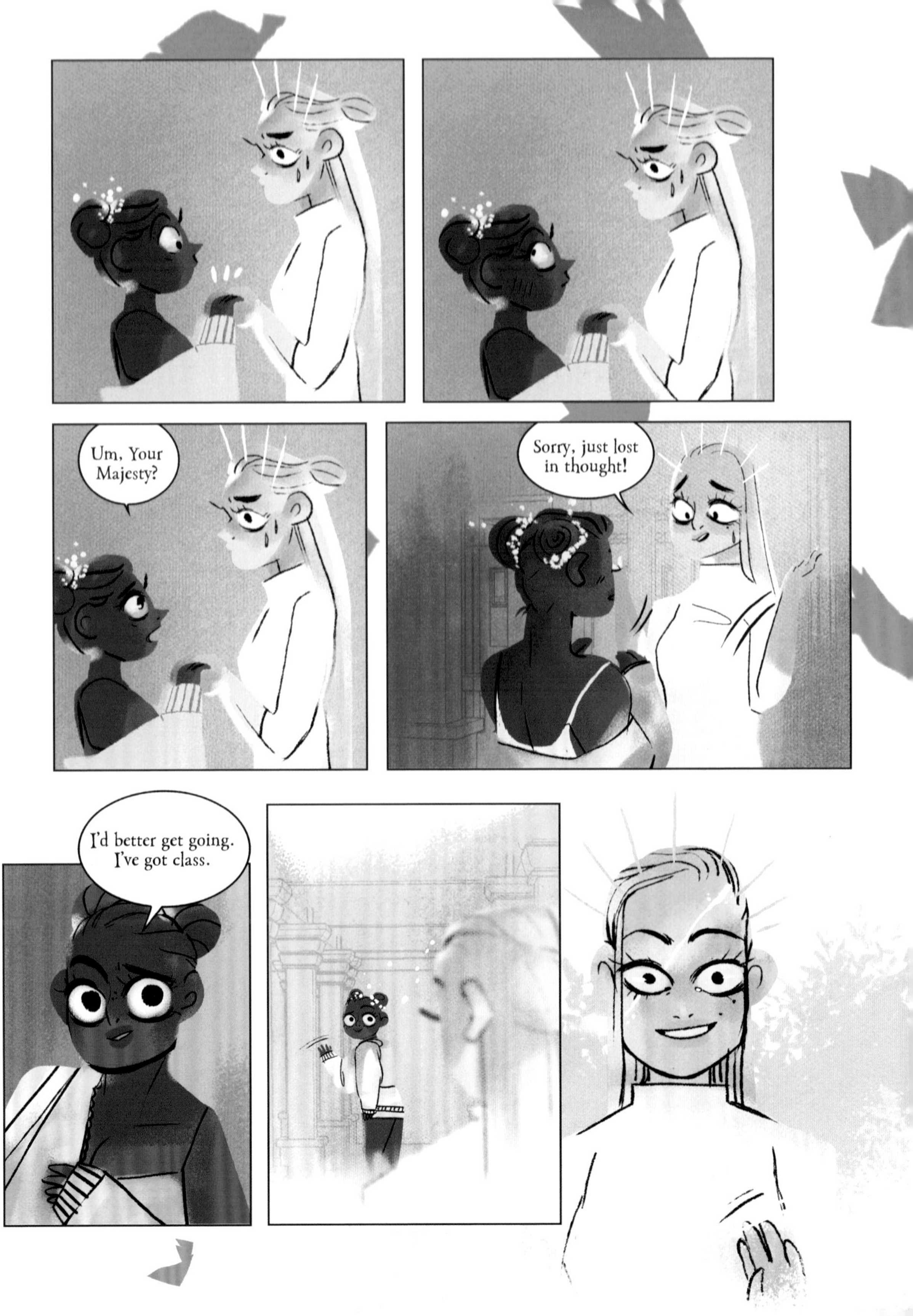
Um, Your Majesty?
Sorry, just lost in thought!
I'd better get going. I've got class.

Who did that
to you?

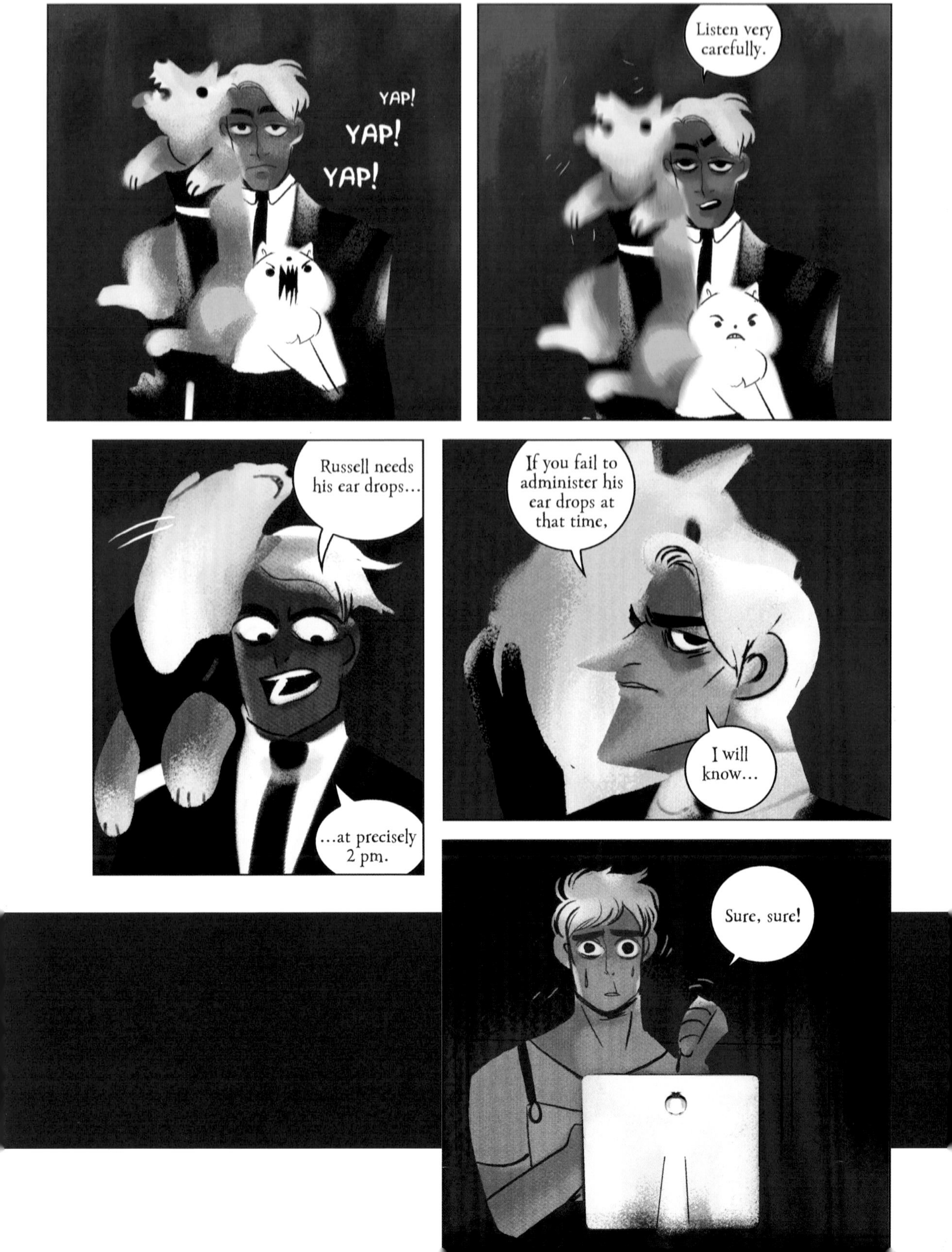
YAP!
YAP!
YAP!
Listen very carefully.
Russell needs his ear drops...
...at precisely 2 pm.
If you fail to administer his ear drops at that time,
I will know...
Sure, sure!

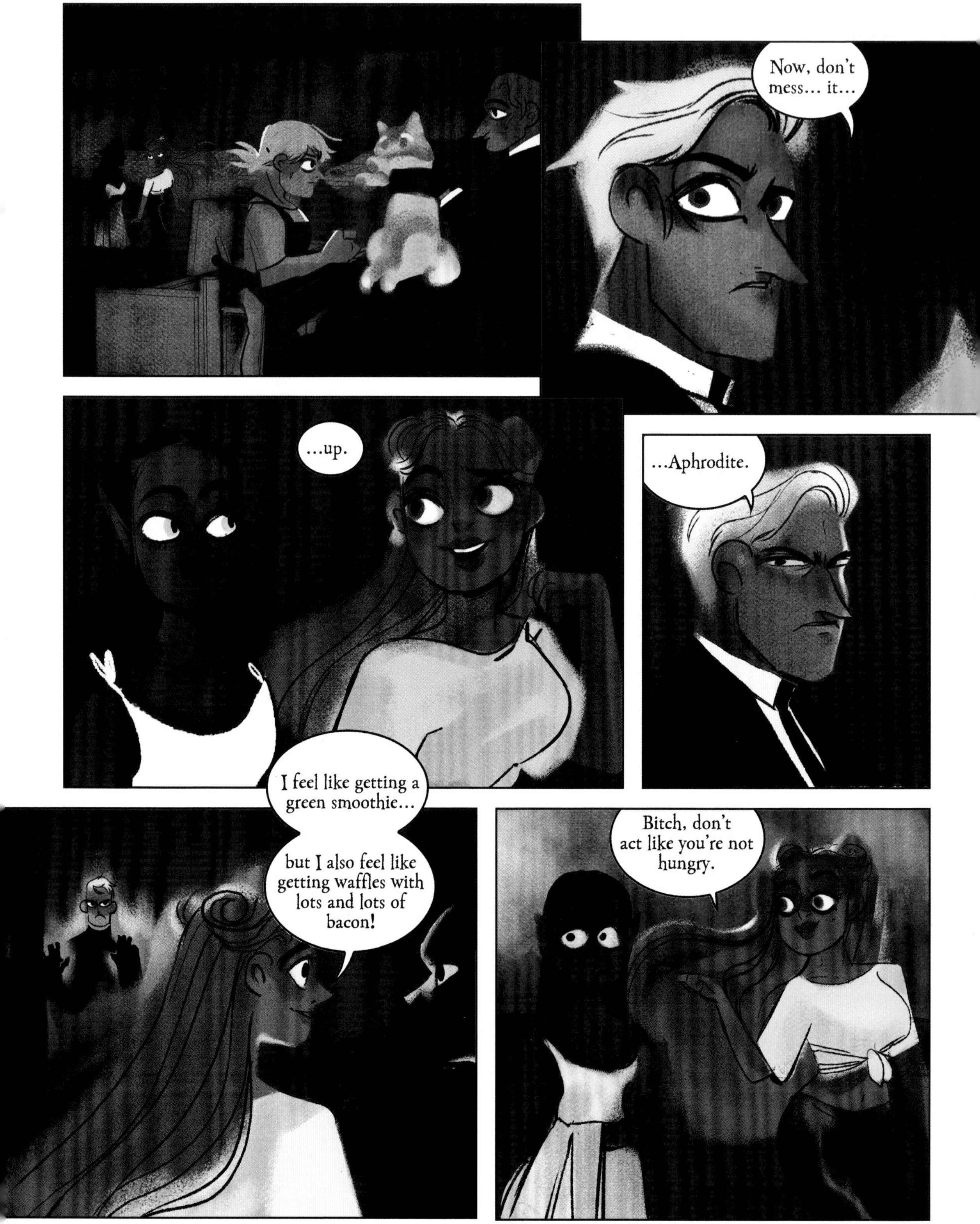
Now, don't mess… it…
…up.
…Aphrodite.
I feel like getting a green smoothie…
but I also feel like getting waffles with lots and lots of bacon!
Bitch, don't act like you're not hungry.

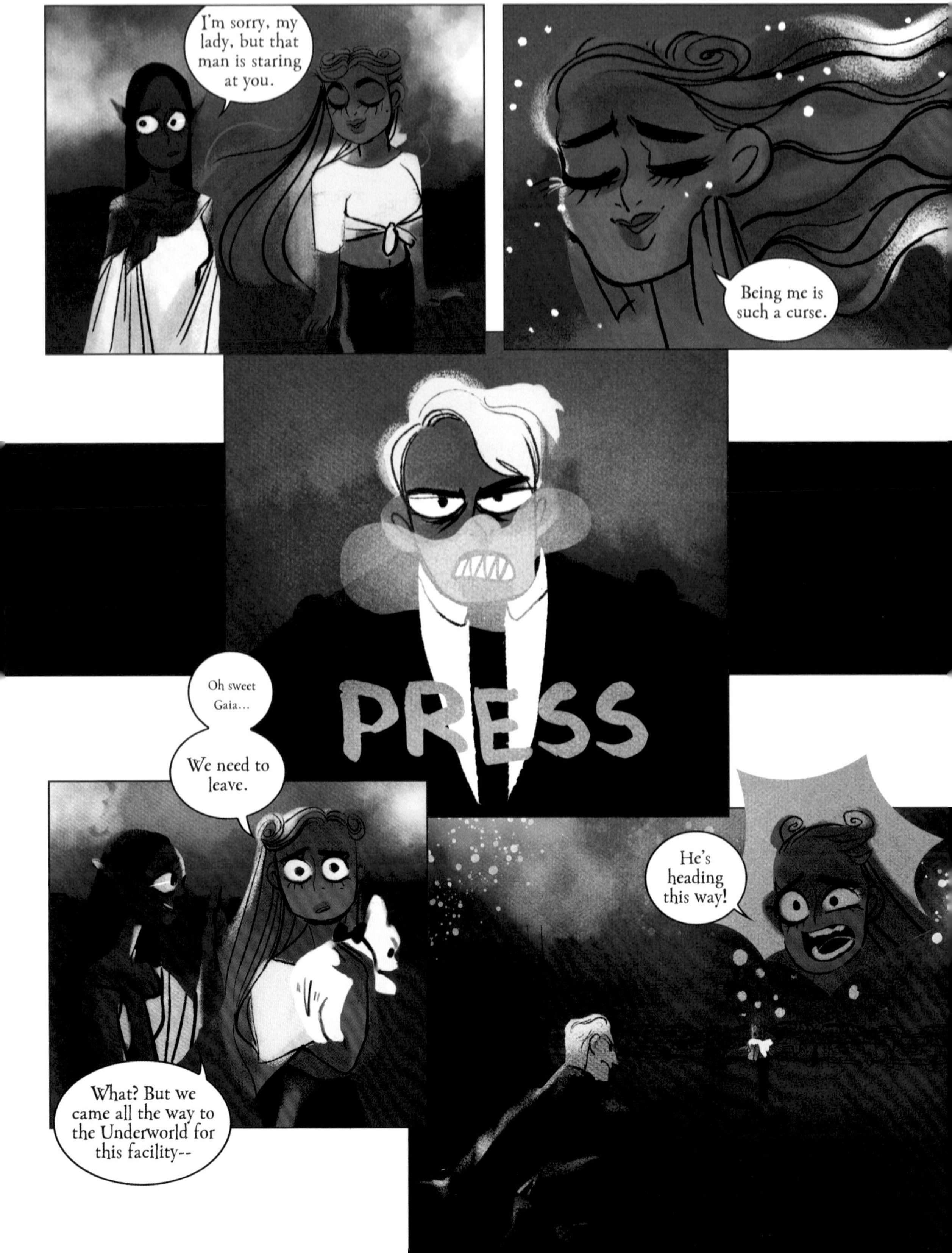

I'm sorry, my lady, but that man is staring at you.
Being me is such a curse.
PRESS
Oh sweet Gaia...
We need to leave.
What? But we came all the way to the Underworld for this facility--
He's heading this way!

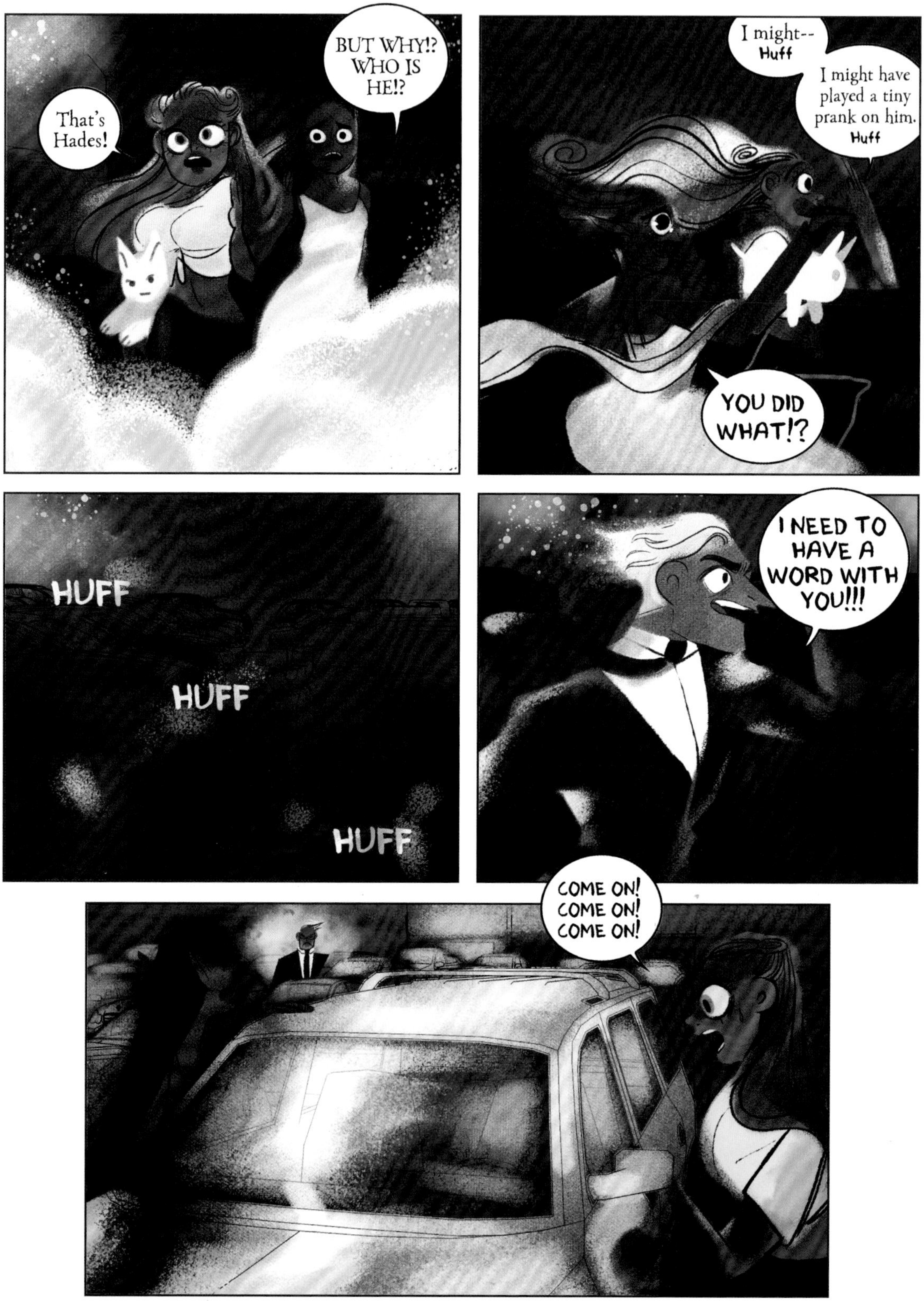
That's Hades!
BUT WHY!? WHO IS HE!?
I might-- Huff
I might have played a tiny prank on him. Huff
YOU DID WHAT!?
HUFF
HUFF
HUFF
I NEED TO HAVE A WORD WITH YOU!!!
COME ON! COME ON! COME ON!

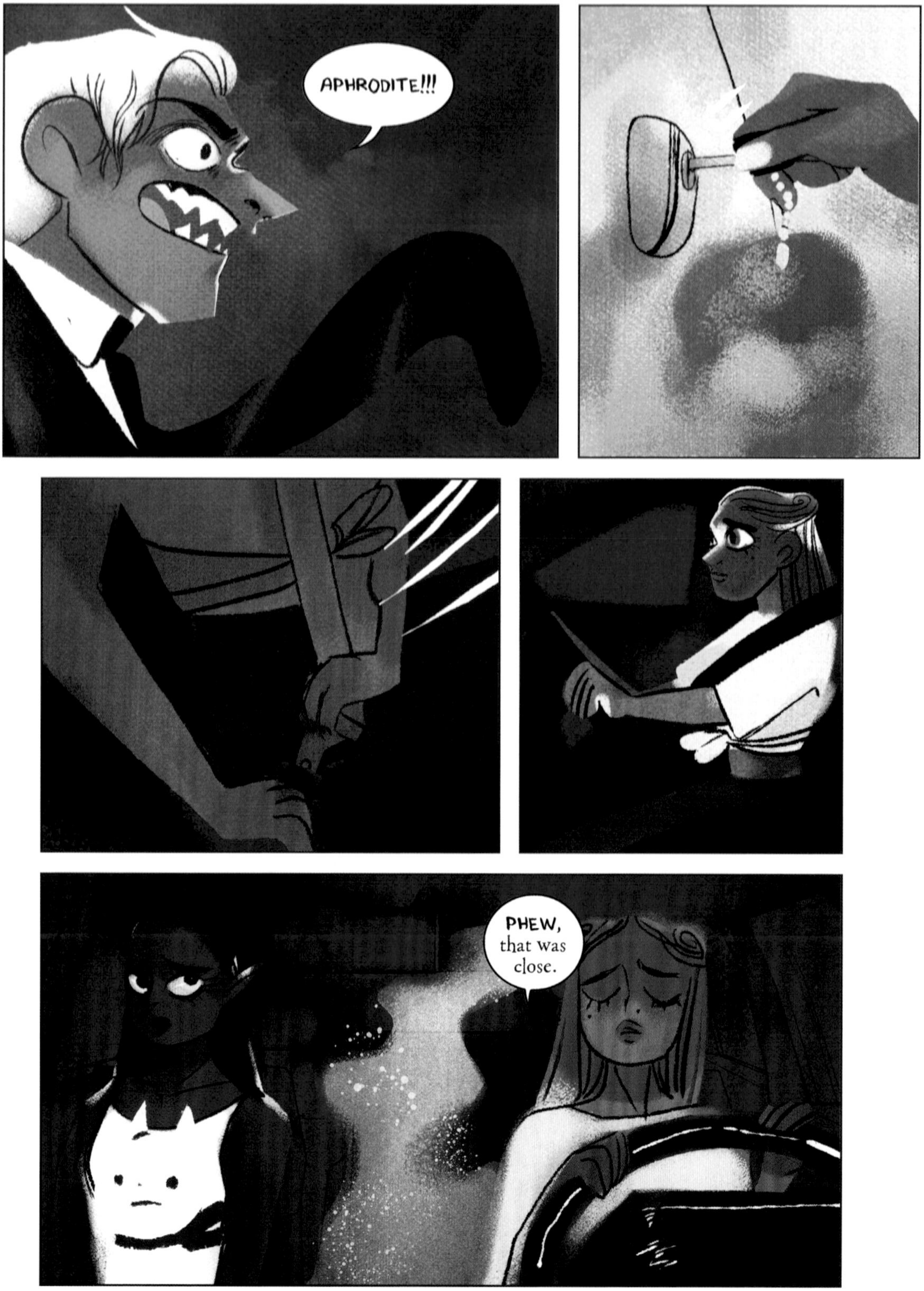
APHRODITE!!!
PHEW, that was close.

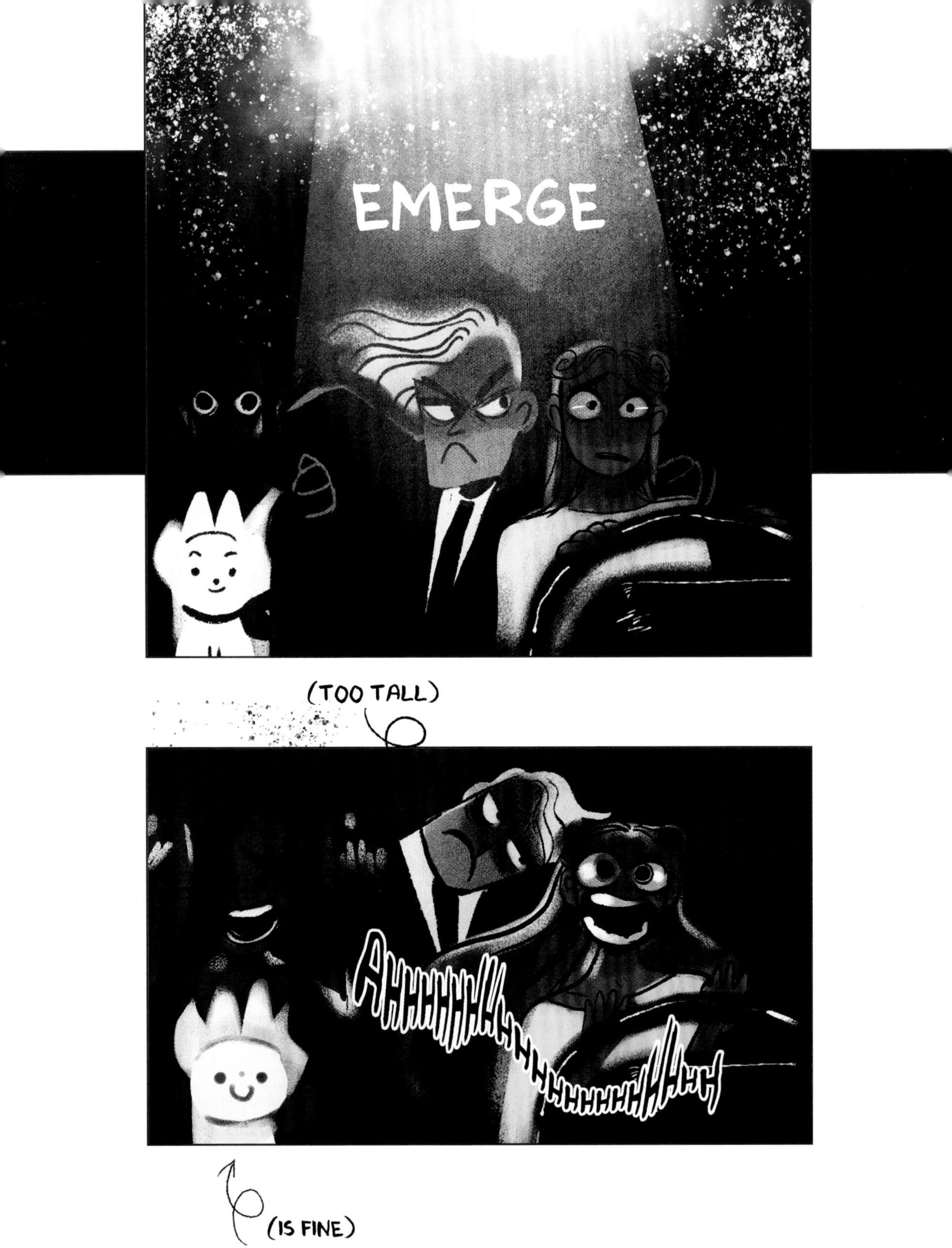
EMERGE
(TOO TALL)
AHHHHHHHHHHHHHHHHHHHHHHHHHHHHH
(IS FINE)

EPISODE 32: SMALL

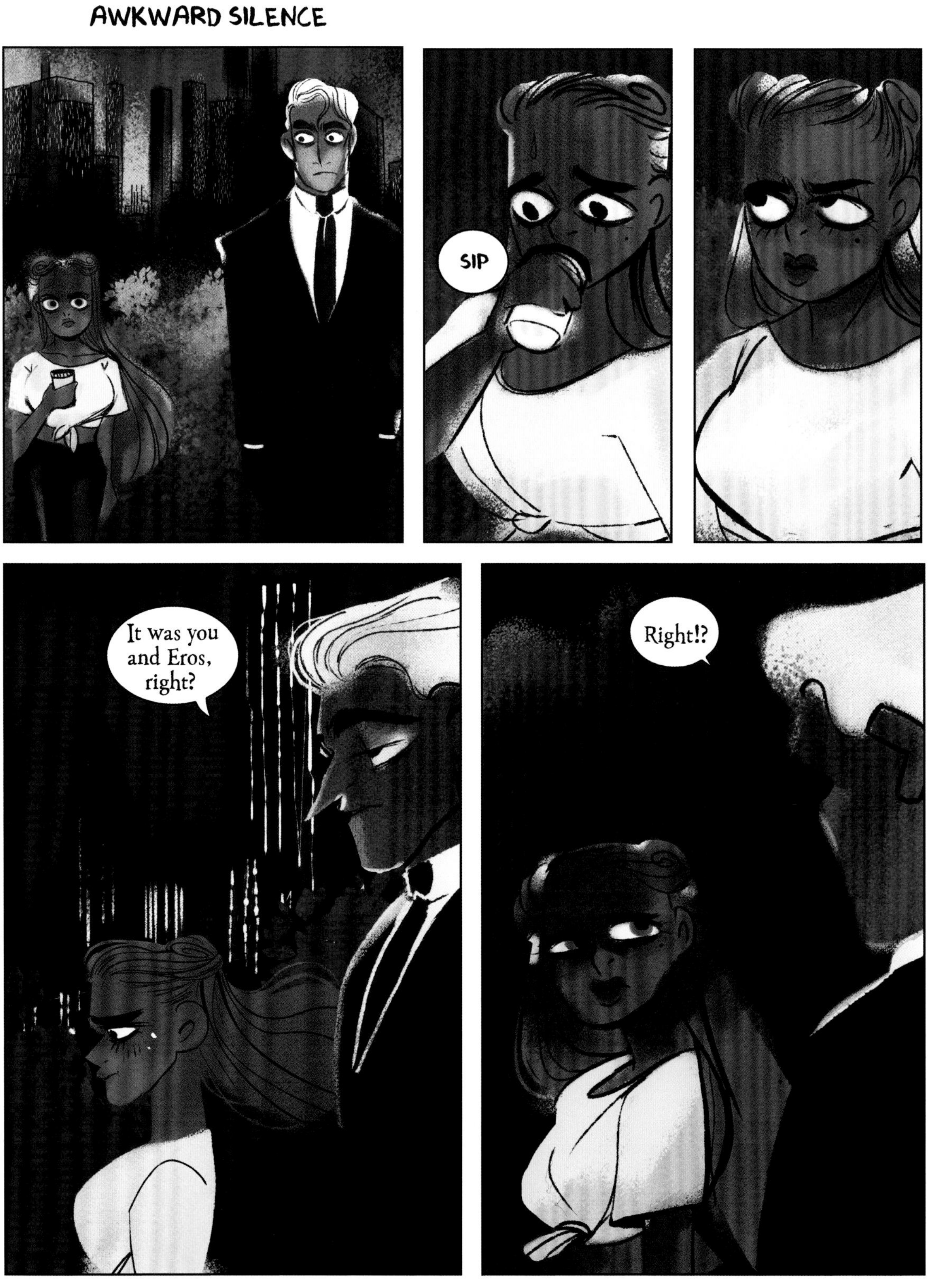
AWKWARD SILENCE
SIP
It was you and Eros, right?
Right!?

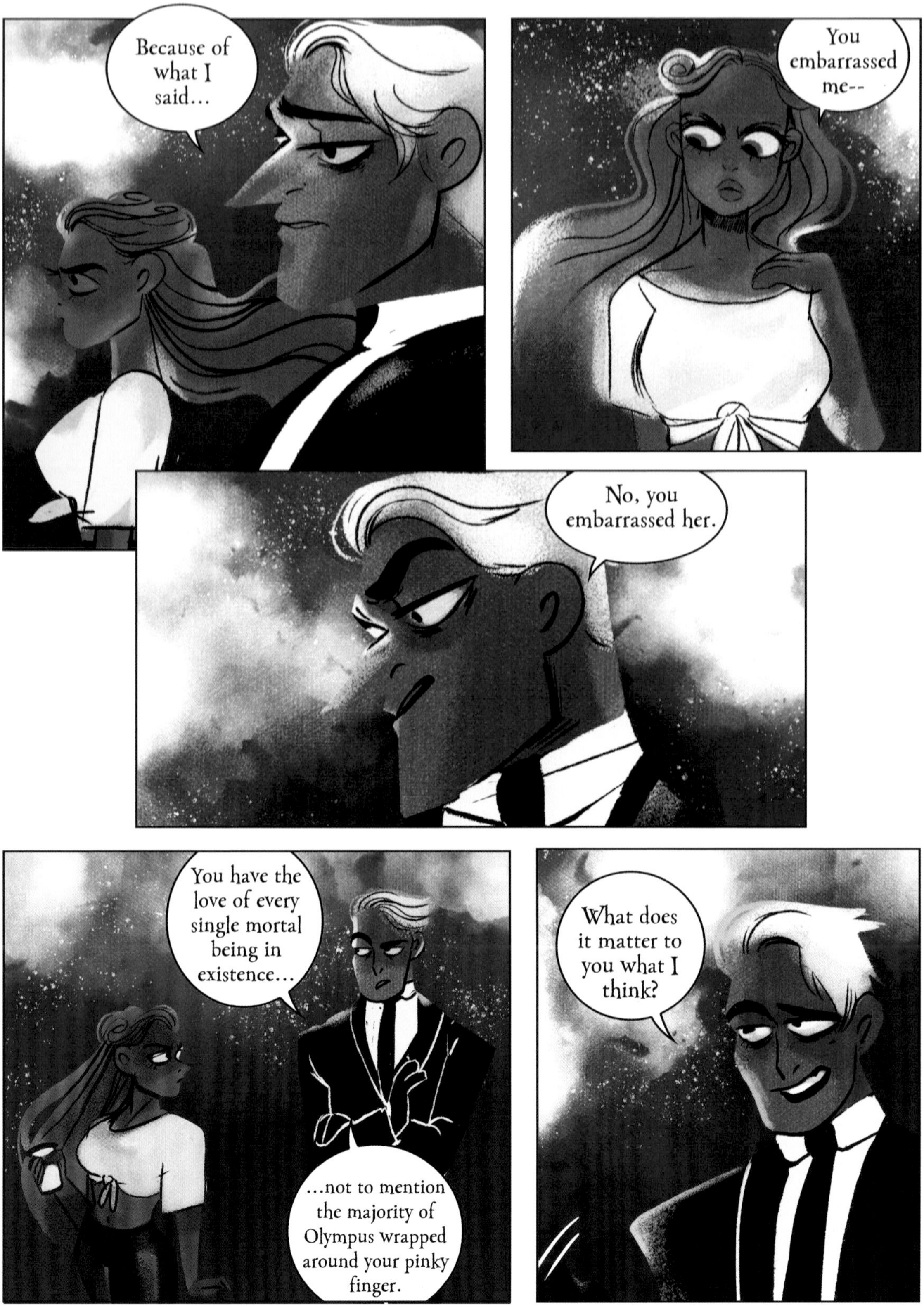
Because of what I said...
You embarrassed me--
No, you embarrassed her.
You have the love of every single mortal being in existence...
...not to mention the majority of Olympus wrapped around your pinky finger.
What does it matter to you what I think?

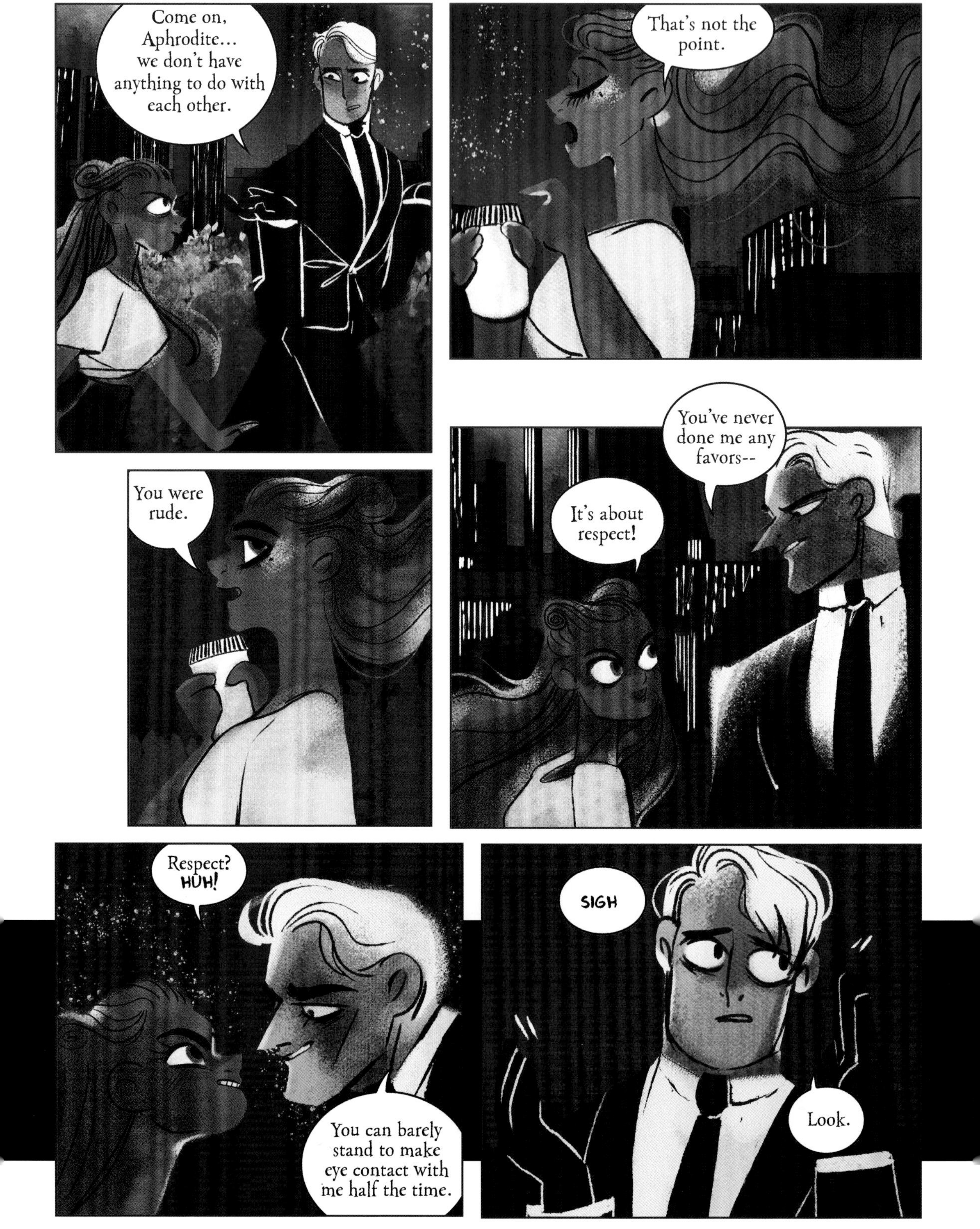
Come on, Aphrodite... we don't have anything to do with each other.
That's not the point.
You were rude.
It's about respect!
You've never done me any favors--
Respect? HUH!
You can barely stand to make eye contact with me half the time.
SIGH
Look.

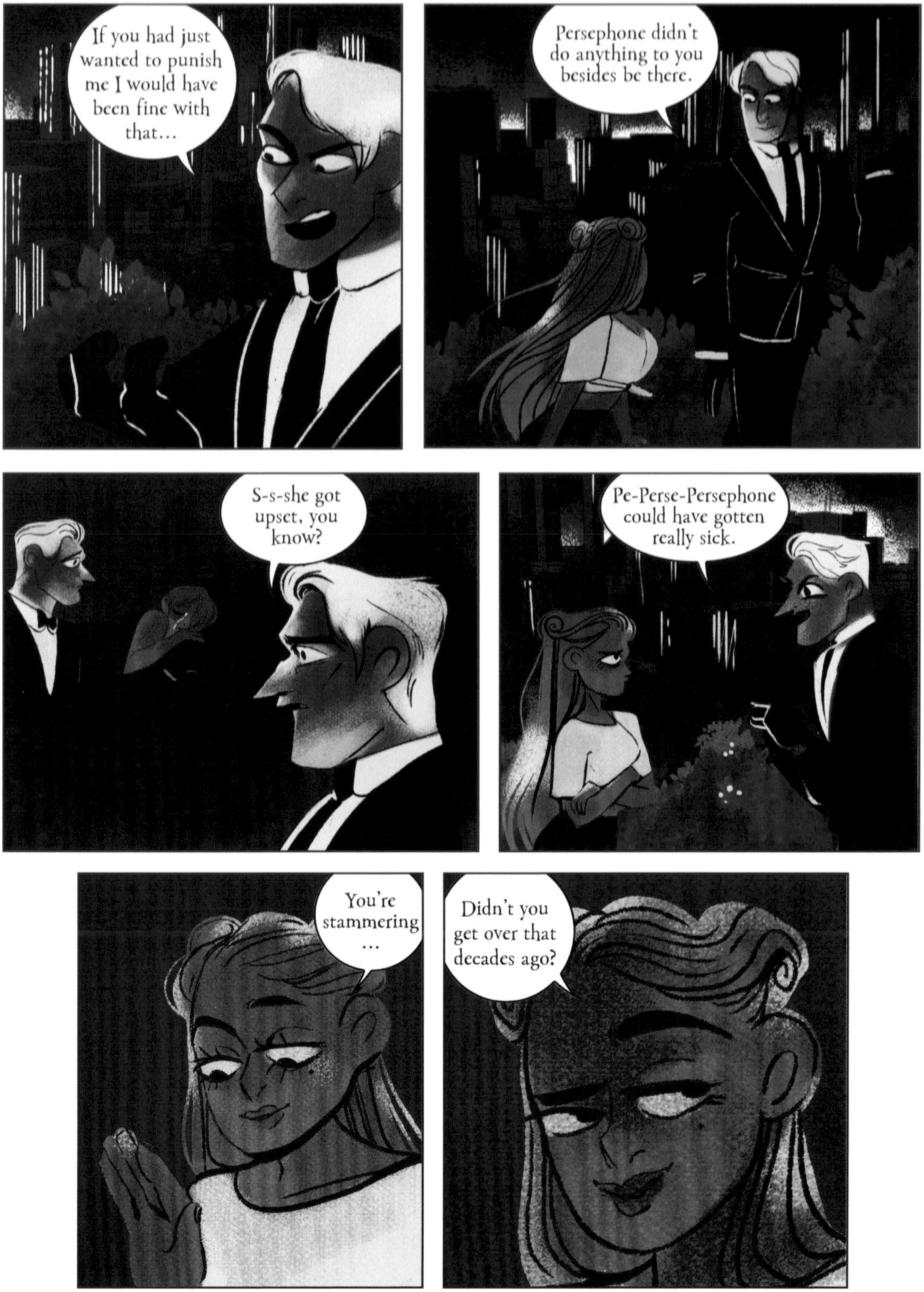
If you had just wanted to punish me I would have been fine with that…
Persephone didn't do anything to you besides be there.
S-s-she got upset, you know?
Pe-Perse-Persephone could have gotten really sick.
You're stammering …
Didn't you get over that decades ago?

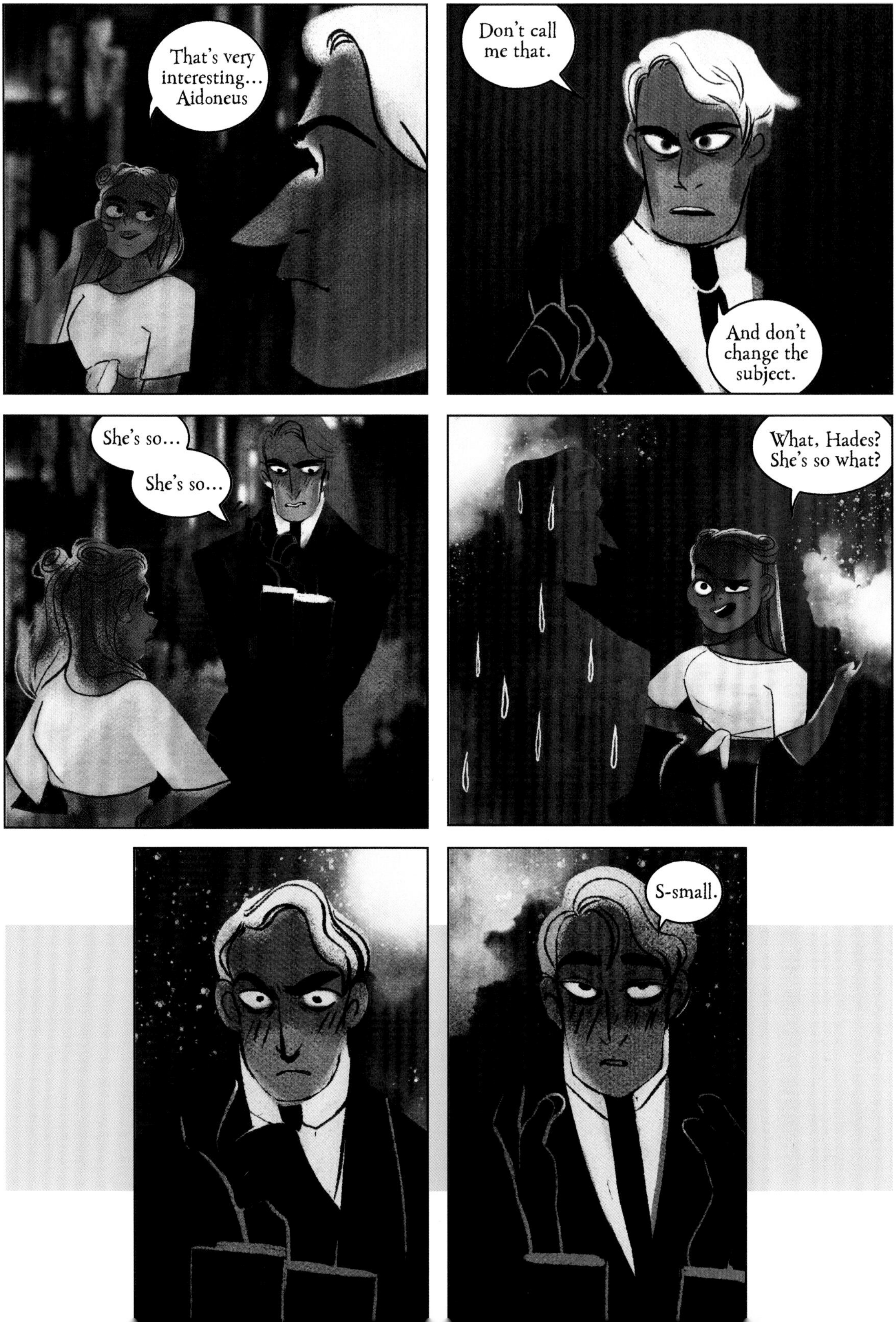
That's very interesting... Aidoneus
Don't call me that.
And don't change the subject.
She's so...
She's so...
What, Hades? She's so what?
S-small.

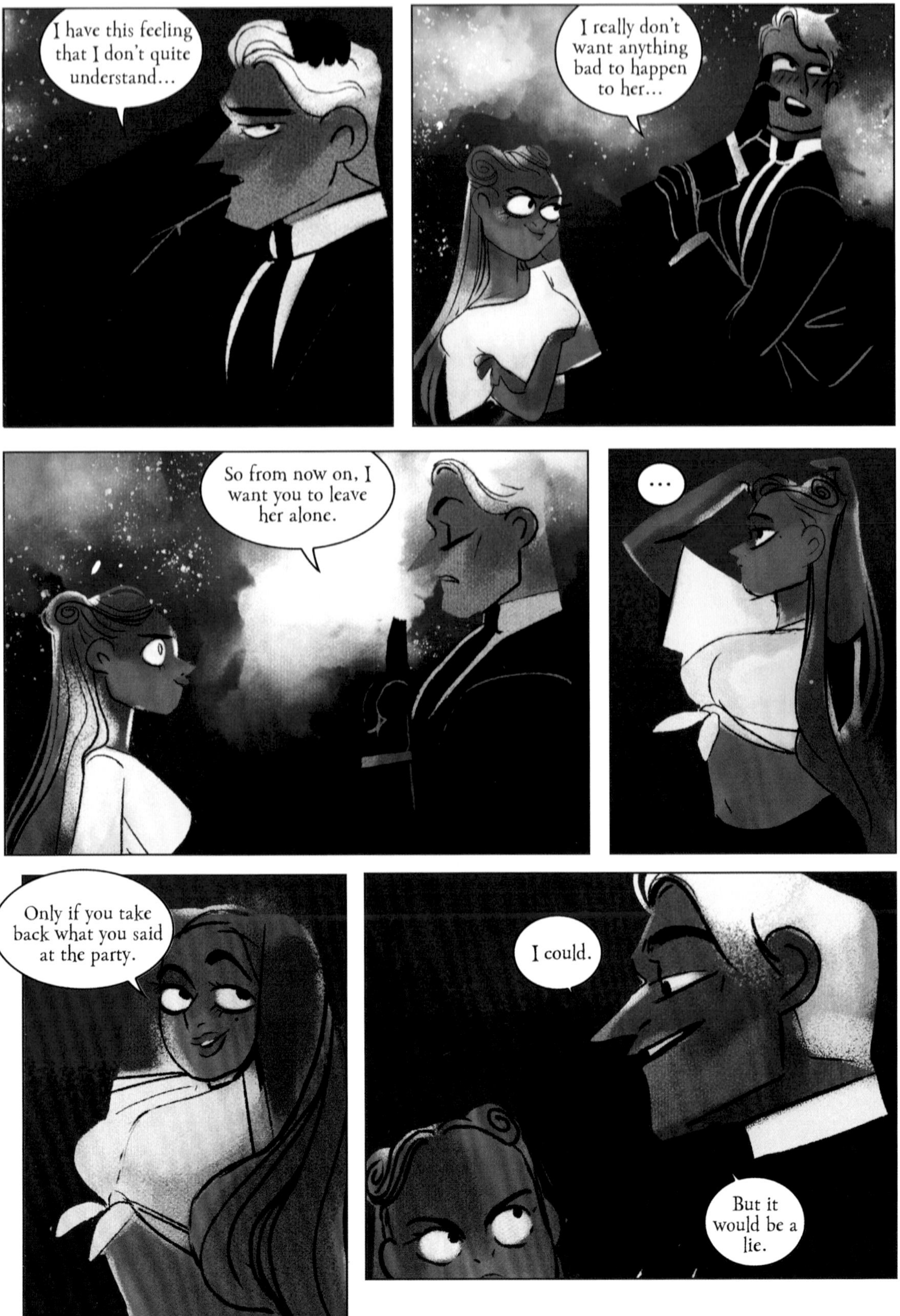
I have this feeling that I don't quite understand...
I really don't want anything bad to happen to her...
So from now on, I want you to leave her alone.
...
Only if you take back what you said at the party.
I could.
But it would be a lie.

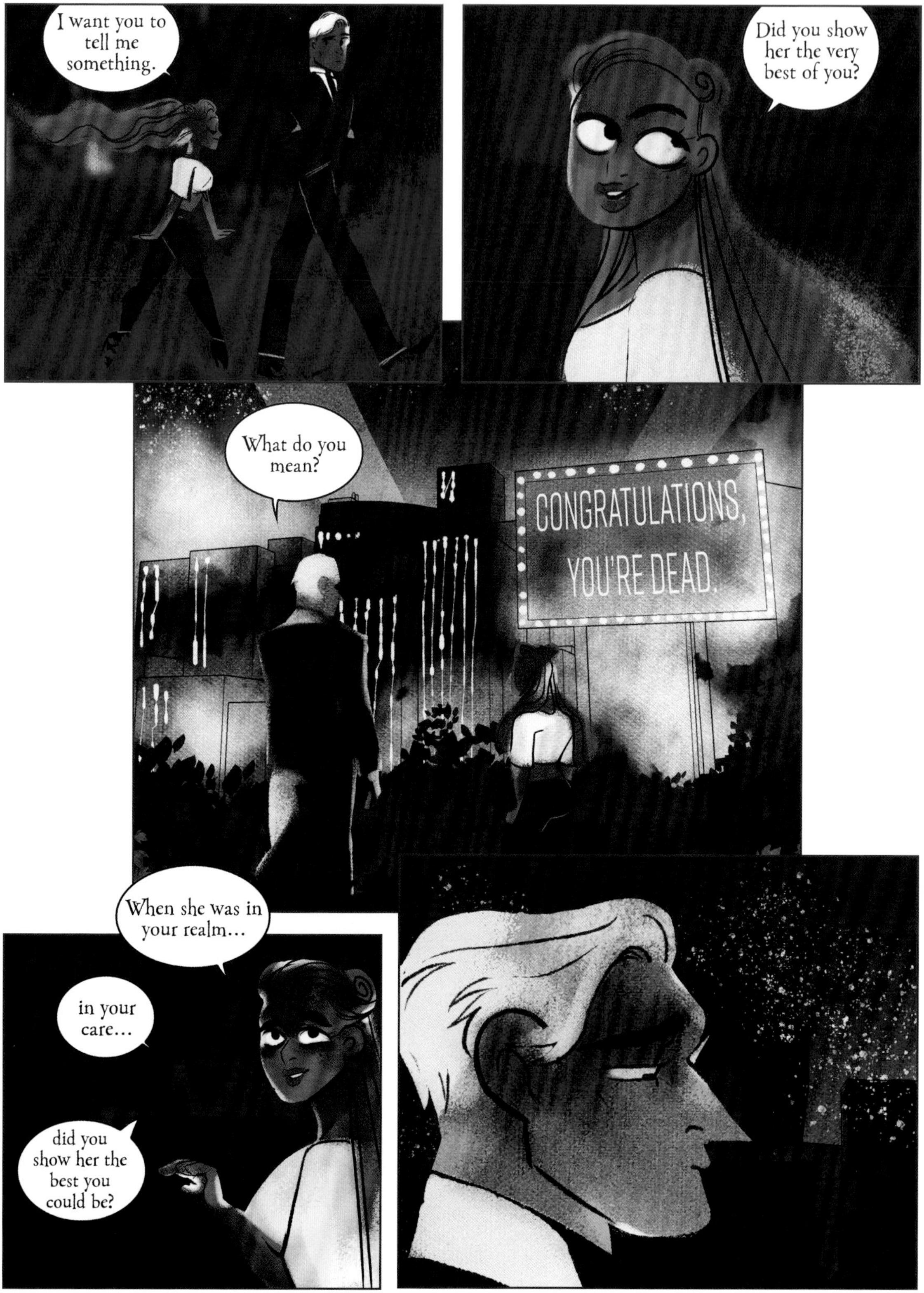

I want you to tell me something.
Did you show her the very best of you?
What do you mean?
CONGRATULATIONS, YOU'RE DEAD.
When she was in your realm...
in your care...
did you show her the best you could be?

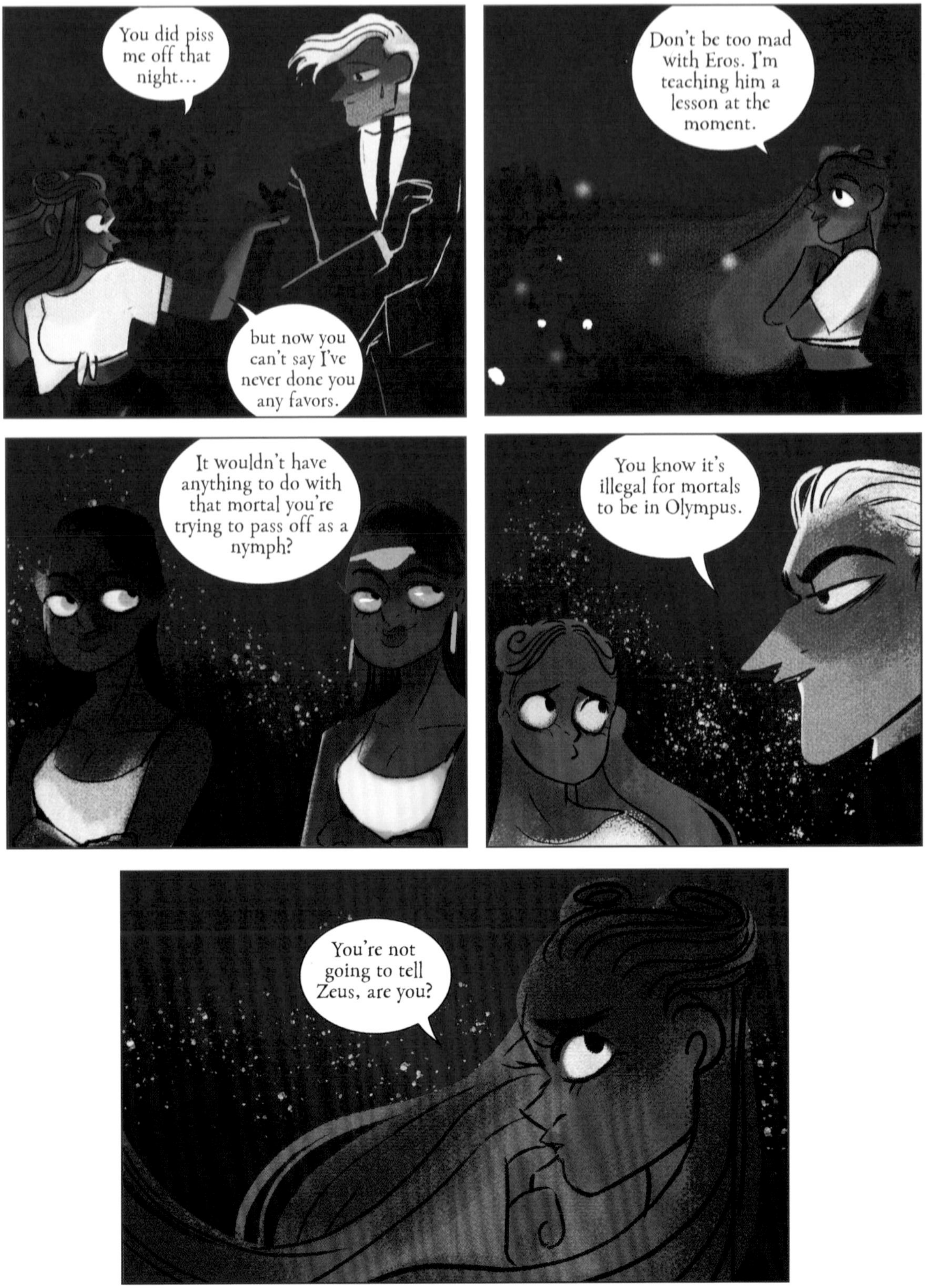
You did piss me off that night...
but now you can't say I've never done you any favors.
Don't be too mad with Eros. I'm teaching him a lesson at the moment.
It wouldn't have anything to do with that mortal you're trying to pass off as a nymph?
You know it's illegal for mortals to be in Olympus.
You're not going to tell Zeus, are you?

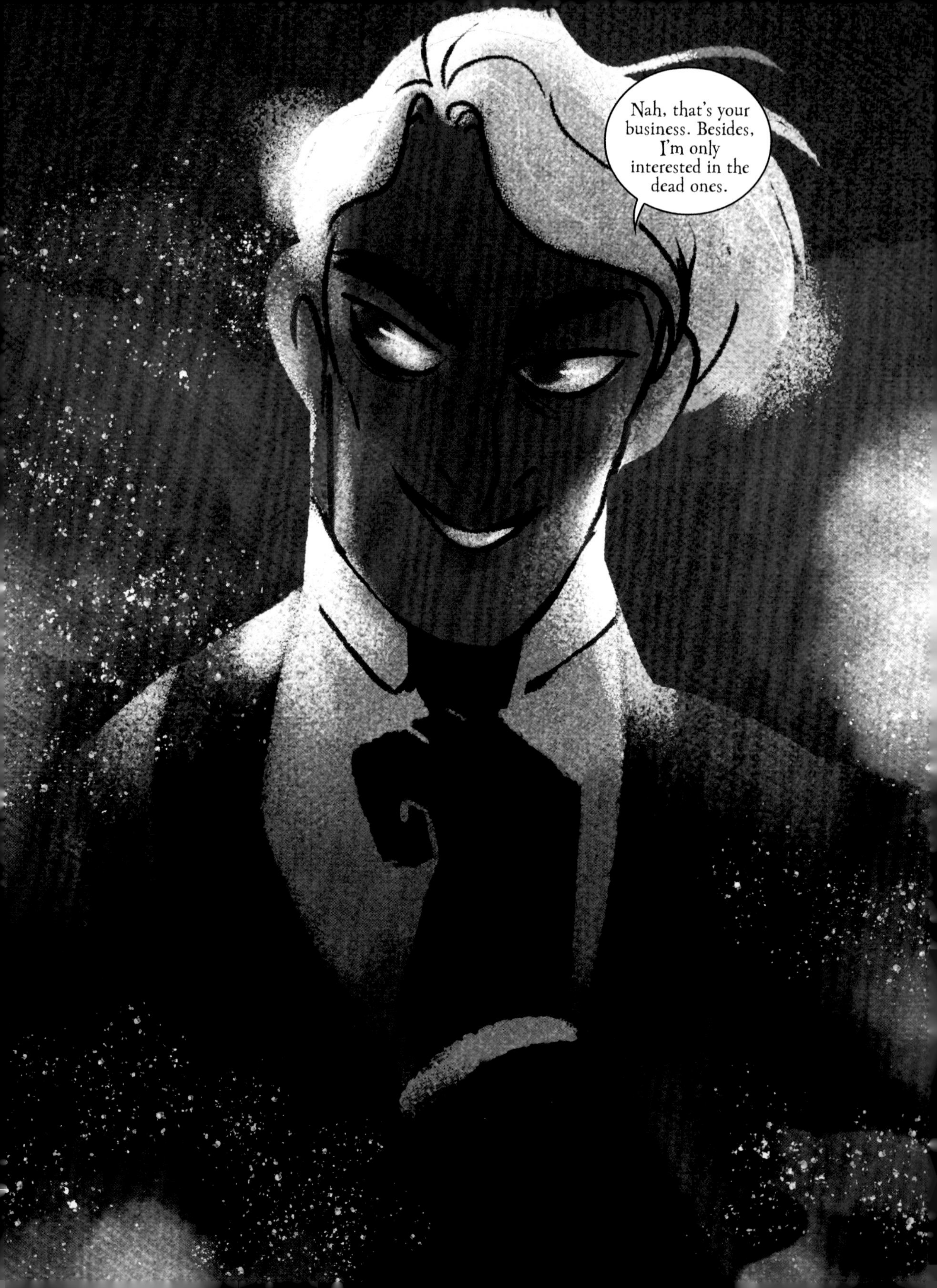
Nah, that's your business. Besides, I'm only interested in the dead ones.

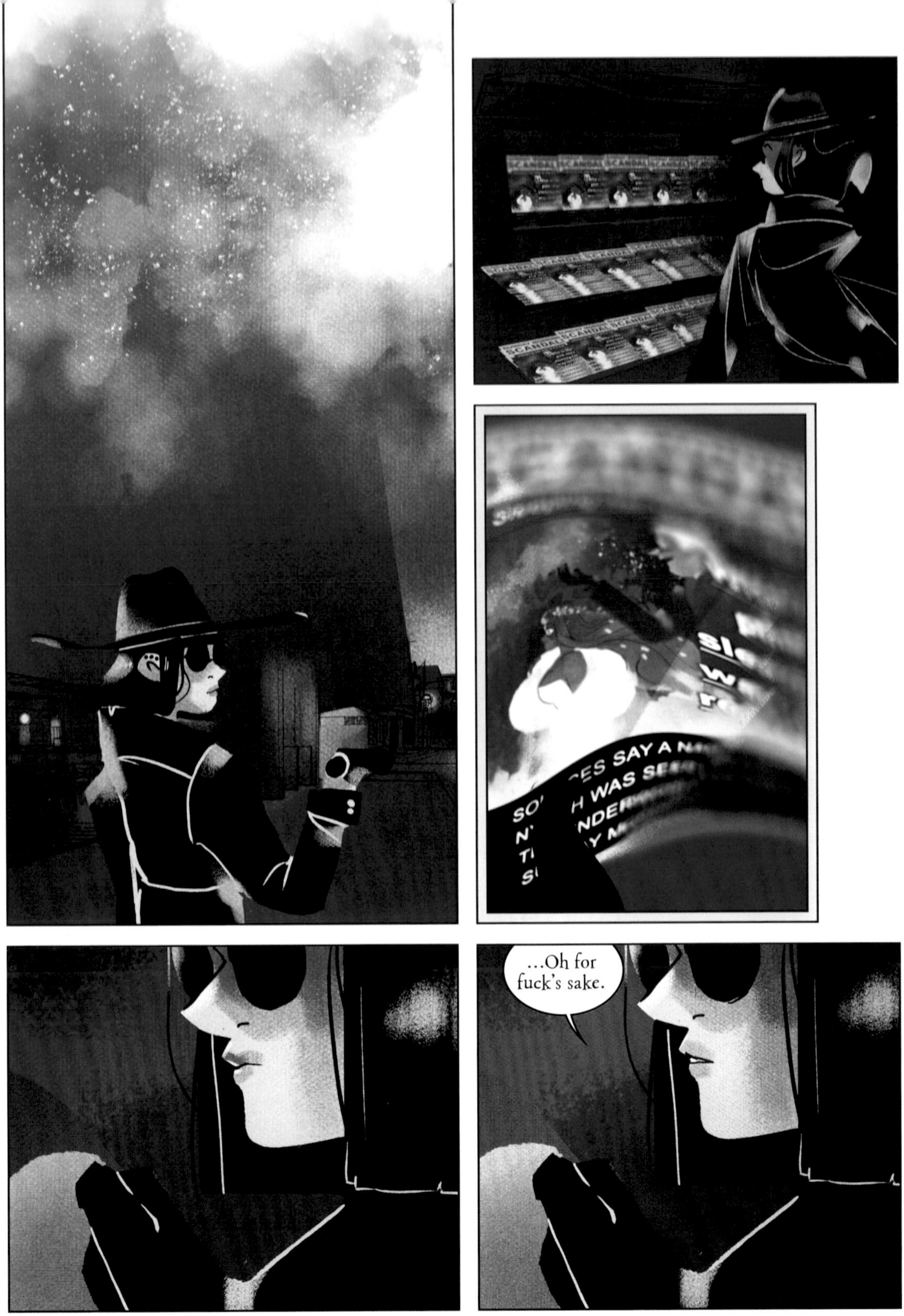
…Oh for fuck's sake.

EPISODE 33: YOUR ROYAL MAJESTY

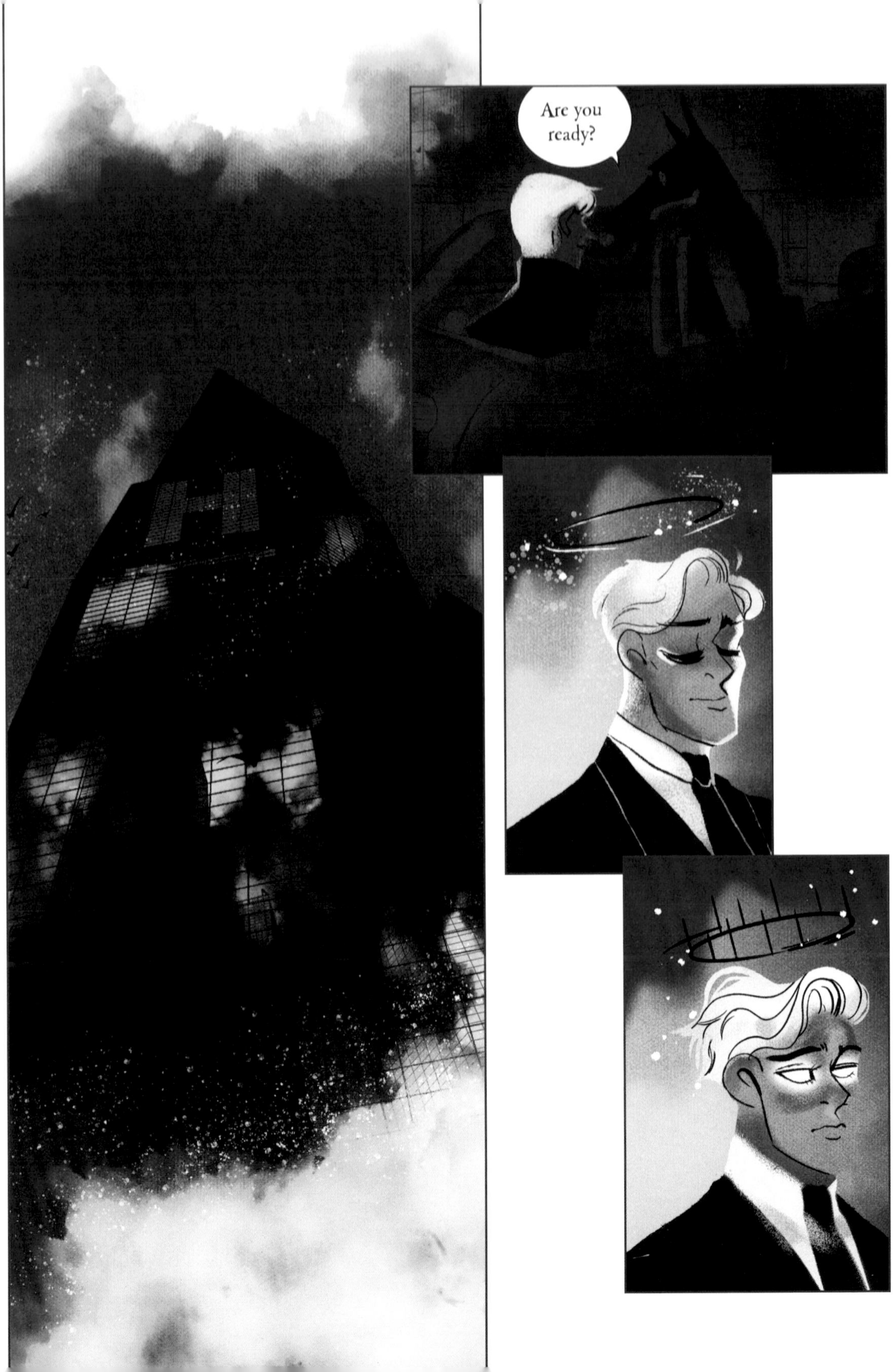
Are you ready?

♪♪ Another daaaaay ♪♪
♪♪Another doooollar♪♪
UNDERWORLD CORP
UNDERWORLD CORP
UNDERWORLD CORP
UNDERWORLD CORP

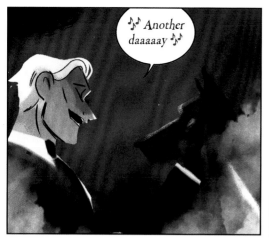

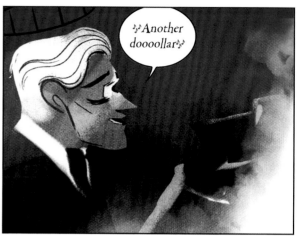

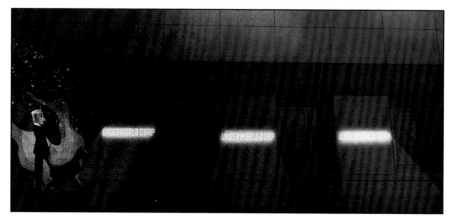

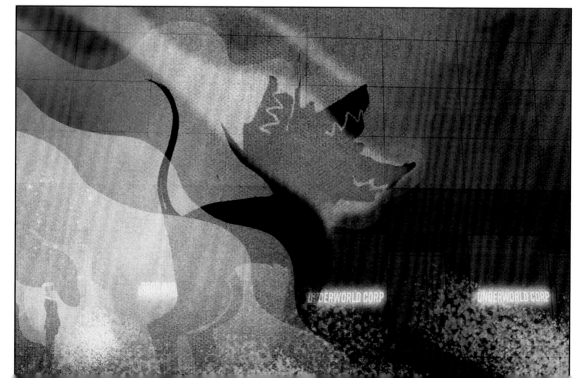

(Self-sufficient.)

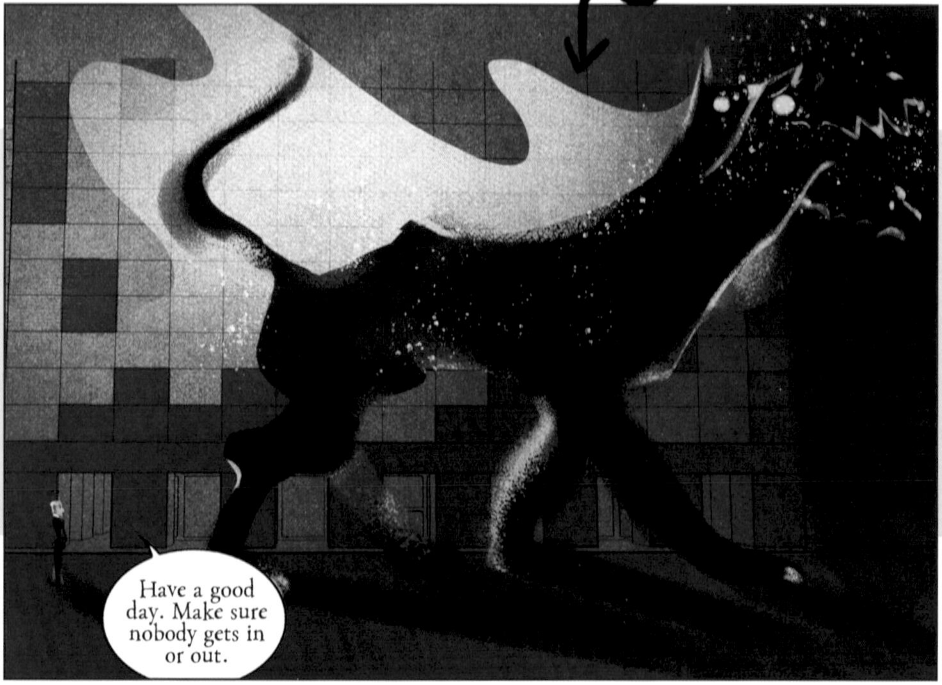
Have a good day. Make sure nobody gets in or out.

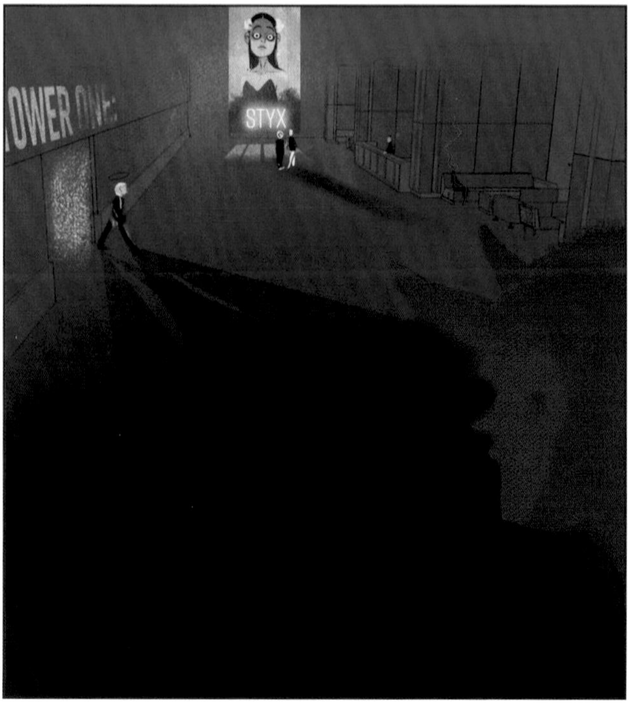
STYX

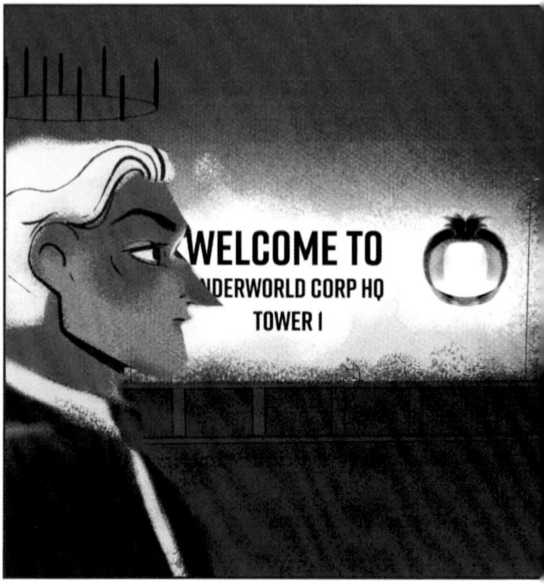
WELCOME TO
TOWER I

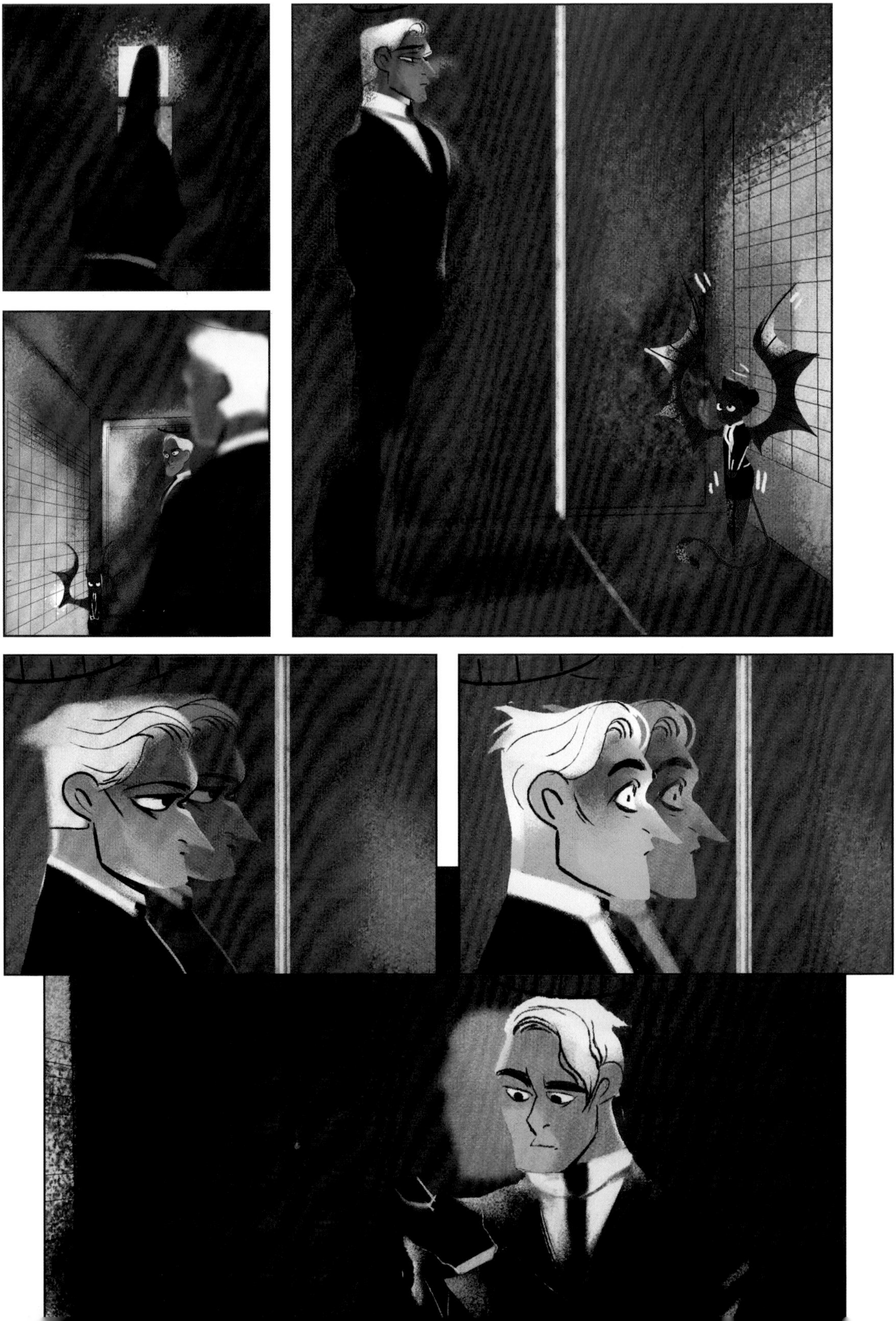

Did you know there is a really dorky portrait of you at Hera's? 🙄

I don't know what to reply.

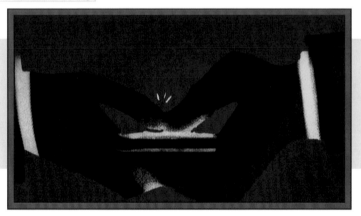

Did you know there is a really dorky portrait of you at Hera's? 🙄

You would make a much better subject for a painting.

Ah! Don't send her that, you idiot.

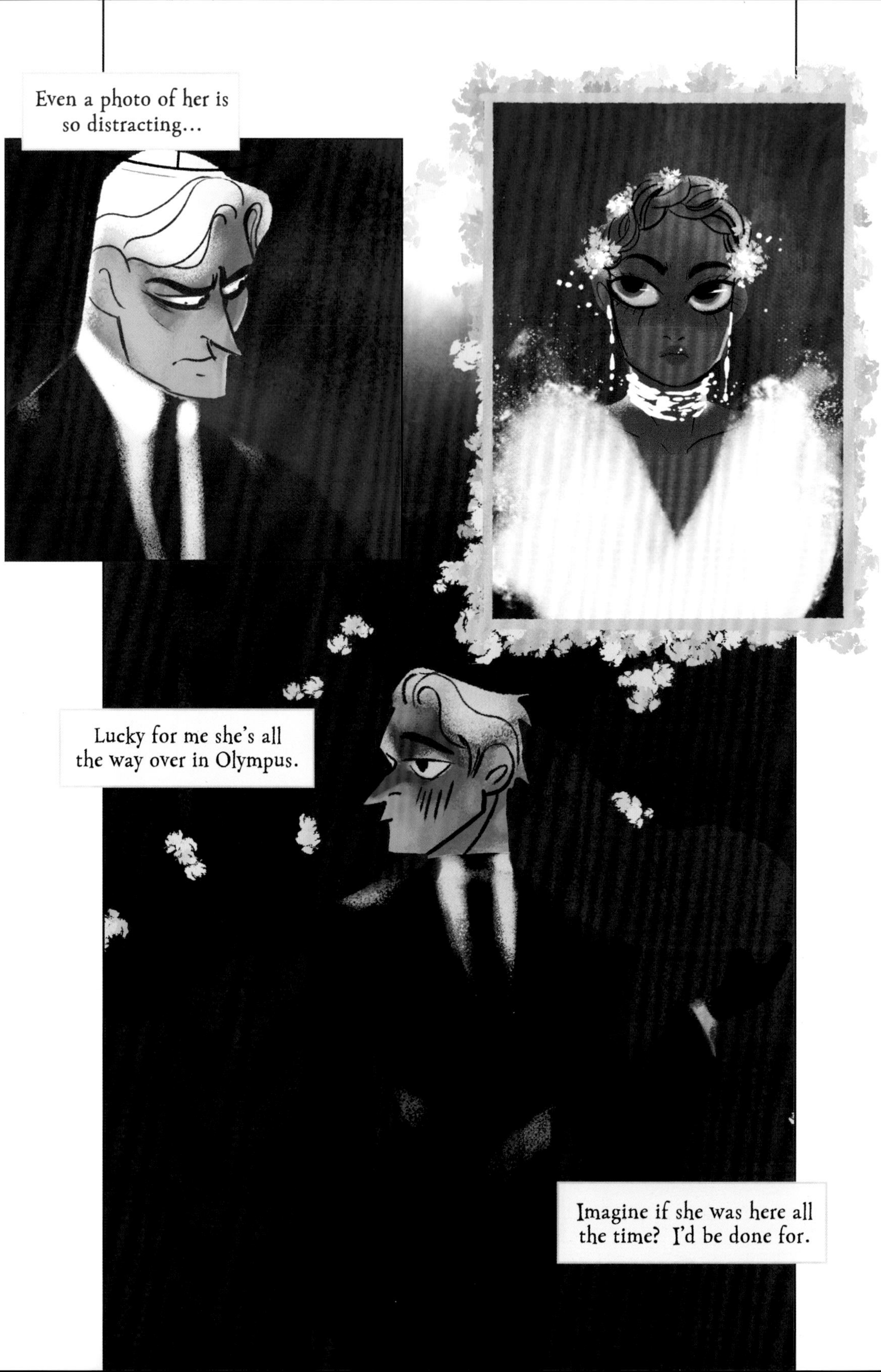
Even a photo of her is so distracting...
Lucky for me she's all the way over in Olympus.
Imagine if she was here all the time? I'd be done for.

Did you know there is a really dorky portrait of you at Hera's?
You would make a muc
Did you know there is a really dorky portrait of you at Hera's?
I don't know why Hera insists on keeping those up. I hope Monday is treating you well.
Why isn't he getting out?
TAP
TAP
TAP
Ummm, Your Majesty.
Oh.
Here.

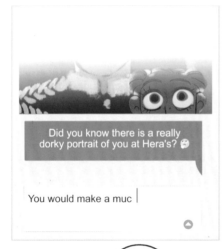

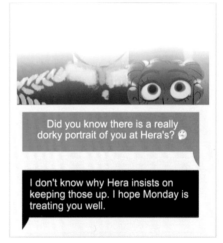

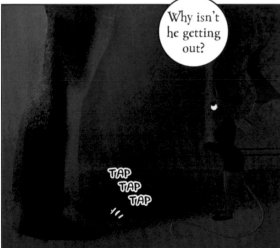

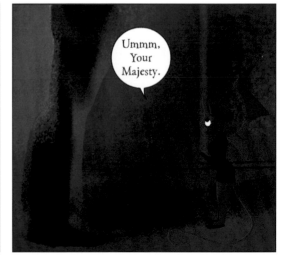

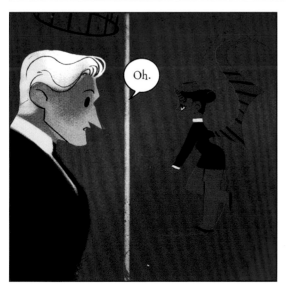

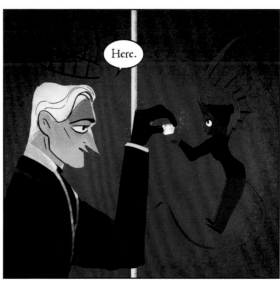

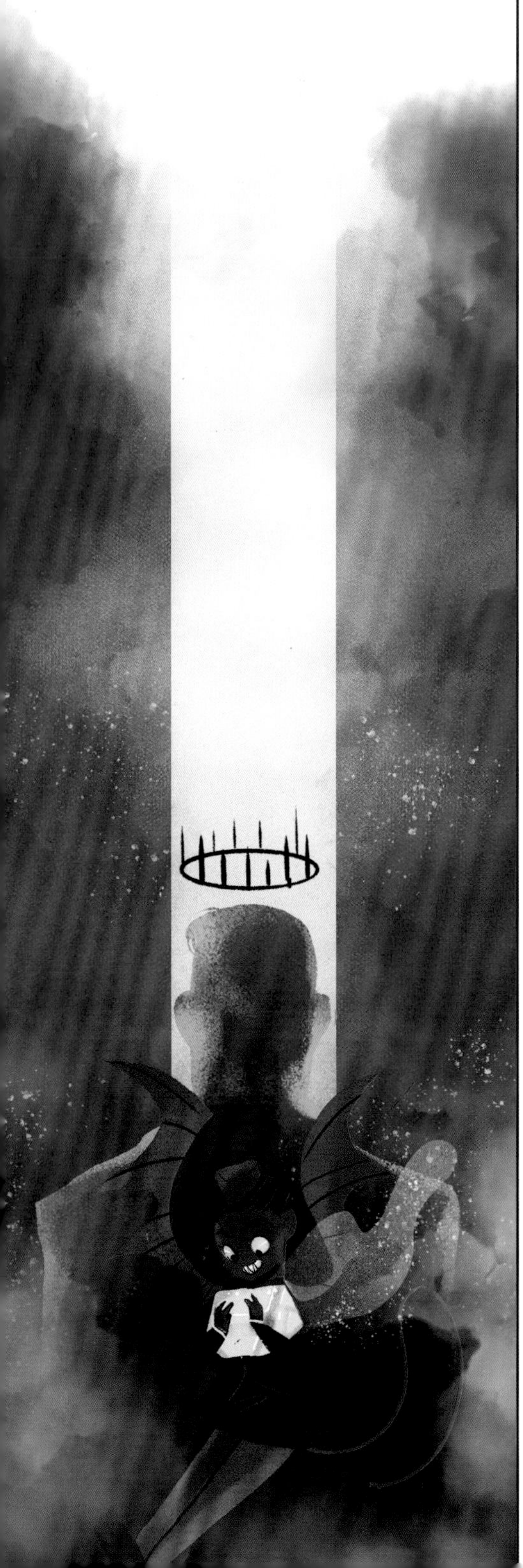

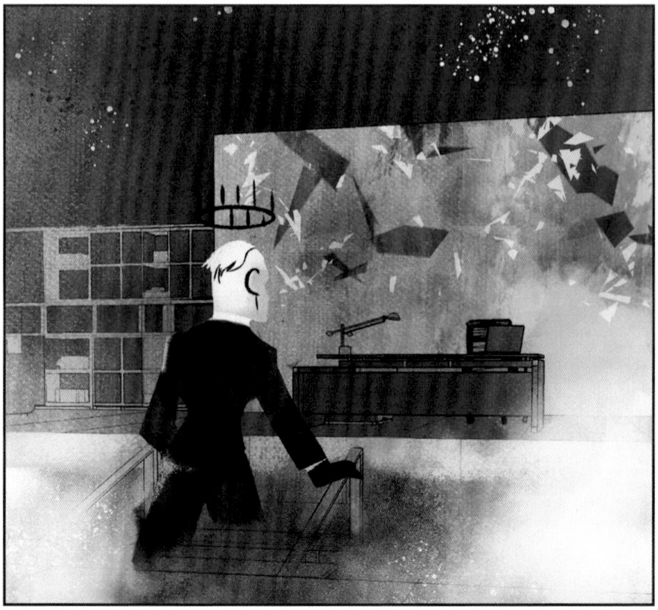

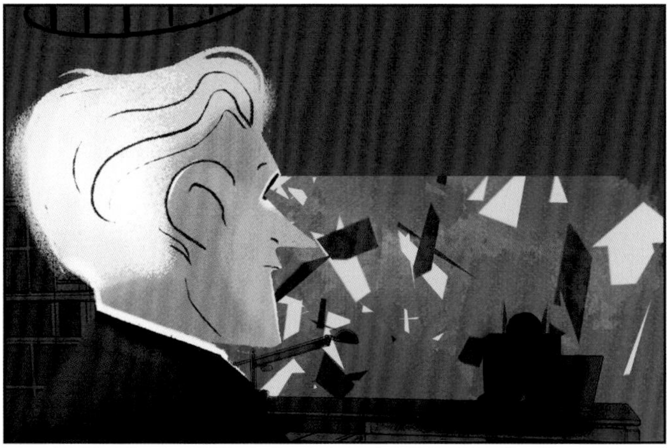

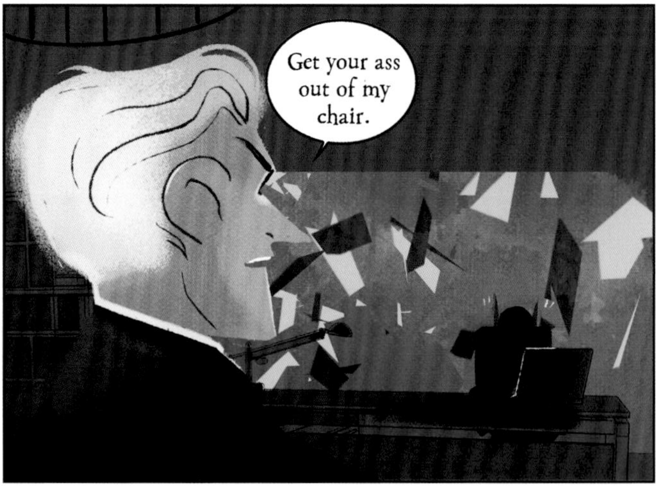
Get your ass
out of my
chair.

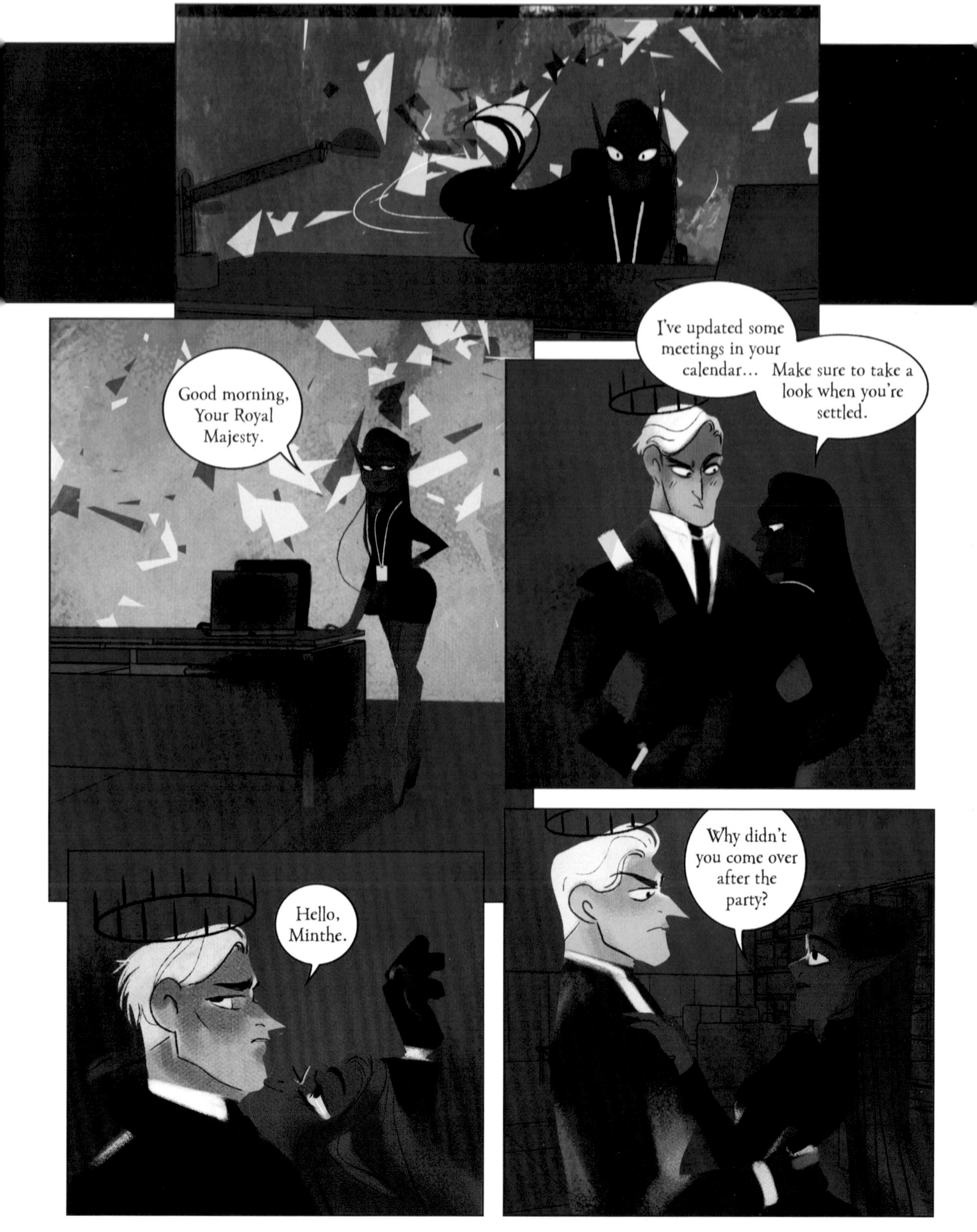
Good morning, Your Royal Majesty.
I've updated some meetings in your calendar... Make sure to take a look when you're settled.
Hello, Minthe.
Why didn't you come over after the party?

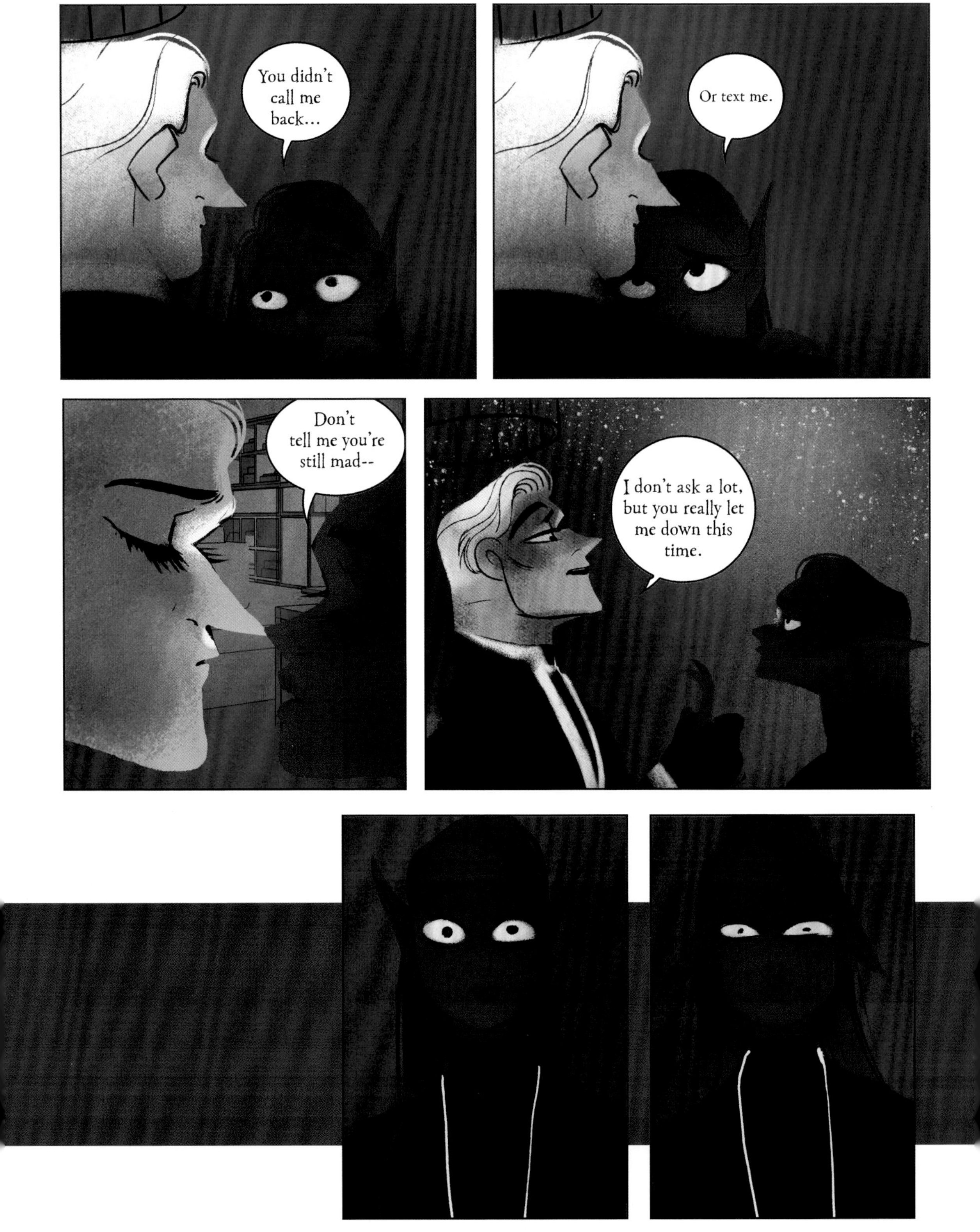
You didn't call me back...
Or text me.
Don't tell me you're still mad--
I don't ask a lot, but you really let me down this time.

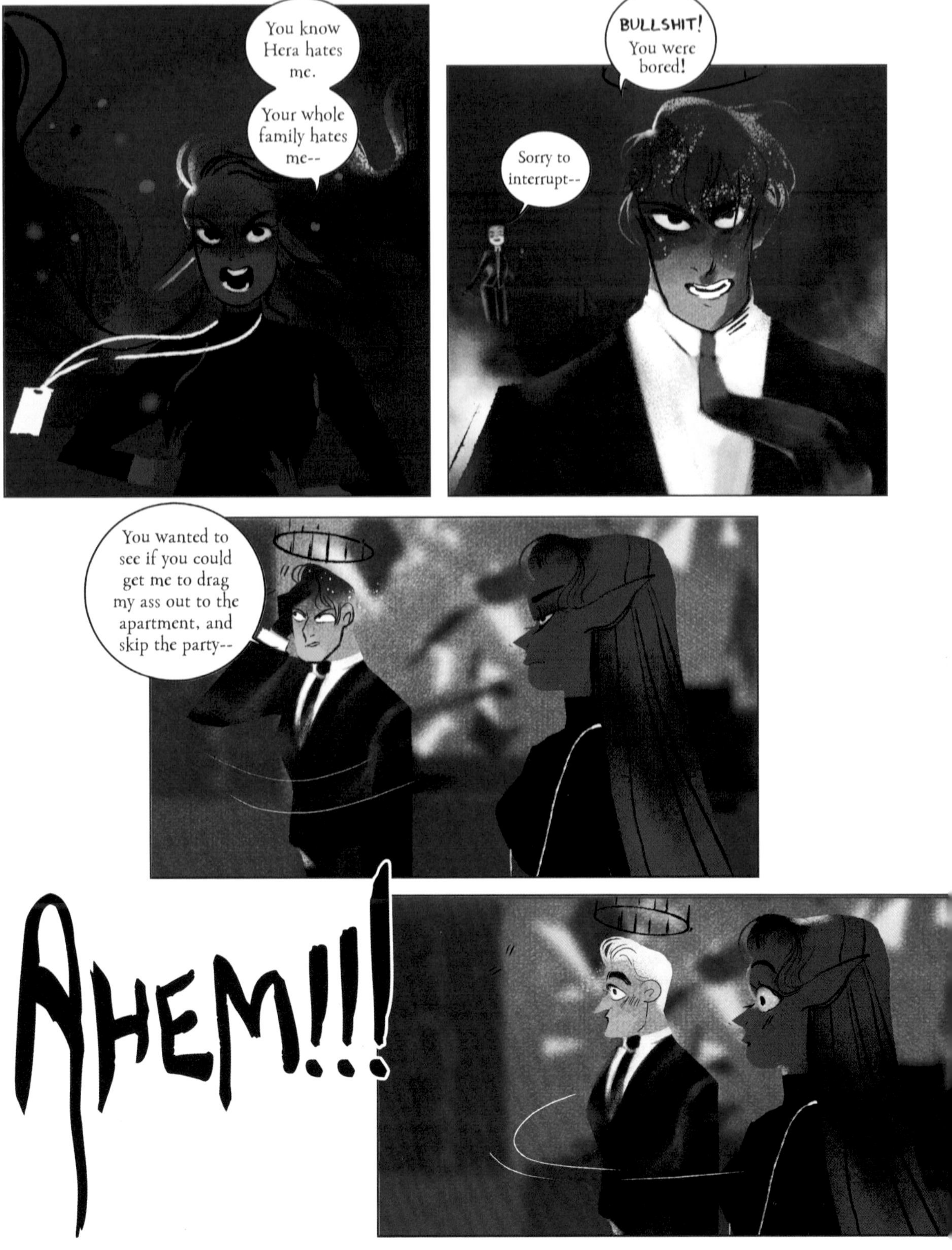
You know Hera hates me.
Your whole family hates me--
BULLSHIT! You were bored!
Sorry to interrupt--
You wanted to see if you could get me to drag my ass out to the apartment, and skip the party--
AHEM!!!

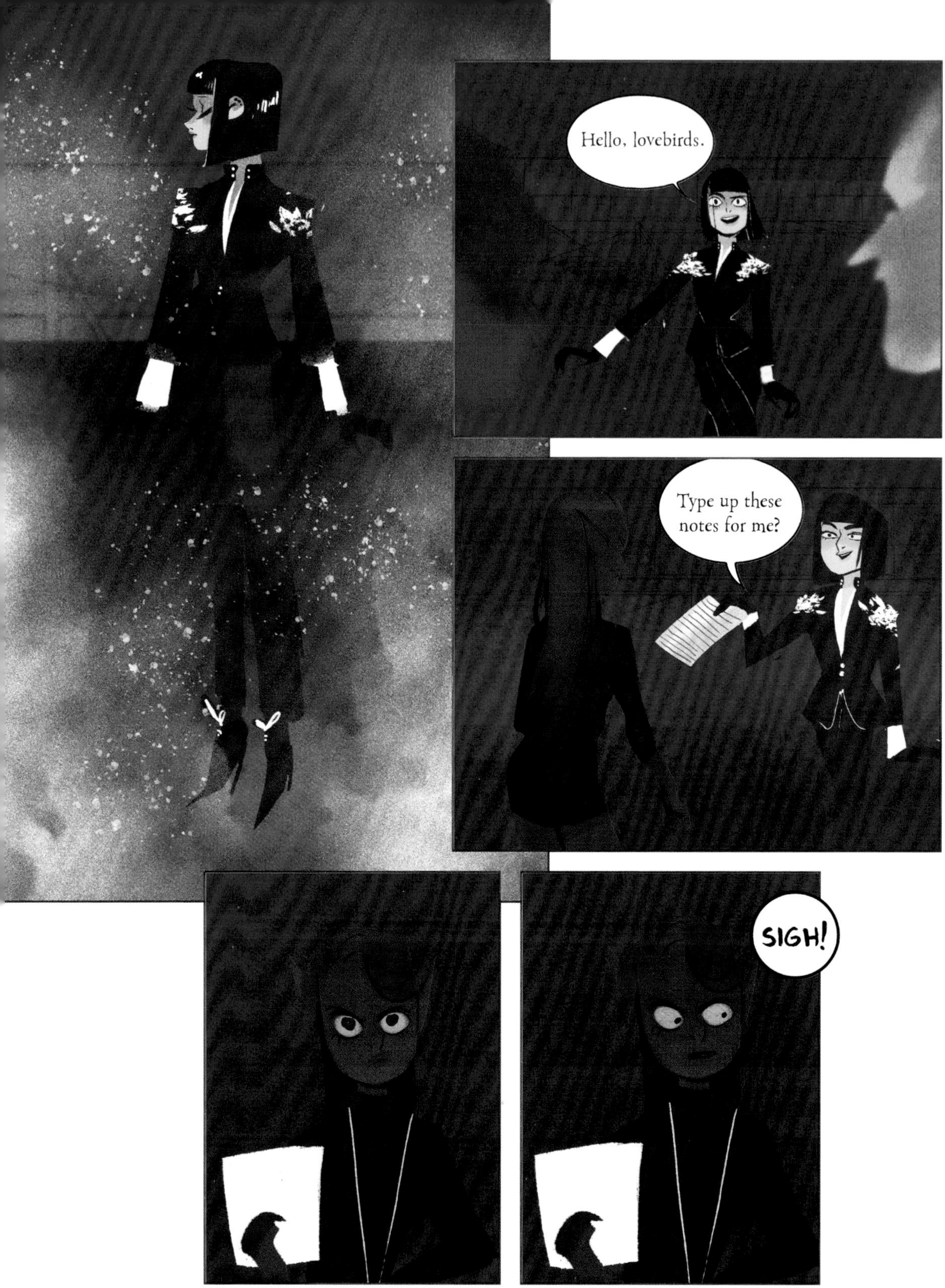
Hello, lovebirds.
Type up these notes for me?
SIGH!

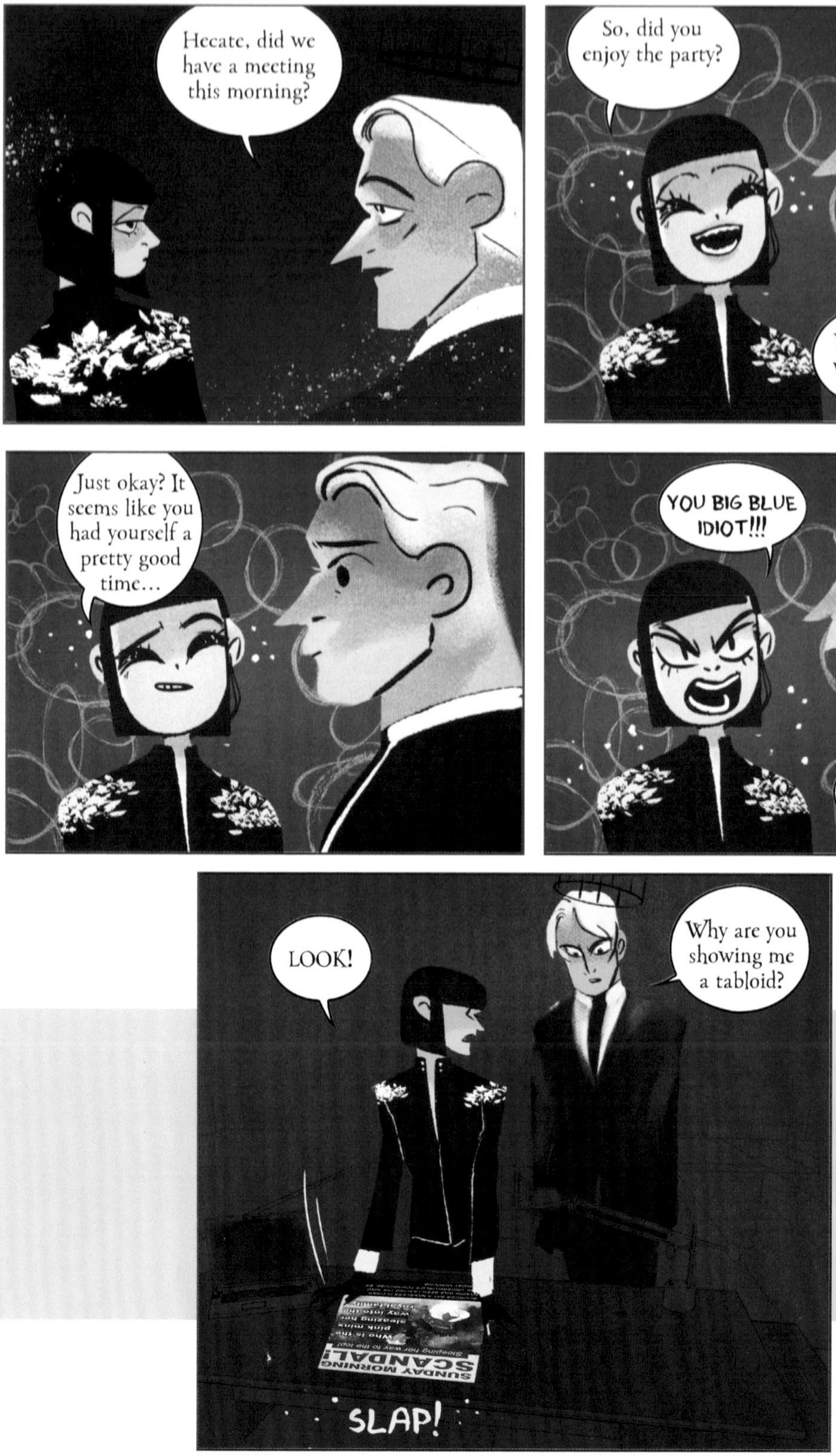
Hecate, did we have a meeting this morning?
So, did you enjoy the party?
Y-yeah, it was okay.
Just okay? It seems like you had yourself a pretty good time...
YOU BIG BLUE IDIOT!!!
WHA???
LOOK!
Why are you showing me a tabloid?
SUNDAY MORNING
SCANDAL!
SLAP!

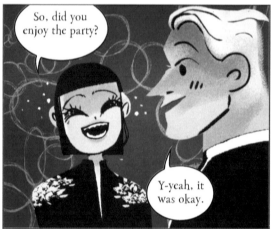

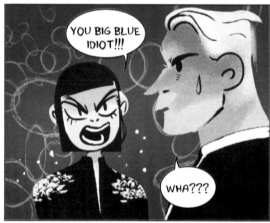

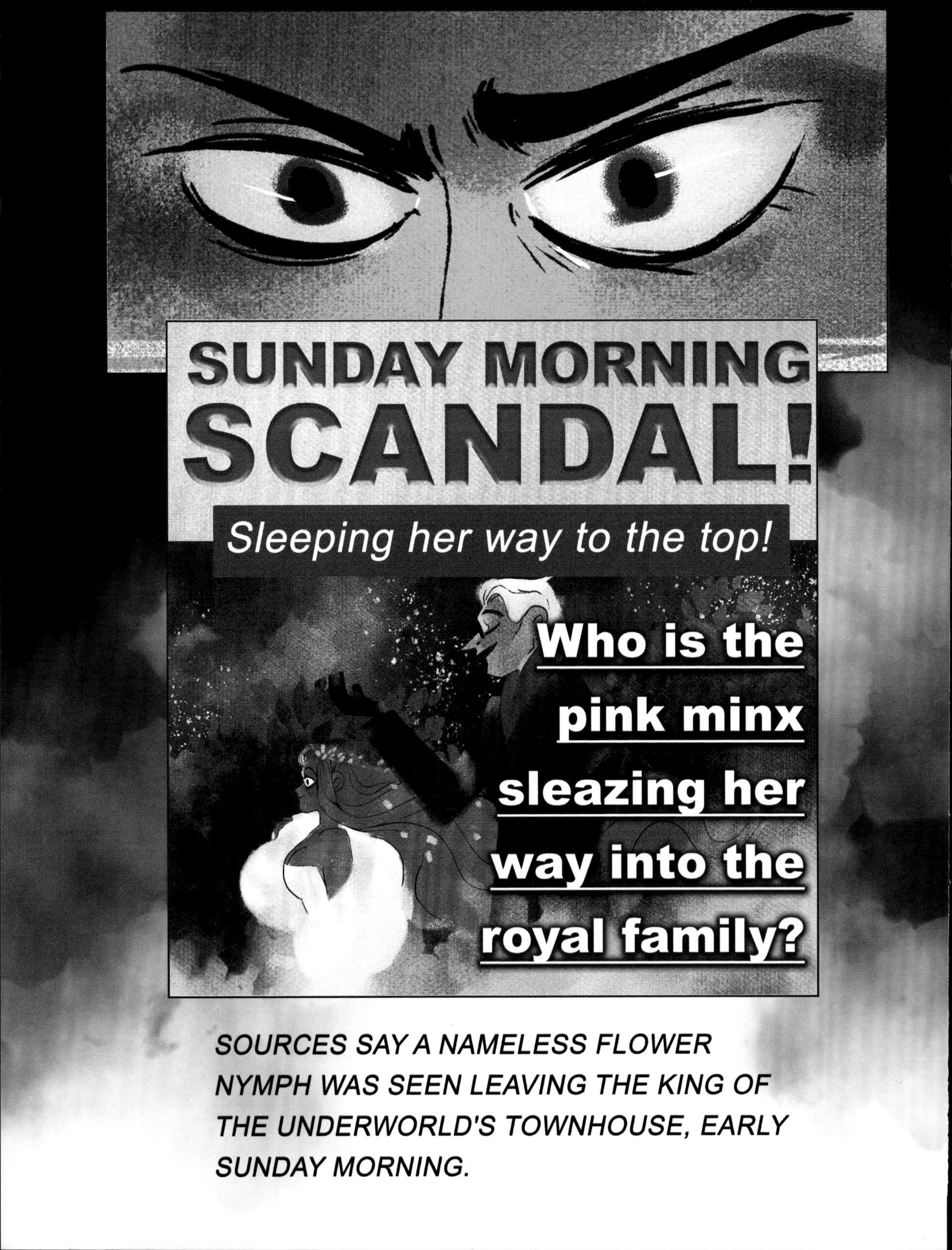
SUNDAY MORNING SCANDAL!
Sleeping her way to the top!
Who is the pink minx sleazing her way into the royal family?
SOURCES SAY A NAMELESS FLOWER NYMPH WAS SEEN LEAVING THE KING OF THE UNDERWORLD'S TOWNHOUSE, EARLY SUNDAY MORNING.

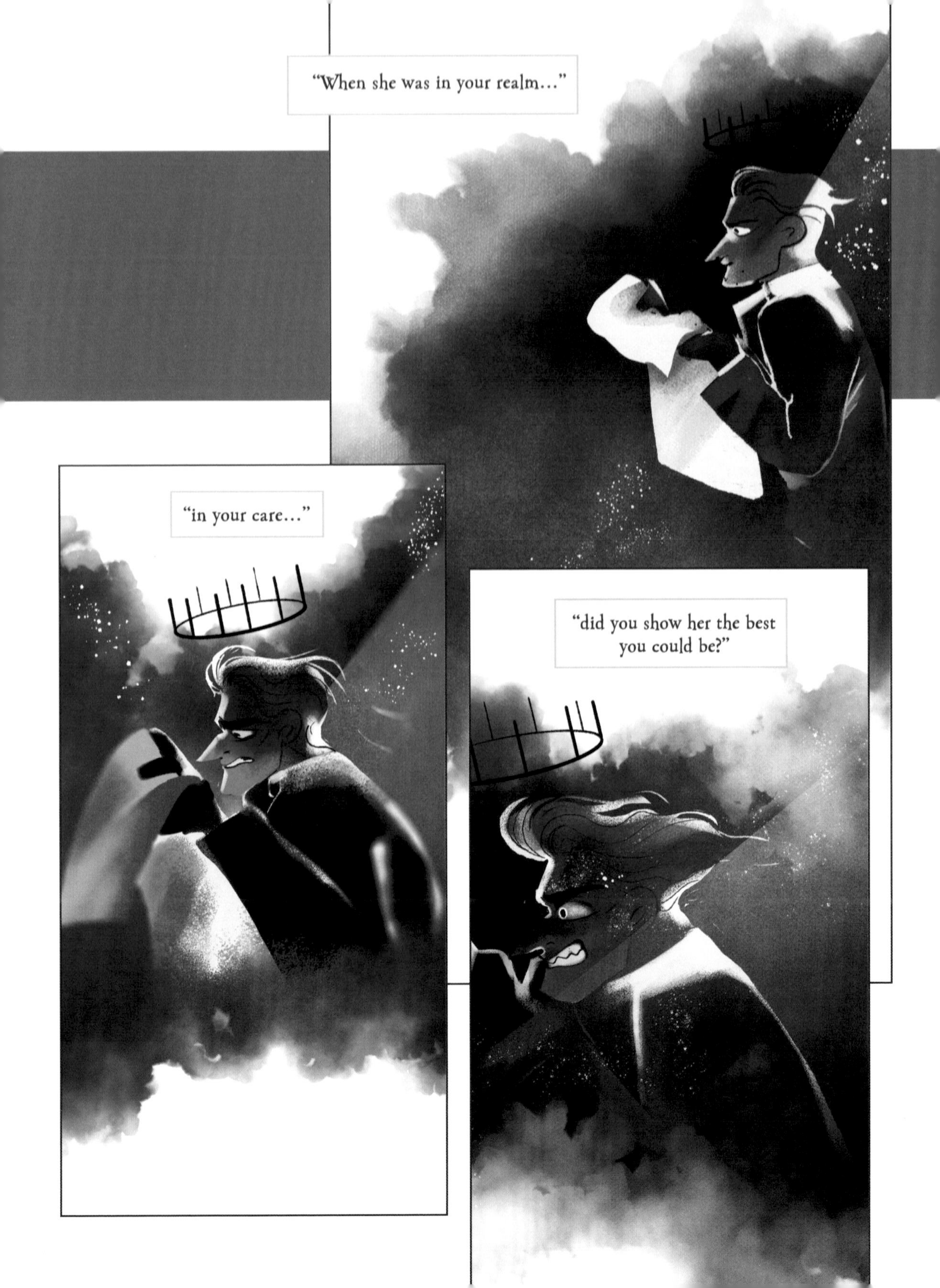
"When she was in your realm..."
"in your care..."
"did you show her the best you could be?"

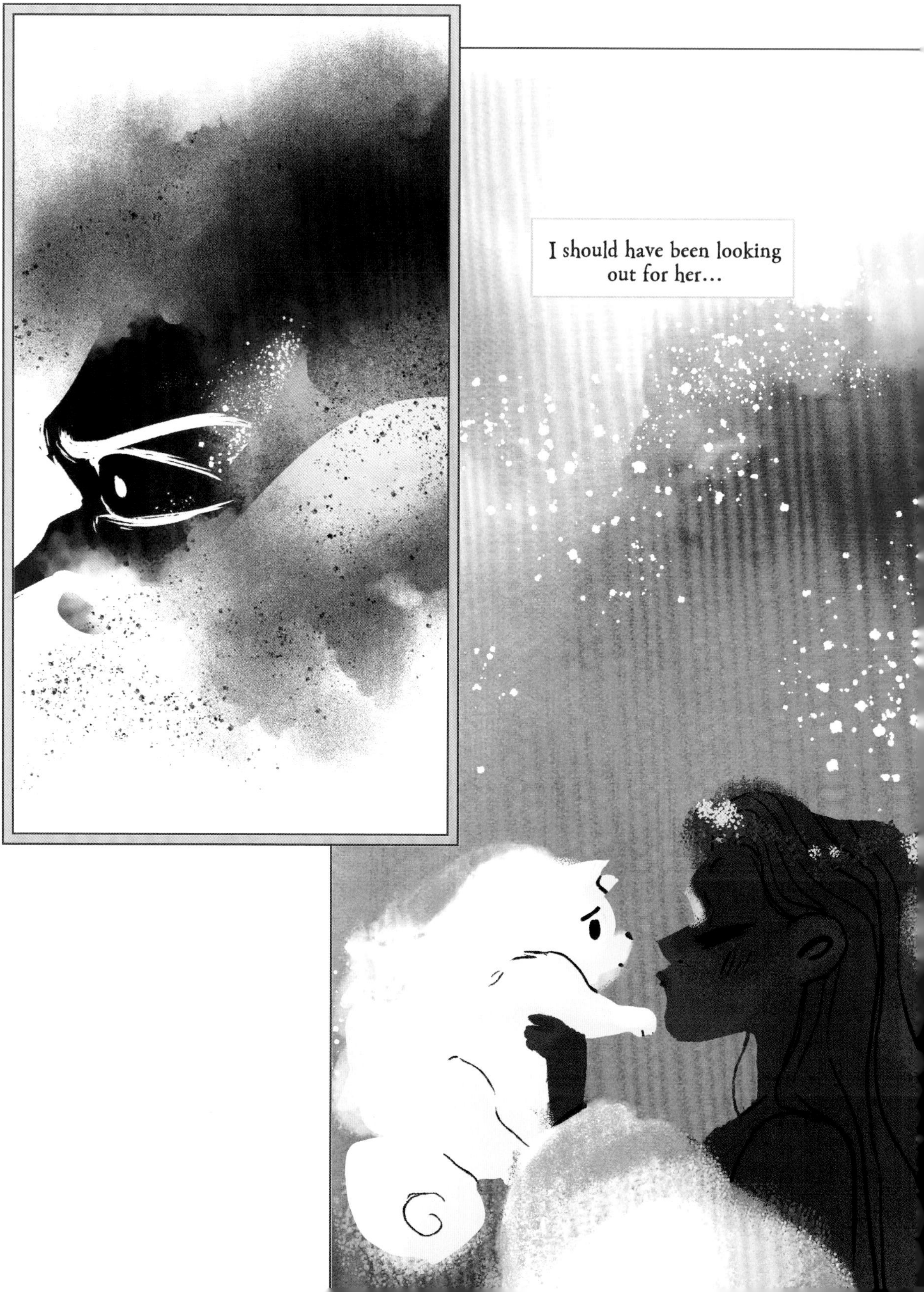
I should have been looking
out for her…

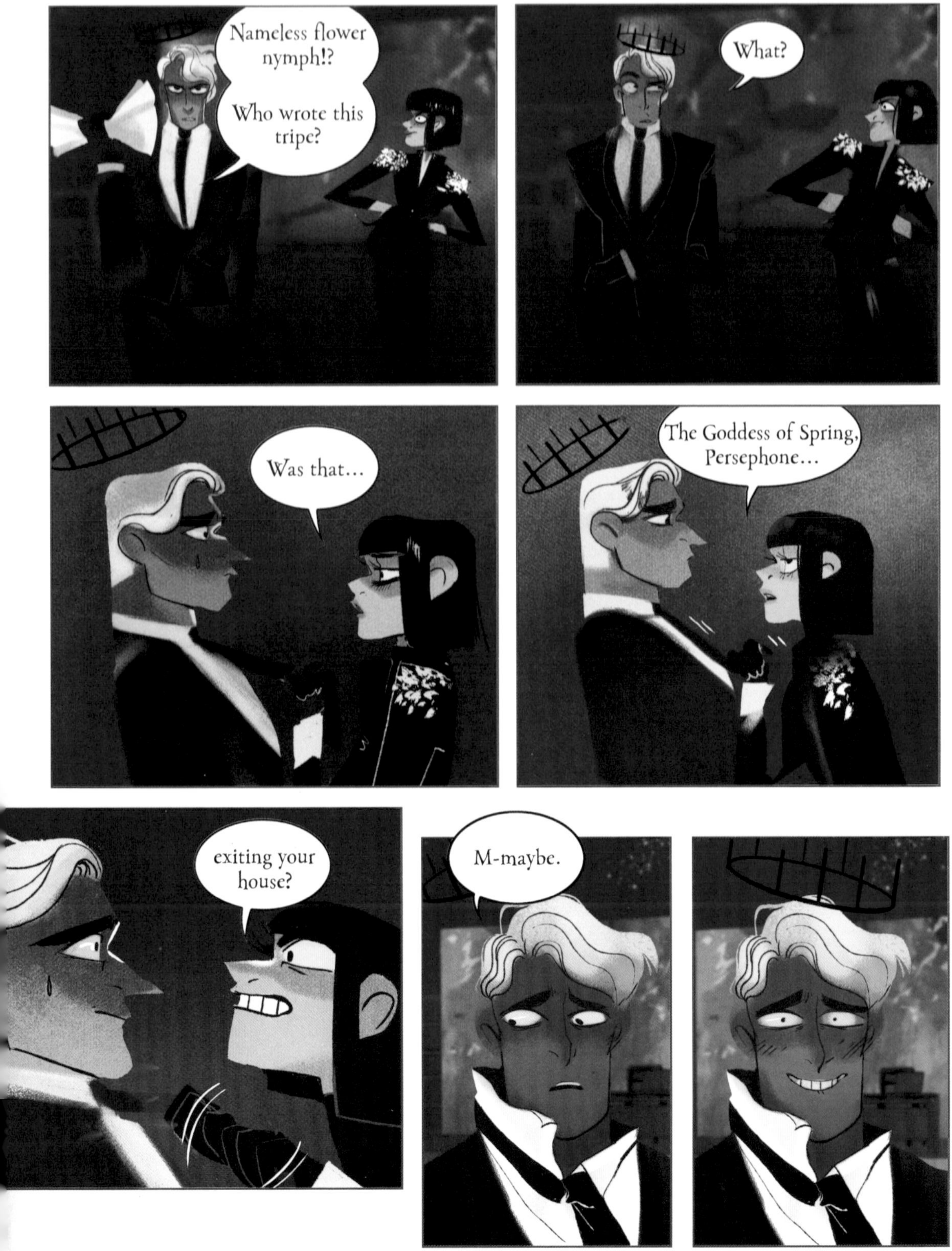
Nameless flower nymph!?
Who wrote this tripe?
What?
Was that...
The Goddess of Spring, Persephone...
exiting your house?
M-maybe.

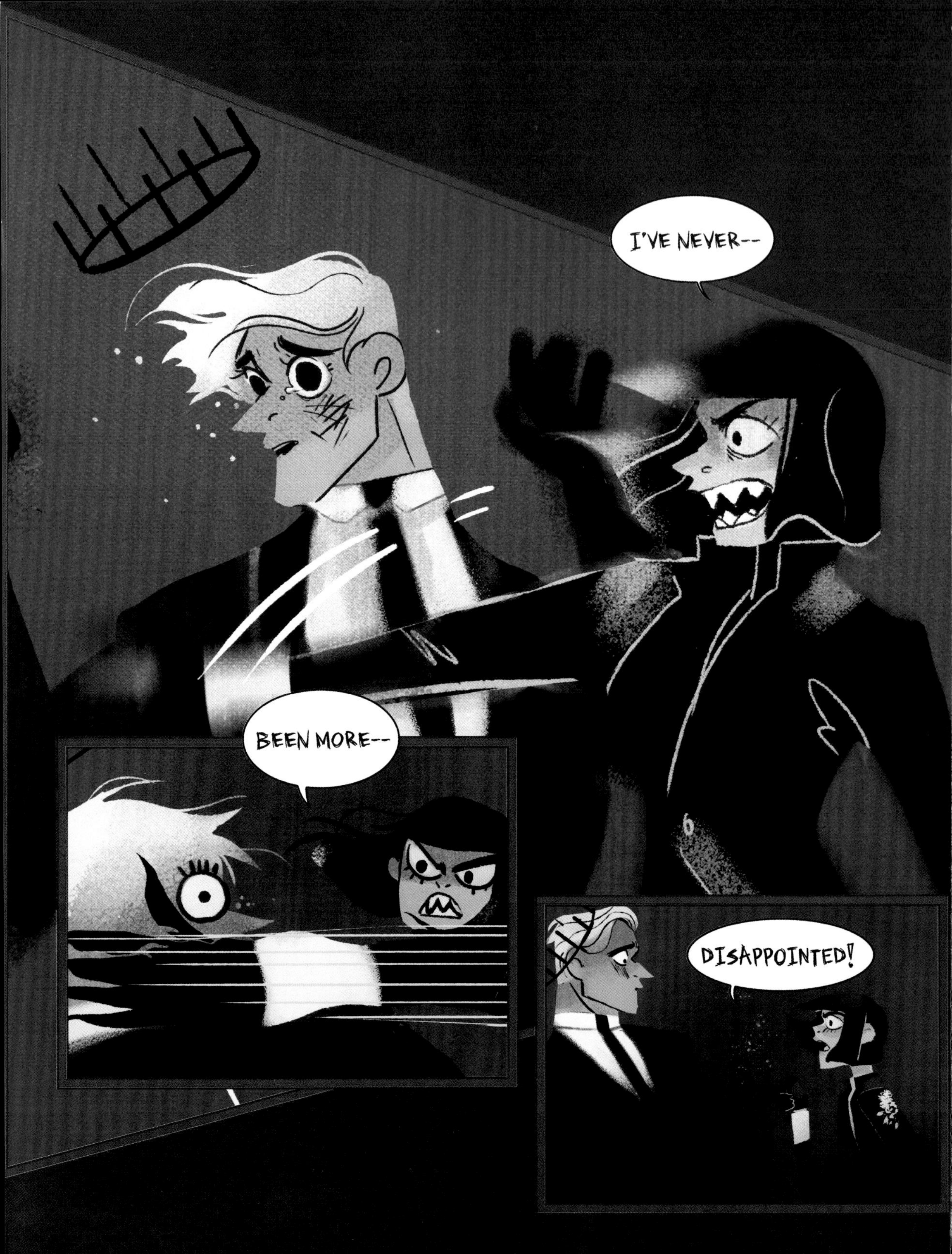
I'VE NEVER--
BEEN MORE--
DISAPPOINTED!

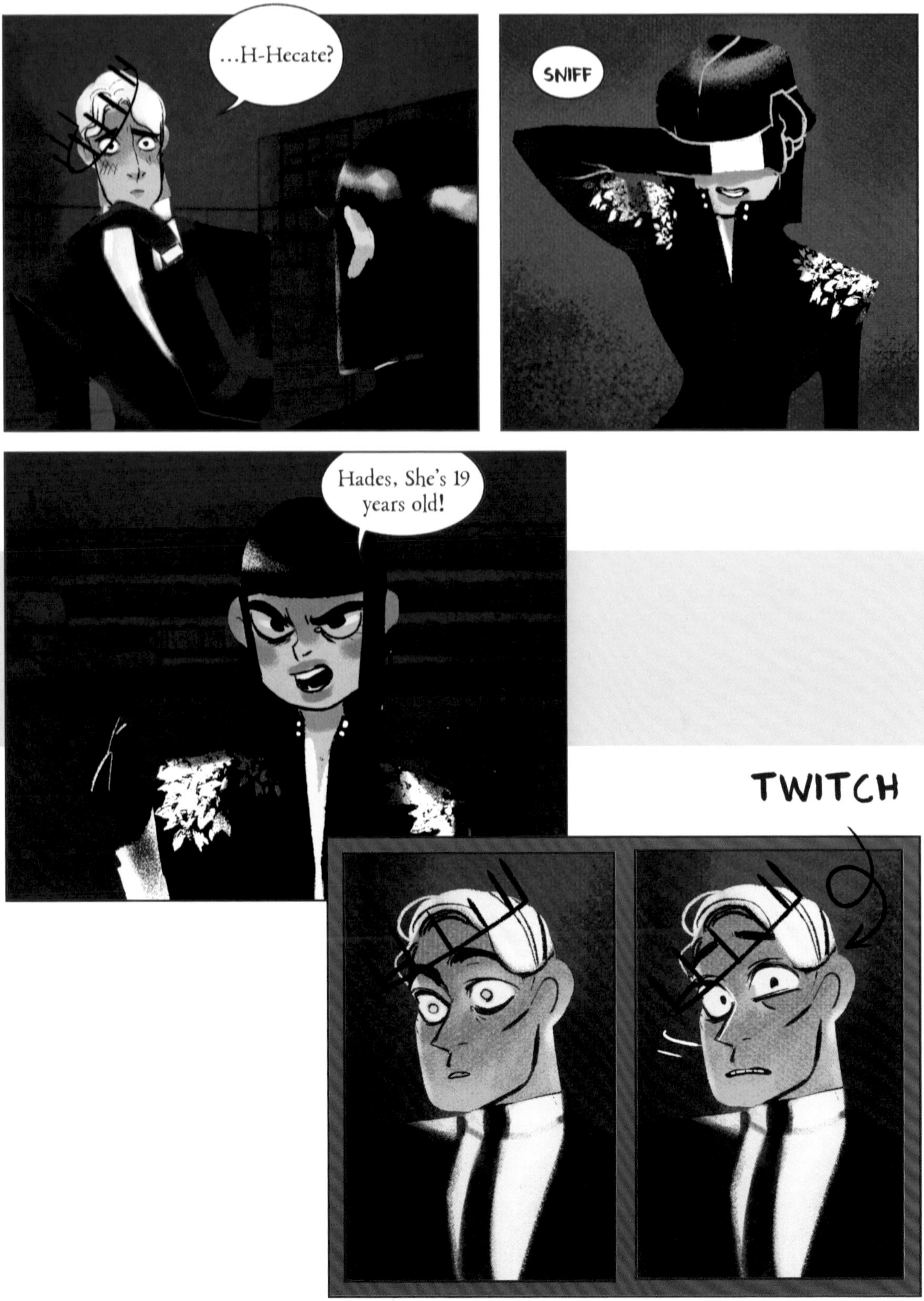
...H-Hecate?
SNIFF
Hades, She's 19 years old!
TWITCH

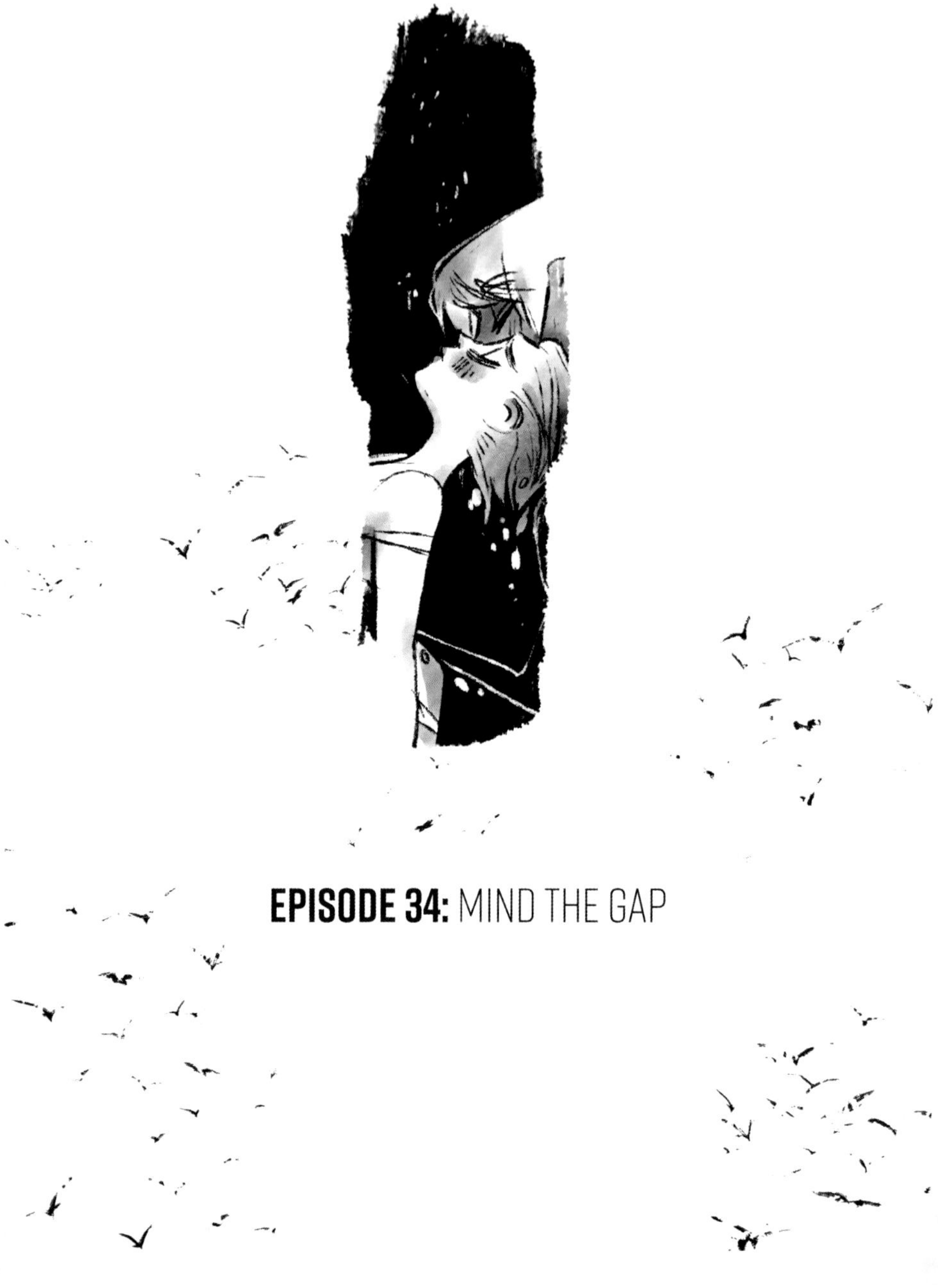

EPISODE 34: MIND THE GAP

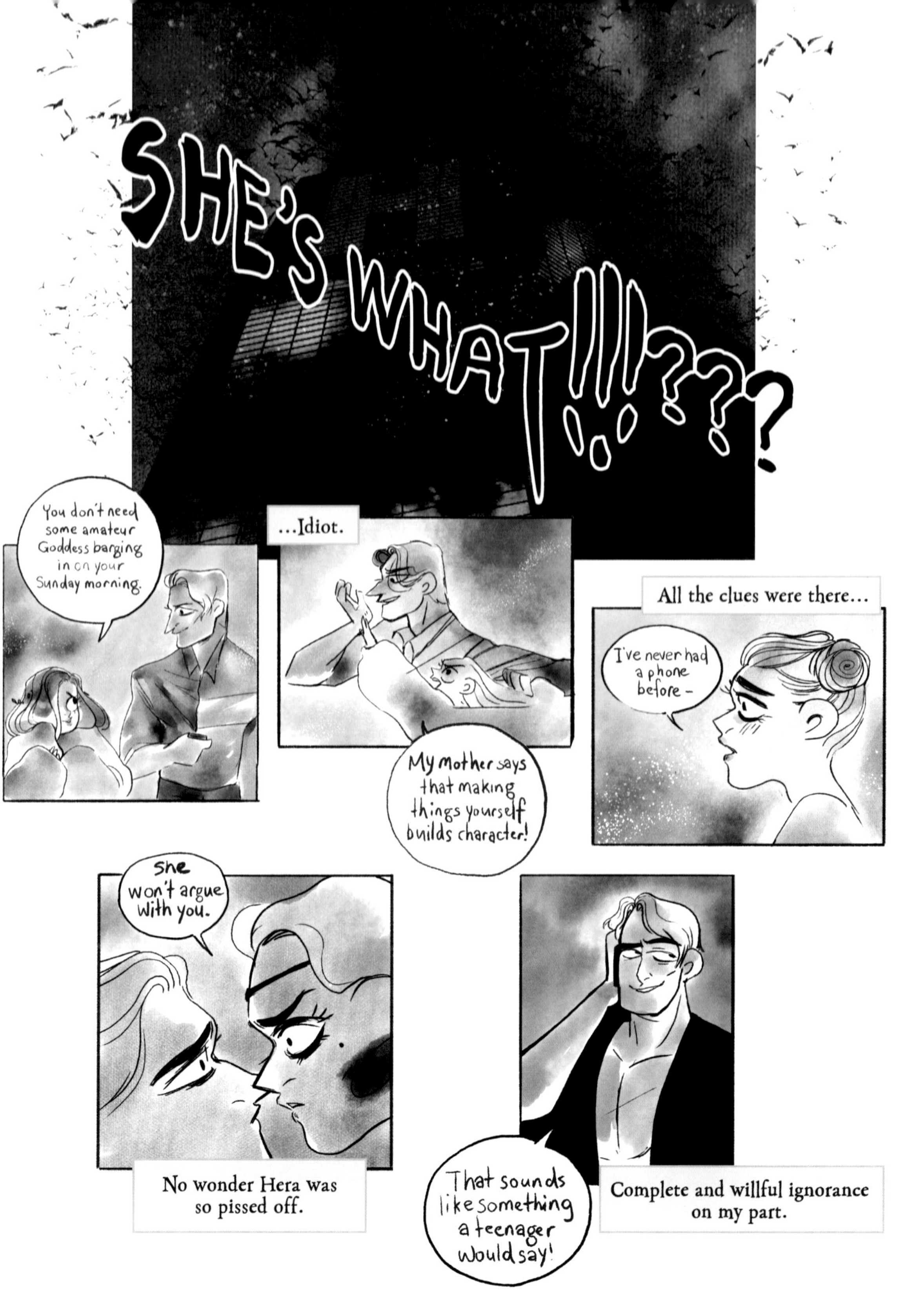
SHE'S WHAT!!!???
You don't need some amateur Goddess barging in on your Sunday morning.
...Idiot.
My mother says that making things yourself builds character!
All the clues were there...
I've never had a phone before –
She won't argue with you.
No wonder Hera was so pissed off.
That sounds like something a teenager would say!
Complete and willful ignorance on my part.

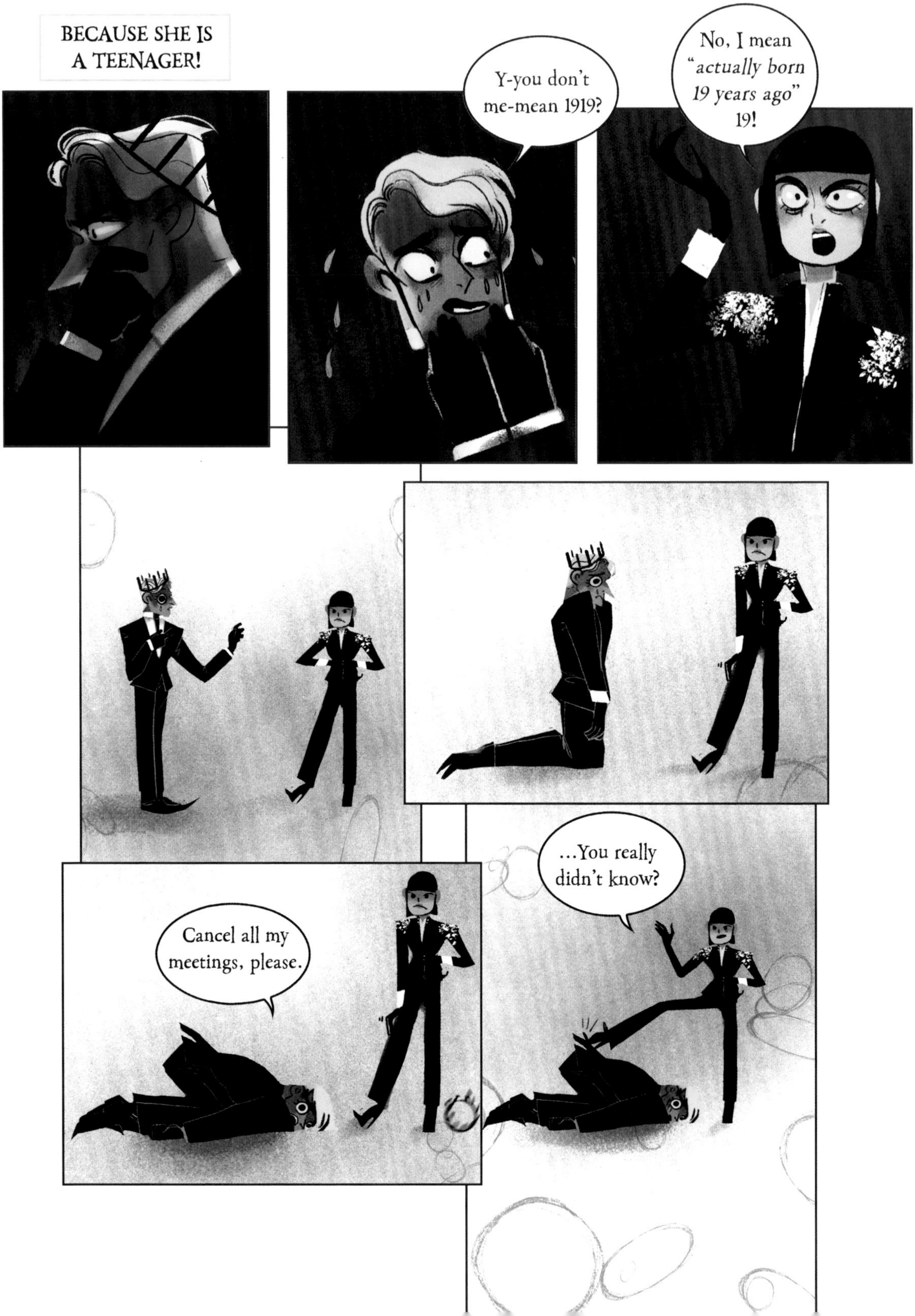
BECAUSE SHE IS A TEENAGER!
Y-you don't me-mean 1919?
No, I mean "actually born 19 years ago" 19!
Cancel all my meetings, please.
...You really didn't know?

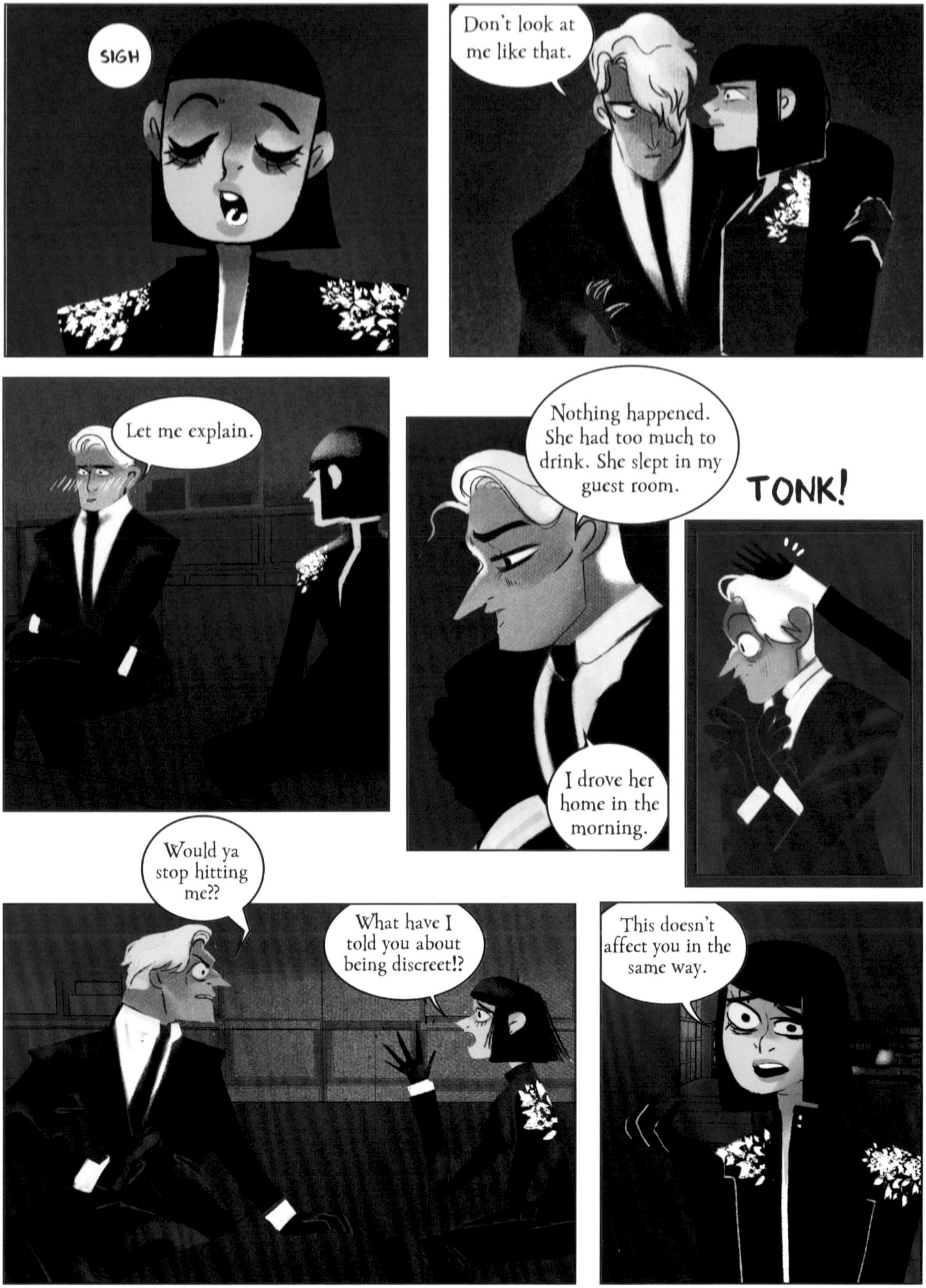
SIGH
Don't look at me like that.
Let me explain.
Nothing happened. She had too much to drink. She slept in my guest room.
I drove her home in the morning.
TONK!
Would ya stop hitting me??
What have I told you about being discreet!?
This doesn't affect you in the same way.

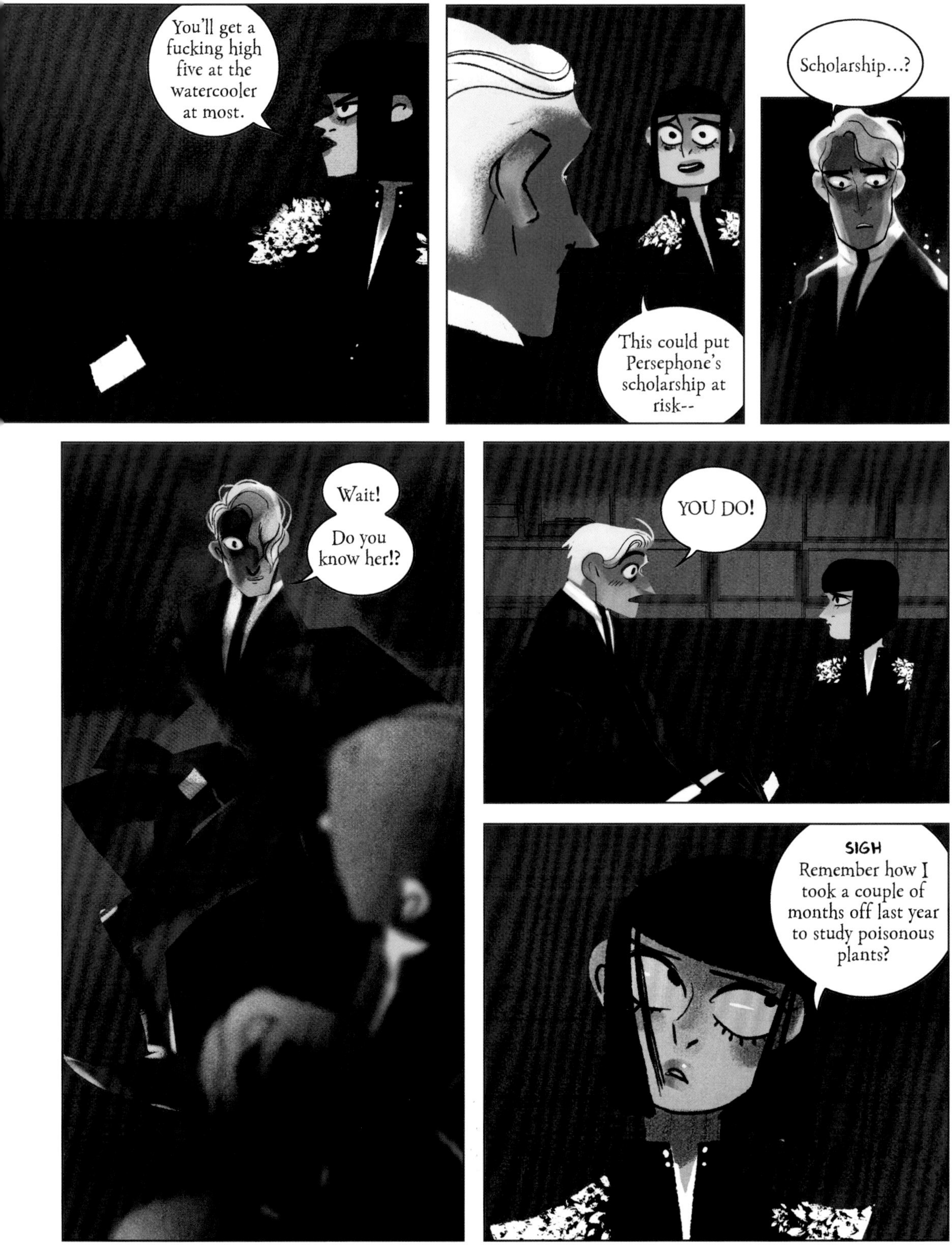
You'll get a fucking high five at the watercooler at most.
This could put Persephone's scholarship at risk--
Scholarship...?
Wait!
Do you know her!?
YOU DO!
SIGH
Remember how I took a couple of months off last year to study poisonous plants?

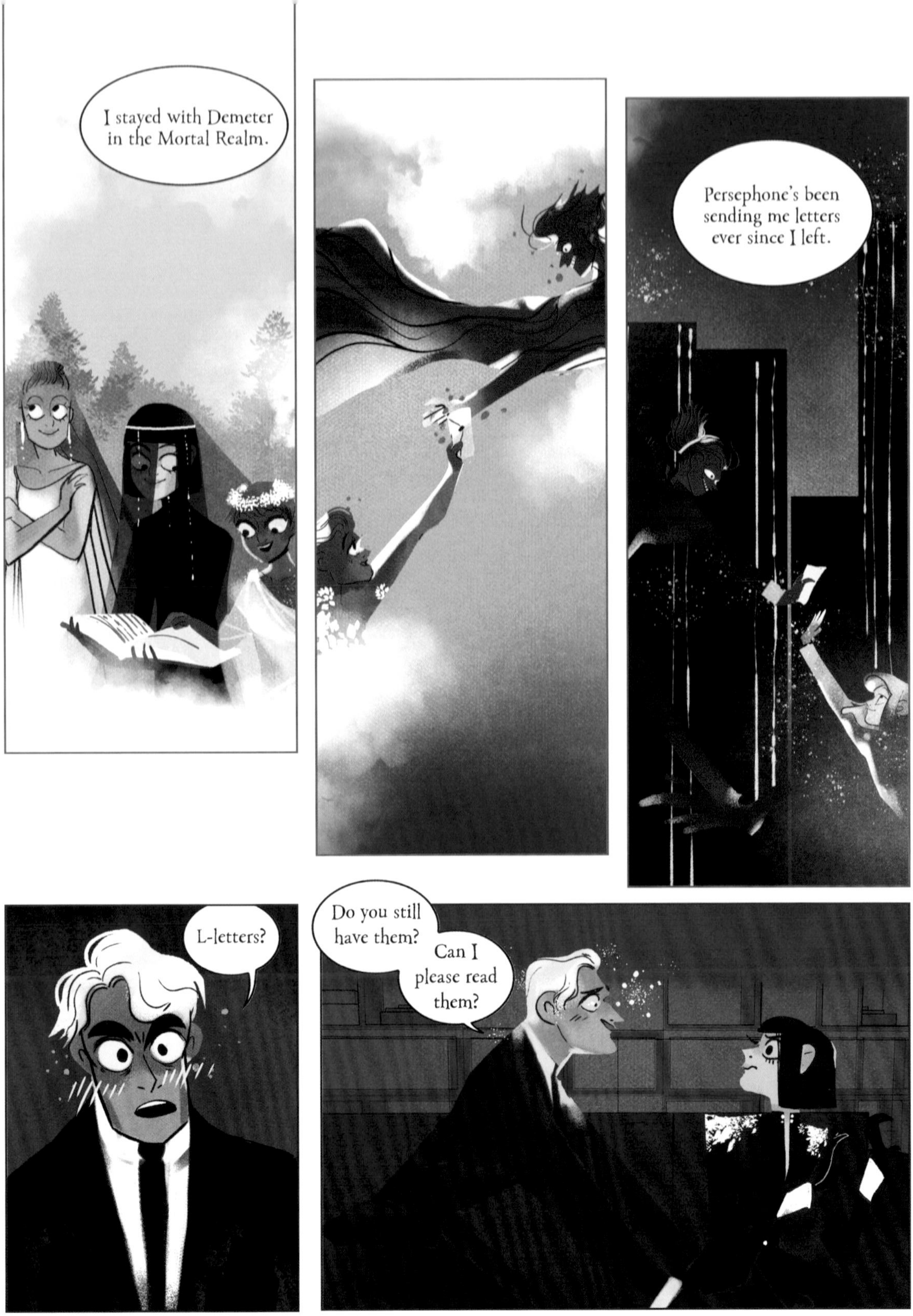

I stayed with Demeter in the Mortal Realm.
Persephone's been sending me letters ever since I left.
L-letters?
Do you still have them?
Can I please read them?

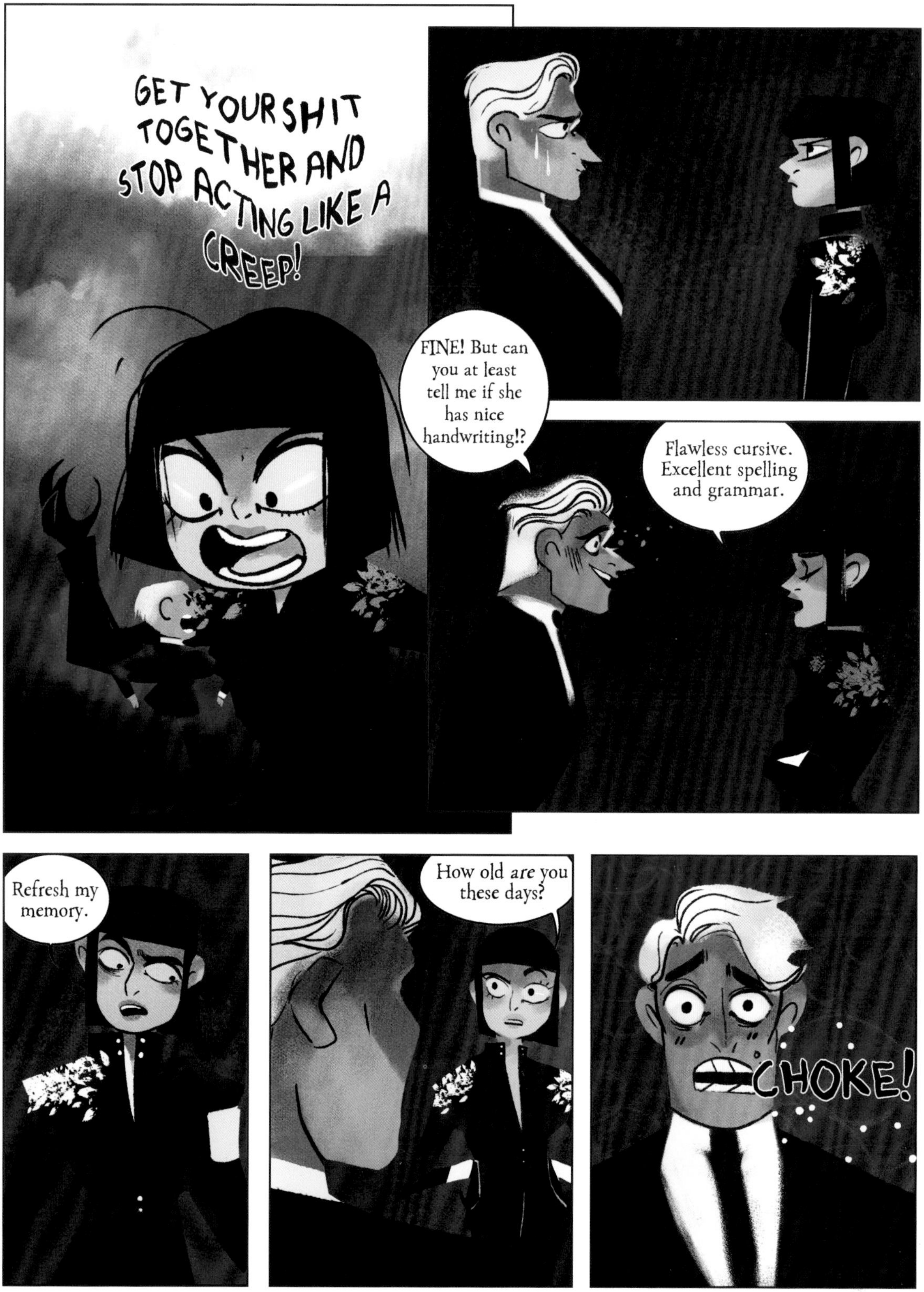
GET YOUR SHIT TOGETHER AND STOP ACTING LIKE A CREEP!
FINE! But can you at least tell me if she has nice handwriting!?
Flawless cursive. Excellent spelling and grammar.
Refresh my memory.
How old *are* you these days?
CHOKE!

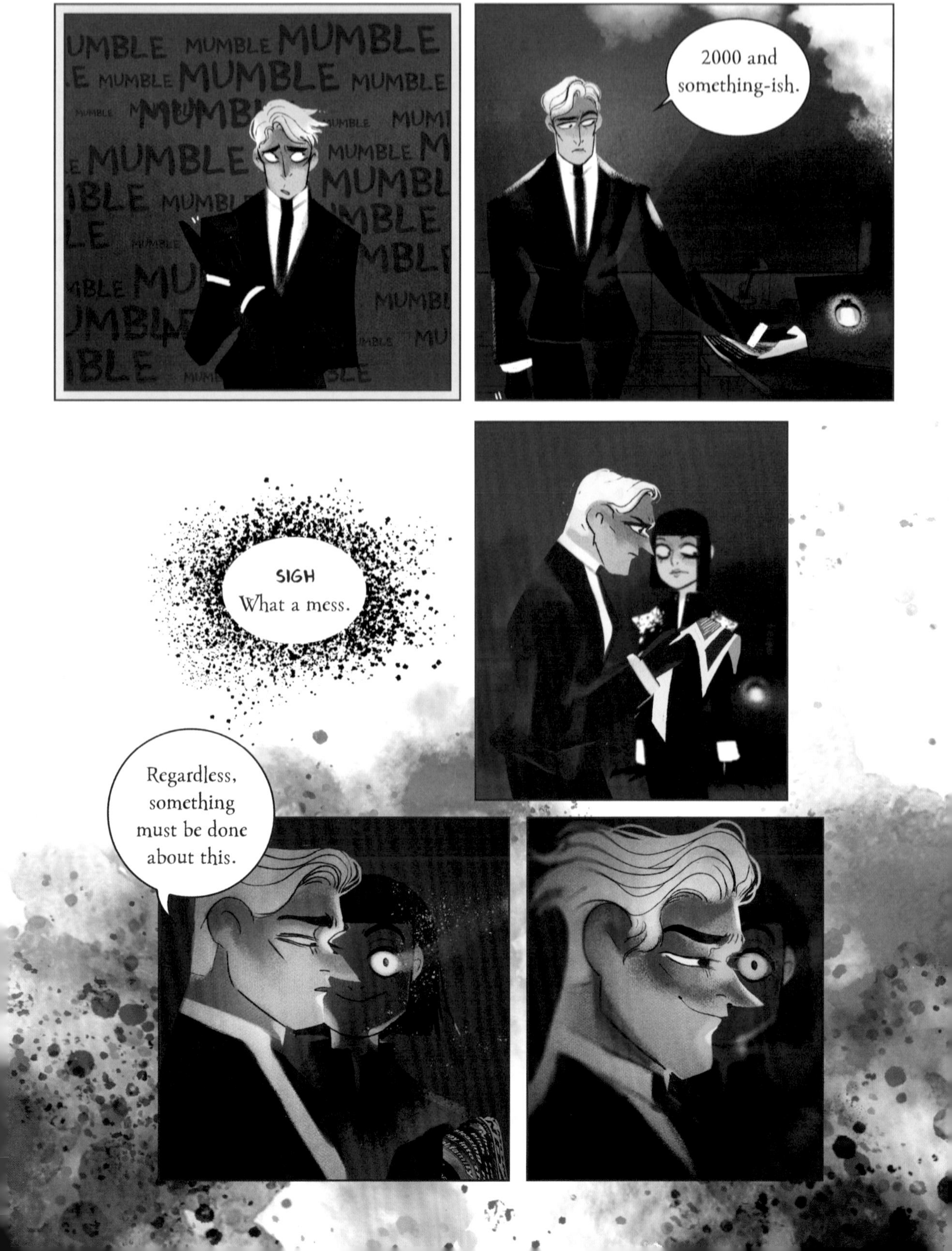
MUMBLE MUMBLE MUMBLE
2000 and something-ish.
SIGH
What a mess.
Regardless, something must be done about this.

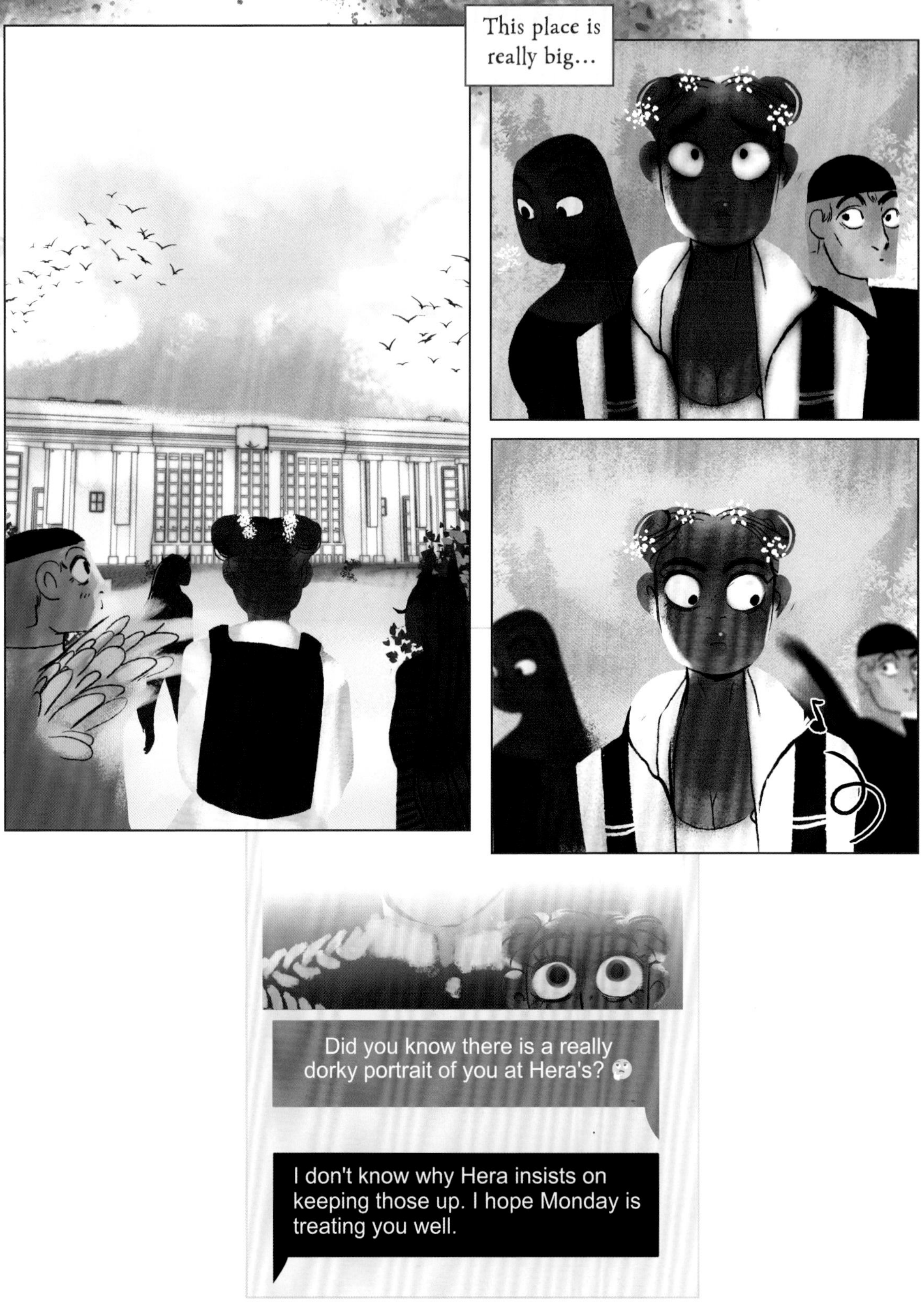
This place is really big...
Did you know there is a really dorky portrait of you at Hera's?
I don't know why Hera insists on keeping those up. I hope Monday is treating you well.

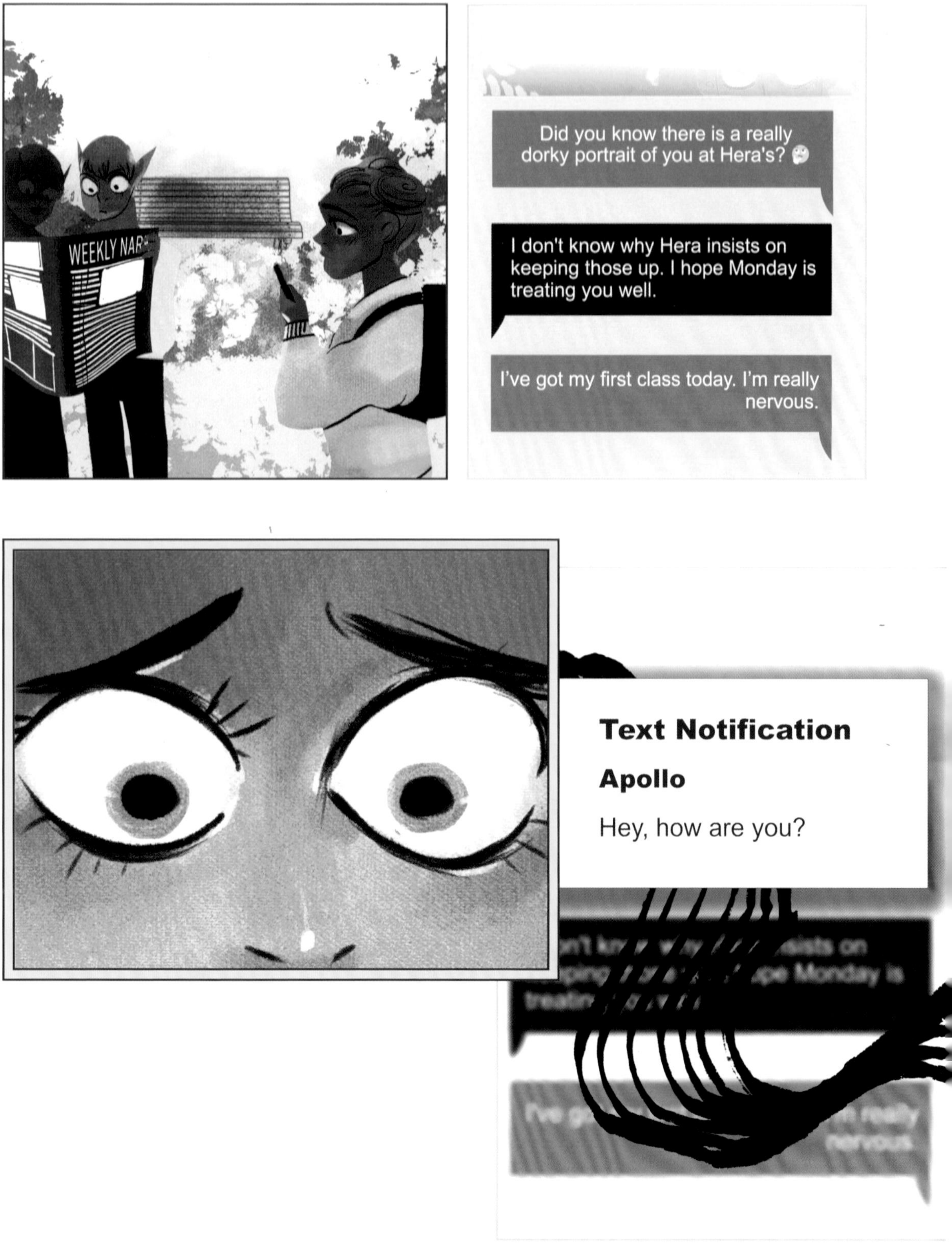
Did you know there is a really dorky portrait of you at Hera's?
I don't know why Hera insists on keeping those up. I hope Monday is treating you well.
I've got my first class today. I'm really nervous.
Text Notification
Apollo
Hey, how are you?

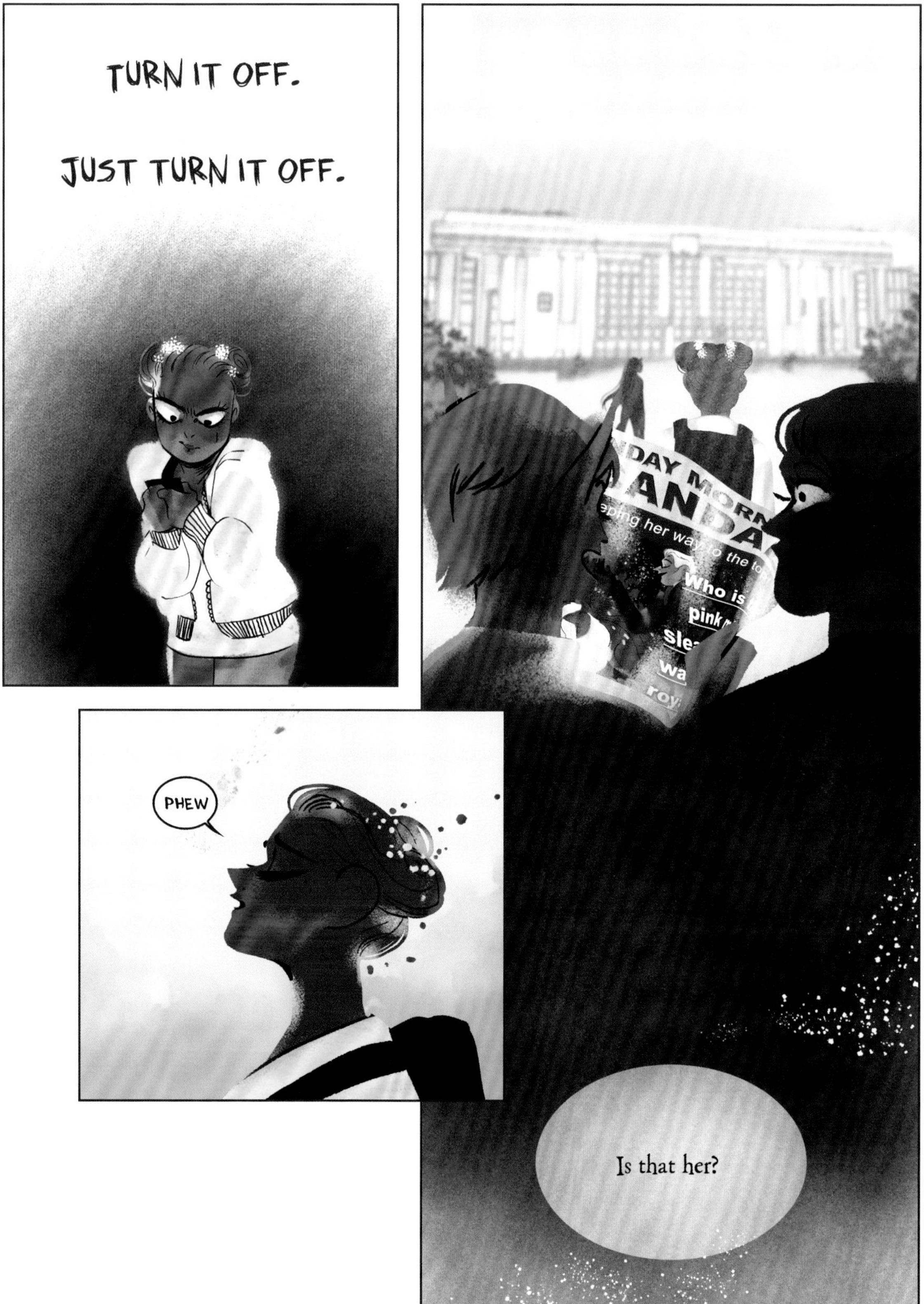
TURN IT OFF.
JUST TURN IT OFF.
PHEW
Is that her?

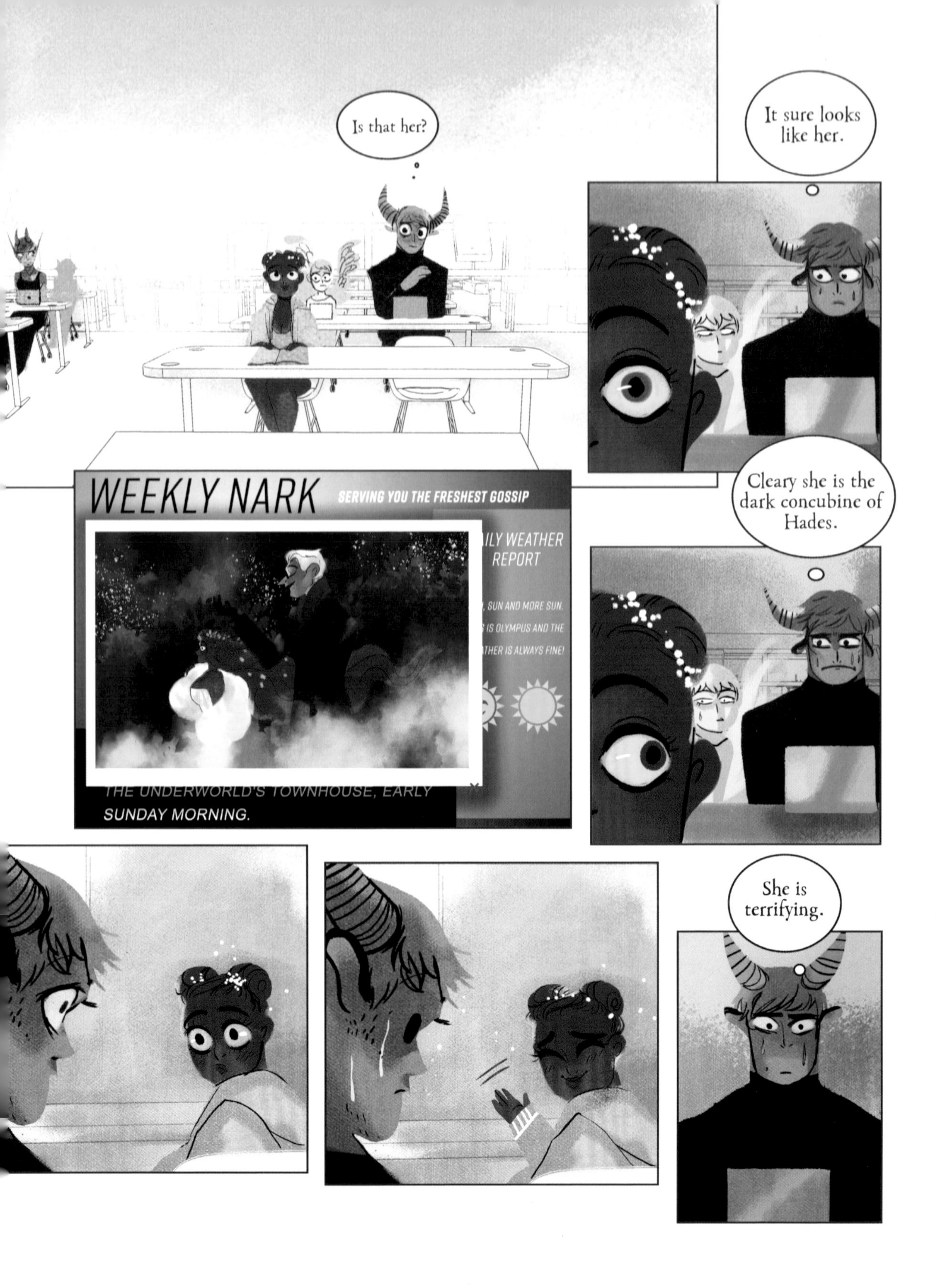

Is that her?
It sure looks like her.
WEEKLY NARK
SERVING YOU THE FRESHEST GOSSIP
ILY WEATHER REPORT
, SUN AND MORE SUN.
S IS OLYMPUS AND THE
THER IS ALWAYS FINE!
THE UNDERWORLD'S TOWNHOUSE, EARLY SUNDAY MORNING.
Cleary she is the dark concubine of Hades.
She is terrifying.

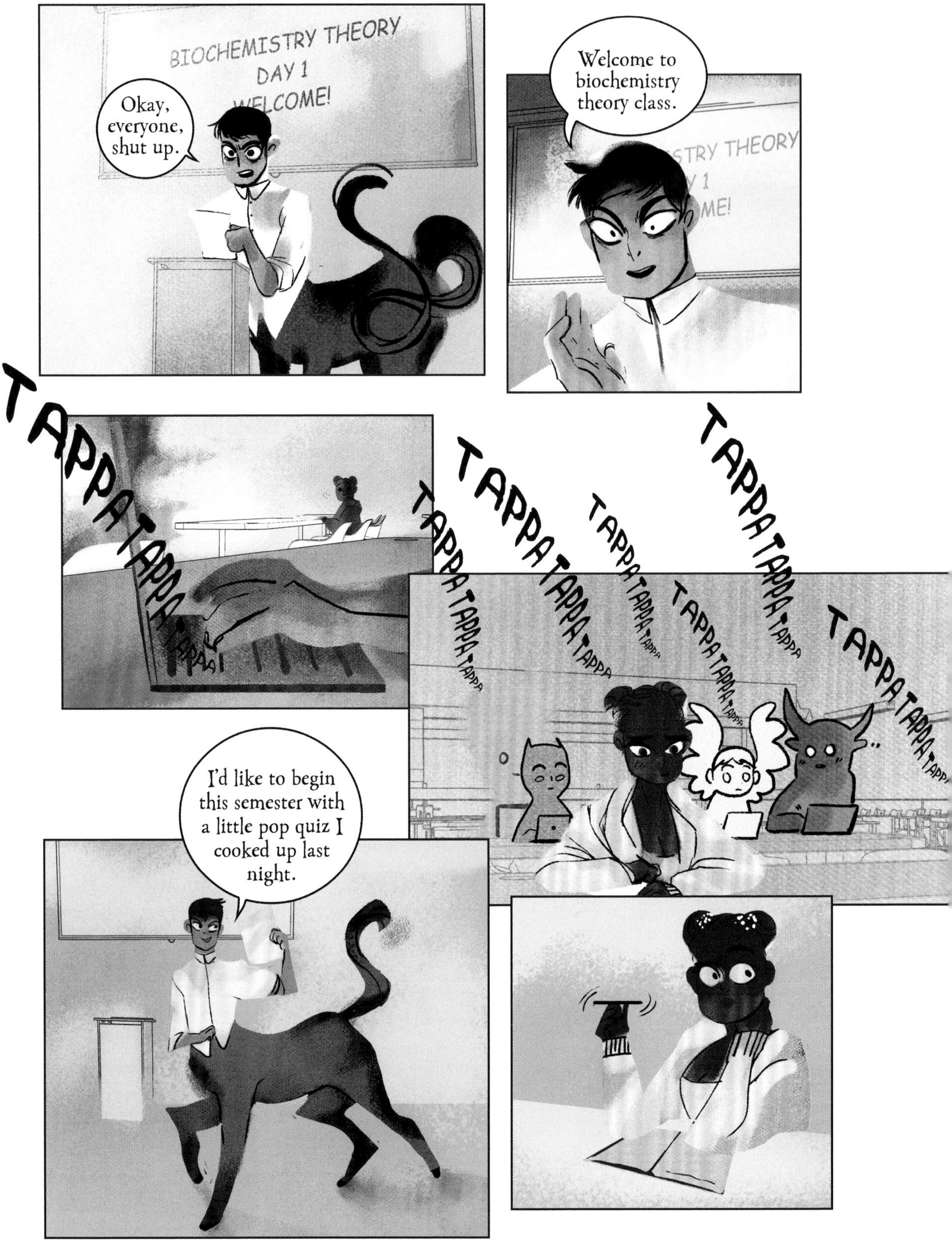
BIOCHEMISTRY THEORY
DAY 1
WELCOME!
Okay, everyone, shut up.
Welcome to biochemistry theory class.
TAPPATAPPATAPPA
TAPPATAPPATAPPA
TAPPATAPPATAPPA
TAPPATAPPATAPPA
TAPPATAPPATAPPA
TAPPATAPPATAPPA
TAPPATAPPATAPPA
I'd like to begin this semester with a little pop quiz I cooked up last night.

EPISODE 35: THE MEAL TICKET

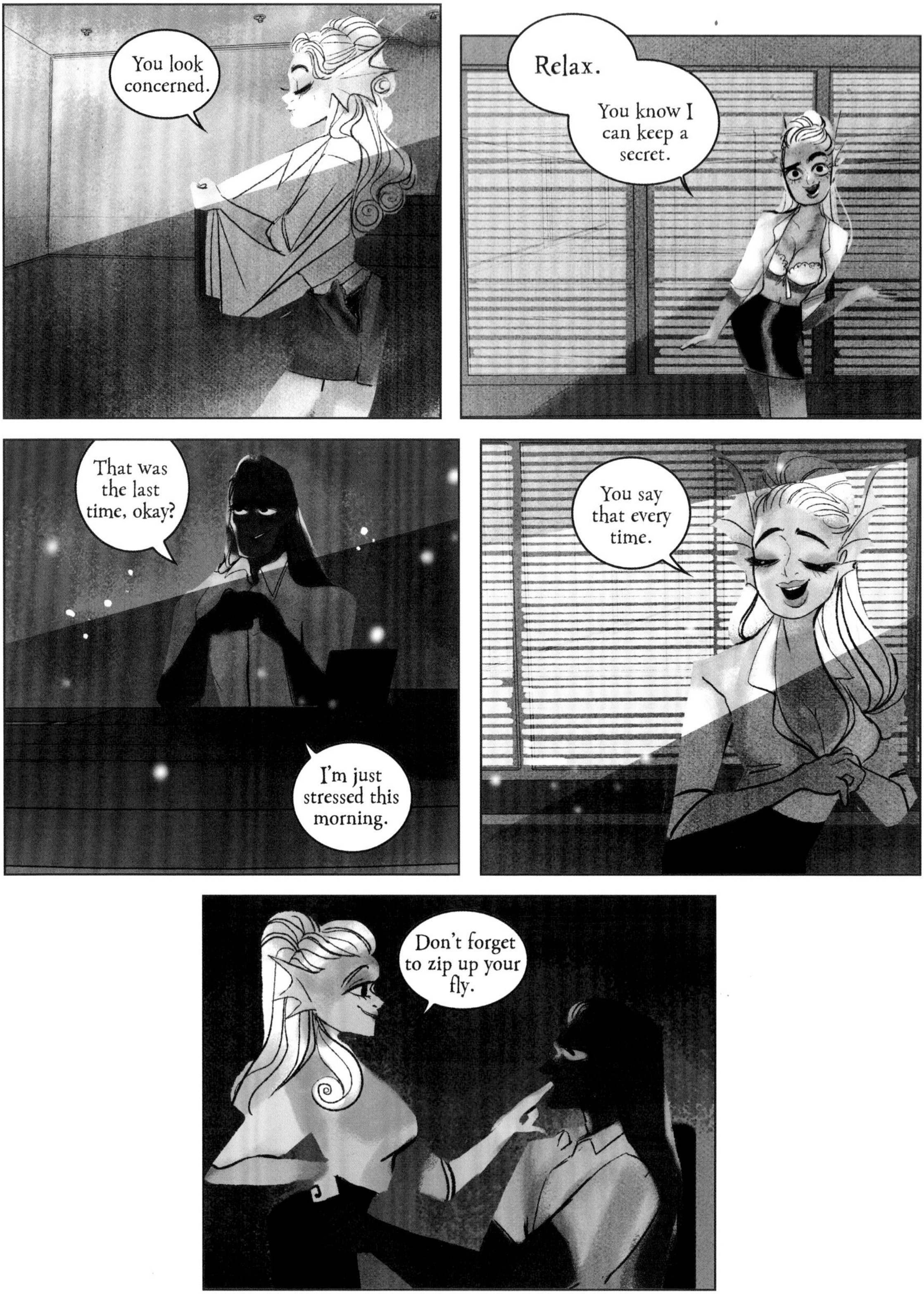
You look concerned.
Relax.
You know I can keep a secret.
That was the last time, okay?
I'm just stressed this morning.
You say that every time.
Don't forget to zip up your fly.

Thanks, Thetis.

You're a star.

I know.

TOSS

Time for 30 minutes of personal browsing before getting to emails...

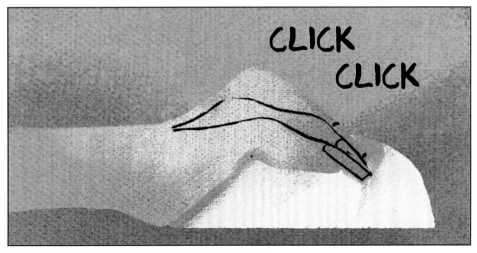

CLICK
CLICK

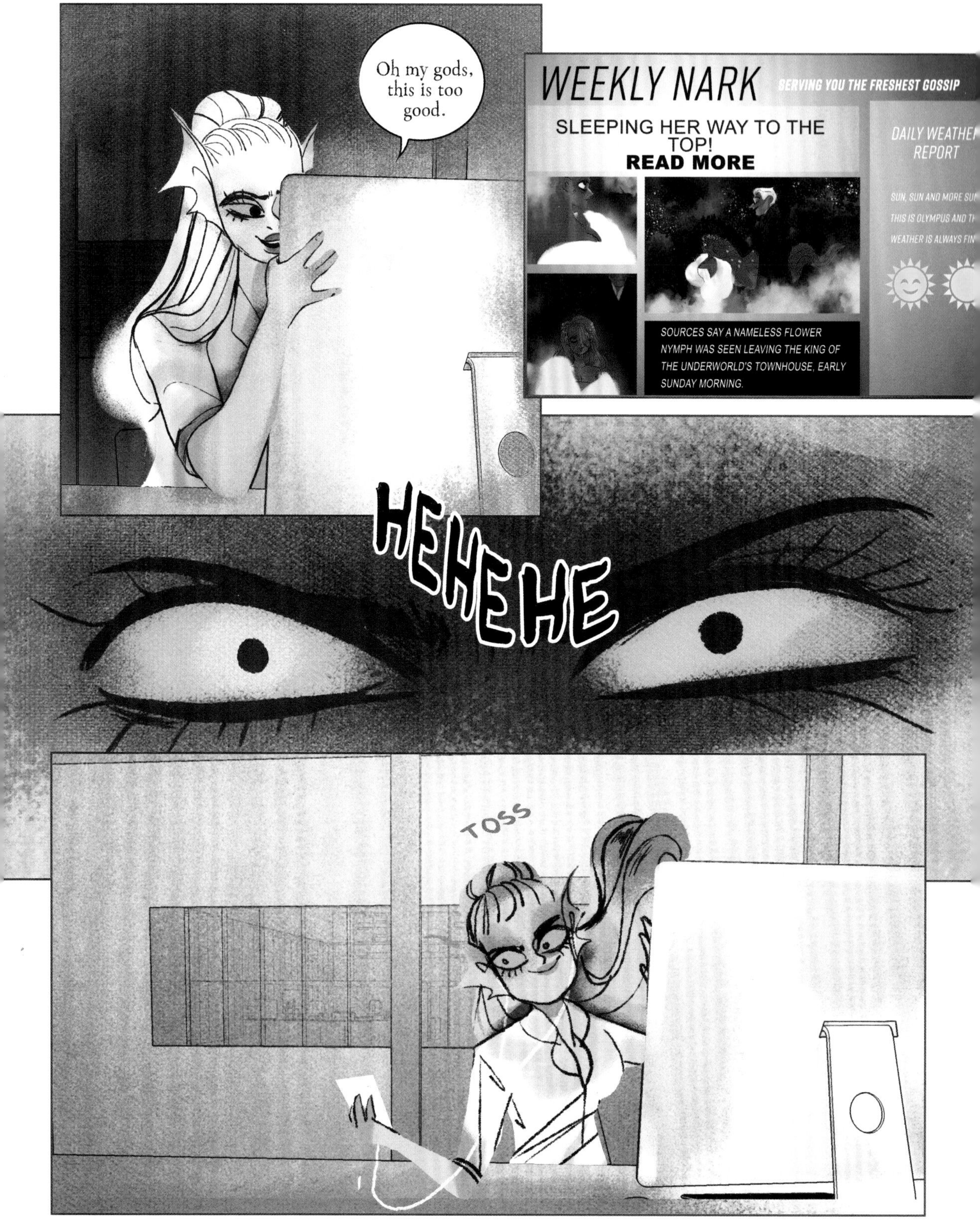
Oh my gods, this is too good.
WEEKLY NARK
SERVING YOU THE FRESHEST GOSSIP
SLEEPING HER WAY TO THE TOP!
READ MORE
SOURCES SAY A NAMELESS FLOWER NYMPH WAS SEEN LEAVING THE KING OF THE UNDERWORLD'S TOWNHOUSE, EARLY SUNDAY MORNING.
HEHEHE
TOSS

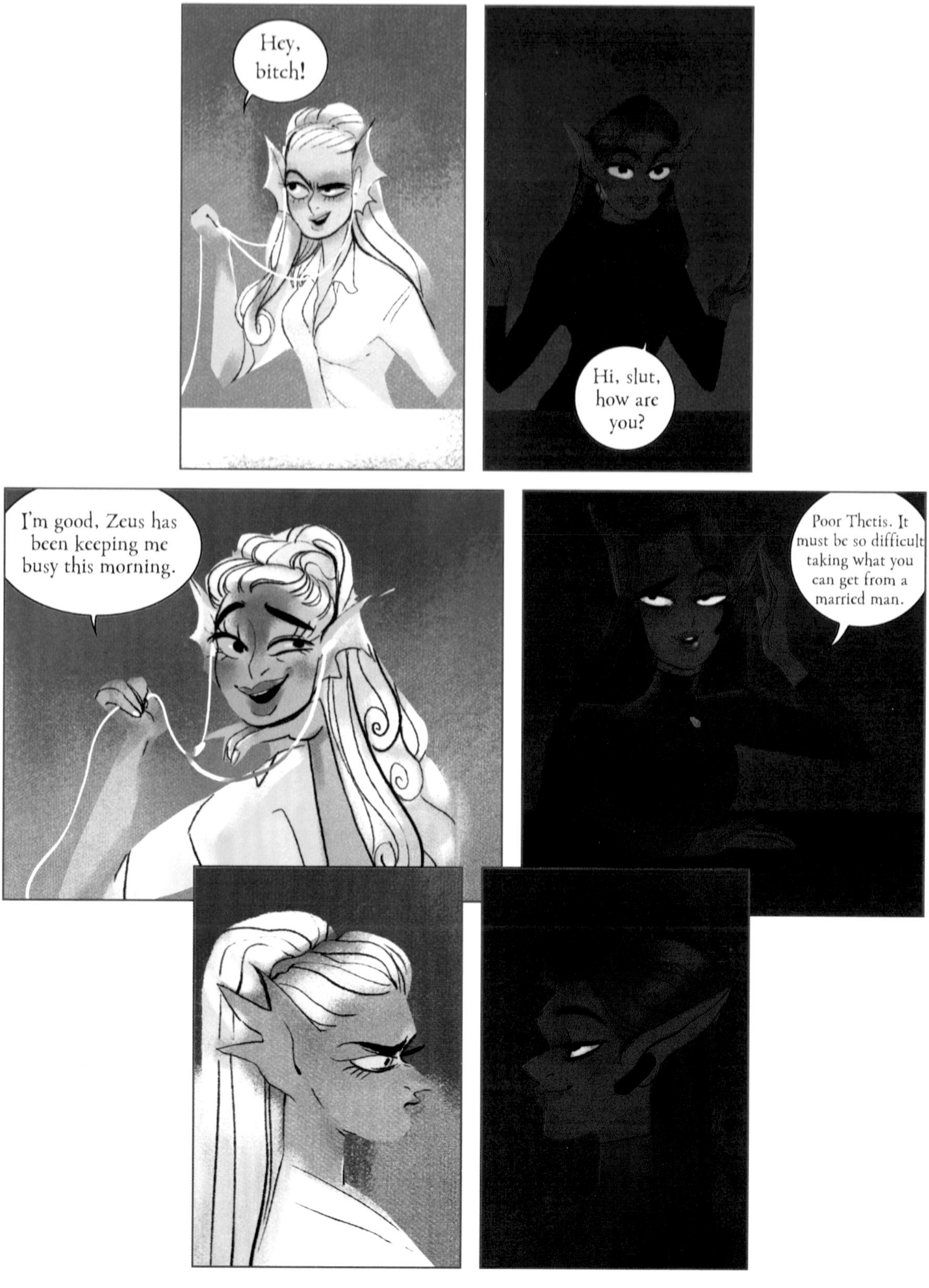
Hey, bitch!
Hi, slut, how are you?
I'm good, Zeus has been keeping me busy this morning.
Poor Thetis. It must be so difficult taking what you can get from a married man.

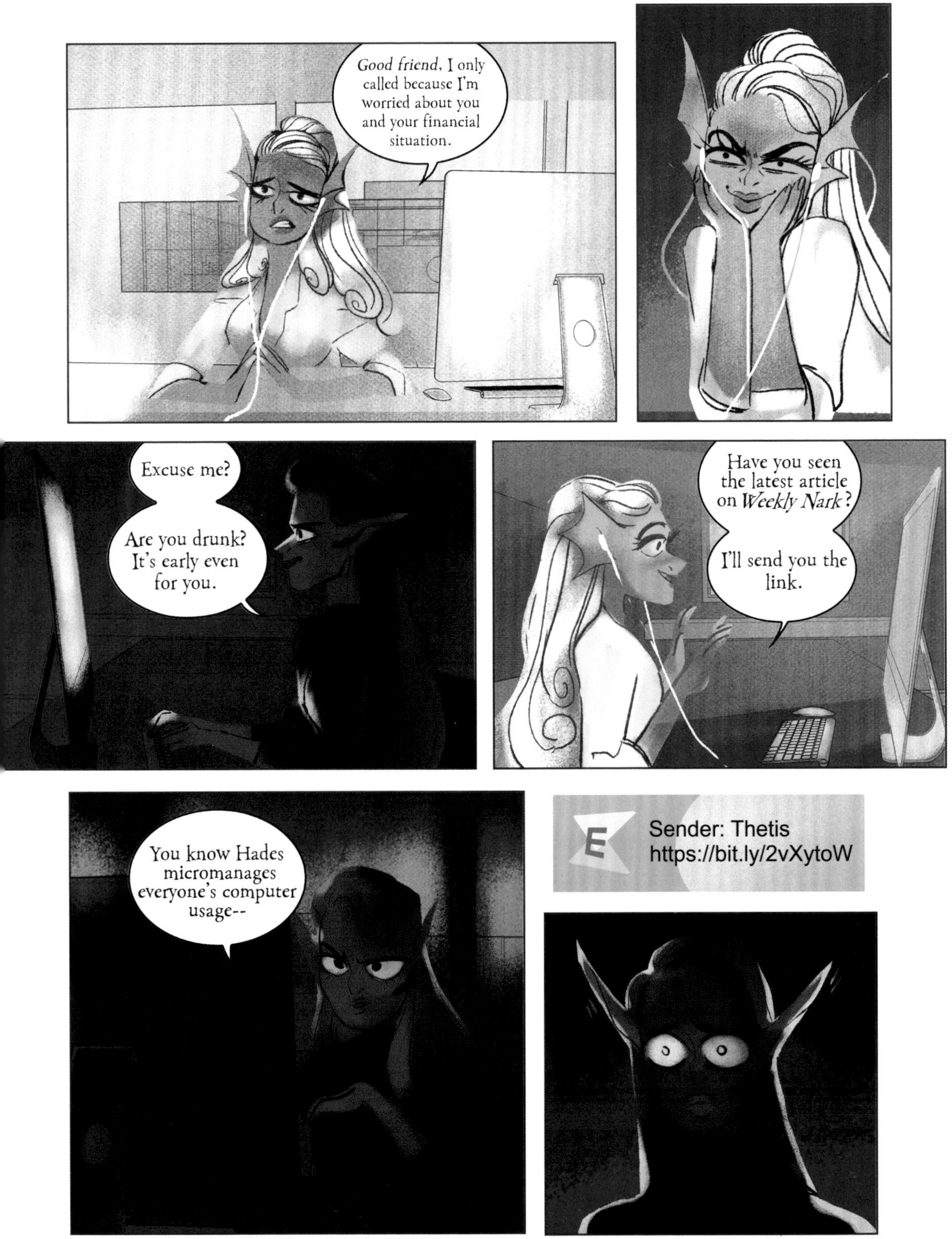
Good friend, I only called because I'm worried about you and your financial situation.
Excuse me?
Are you drunk? It's early even for you.
Have you seen the latest article on *Weekly Nark*?
I'll send you the link.
You know Hades micromanages everyone's computer usage--
Sender: Thetis
https://bit.ly/2vXytoW

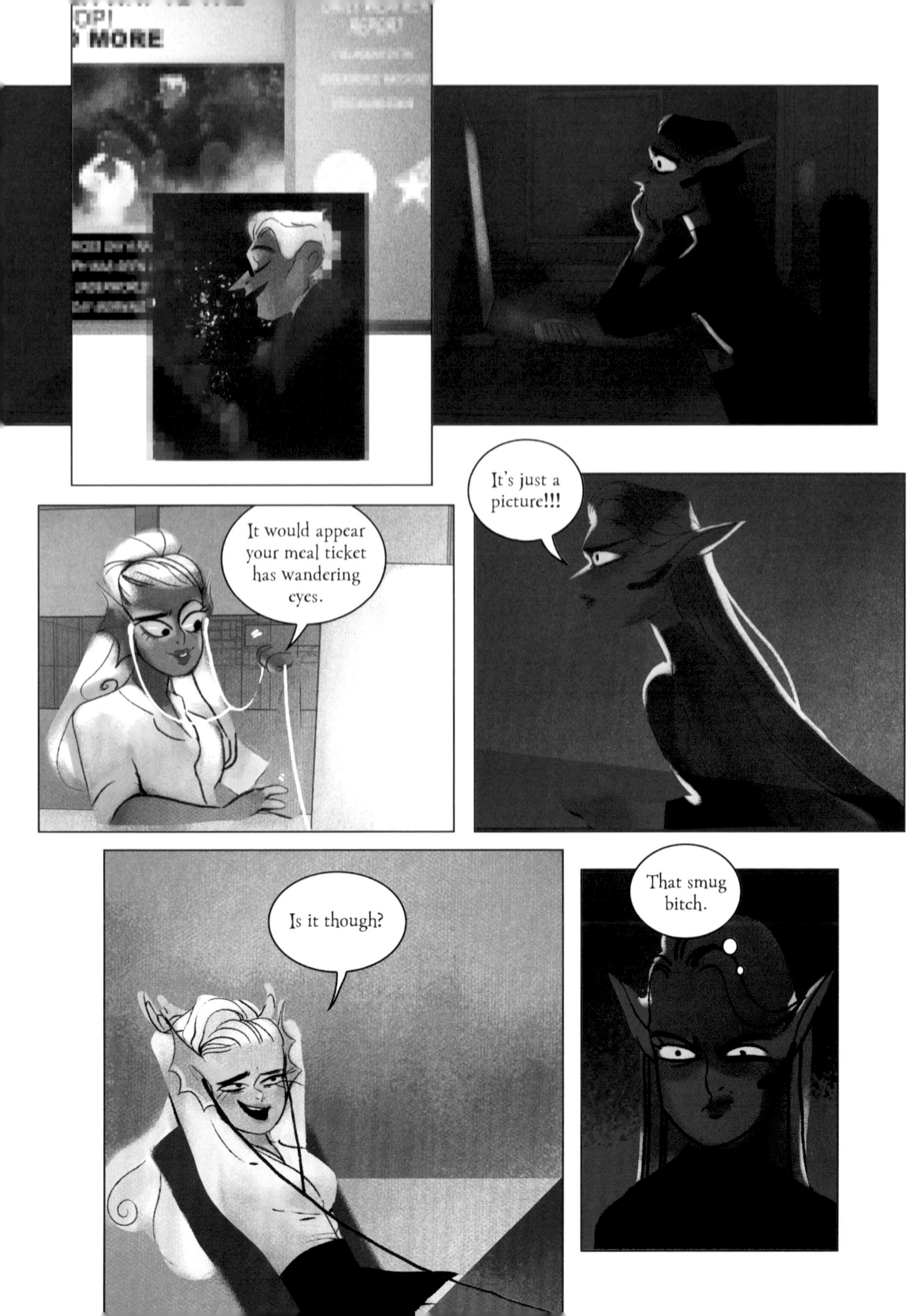

OP!
MORE
It would appear your meal ticket has wandering eyes.
It's just a picture!!!
Is it though?
That smug bitch.

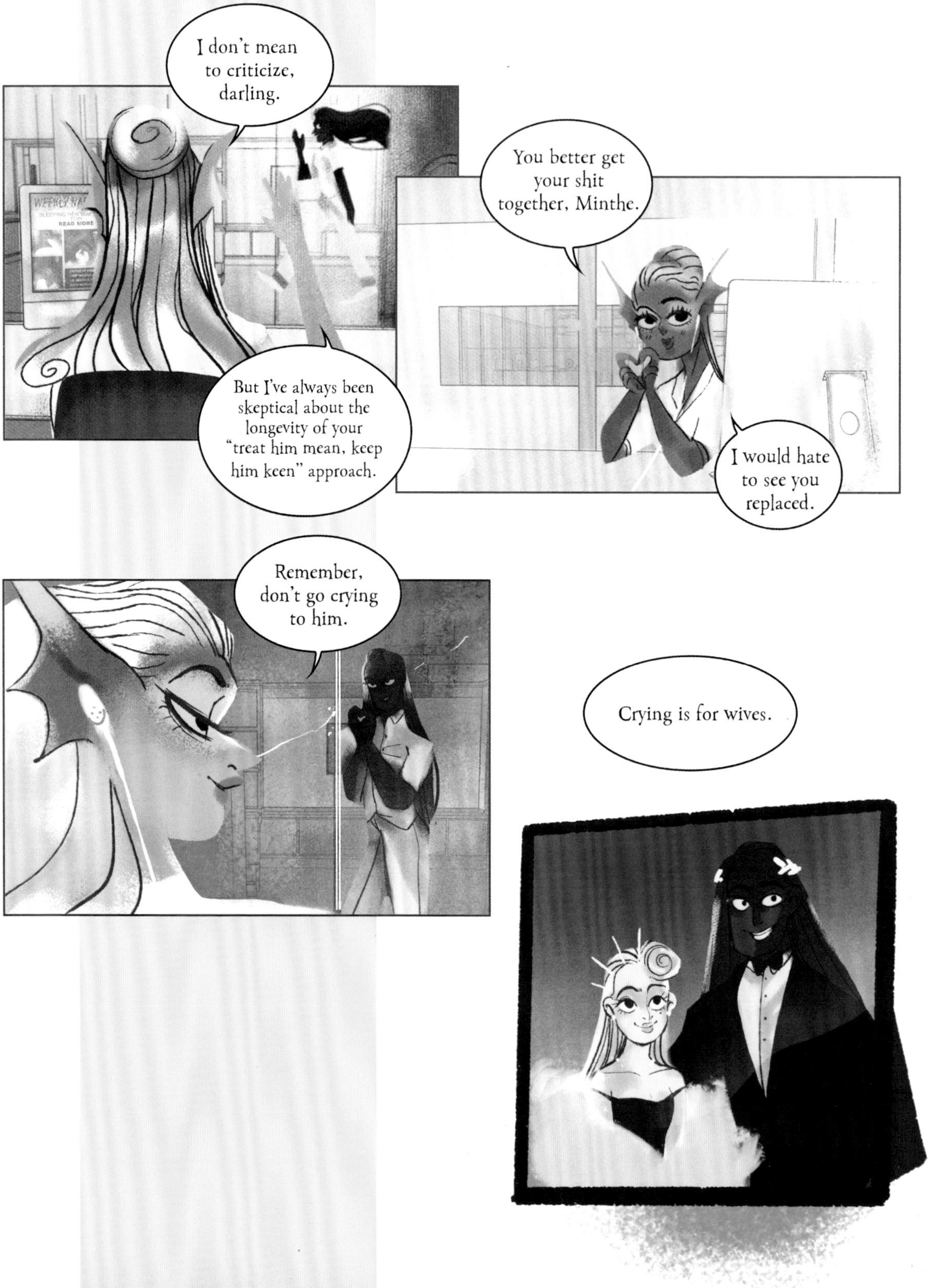

I don't mean to criticize, darling.
But I've always been skeptical about the longevity of your "treat him mean, keep him keen" approach.
You better get your shit together, Minthe.
I would hate to see you replaced.
Remember, don't go crying to him.
Crying is for wives.

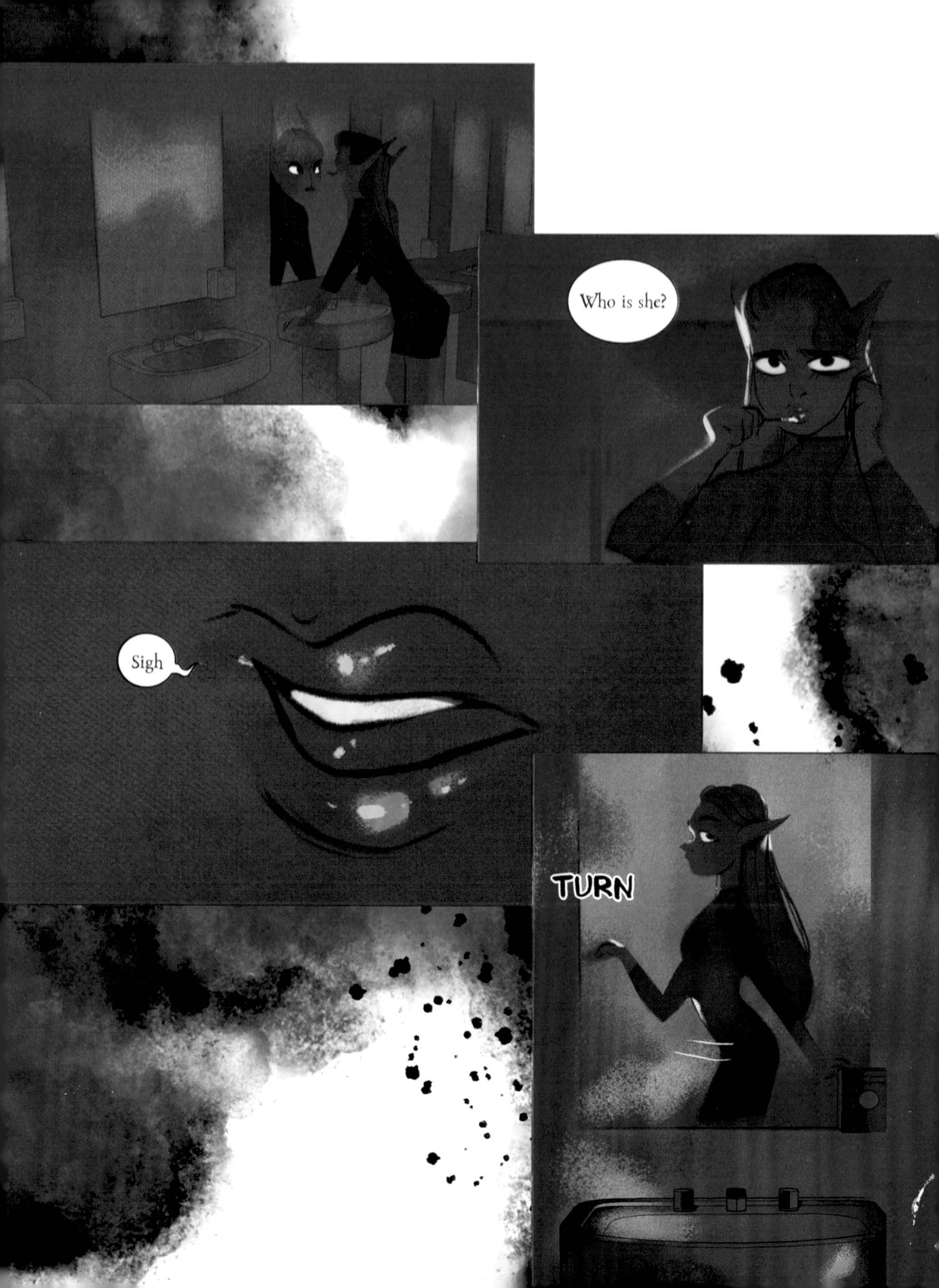
Who is she?
Sigh
TURN

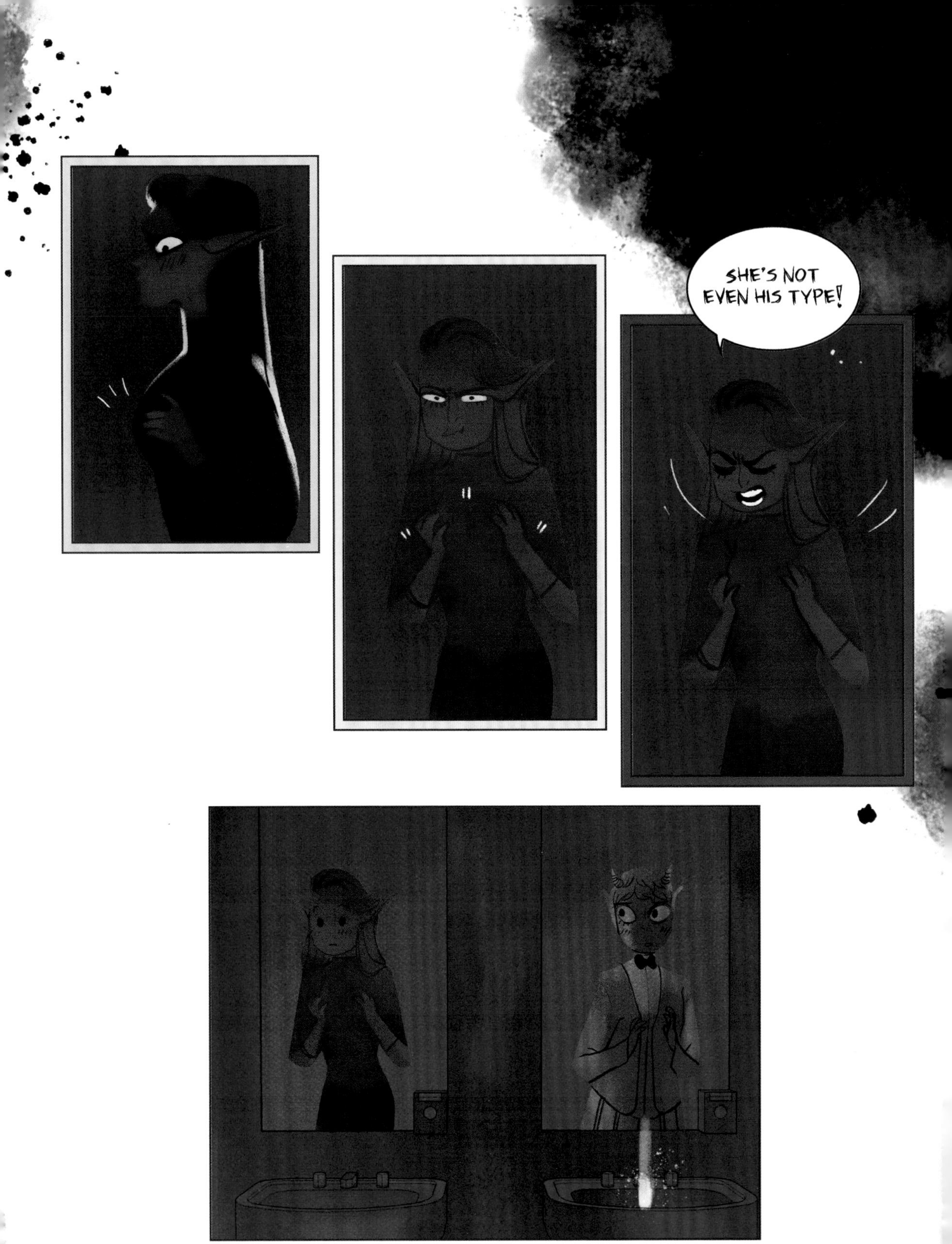
SHE'S NOT EVEN HIS TYPE!

Artemis,
do I start
talking now?

Yes! It's already
recording.

OH! Oops! Hello, Ko-- I mean,
Persephone here! I'm sorry,
I can't take your call right now.

Please leave a message
and I'll get back to you
as soon as I can.

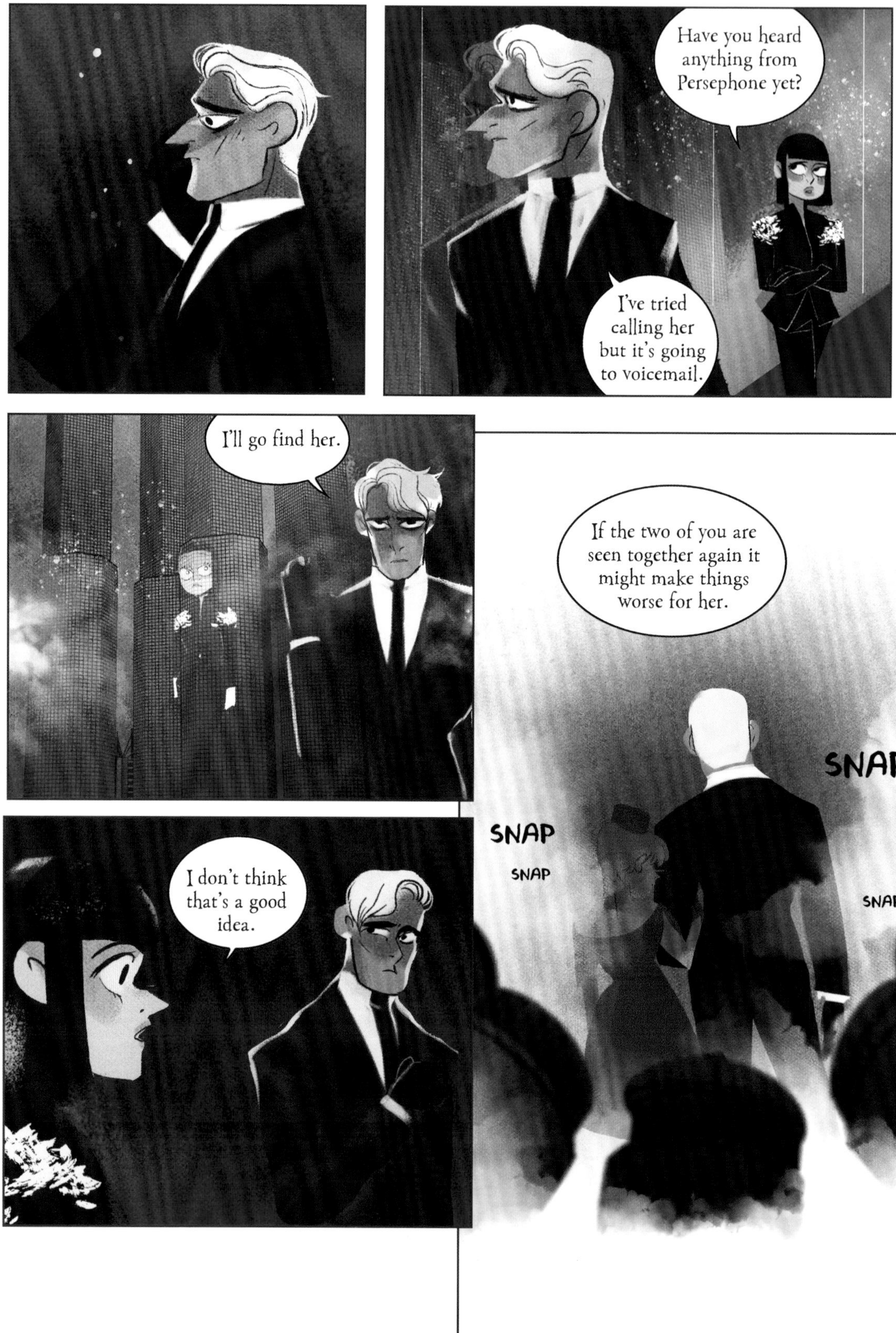
Have you heard anything from Persephone yet?
I've tried calling her but it's going to voicemail.
I'll go find her.
I don't think that's a good idea.
If the two of you are seen together again it might make things worse for her.
SNAP
SNAP
SNAP
SNAP

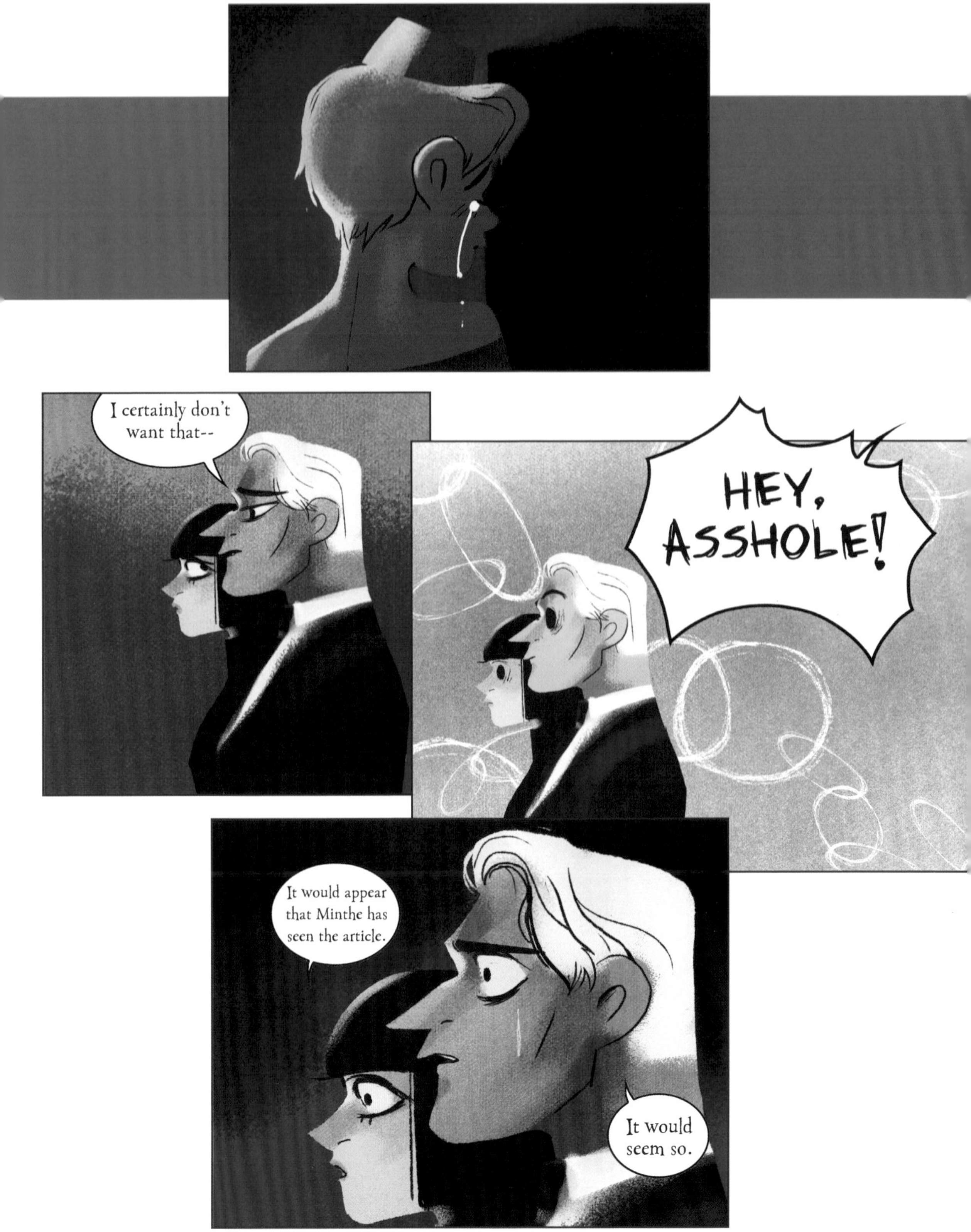

I certainly don't want that--
HEY, ASSHOLE!
It would appear that Minthe has seen the article.
It would seem so.

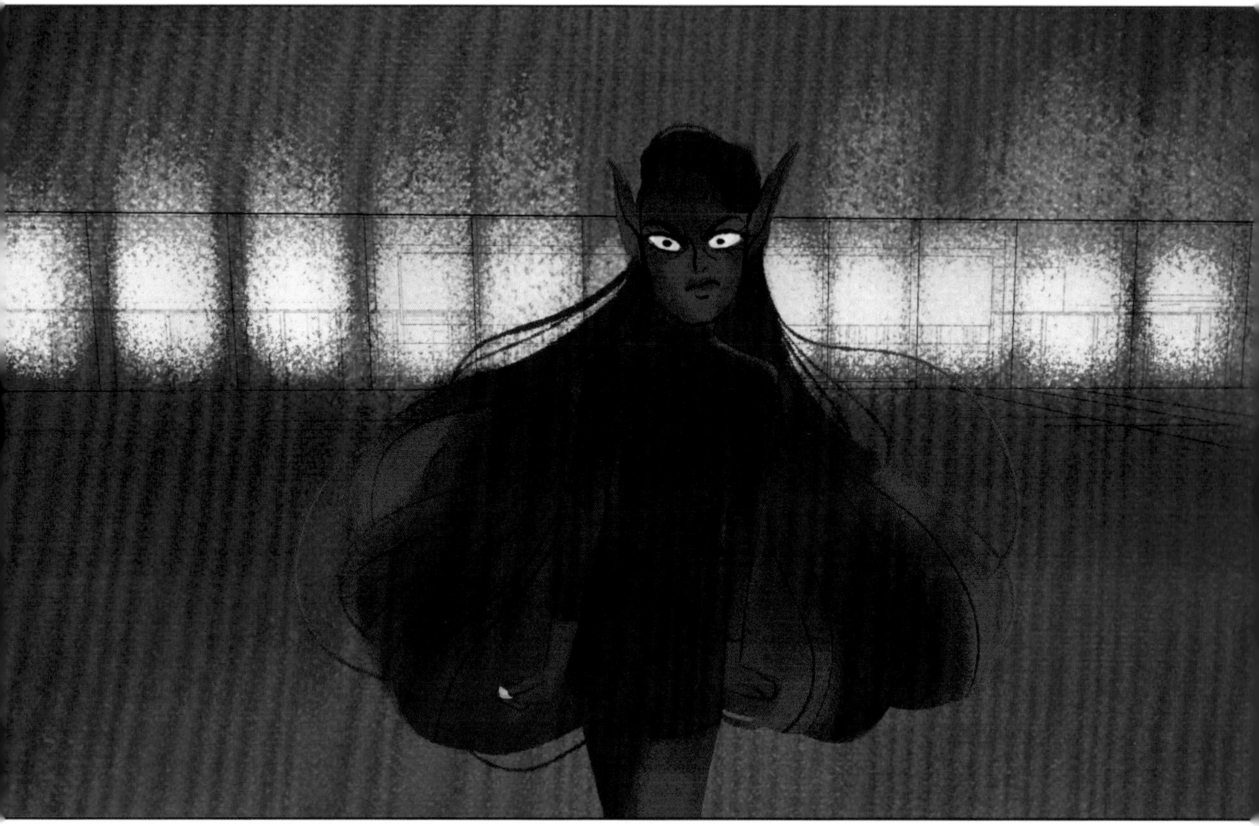
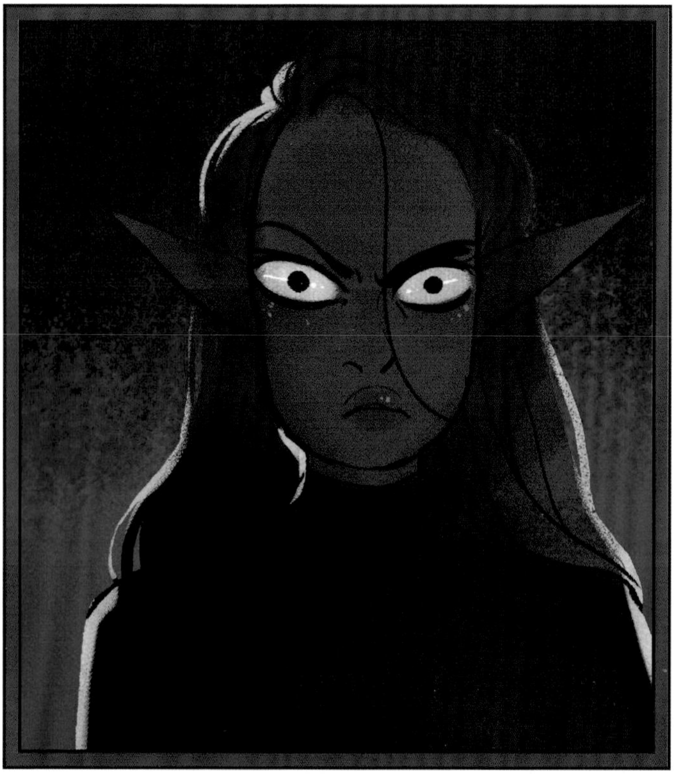

EPISODE 36: SMARTY PANTS

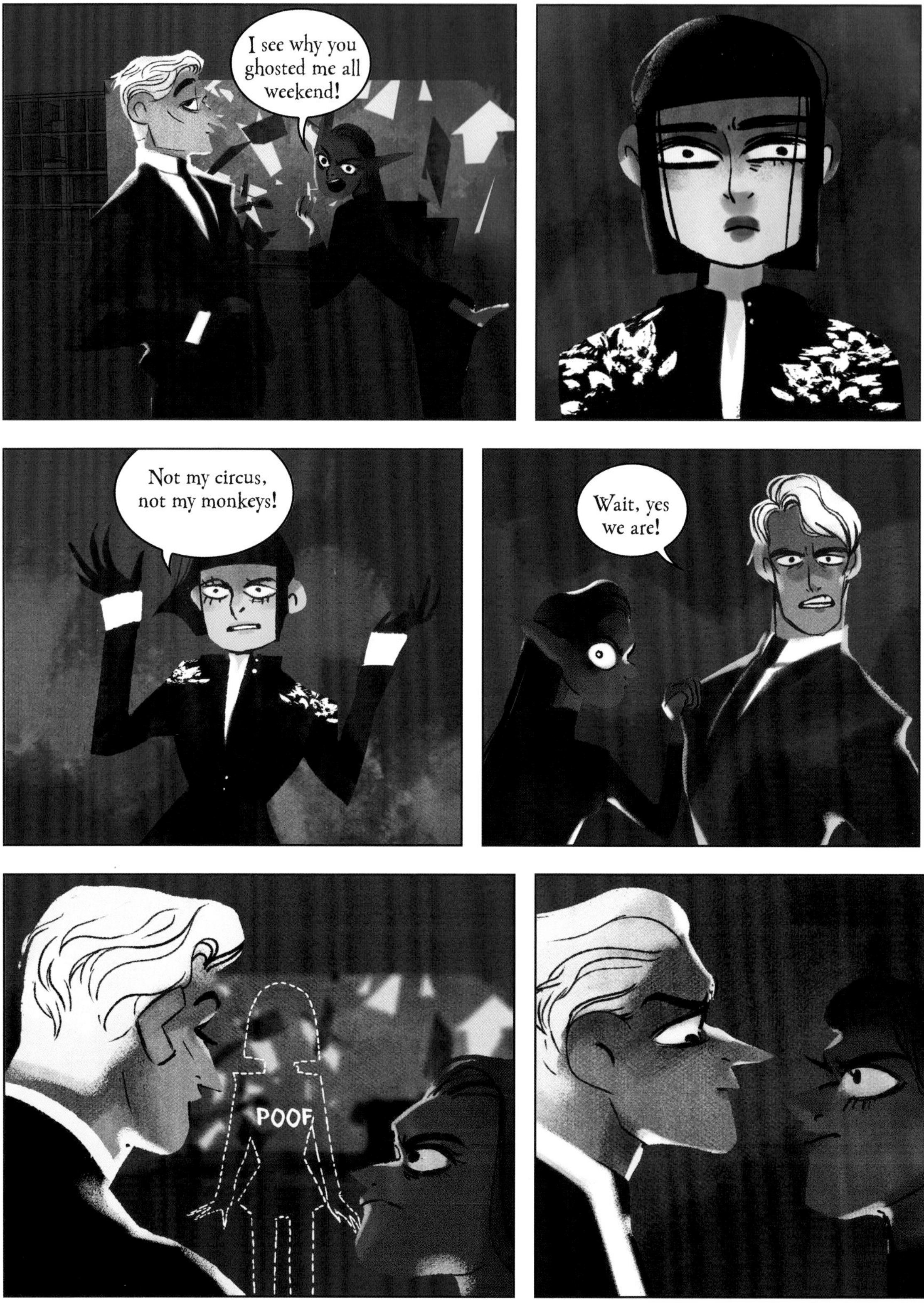
I see why you ghosted me all weekend!
Not my circus, not my monkeys!
Wait, yes we are!
POOF

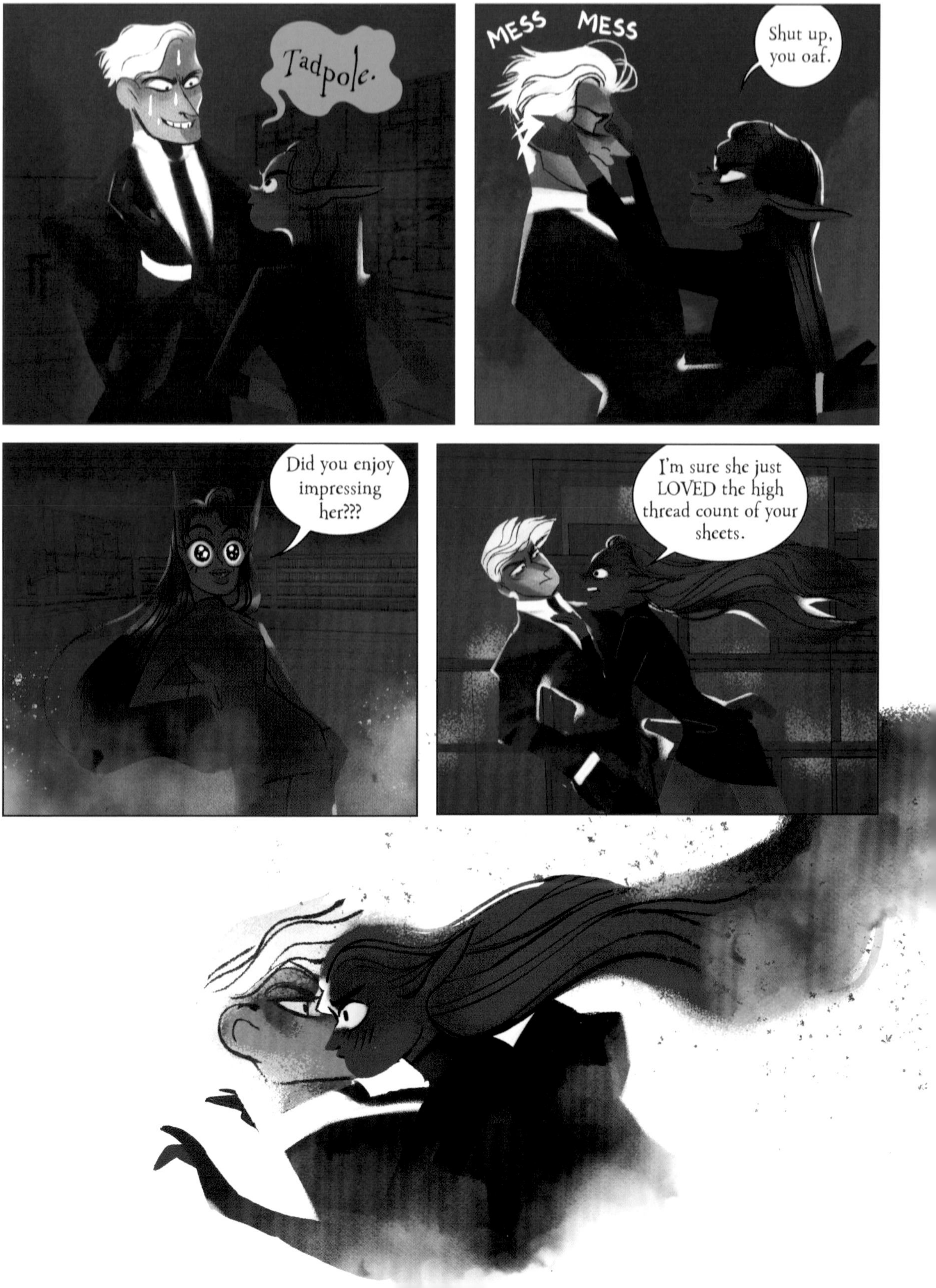
Tadpole.
MESS MESS
Shut up, you oaf.
Did you enjoy impressing her???
I'm sure she just LOVED the high thread count of your sheets.

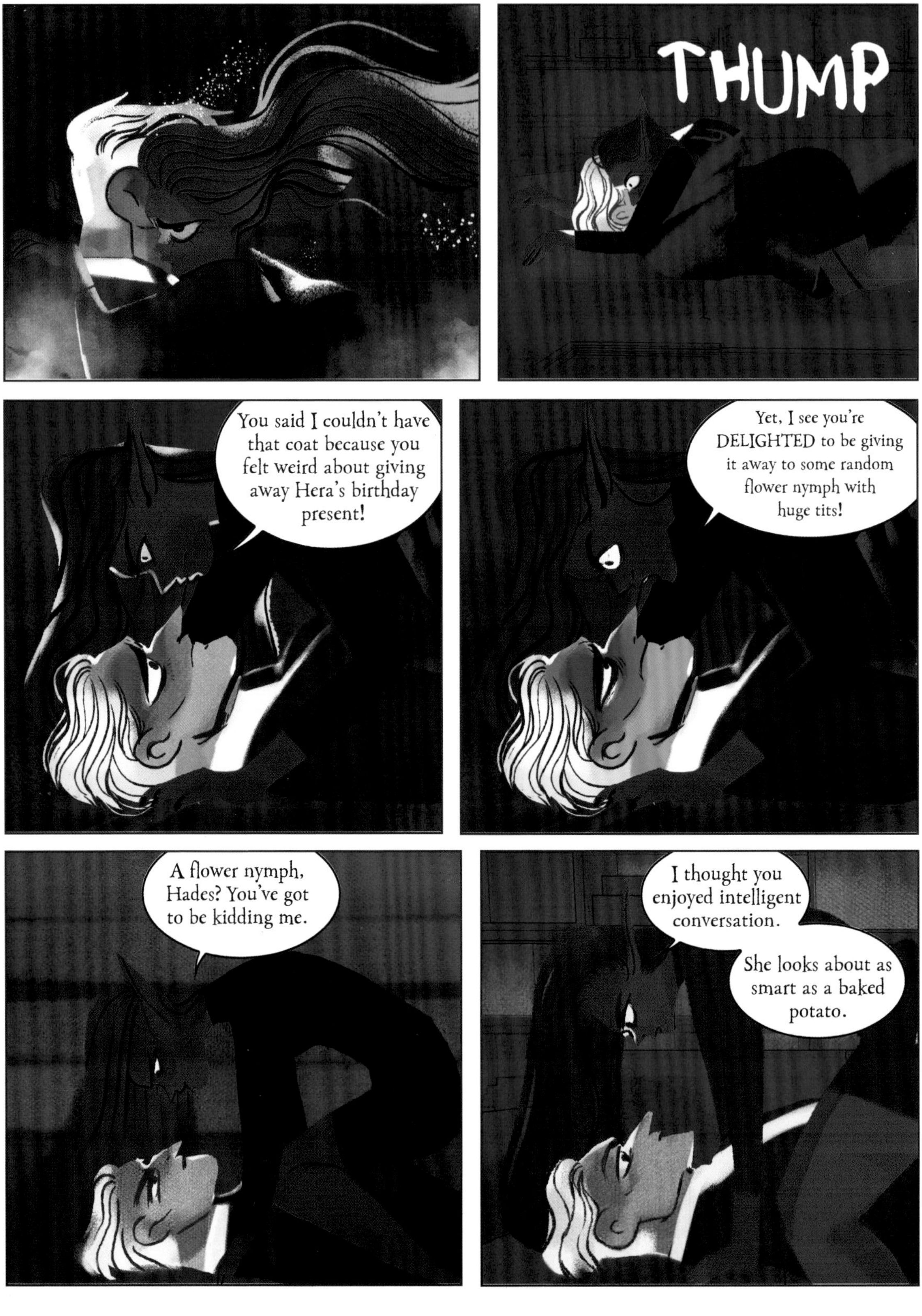
THUMP
You said I couldn't have that coat because you felt weird about giving away Hera's birthday present!
Yet, I see you're DELIGHTED to be giving it away to some random flower nymph with huge tits!
A flower nymph, Hades? You've got to be kidding me.
I thought you enjoyed intelligent conversation.
She looks about as smart as a baked potato.

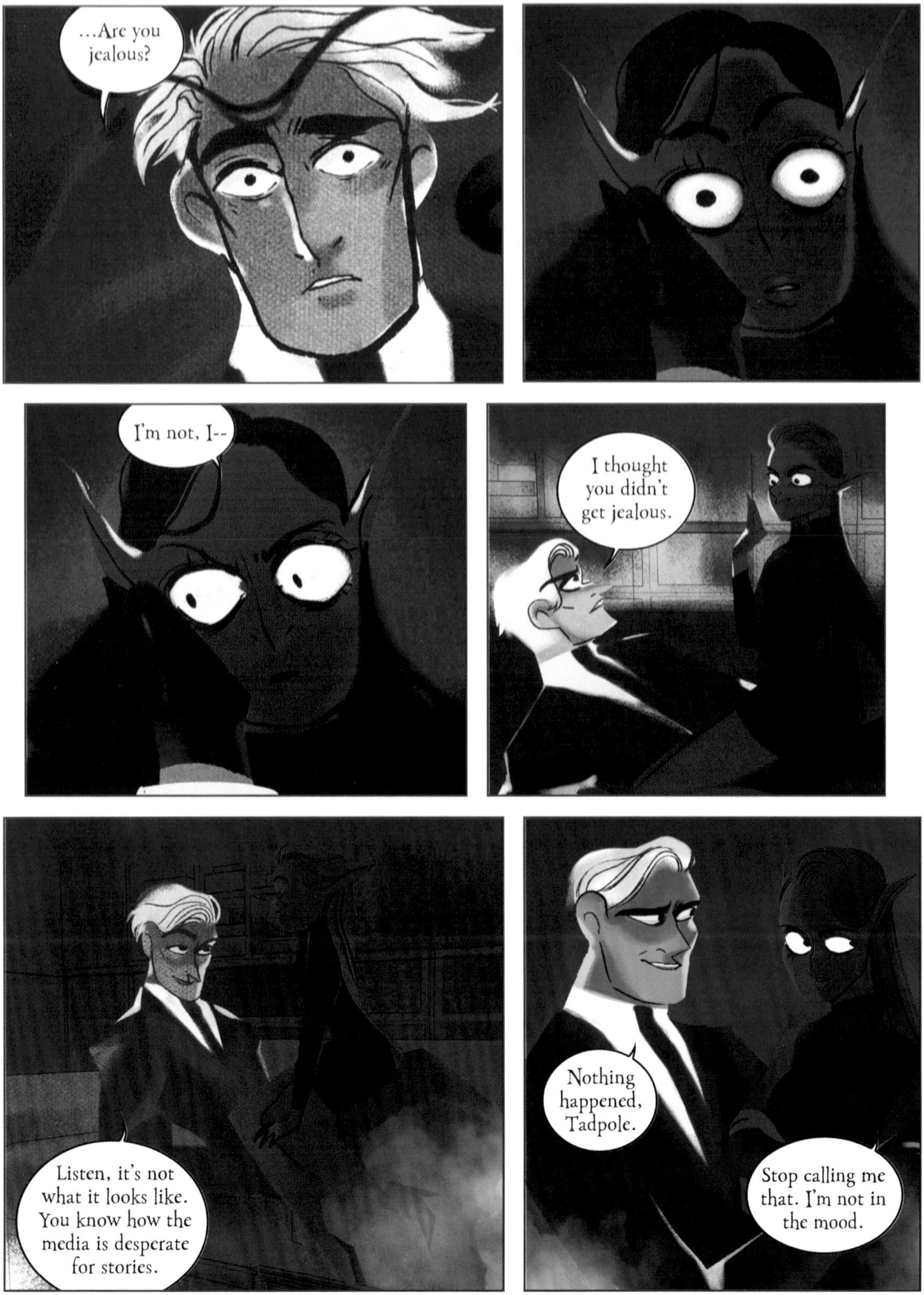
...Are you jealous?
I'm not, I--
I thought you didn't get jealous.
Listen, it's not what it looks like. You know how the media is desperate for stories.
Nothing happened, Tadpole.
Stop calling me that. I'm not in the mood.

She's actually a goddess from the Mortal Realm.

The daughter of an old friend.

...Oh

Minthe.

What happened?

...

Why didn't you come to the party?

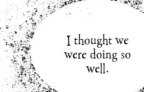

I thought we were doing so well.

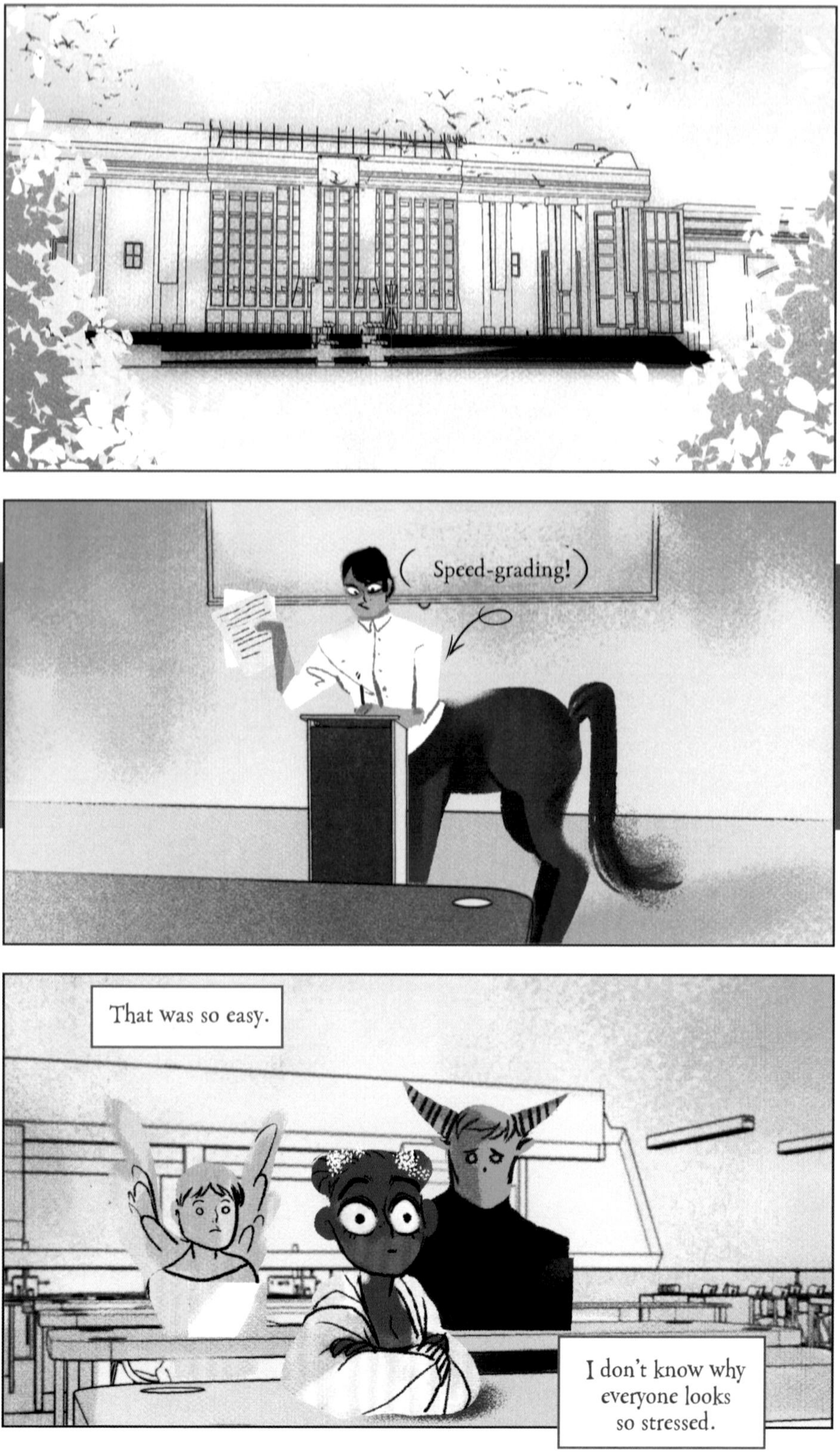
Speed-grading!
That was so easy.
I don't know why everyone looks so stressed.

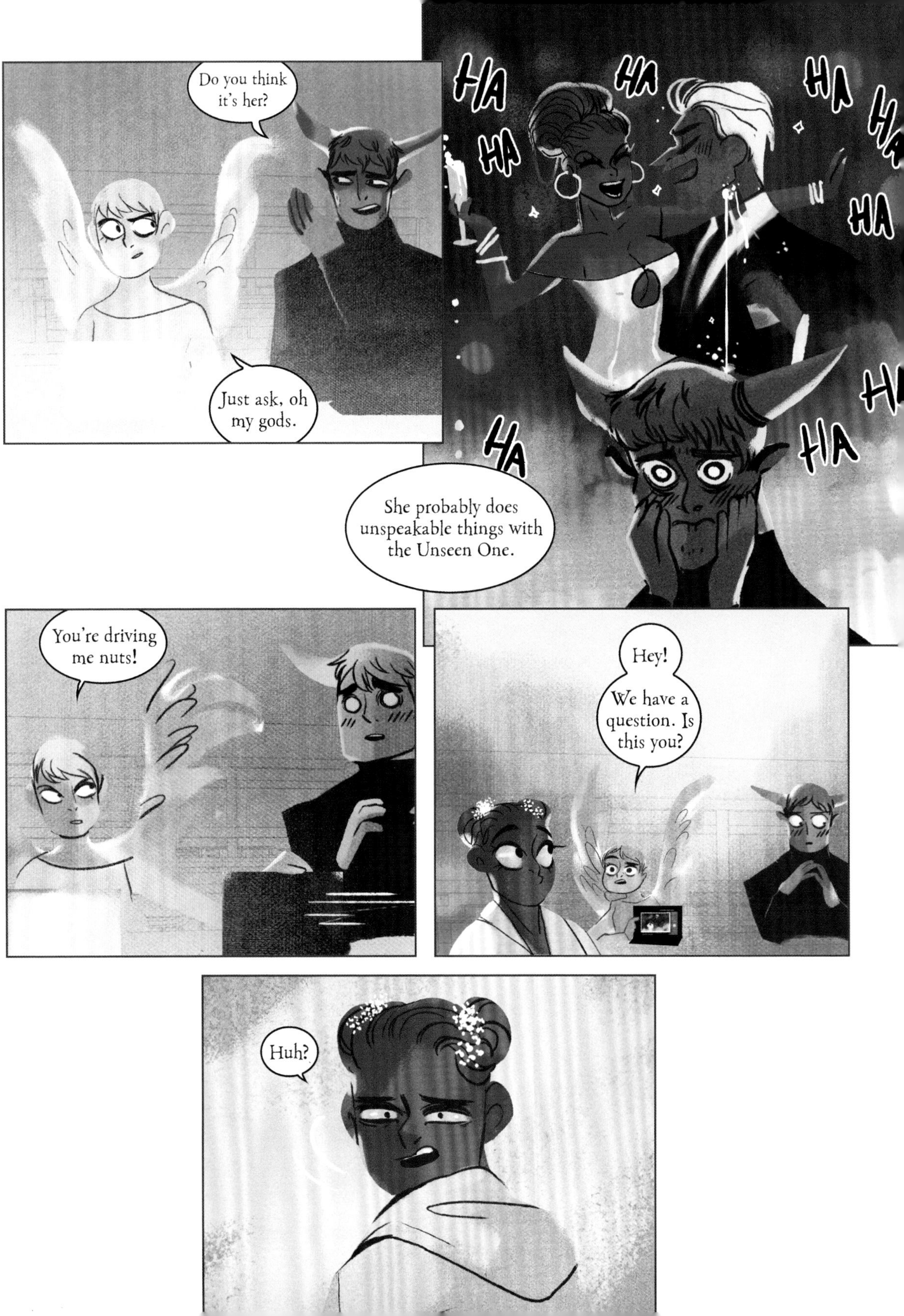

Do you think it's her?
Just ask, oh my gods.
HA HA HA HA HA HA HA HA HA HA HA
She probably does unspeakable things with the Unseen One.
You're driving me nuts!
Hey!
We have a question. Is this you?
Huh?

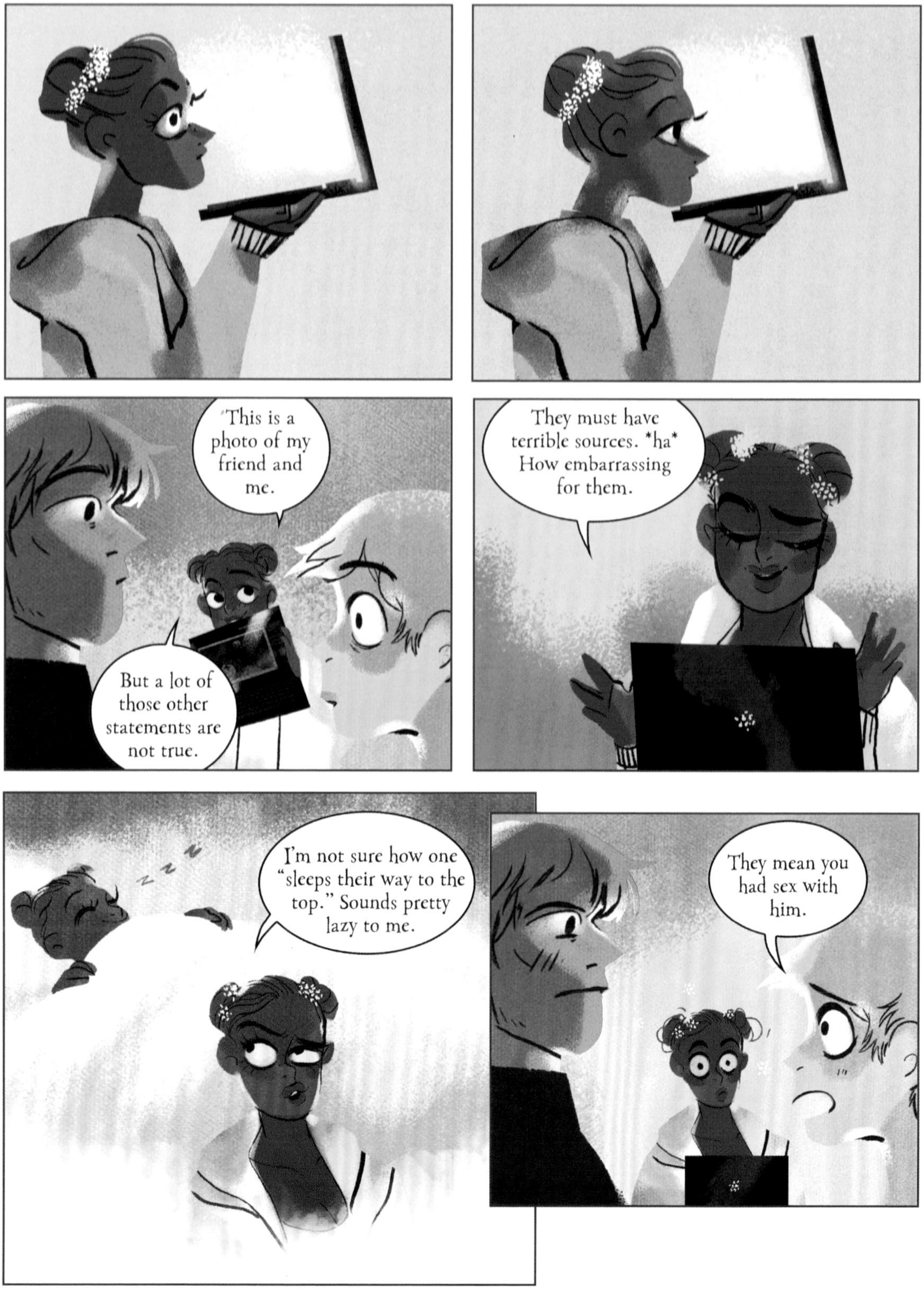
This is a photo of my friend and me.
But a lot of those other statements are not true.
They must have terrible sources. *ha* How embarrassing for them.
Z Z Z
I'm not sure how one "sleeps their way to the top." Sounds pretty lazy to me.
They mean you had sex with him.

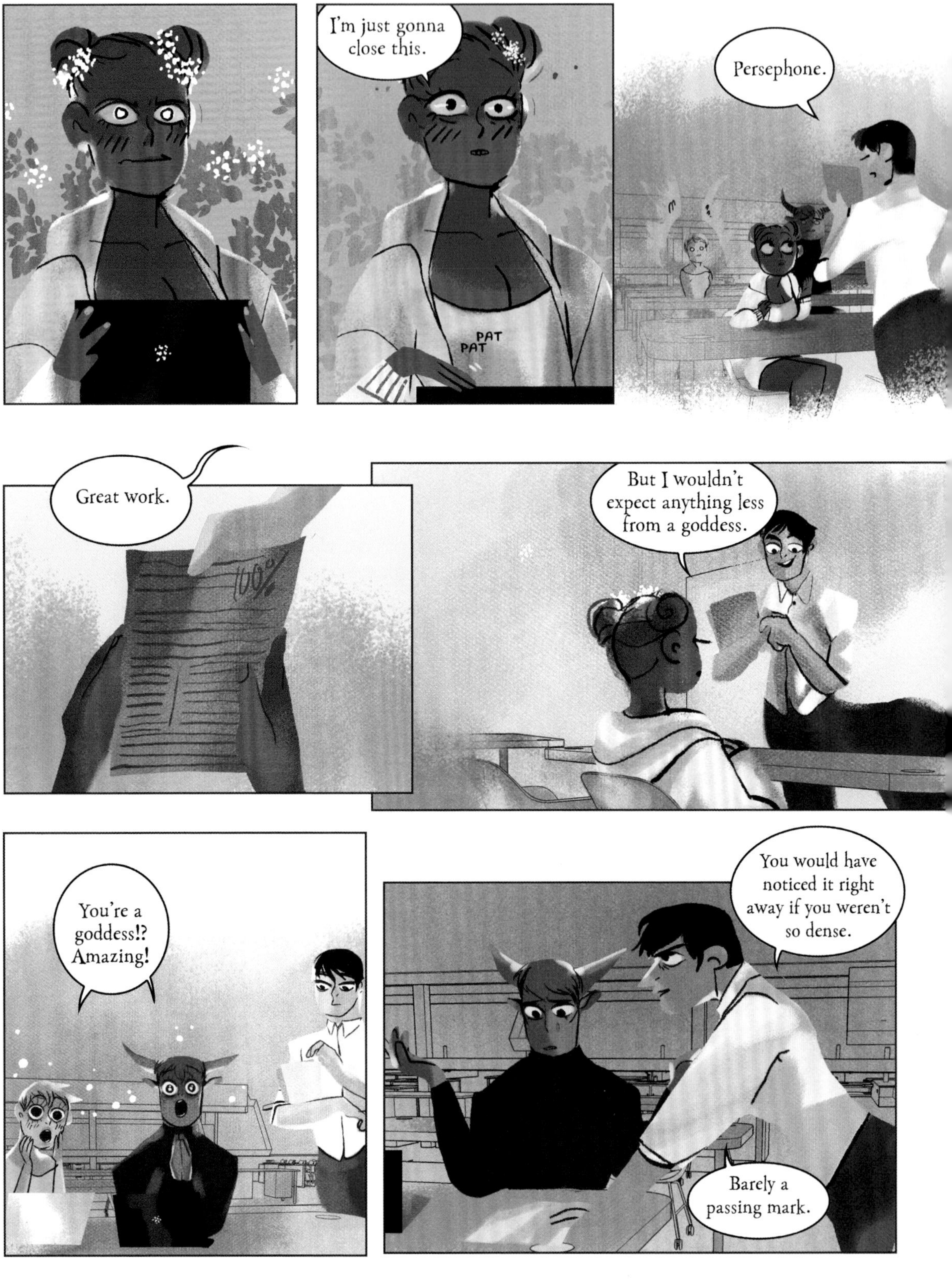

I'm just gonna close this.
PAT PAT
Persephone.
Great work.
100%
But I wouldn't expect anything less from a goddess.
You're a goddess!? Amazing!
You would have noticed it right away if you weren't so dense.
Barely a passing mark.

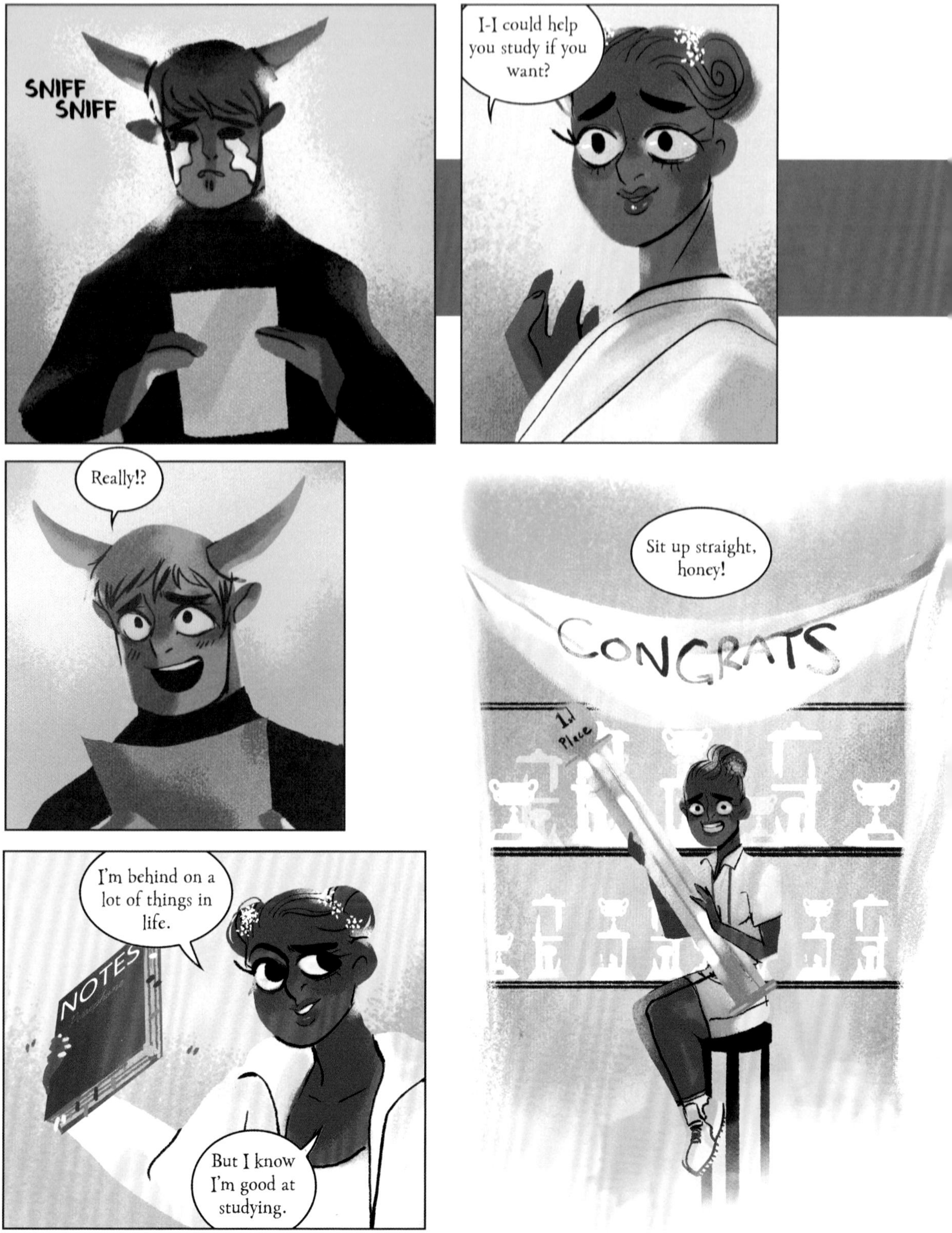
SNIFF SNIFF
I-I could help you study if you want?
Really!?
I'm behind on a lot of things in life.
NOTES
But I know I'm good at studying.
Sit up straight, honey!
CONGRATS
1st Place

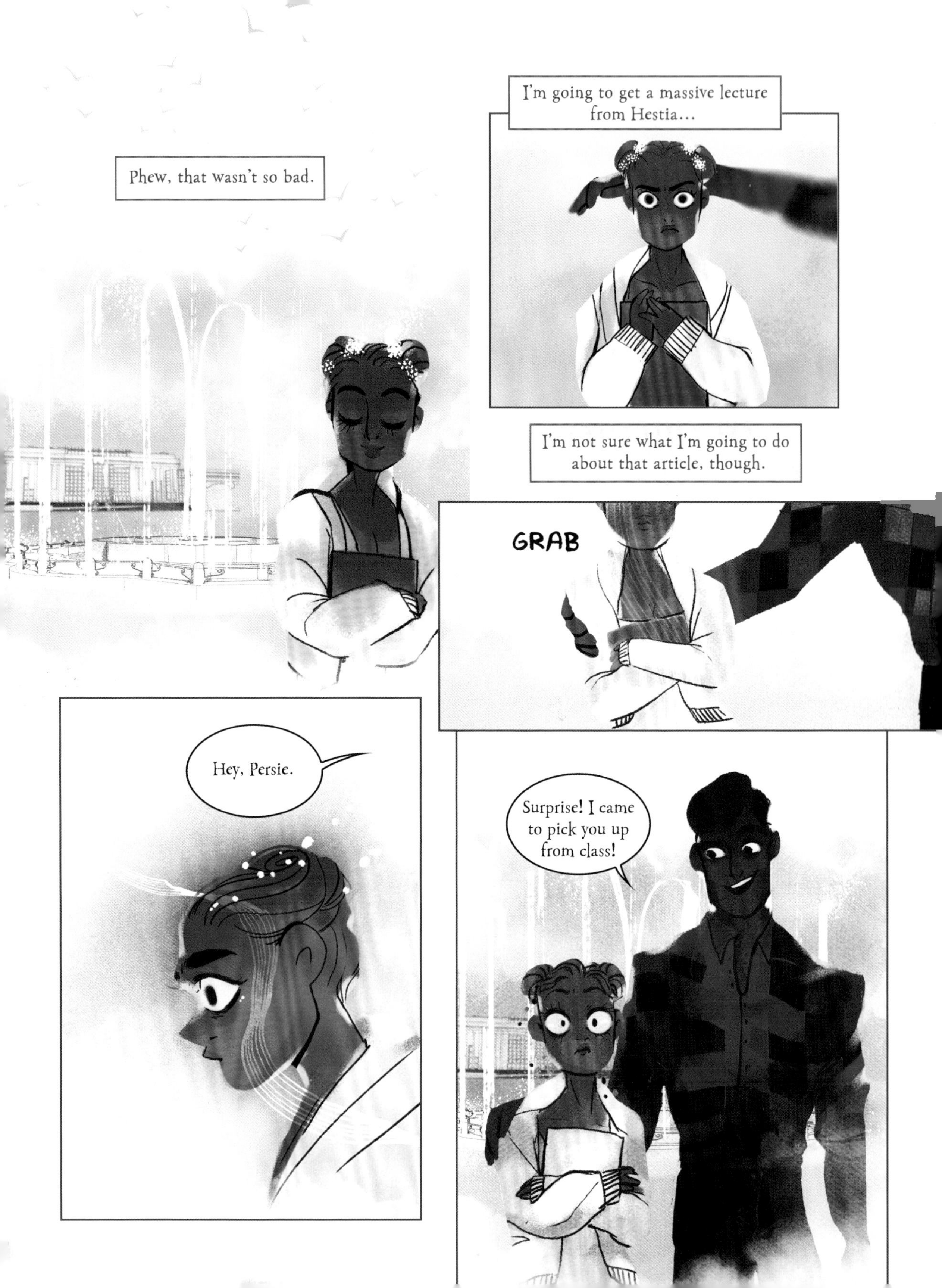
Phew, that wasn't so bad.
I'm going to get a massive lecture from Hestia...
I'm not sure what I'm going to do about that article, though.
GRAB
Hey, Persie.
Surprise! I came to pick you up from class!

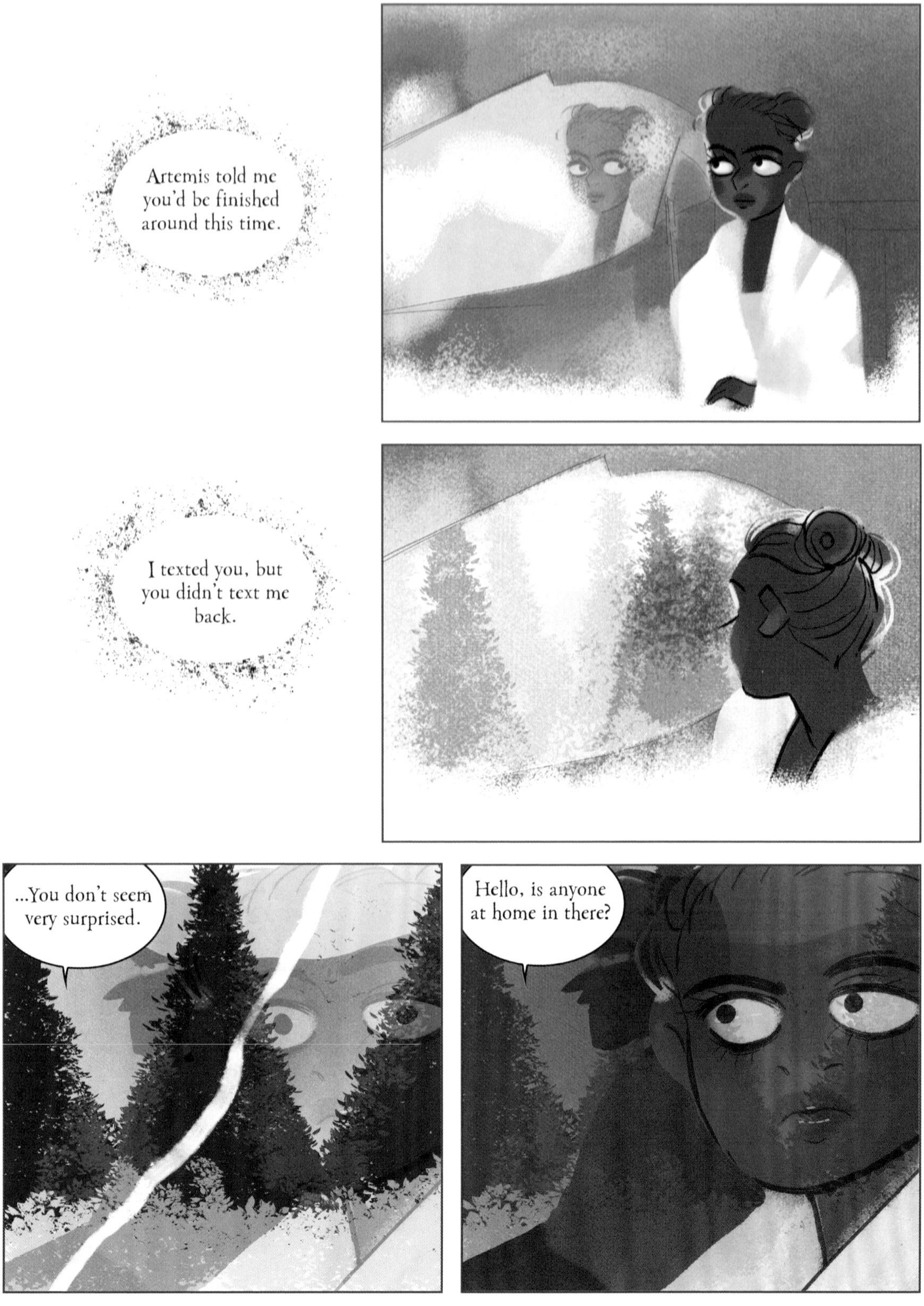
Artemis told me you'd be finished around this time.
I texted you, but you didn't text me back.
...You don't seem very surprised.
Hello, is anyone at home in there?

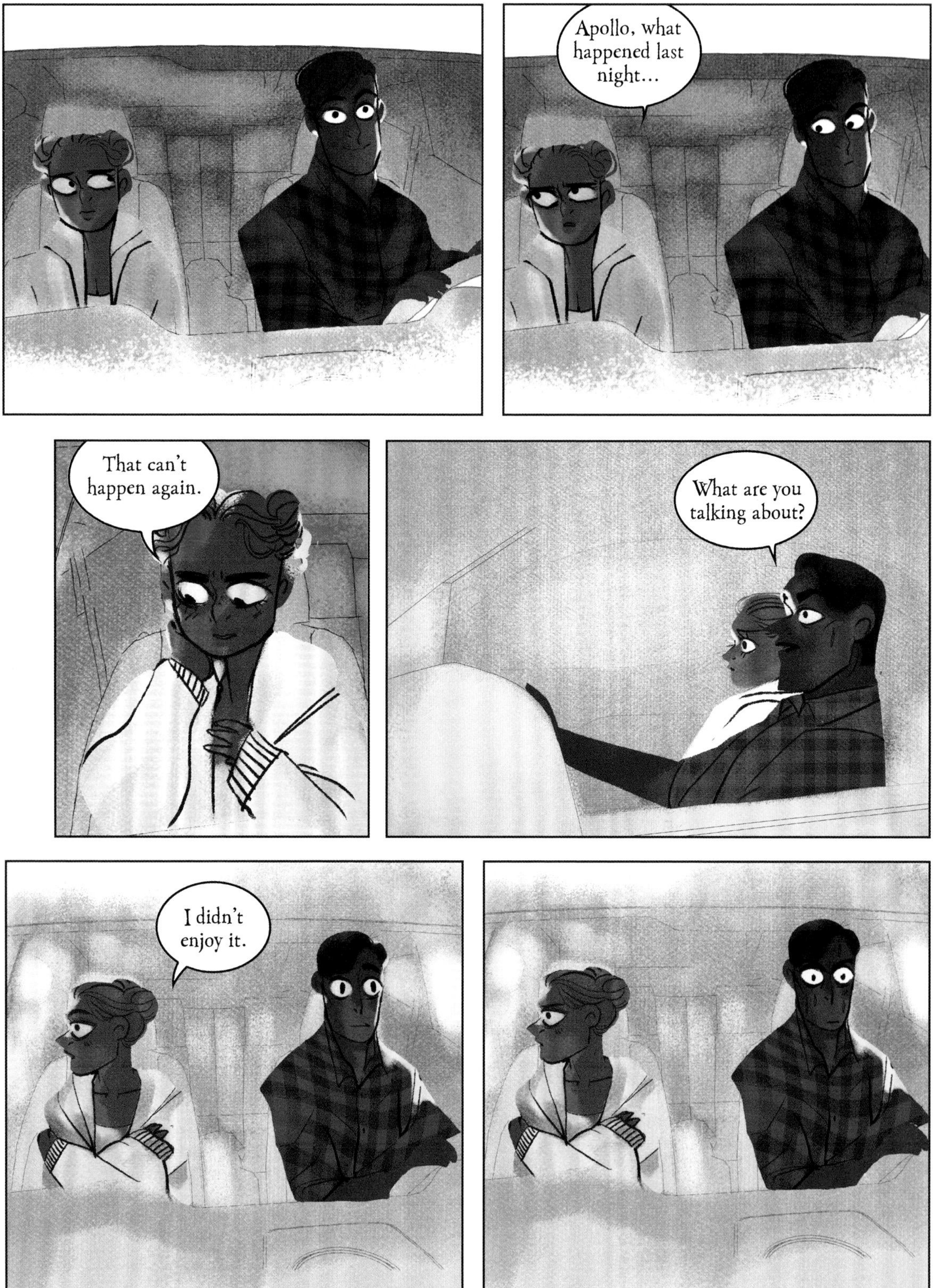
Apollo, what happened last night...
That can't happen again.
What are you talking about?
I didn't enjoy it.

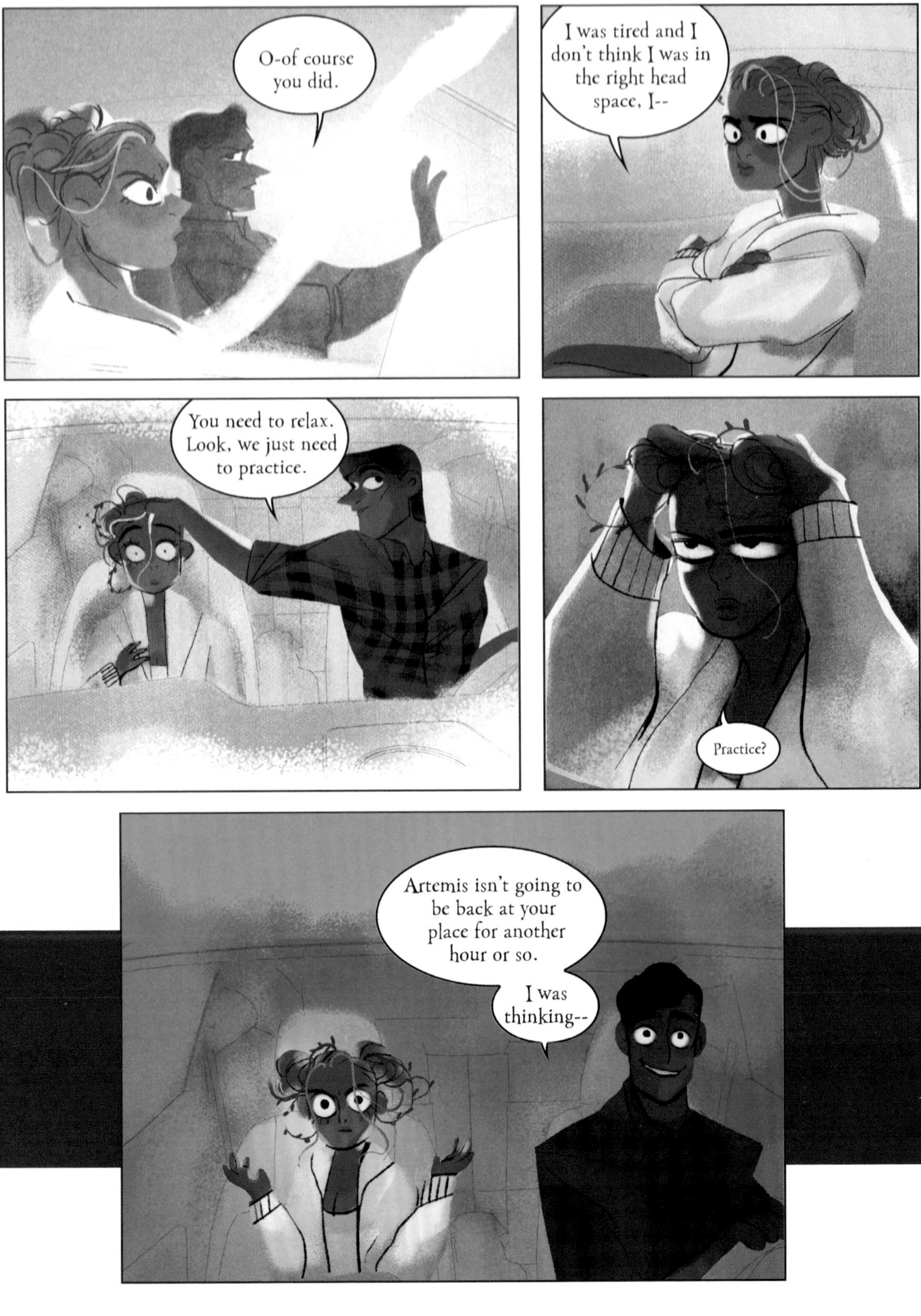
O-of course you did.
I was tired and I don't think I was in the right head space, I--
You need to relax. Look, we just need to practice.
Practice?
Artemis isn't going to be back at your place for another hour or so.
I was thinking--

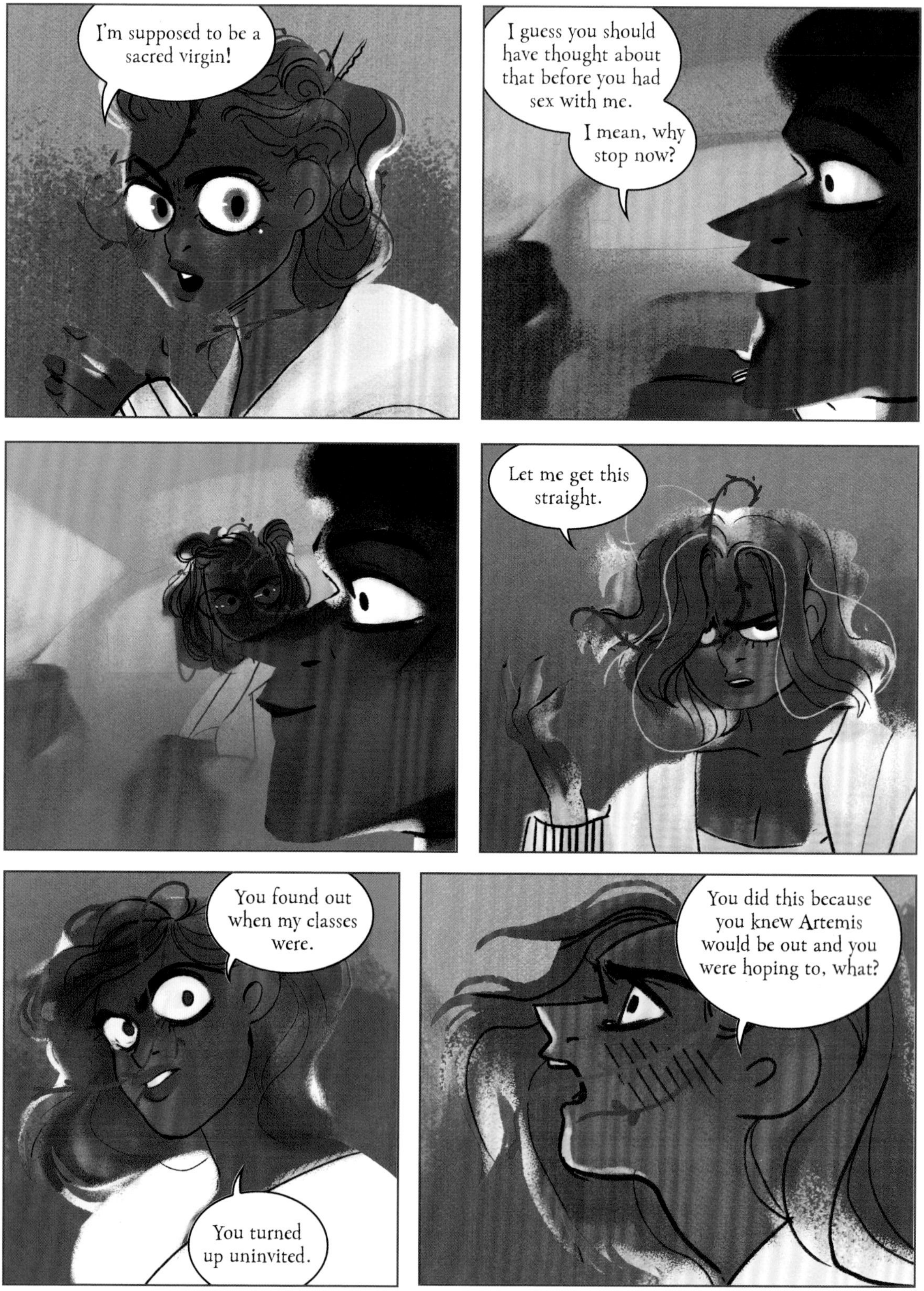
I'm supposed to be a sacred virgin!
I guess you should have thought about that before you had sex with me.
I mean, why stop now?
Let me get this straight.
You found out when my classes were.
You turned up uninvited.
You did this because you knew Artemis would be out and you were hoping to, what?

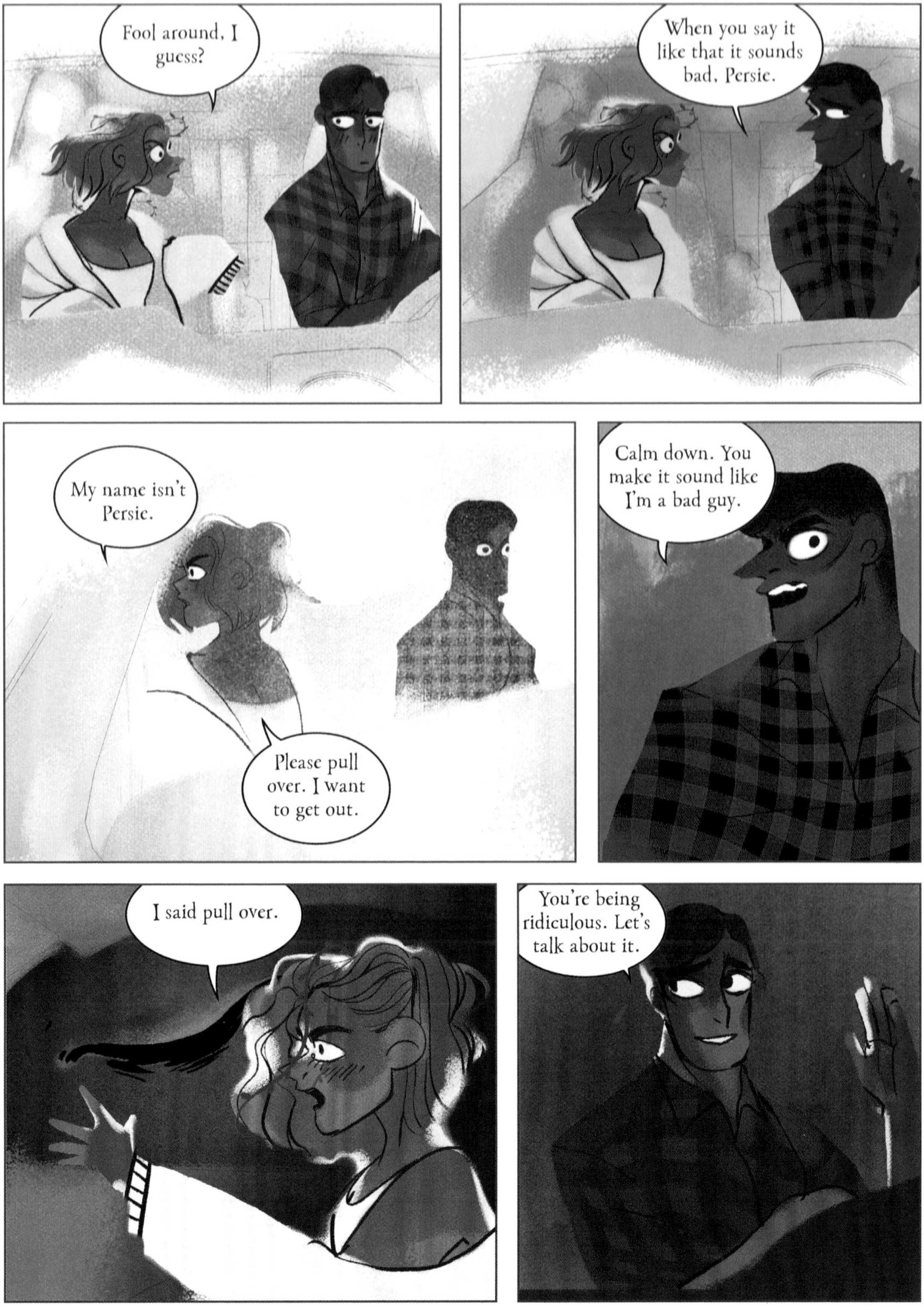
Fool around, I guess?
When you say it like that it sounds bad, Persie.
My name isn't Persie.
Please pull over. I want to get out.
Calm down. You make it sound like I'm a bad guy.
I said pull over.
You're being ridiculous. Let's talk about it.

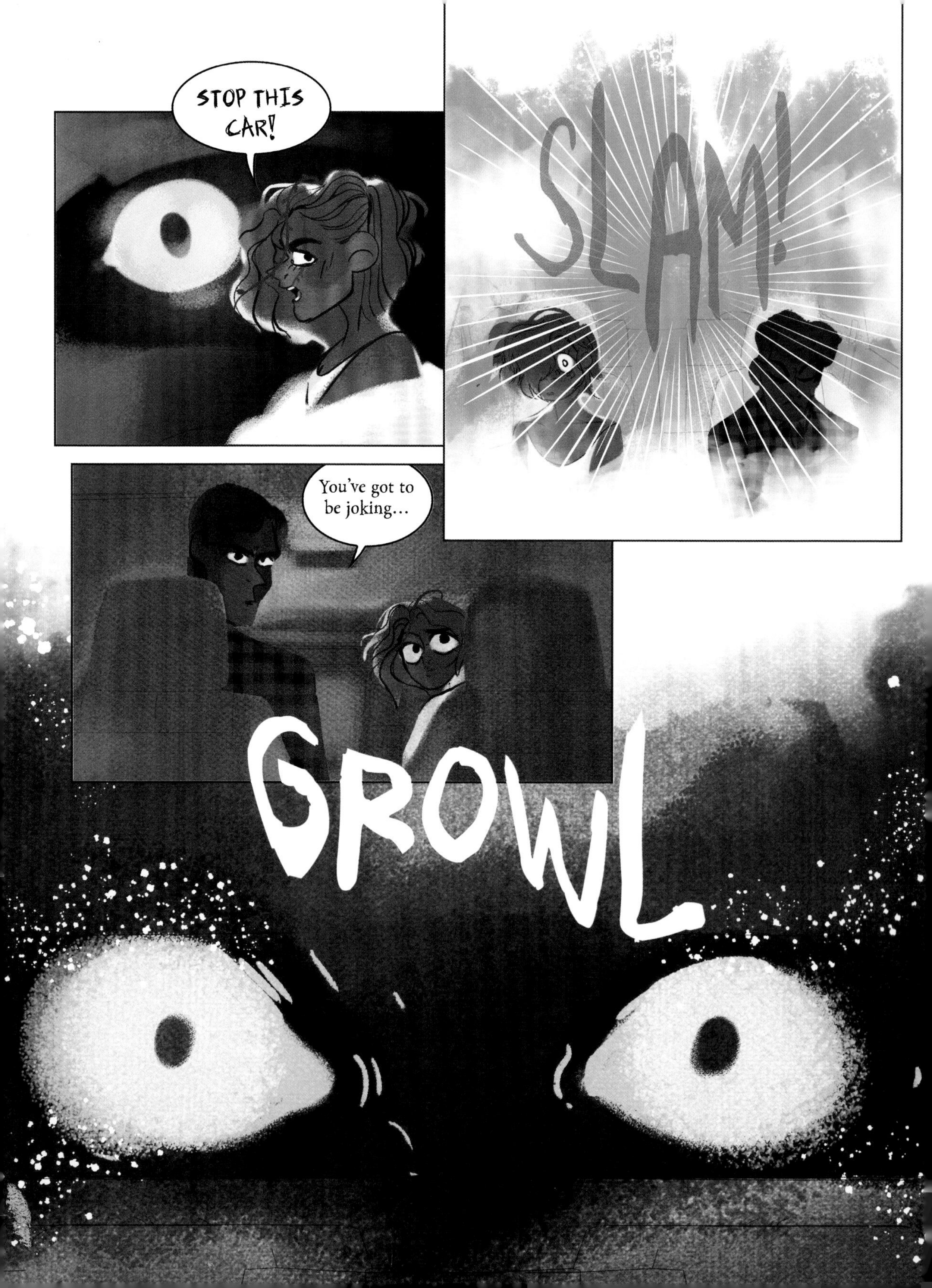
STOP THIS CAR!
SLAM!
You've got to be joking...
GROWL

EPISODE 37: A PRINCE IN DARK VELVET

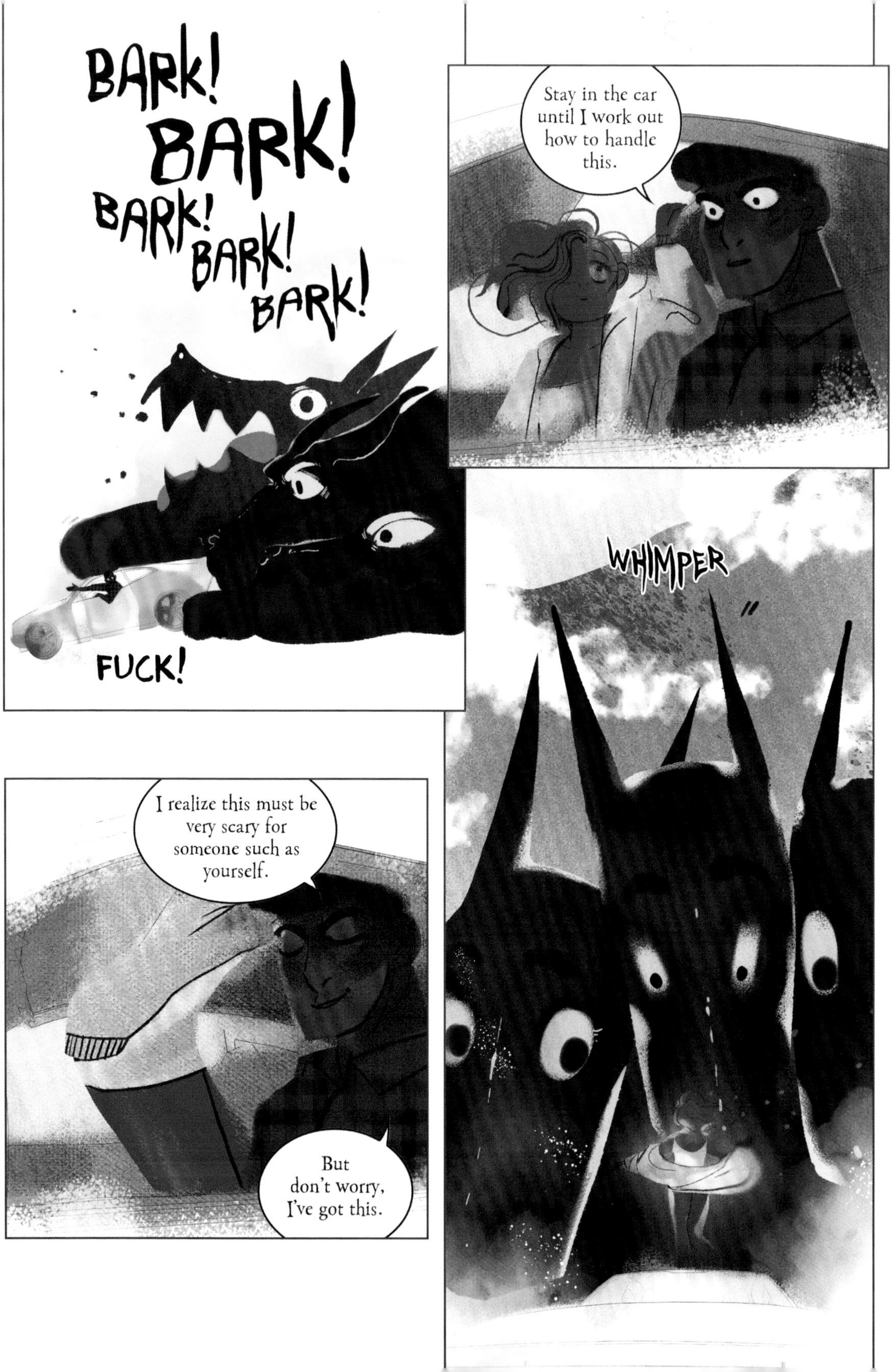
BARK! BARK! BARK! BARK! BARK!
FUCK!
Stay in the car until I work out how to handle this.
WHIMPER
I realize this must be very scary for someone such as yourself.
But don't worry, I've got this.

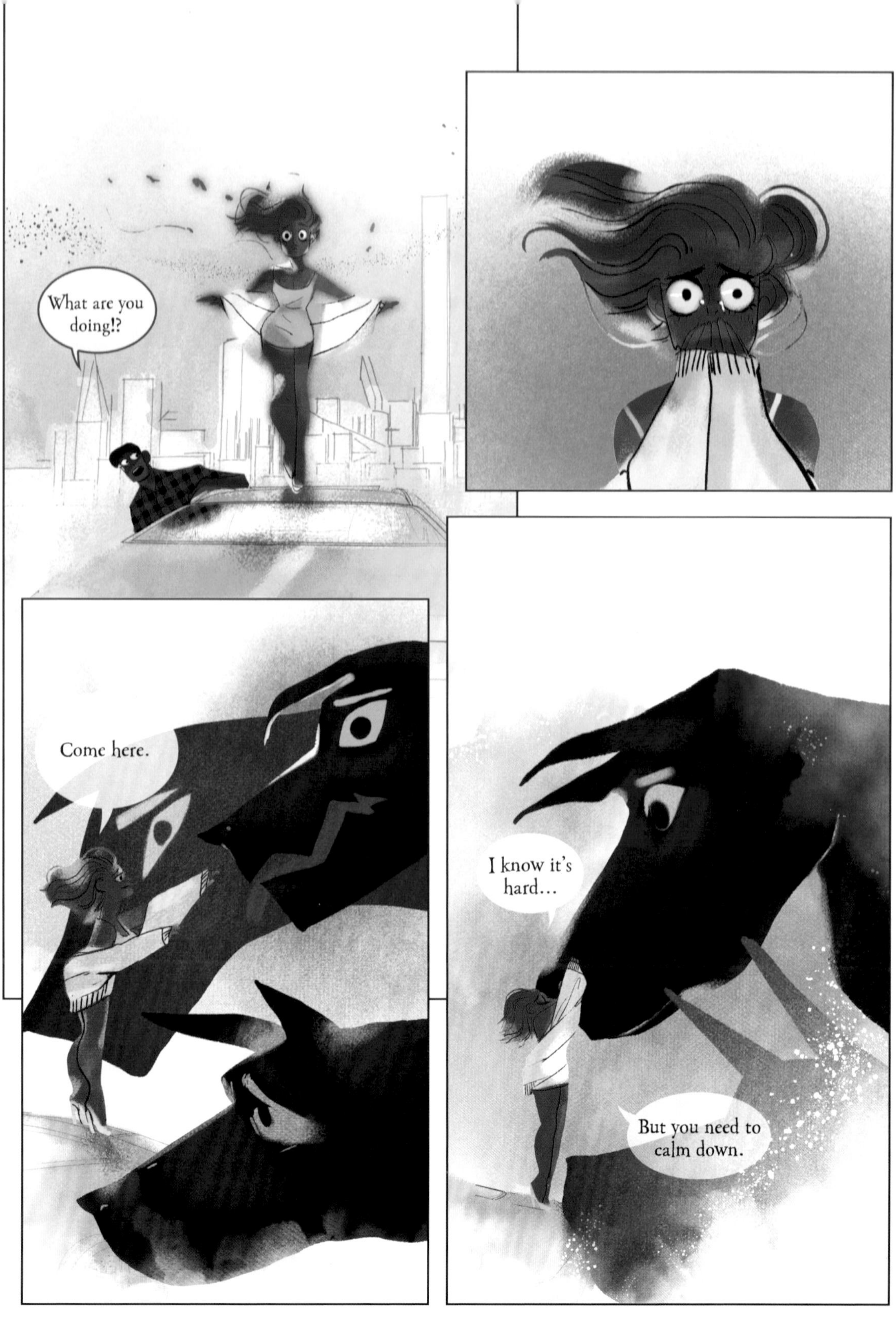
What are you doing!?
Come here.
I know it's hard…
But you need to calm down.

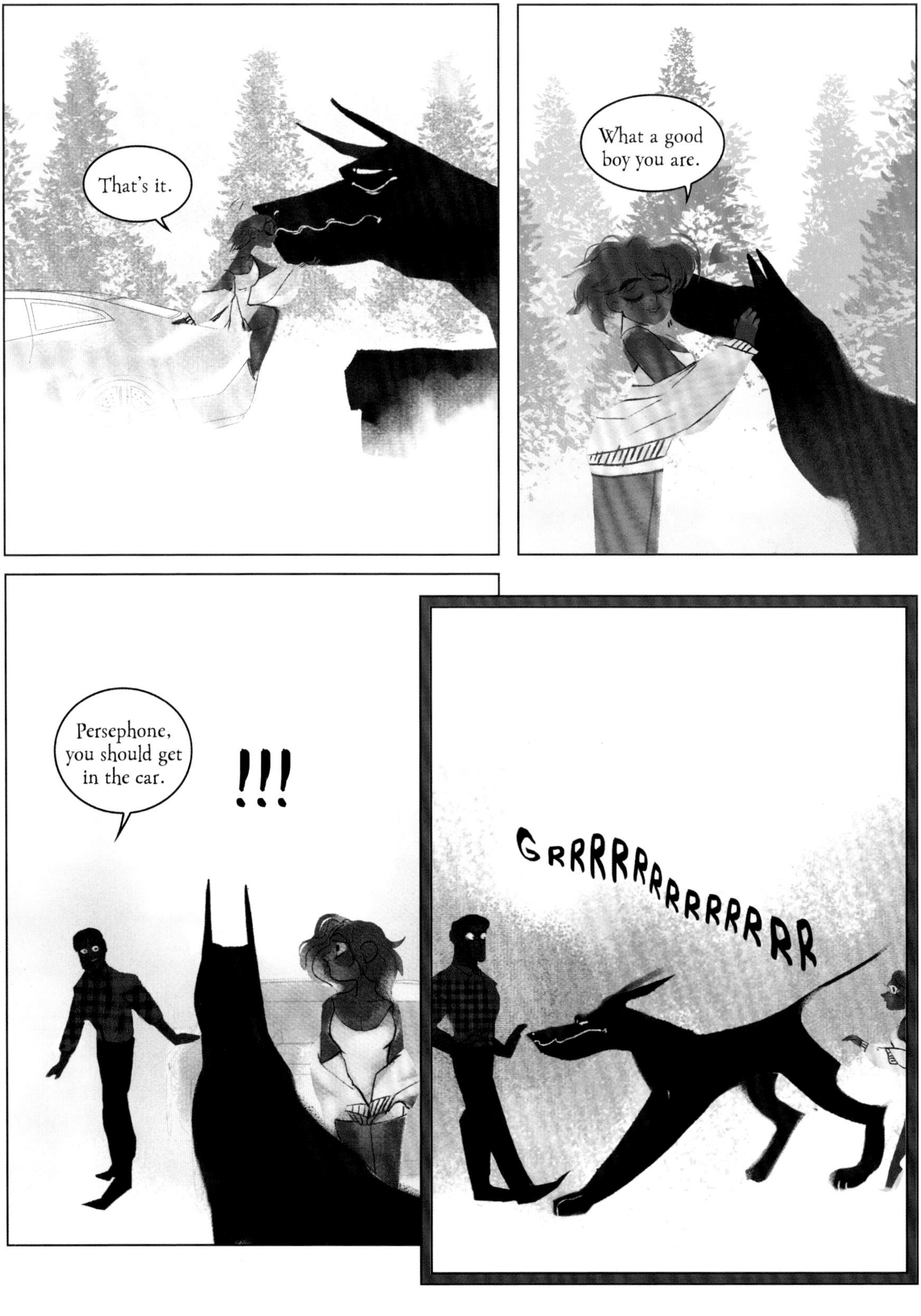
That's it.
What a good boy you are.
Persephone, you should get in the car.
!!!
GRRRRRRRRRRRRR

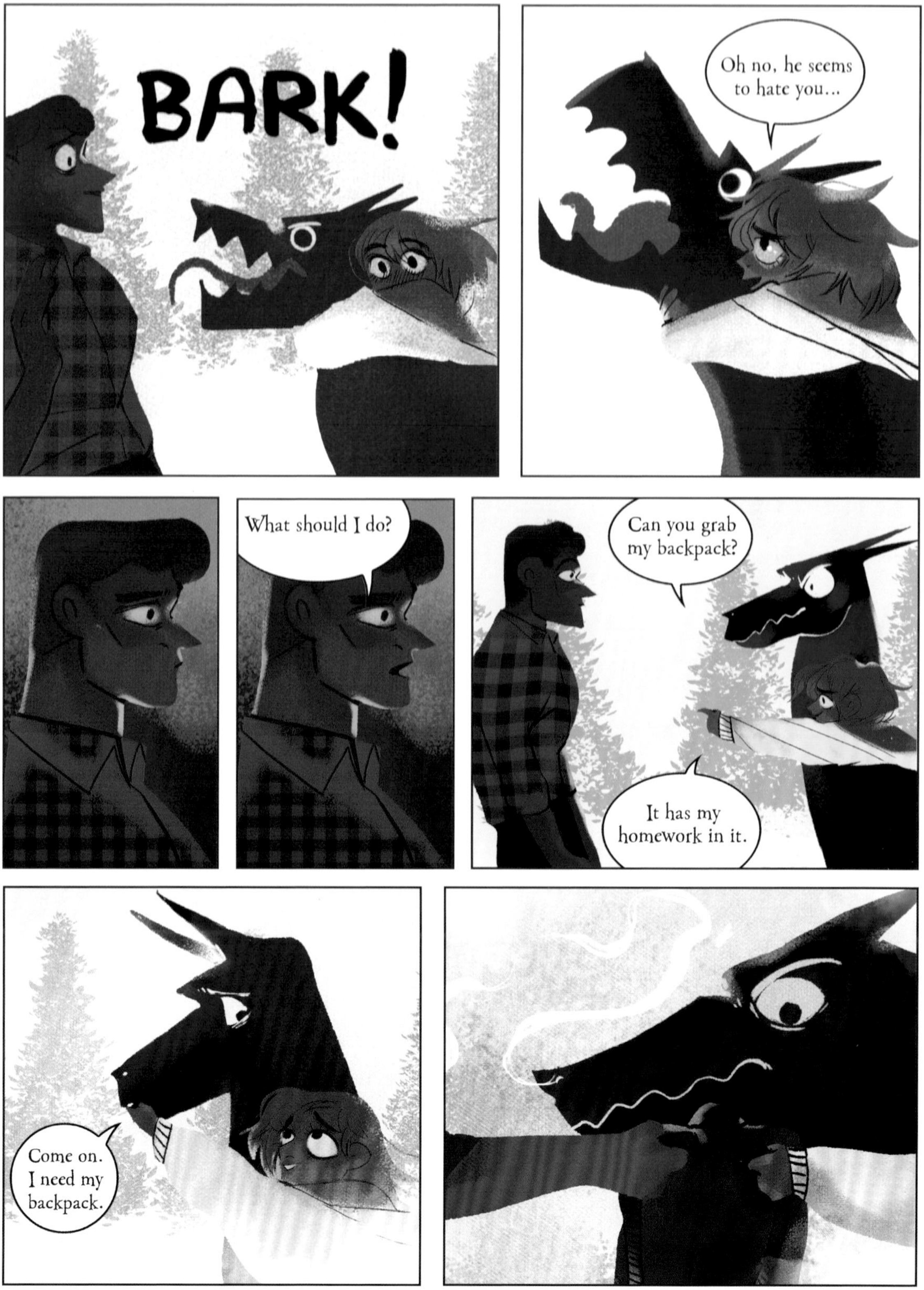

BARK!
Oh no, he seems to hate you...
What should I do?
Can you grab my backpack?
It has my homework in it.
Come on. I need my backpack.

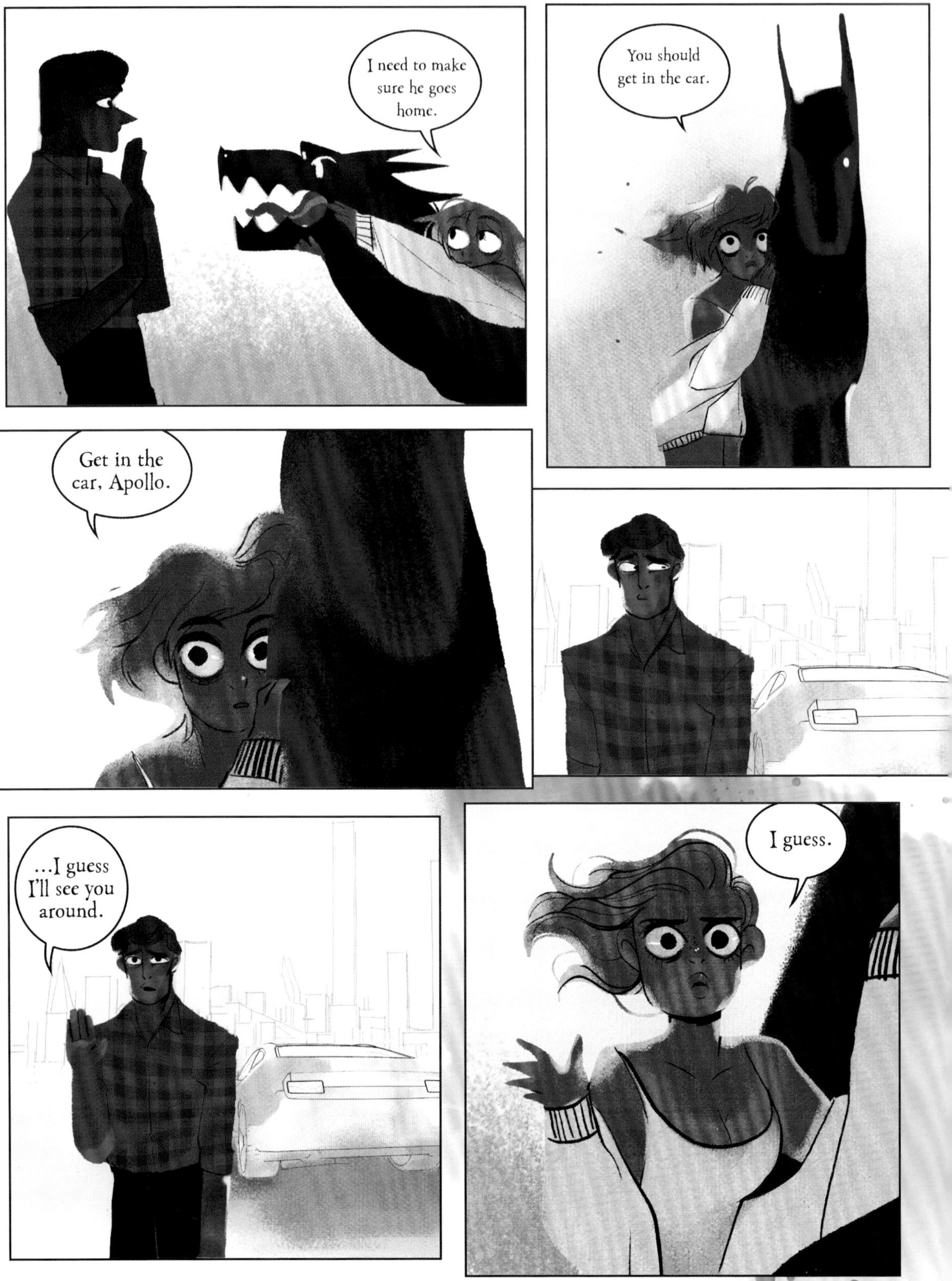
I need to make sure he goes home.
You should get in the car.
Get in the car, Apollo.
...I guess I'll see you around.
I guess.

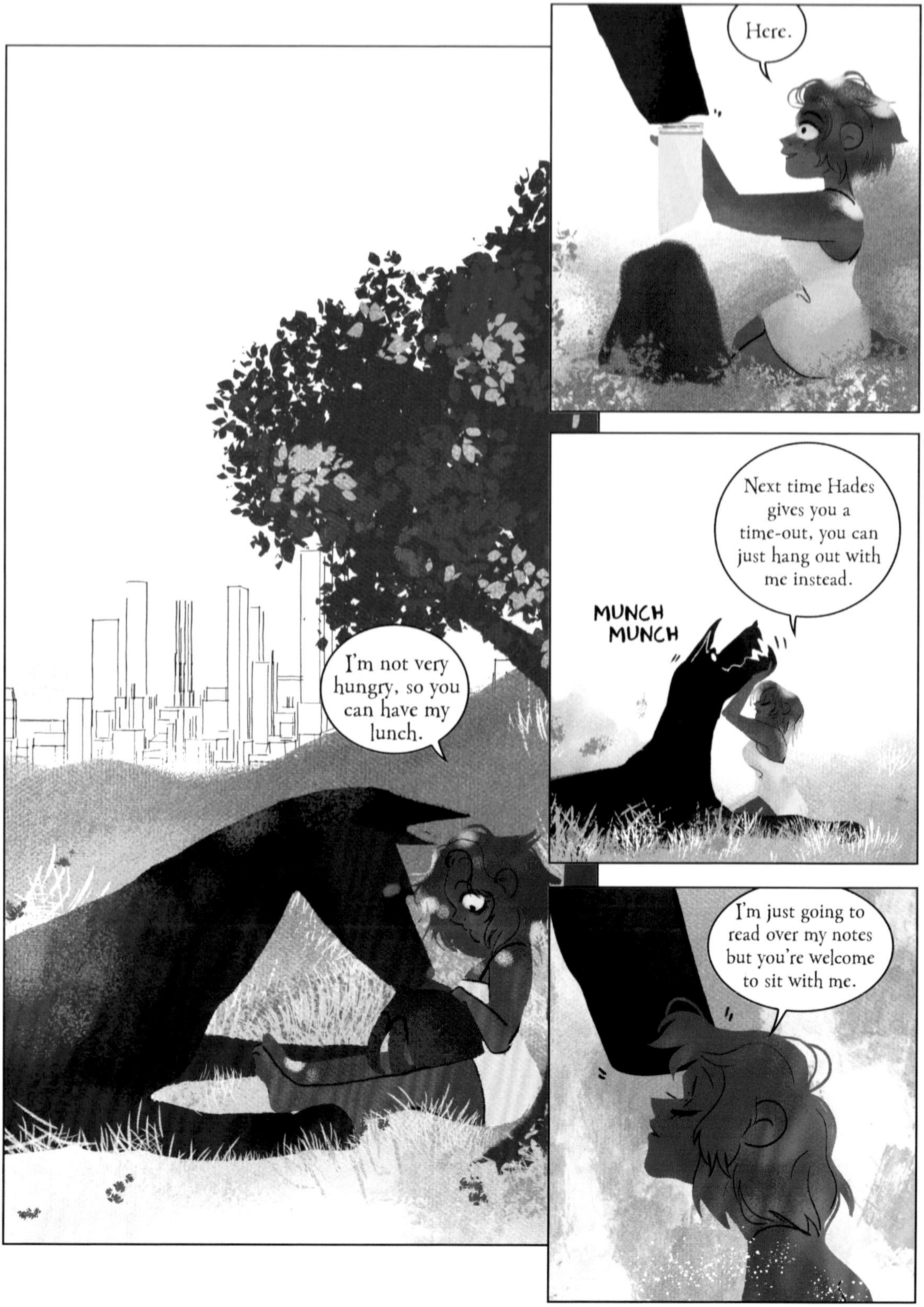
Here.
I'm not very hungry, so you can have my lunch.
Next time Hades gives you a time-out, you can just hang out with me instead.
MUNCH MUNCH
I'm just going to read over my notes but you're welcome to sit with me.

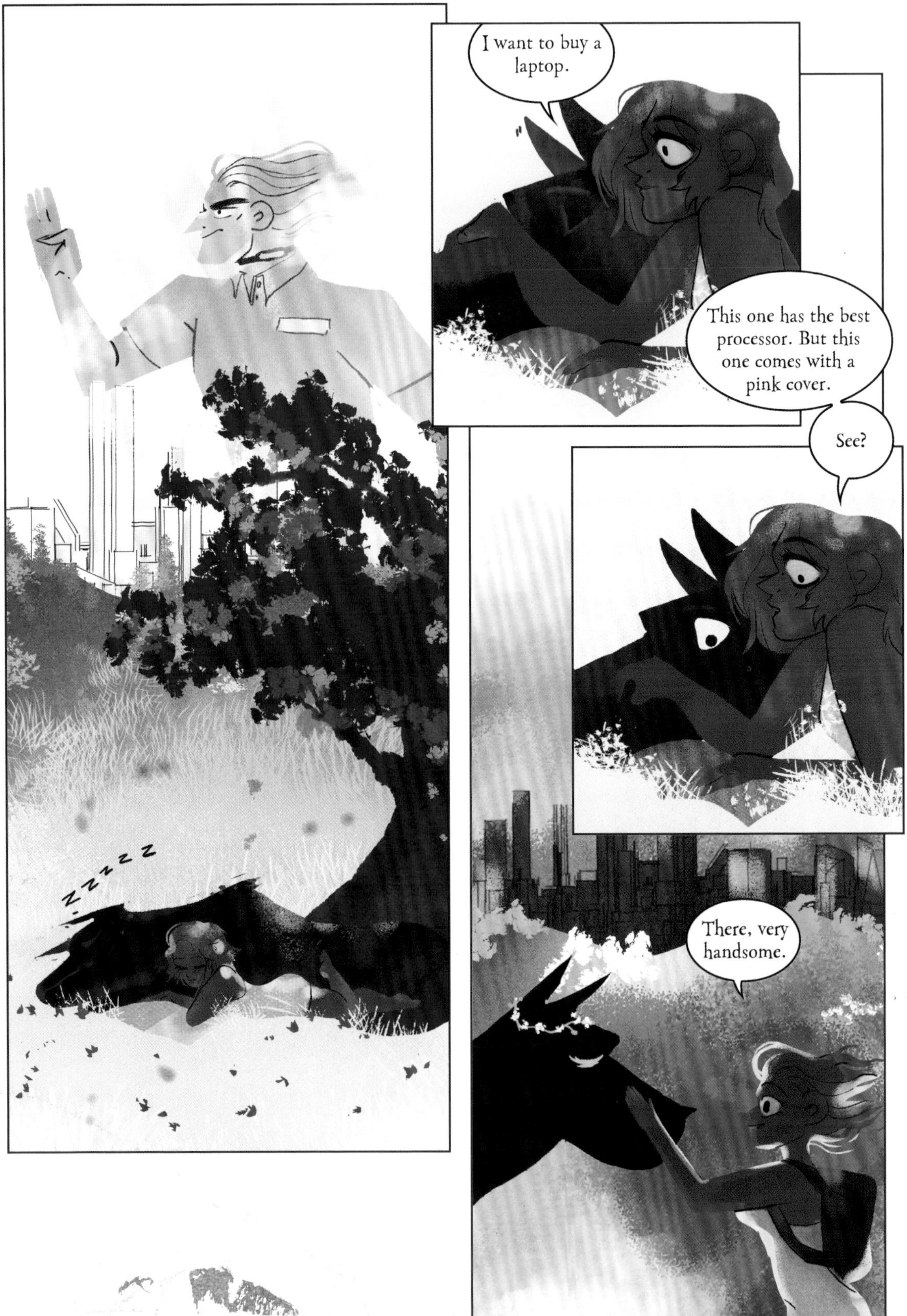
ZZZZZ
I want to buy a laptop.
This one has the best processor. But this one comes with a pink cover.
See?
There, very handsome.

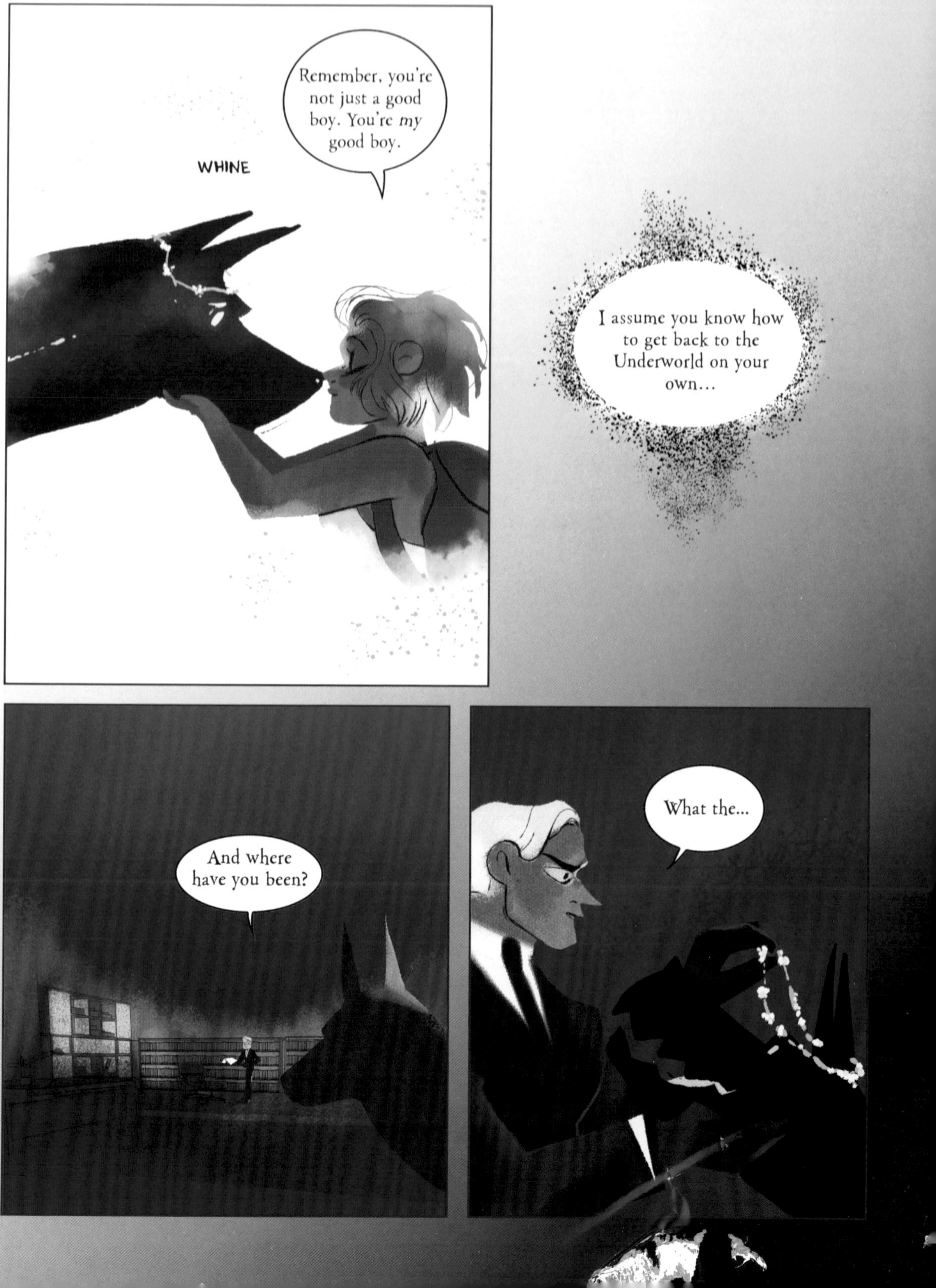
Remember, you're not just a good boy. You're *my* good boy.
WHINE
I assume you know how to get back to the Underworld on your own...
And where have you been?
What the...

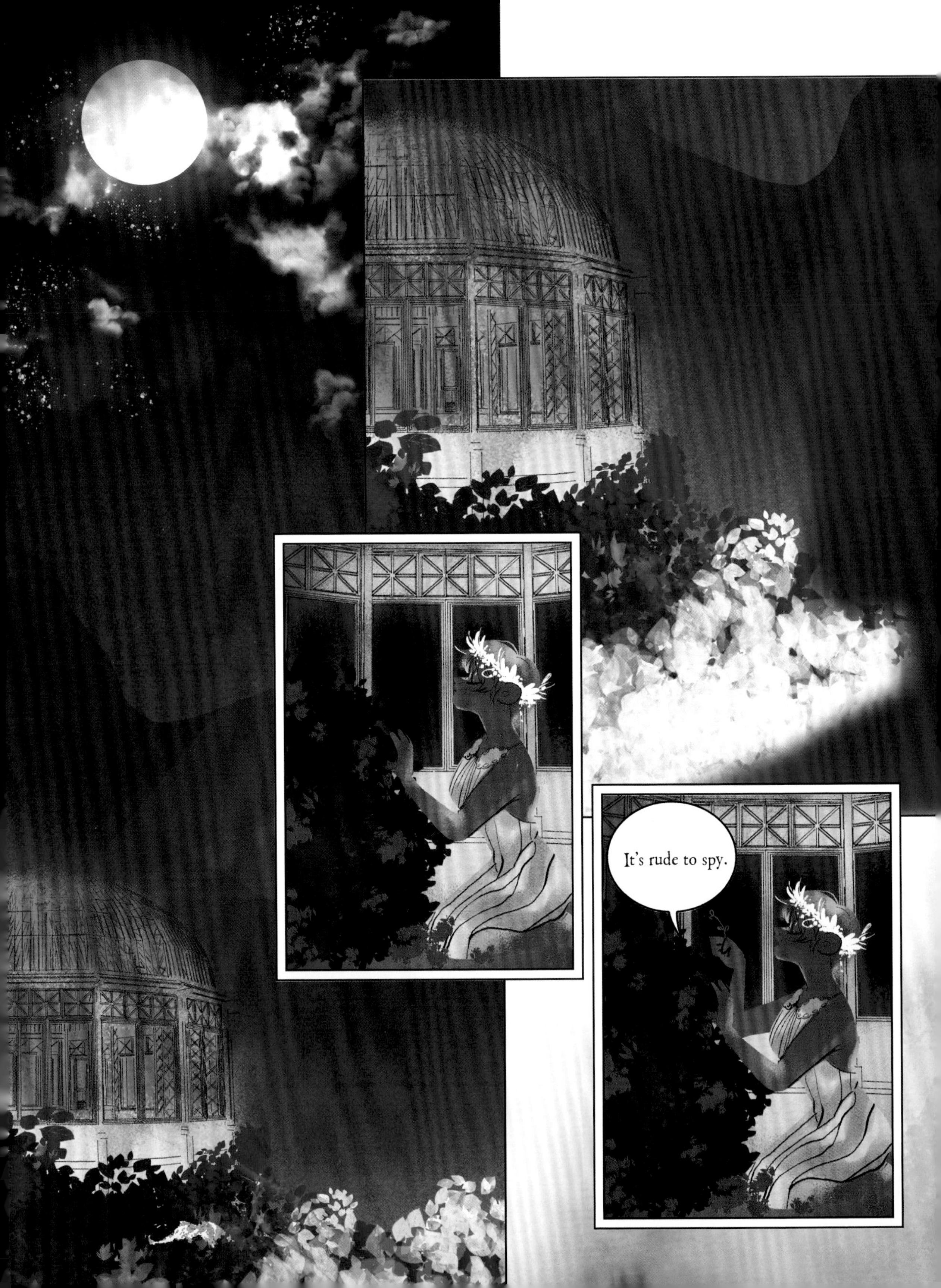
It's rude to spy.

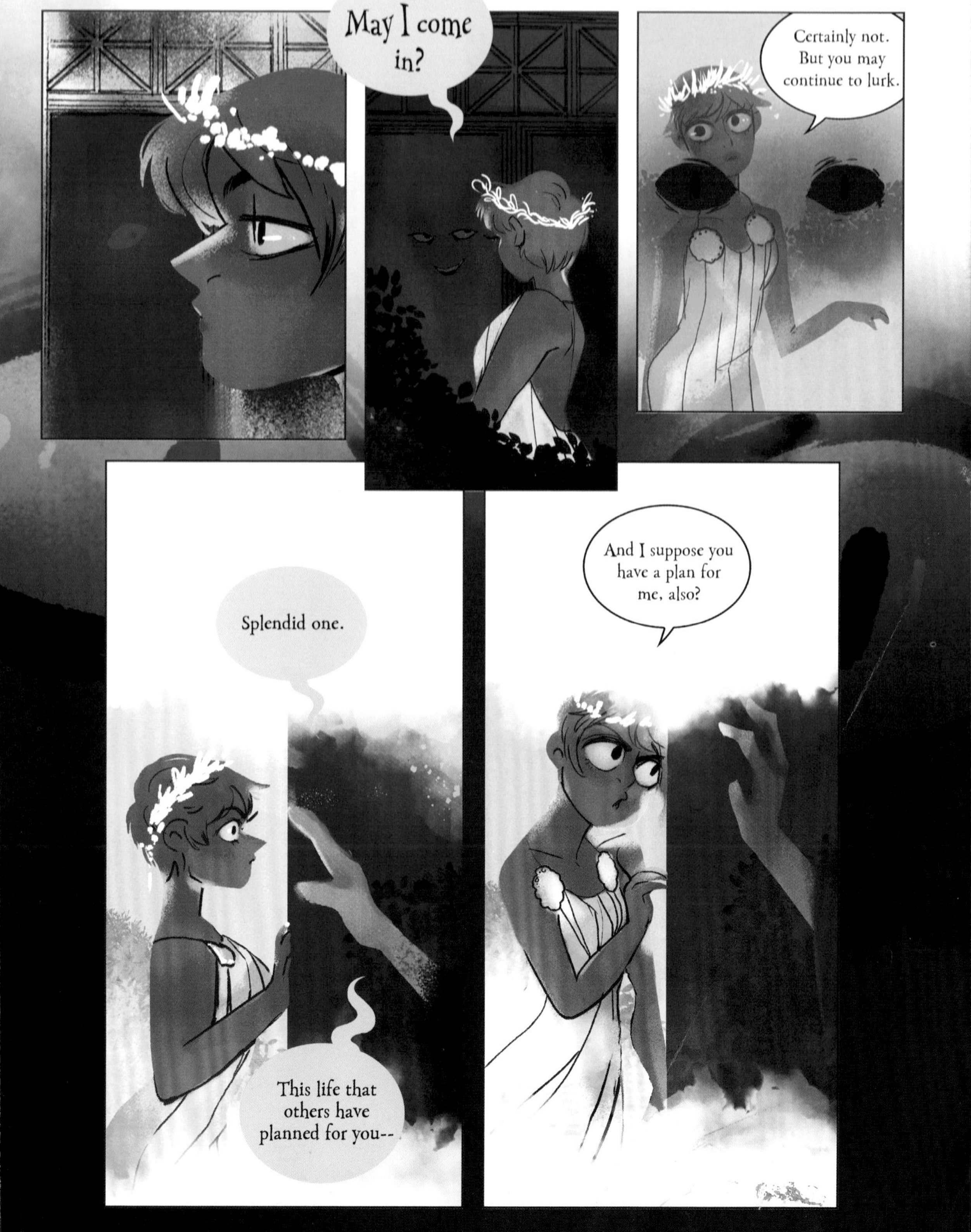
May I come in?
Certainly not. But you may continue to lurk.
Splendid one.
This life that others have planned for you--
And I suppose you have a plan for me, also?

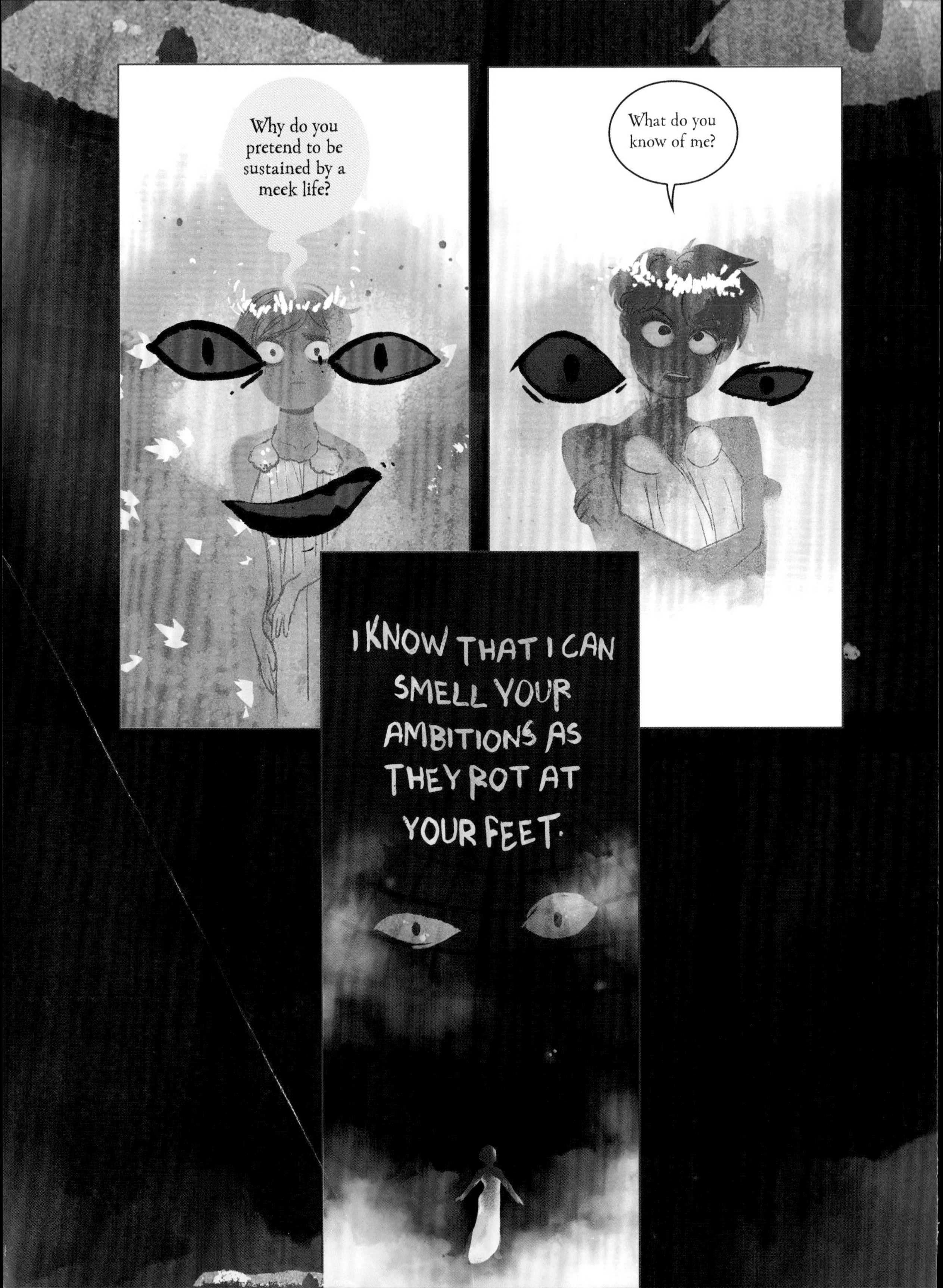
Why do you pretend to be sustained by a meek life?
What do you know of me?
I KNOW THAT I CAN SMELL YOUR AMBITIONS AS THEY ROT AT YOUR FEET.

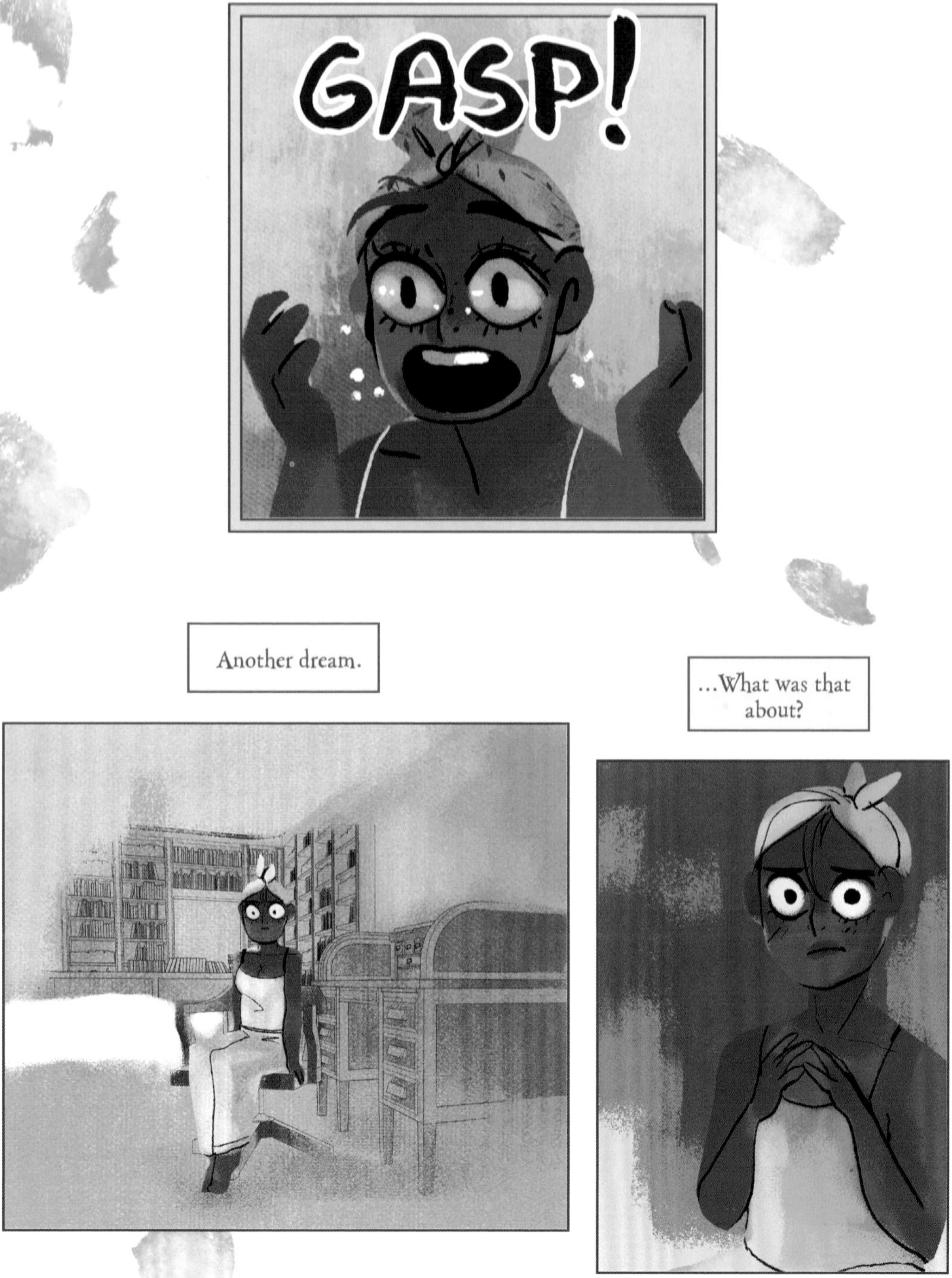
GASP!
Another dream.
...What was that about?

EPISODE 38: MEETING READY

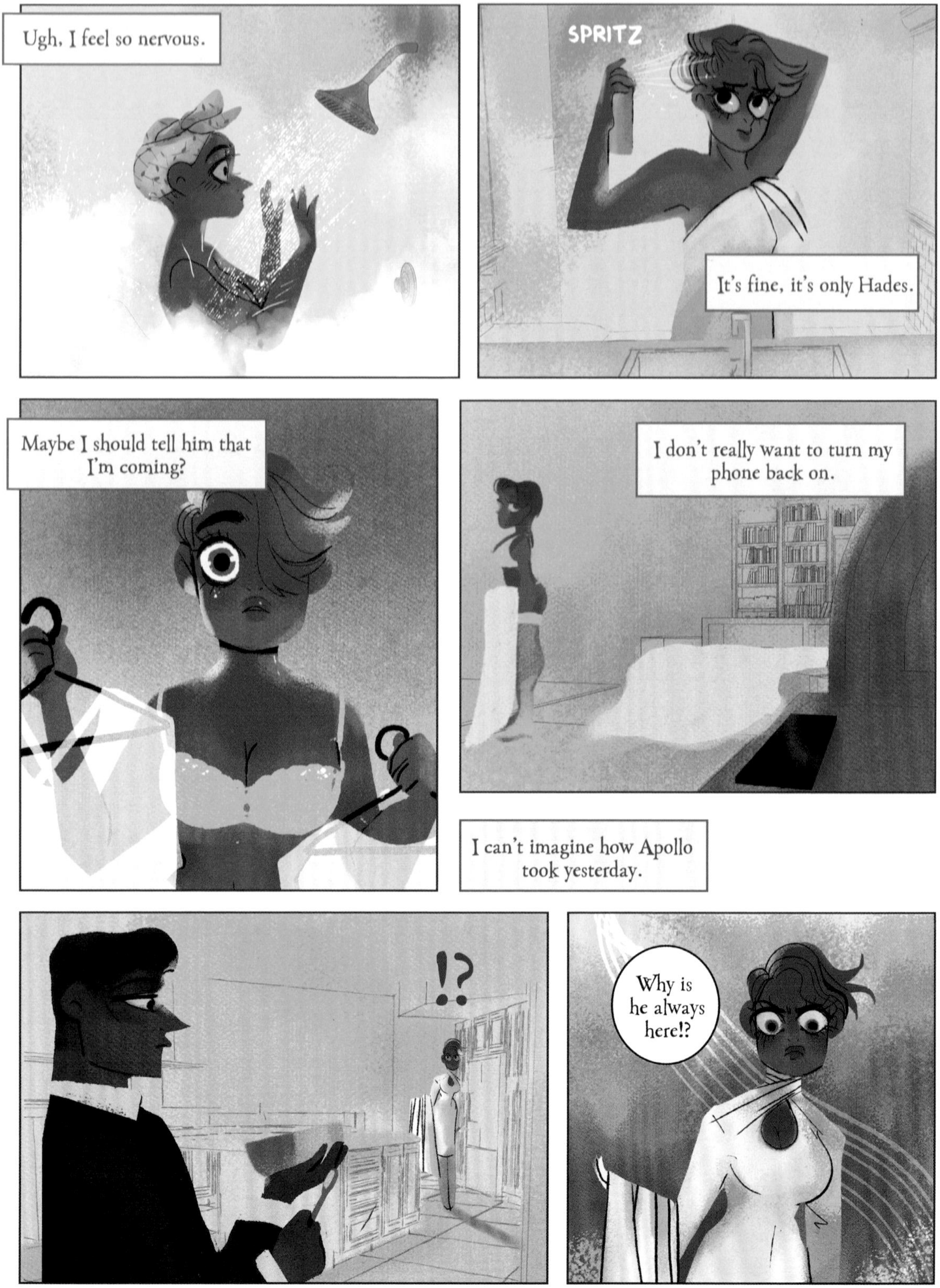
Ugh, I feel so nervous.
SPRITZ
It's fine, it's only Hades.
Maybe I should tell him that I'm coming?
I don't really want to turn my phone back on.
I can't imagine how Apollo took yesterday.
!?
Why is he always here!?

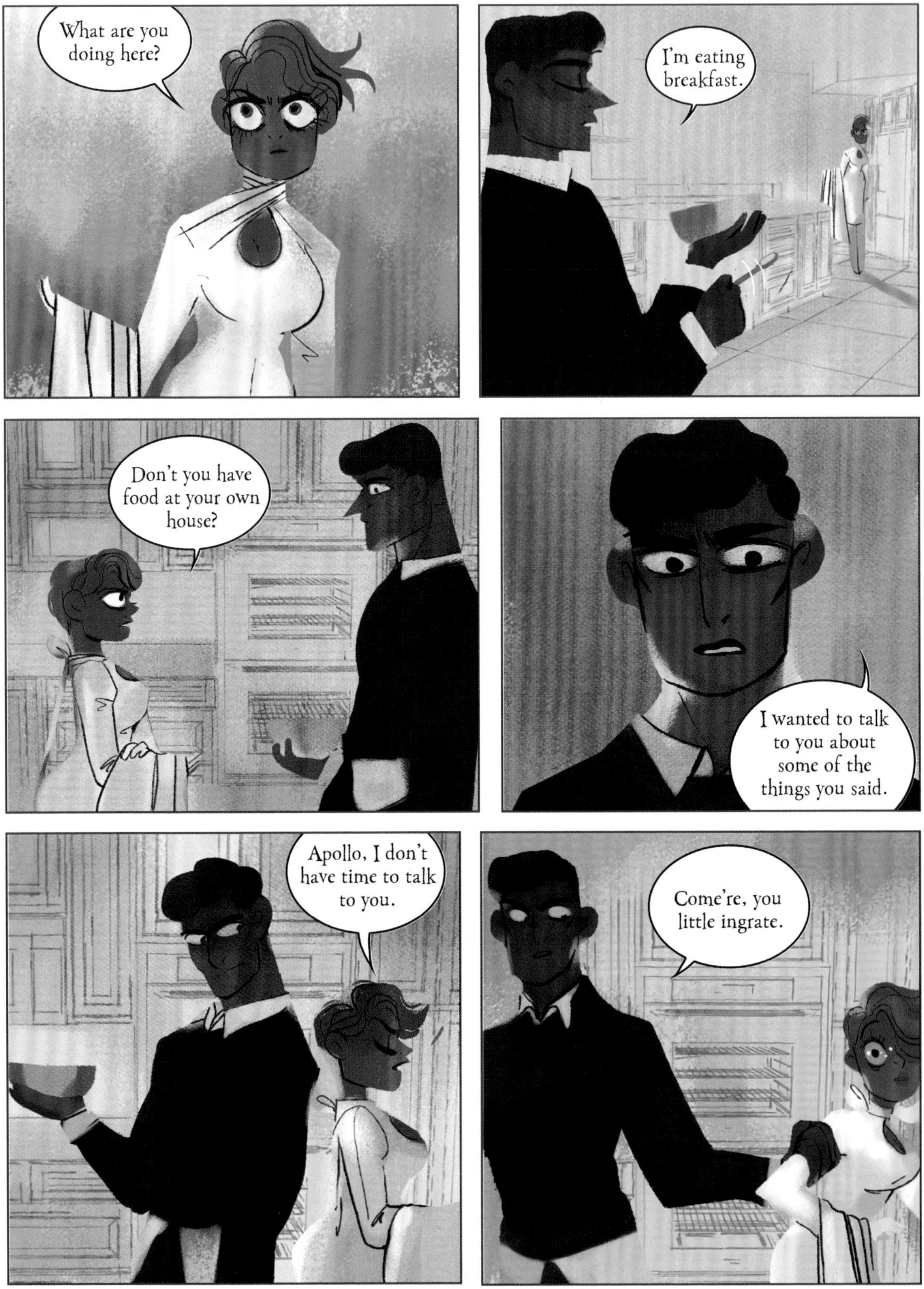
What are you doing here?
I'm eating breakfast.
Don't you have food at your own house?
I wanted to talk to you about some of the things you said.
Apollo, I don't have time to talk to you.
Come're, you little ingrate.

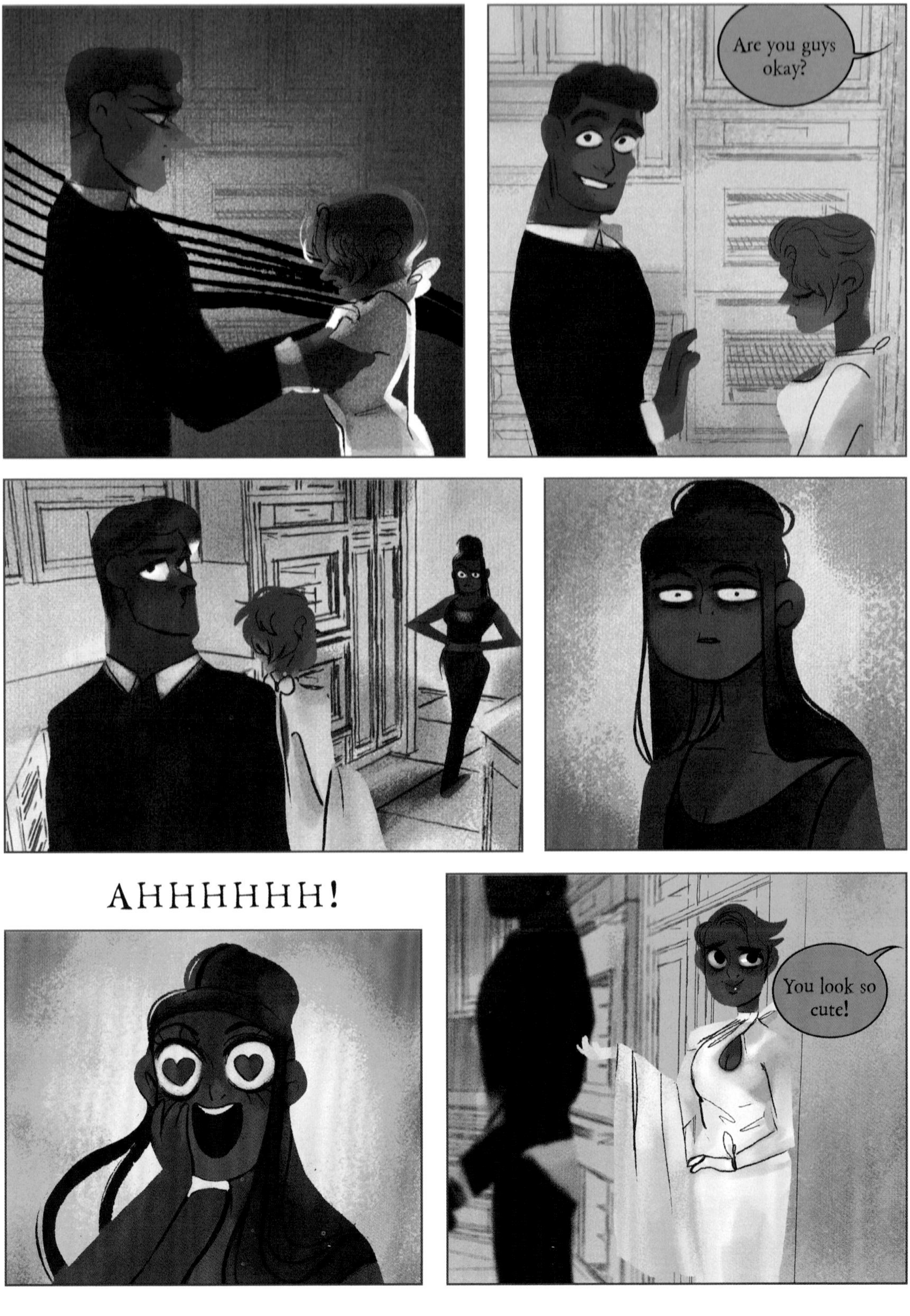
Are you guys okay?
AHHHHHH!
You look so cute!

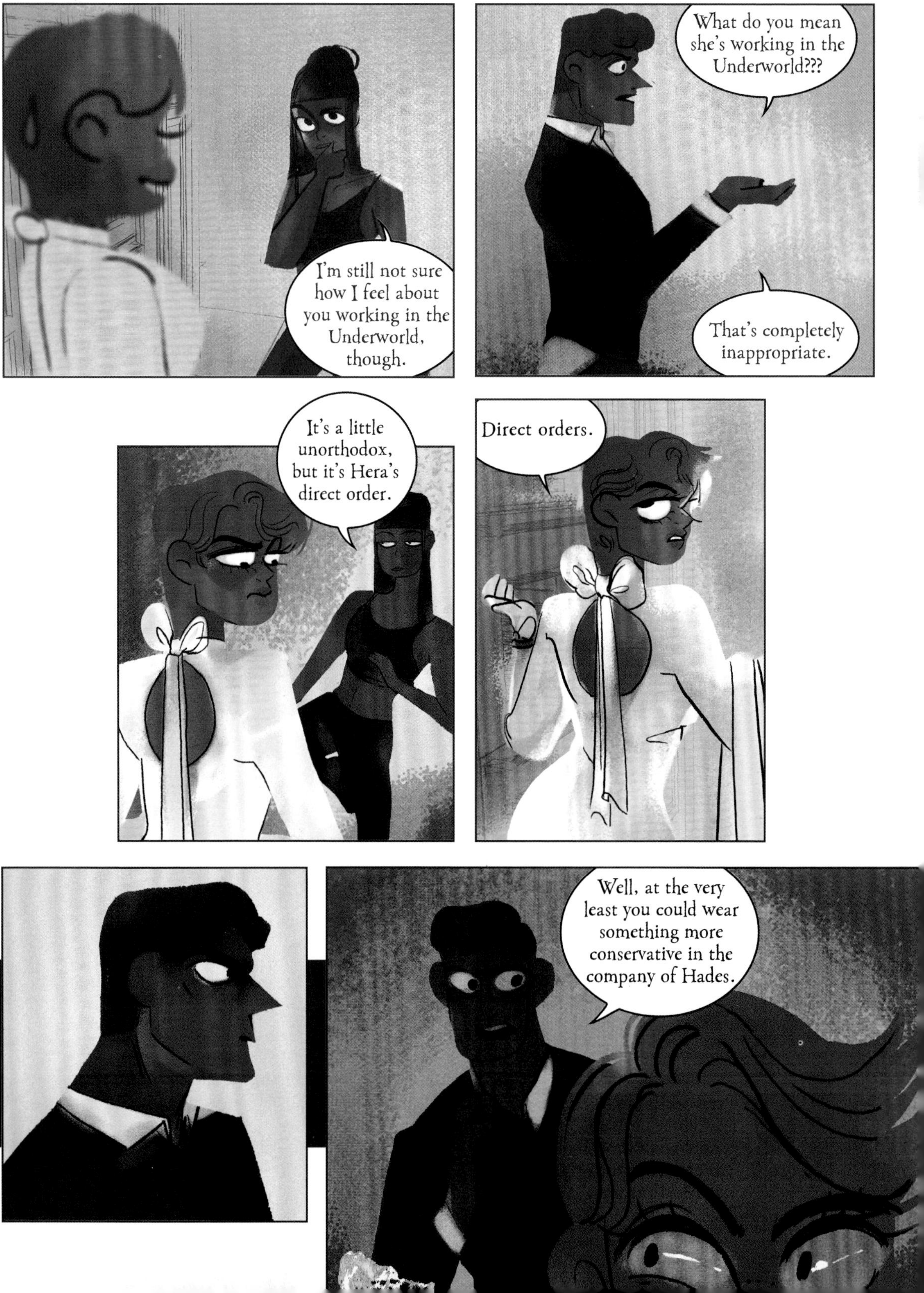
I'm still not sure how I feel about you working in the Underworld, though.
What do you mean she's working in the Underworld???
That's completely inappropriate.
It's a little unorthodox, but it's Hera's direct order.
Direct orders.
Well, at the very least you could wear something more conservative in the company of Hades.

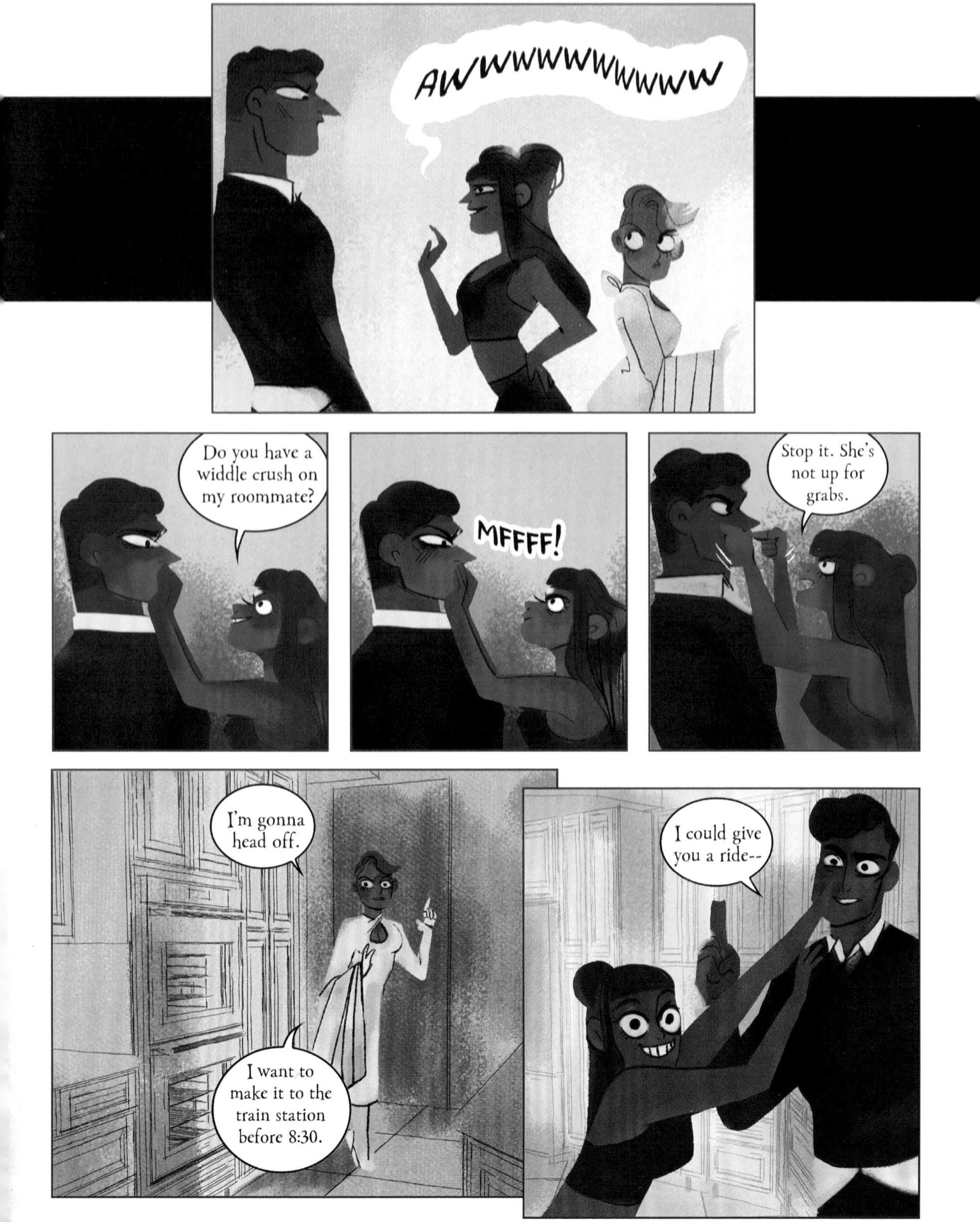
AWWWWWWWWWWW
Do you have a widdle crush on my roommate?
MFFFF!
Stop it. She's not up for grabs.
I'm gonna head off.
I want to make it to the train station before 8:30.
I could give you a ride--

NO!

...

I'd prefer to walk.

Helps me clear my head.

Okay then, good luck for today.

Yes, good luck.

Don't let him rattle you.

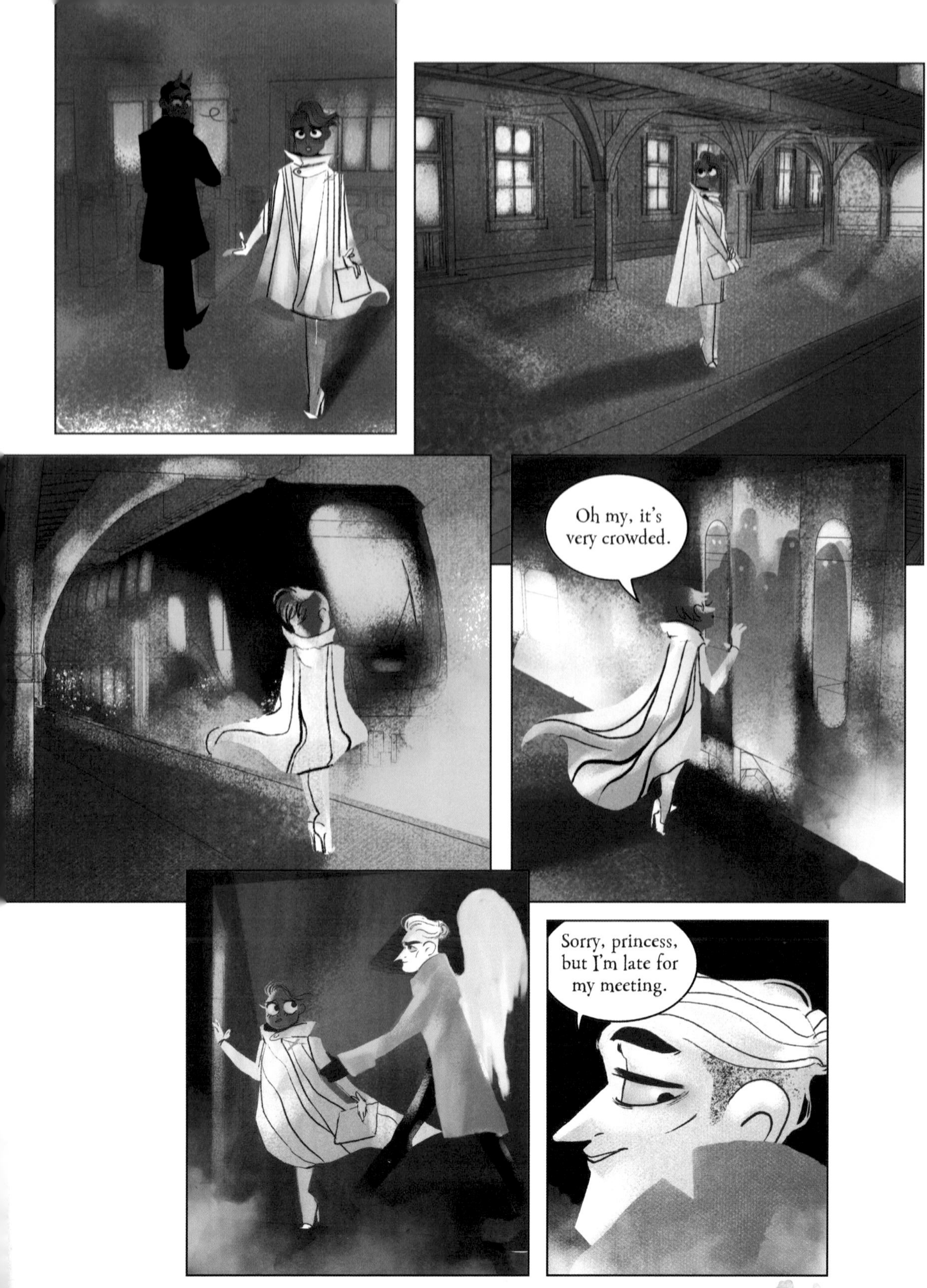

Oh my, it's very crowded.
Sorry, princess, but I'm late for my meeting.

SHOVE

Wings!?

But you've got wings!!!

Y-YOU LAZY BONES!!!

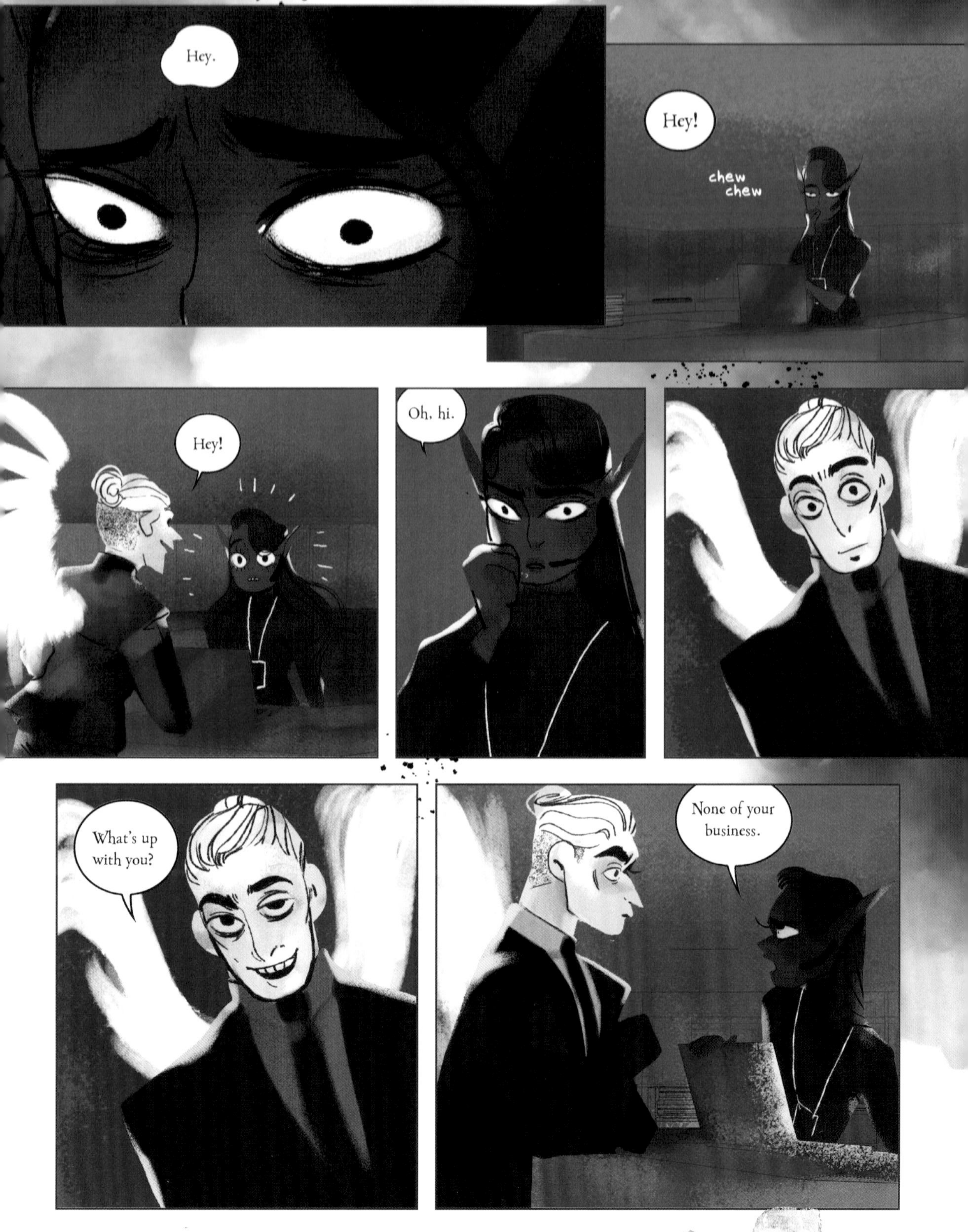
Hey.
Hey!
chew chew
Hey!
Oh, hi.
What's up with you?
None of your business.

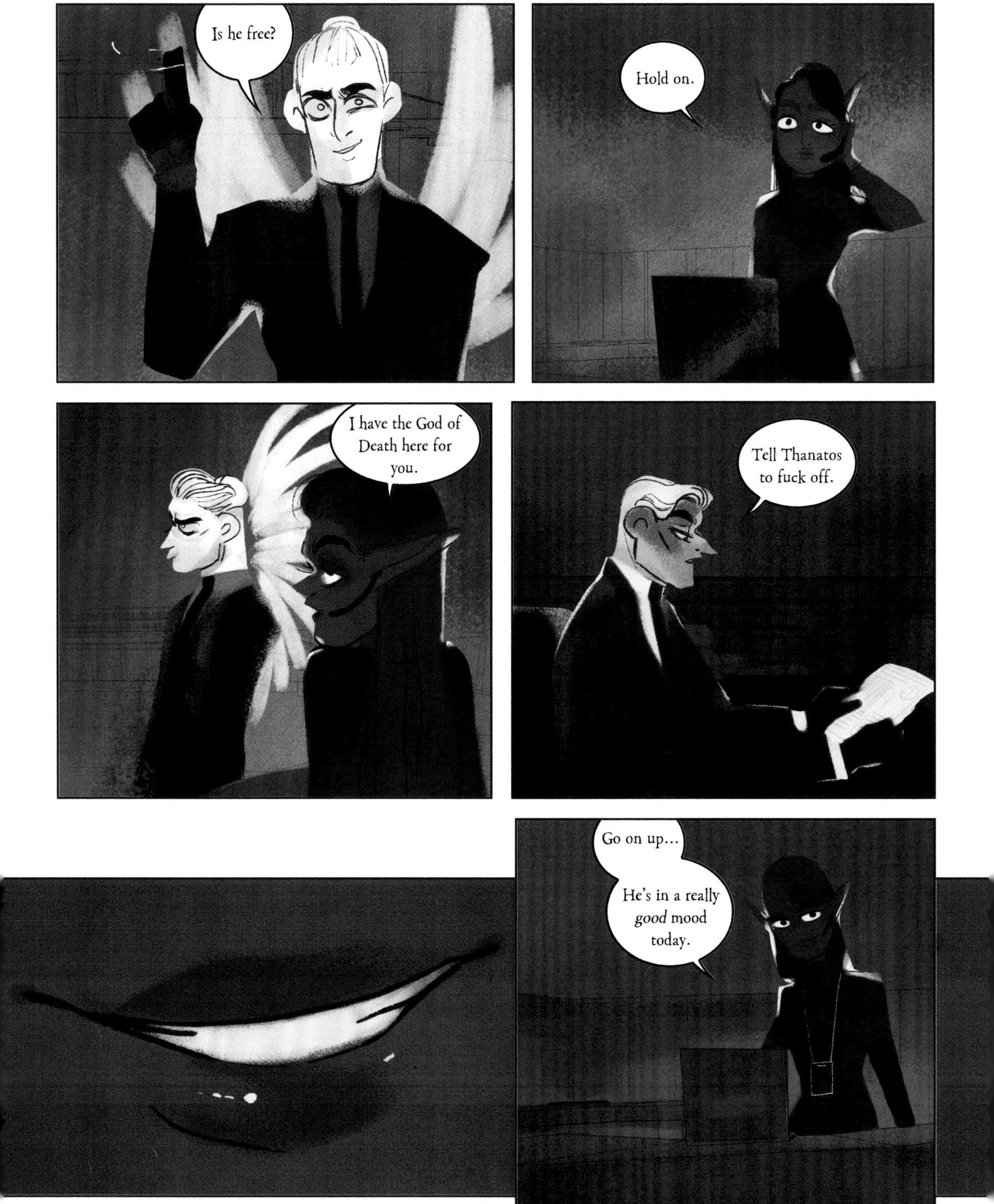
Is he free?
Hold on.
I have the God of Death here for you.
Tell Thanatos to fuck off.
Go on up...
He's in a really *good* mood today.

EPISODE 39: TOWER 4

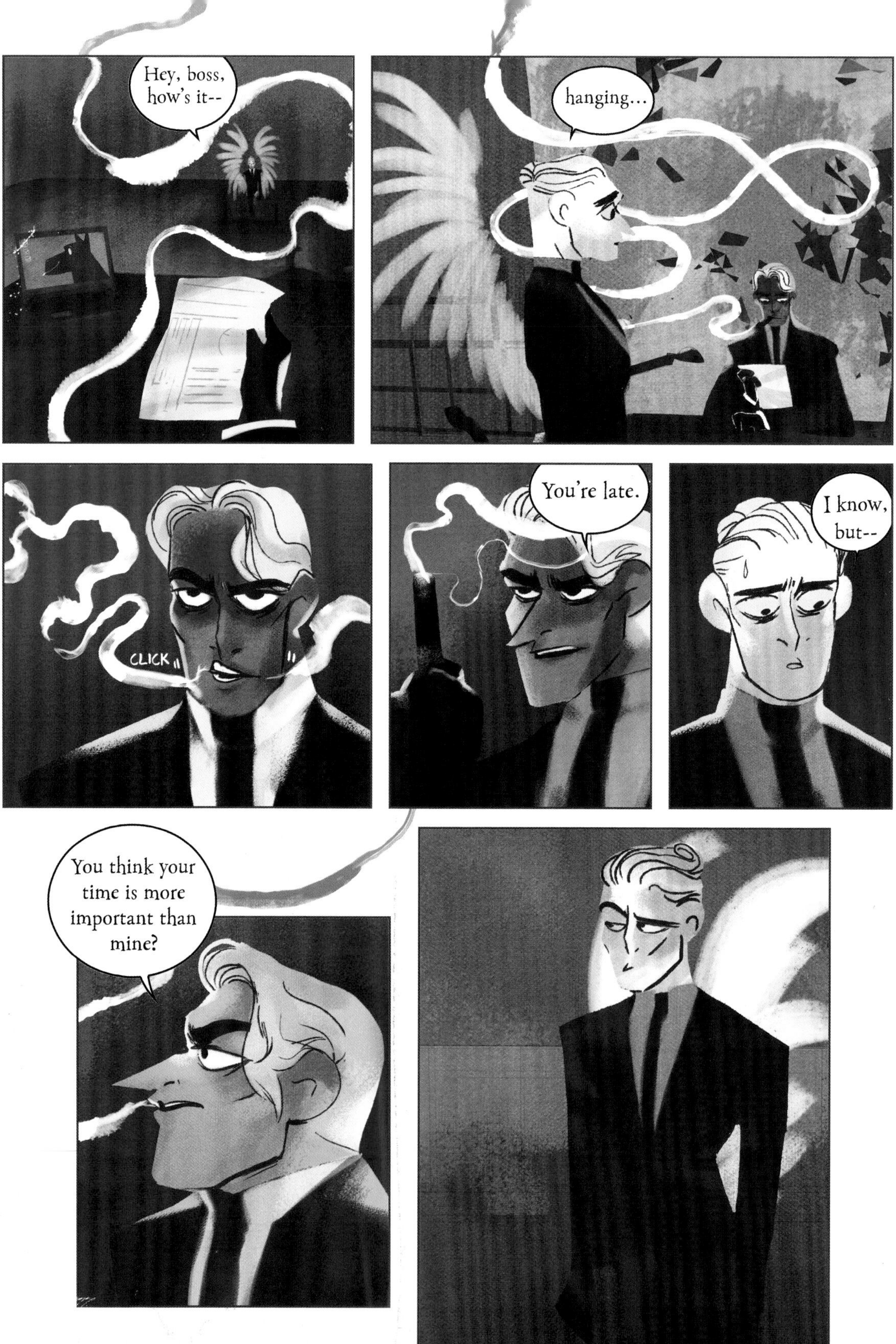
Hey, boss, how's it--
hanging...
CLICK
You're late.
I know, but--
You think your time is more important than mine?

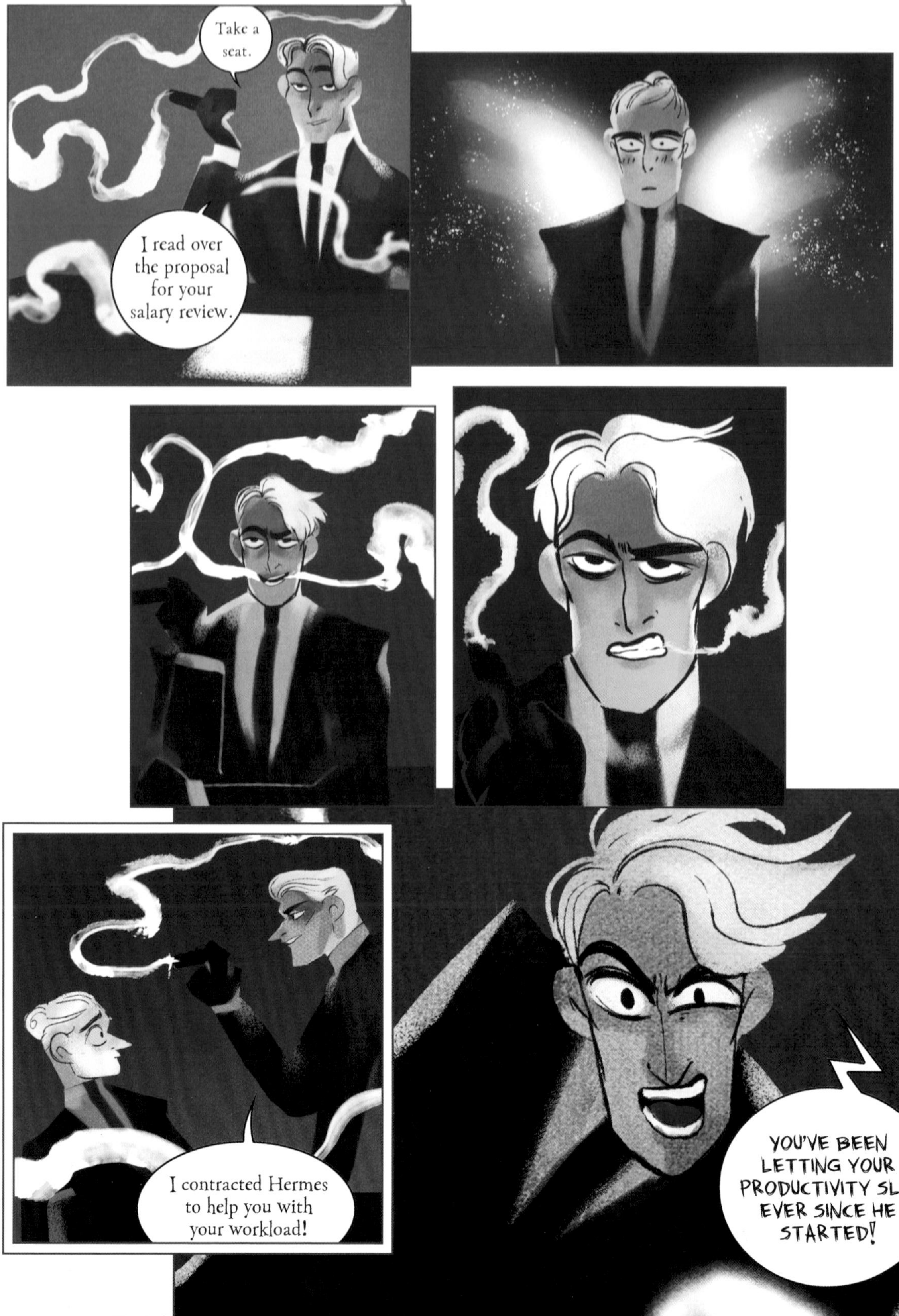
Take a seat.
I read over the proposal for your salary review.
I contracted Hermes to help you with your workload!
YOU'VE BEEN LETTING YOUR PRODUCTIVITY SLIP EVER SINCE HE STARTED!

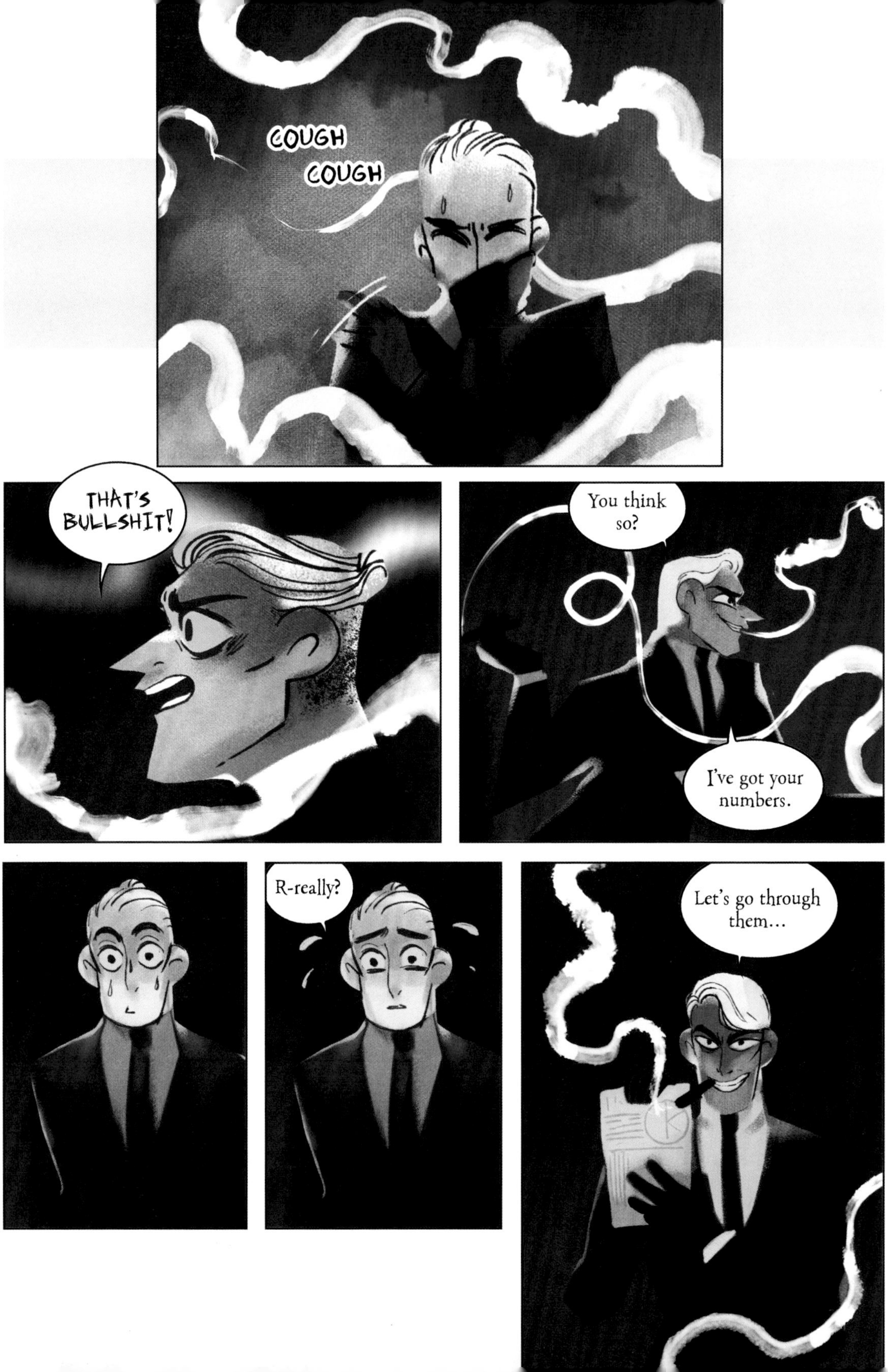
COUGH
COUGH
THAT'S BULLSHIT!
You think so?
I've got your numbers.
R-really?
Let's go through them...

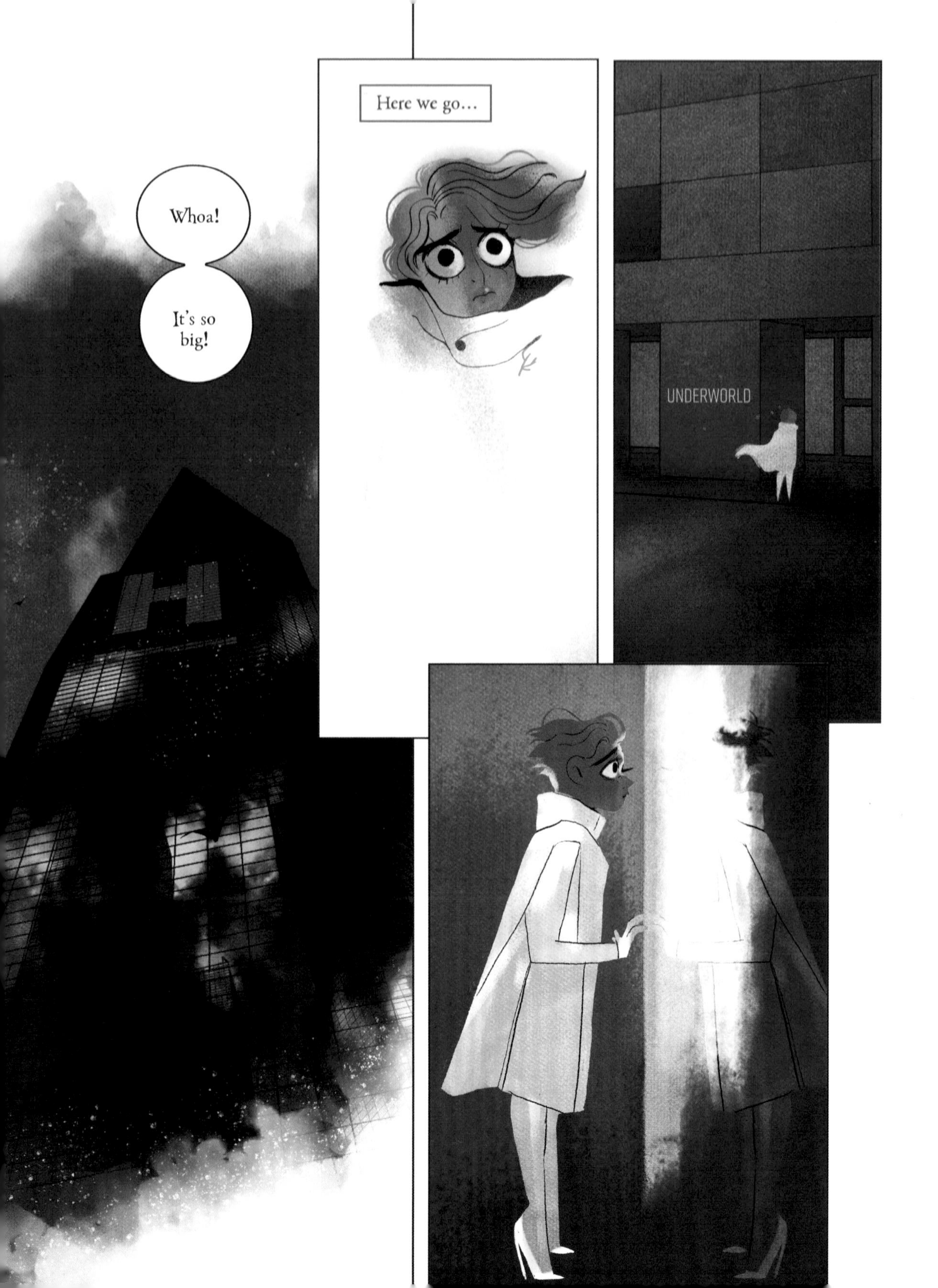
Whoa!
It's so big!
Here we go...
UNDERWORLD

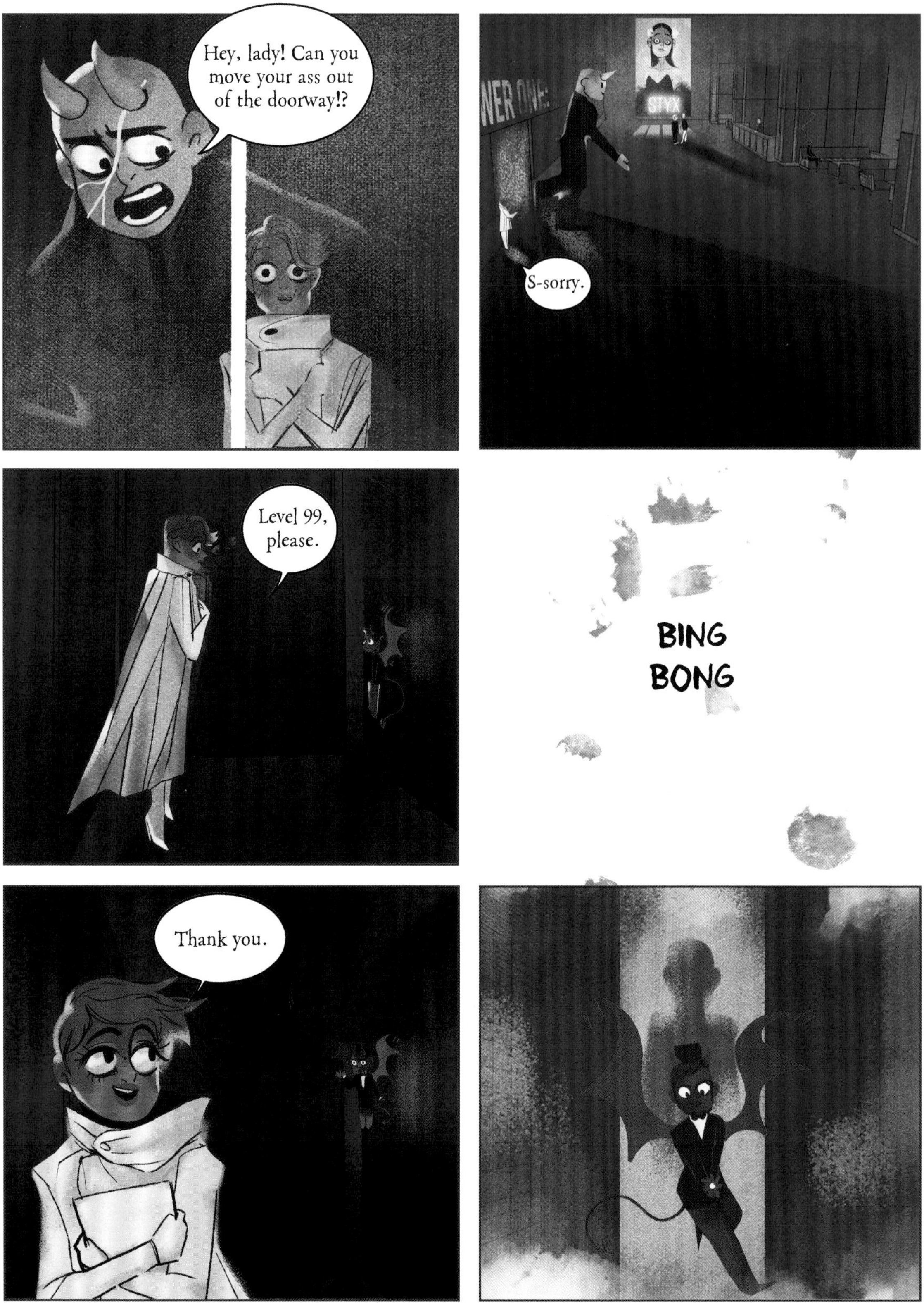
Hey, lady! Can you move your ass out of the doorway!?
STYX
S-sorry.
Level 99, please.
BING
BONG
Thank you.

Oh my...

She's so beautiful and thin.

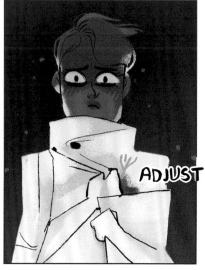

ADJUST

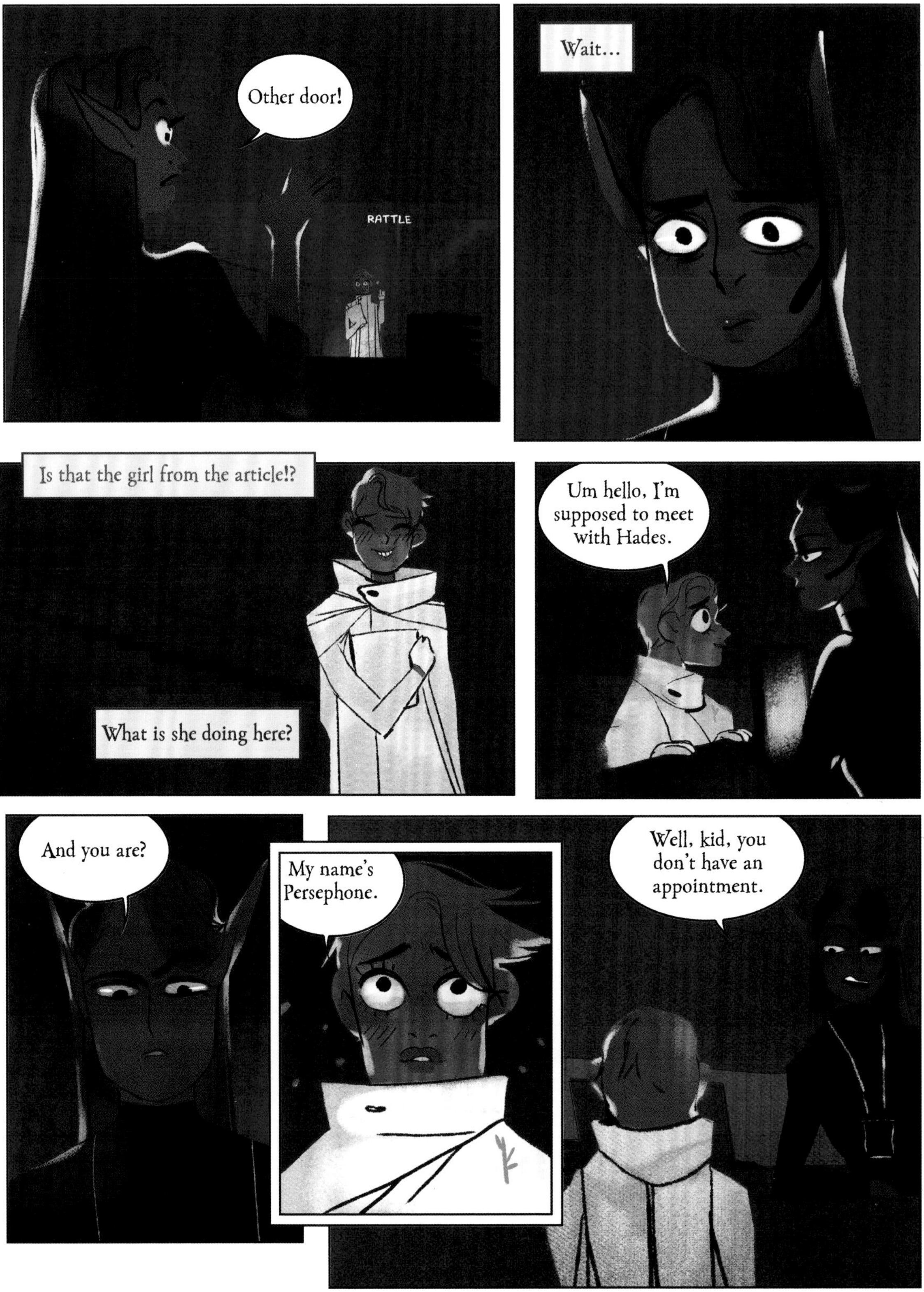
Other door!
RATTLE
Wait...
Is that the girl from the article!?
What is she doing here?
Um hello, I'm supposed to meet with Hades.
And you are?
My name's Persephone.
Well, kid, you don't have an appointment.

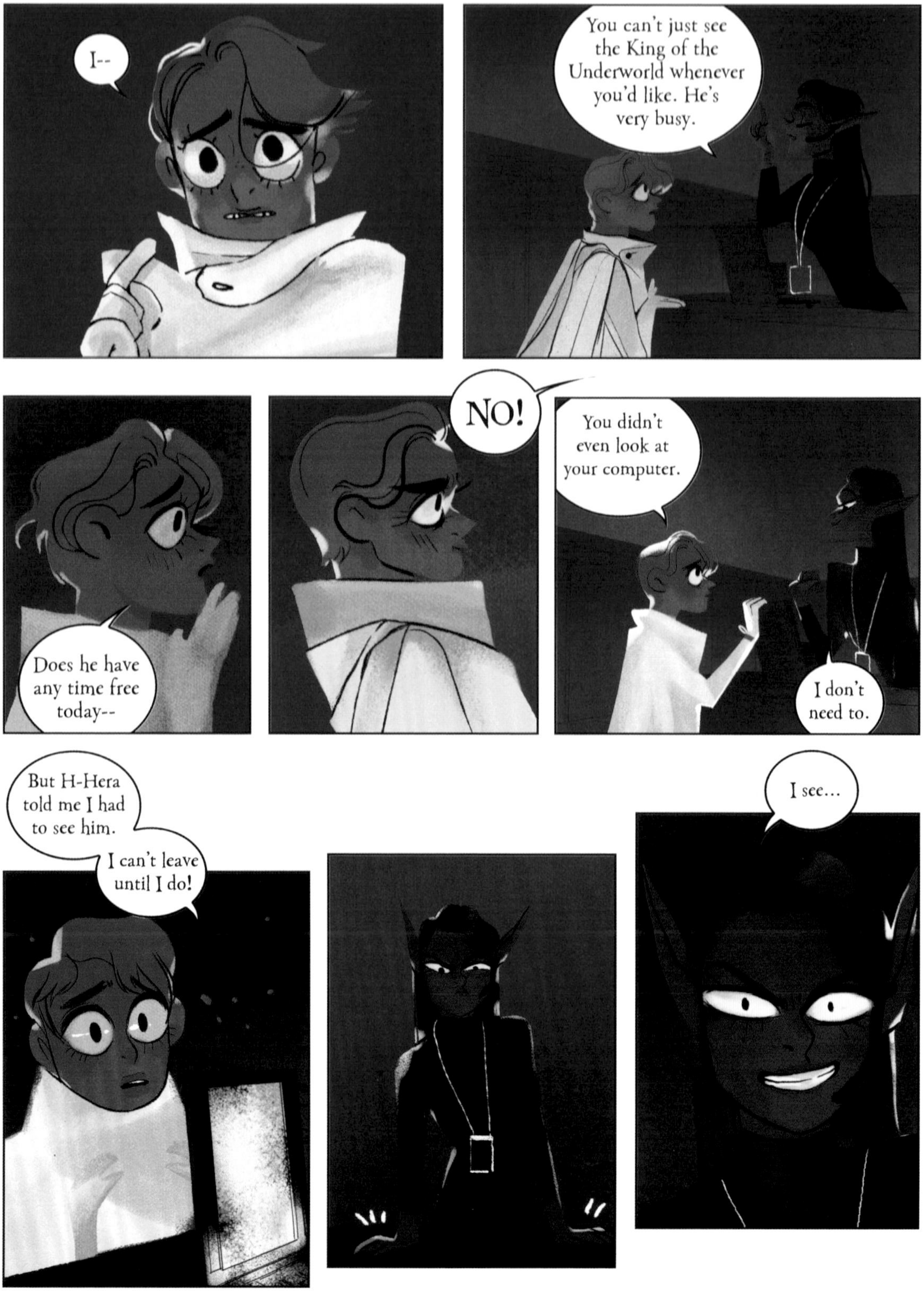
I--
You can't just see the King of the Underworld whenever you'd like. He's very busy.
Does he have any time free today--
NO!
You didn't even look at your computer.
I don't need to.
But H-Hera told me I had to see him.
I can't leave until I do!
I see...

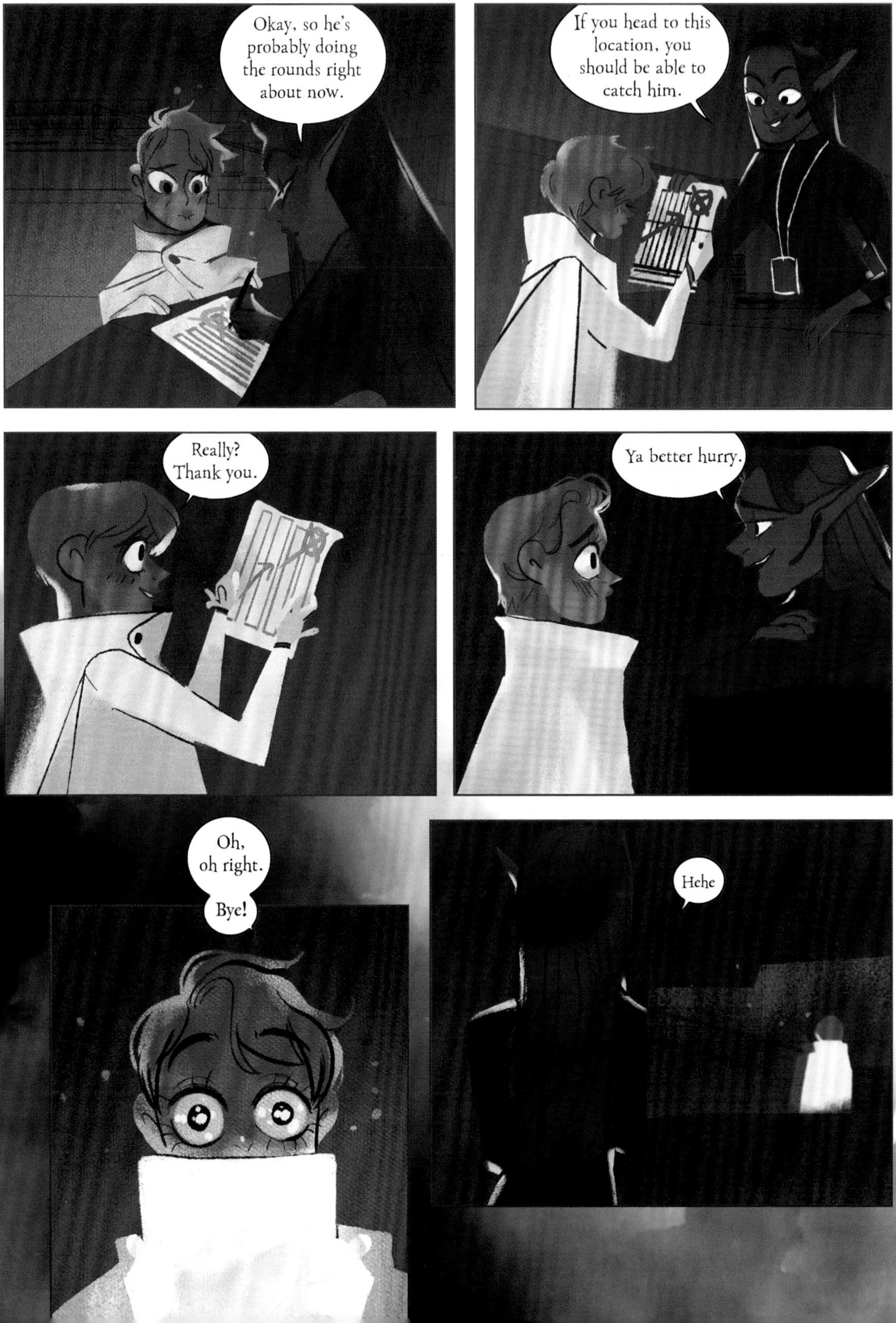
Okay, so he's probably doing the rounds right about now.
If you head to this location, you should be able to catch him.
Really? Thank you.
Ya better hurry.
Oh, oh right.
Bye!
Hehe

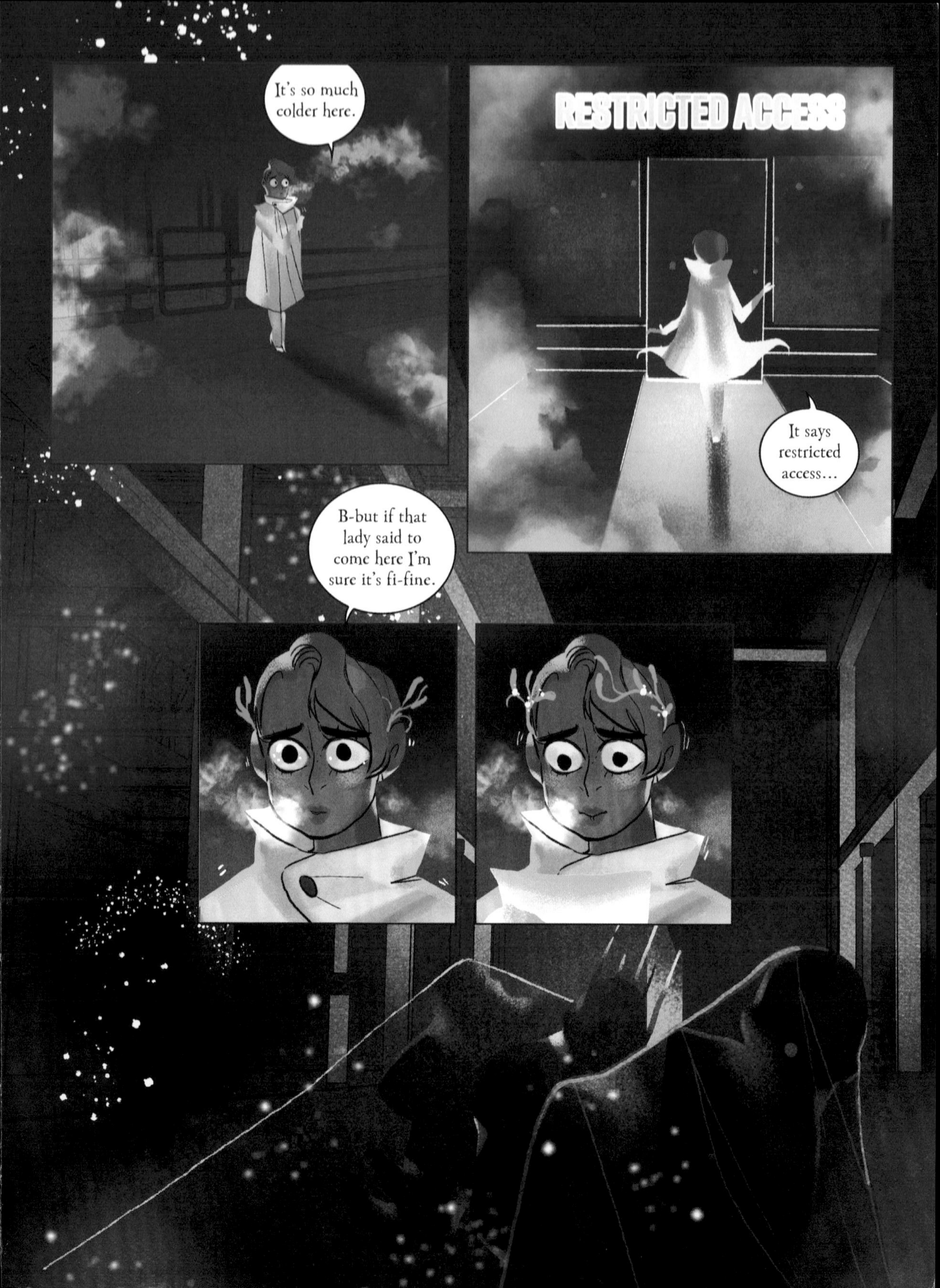
It's so much colder here.
RESTRICTED ACCESS
It says restricted access…
B-but if that lady said to come here I'm sure it's fi-fine.

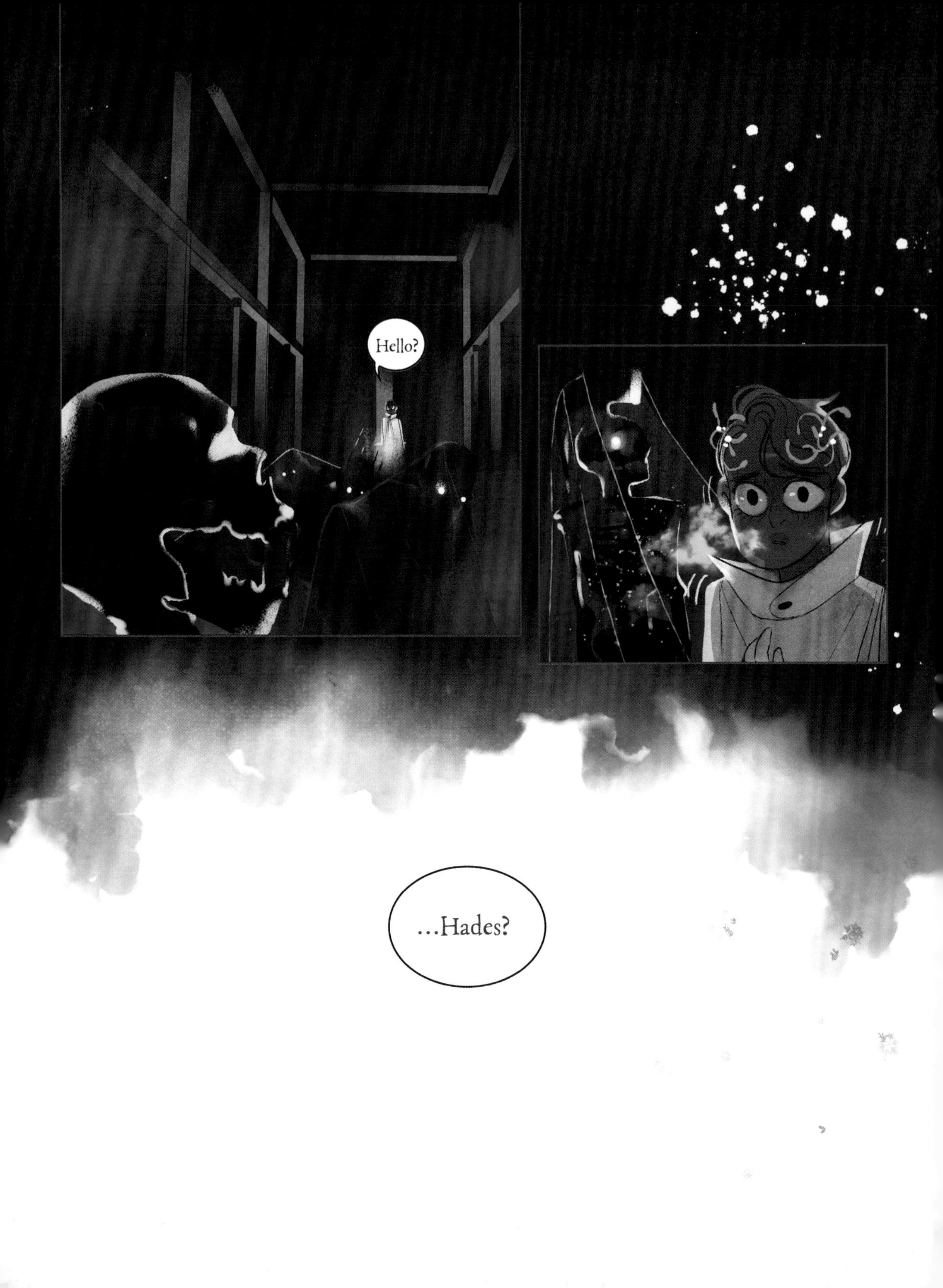
Hello?
...Hades?

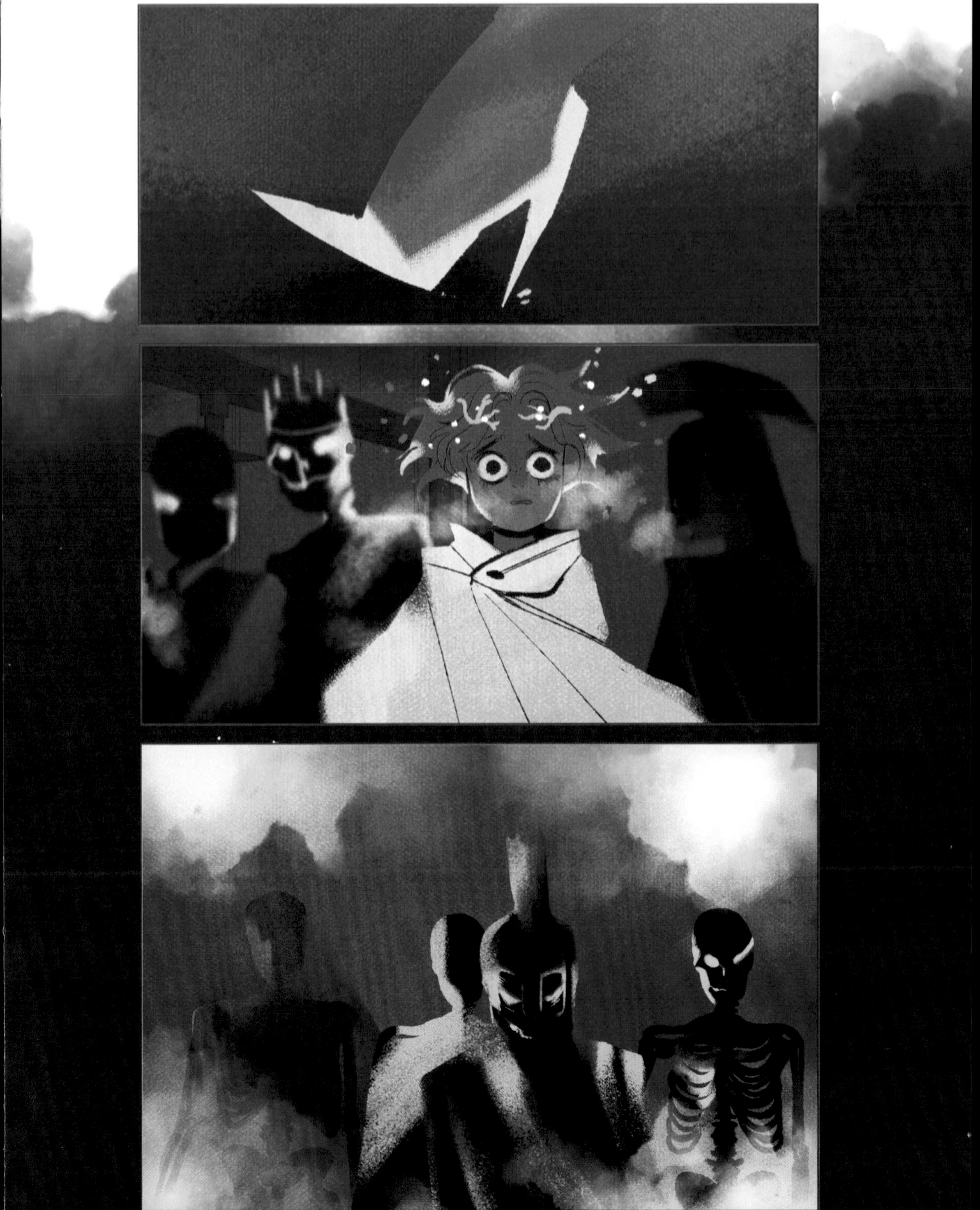

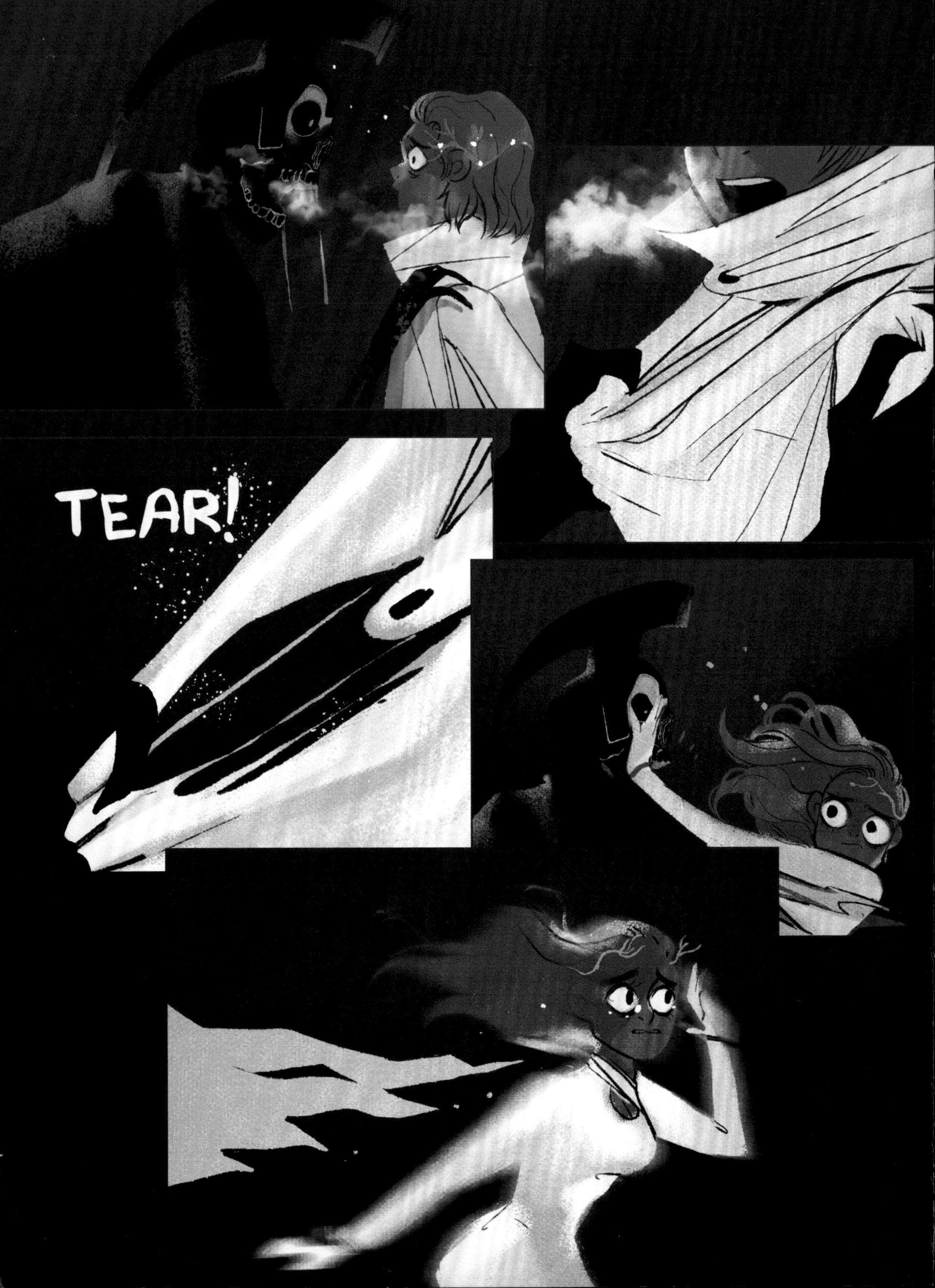
TEAR!

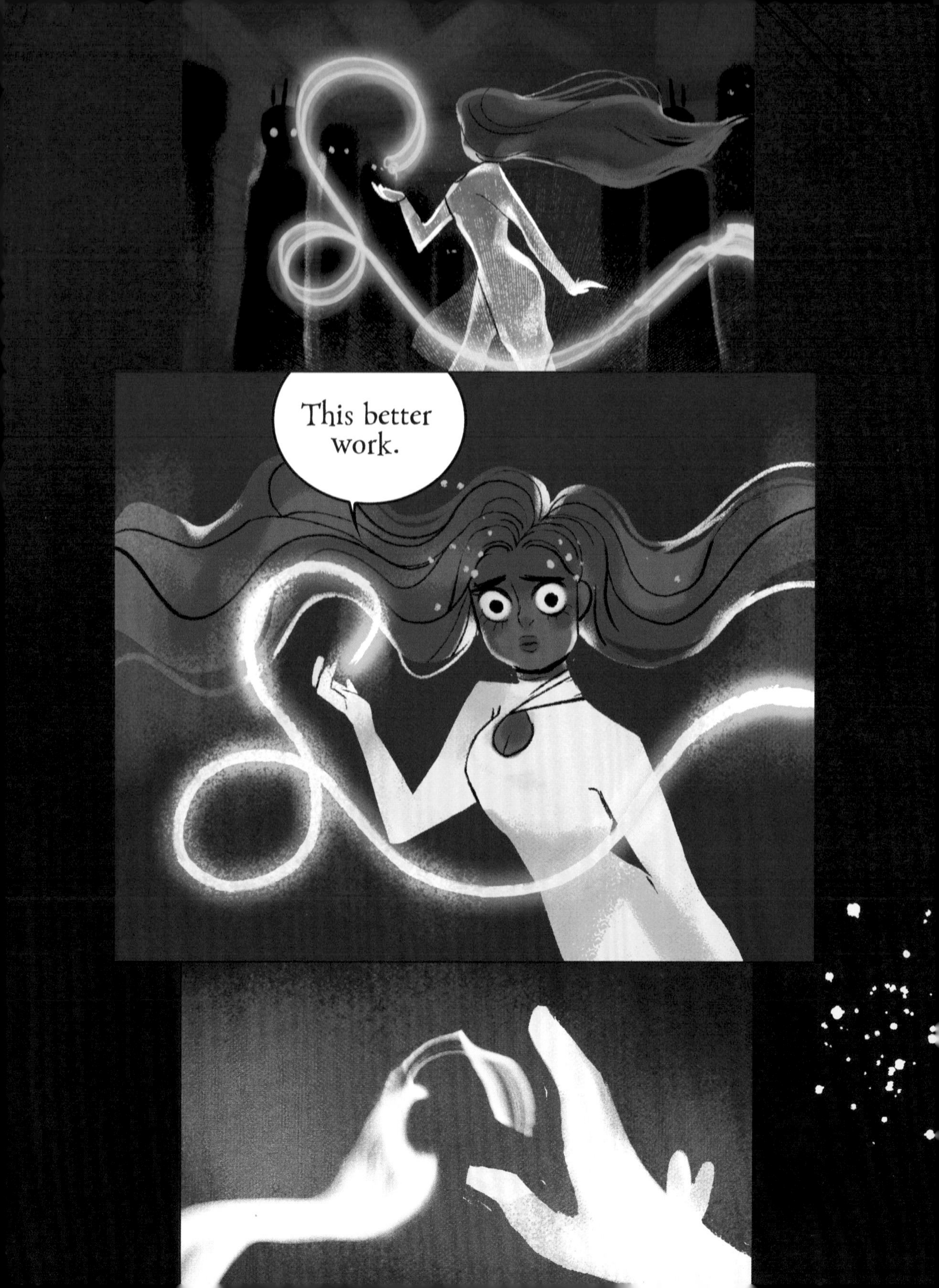
This better work.

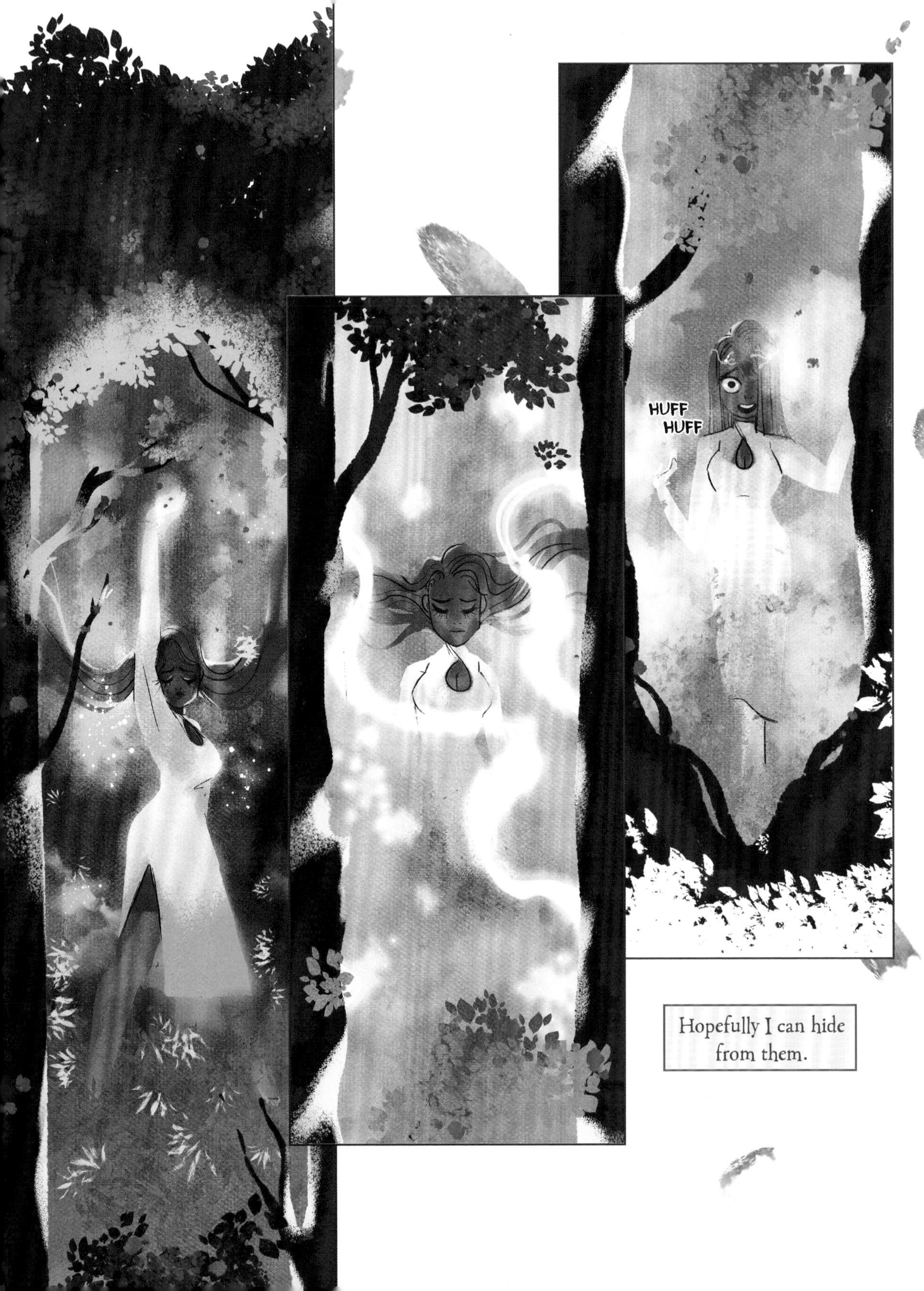
HUFF
HUFF

Hopefully I can hide from them.

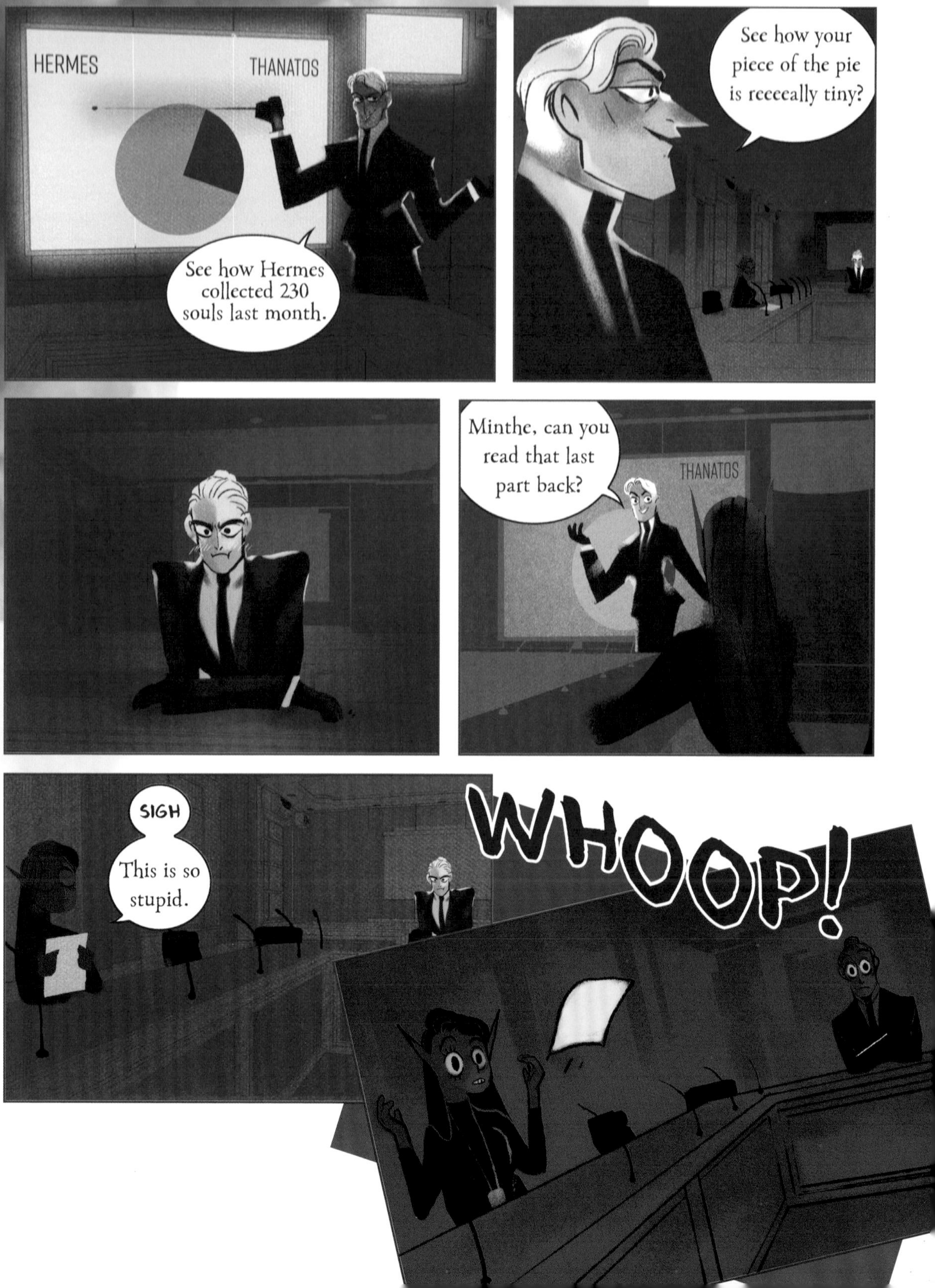
HERMES
THANATOS
See how Hermes collected 230 souls last month.
See how your piece of the pie is reeeeally tiny?
Minthe, can you read that last part back?
THANATOS
SIGH
This is so stupid.
WHOOP!

WHOOP!

THERE'S BEEN A SECURITY BREACH IN TARTARUS!

WHOOP!

HOW IS THAT EVEN POSSIBLE!?

WHOOP!

I'LL PUT ON THE LIVE FEED!

THEN WE'LL KNOW IF IT'S A FALSE ALARM!

GOOD IDEA!

WHOOP!

WHOOP!

WHOOP!

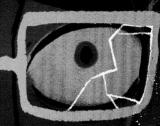

WHOOP!

EPISODE 40: HIDE AND SNEAK

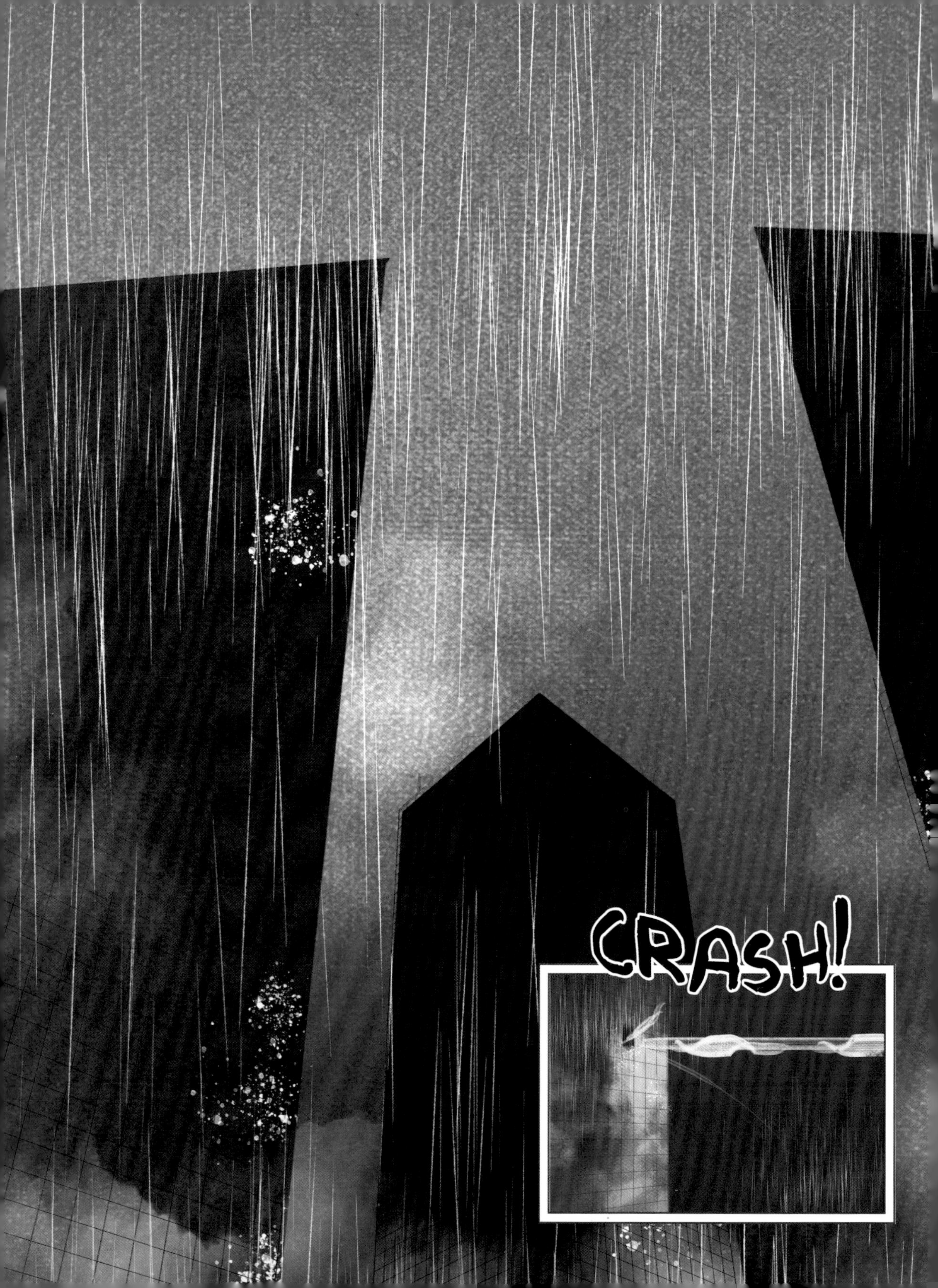
CRASH!

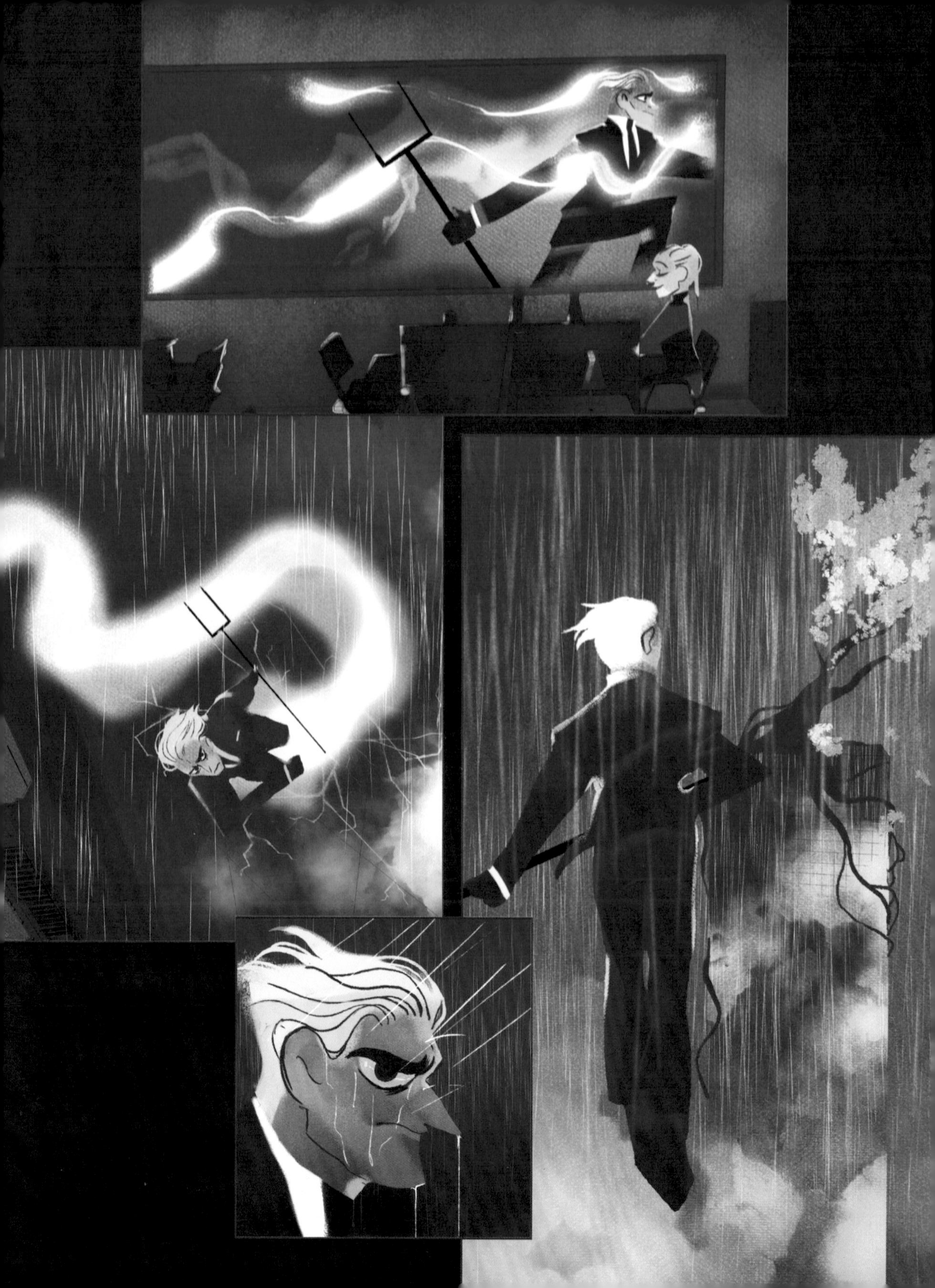

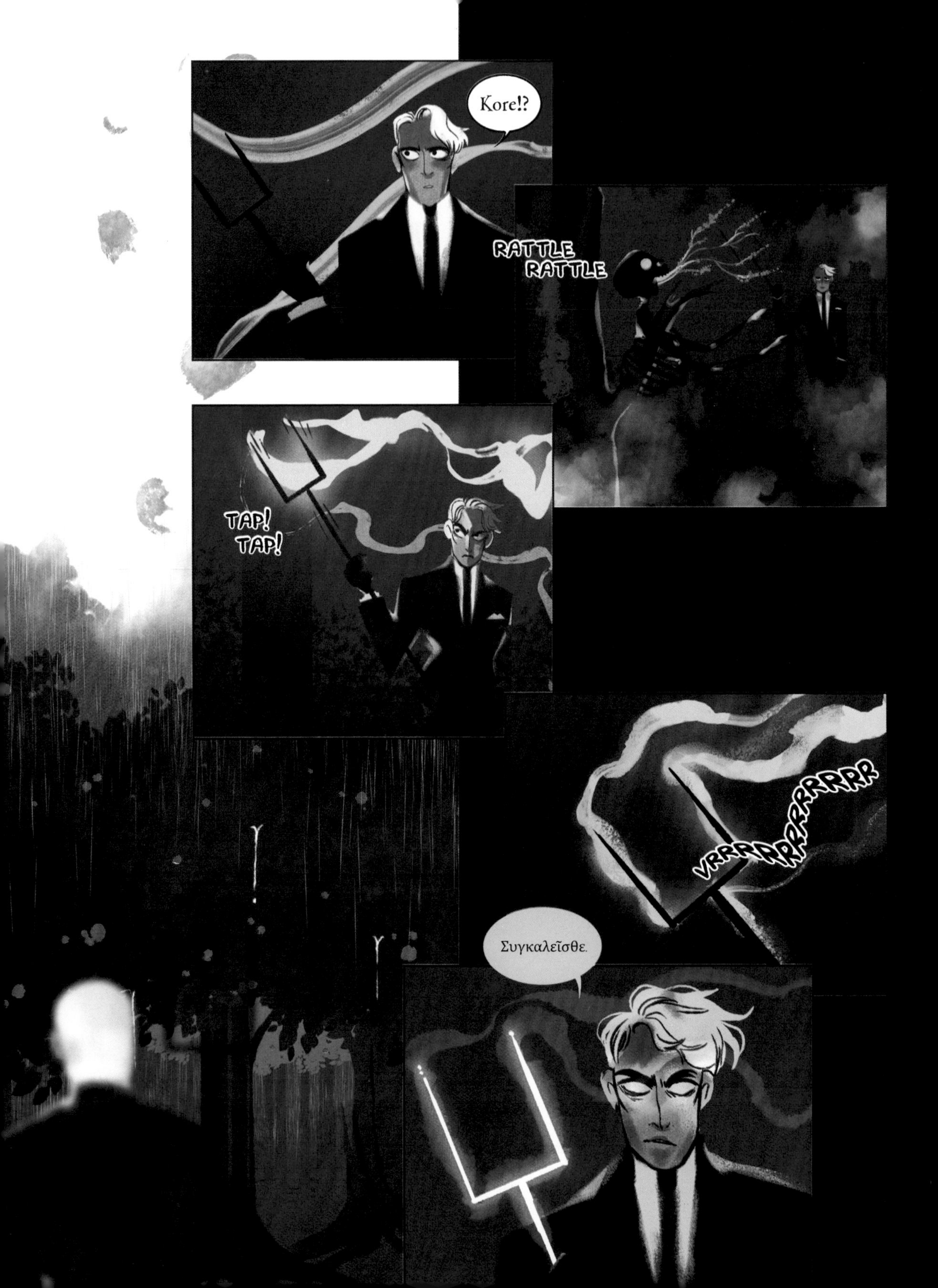
Kore!?
RATTLE RATTLE
TAP! TAP!
VRRRRRRRRRRRRR
Συγκαλεῖσθε.

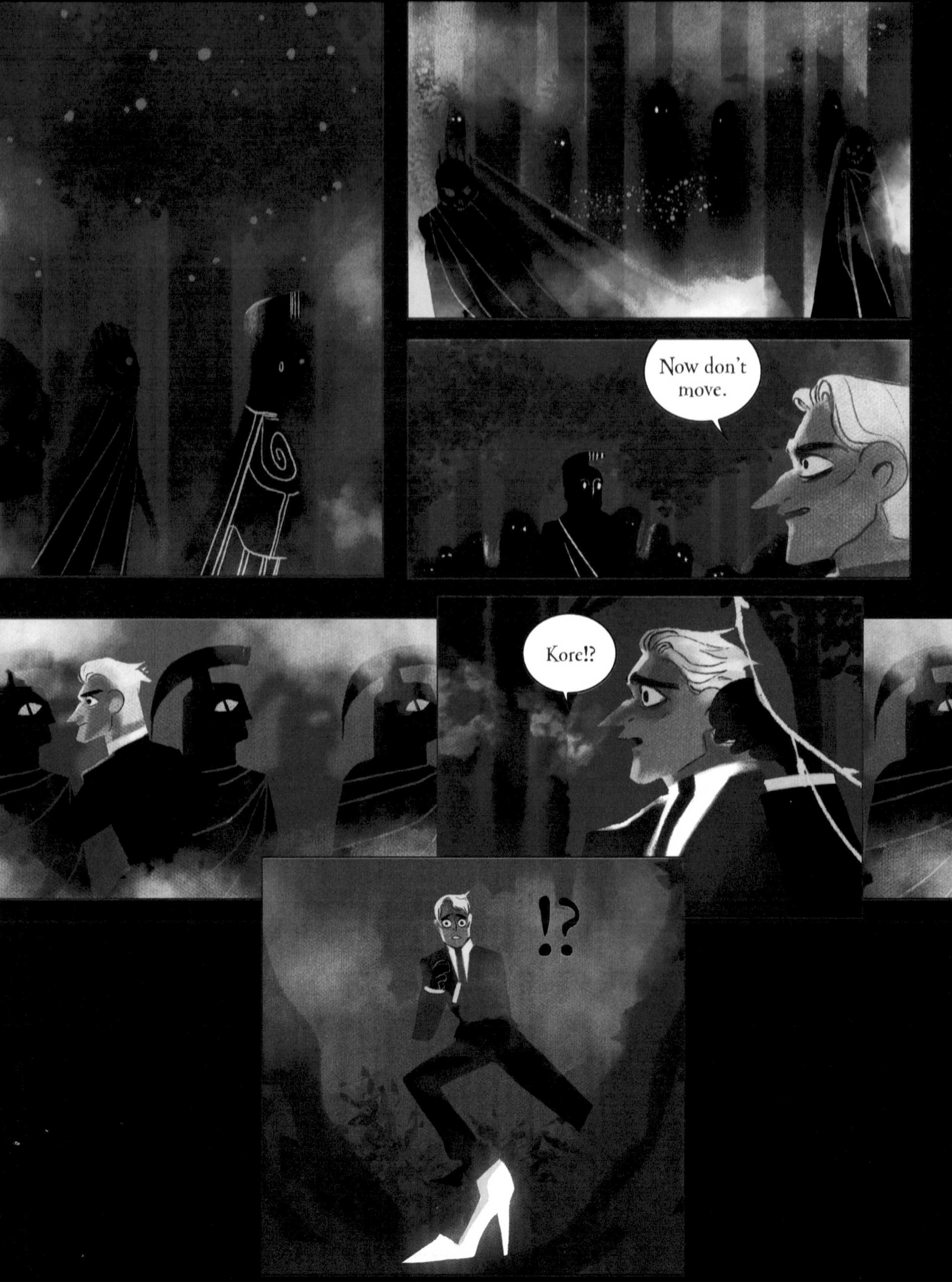
Now don't move.
Kore!?
!?

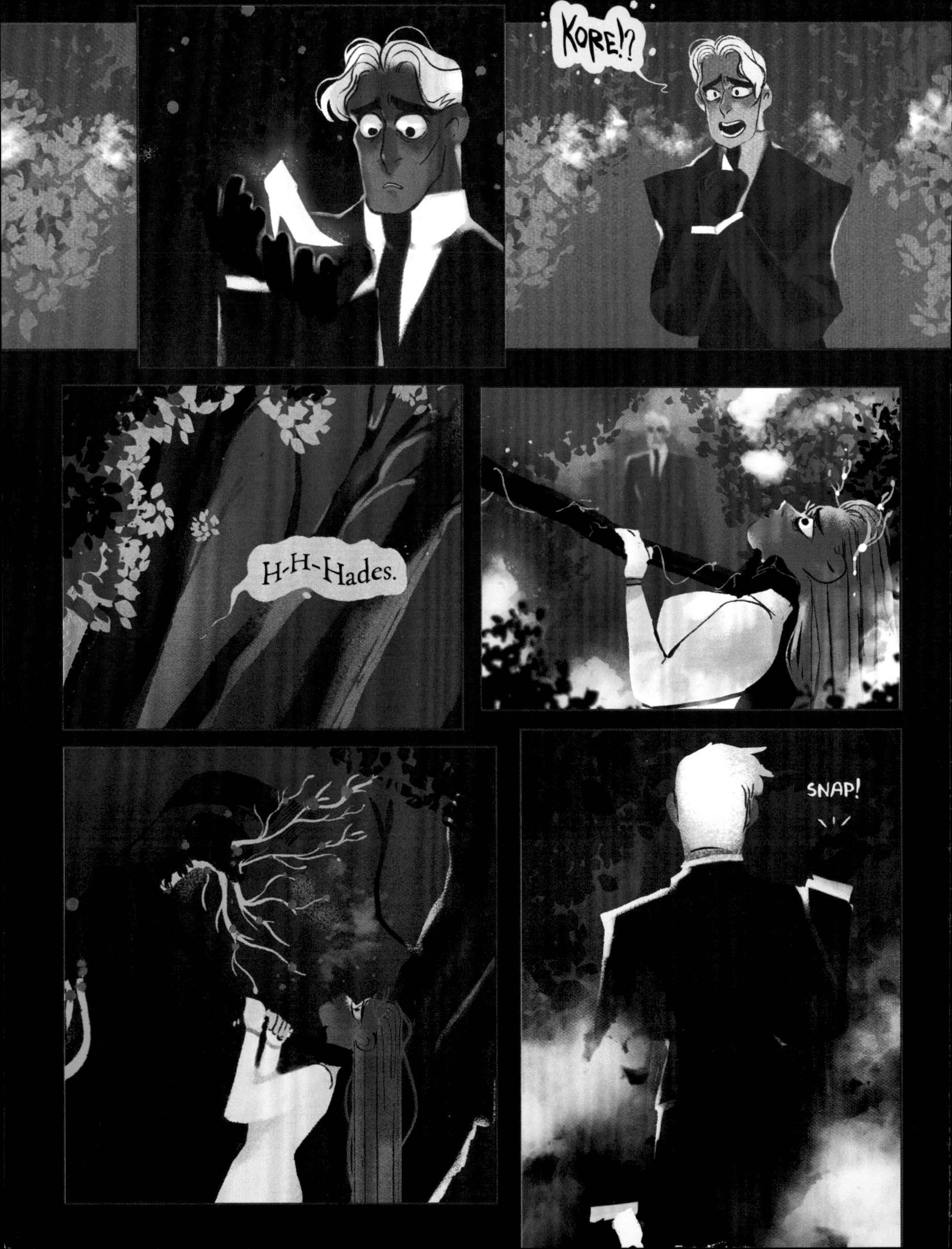
KORE!?
H-H-Hades.
SNAP!

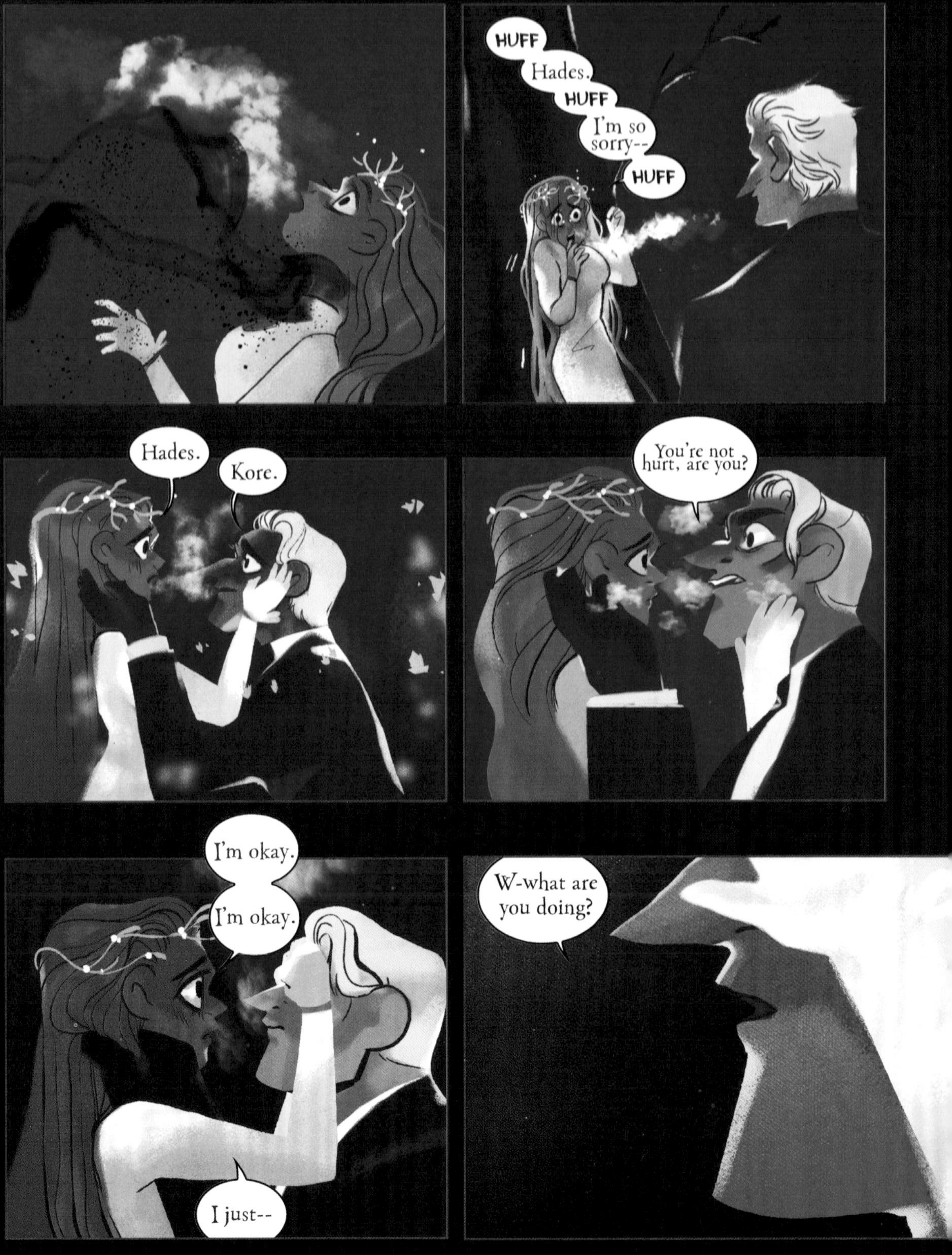
HUFF
Hades.
HUFF
I'm so sorry--
HUFF
Hades.
Kore.
You're not hurt, are you?
I'm okay.
I'm okay.
I just--
W-what are you doing?

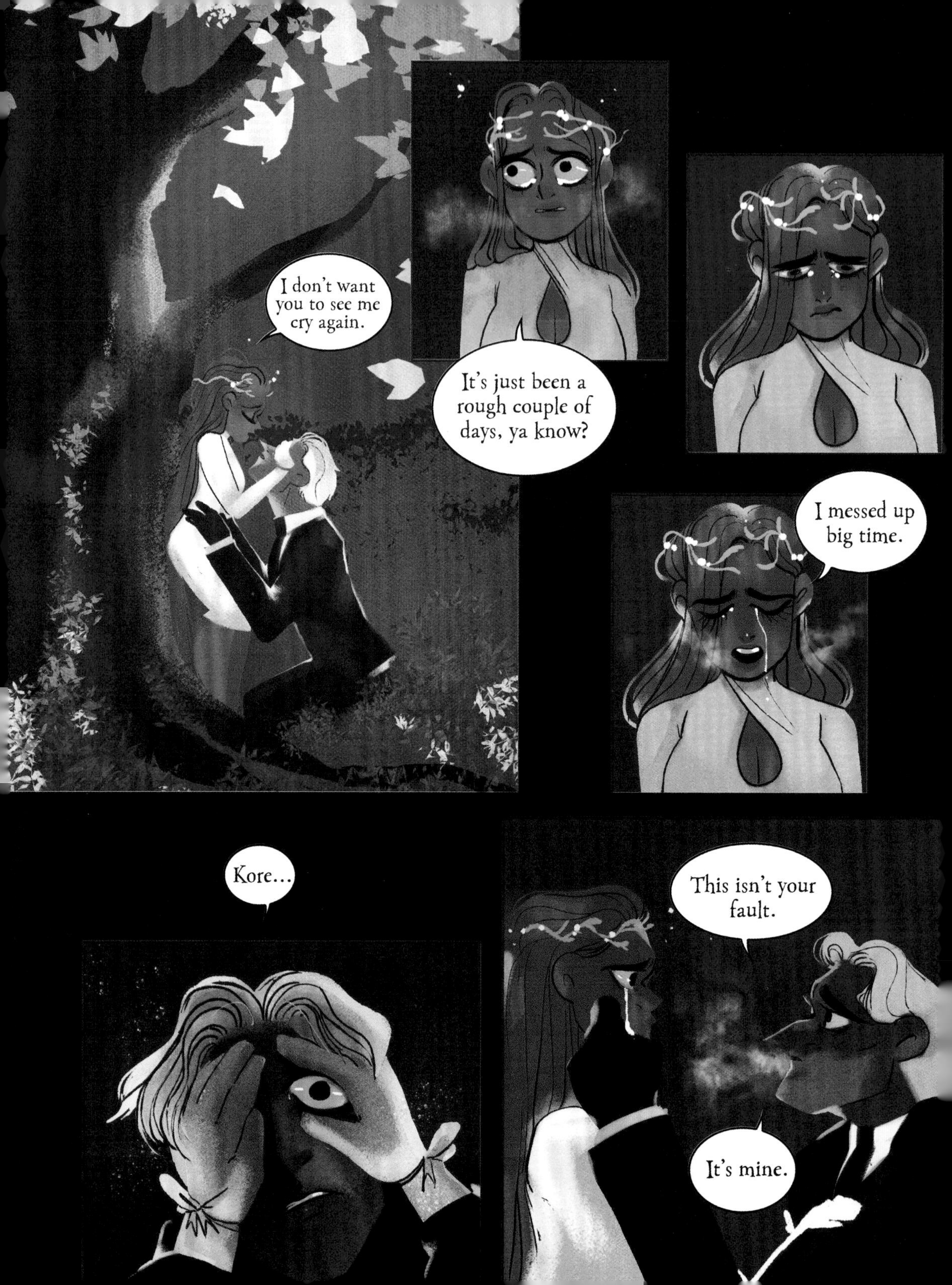
I don't want you to see me cry again.
It's just been a rough couple of days, ya know?
I messed up big time.
Kore...
This isn't your fault.
It's mine.

Εἰμί βασιλεύς ἀπαίσιος.

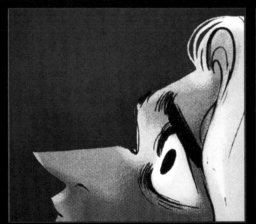

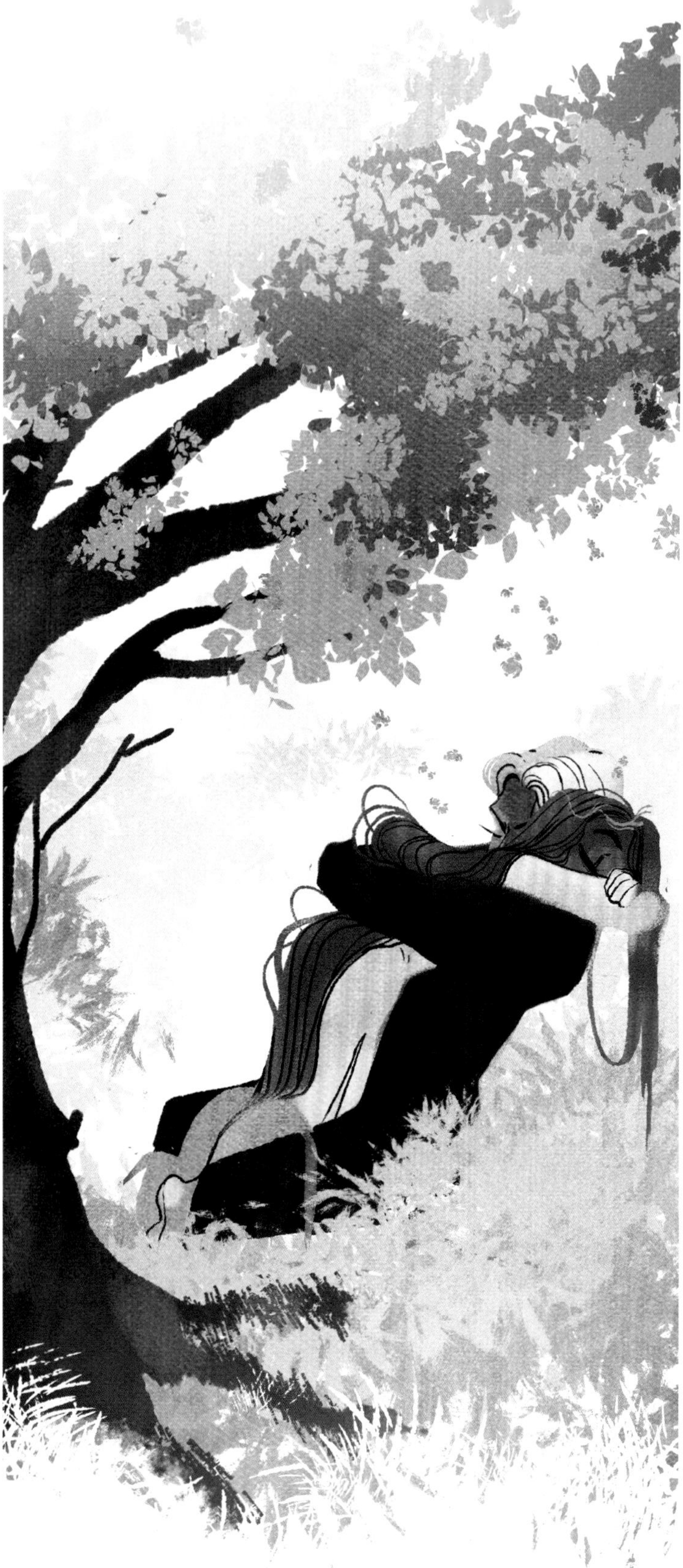

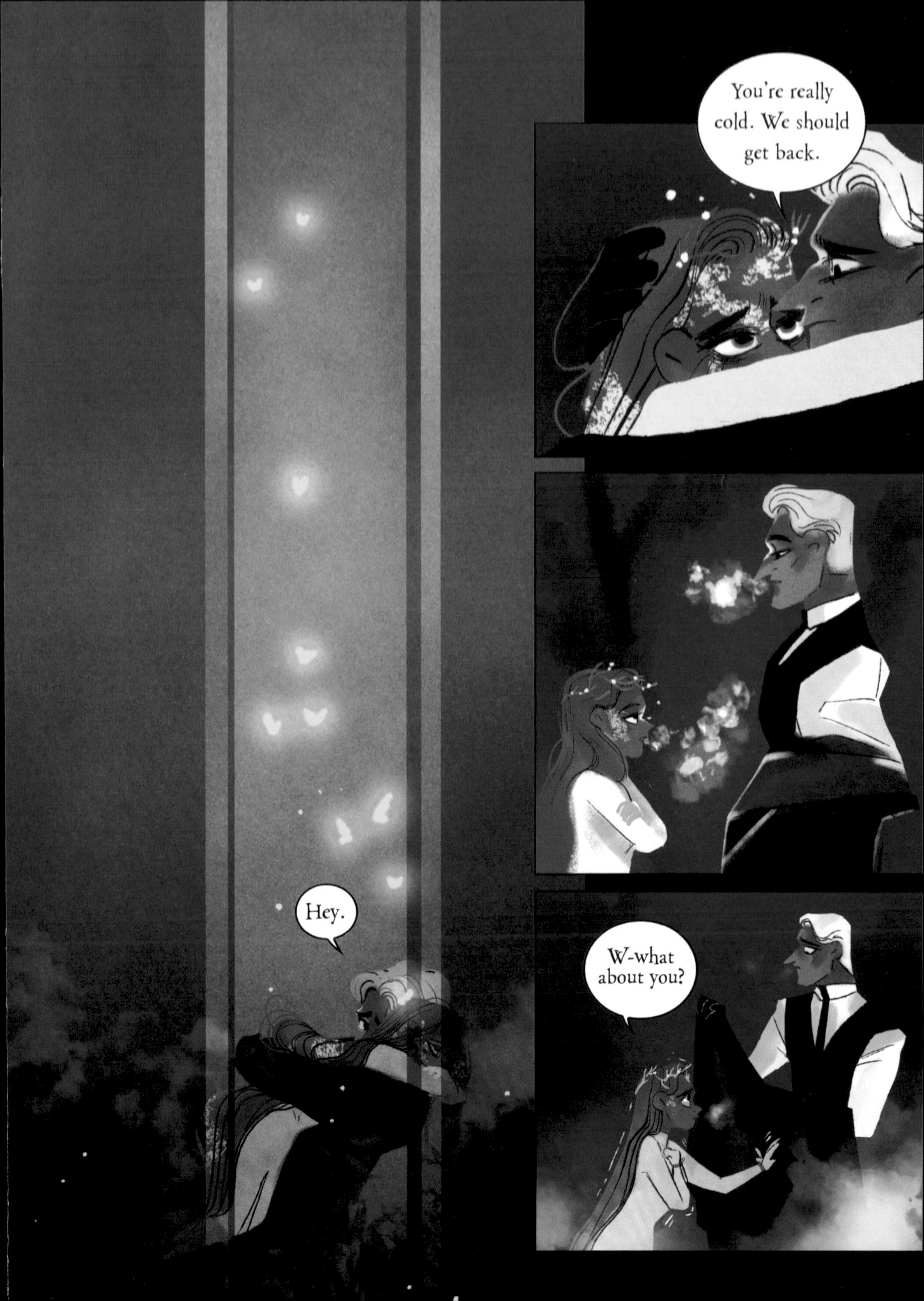
Hey.
You're really cold. We should get back.
W-what about you?

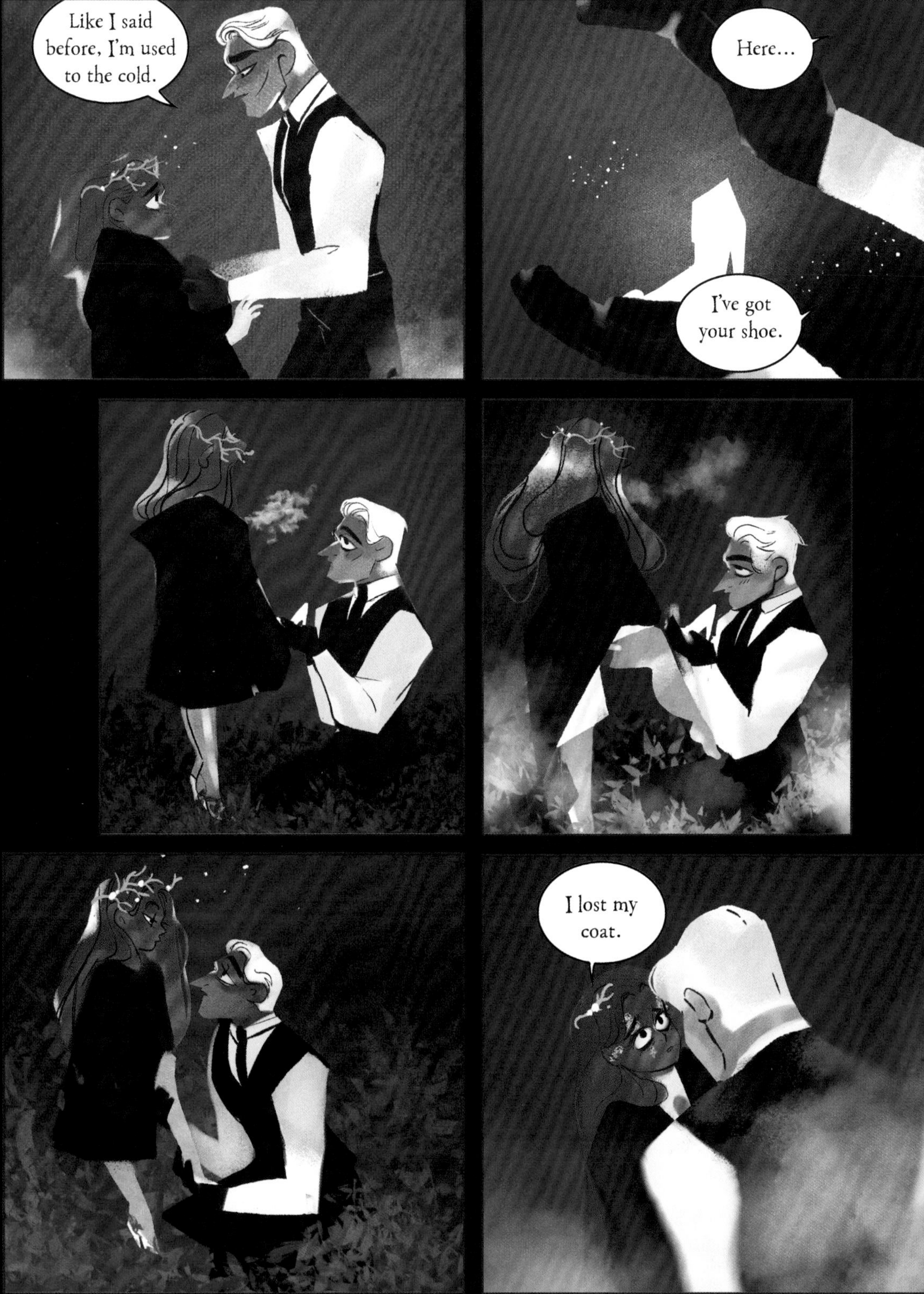
Like I said before, I'm used to the cold.
Here...
I've got your shoe.
I lost my coat.

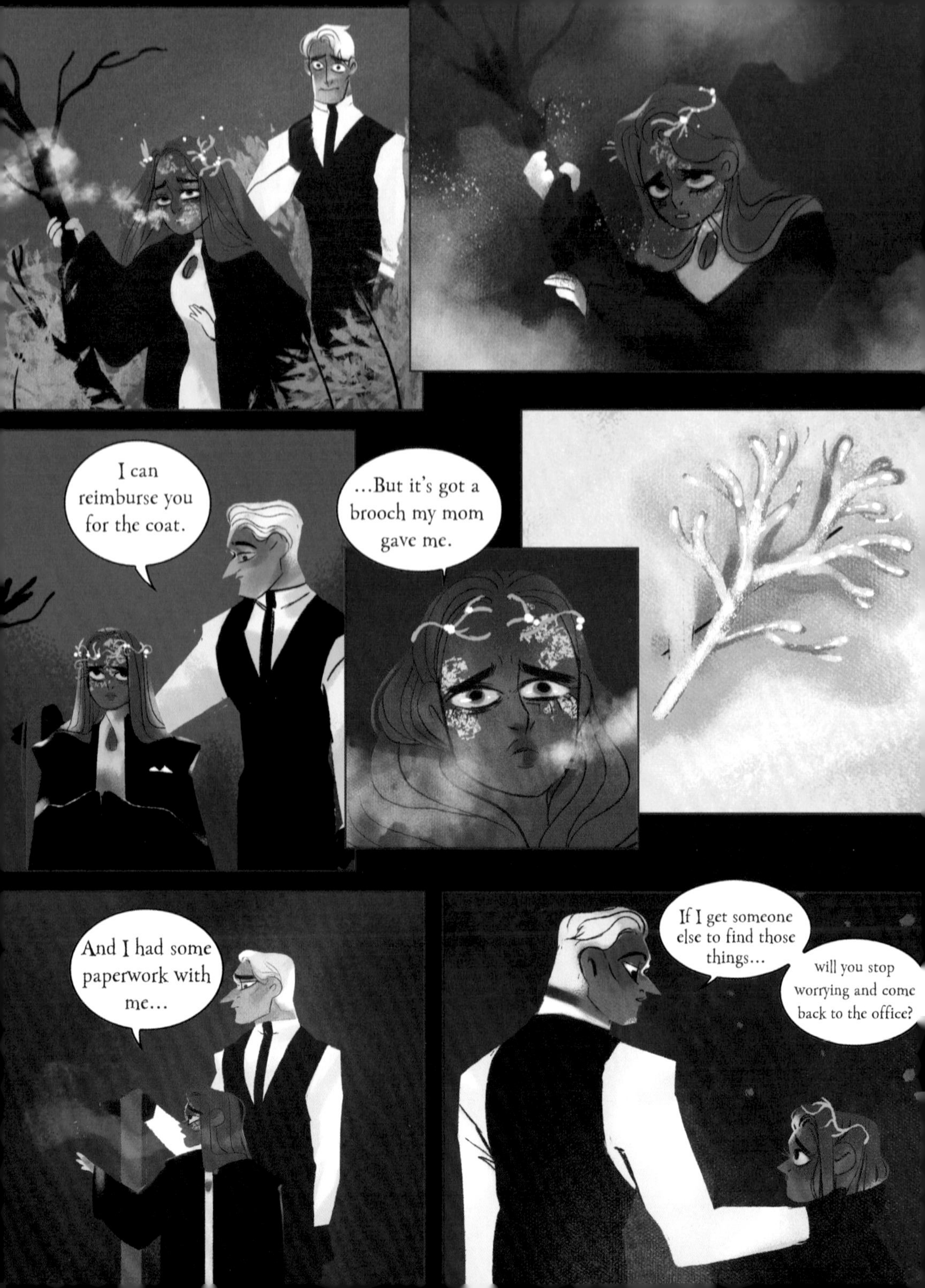
I can reimburse you for the coat.
...But it's got a brooch my mom gave me.
And I had some paperwork with me...
If I get someone else to find those things...
will you stop worrying and come back to the office?

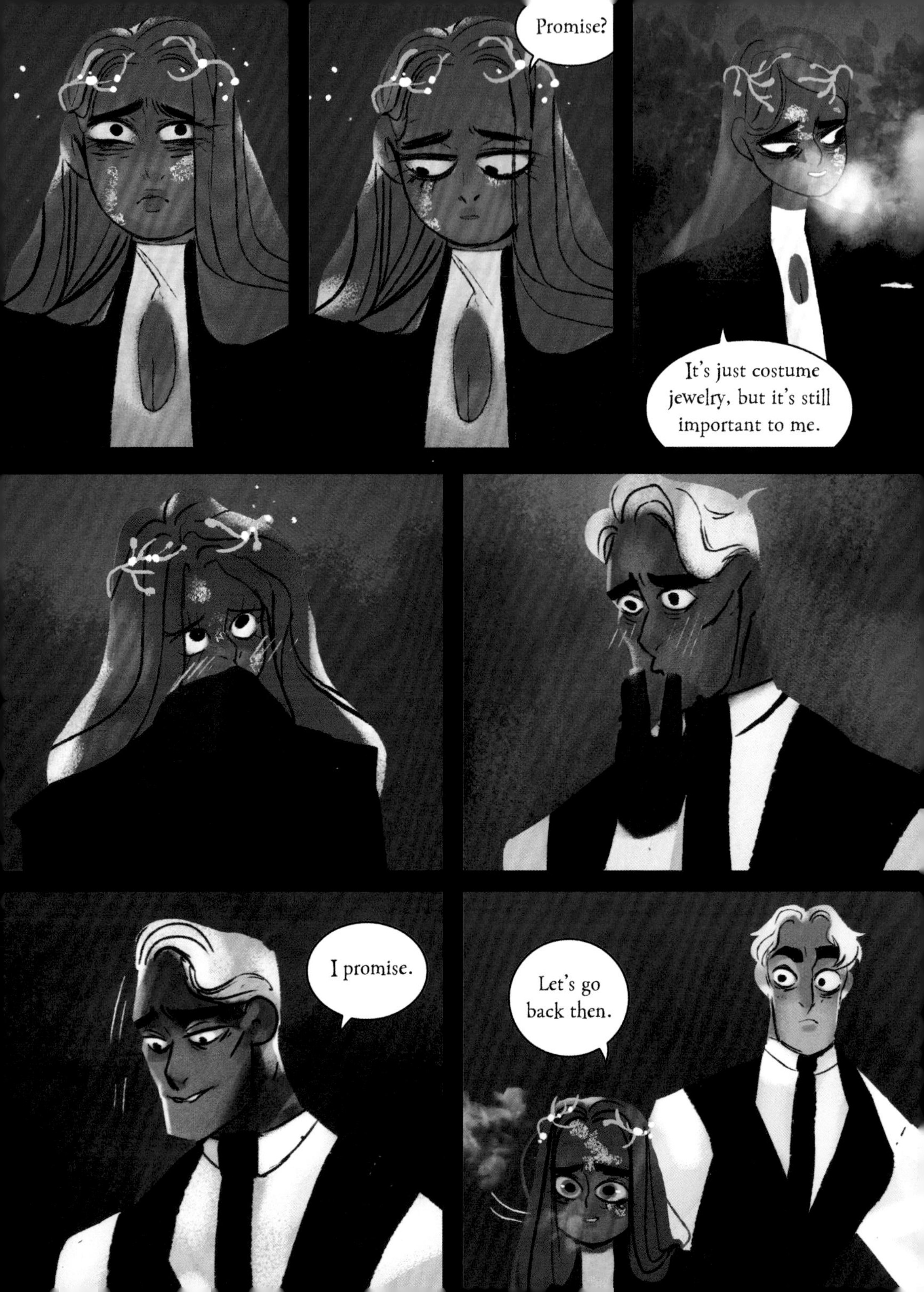
Promise?
It's just costume jewelry, but it's still important to me.
I promise.
Let's go back then.

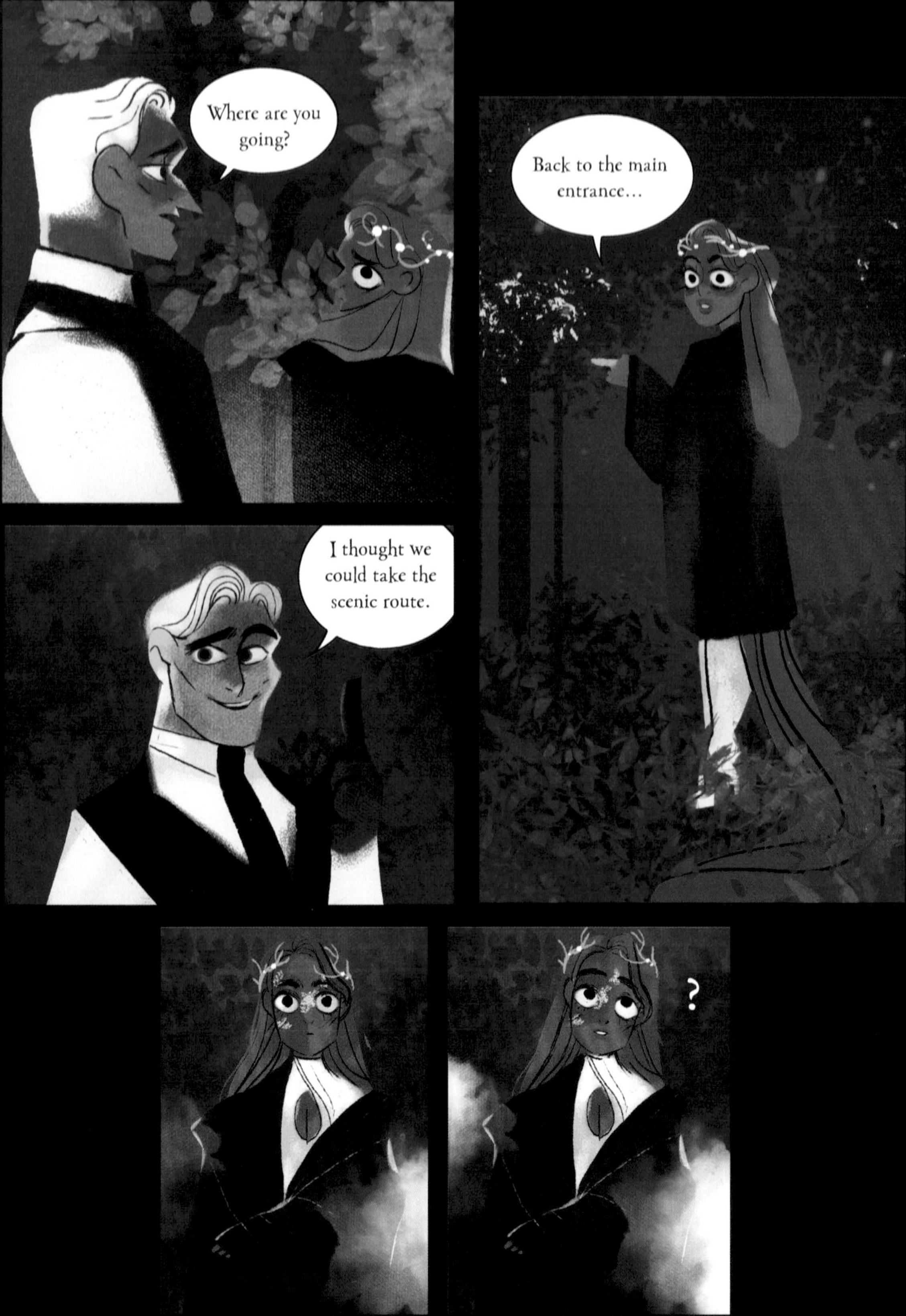
Where are you going?
Back to the main entrance...
I thought we could take the scenic route.
?

EPISODE 41: RETURN OF THE PRINCESS

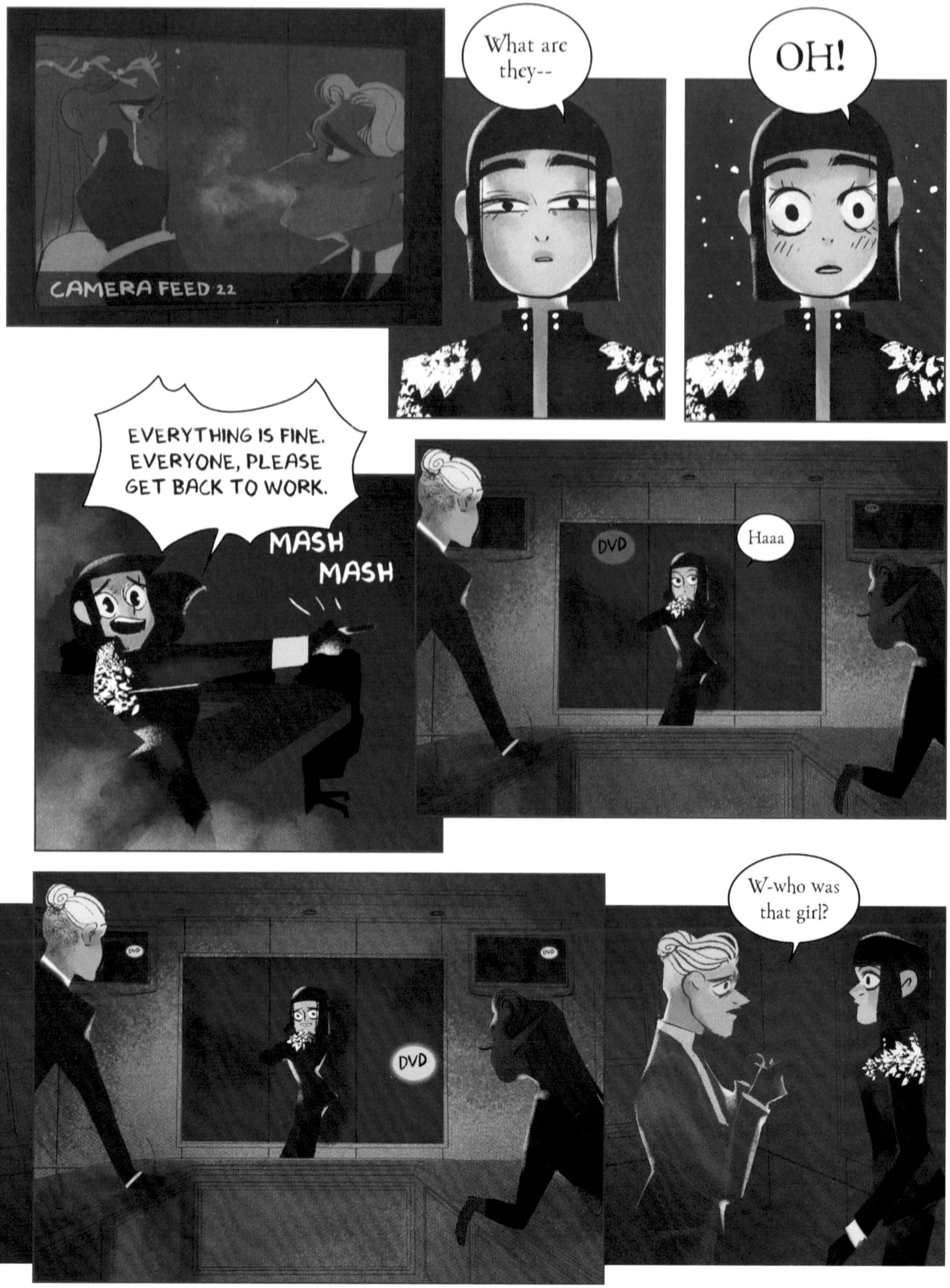
CAMERA FEED 22
What are they--
OH!
EVERYTHING IS FINE. EVERYONE, PLEASE GET BACK TO WORK.
MASH MASH
DVD
Haaa
DVD
DVD
DVD
W-who was that girl?

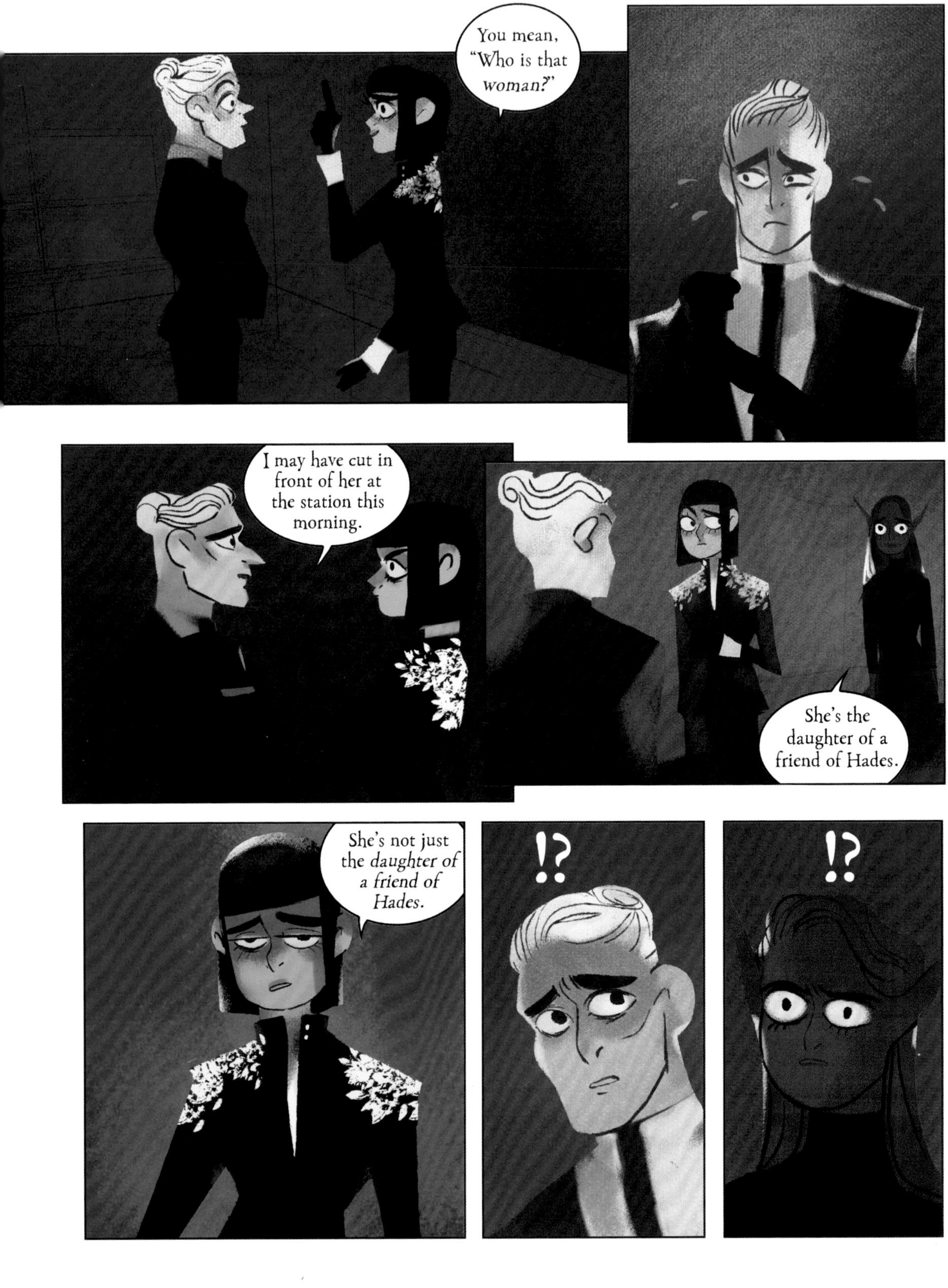
You mean, "Who is that *woman?*"
I may have cut in front of her at the station this morning.
She's the daughter of a friend of Hades.
She's not just the *daughter of a friend of Hades.*
!?
!?

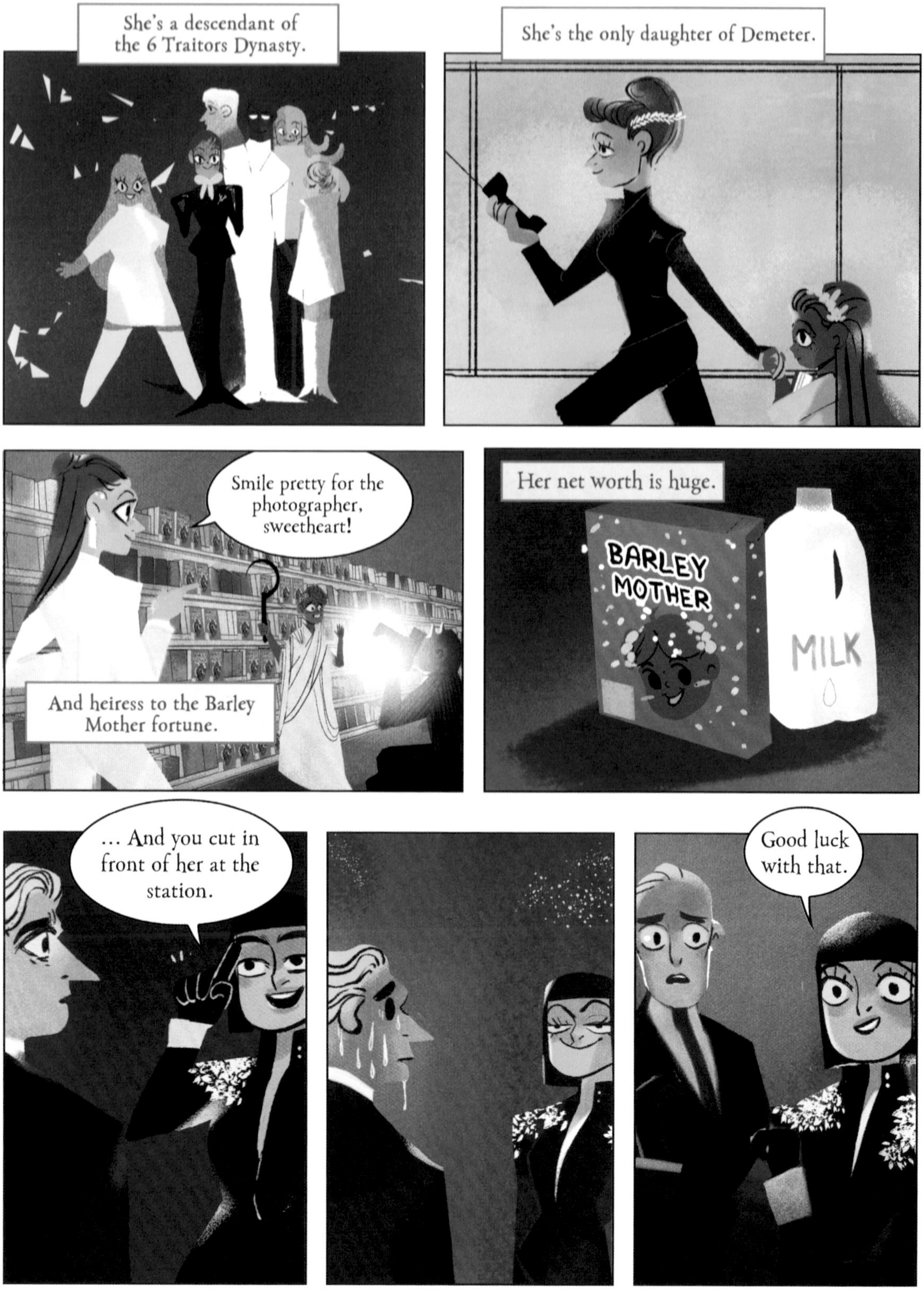
She's a descendant of the 6 Traitors Dynasty.
She's the only daughter of Demeter.
Smile pretty for the photographer, sweetheart!
And heiress to the Barley Mother fortune.
Her net worth is huge.
BARLEY MOTHER
MILK
... And you cut in front of her at the station.
Good luck with that.

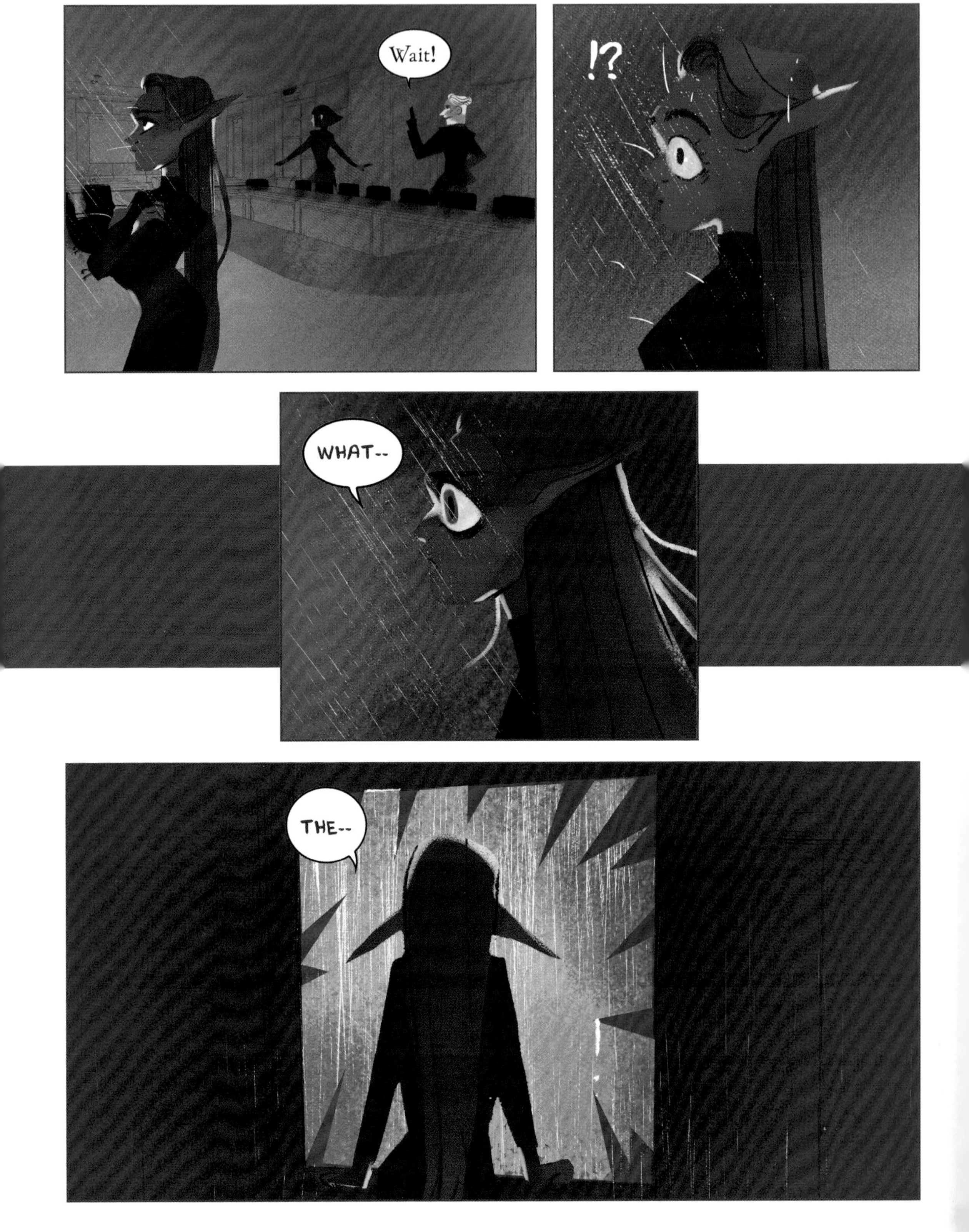
Wait!
!?
WHAT--
THE--

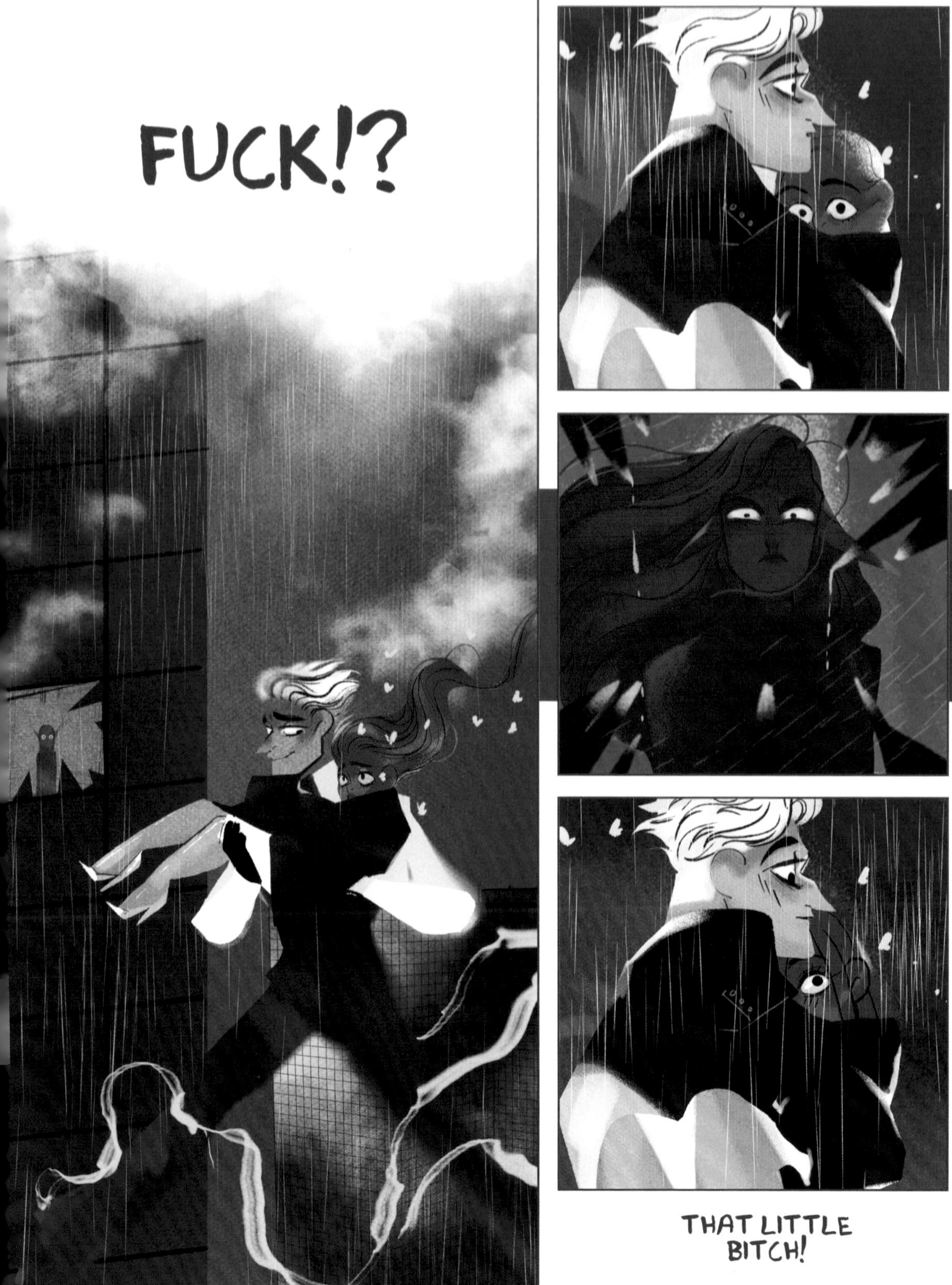
FUCK!?
THAT LITTLE BITCH!

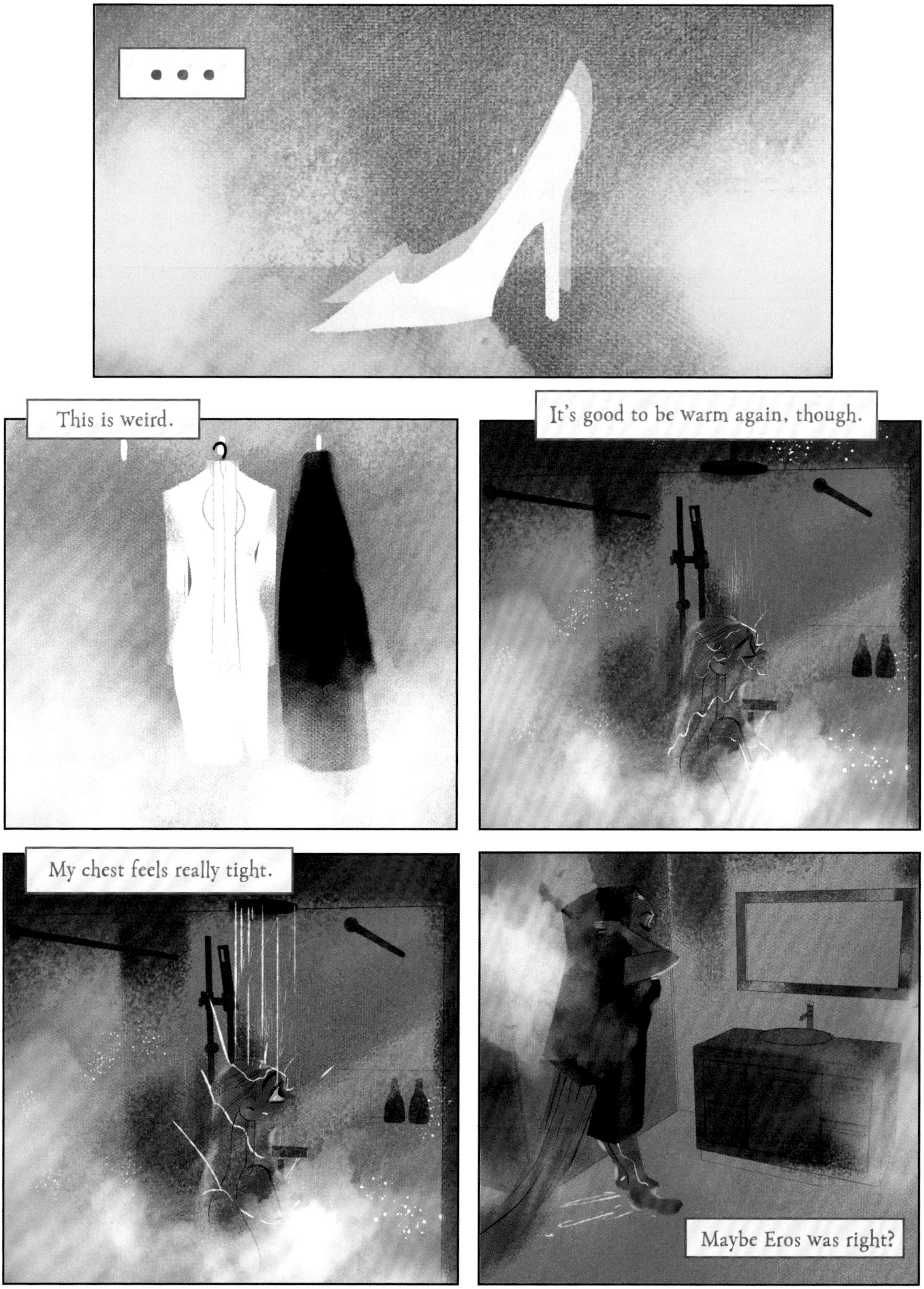
...
This is weird.
It's good to be warm again, though.
My chest feels really tight.
Maybe Eros was right?

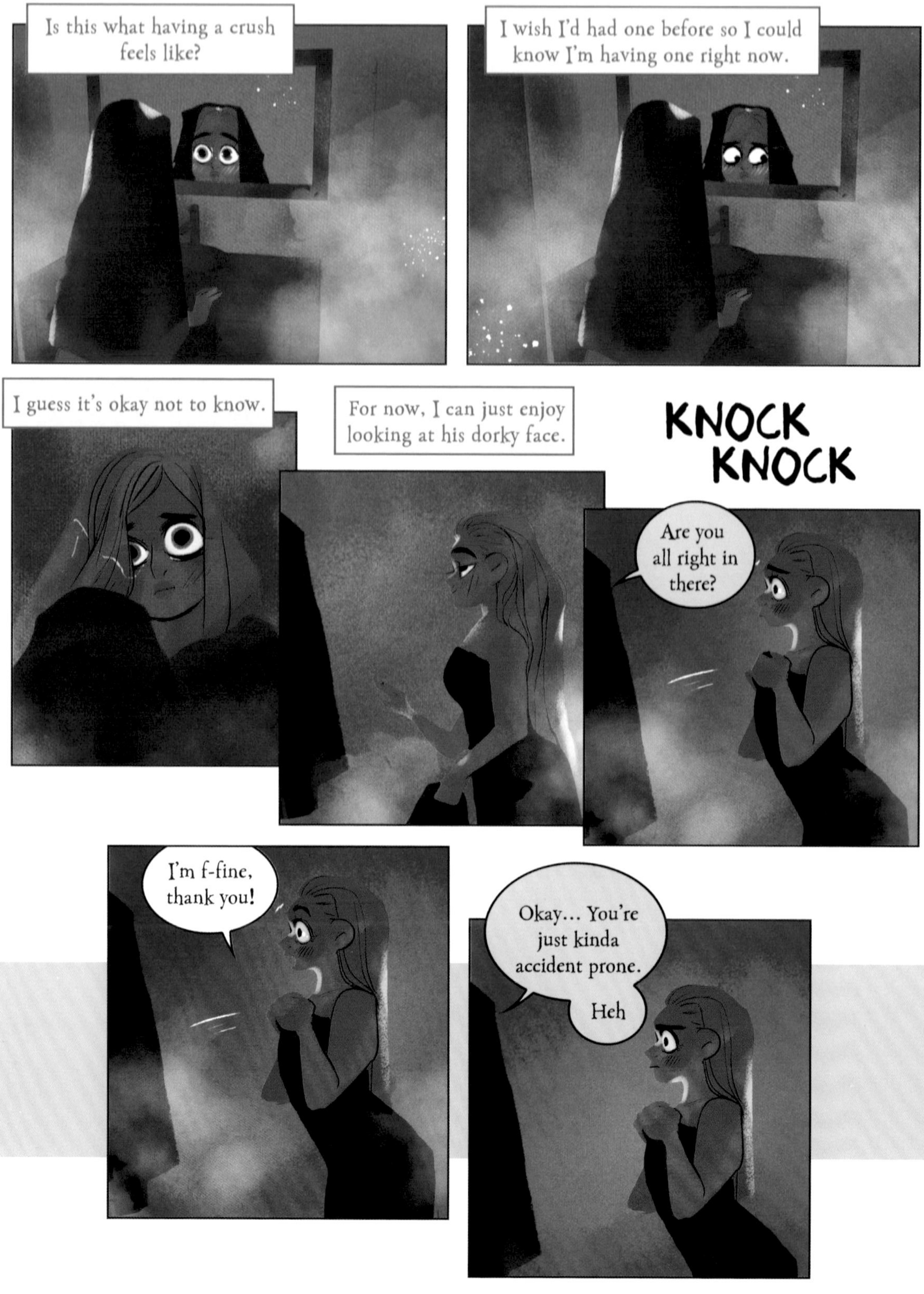
Is this what having a crush feels like?
I wish I'd had one before so I could know I'm having one right now.
I guess it's okay not to know.
For now, I can just enjoy looking at his dorky face.
KNOCK KNOCK
Are you all right in there?
I'm f-fine, thank you!
Okay... You're just kinda accident prone.
Heh

EPISODE 42: THE WAY SHE LOOKED AT ME

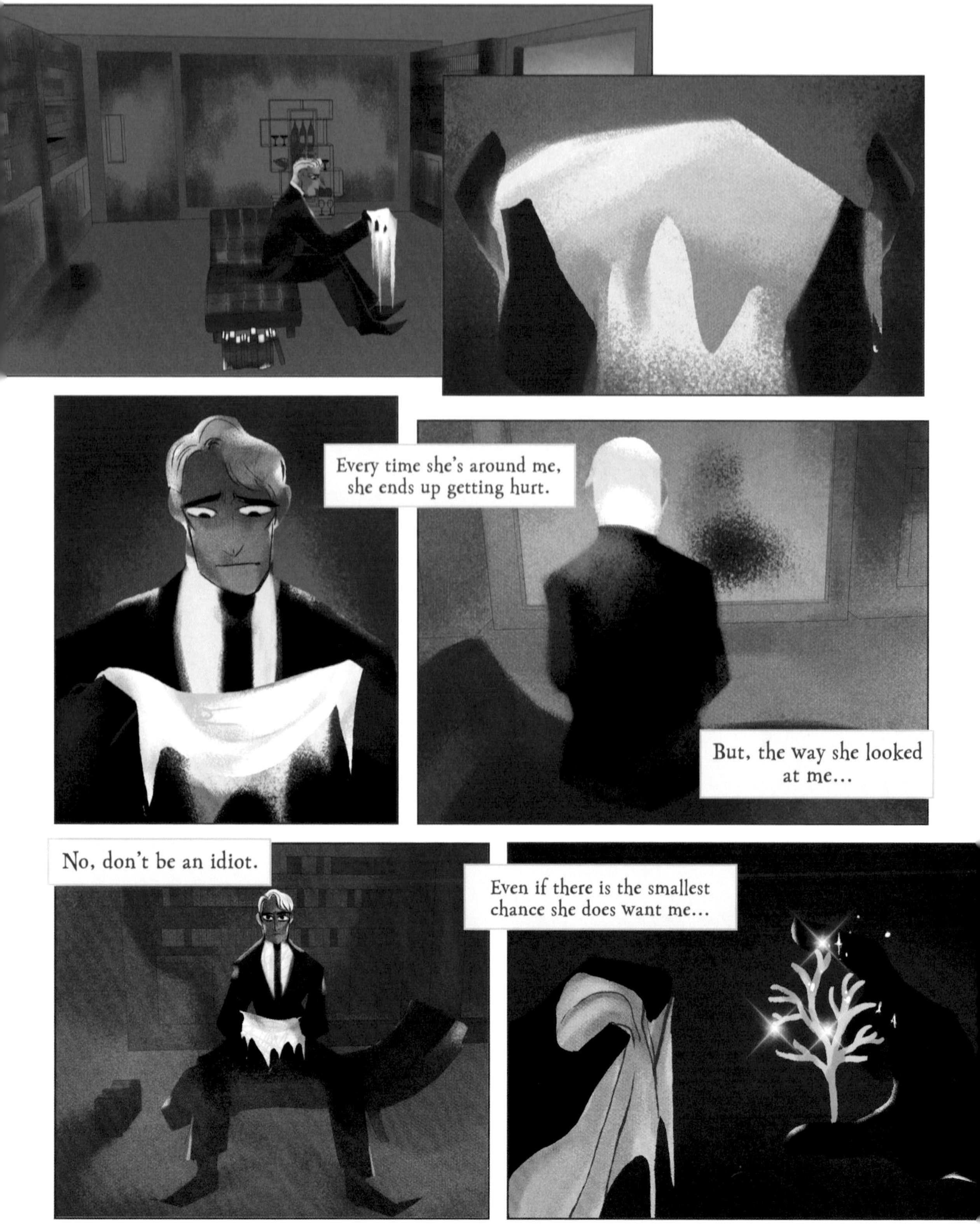
Every time she's around me, she ends up getting hurt.
But, the way she looked at me...
No, don't be an idiot.
Even if there is the smallest chance she does want me...

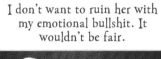

...she's still too young, and I'm still a complete mess.

I don't want to ruin her with my emotional bullshit. It wouldn't be fair.

The sooner she can get away from me, the better.

Um, excuse me, don't you have a gateway to guard?

I see I'm old news, huh?

Would you cut that out?

BARK! BARK! BARK! BARK!

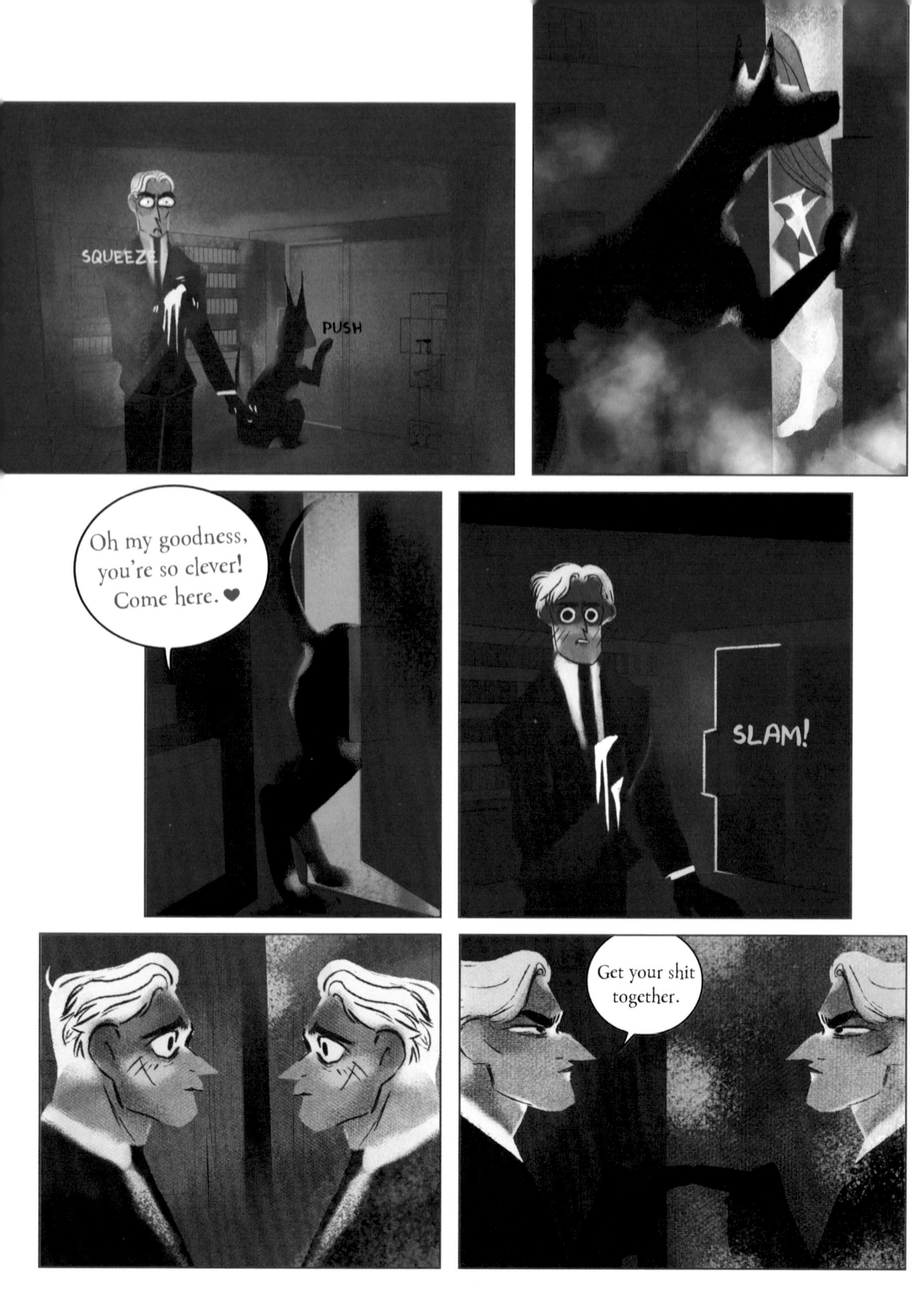
SQUEEZE
PUSH
Oh my goodness, you're so clever! Come here. ❤
SLAM!
Get your shit together.

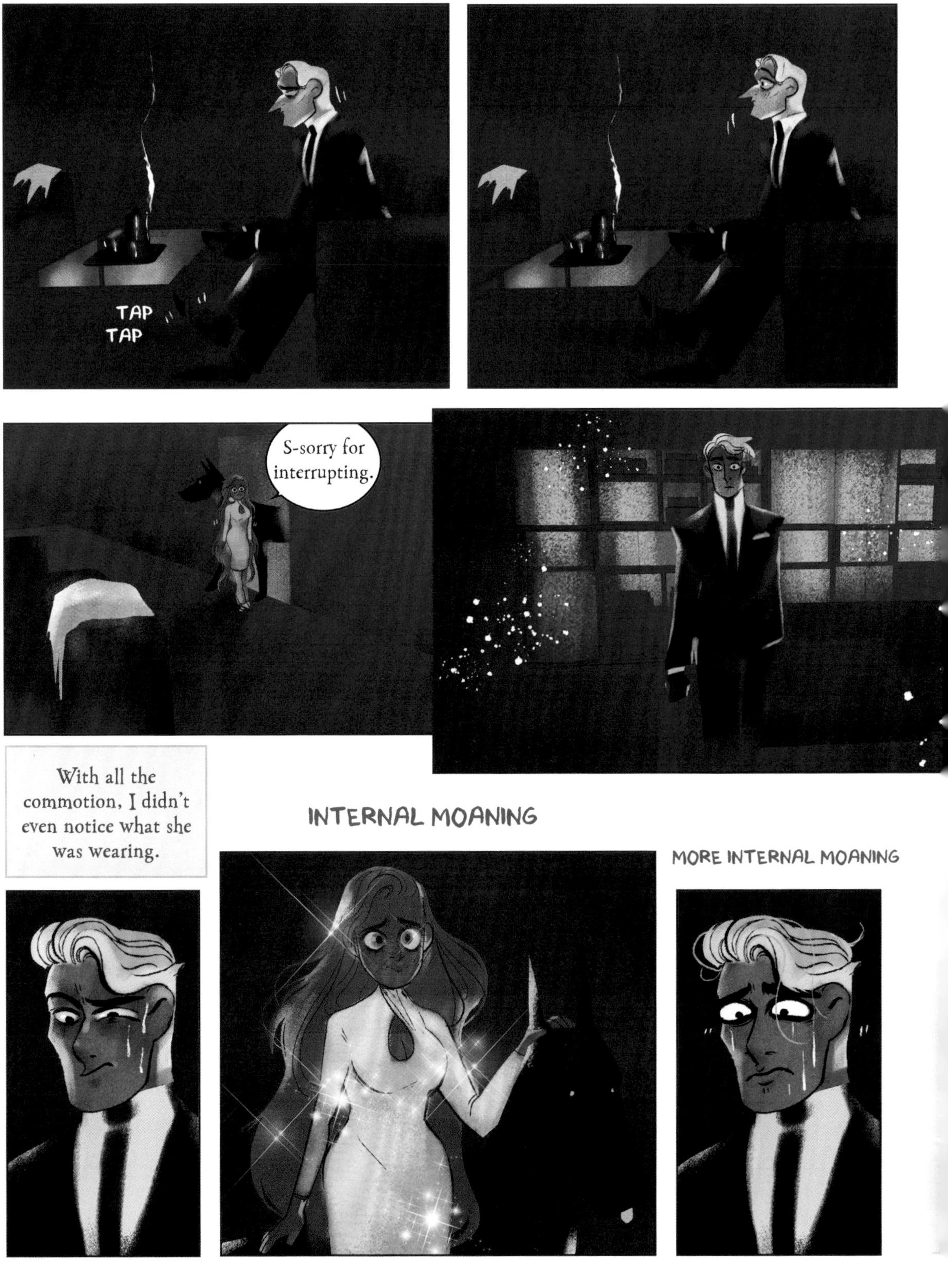
TAP
TAP
S-sorry for interrupting.
With all the commotion, I didn't even notice what she was wearing.
INTERNAL MOANING
MORE INTERNAL MOANING

Ugh, is it my hair? It goes frizzy when it air dries.

No, no, I was just lost in thought.

Please, take a seat.

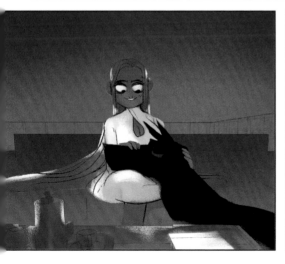

DIG DIG

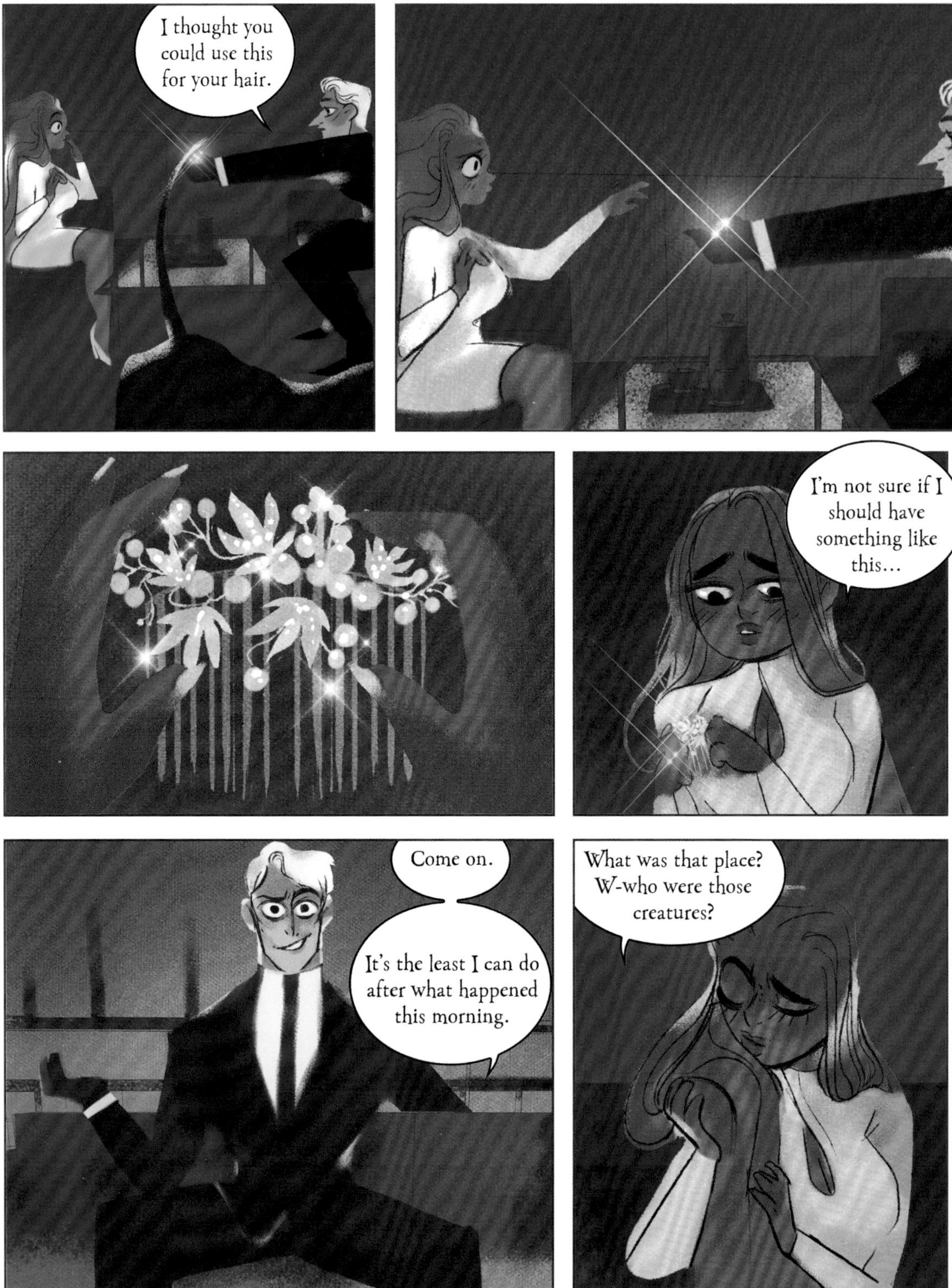
I thought you could use this for your hair.
I'm not sure if I should have something like this...
Come on.
It's the least I can do after what happened this morning.
What was that place? W-who were those creatures?

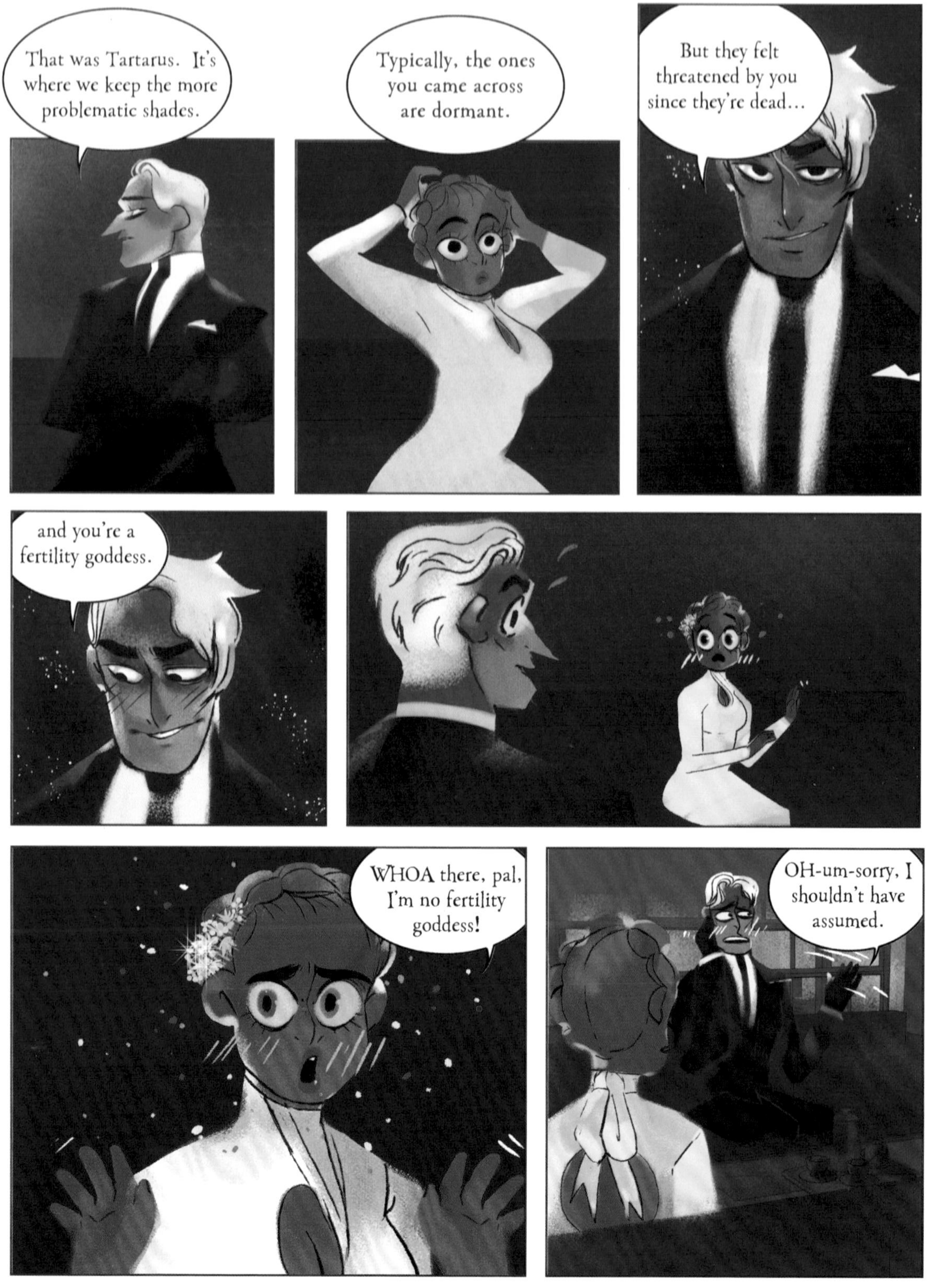
That was Tartarus. It's where we keep the more problematic shades.
Typically, the ones you came across are dormant.
But they felt threatened by you since they're dead...
and you're a fertility goddess.
WHOA there, pal, I'm no fertility goddess!
OH-um-sorry, I shouldn't have assumed.

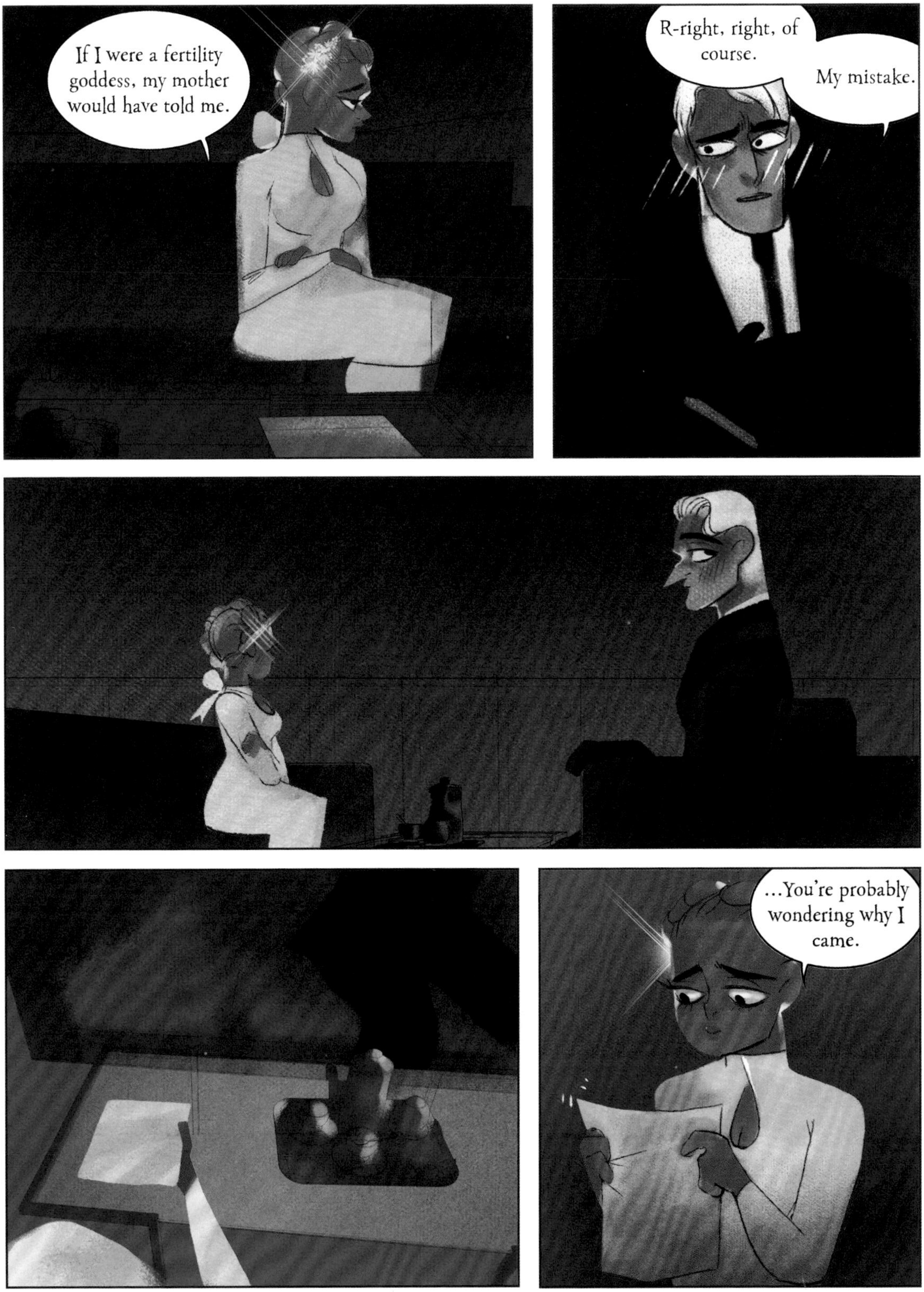
If I were a fertility goddess, my mother would have told me.
R-right, right, of course.
My mistake.
...You're probably wondering why I came.

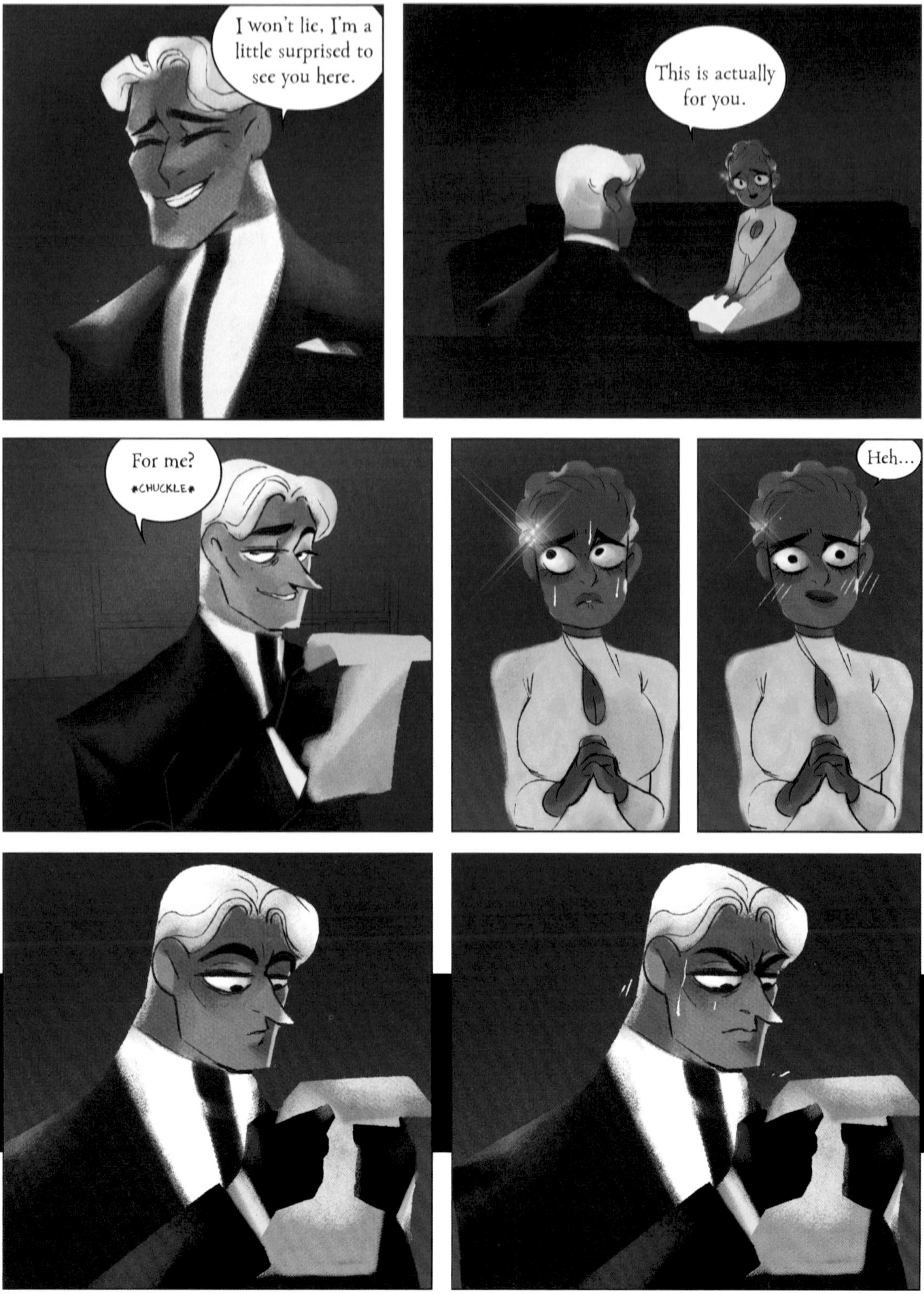
I won't lie, I'm a little surprised to see you here.
This is actually for you.
For me?
CHUCKLE
Heh...

No…

No!

APPLICANT: PERSEPHONE (KORE)
REPORT TO: HADES, GOD/KING OF THE DEAD/UNDERWORLD
LOCATION: UNDERWORLD CORP, TOWER I, LV 99
TIME: ASAP
INTERNSHIP ROLE:
STATUS:

OH N-NO, NO!

Who is responsible for this!?

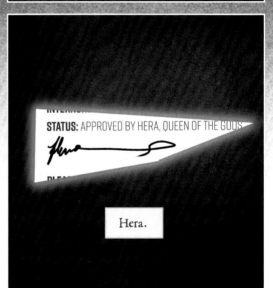

STATUS: APPROVED BY HERA, QUEEN OF THE GODS

Hera.

FUCKING HERA!

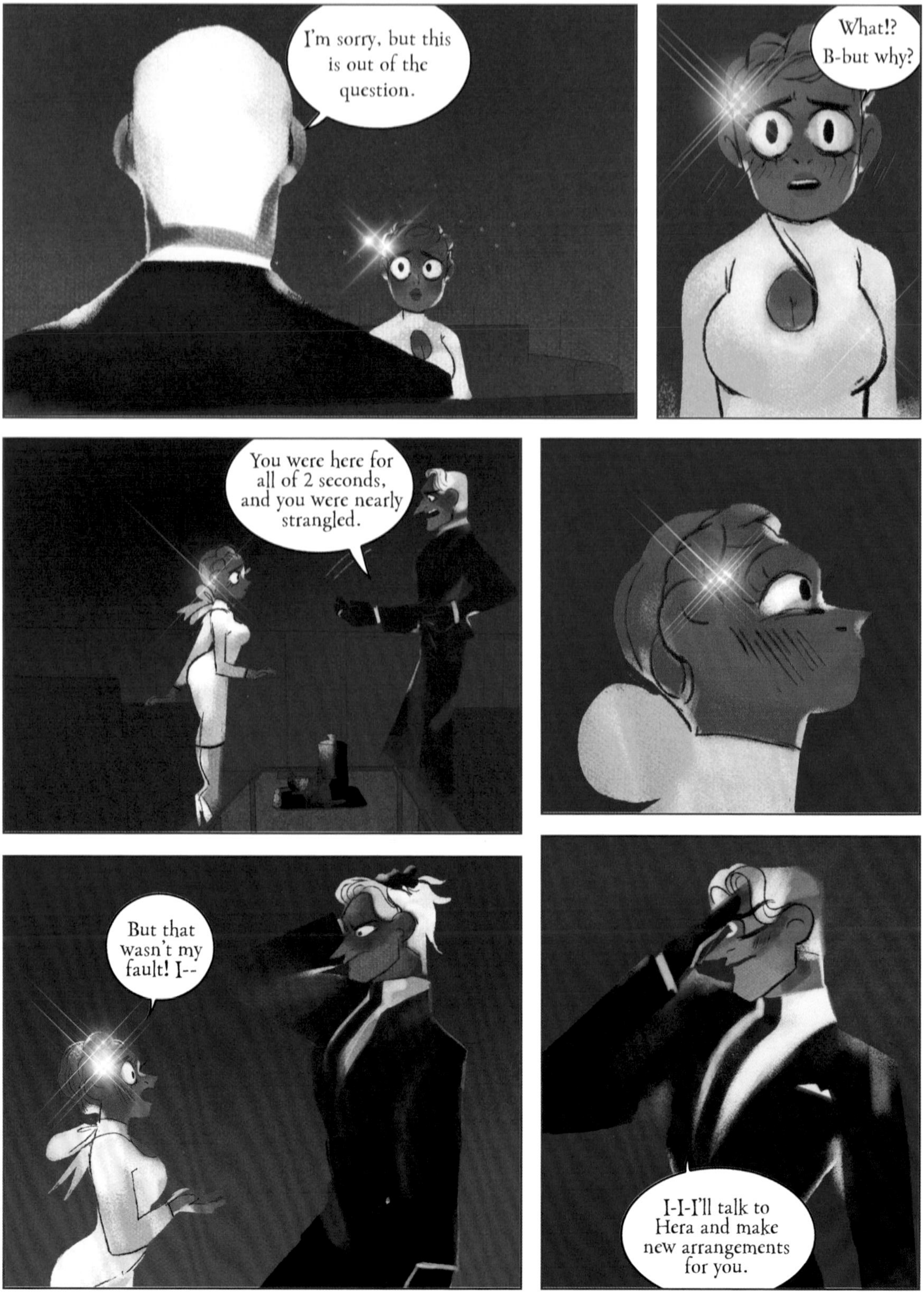
I'm sorry, but this is out of the question.
What!? B-but why?
You were here for all of 2 seconds, and you were nearly strangled.
But that wasn't my fault! I--
I-I-I'll talk to Hera and make new arrangements for you.

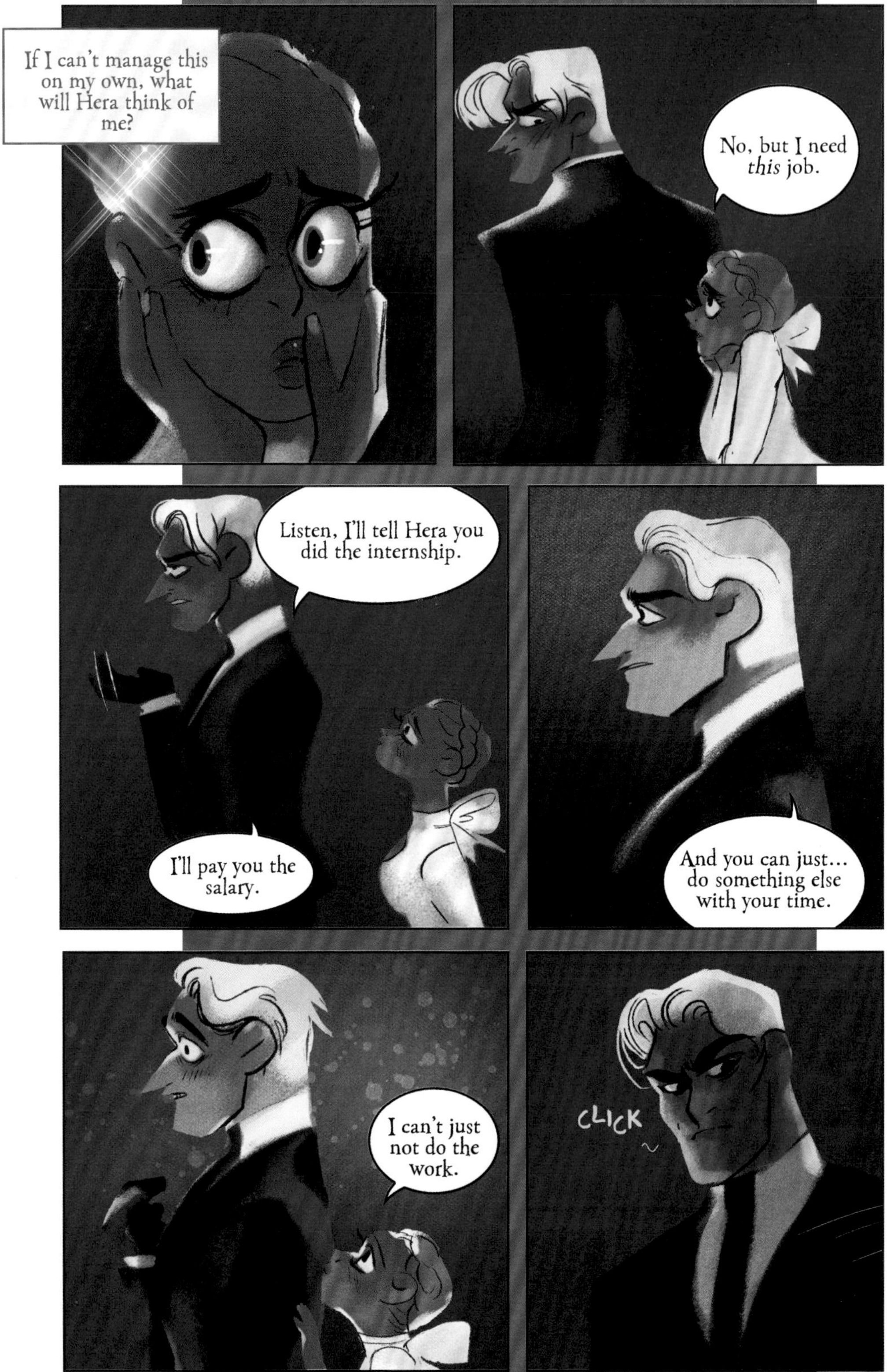
If I can't manage this on my own, what will Hera think of me?
No, but I need *this* job.
Listen, I'll tell Hera you did the internship.
I'll pay you the salary.
And you can just... do something else with your time.
I can't just not do the work.
CLICK

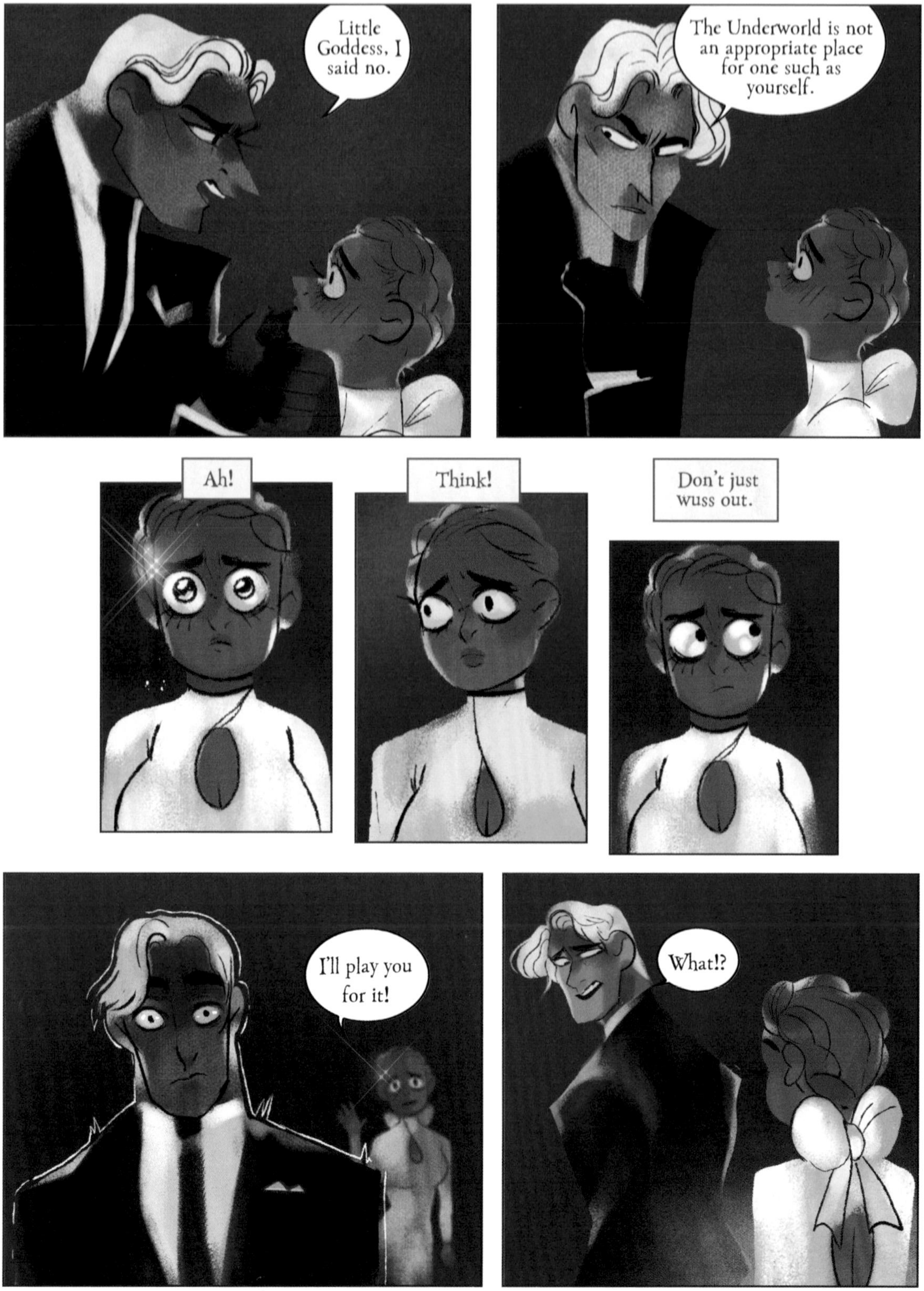
Little Goddess, I said no.
The Underworld is not an appropriate place for one such as yourself.
Ah!
Think!
Don't just wuss out.
I'll play you for it!
What!?

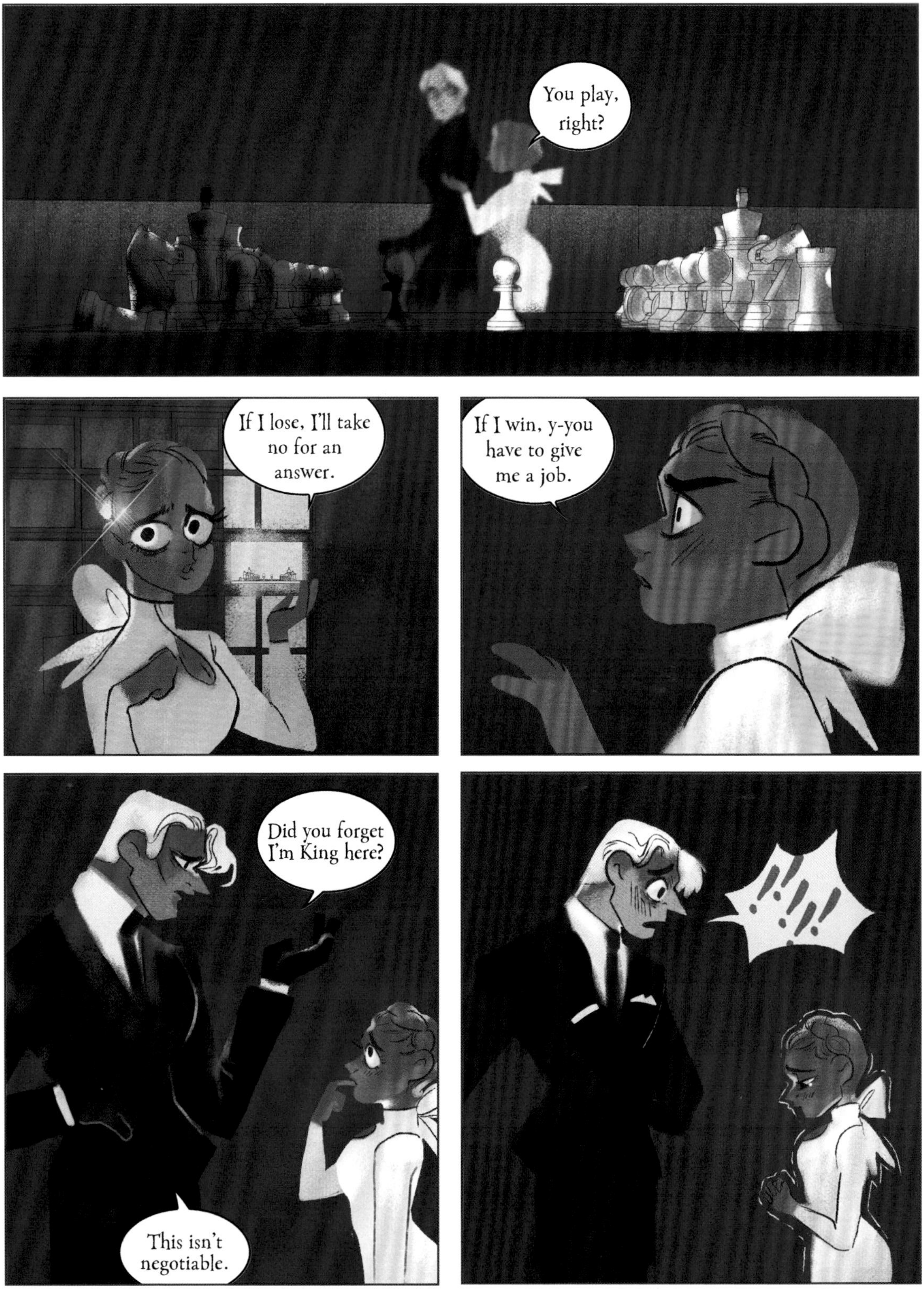
You play, right?
If I lose, I'll take no for an answer.
If I win, y-you have to give me a job.
Did you forget I'm King here?
This isn't negotiable.
!!!!

EPISODE 43: THE WAGER

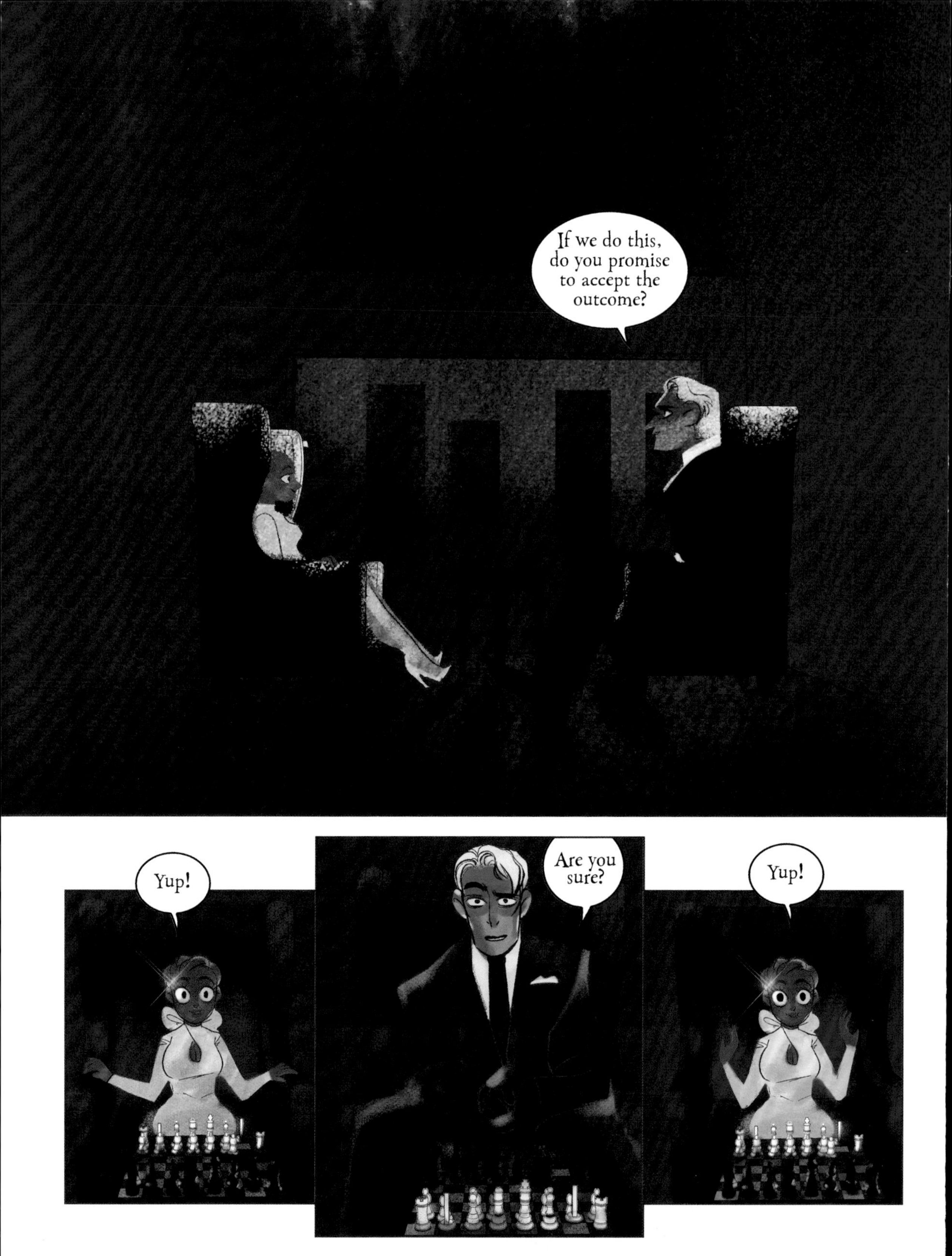
If we do this, do you promise to accept the outcome?
Yup!
Are you sure?
Yup!

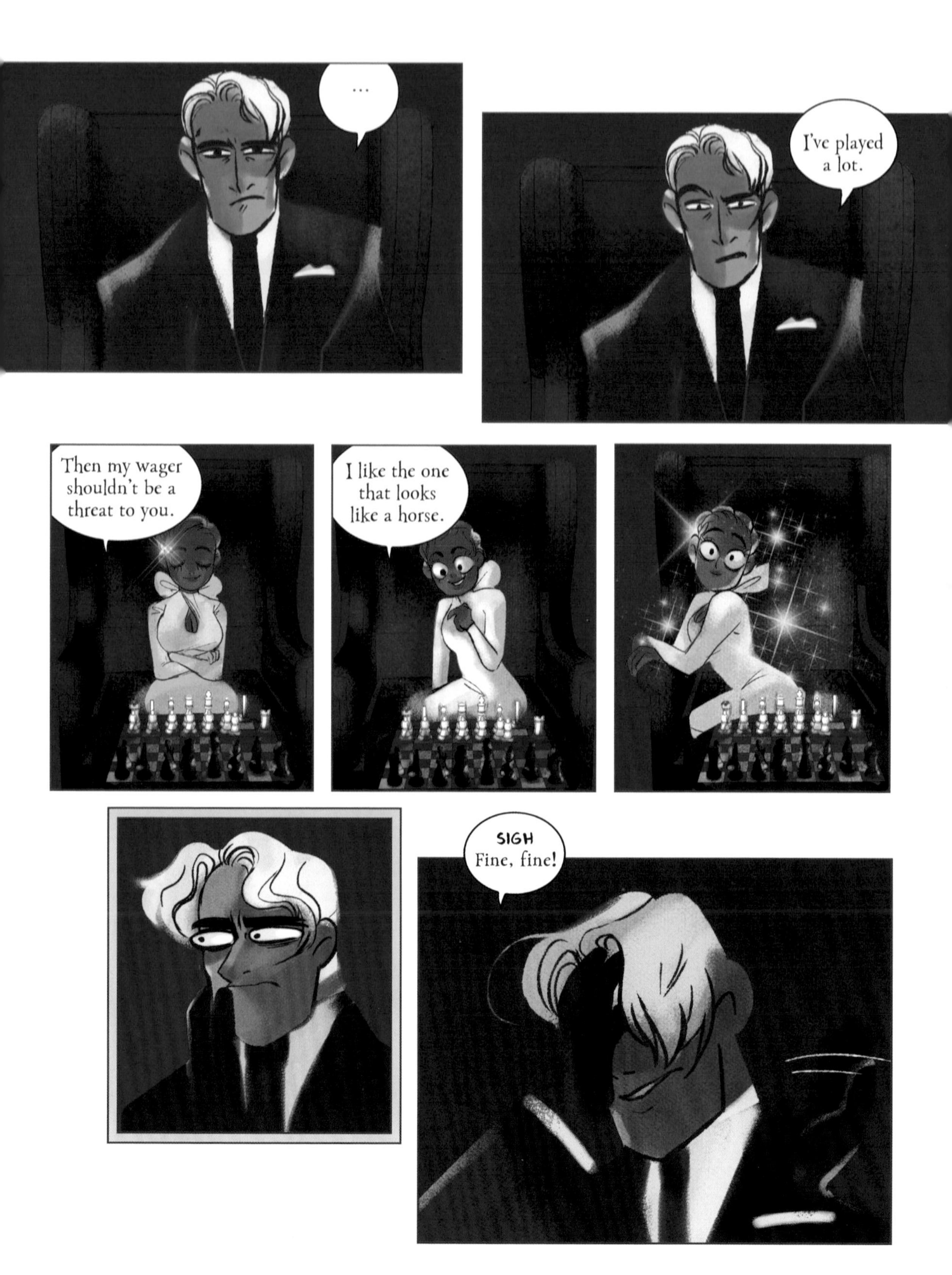
...
I've played a lot.
Then my wager shouldn't be a threat to you.
I like the one that looks like a horse.
SIGH
Fine, fine!

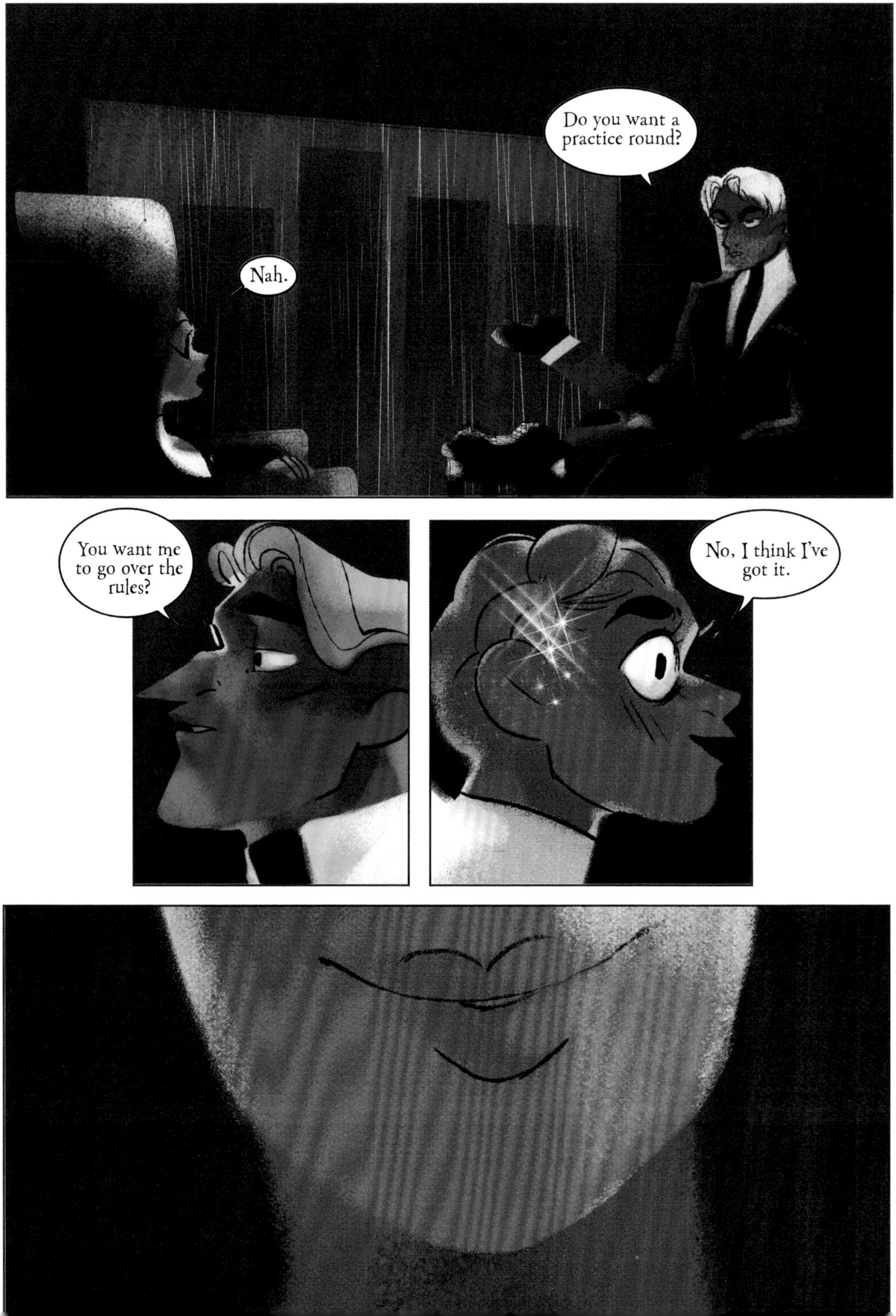
Do you want a practice round?
Nah.
You want me to go over the rules?
No, I think I've got it.

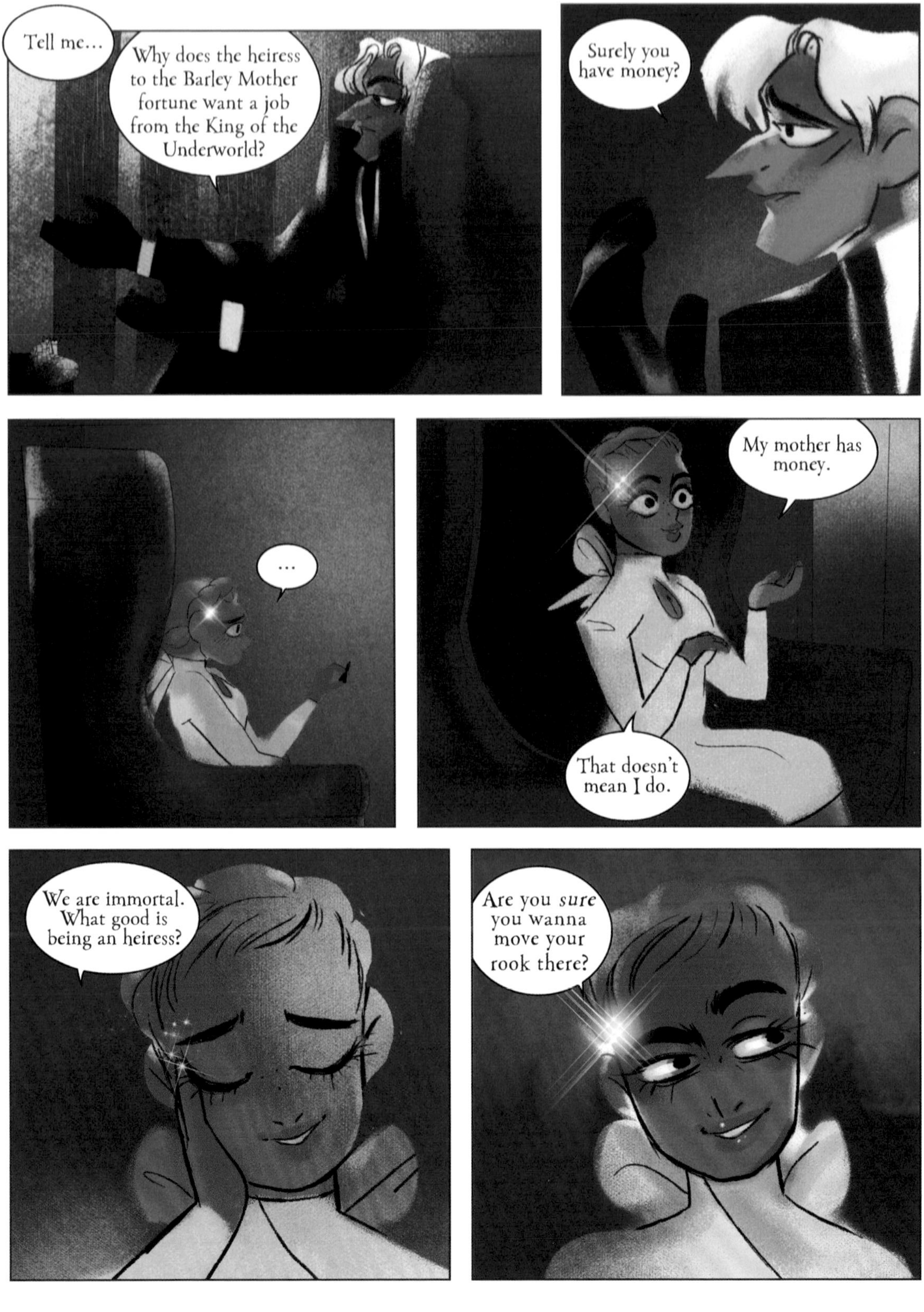
Tell me...
Why does the heiress to the Barley Mother fortune want a job from the King of the Underworld?
Surely you have money?
...
My mother has money.
That doesn't mean I do.
We are immortal. What good is being an heiress?
Are you *sure* you wanna move your rook there?

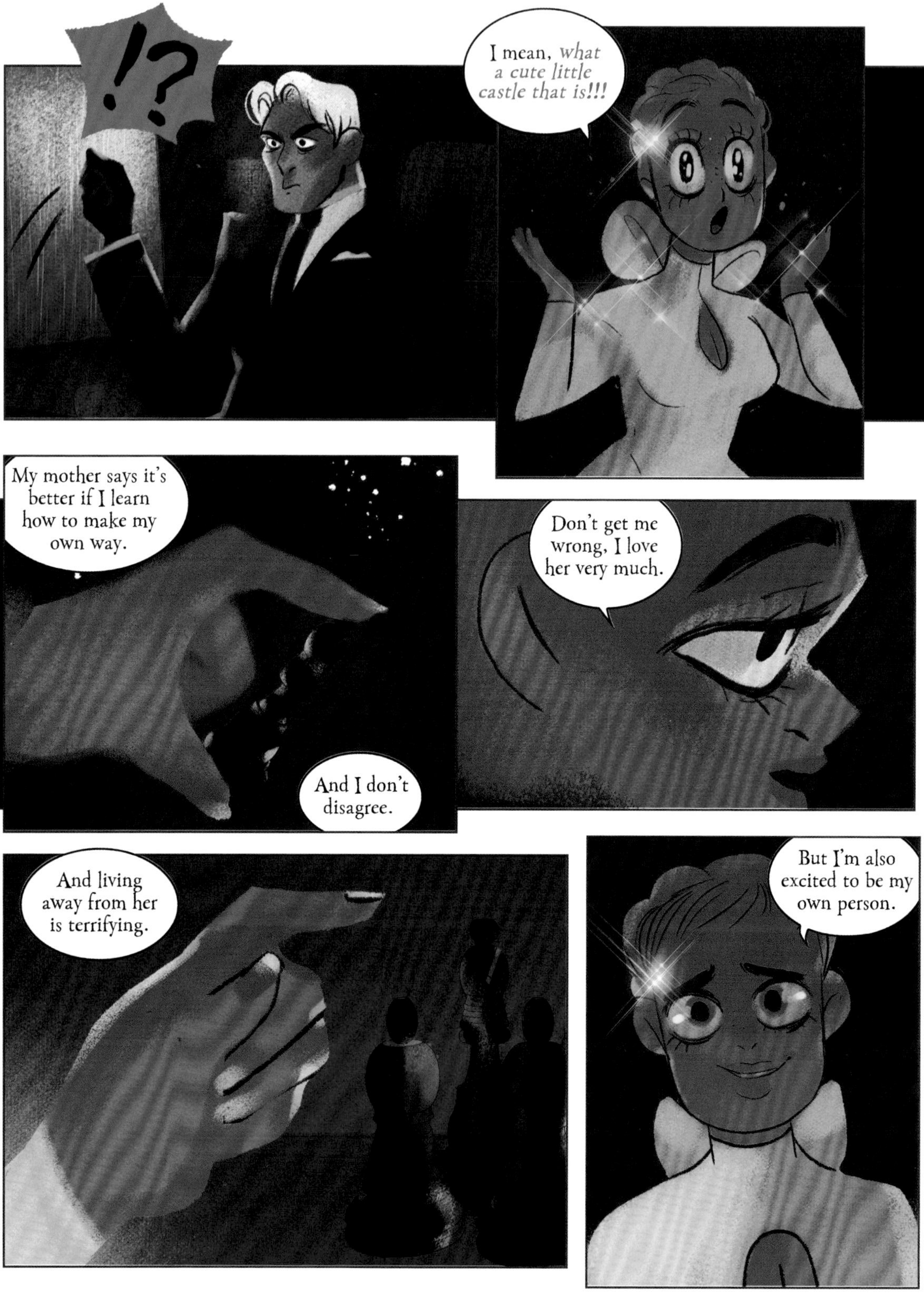
!?
I mean, what a cute little castle that is!!!
My mother says it's better if I learn how to make my own way.
Don't get me wrong, I love her very much.
And I don't disagree.
And living away from her is terrifying.
But I'm also excited to be my own person.

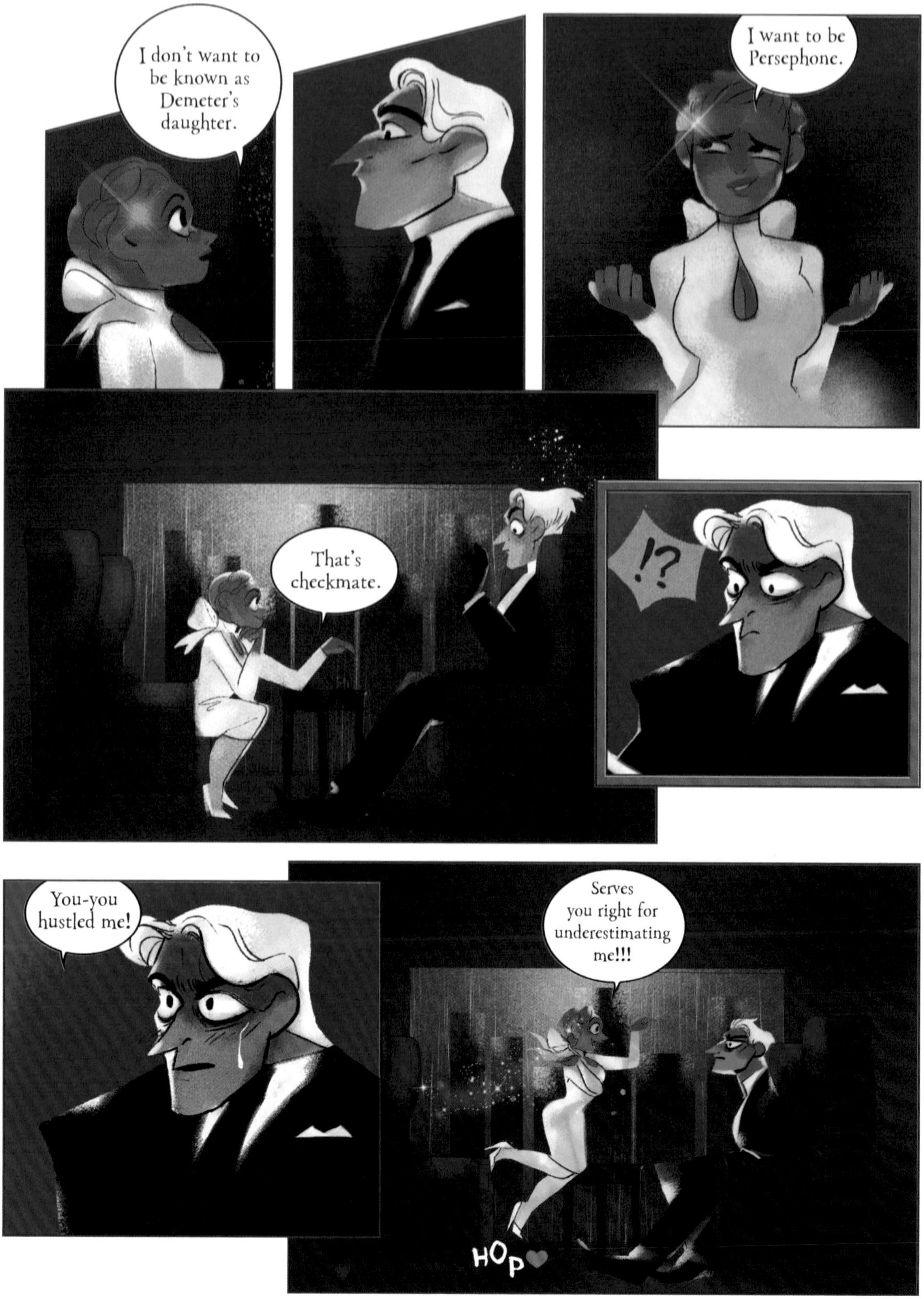
I don't want to be known as Demeter's daughter.
I want to be Persephone.
That's checkmate.
!?
You-you hustled me!
Serves you right for underestimating me!!!
HOP

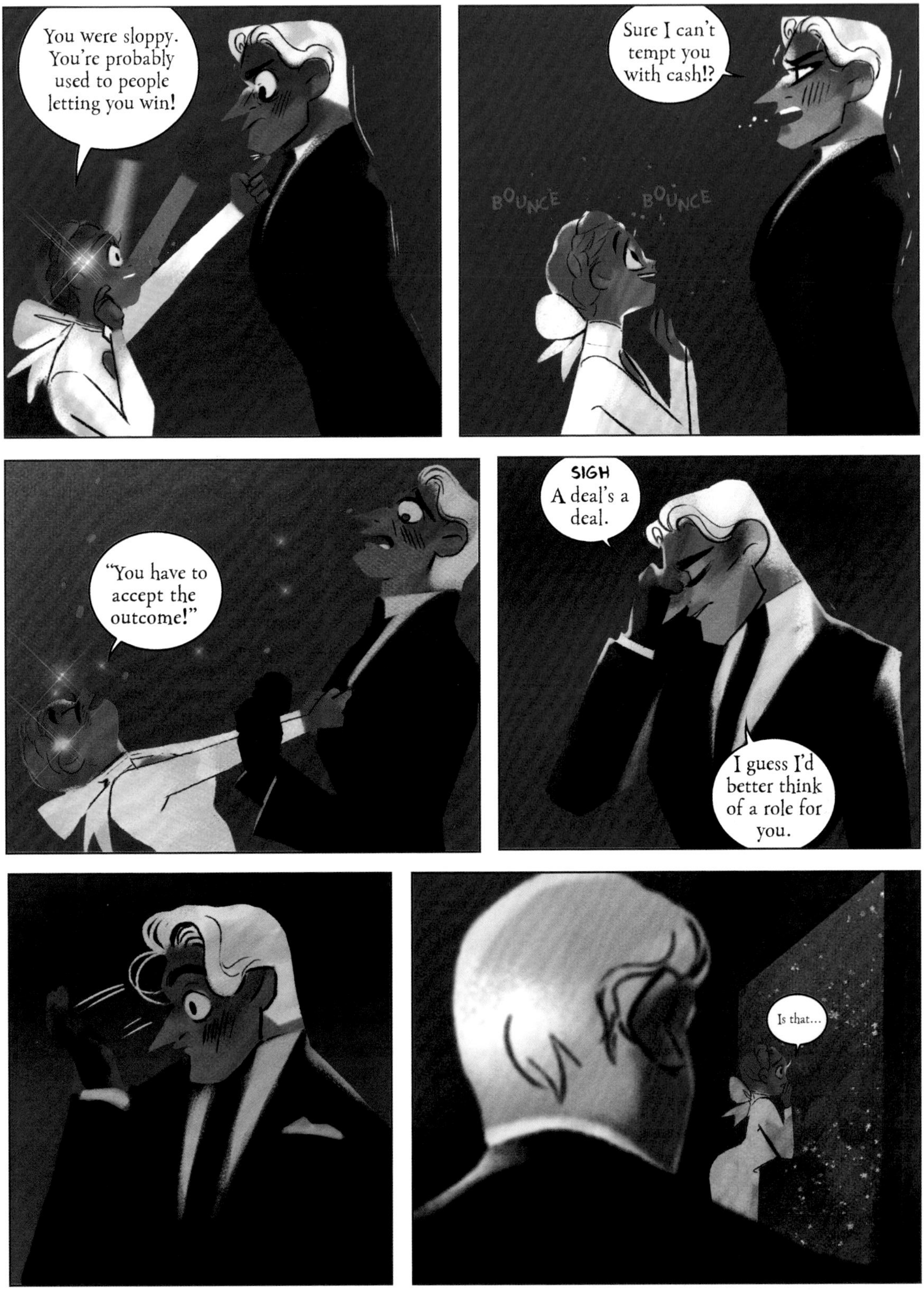
You were sloppy. You're probably used to people letting you win!
Sure I can't tempt you with cash!?
BOUNCE
BOUNCE
"You have to accept the outcome!"
SIGH
A deal's a deal.
I guess I'd better think of a role for you.
Is that...

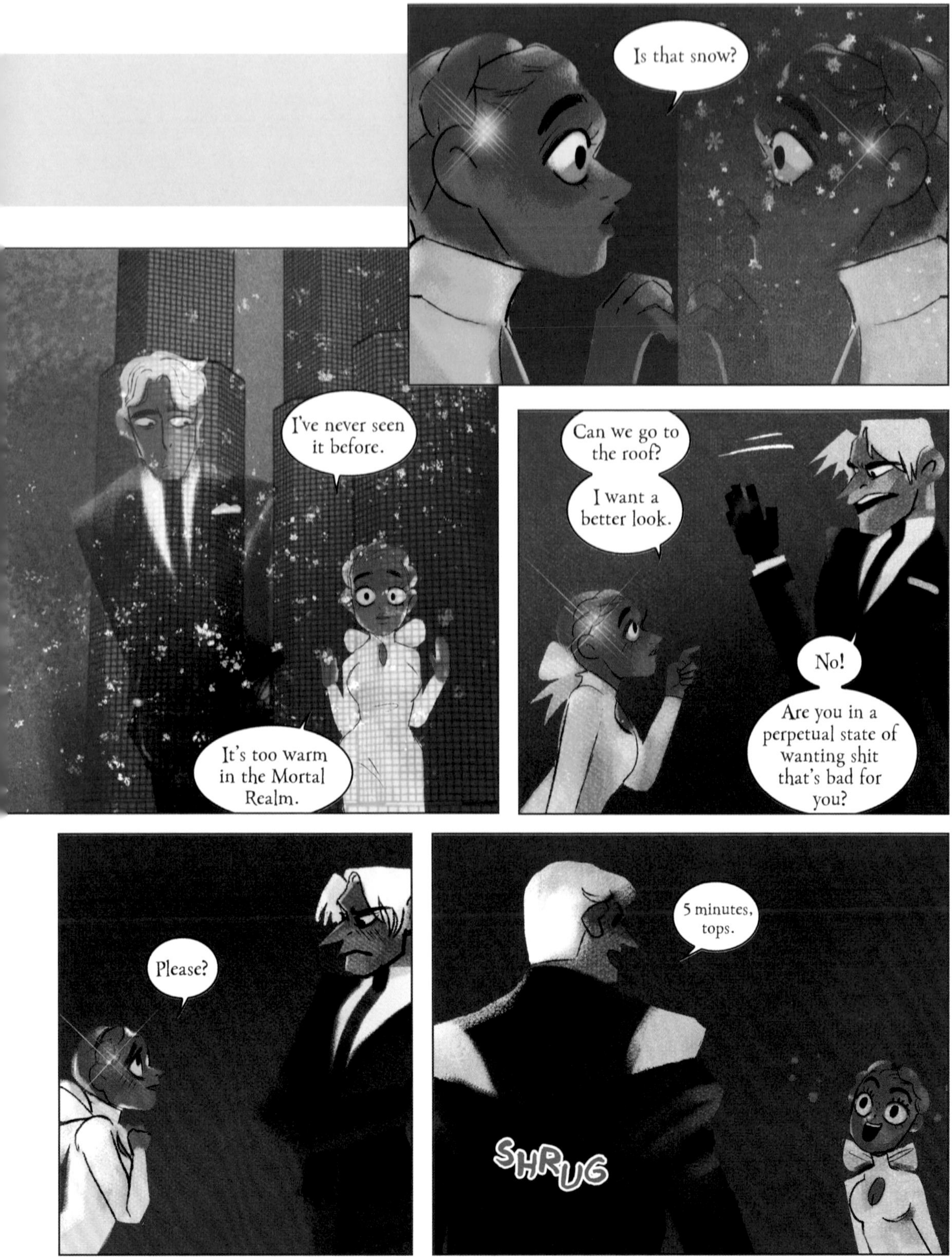
Is that snow?
I've never seen it before.
It's too warm in the Mortal Realm.
Can we go to the roof?
I want a better look.
No!
Are you in a perpetual state of wanting shit that's bad for you?
Please?
5 minutes, tops.
SHRUG

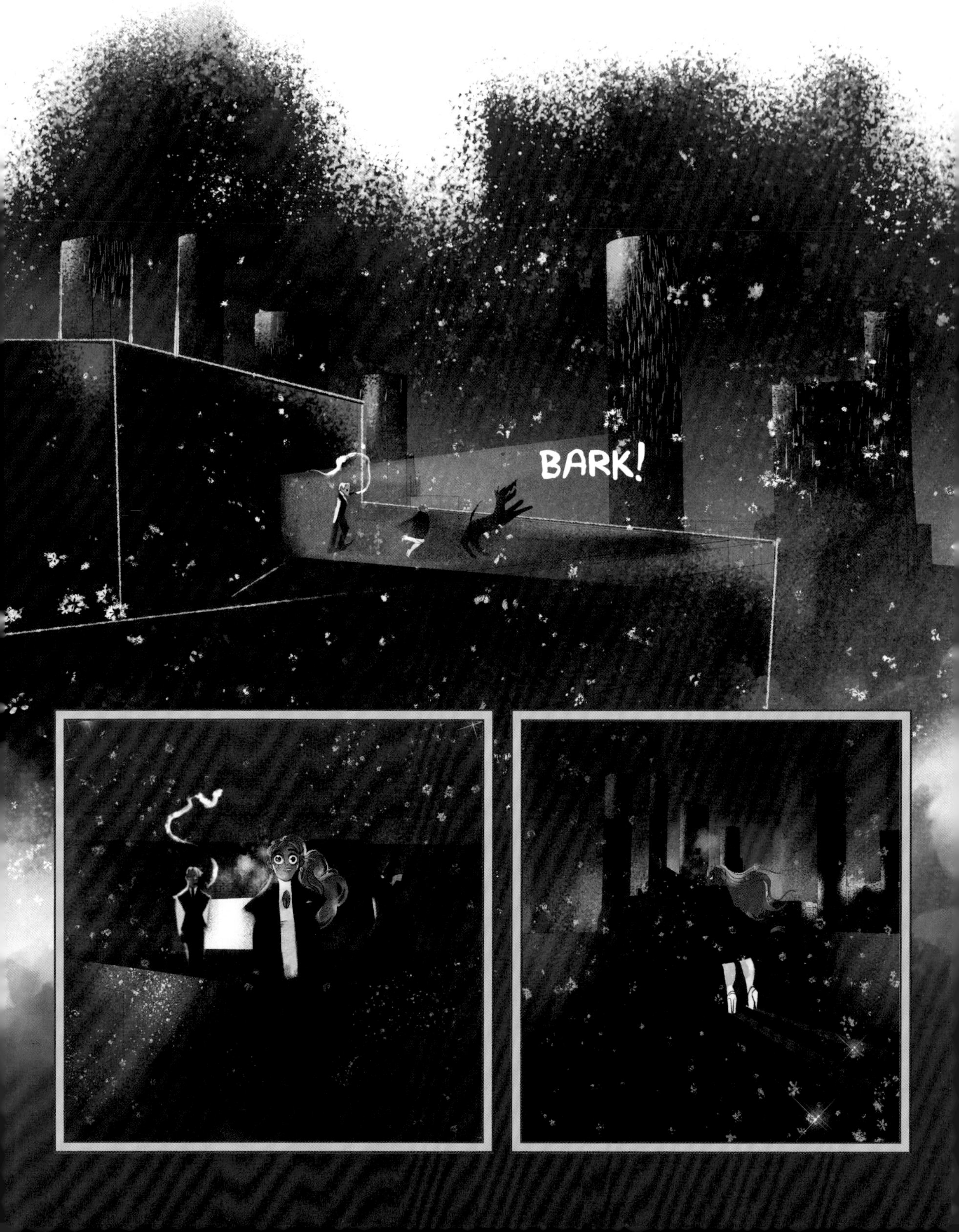
BARK!

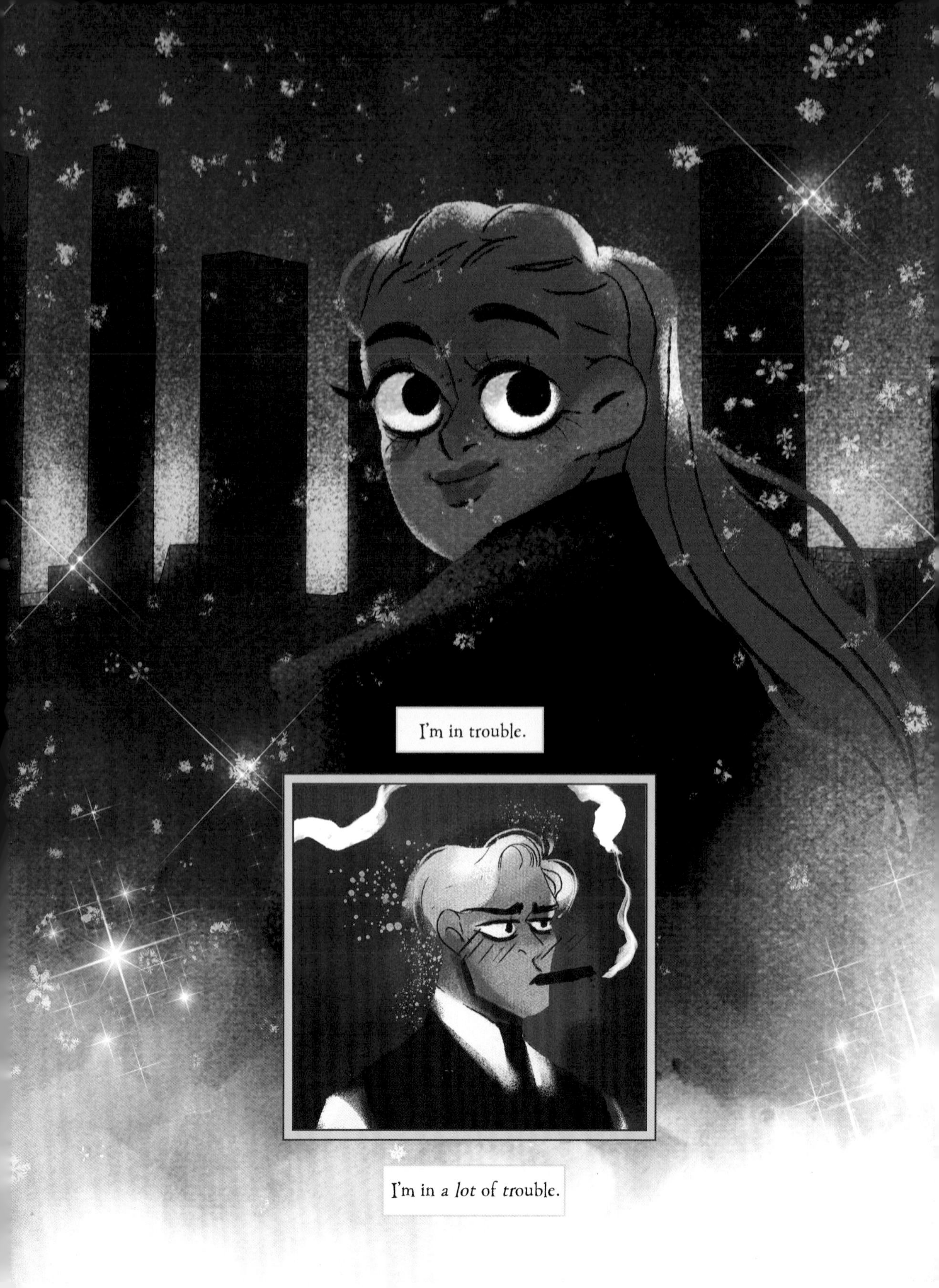
I'm in trouble.
I'm in a *lot* of trouble.

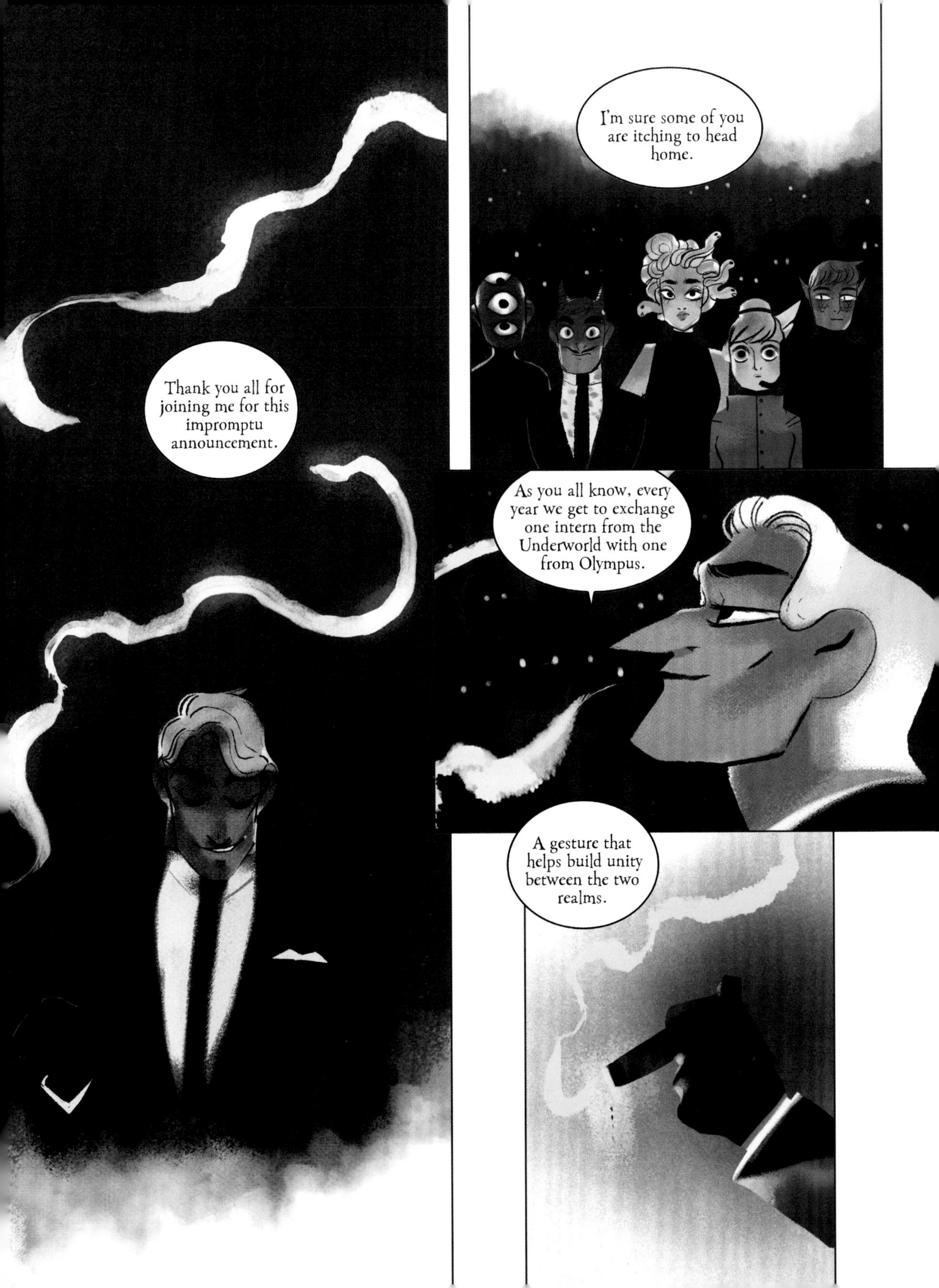
Thank you all for joining me for this impromptu announcement.
I'm sure some of you are itching to head home.
As you all know, every year we get to exchange one intern from the Underworld with one from Olympus.
A gesture that helps build unity between the two realms.

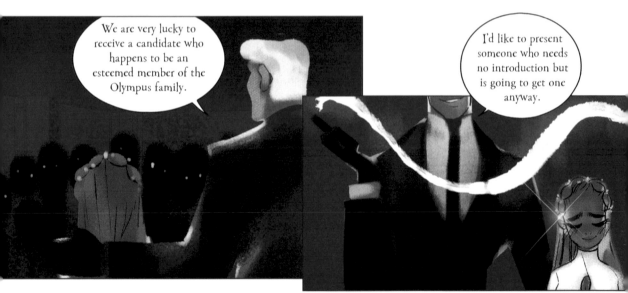

We are very lucky to receive a candidate who happens to be an esteemed member of the Olympus family.

I'd like to present someone who needs no introduction but is going to get one anyway.

Give a warm welcome to our newest intern, Persephone, the Goddess of Spring.

CLAP
CLAP

CLAP
CLAP

...

Since when did interns receive all staff, formal introductions?

EPISODE 44: SOFT

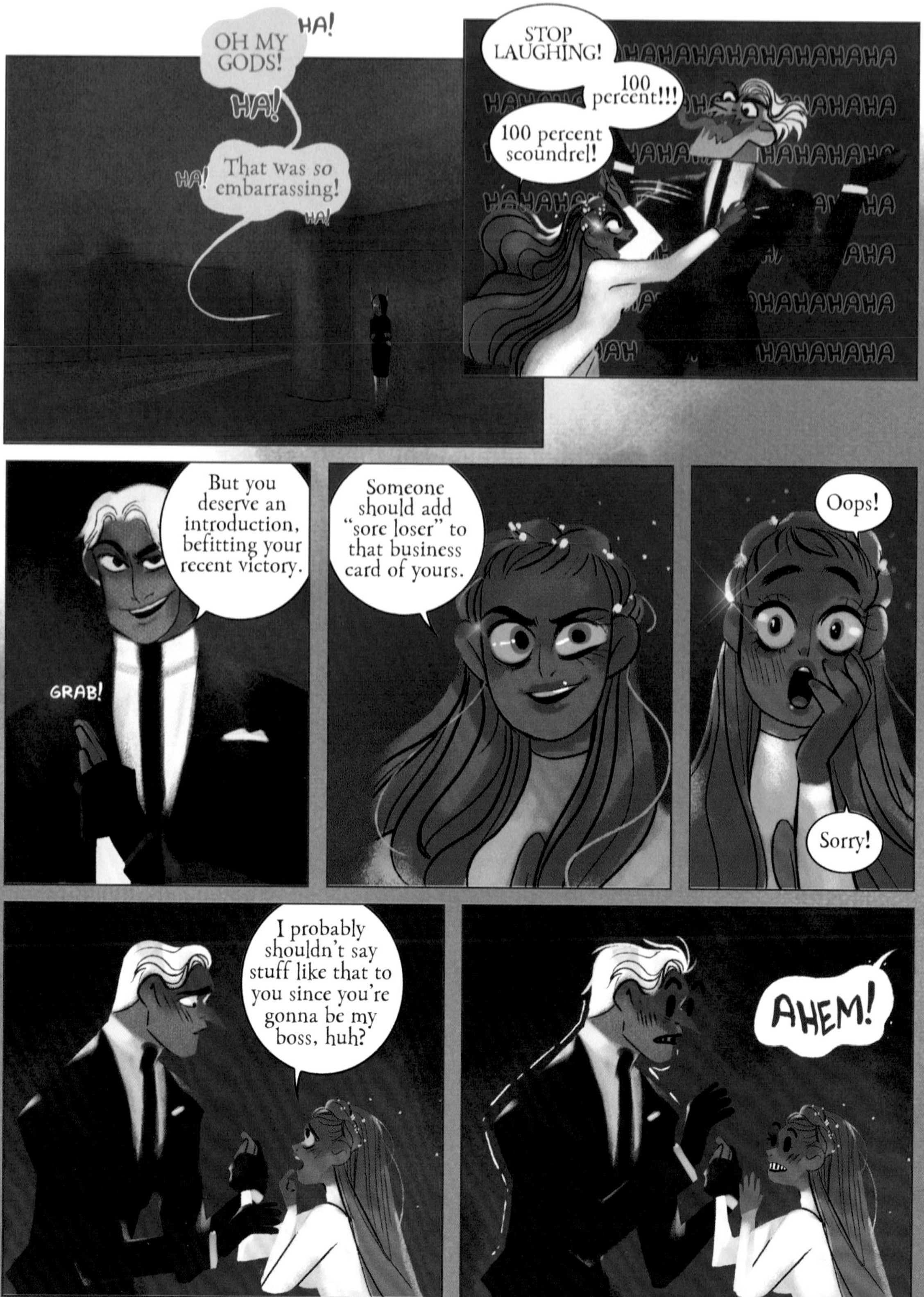
HA!
OH MY GODS!
HA!
HA!
That was *so* embarrassing!
HA!
STOP LAUGHING!
100 percent!!!
100 percent scoundrel!
But you deserve an introduction, befitting your recent victory.
GRAB!
Someone should add "sore loser" to that business card of yours.
Oops!
Sorry!
I probably shouldn't say stuff like that to you since you're gonna be my boss, huh?
AHEM!

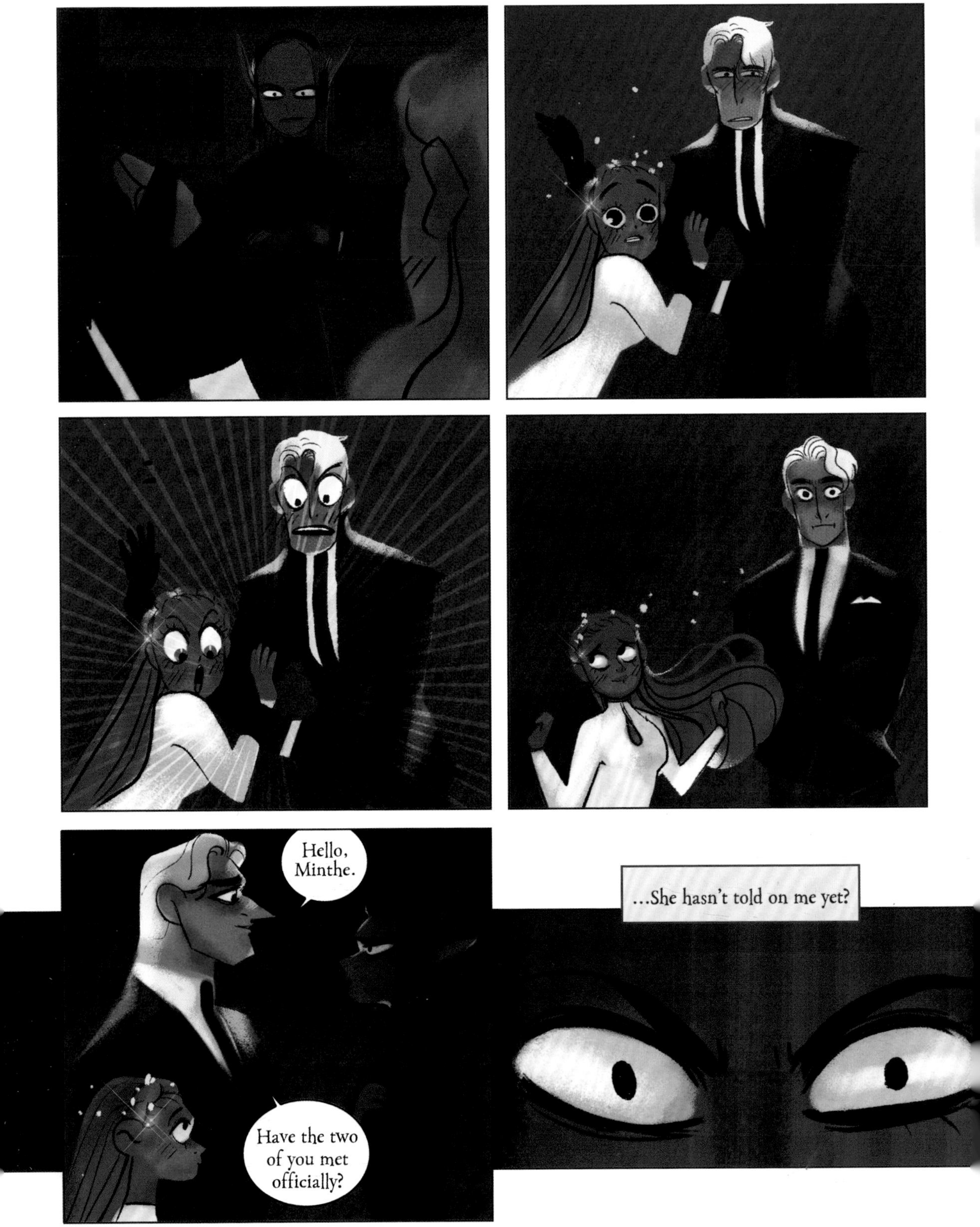
Hello, Minthe.
Have the two of you met officially?
...She hasn't told on me yet?

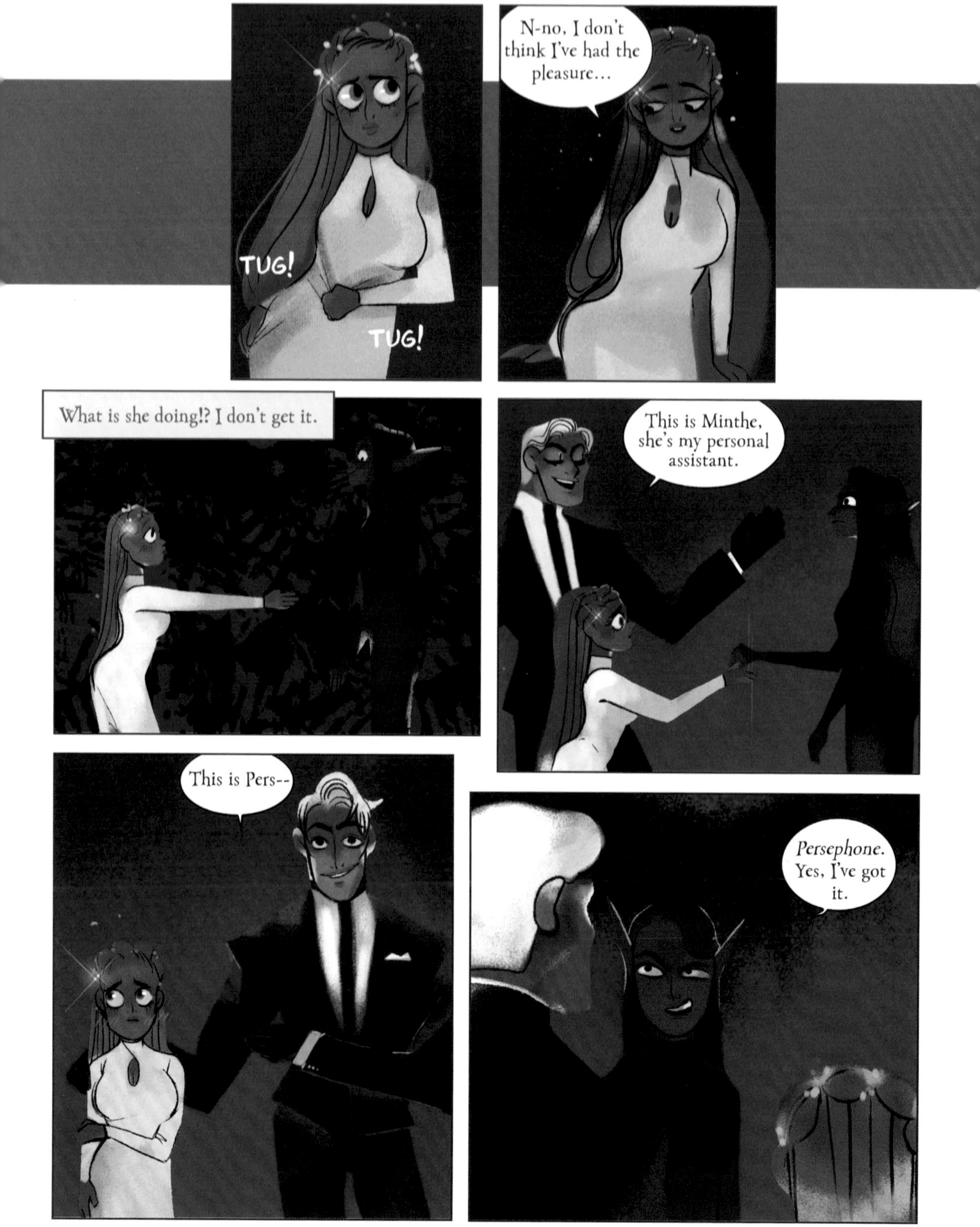
TUG!
TUG!
N-no, I don't think I've had the pleasure...
What is she doing!? I don't get it.
This is Minthe, she's my personal assistant.
This is Pers--
Persephone. Yes, I've got it.

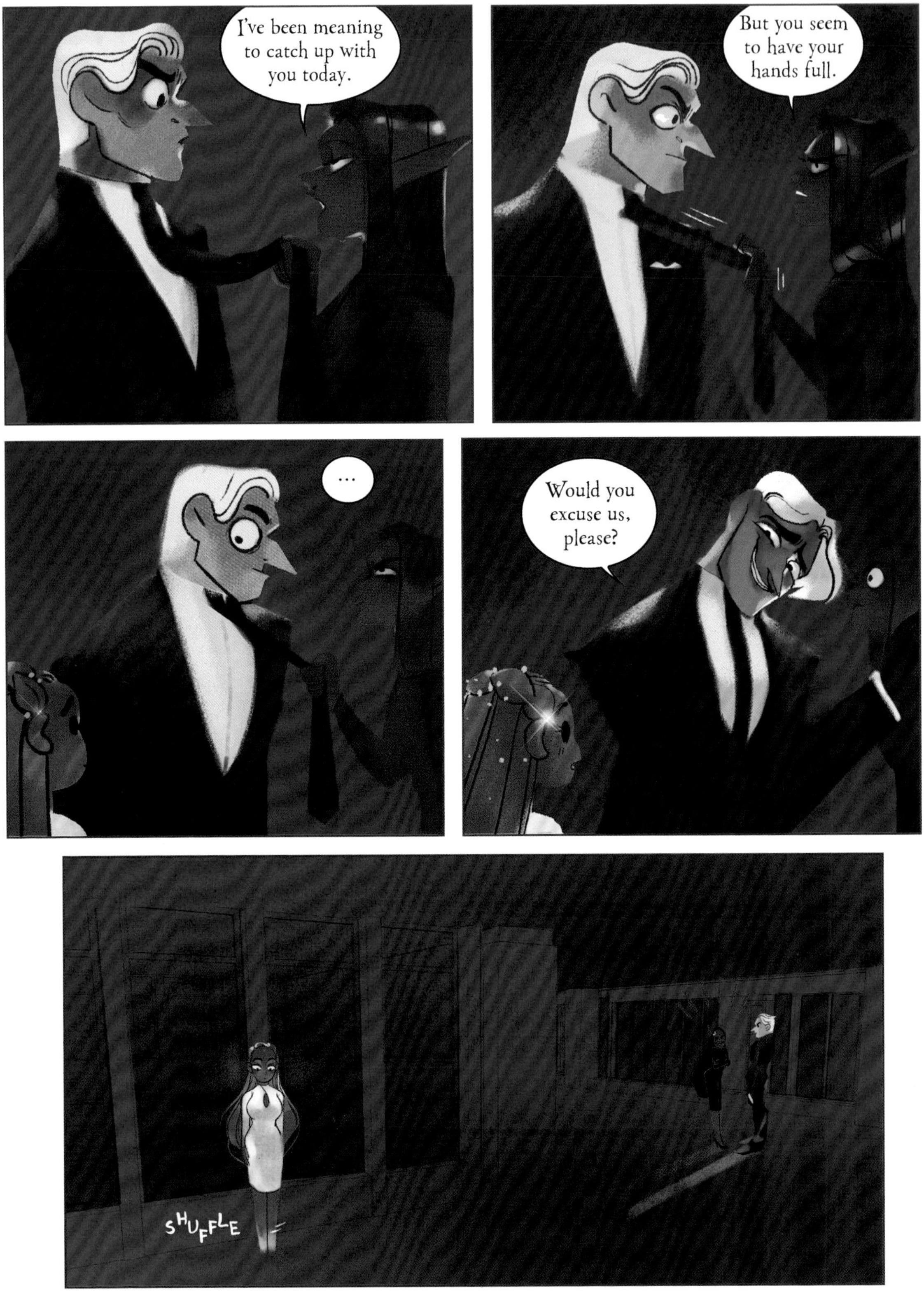
I've been meaning to catch up with you today.
But you seem to have your hands full.
...
Would you excuse us, please?
SHUFFLE

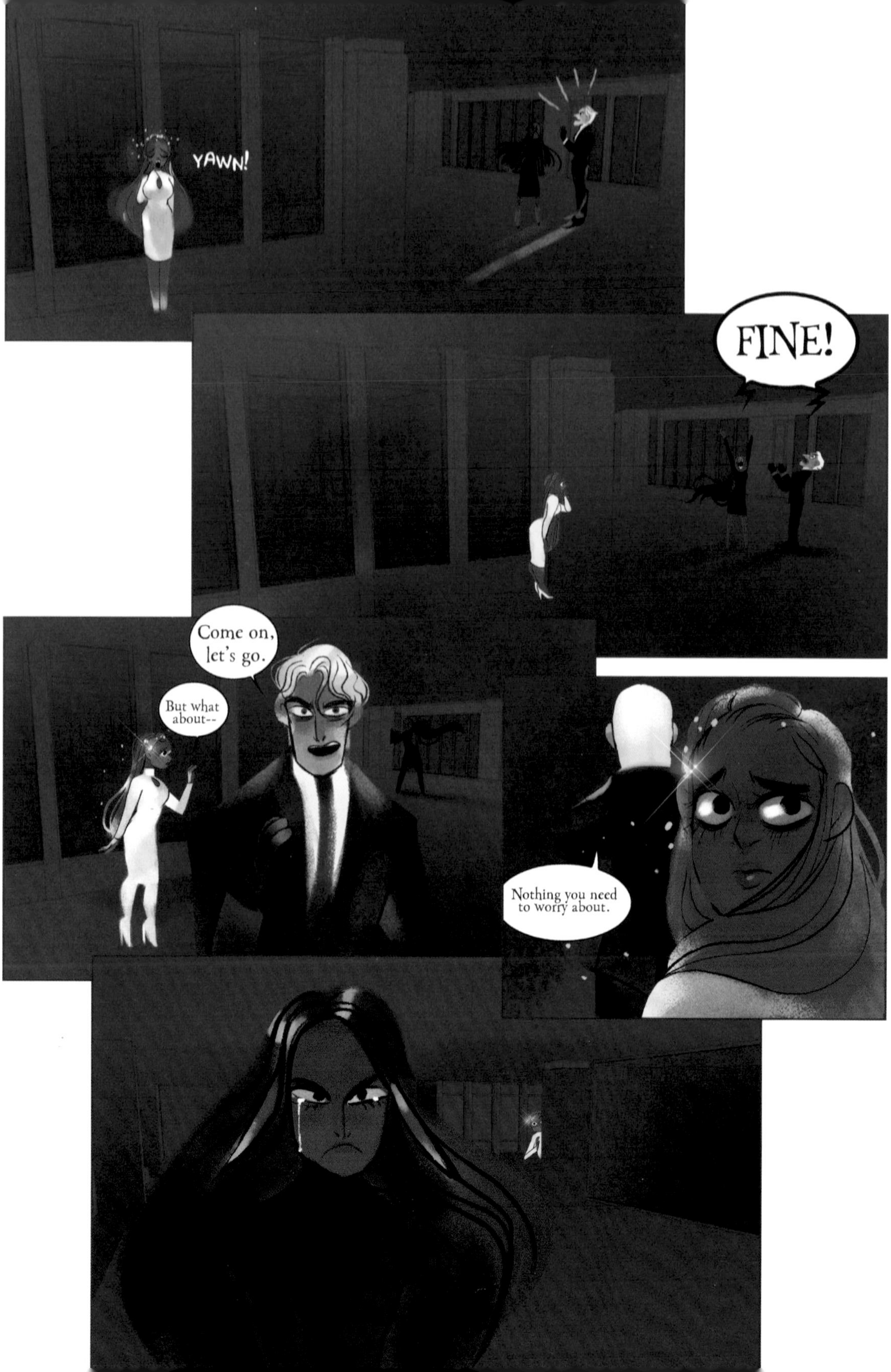
YAWN!
FINE!
Come on, let's go.
But what about--
Nothing you need to worry about.

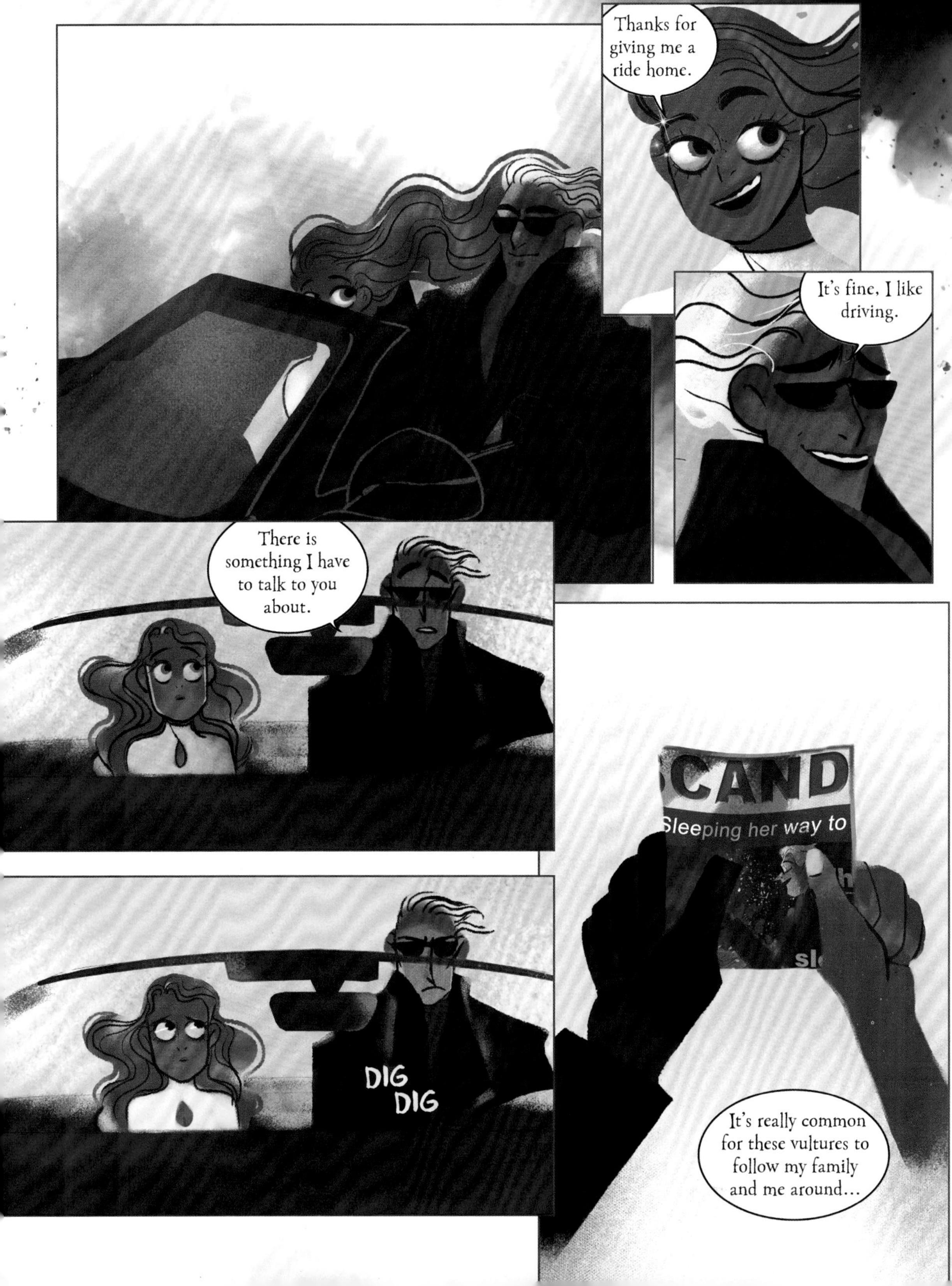
Thanks for giving me a ride home.
It's fine, I like driving.
There is something I have to talk to you about.
DIG DIG
CAND
Sleeping her way to
It's really common for these vultures to follow my family and me around...

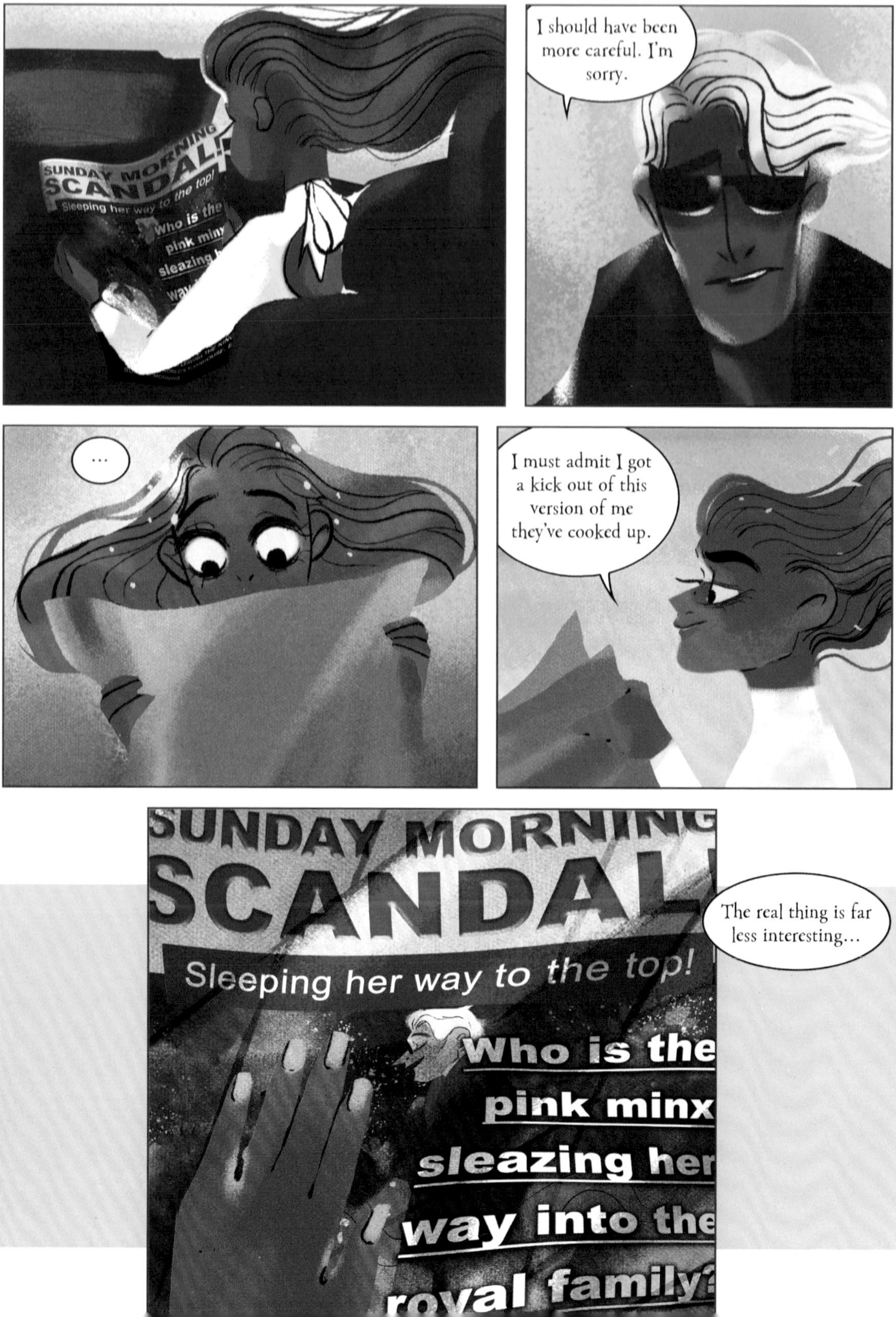
SUNDAY MORNING
SCANDAL!
Sleeping her way to the top!
I should have been more careful. I'm sorry.
...
I must admit I got a kick out of this version of me they've cooked up.
SUNDAY MORNING
SCANDAL
Sleeping her way to the top!
Who is the pink minx sleazing her way into the royal family?
The real thing is far less interesting...

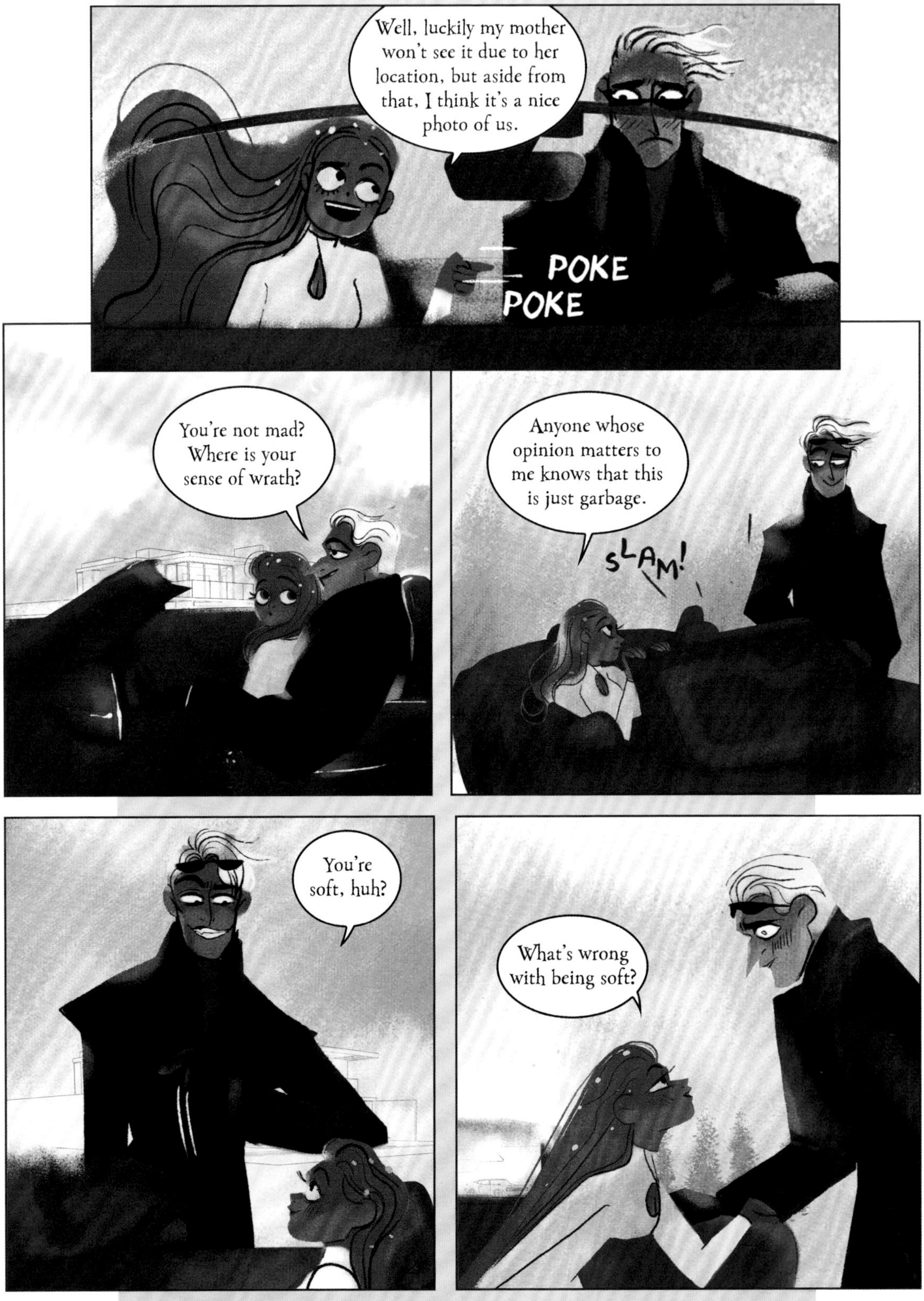
Well, luckily my mother won't see it due to her location, but aside from that, I think it's a nice photo of us.
POKE
POKE
You're not mad? Where is your sense of wrath?
Anyone whose opinion matters to me knows that this is just garbage.
SLAM!
You're soft, huh?
What's wrong with being soft?

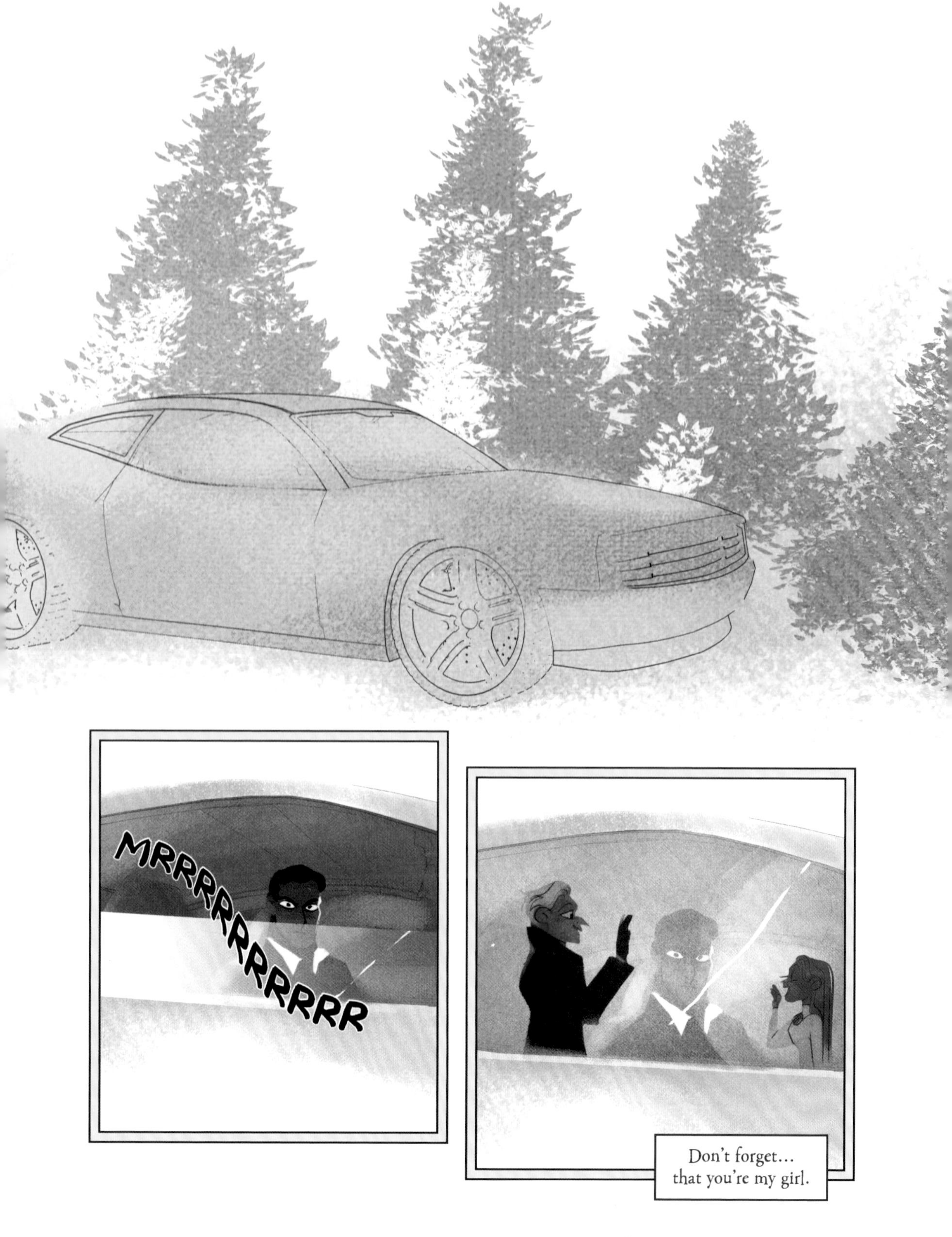
MRRRRRRRRRRRRRR
Don't forget...
that you're my girl.

EPISODE 45: CRUSHED

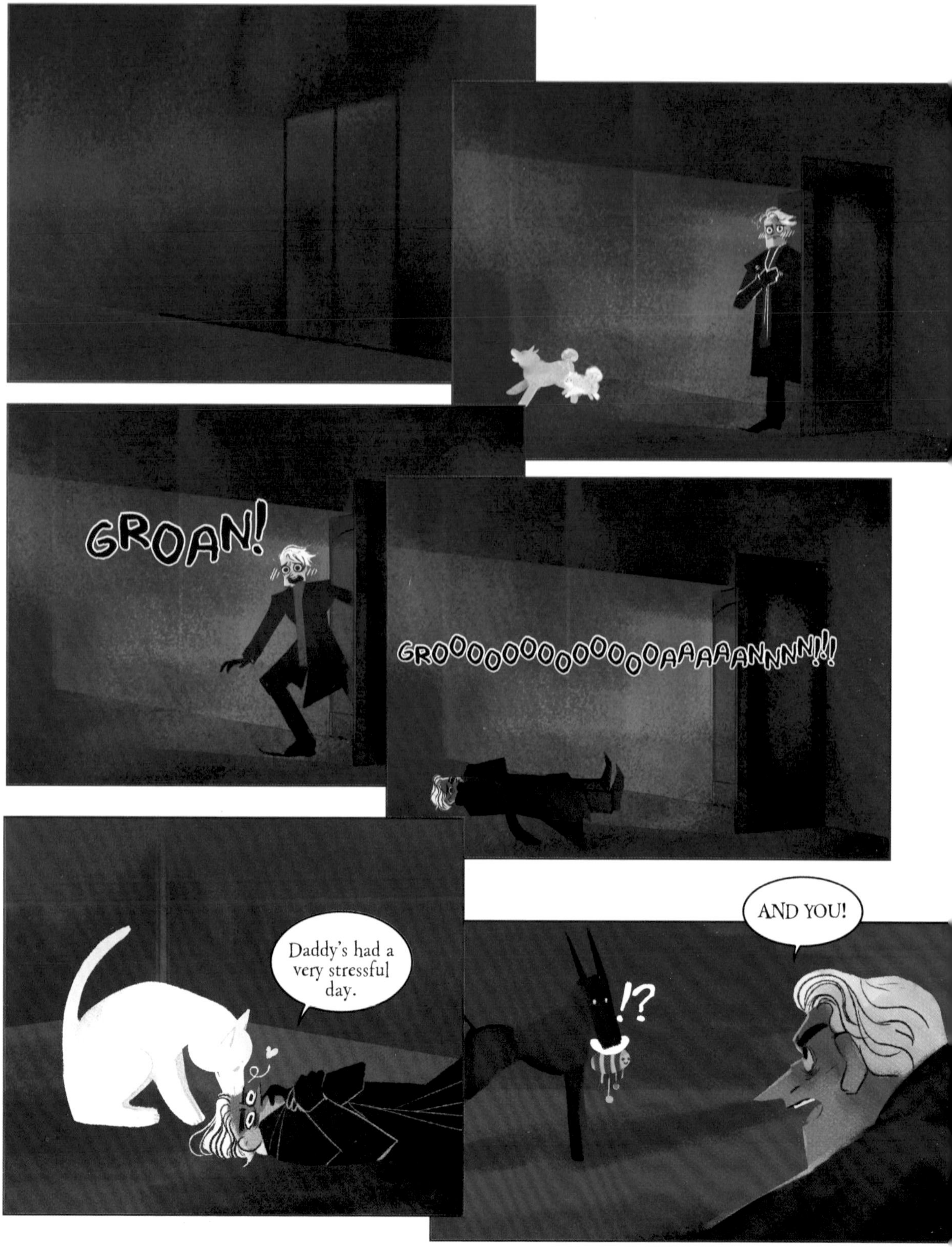
GROAN!
GROOOOOOOOOOOOOOOAAAAANNNN!!!
Daddy's had a very stressful day.
AND YOU!
!?

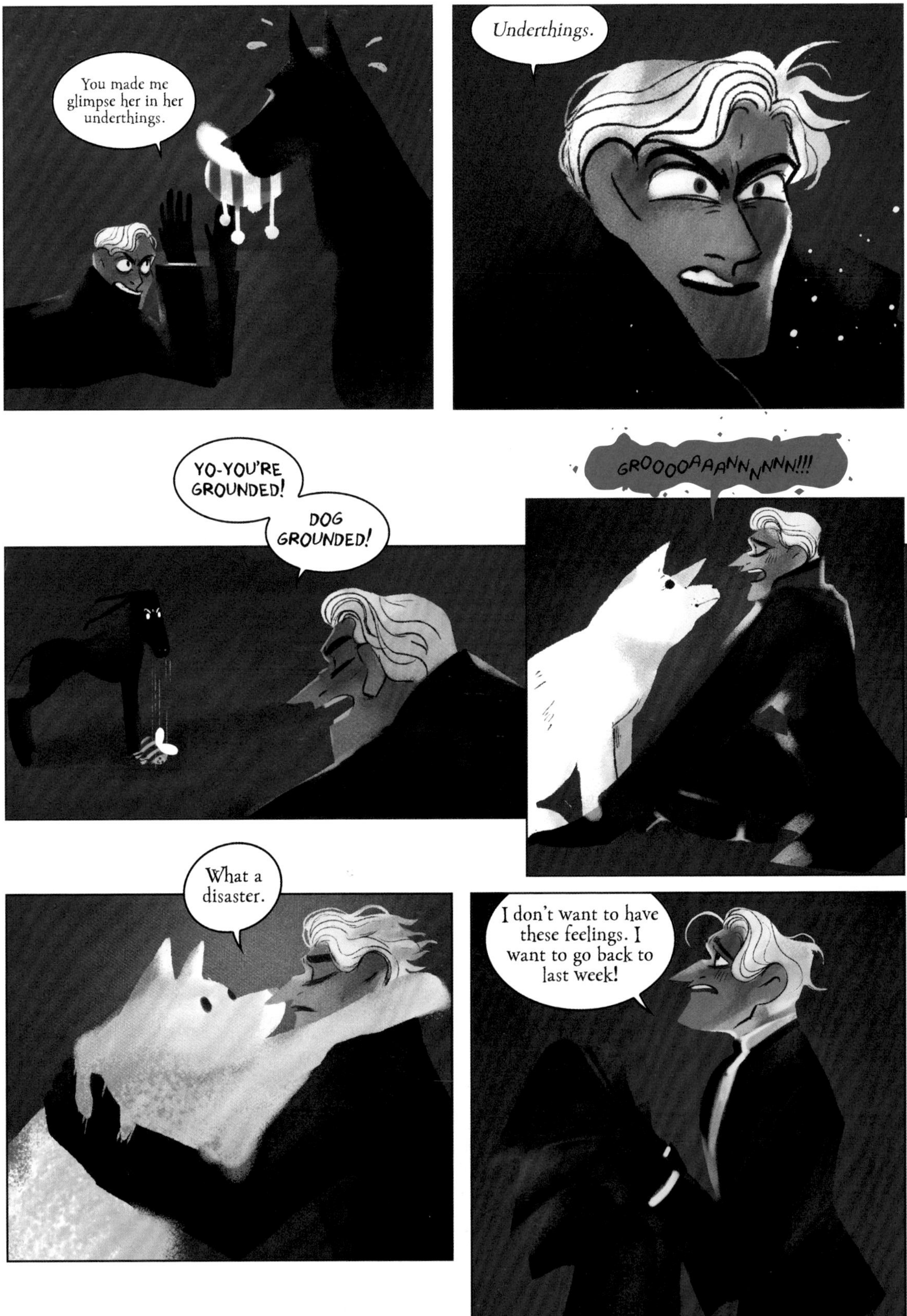

You made me glimpse her in her underthings.
Underthings.
YO-YOU'RE GROUNDED!
DOG GROUNDED!
GROOOOAAANNNNNN!!!
What a disaster.
I don't want to have these feelings. I want to go back to last week!

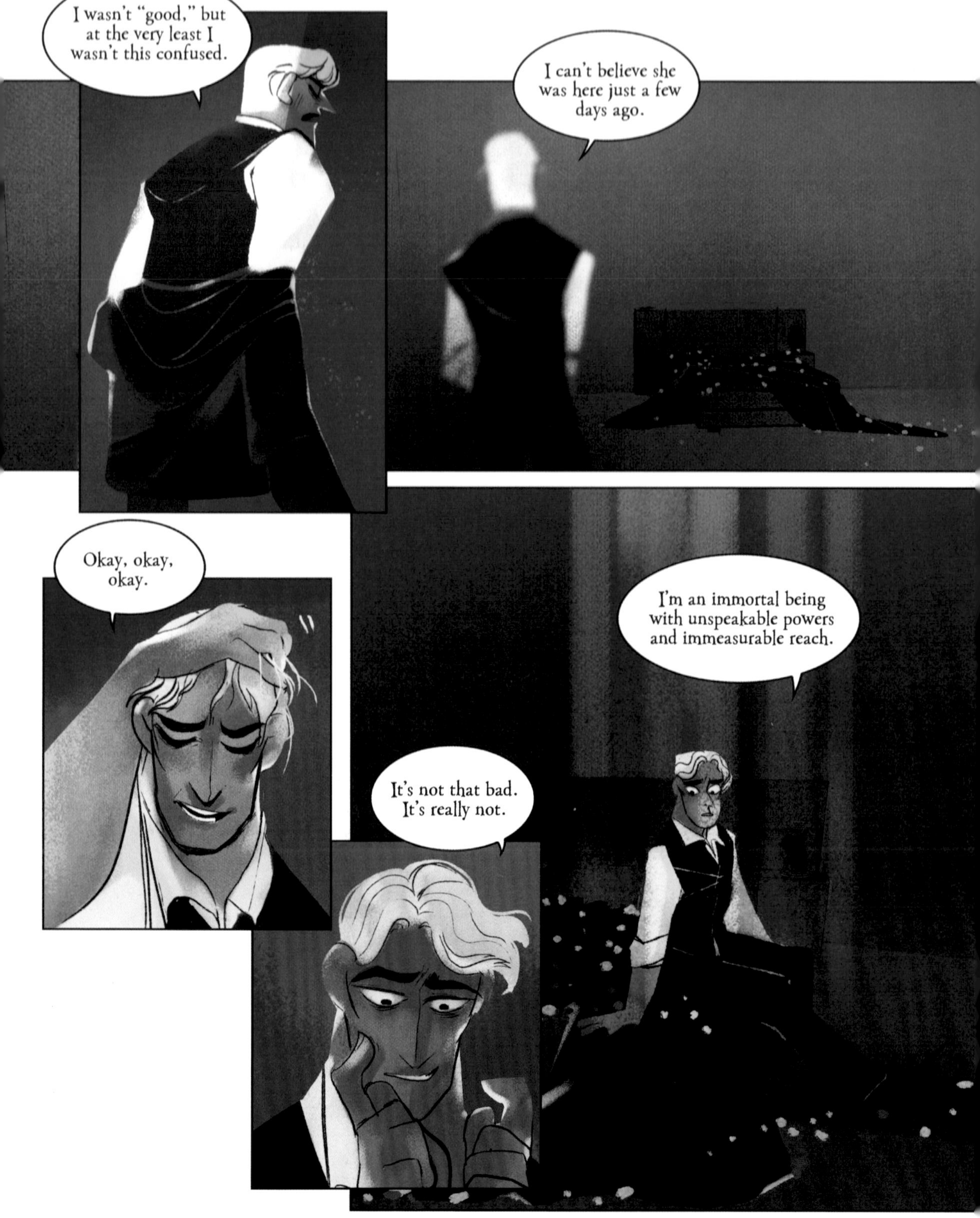
I wasn't "good," but at the very least I wasn't this confused.
I can't believe she was here just a few days ago.
Okay, okay, okay.
I'm an immortal being with unspeakable powers and immeasurable reach.
It's not that bad. It's really not.

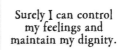

Surely I can control my feelings and maintain my dignity.

PULL

She's not *that* great.

She just makes me feel all warm and snuggly inside when I think about her.

Do I even like feeling warm and snuggly?

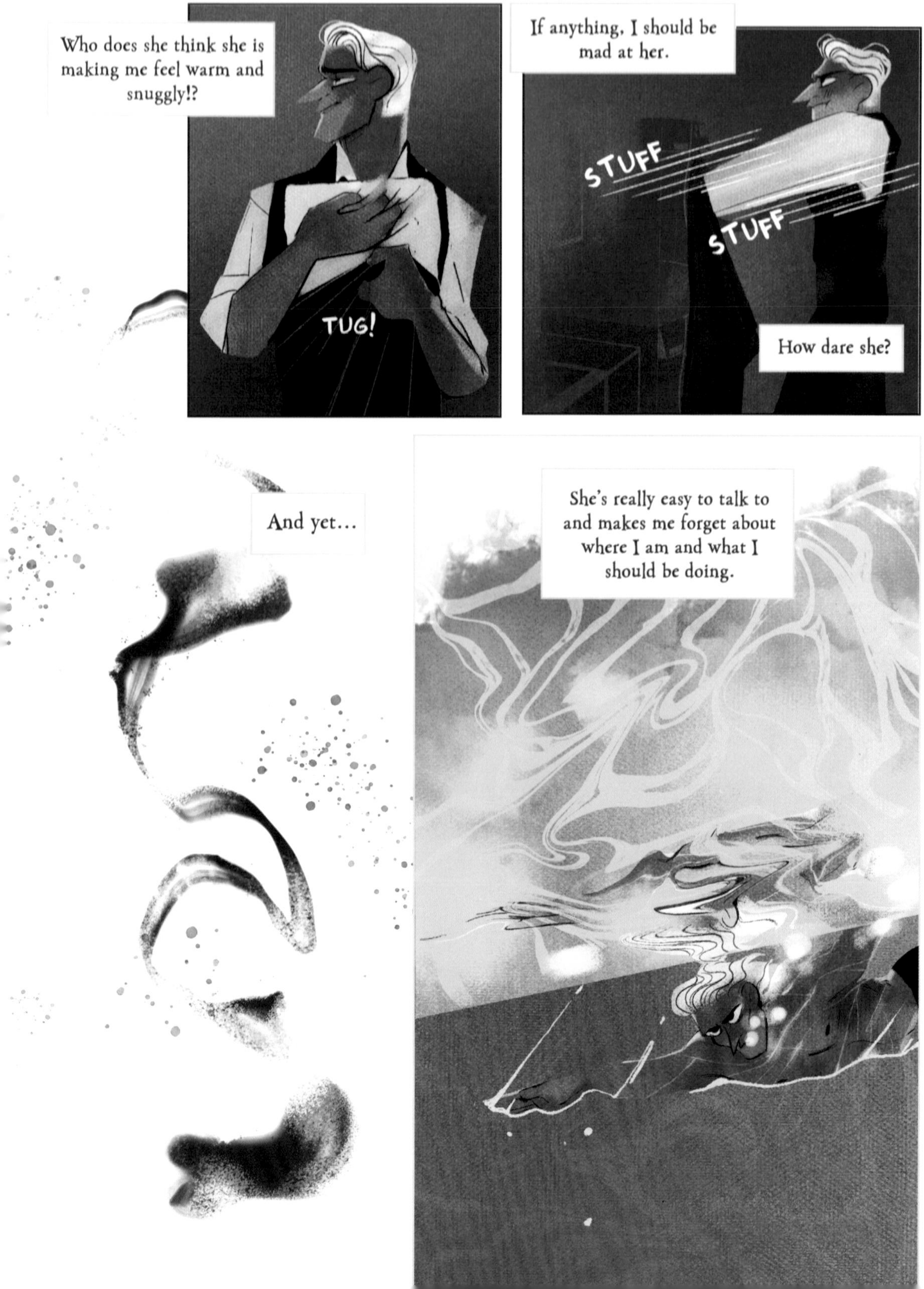
Who does she think she is making me feel warm and snuggly!?
TUG!
If anything, I should be mad at her.
STUFF
STUFF
How dare she?
And yet...
She's really easy to talk to and makes me forget about where I am and what I should be doing.

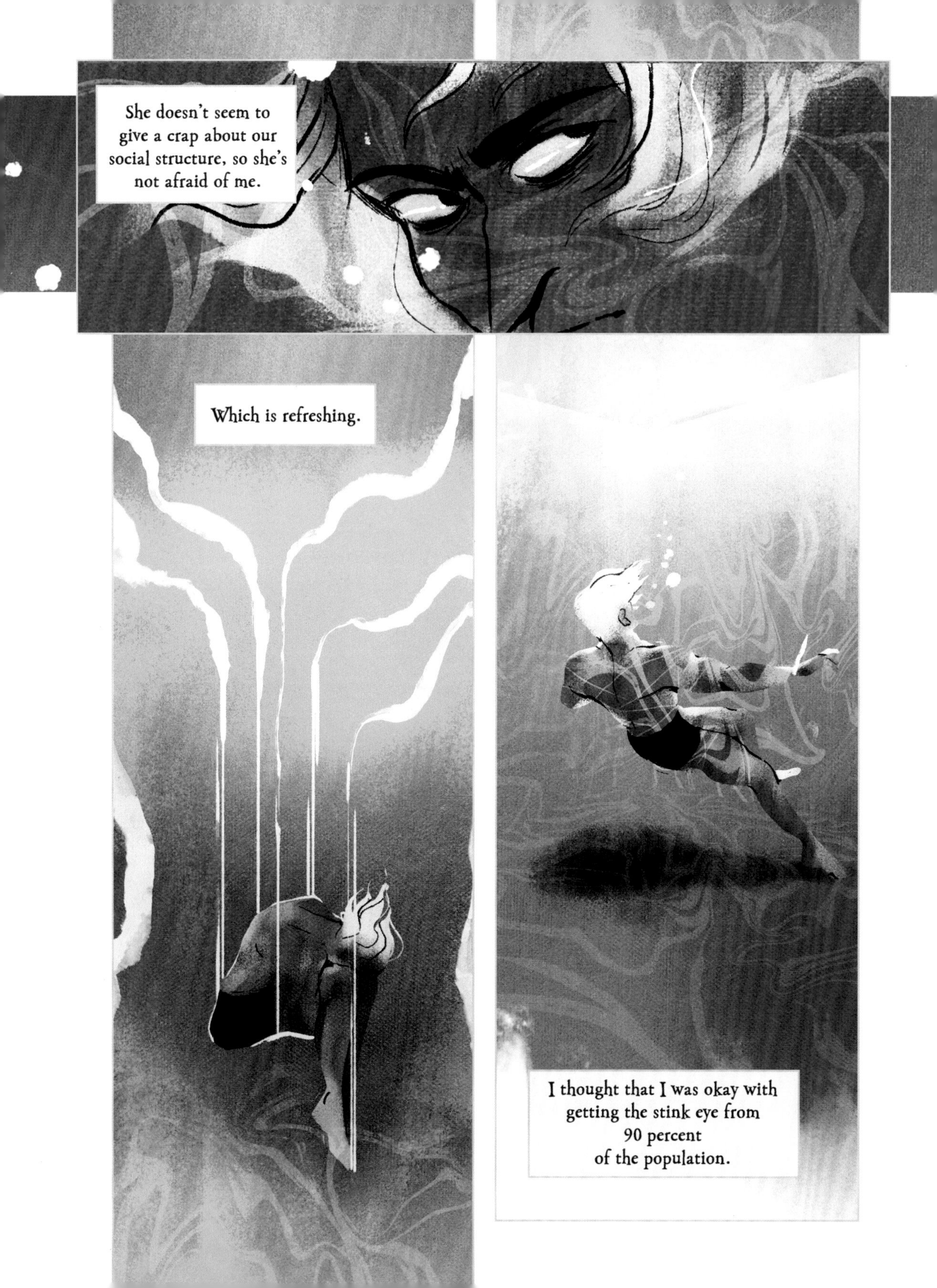
She doesn't seem to give a crap about our social structure, so she's not afraid of me.
Which is refreshing.
I thought that I was okay with getting the stink eye from 90 percent of the population.

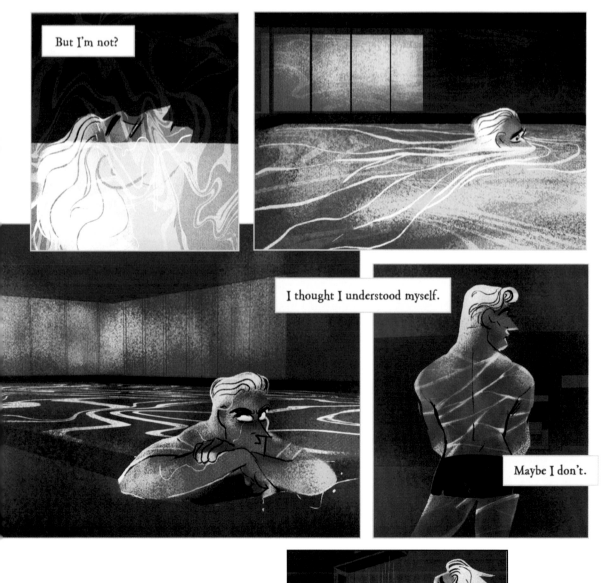

But I'm not?

I thought I understood myself.

Maybe I don't.

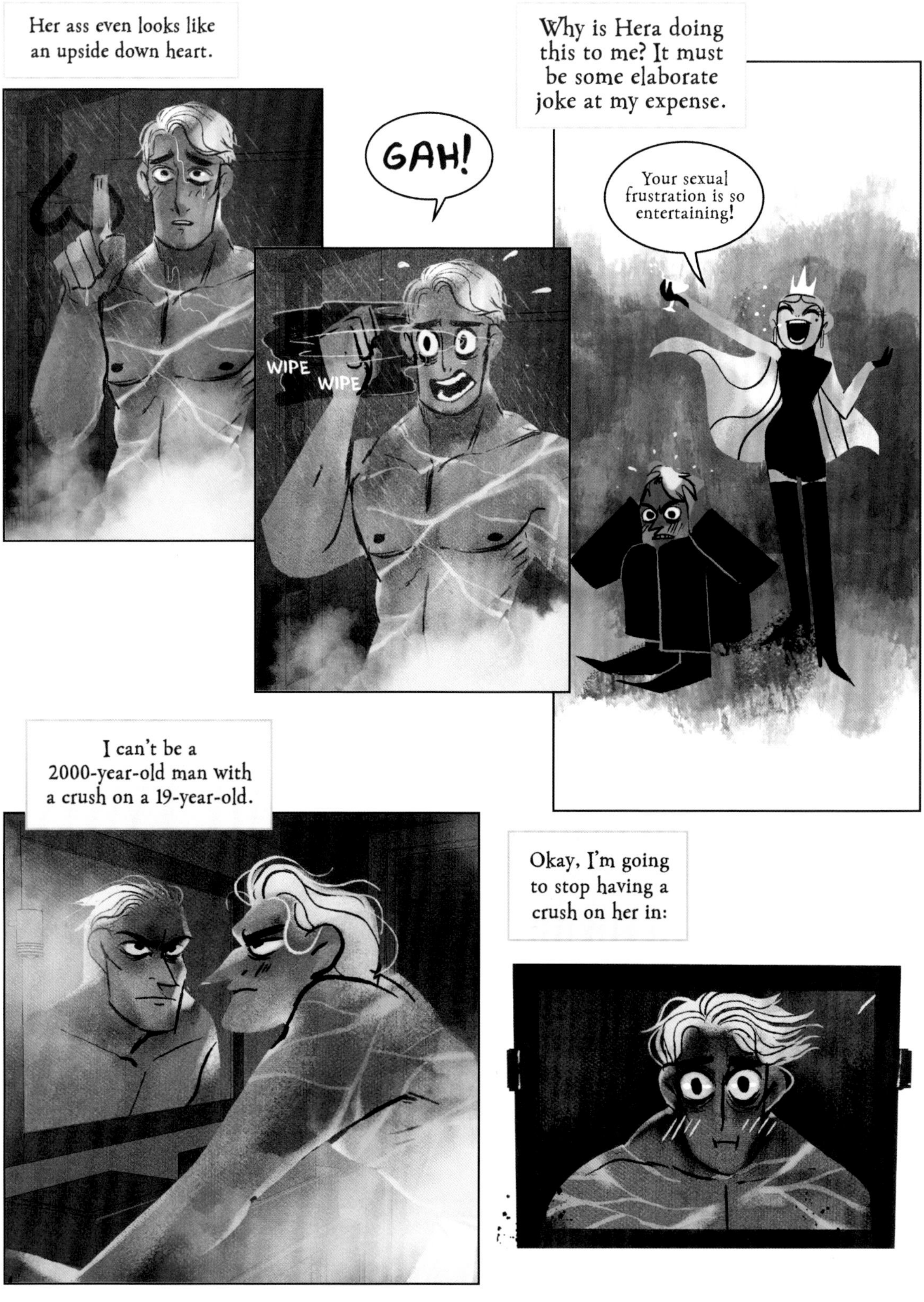
Her ass even looks like an upside down heart.
GAH!
WIPE
WIPE
Why is Hera doing this to me? It must be some elaborate joke at my expense.
Your sexual frustration is so entertaining!
I can't be a 2000-year-old man with a crush on a 19-year-old.
Okay, I'm going to stop having a crush on her in:

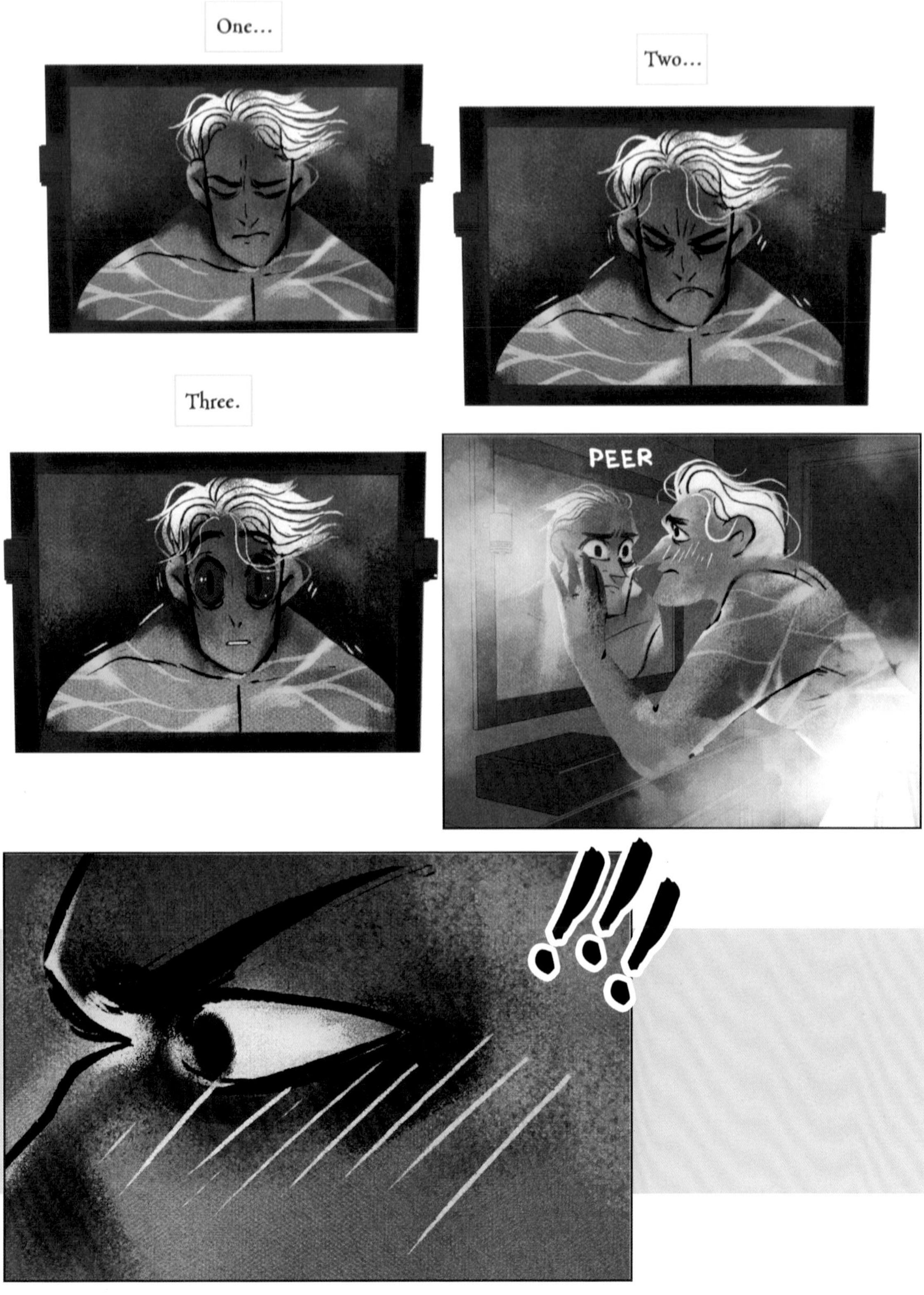
One...
Two...
Three.
PEER
!!!

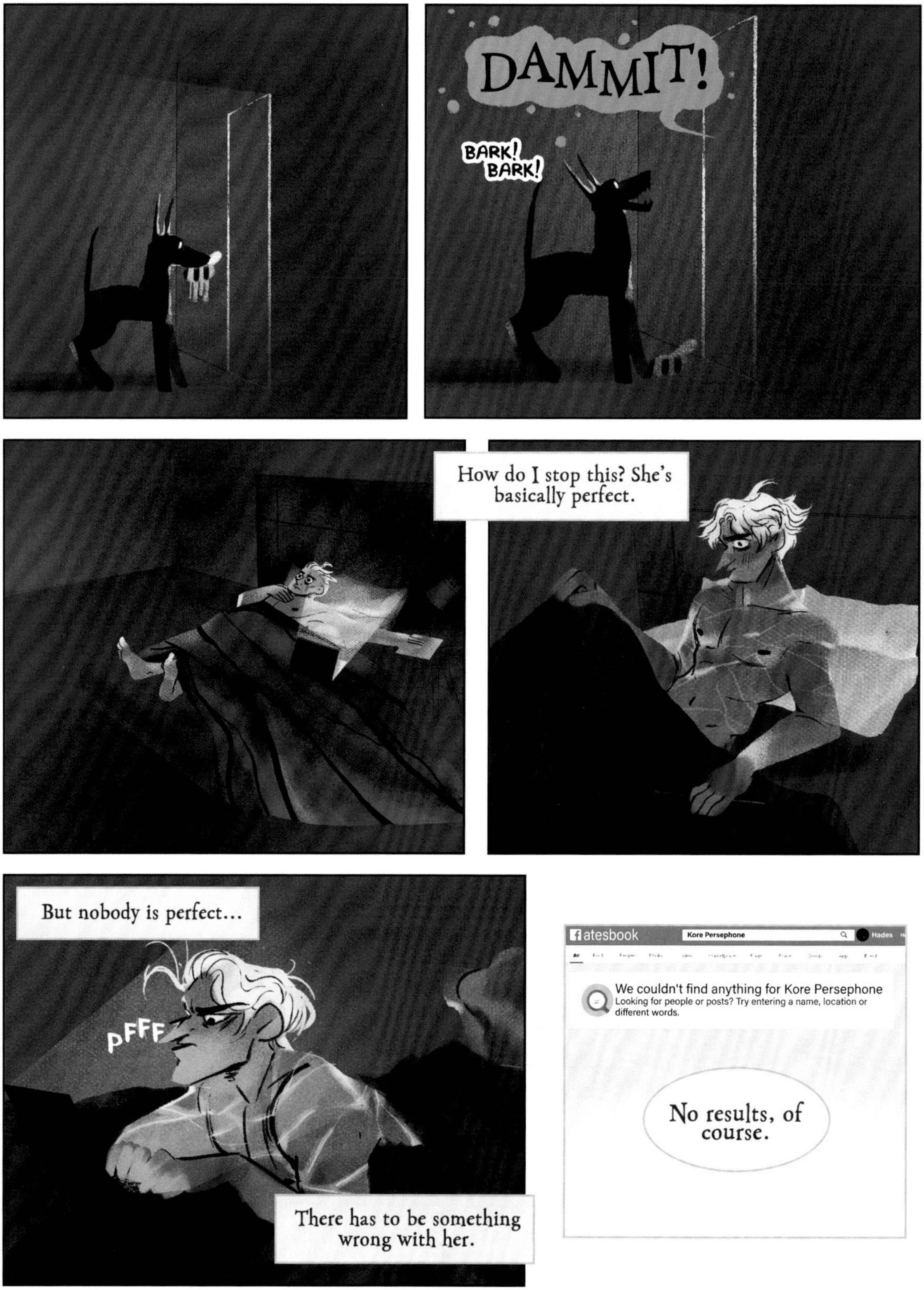
DAMMIT!
BARK! BARK!
How do I stop this? She's basically perfect.
But nobody is perfect...
PFFF
There has to be something wrong with her.
fatesbook
Kore Persephone
Hades
We couldn't find anything for Kore Persephone
Looking for people or posts? Try entering a name, location or different words.
No results, of course.

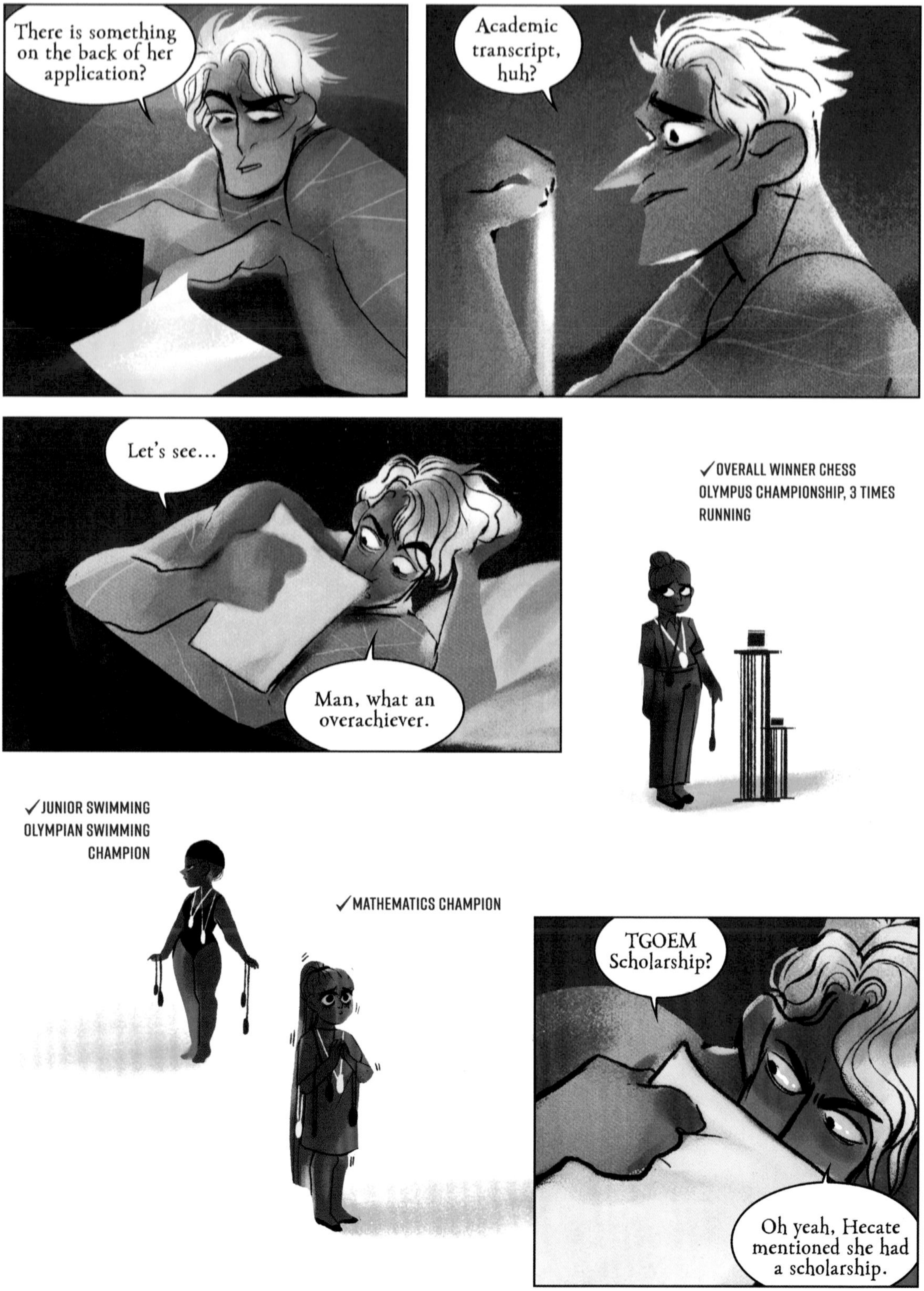
There is something on the back of her application?
Academic transcript, huh?
Let's see...
Man, what an overachiever.
✓OVERALL WINNER CHESS OLYMPUS CHAMPIONSHIP, 3 TIMES RUNNING
✓JUNIOR SWIMMING OLYMPIAN SWIMMING CHAMPION
✓MATHEMATICS CHAMPION
TGOEM Scholarship?
Oh yeah, Hecate mentioned she had a scholarship.

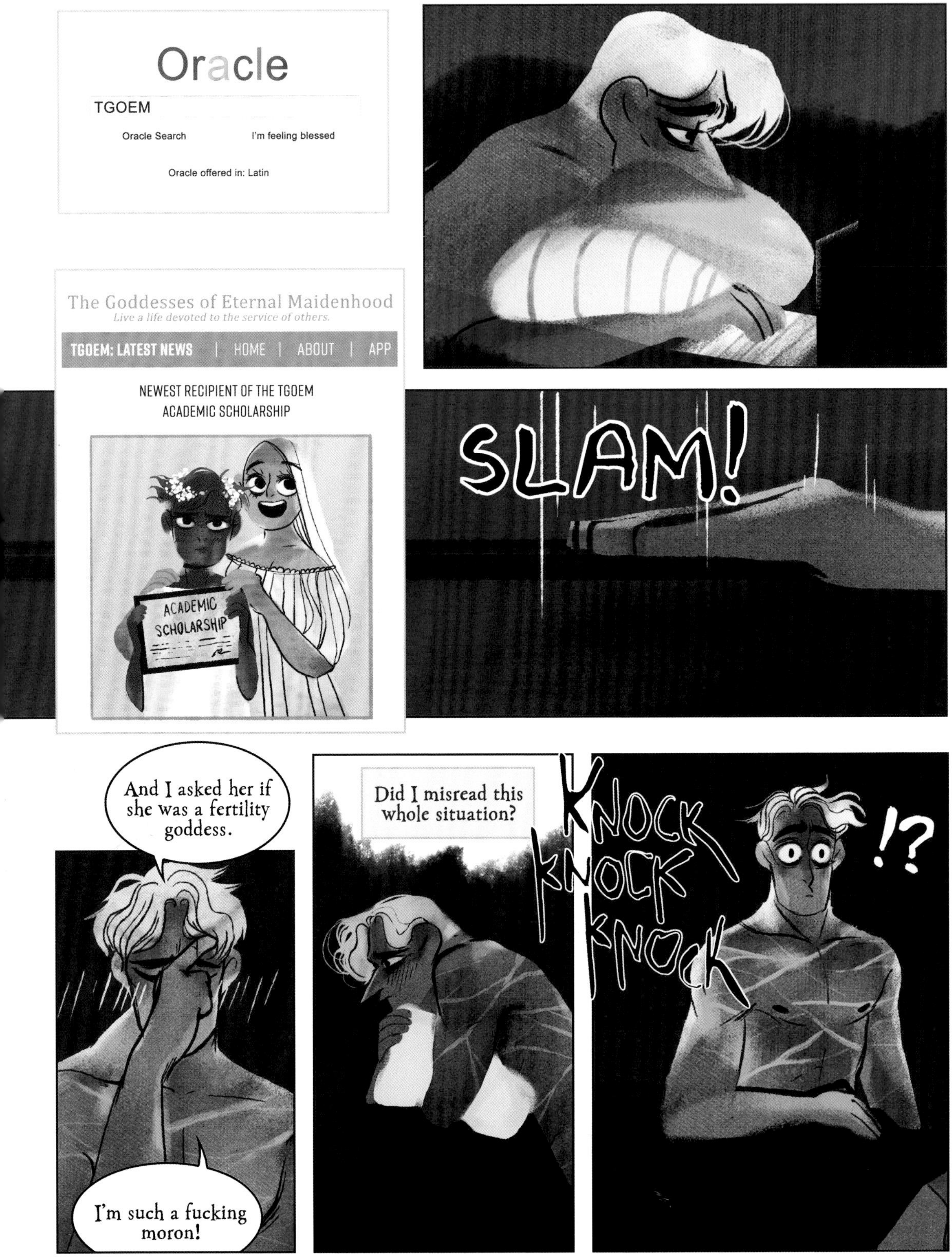
Oracle
TGOEM
Oracle Search
I'm feeling blessed
Oracle offered in: Latin
The Goddesses of Eternal Maidenhood
Live a life devoted to the service of others.
TGOEM: LATEST NEWS | HOME | ABOUT | APP
NEWEST RECIPIENT OF THE TGOEM ACADEMIC SCHOLARSHIP
ACADEMIC SCHOLARSHIP
SLAM!
And I asked her if she was a fertility goddess.
I'm such a fucking moron!
Did I misread this whole situation?
KNOCK KNOCK KNOCK
!?

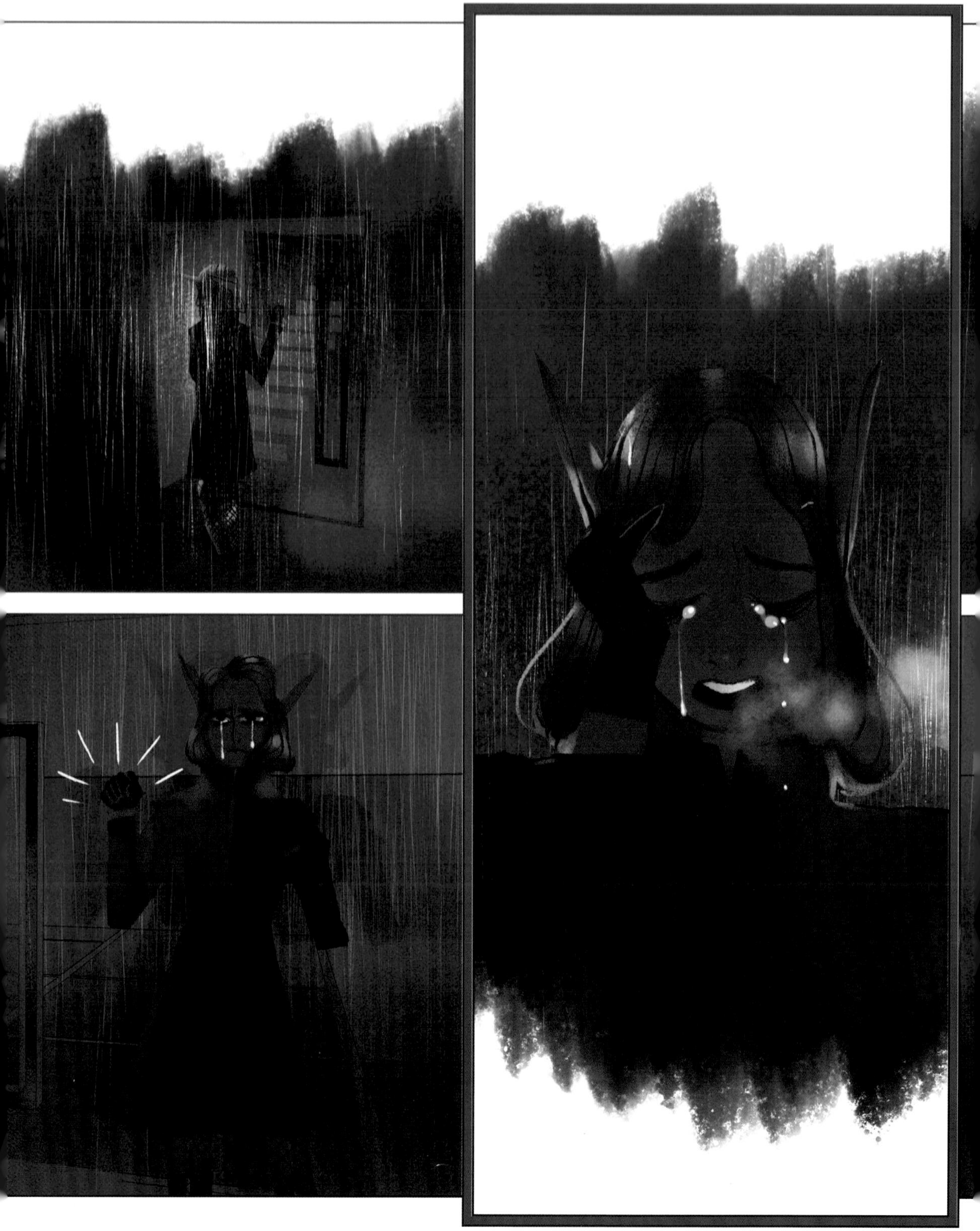

4 DAYS AGO!
(THE DAY OF THE PARTY)

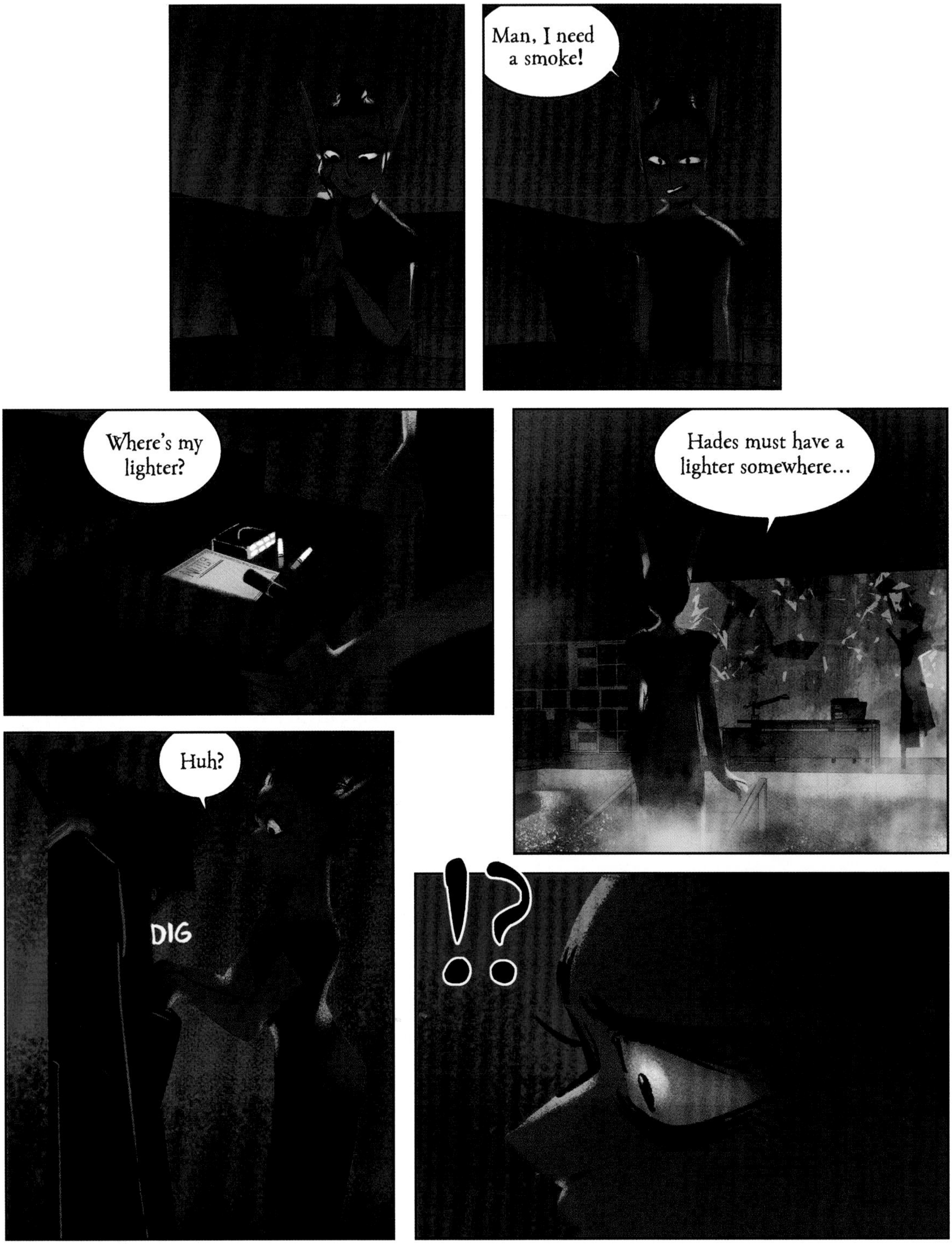
Man, I need a smoke!
Where's my lighter?
Hades must have a lighter somewhere...
Huh?
DIG
!?

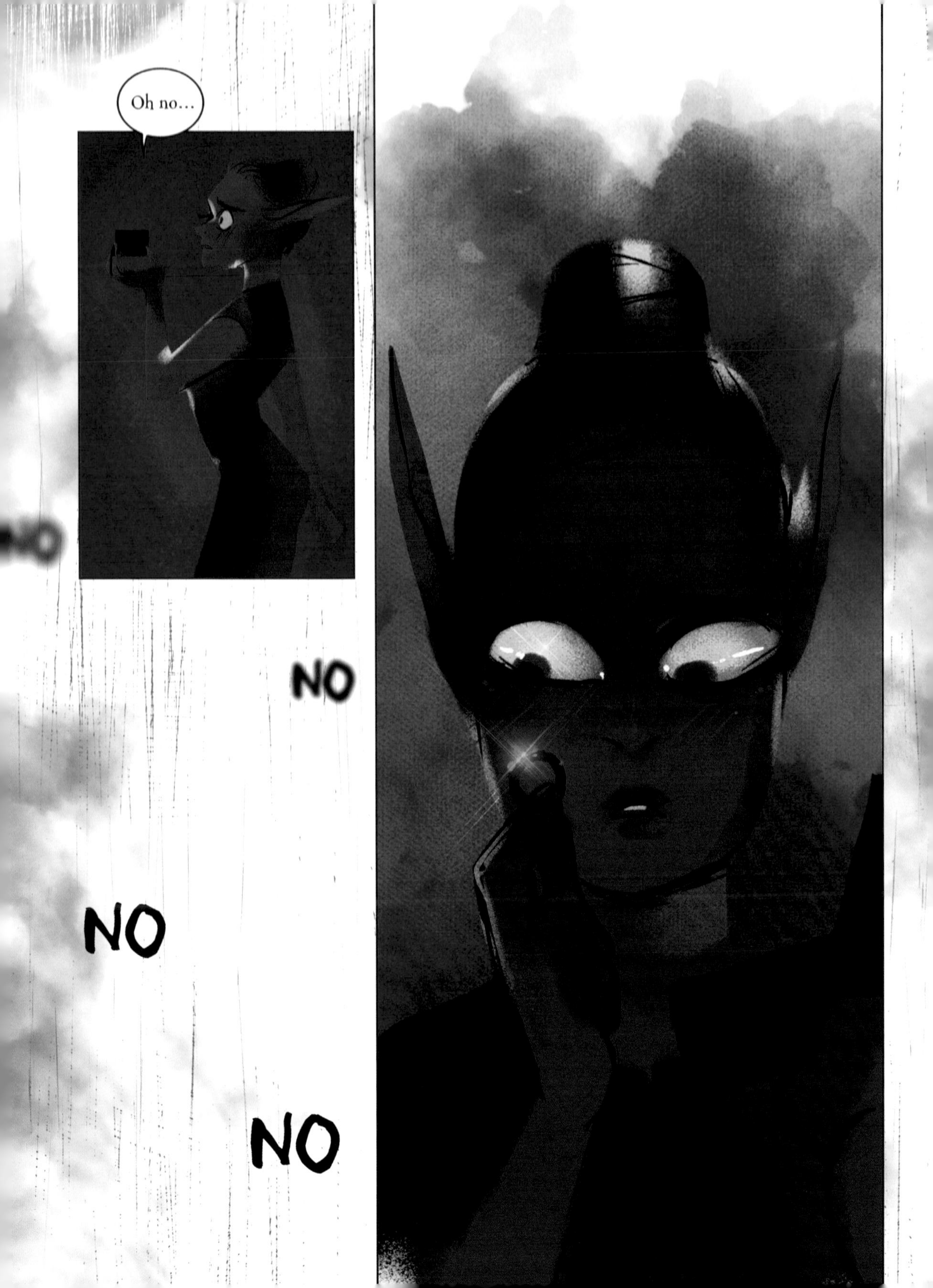
Oh no…
NO
NO
NO

EPISODE 46: RED RAW

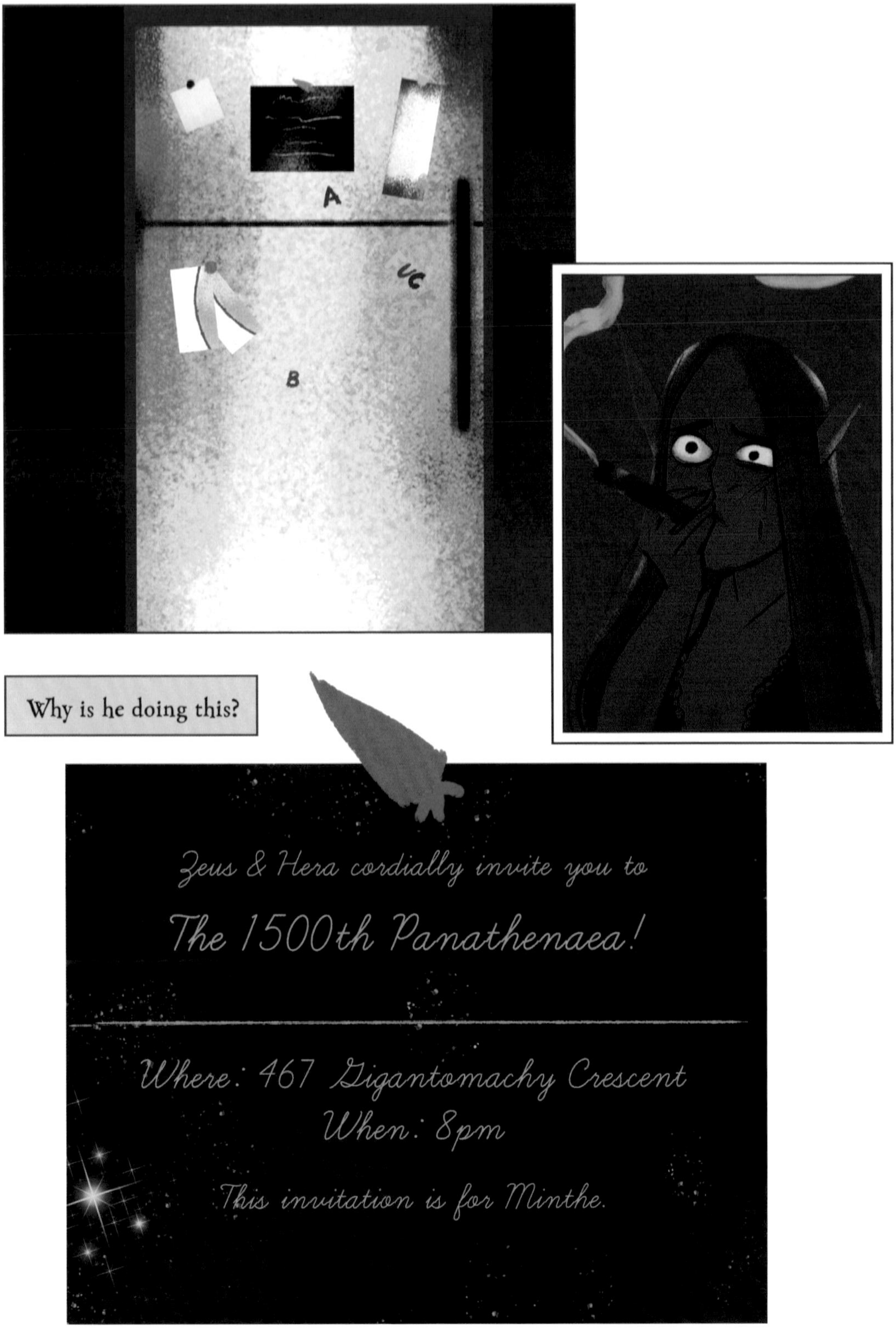
Why is he doing this?
Zeus & Hera cordially invite you to
The 1500th Panathenaea!
Where: 467 Gigantomachy Crescent
When: 8pm
This invitation is for Minthe.

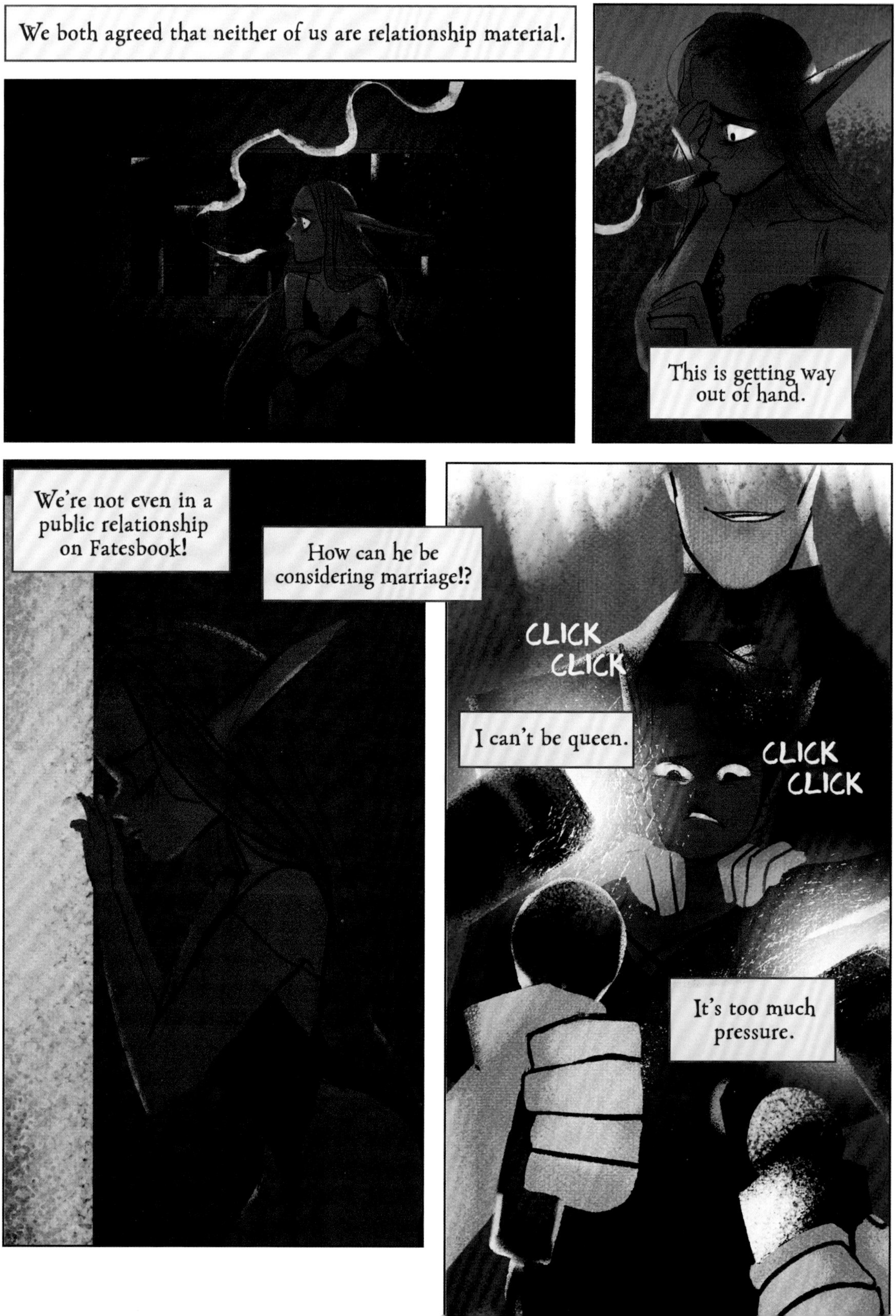
We both agreed that neither of us are relationship material.
This is getting way out of hand.
We're not even in a public relationship on Fatesbook!
How can he be considering marriage!?
CLICK CLICK
I can't be queen.
CLICK CLICK
It's too much pressure.

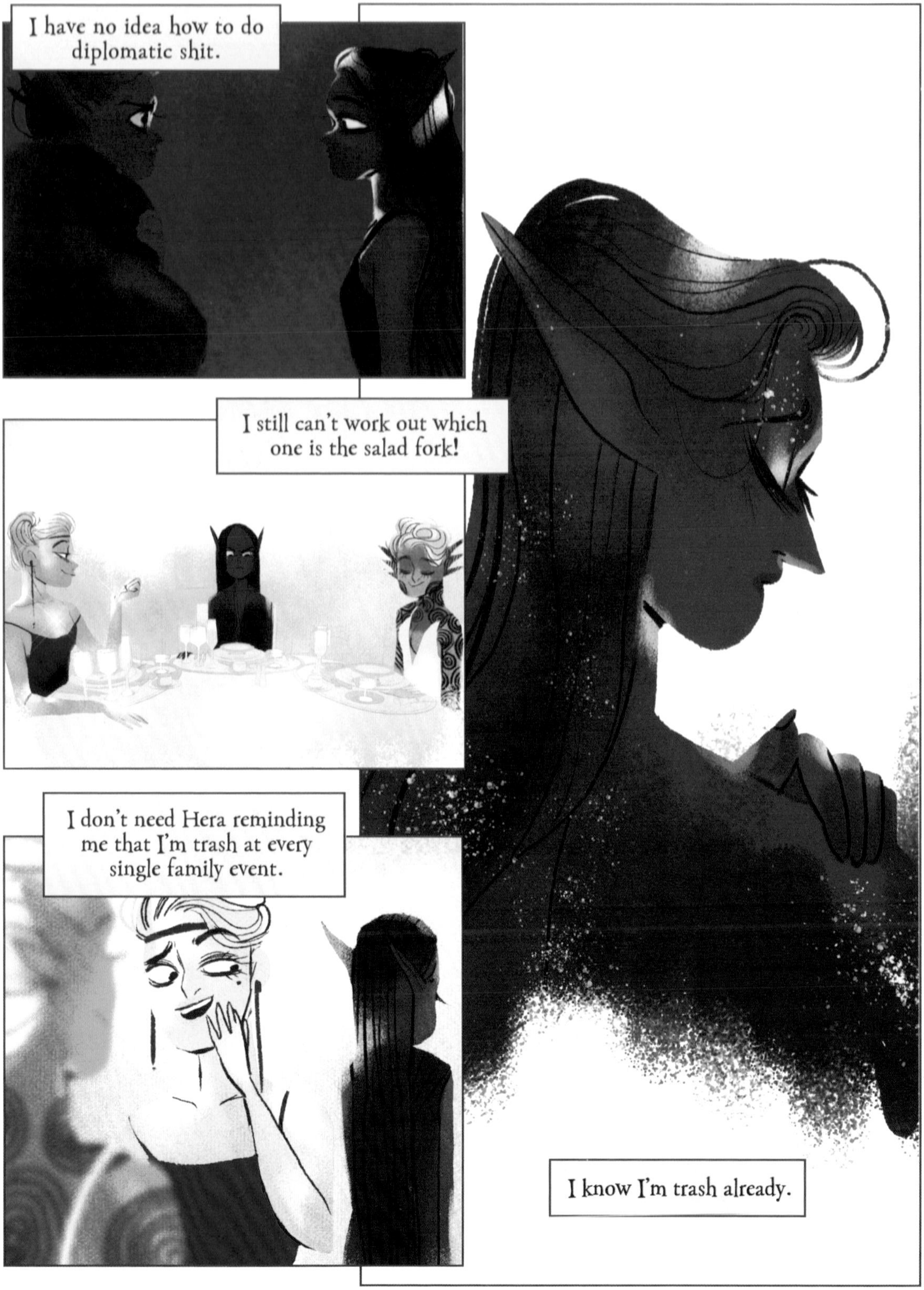
I have no idea how to do diplomatic shit.
I still can't work out which one is the salad fork!
I don't need Hera reminding me that I'm trash at every single family event.
I know I'm trash already.

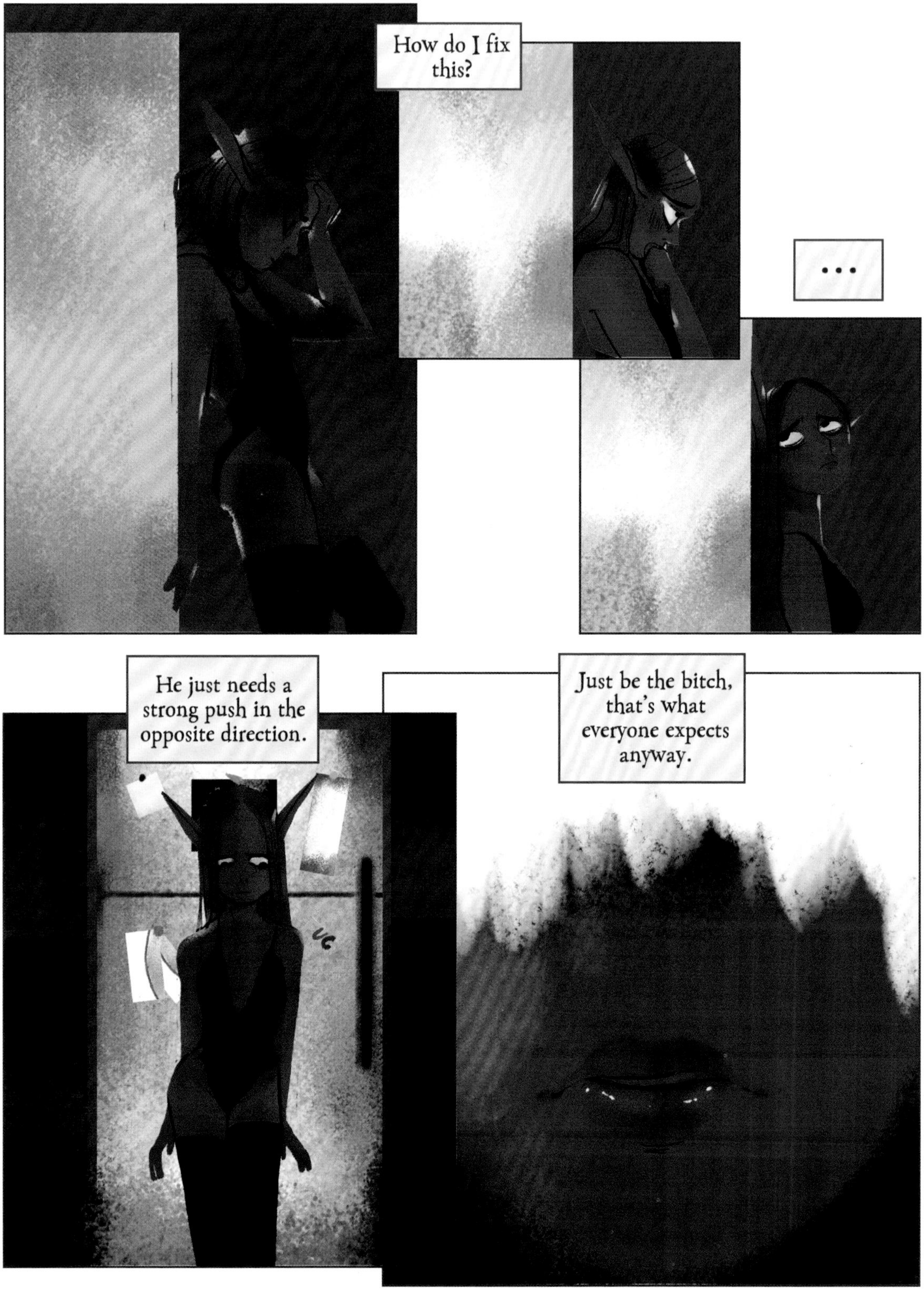
How do I fix this?
...
He just needs a strong push in the opposite direction.
Just be the bitch, that's what everyone expects anyway.

PRESENT DAY

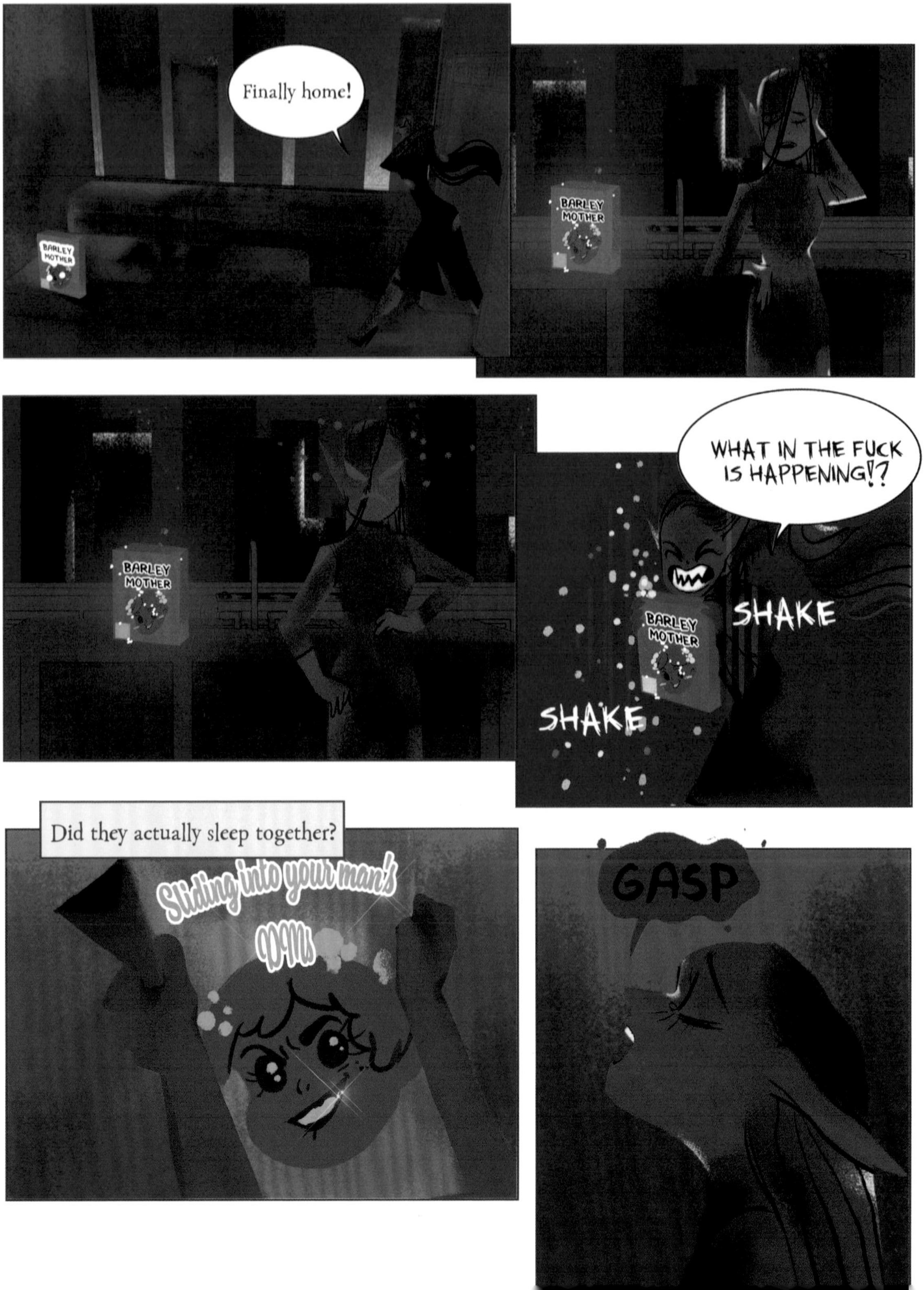
Finally home!
BARLEY MOTHER
BARLEY MOTHER
BARLEY MOTHER
WHAT IN THE FUCK IS HAPPENING!?
SHAKE
SHAKE
BARLEY MOTHER
Did they actually sleep together?
Sliding into your man's DMs
GASP

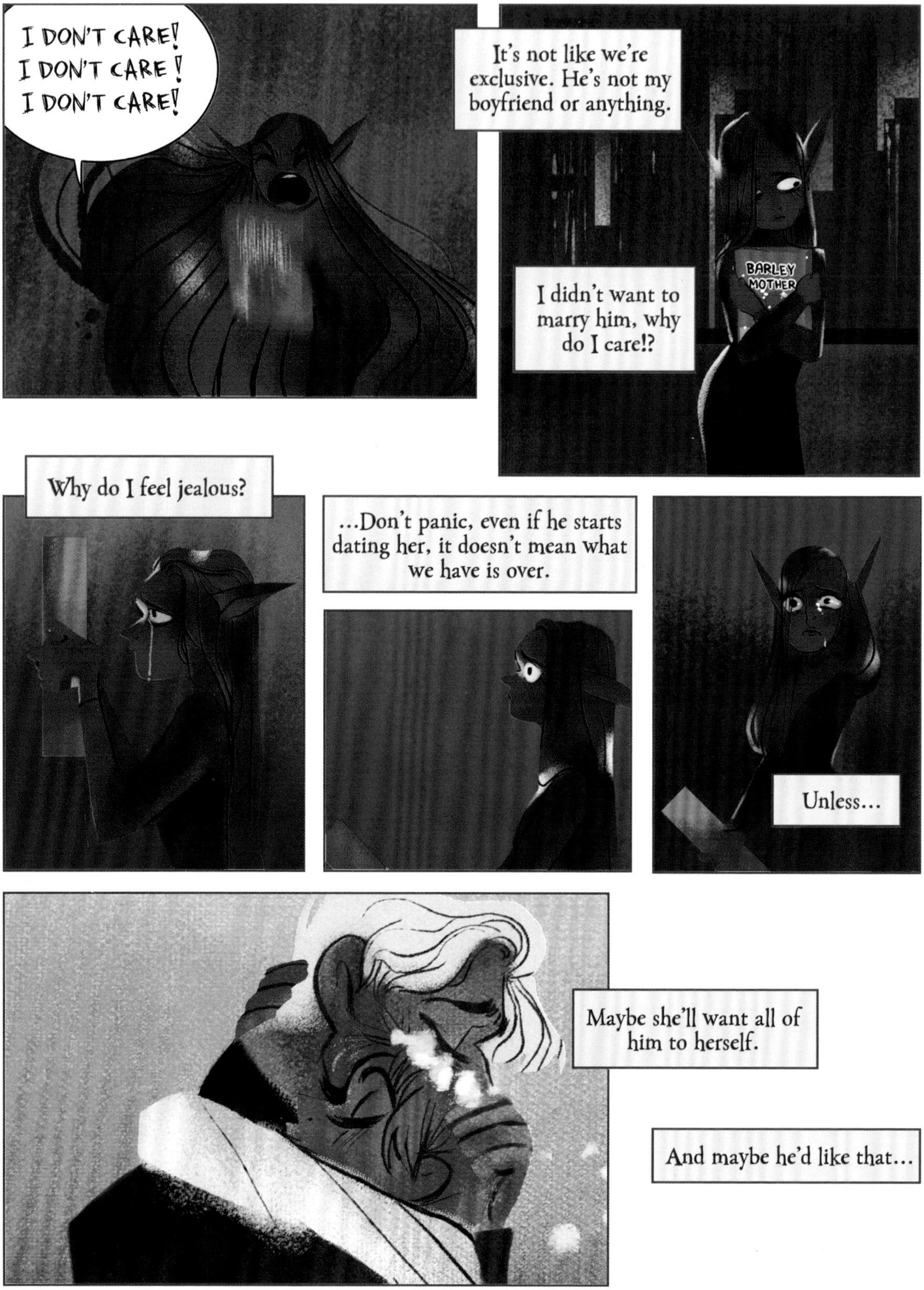
I DON'T CARE! I DON'T CARE! I DON'T CARE!
It's not like we're exclusive. He's not my boyfriend or anything.
BARLEY MOTHER
I didn't want to marry him, why do I care!?
Why do I feel jealous?
...Don't panic, even if he starts dating her, it doesn't mean what we have is over.
Unless...
Maybe she'll want all of him to herself.
And maybe he'd like that...

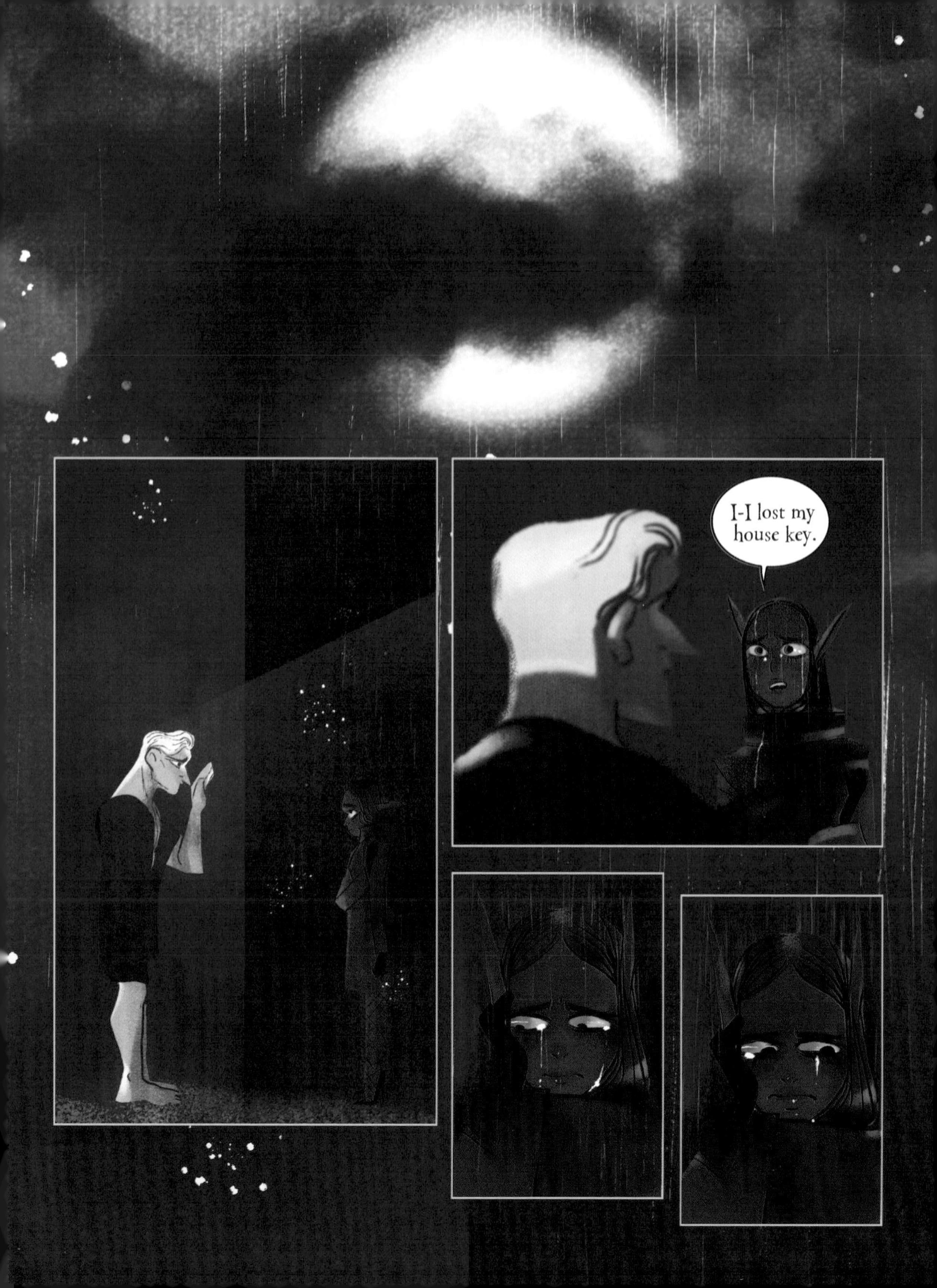
I-I lost my house key.

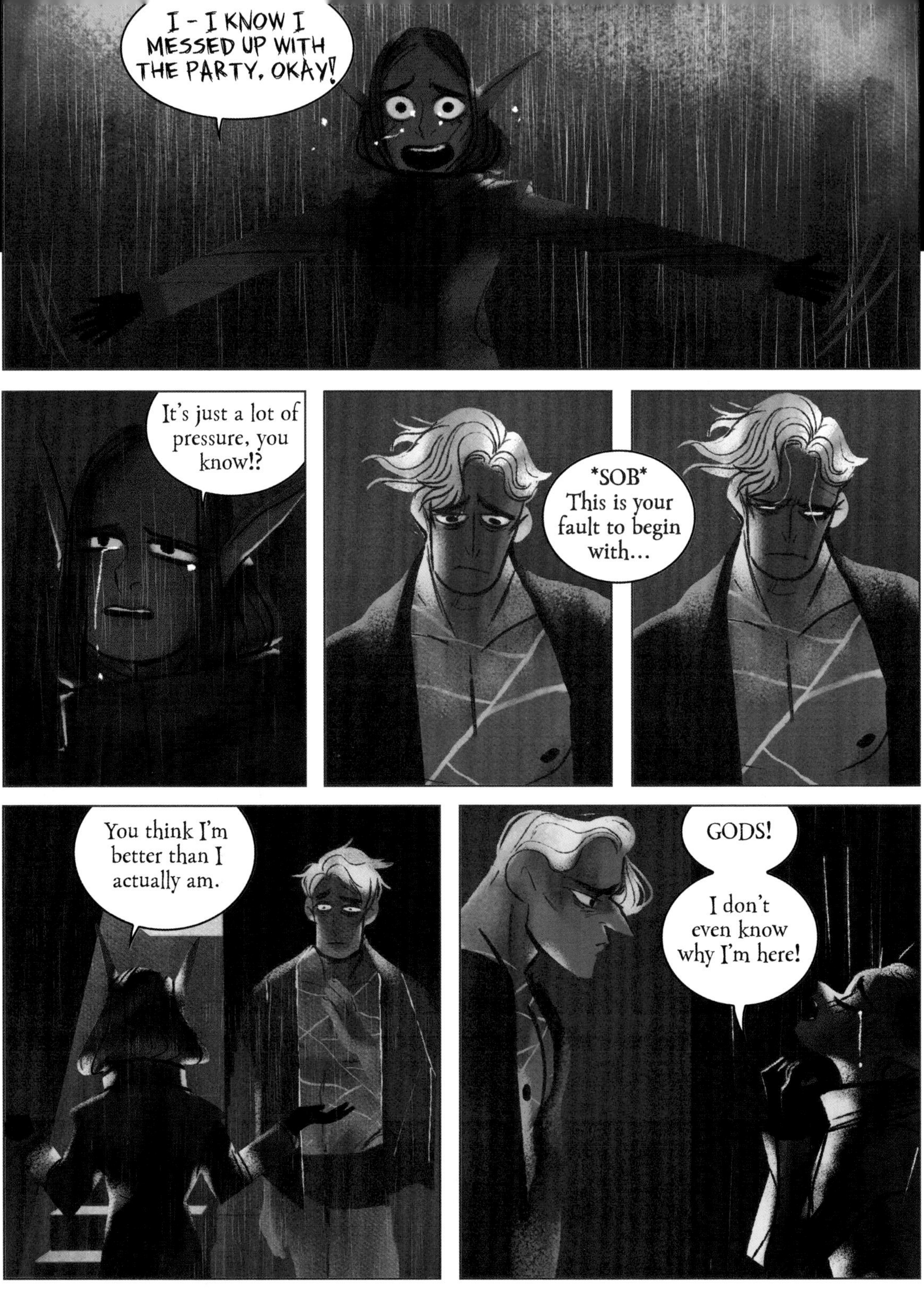
I - I KNOW I MESSED UP WITH THE PARTY, OKAY!
It's just a lot of pressure, you know!?
SOB This is your fault to begin with...
You think I'm better than I actually am.
GODS!
I don't even know why I'm here!

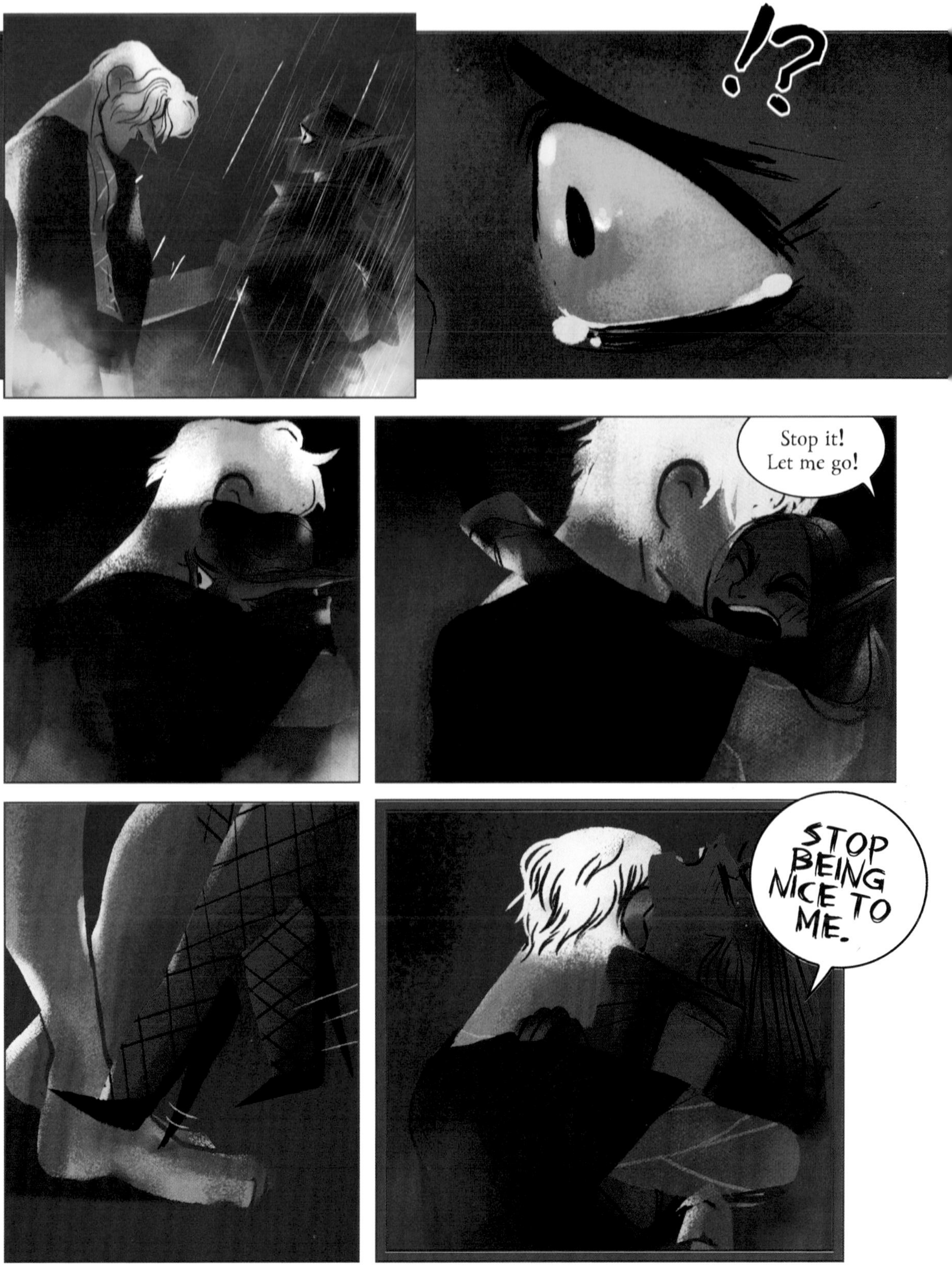
!?
Stop it! Let me go!
STOP BEING NICE TO ME.

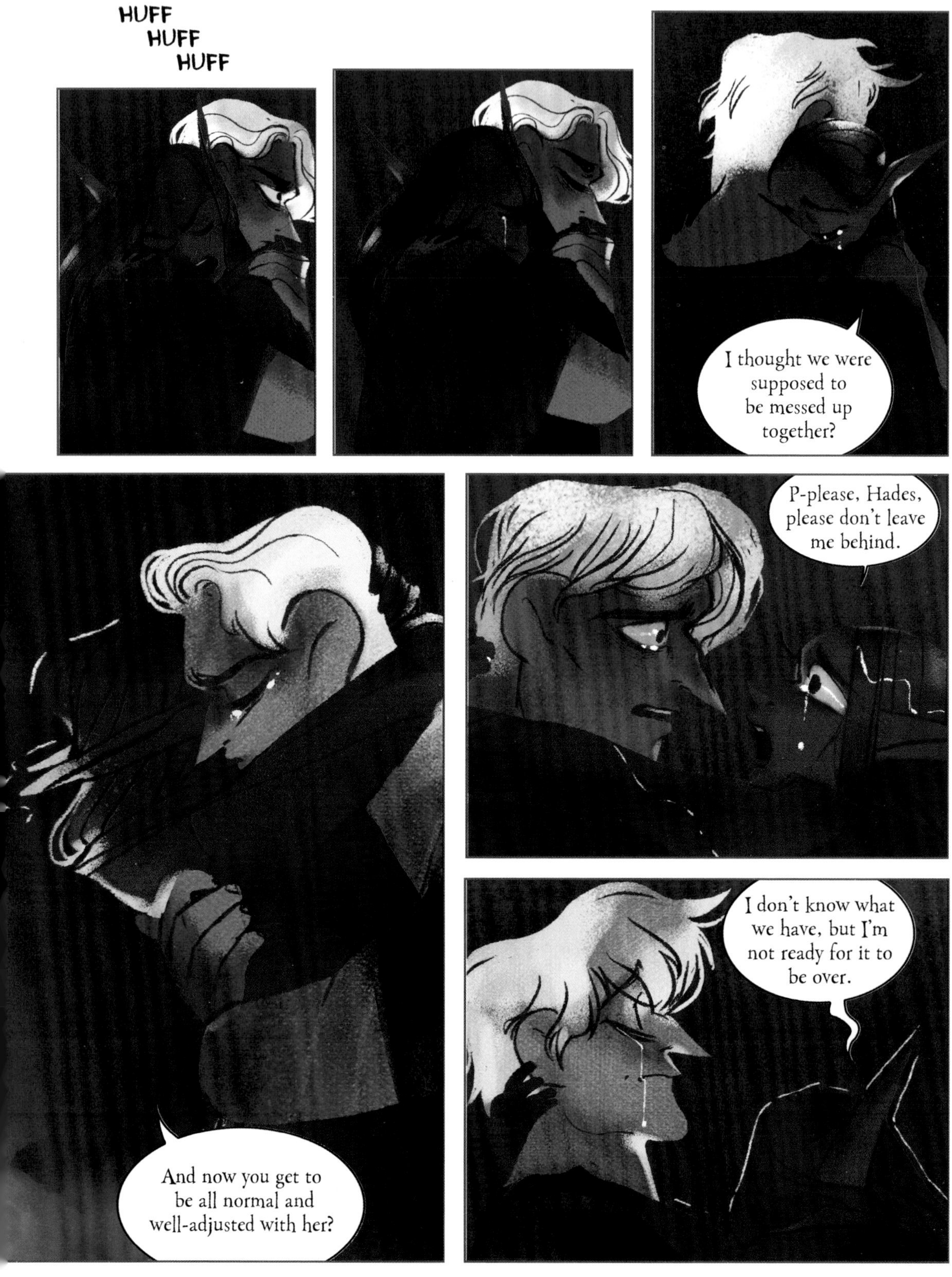
HUFF
HUFF
HUFF
I thought we were supposed to be messed up together?
P-please, Hades, please don't leave me behind.
And now you get to be all normal and well-adjusted with her?
I don't know what we have, but I'm not ready for it to be over.

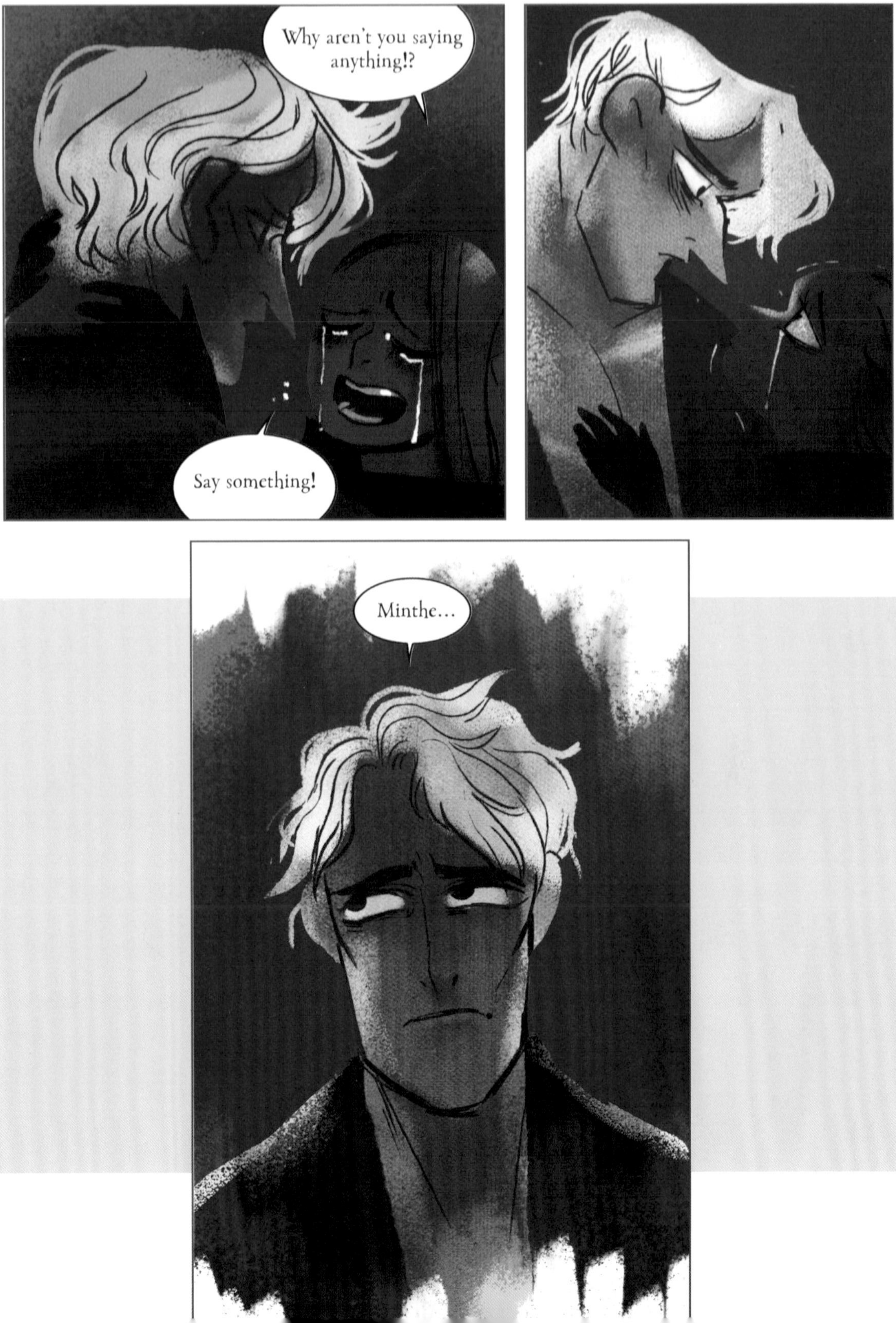
Why aren't you saying anything!?
Say something!
Minthe...

EPISODE 47: NEEDED

Dear Persephone,

My therapist assigned me the exercise of writing letters of what I would hypothetically tell others about what I'm feeling.

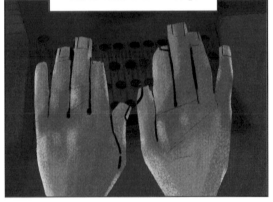

Apparently doing this will help me "UNPACK MY EMOTIONS AND GAIN A GREATER UNDERSTANDING OF MYSELF."

Gods, why do I pay that hack?

Luckily I never have to show anybody these letters so I guess it doesn't hurt to try.

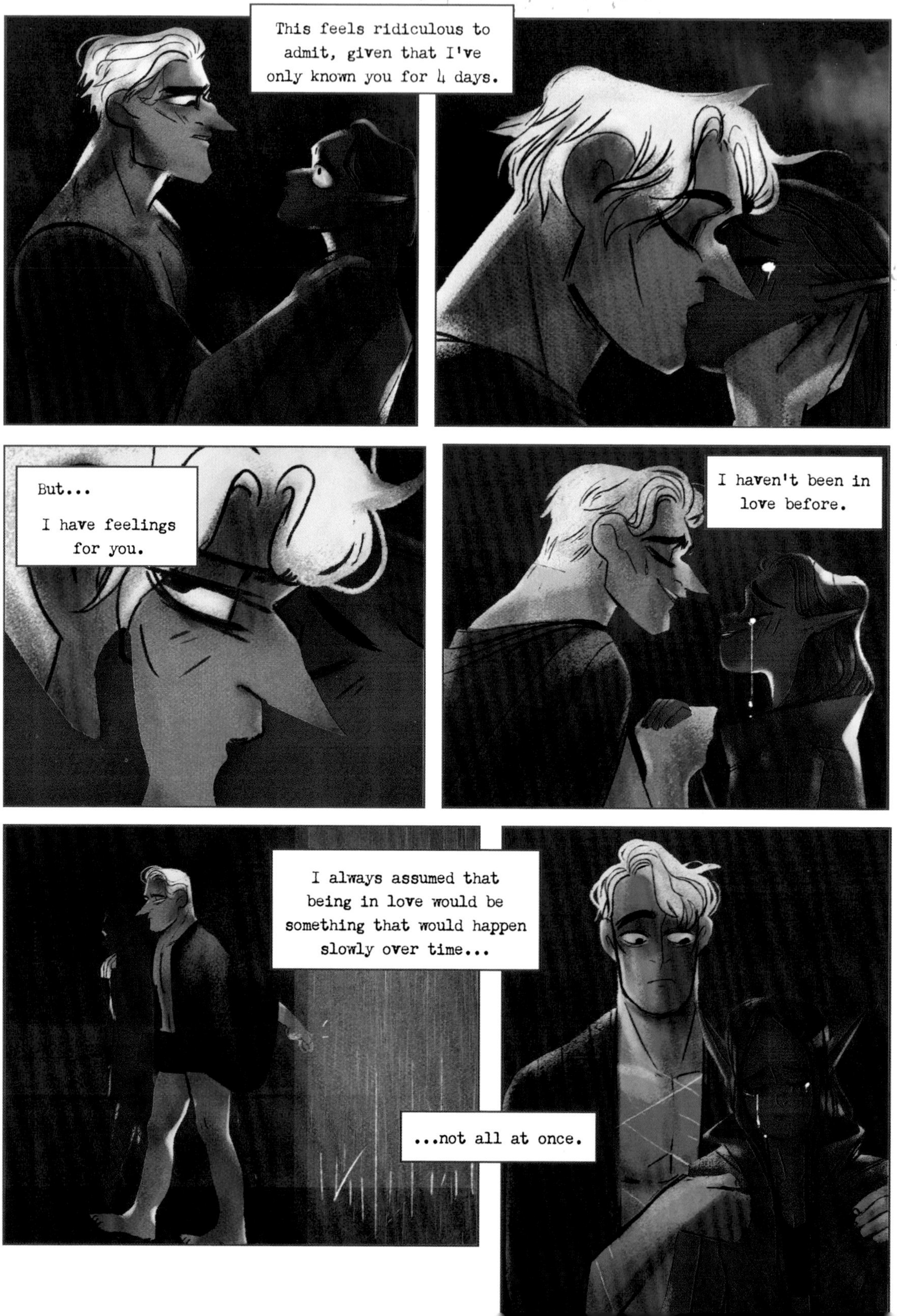
This feels ridiculous to admit, given that I've only known you for 4 days.
But...
I have feelings for you.
I haven't been in love before.
I always assumed that being in love would be something that would happen slowly over time...
...not all at once.

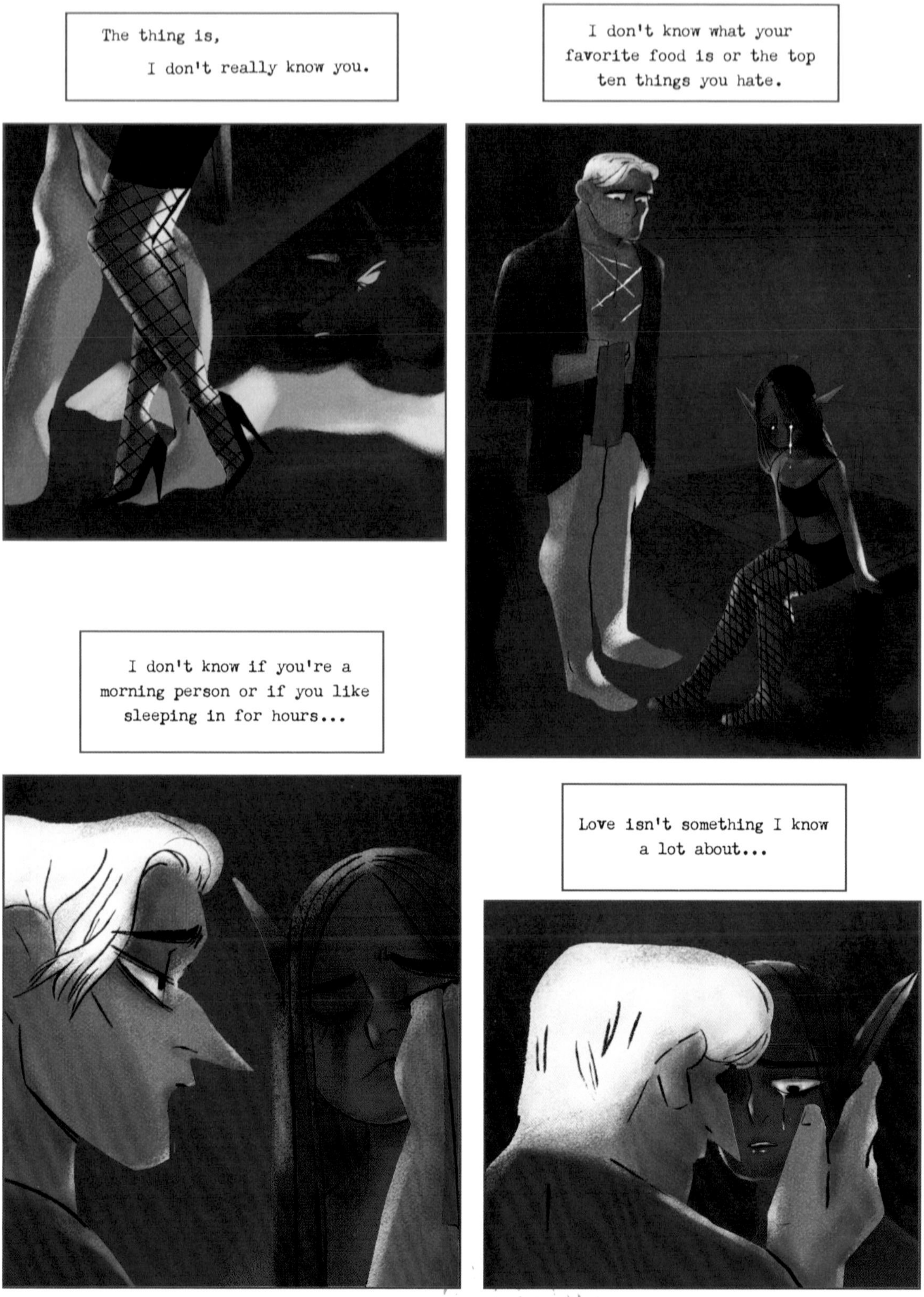
The thing is, I don't really know you.
I don't know what your favorite food is or the top ten things you hate.
I don't know if you're a morning person or if you like sleeping in for hours...
Love isn't something I know a lot about...

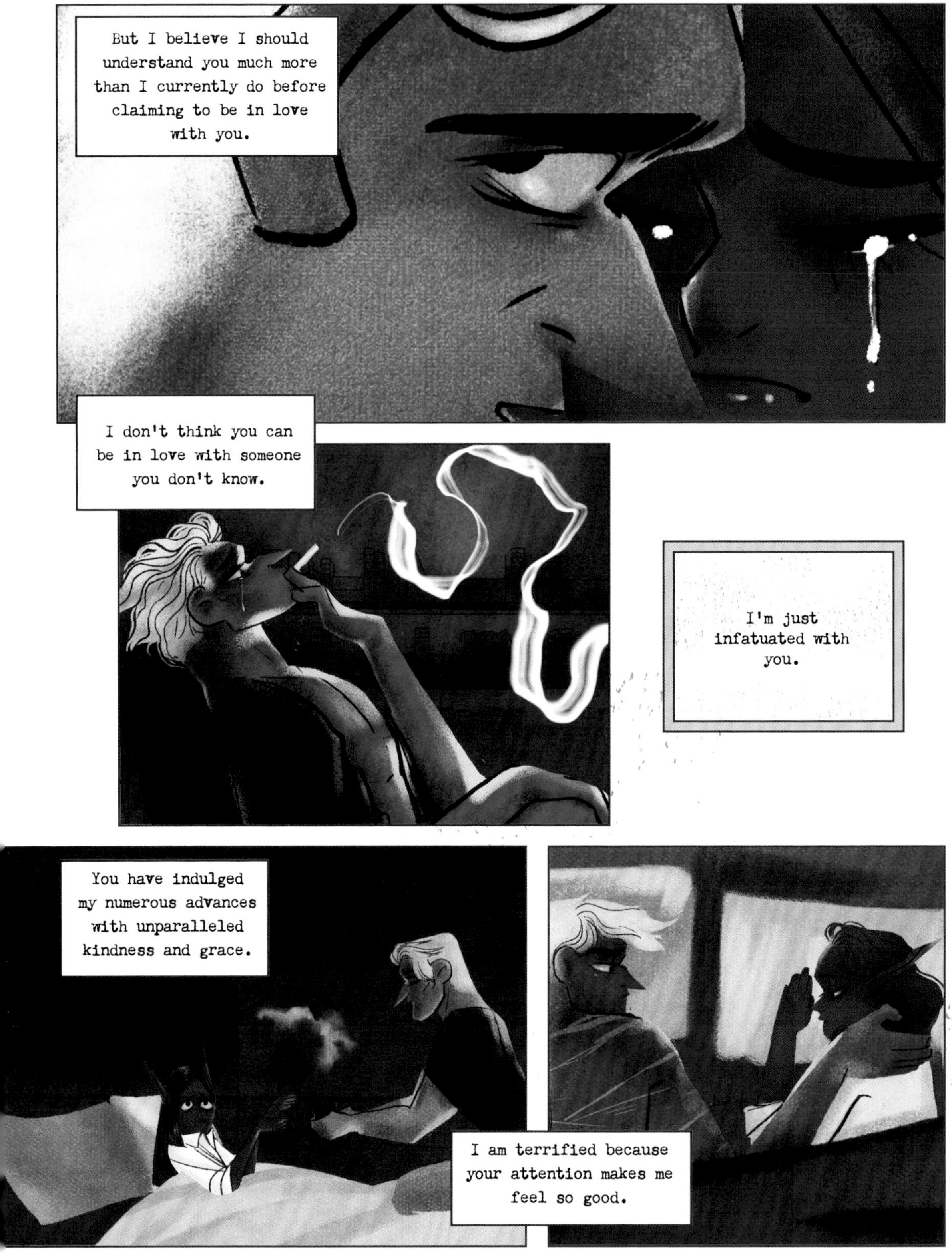

But I believe I should understand you much more than I currently do before claiming to be in love with you.
I don't think you can be in love with someone you don't know.
I'm just infatuated with you.
You have indulged my numerous advances with unparalleled kindness and grace.
I am terrified because your attention makes me feel so good.

The concept of not being able to feel that way again is devastating.

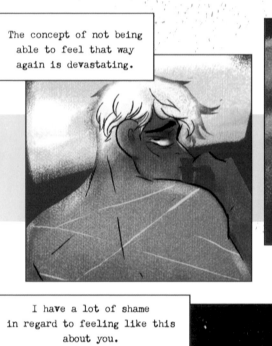

I have a lot of shame in regard to feeling like this about you.

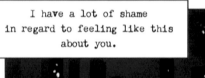

That's a lot to put on someone who is so young.

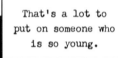

It goes without saying, I have a lot of baggage.

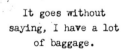

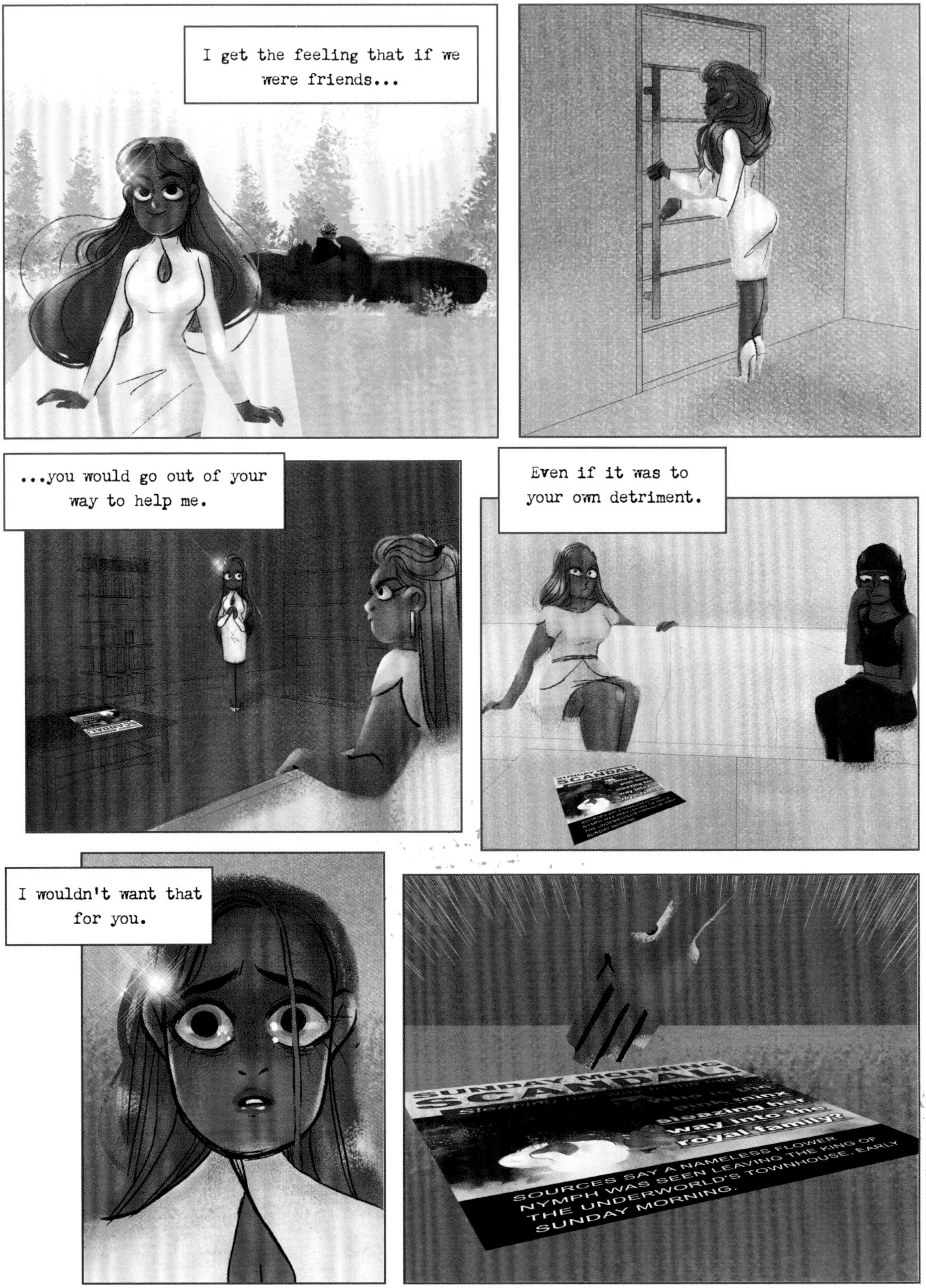
I get the feeling that if we were friends...
...you would go out of your way to help me.
Even if it was to your own detriment.
I wouldn't want that for you.
SUNDAY MORNING
SCANDAL
pink minx
sleazing her
way into the
royal family?
SOURCES SAY A NAMELESS FLOWER NYMPH WAS SEEN LEAVING THE KING OF THE UNDERWORLD'S TOWNHOUSE, EARLY SUNDAY MORNING.

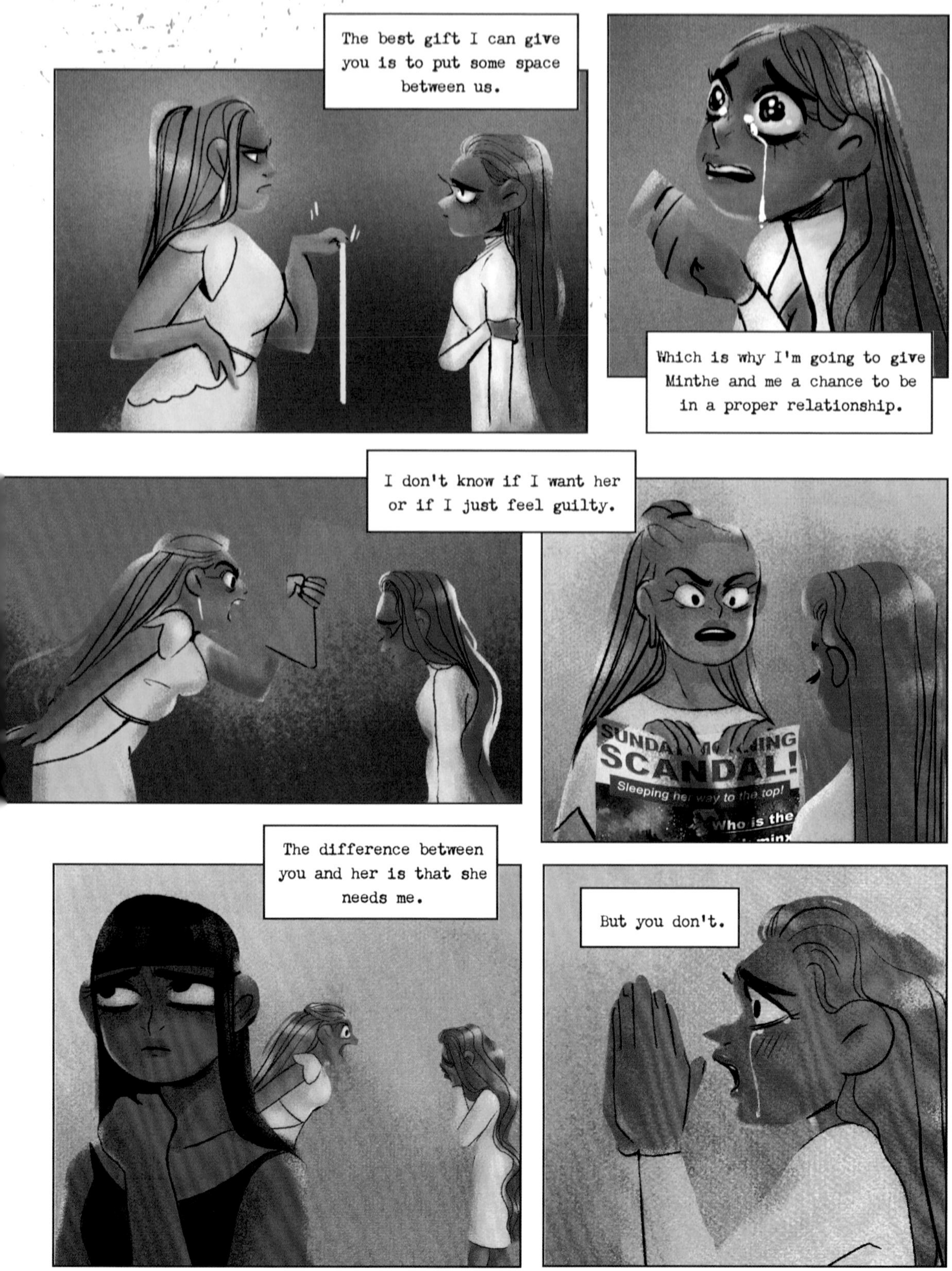
The best gift I can give you is to put some space between us.
Which is why I'm going to give Minthe and me a chance to be in a proper relationship.
I don't know if I want her or if I just feel guilty.
SUNDAY MORNING SCANDAL!
Sleeping her way to the top!
Who is the
The difference between you and her is that she needs me.
But you don't.

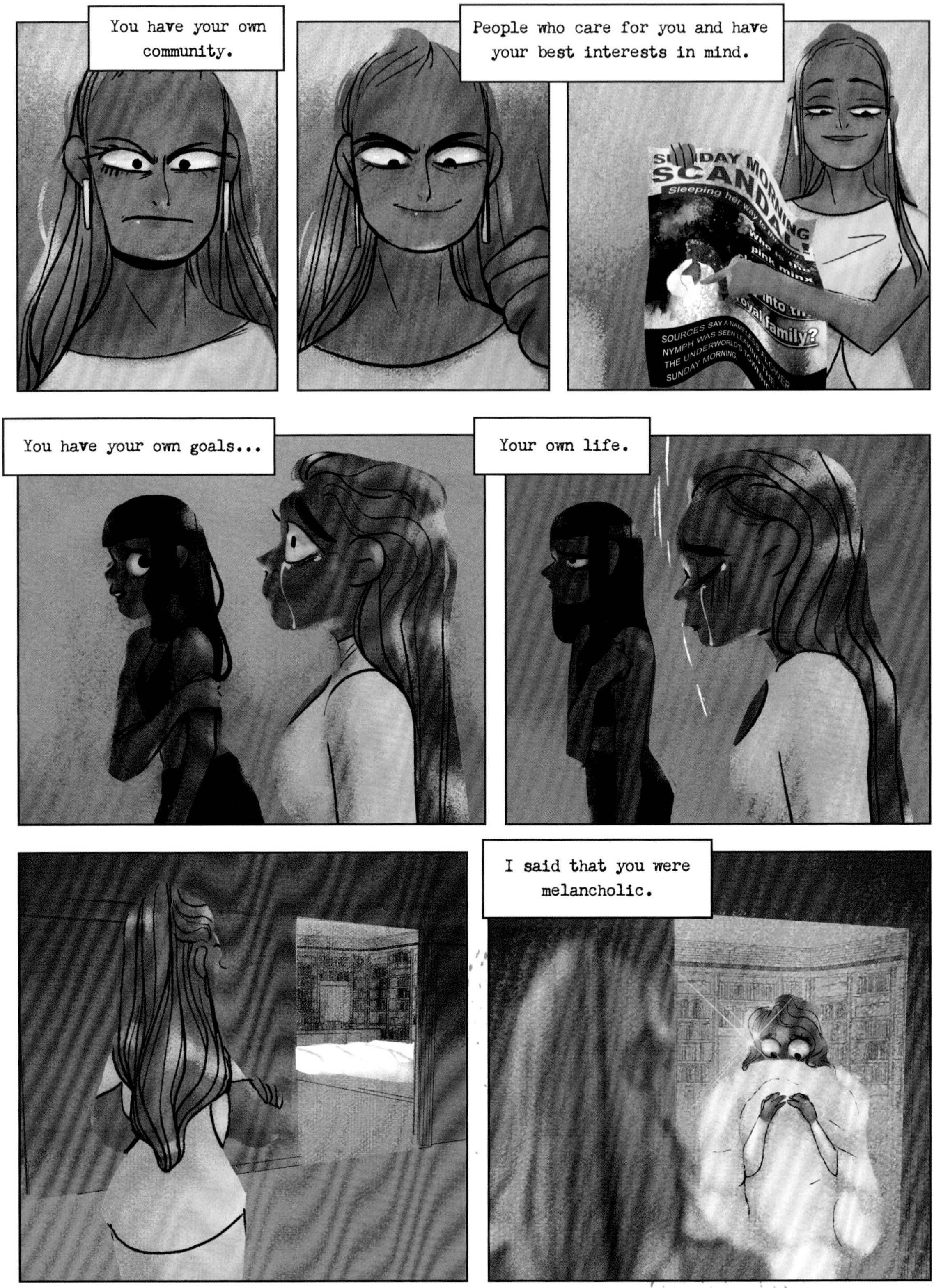
You have your own community.
People who care for you and have your best interests in mind.
SCANDAL
pink minx
royal family?
You have your own goals...
Your own life.
I said that you were melancholic.

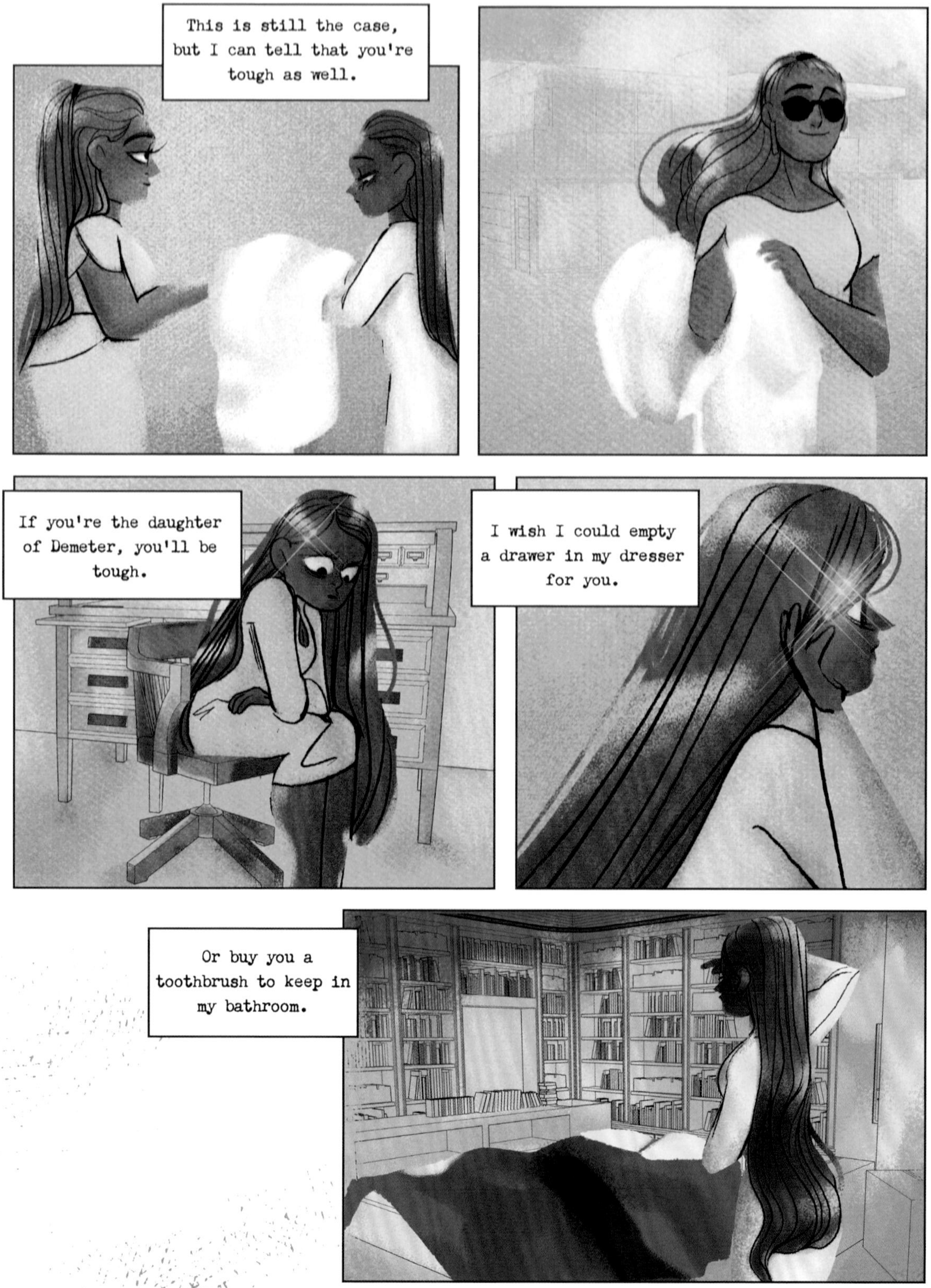
This is still the case, but I can tell that you're tough as well.
If you're the daughter of Demeter, you'll be tough.
I wish I could empty a drawer in my dresser for you.
Or buy you a toothbrush to keep in my bathroom.

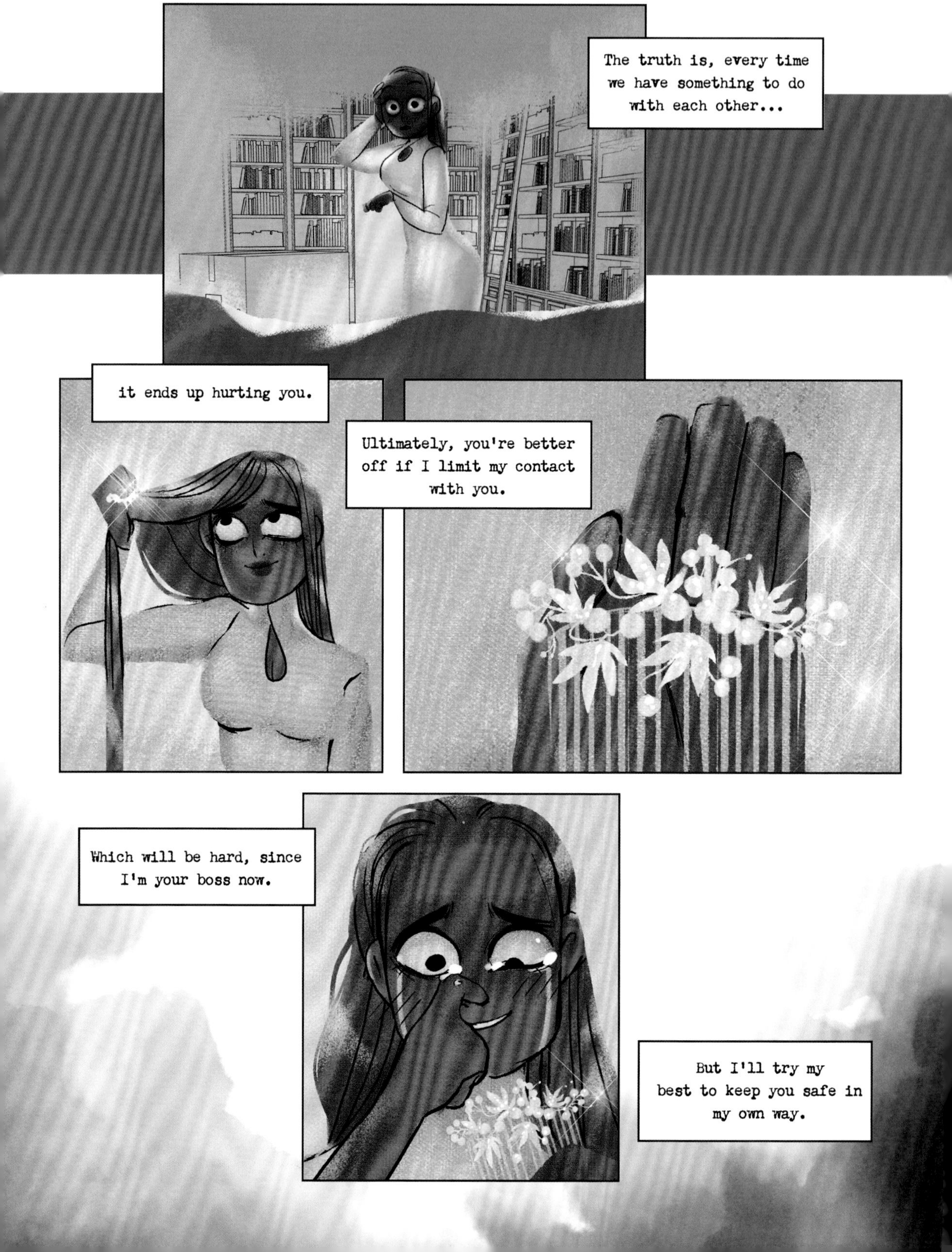
The truth is, every time we have something to do with each other...
it ends up hurting you.
Ultimately, you're better off if I limit my contact with you.
Which will be hard, since I'm your boss now.
But I'll try my best to keep you safe in my own way.

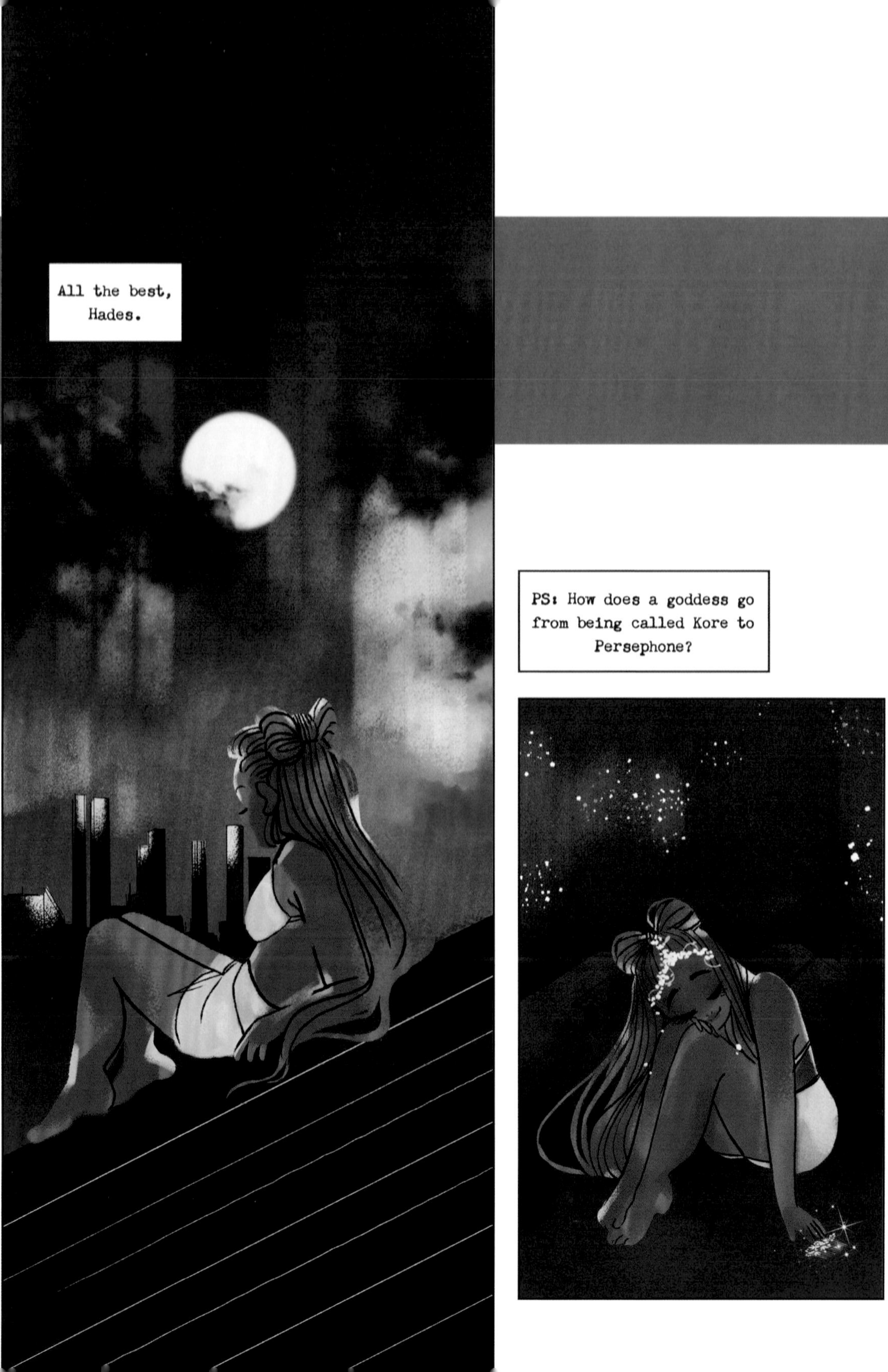
All the best,
Hades.
PS: How does a goddess go from being called Kore to Persephone?

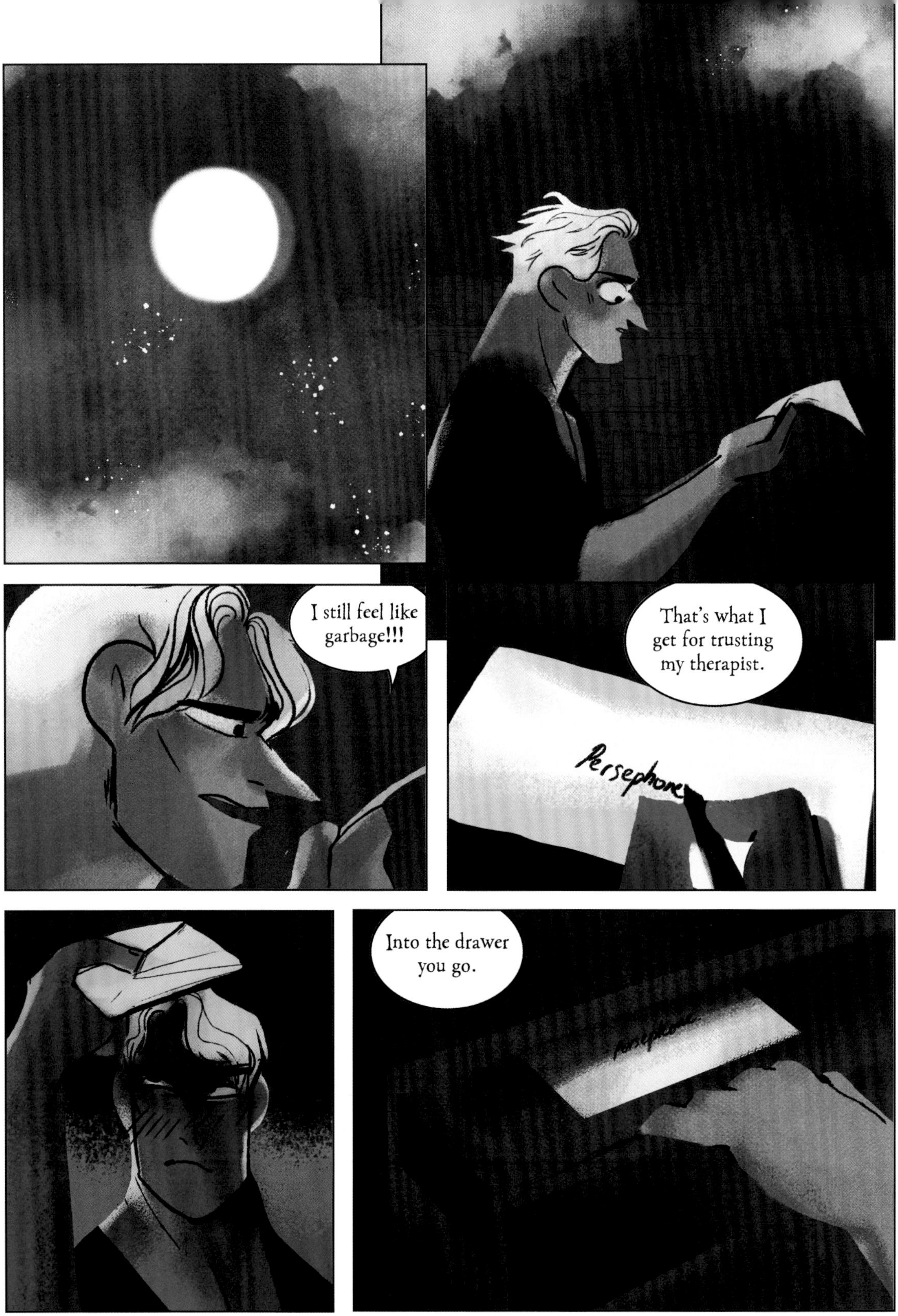
I still feel like garbage!!!
That's what I get for trusting my therapist.
Persephone
Into the drawer you go.

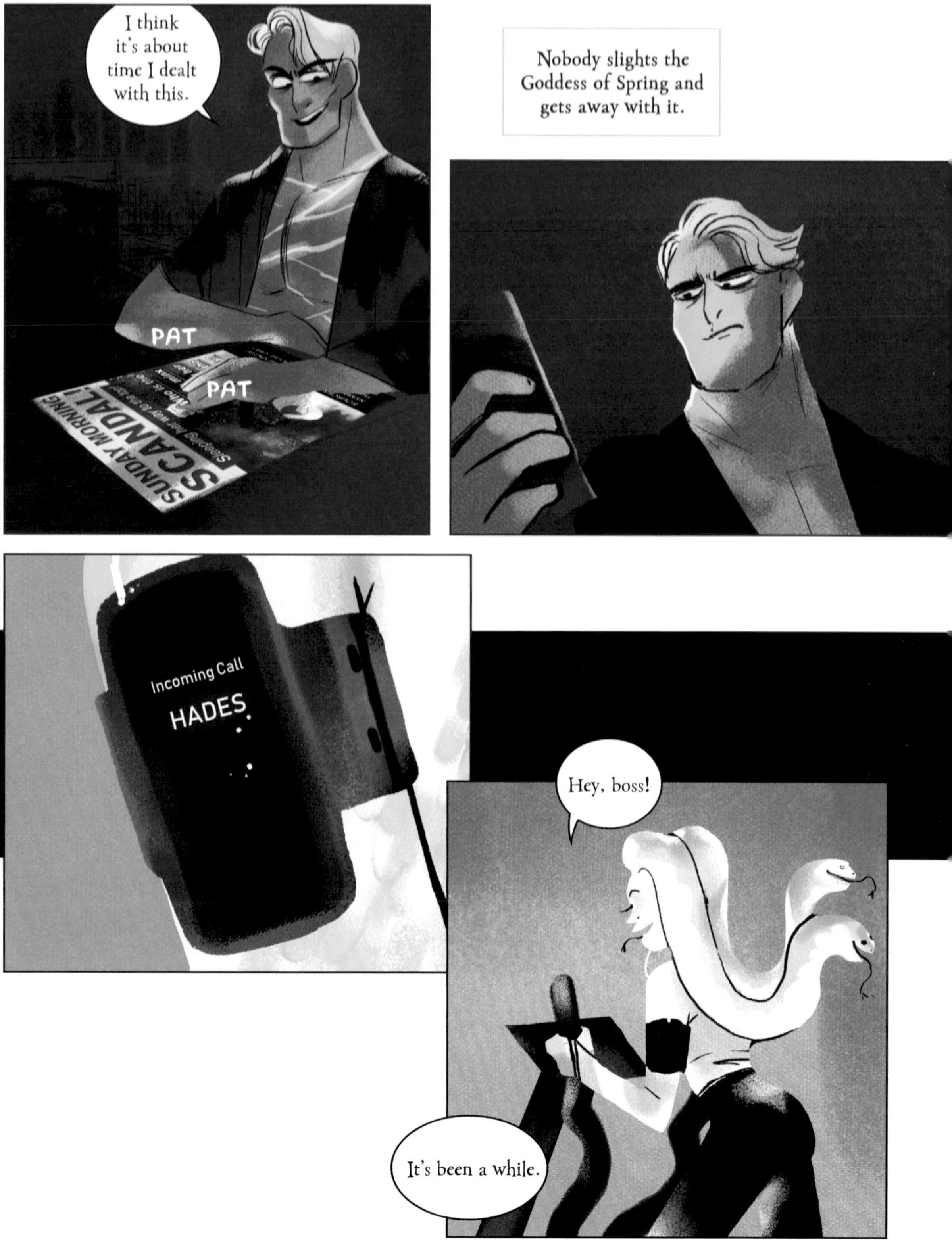

I think it's about time I dealt with this.
PAT
PAT
SUNDAY MORNING
SCANDAL!!
Nobody slights the Goddess of Spring and gets away with it.
Incoming Call
HADES
Hey, boss!
It's been a while.

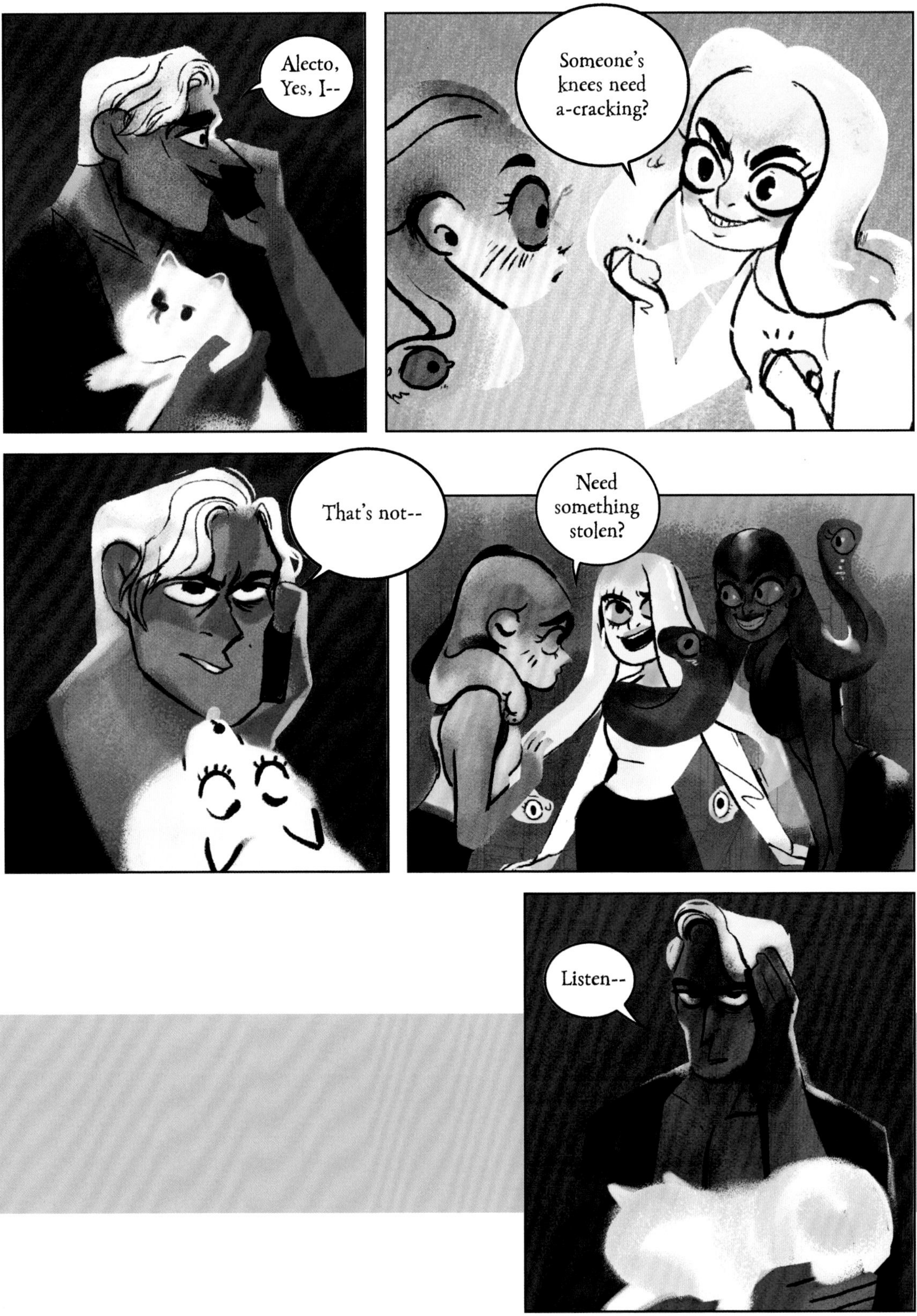

Alecto, Yes, I--
Someone's knees need a-cracking?
That's not--
Need something stolen?
Listen--

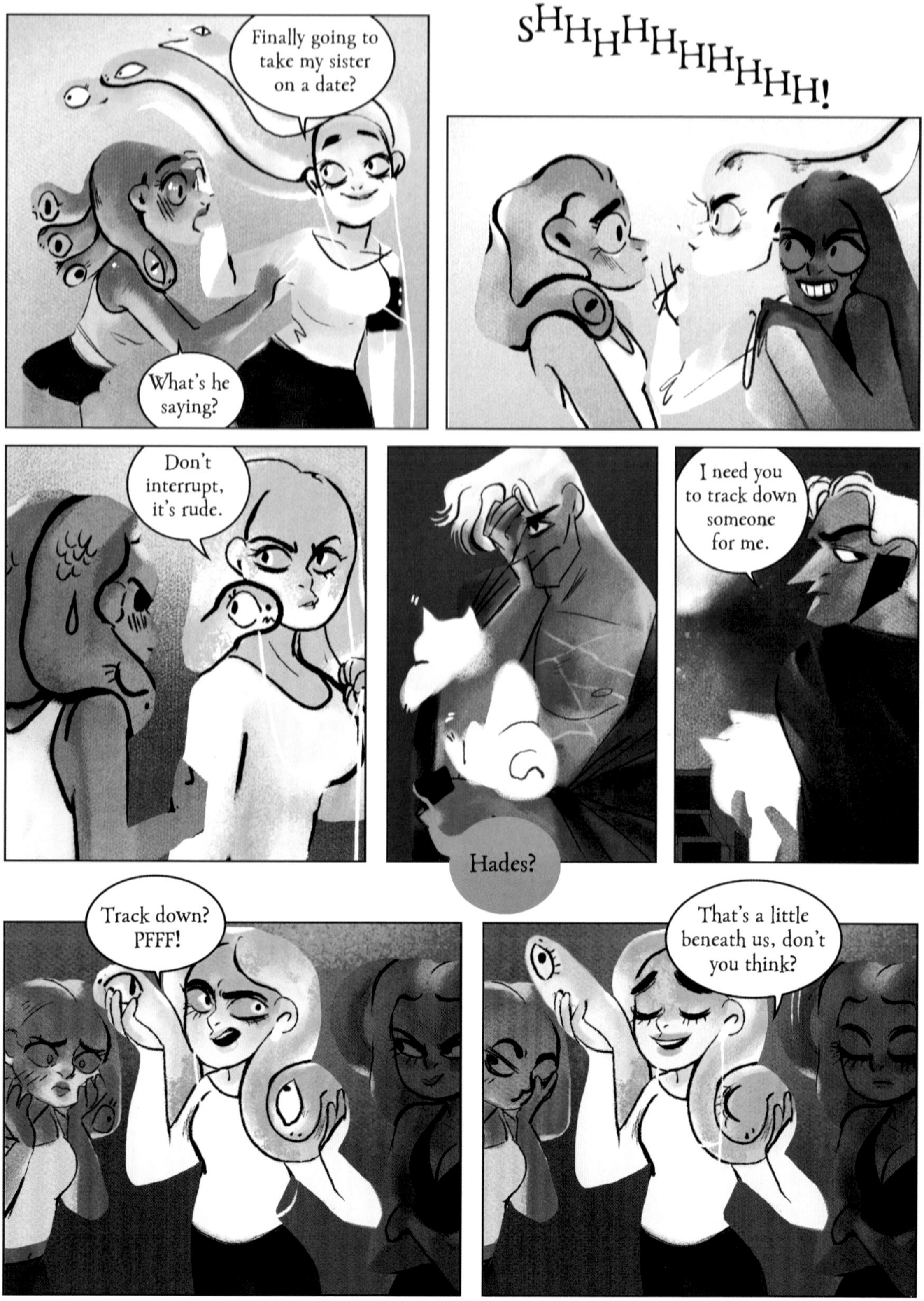
Finally going to take my sister on a date?
What's he saying?
SHHHHHHHHHH!
Don't interrupt, it's rude.
I need you to track down someone for me.
Hades?
Track down? PFFF!
That's a little beneath us, don't you think?

2 WEEKS AGO.

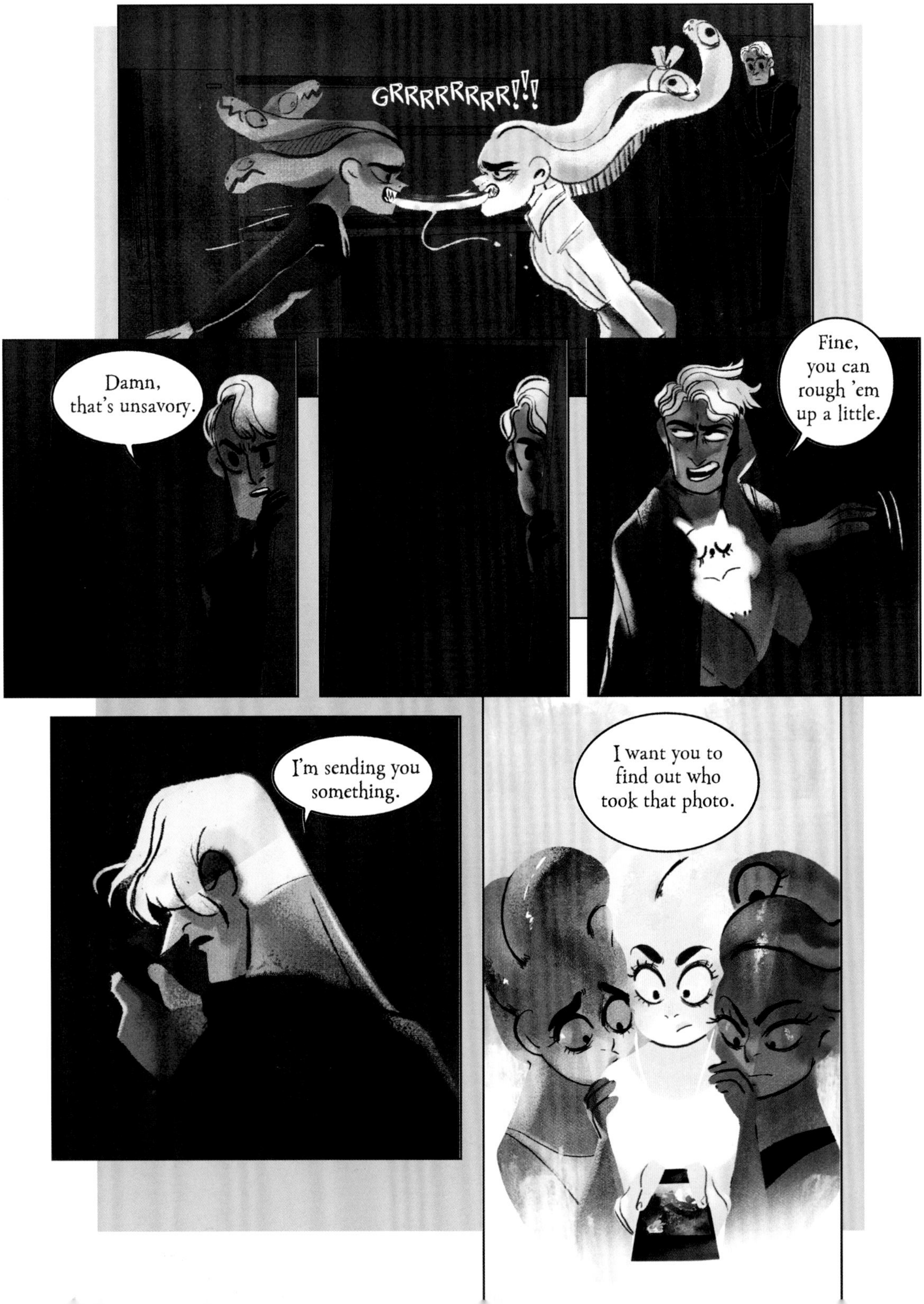
GRRRRRRRR!!!
Damn, that's unsavory.
Fine, you can rough 'em up a little.
I'm sending you something.
I want you to find out who took that photo.

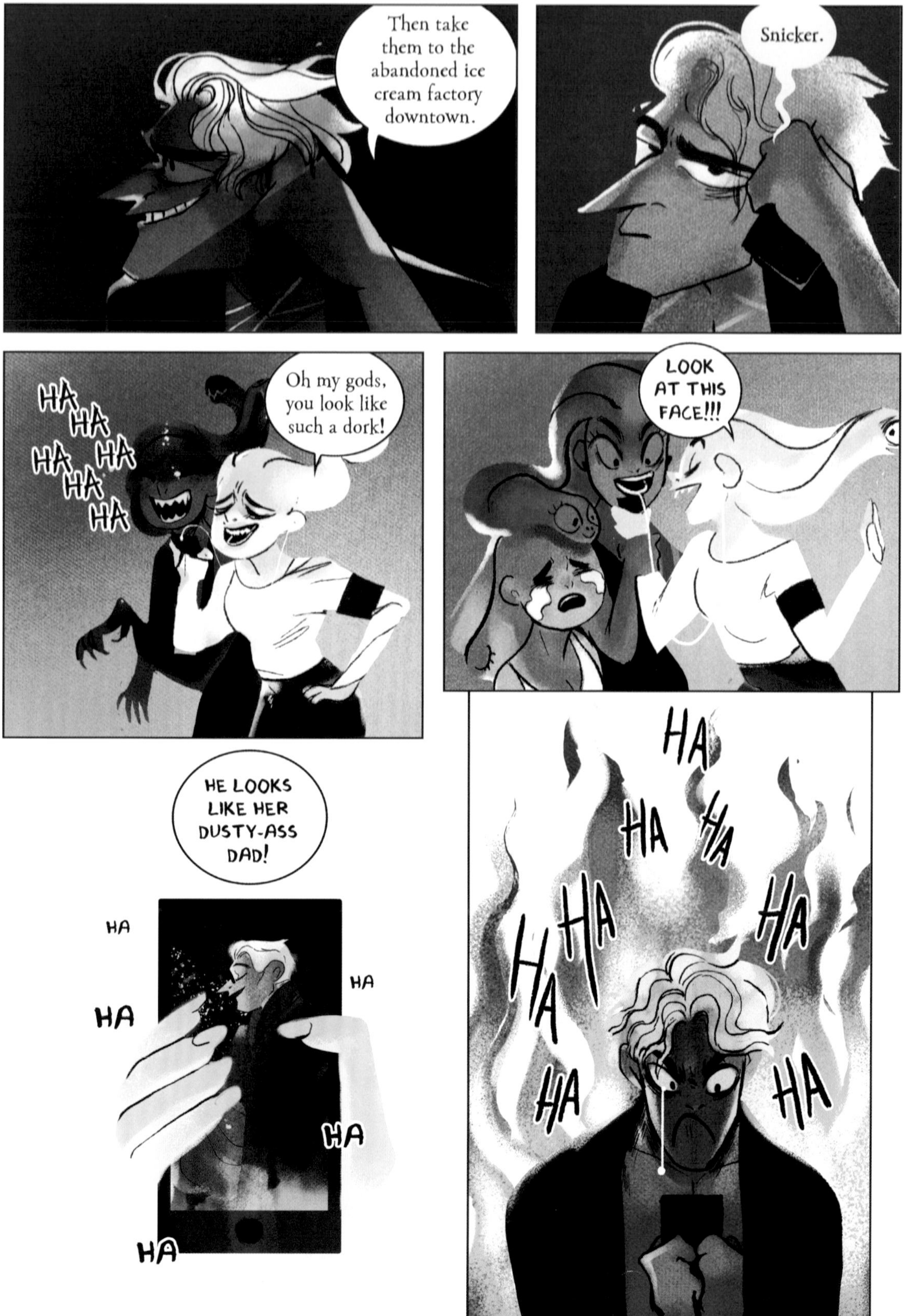
Then take them to the abandoned ice cream factory downtown.
Snicker.
HA HA HA HA HA HA
Oh my gods, you look like such a dork!
LOOK AT THIS FACE!!!
HE LOOKS LIKE HER DUSTY-ASS DAD!
HA
HA
HA
HA
HA
HA HA HA HA HA HA HA HA

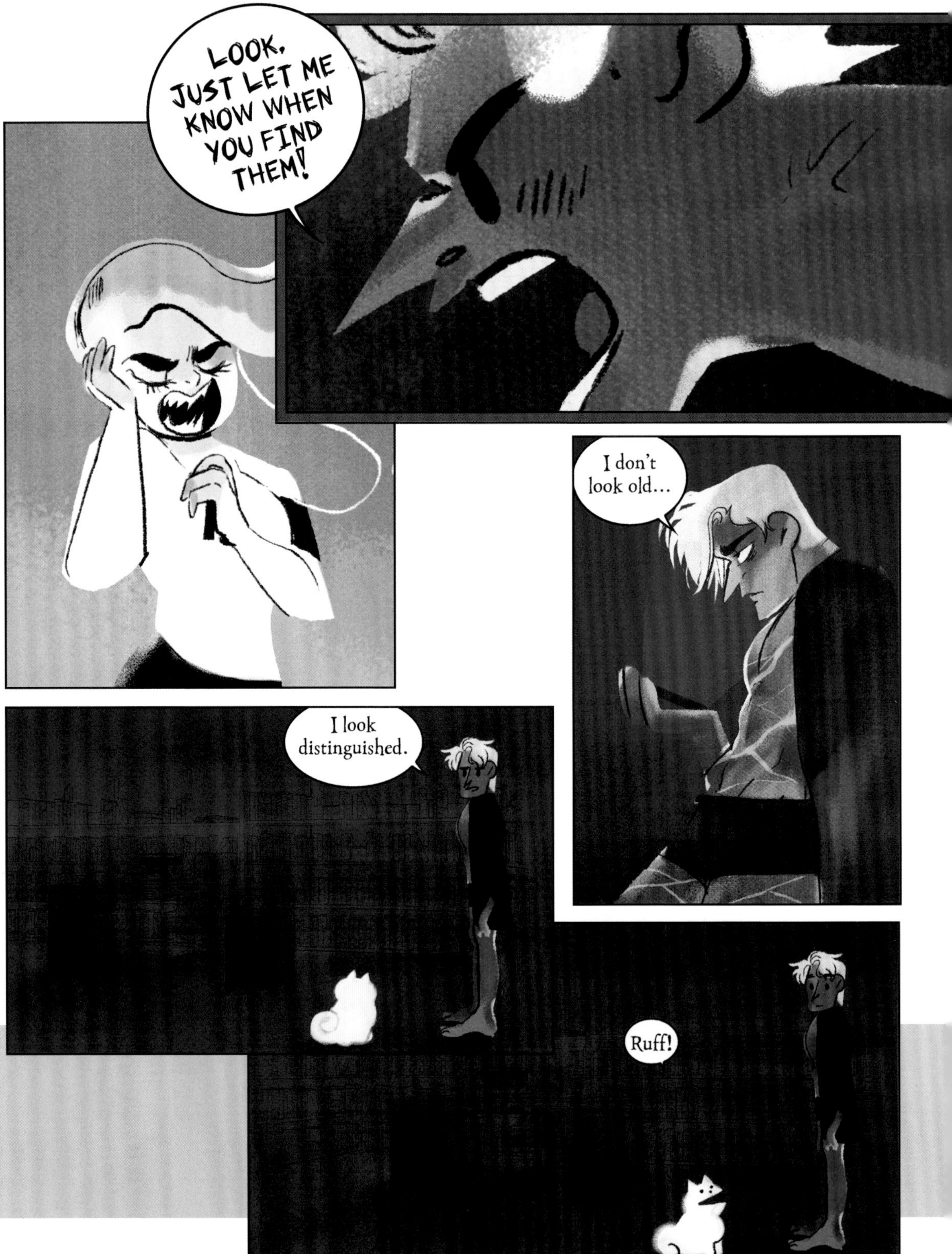
LOOK, JUST LET ME KNOW WHEN YOU FIND THEM!
I don't look old…
I look distinguished.
Ruff!

EPISODE 48: SISSSS

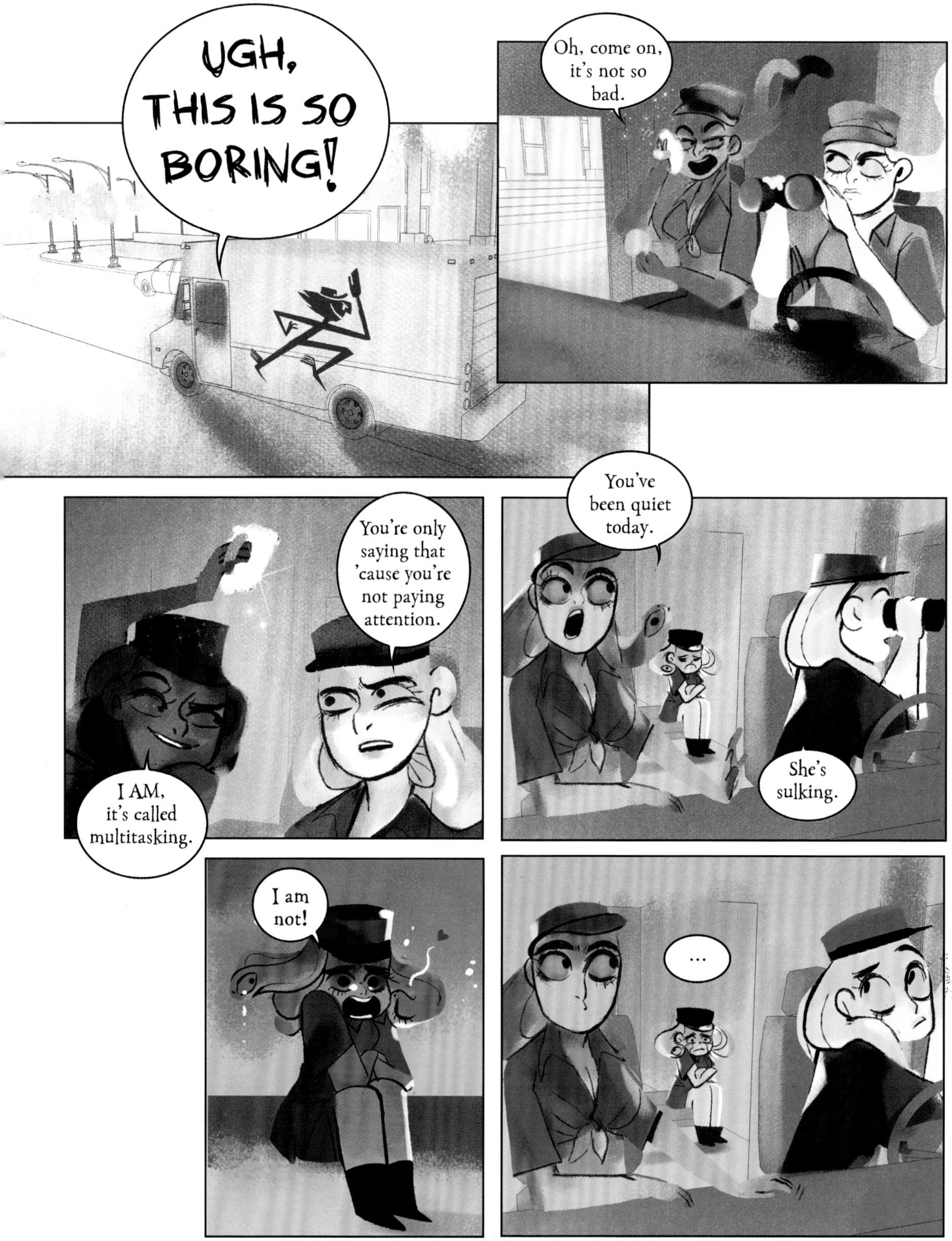
UGH, THIS IS SO BORING!
Oh, come on, it's not so bad.
You're only saying that 'cause you're not paying attention.
I AM, it's called multitasking.
You've been quiet today.
She's sulking.
I am not!
...

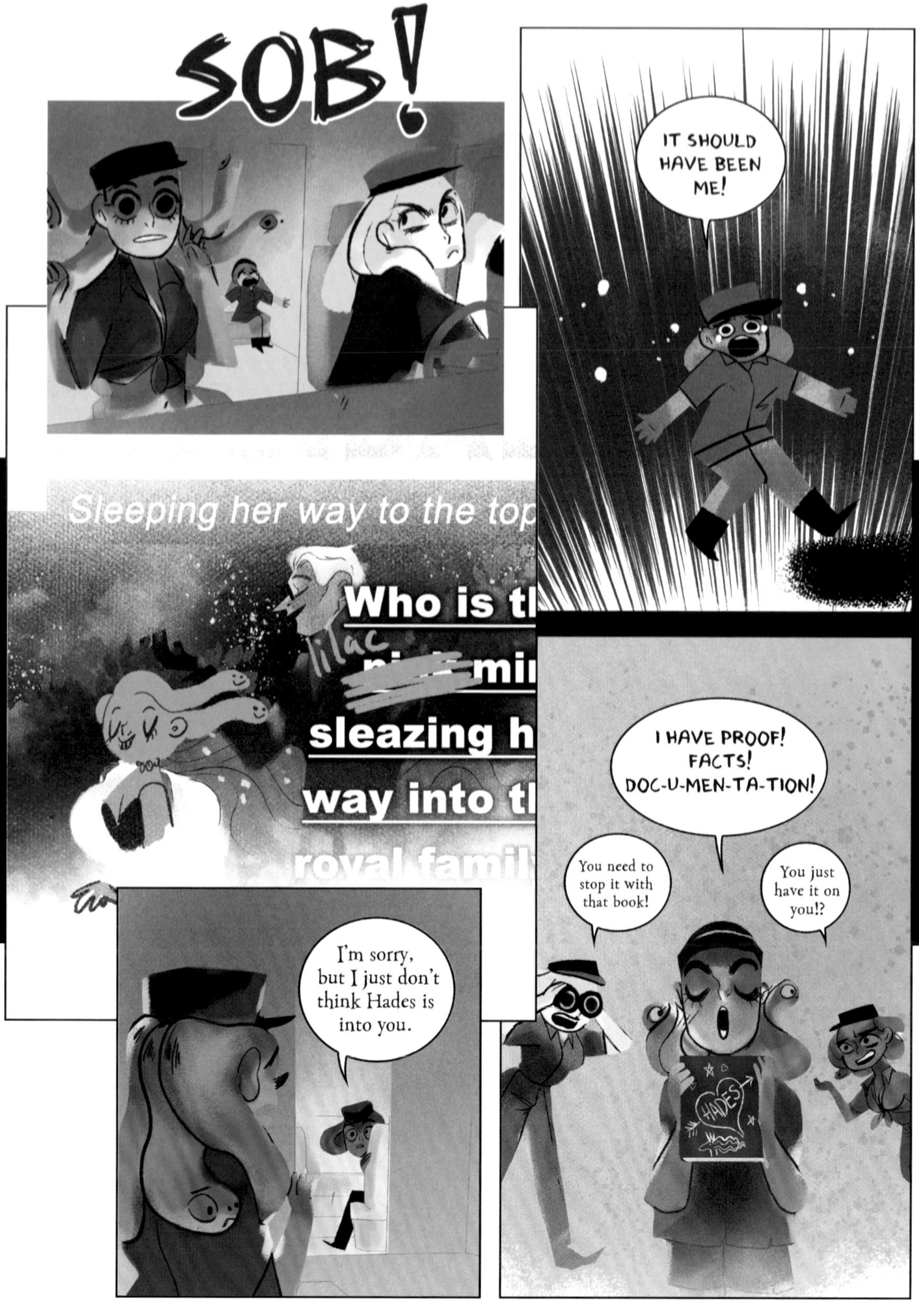
SOB!
IT SHOULD HAVE BEEN ME!
Sleeping her way to the top
Who is th
lilac
min
sleazing h
way into th
royal famil
I HAVE PROOF! FACTS! DOC-U-MEN-TA-TION!
You need to stop it with that book!
You just have it on you!?
HADES
I'm sorry, but I just don't think Hades is into you.

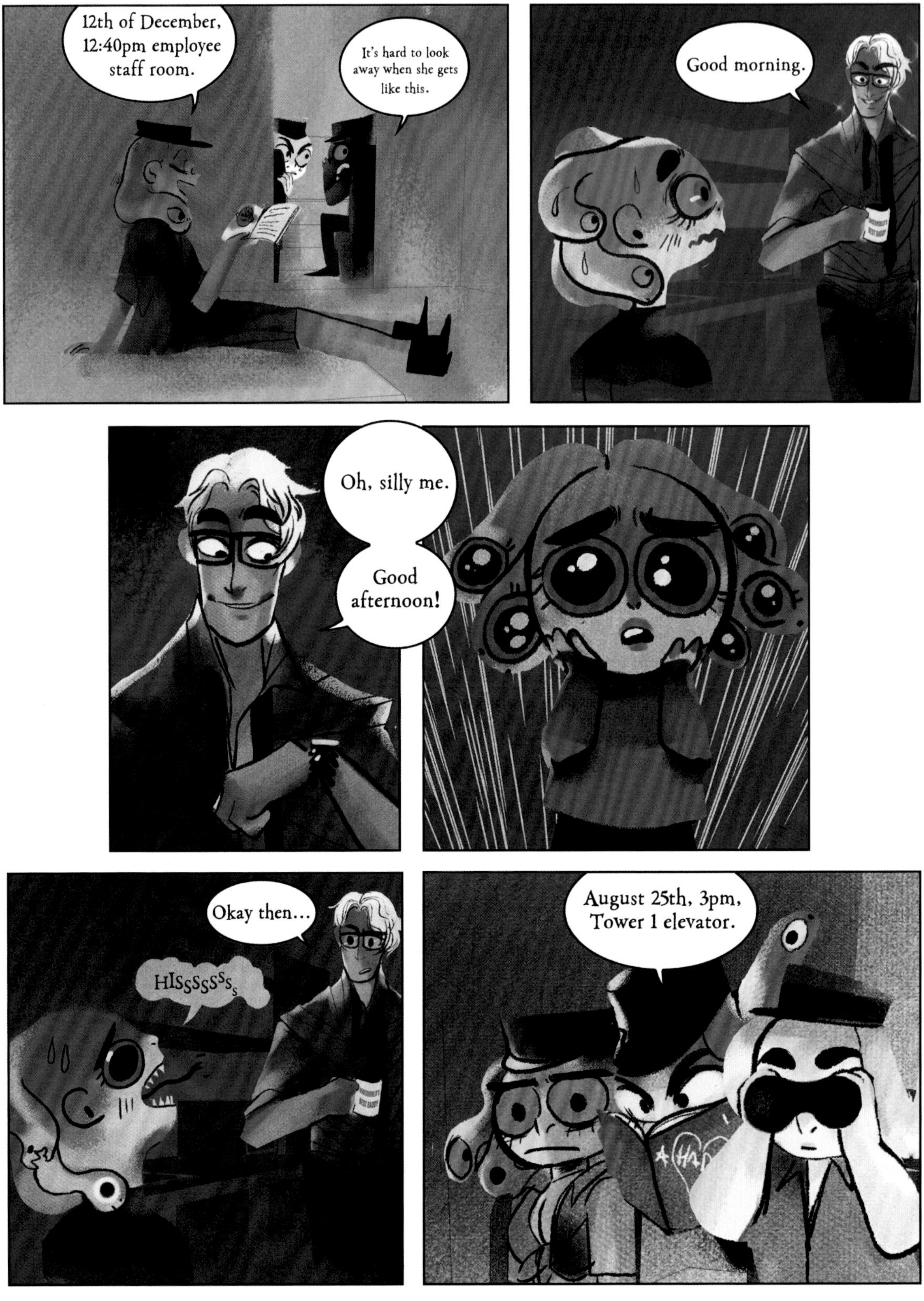
12th of December, 12:40pm employee staff room.
It's hard to look away when she gets like this.
Good morning.
Oh, silly me.
Good afternoon!
Okay then...
HISSSSSSSs
August 25th, 3pm, Tower 1 elevator.

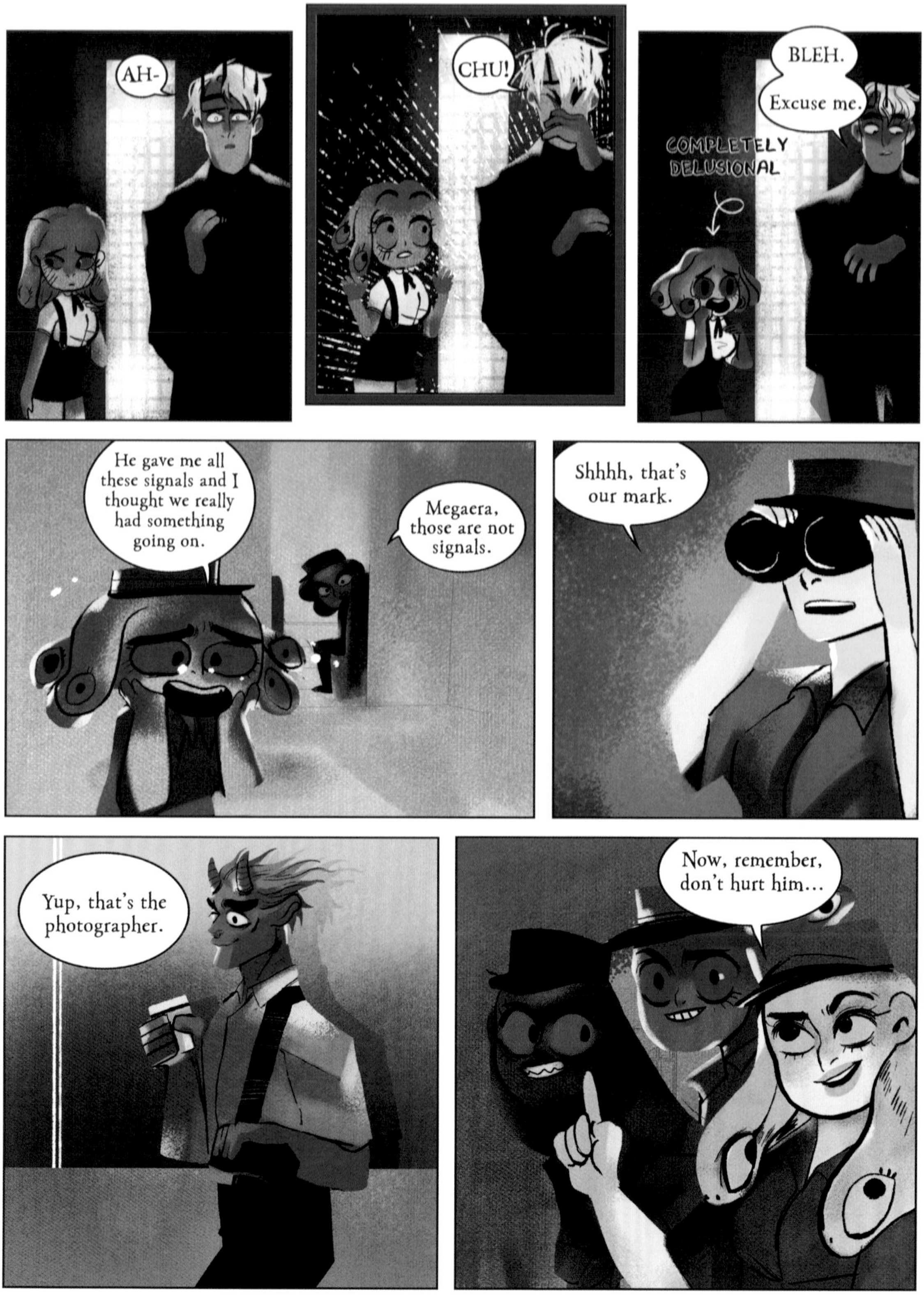
AH-
CHU!
BLEH.
Excuse me.
COMPLETELY DELUSIONAL
He gave me all these signals and I thought we really had something going on.
Megaera, those are not signals.
Shhhh, that's our mark.
Yup, that's the photographer.
Now, remember, don't hurt him...

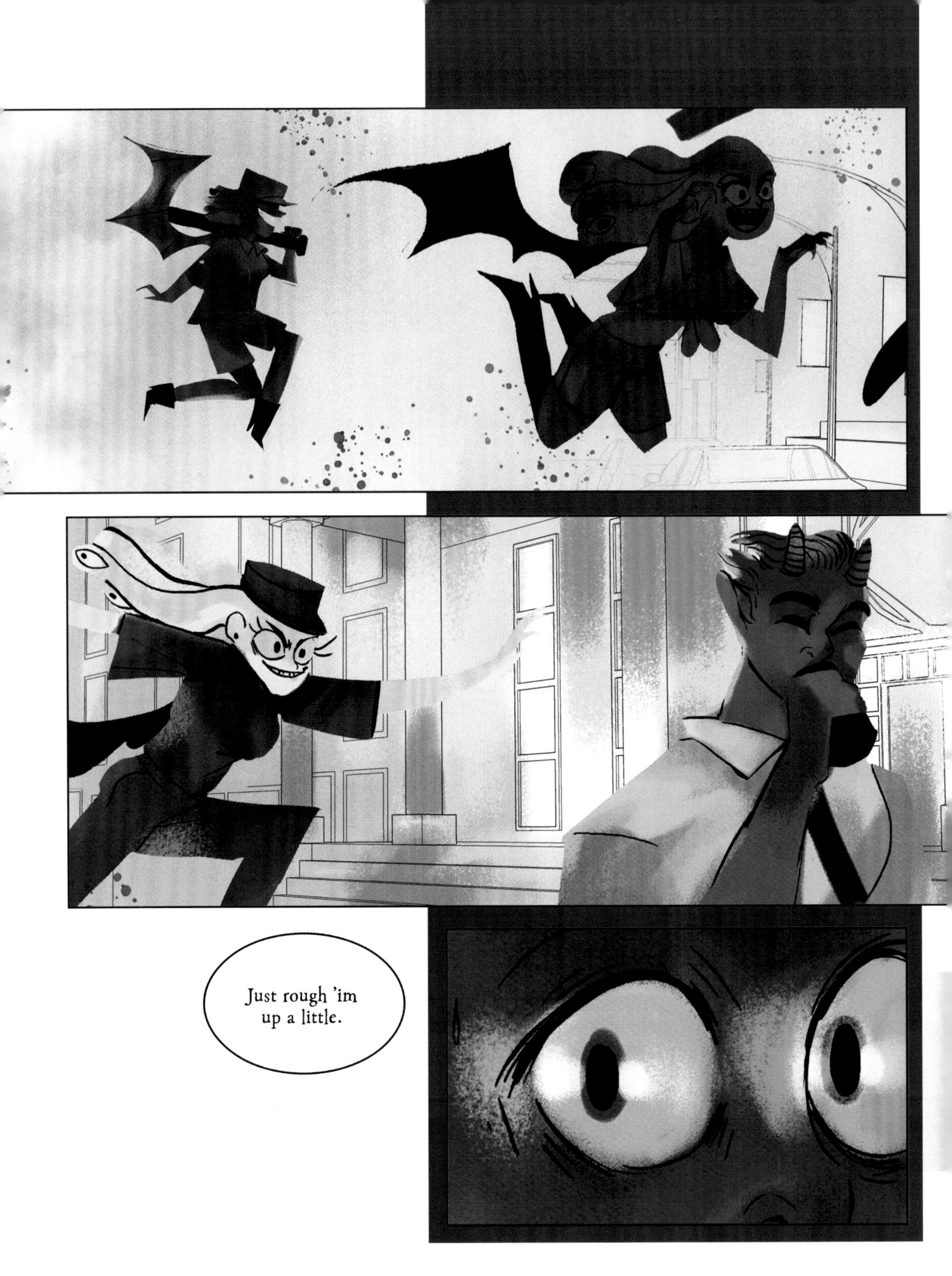
Just rough 'im up a little.

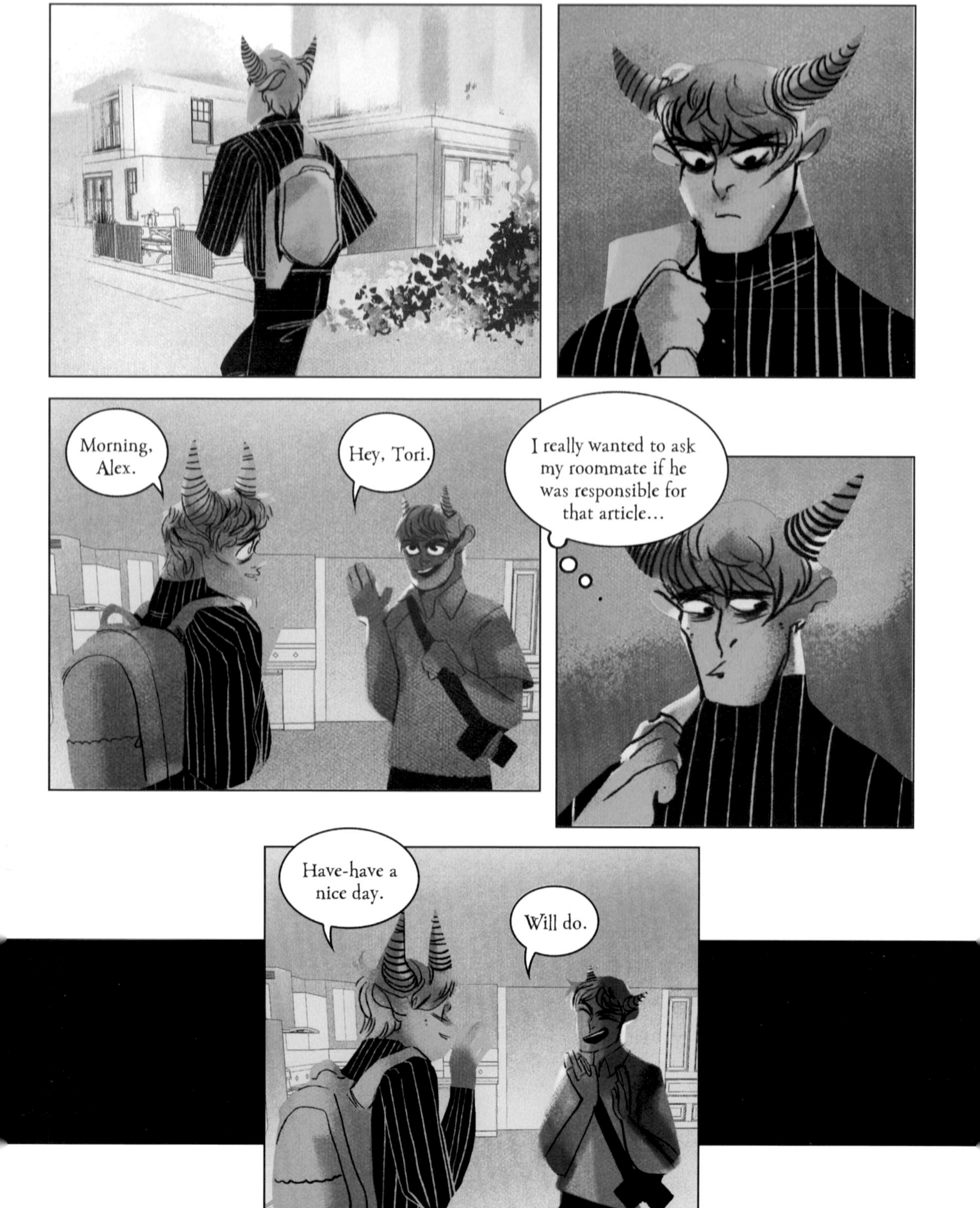
Morning, Alex.
Hey, Tori.
I really wanted to ask my roommate if he was responsible for that article...
Have-have a nice day.
Will do.

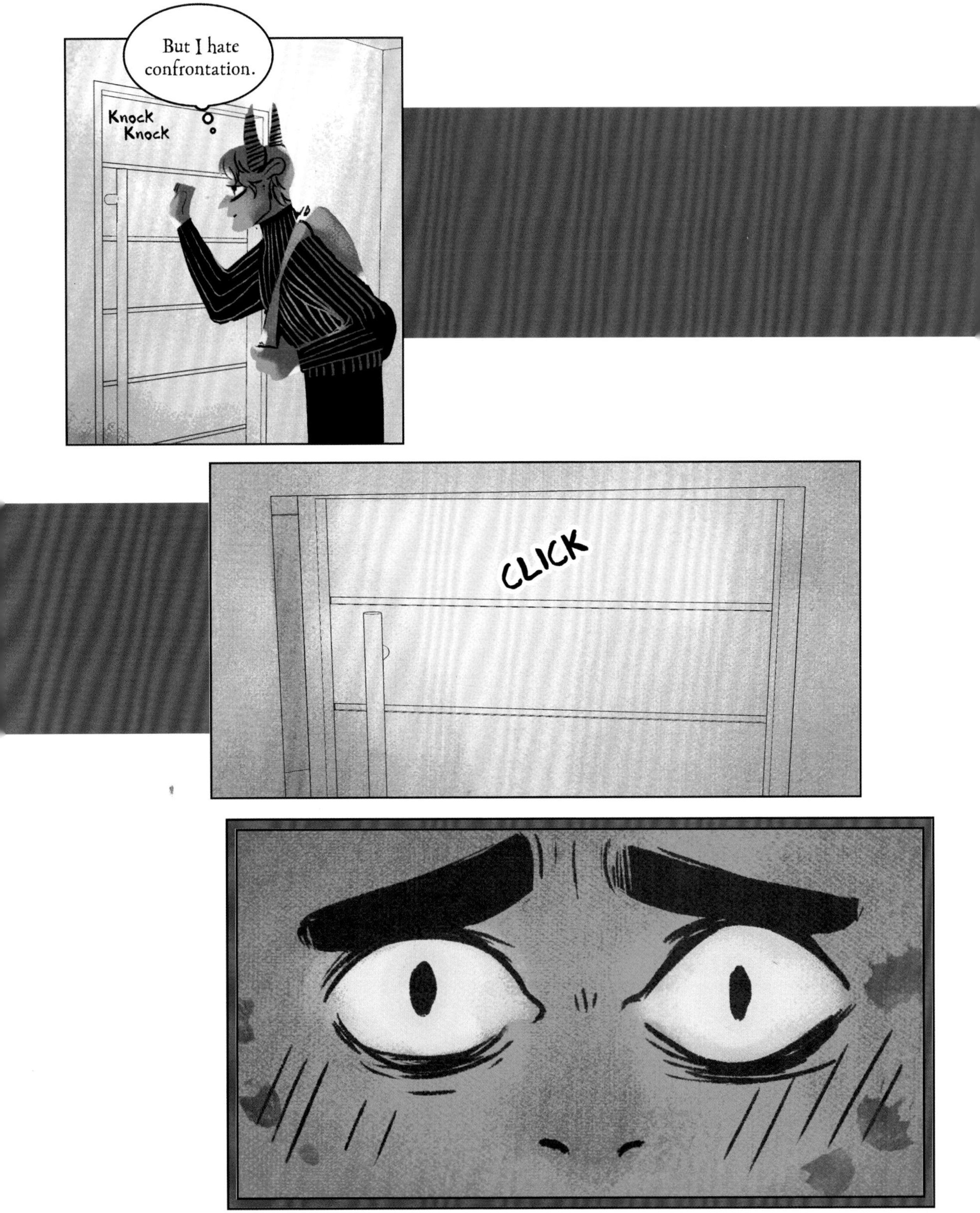

Knock
Knock
But I hate confrontation.
CLICK

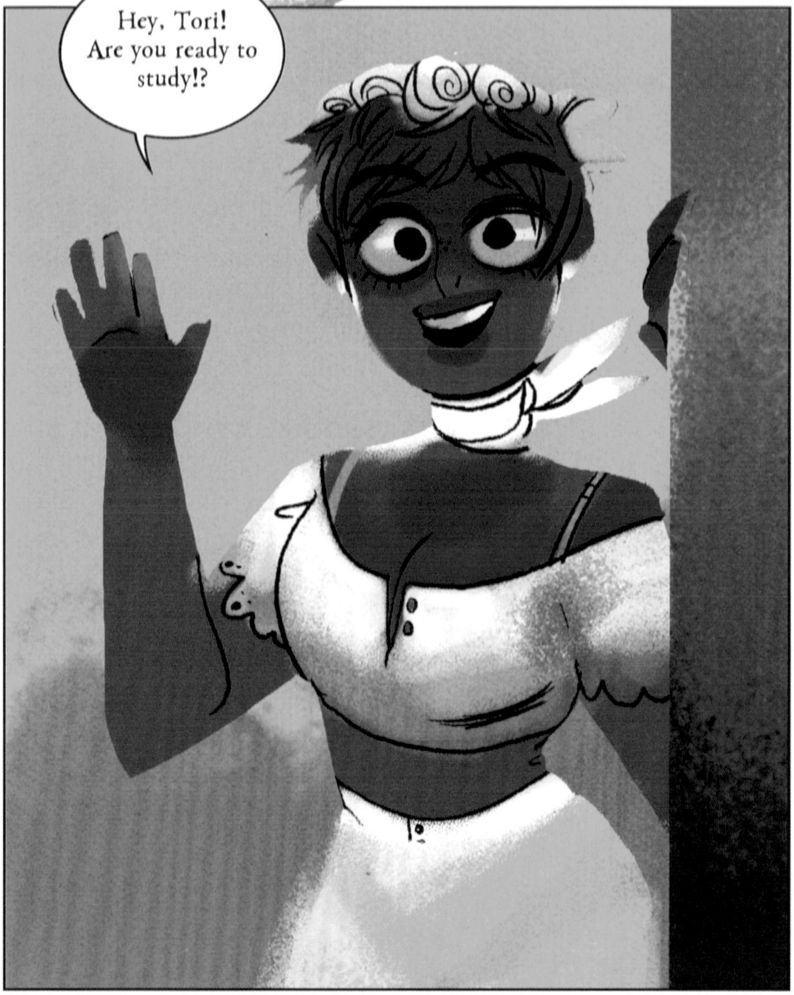
Hey, Tori!
Are you ready to
study!?

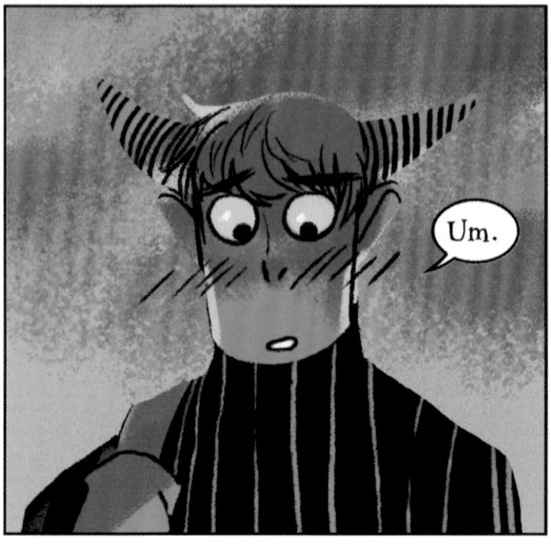
Um.

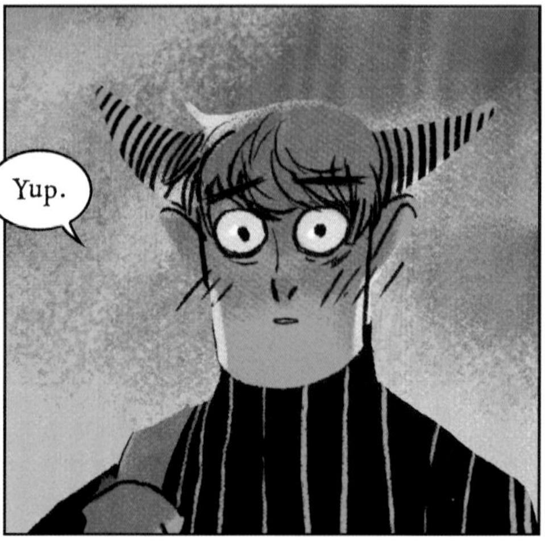
Yup.

EPISODE 49: EYE FOR AN EYE

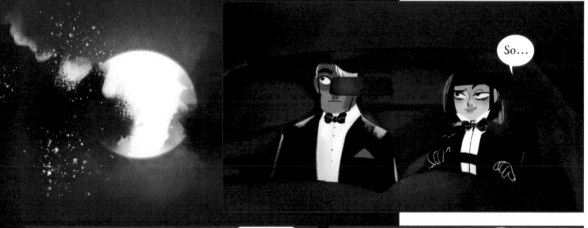

So...

...Minthe.

That's an interesting turn of events.

You know already?

Please, I know everything.

Plus Minthe put it on Fatesbook.

I thought you'd be happy with my decision.

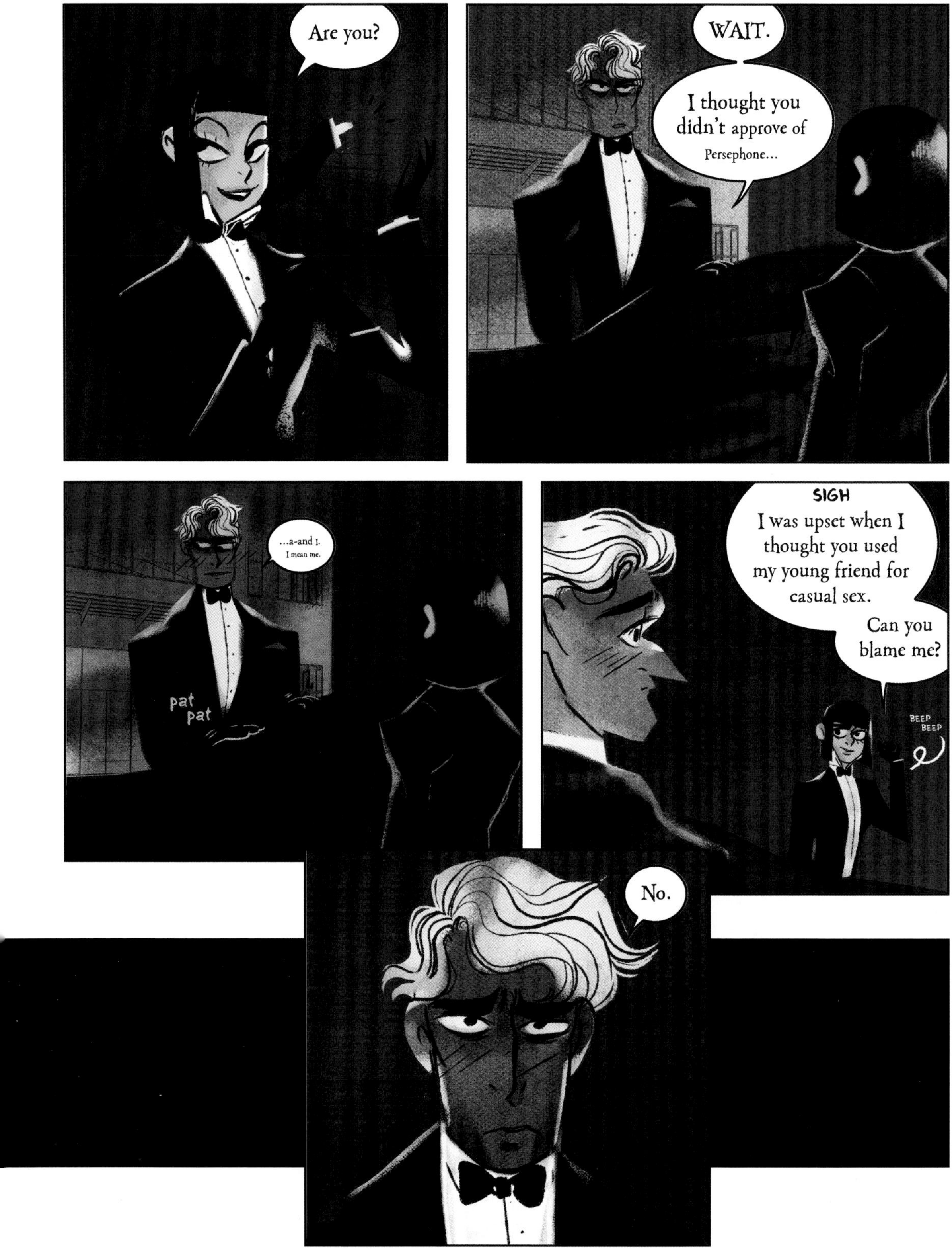
Are you?
WAIT.
I thought you didn't approve of Persephone...
...a-and I. I mean me.
pat pat
SIGH
I was upset when I thought you used my young friend for casual sex.
Can you blame me?
BEEP BEEP
No.

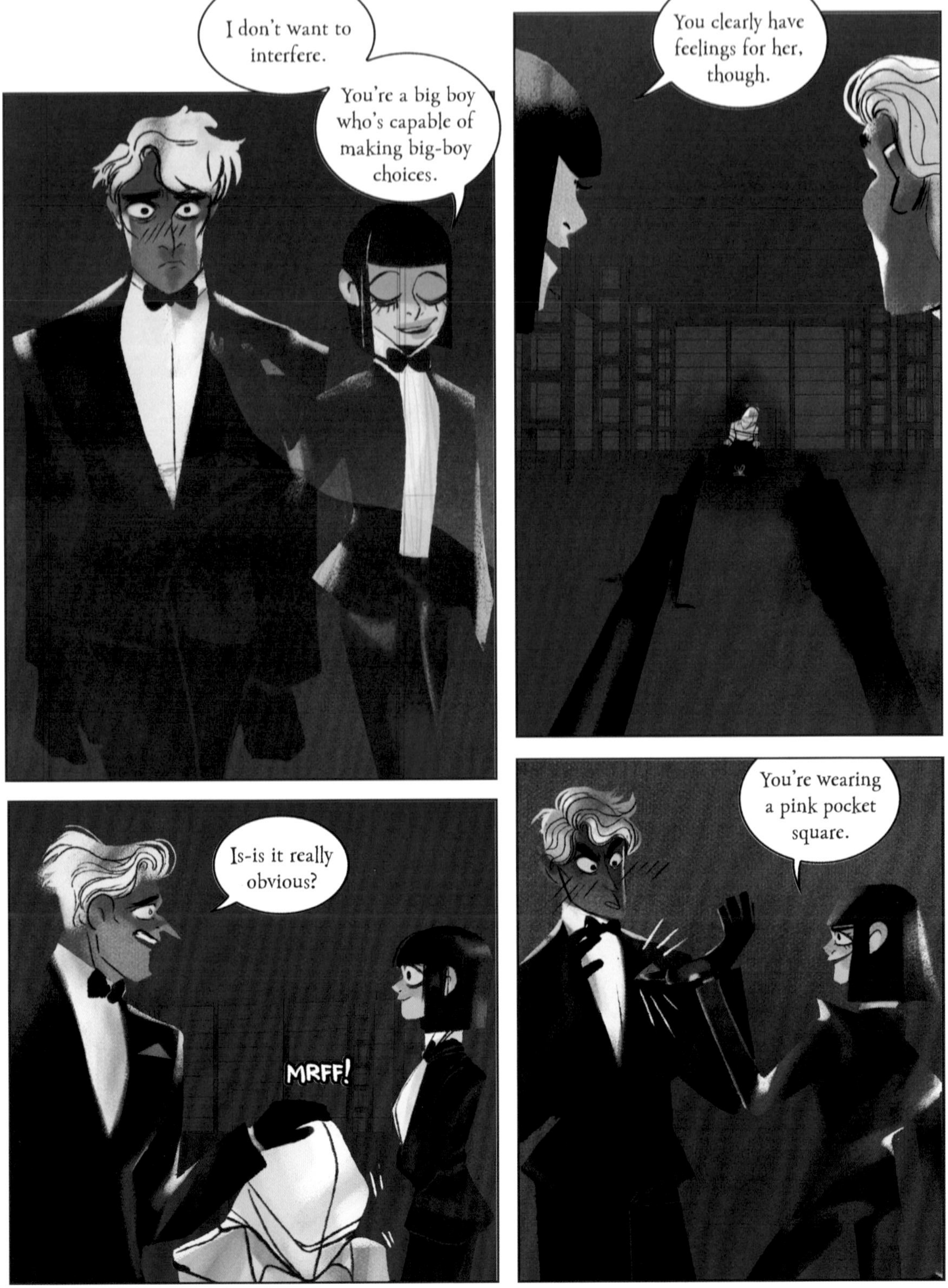
I don't want to interfere.
You're a big boy who's capable of making big-boy choices.
You clearly have feelings for her, though.
Is-is it really obvious?
MRFF!
You're wearing a pink pocket square.

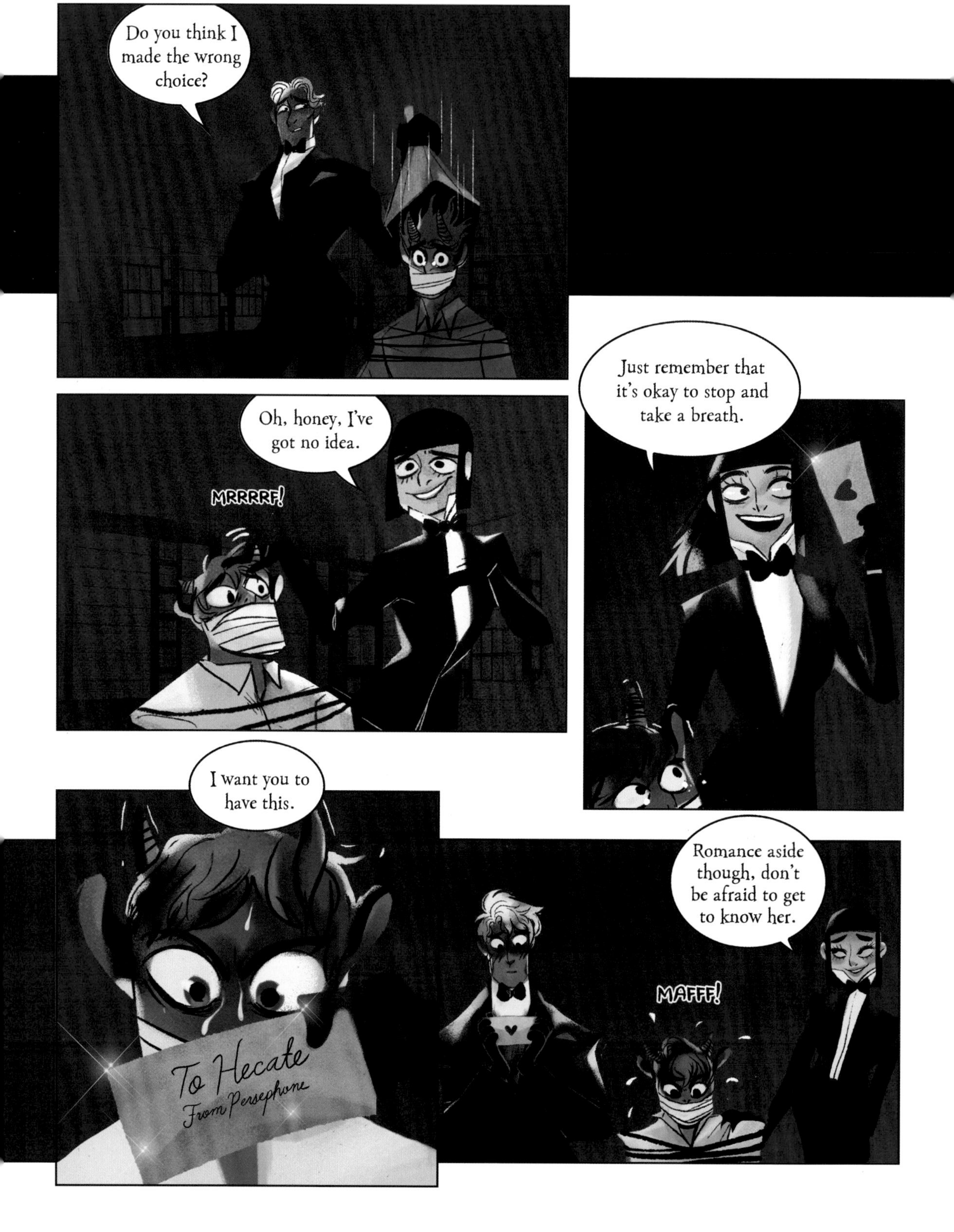
Do you think I made the wrong choice?
Oh, honey, I've got no idea.
MRRRRF!
Just remember that it's okay to stop and take a breath.
I want you to have this.
To Hecate
From Persephone
Romance aside though, don't be afraid to get to know her.
MAFFF!

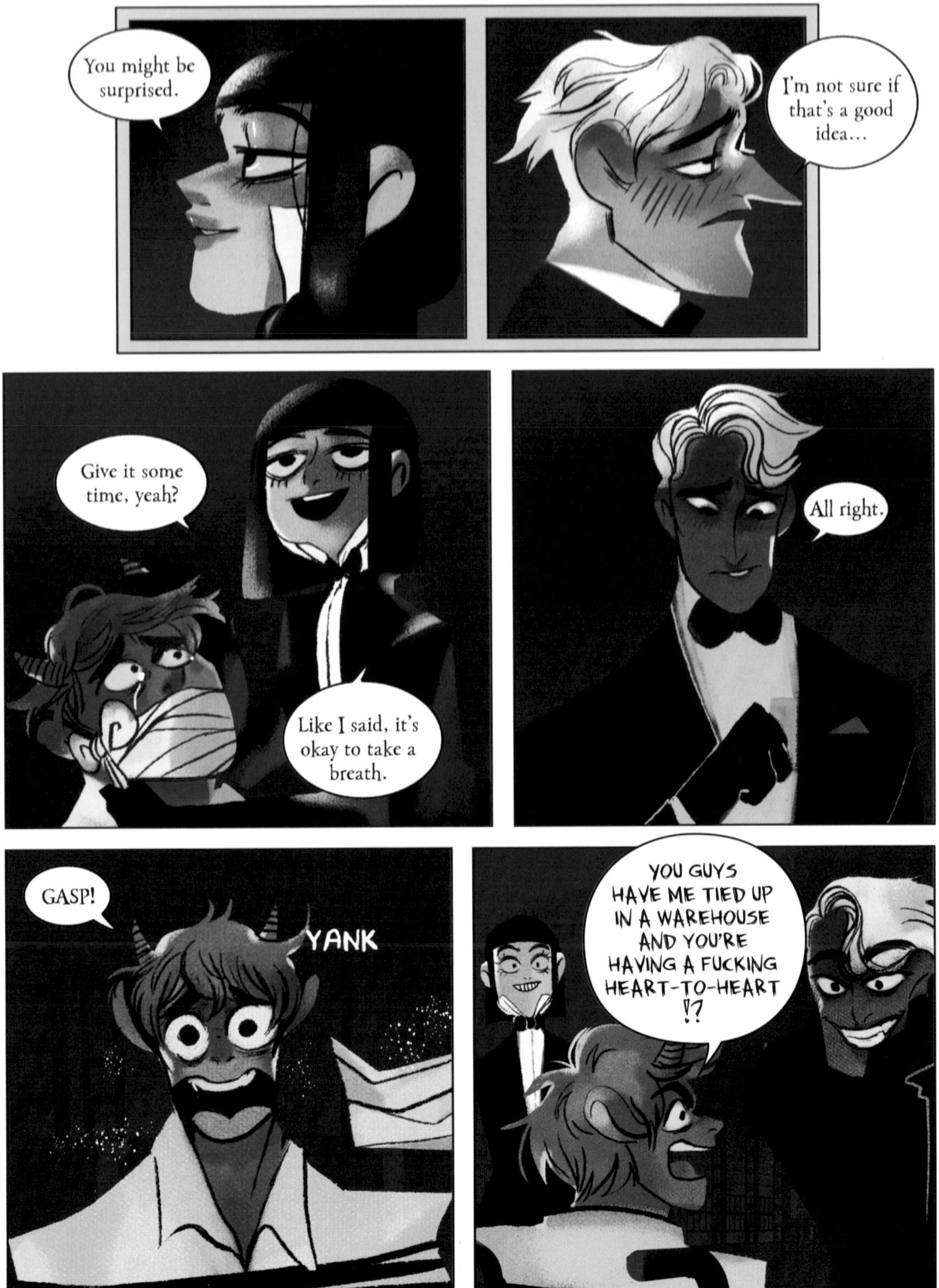
You might be surprised.
I'm not sure if that's a good idea…
Give it some time, yeah?
Like I said, it's okay to take a breath.
All right.
GASP!
YANK
YOU GUYS HAVE ME TIED UP IN A WAREHOUSE AND YOU'RE HAVING A FUCKING HEART-TO-HEART!?

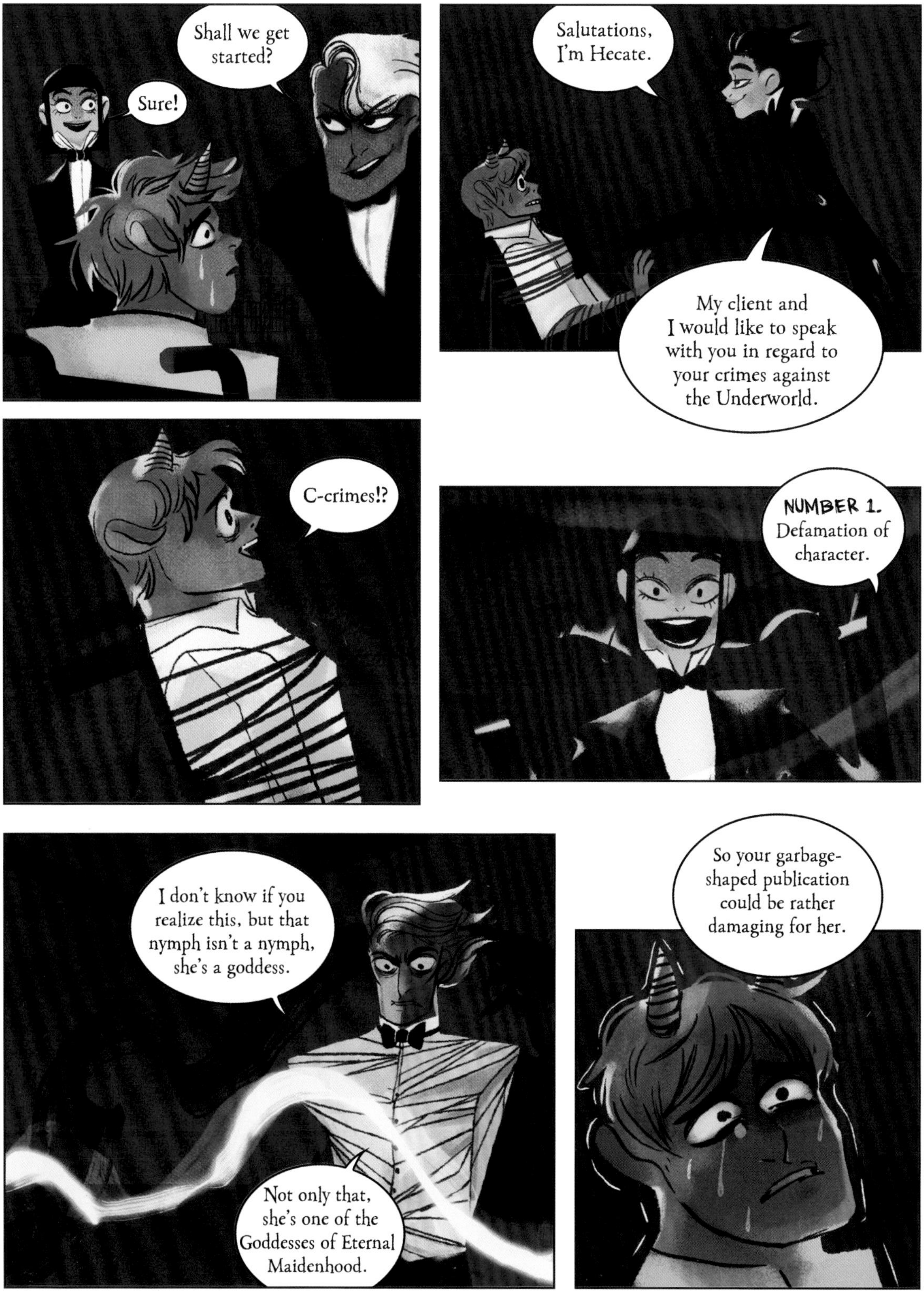
Shall we get started?
Sure!
Salutations, I'm Hecate.
My client and I would like to speak with you in regard to your crimes against the Underworld.
C-crimes!?
NUMBER 1. Defamation of character.
I don't know if you realize this, but that nymph isn't a nymph, she's a goddess.
Not only that, she's one of the Goddesses of Eternal Maidenhood.
So your garbage-shaped publication could be rather damaging for her.

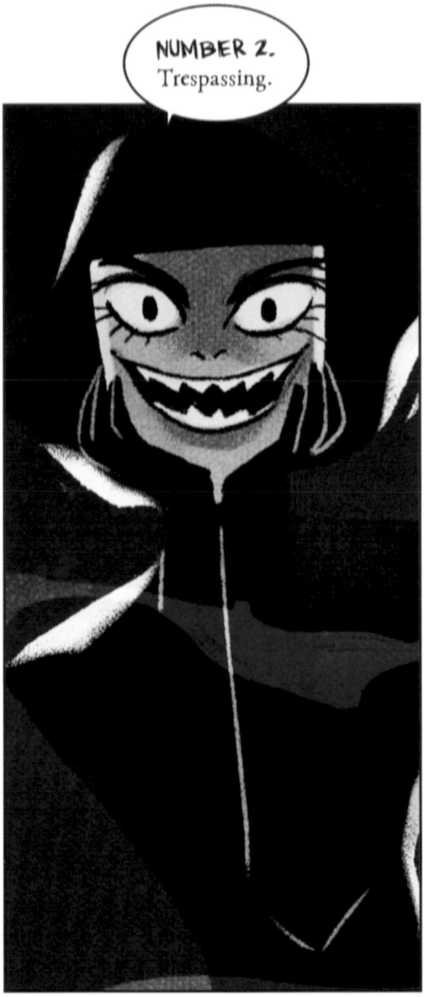
NUMBER 2.
Trespassing.
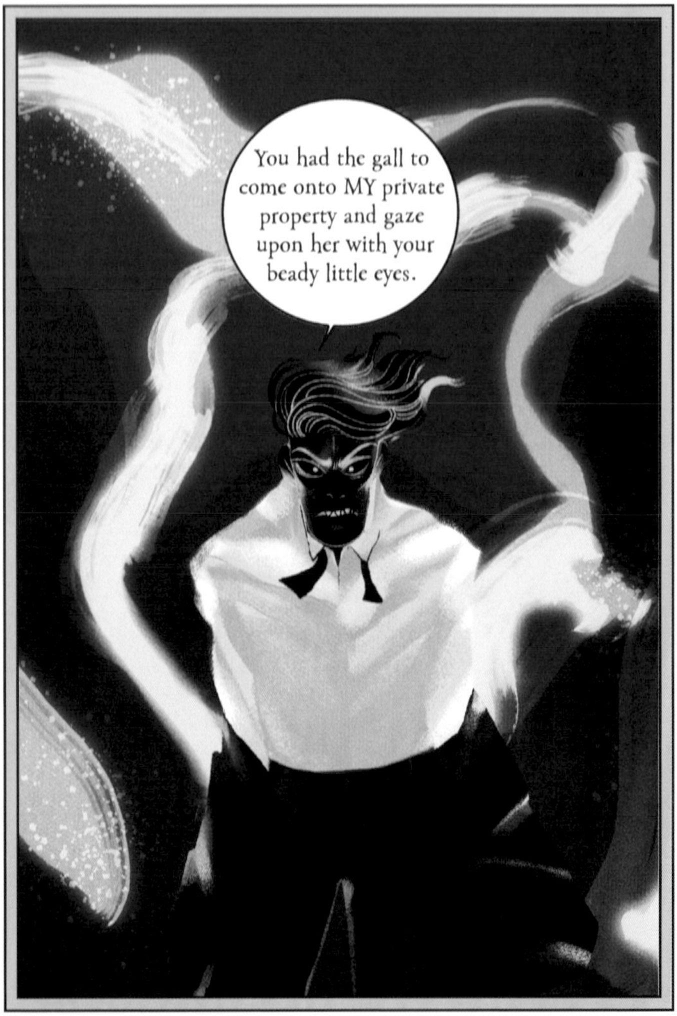
You had the gall to come onto MY private property and gaze upon her with your beady little eyes.
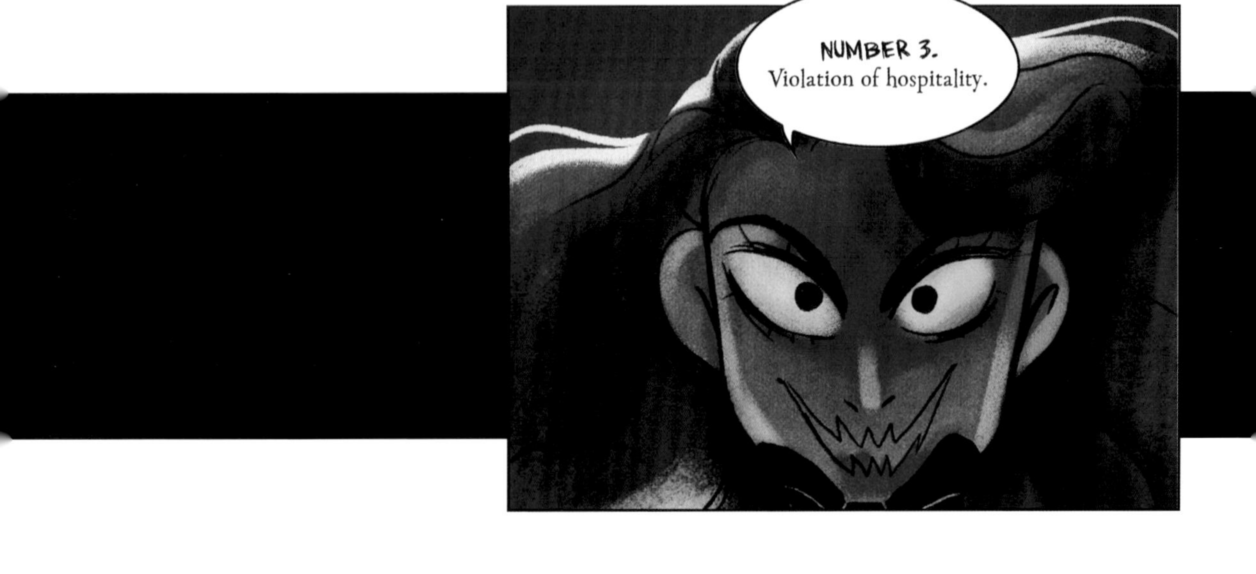
NUMBER 3.
Violation of hospitality.

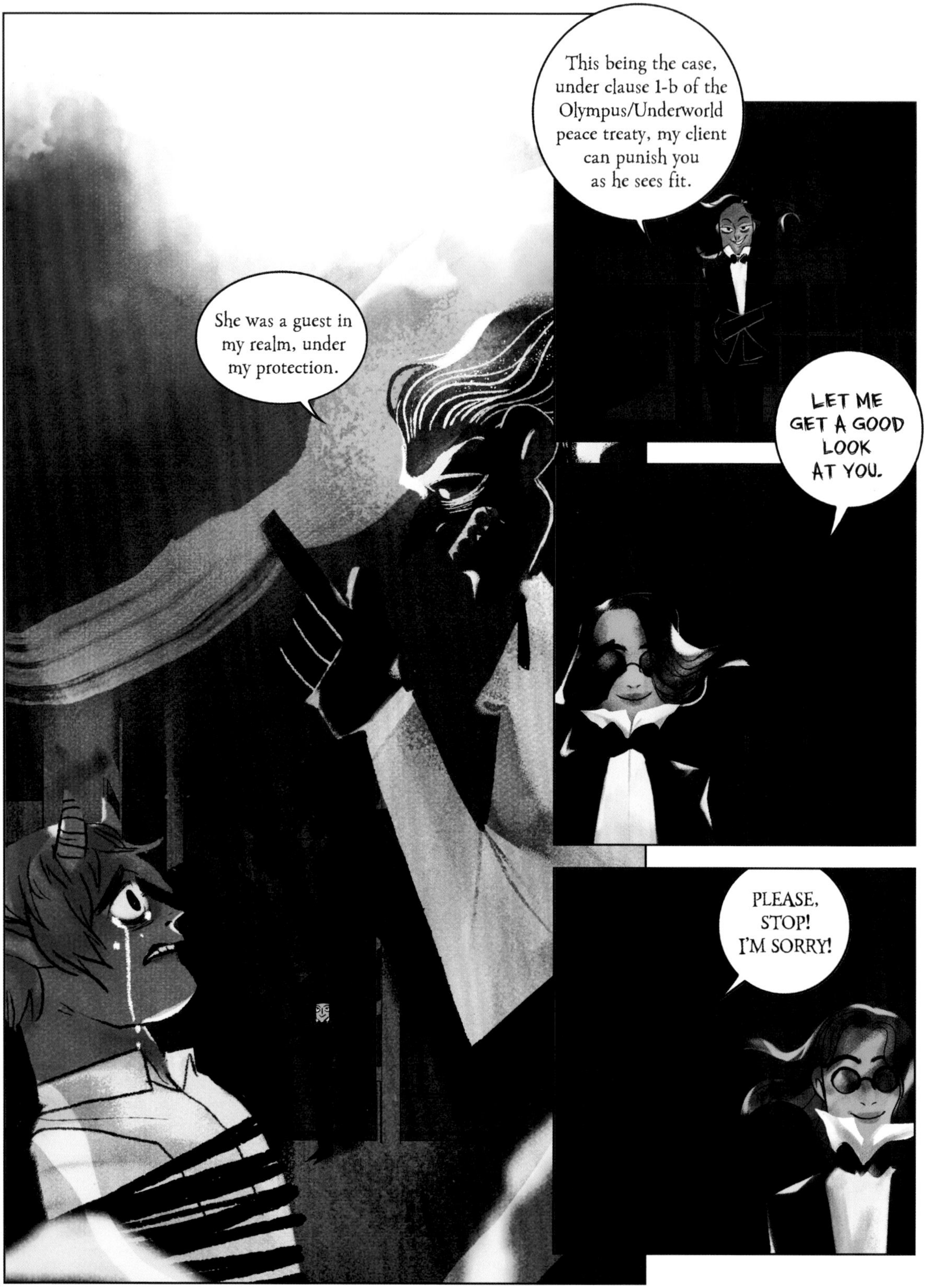
She was a guest in my realm, under my protection.
This being the case, under clause 1-b of the Olympus/Underworld peace treaty, my client can punish you as he sees fit.
LET ME GET A GOOD LOOK AT YOU.
PLEASE, STOP! I'M SORRY!

You know
what they say...

...an eye
for an eye.

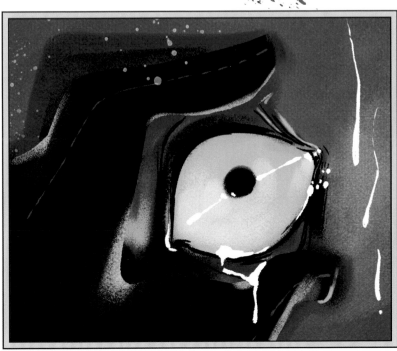

This chapter takes place before Persephone's coat was confiscated by Hestia.

I was initially planning to include this, but I was unable to structure in the concept at the time. In some ways I think that contextualizing Hestia's seemingly cruel behavior takes away from the emotional impact of episode 47, "Needed," which to this day, is one of my favorite pieces of work.

With all that being said, part of me still really wants the readers of *Lore Olympus* to know this missing part of the story.

Edited by Kathleen Wisneski
Art Assistants Jaki Haboon & Amy Kim

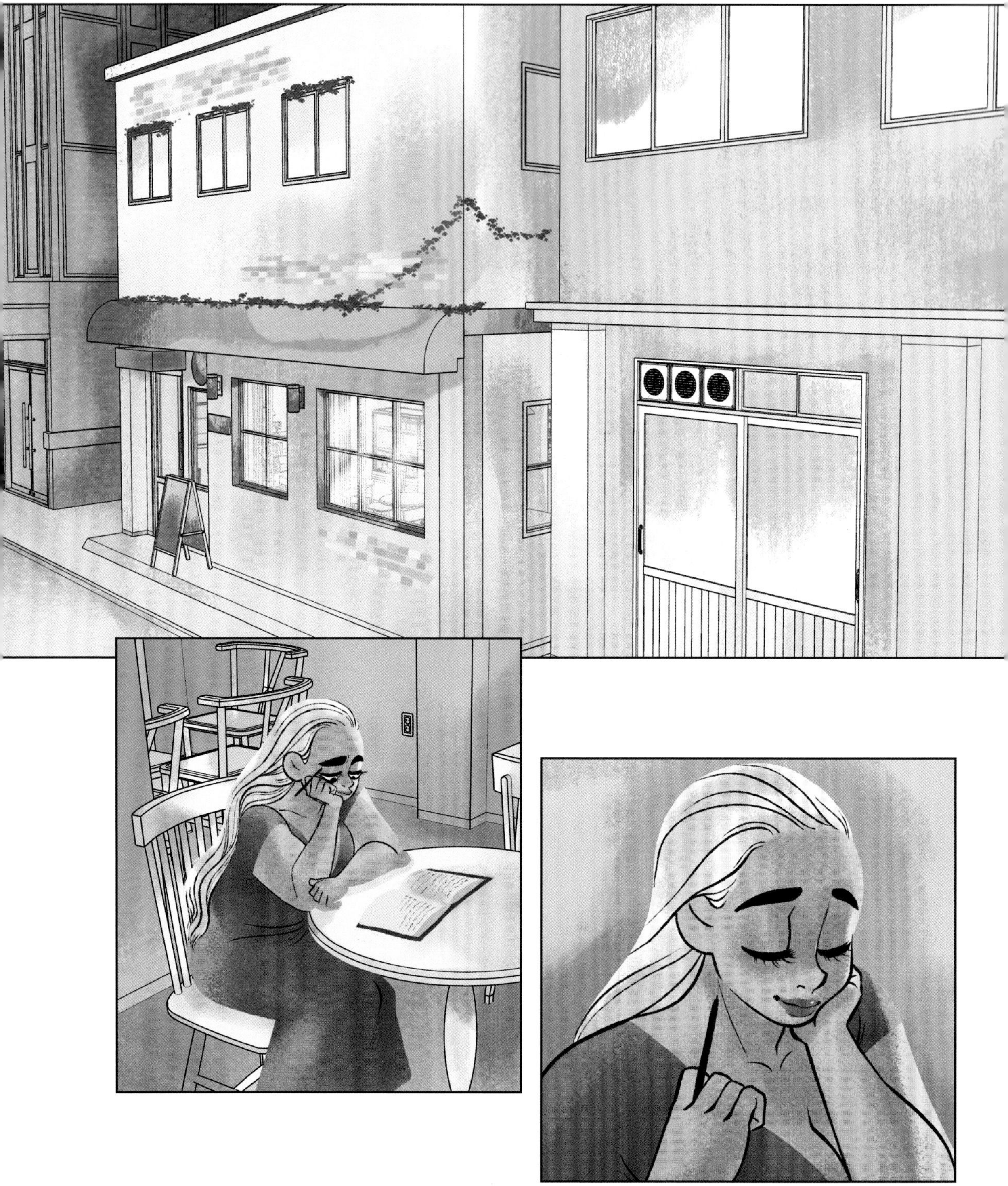

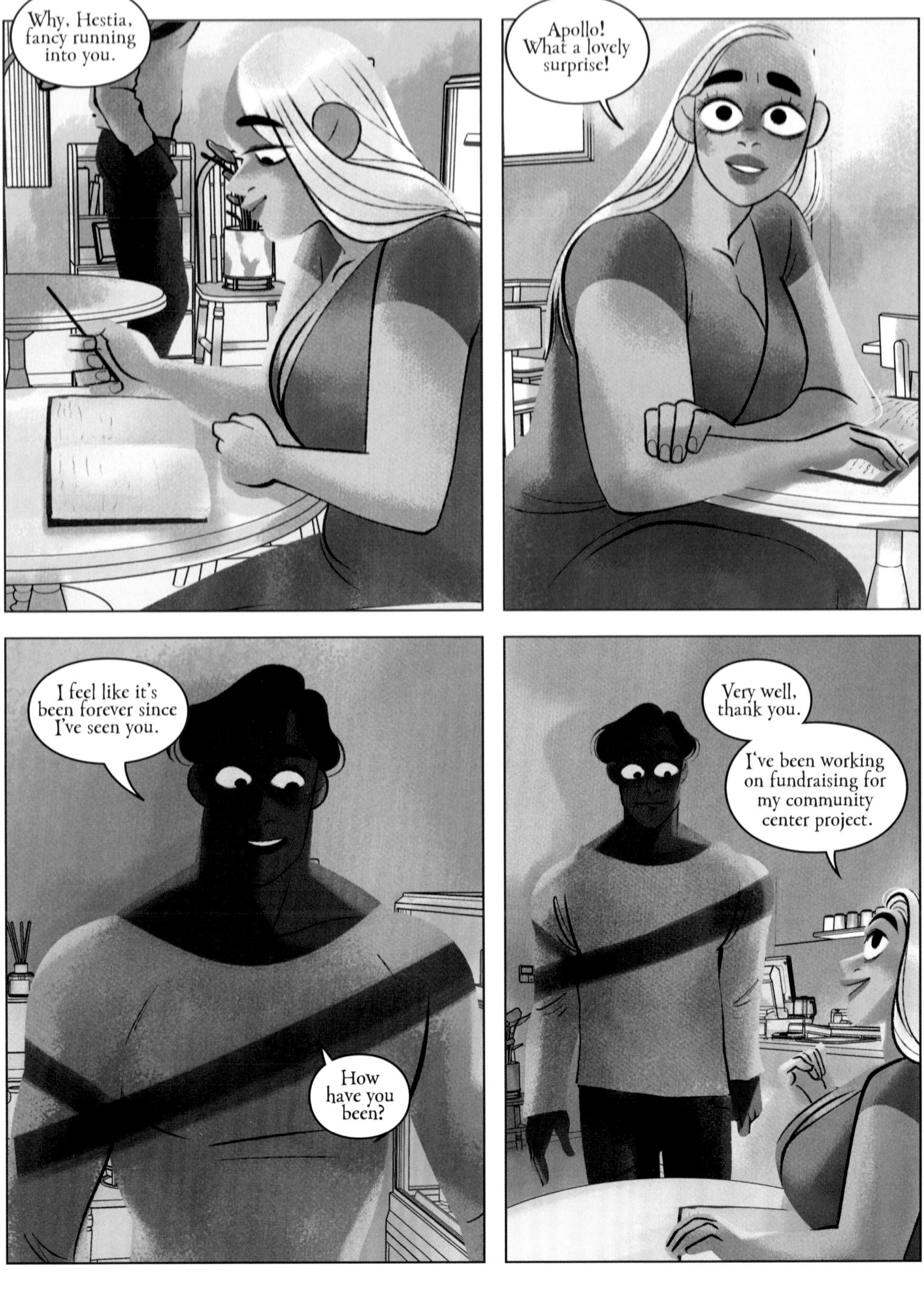
Why, Hestia, fancy running into you.
Apollo! What a lovely surprise!
I feel like it's been forever since I've seen you.
How have you been?
Very well, thank you.
I've been working on fundraising for my community center project.

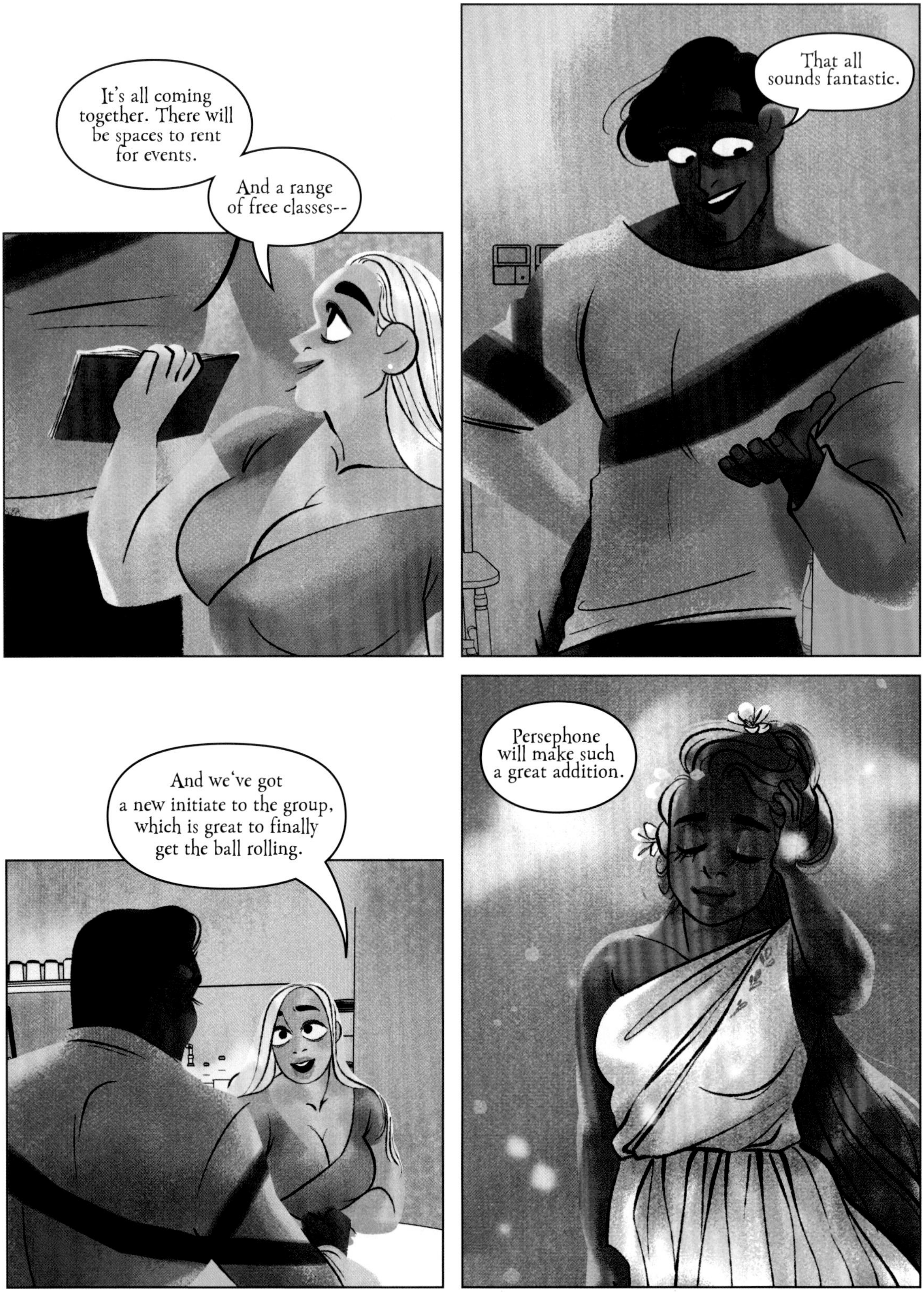

It's all coming together. There will be spaces to rent for events.
And a range of free classes--
That all sounds fantastic.
And we've got a new initiate to the group, which is great to finally get the ball rolling.
Persephone will make such a great addition.

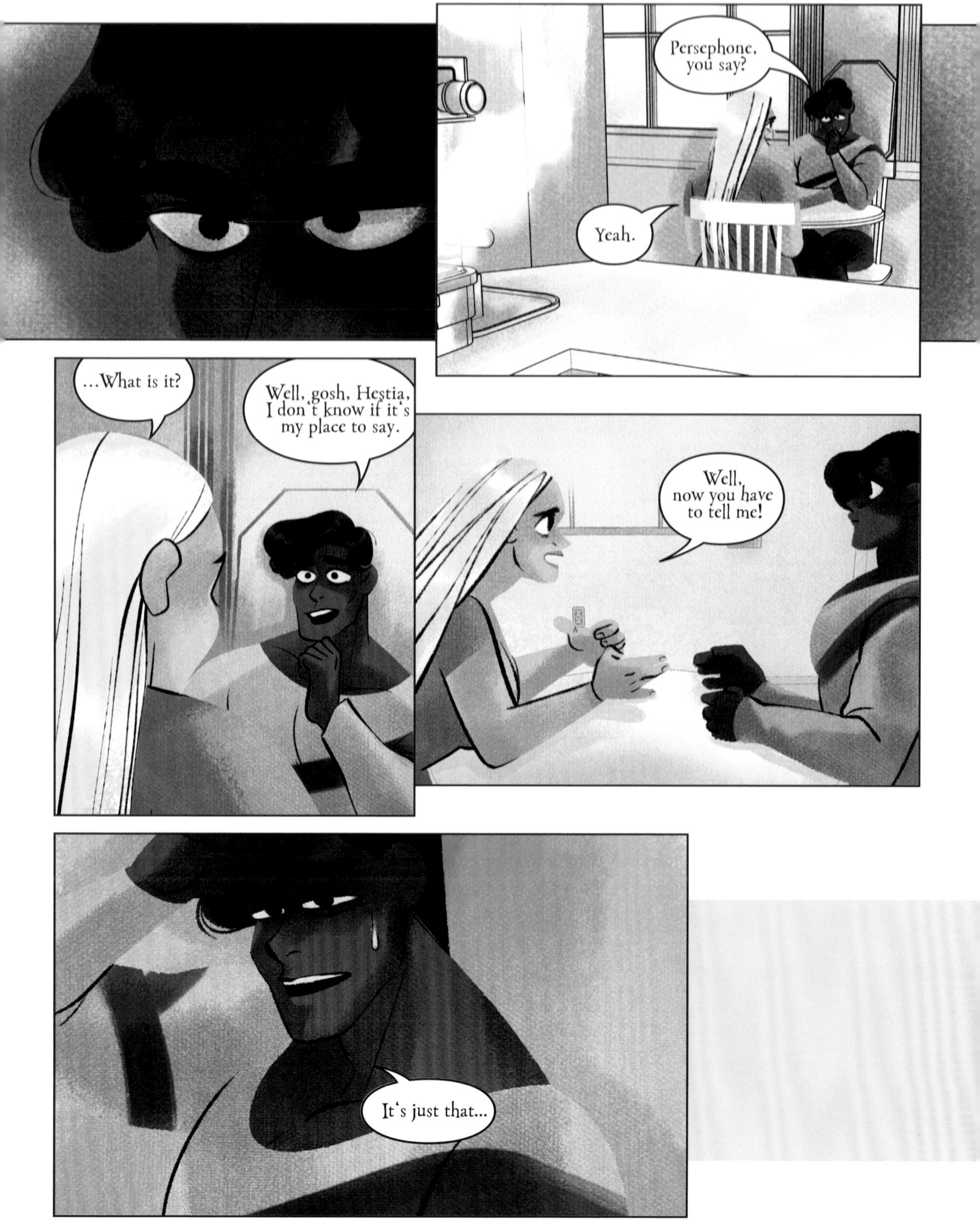
Persephone, you say?
Yeah.
...What is it?
Well, gosh, Hestia, I don't know if it's my place to say.
Well, now you have to tell me!
It's just that...

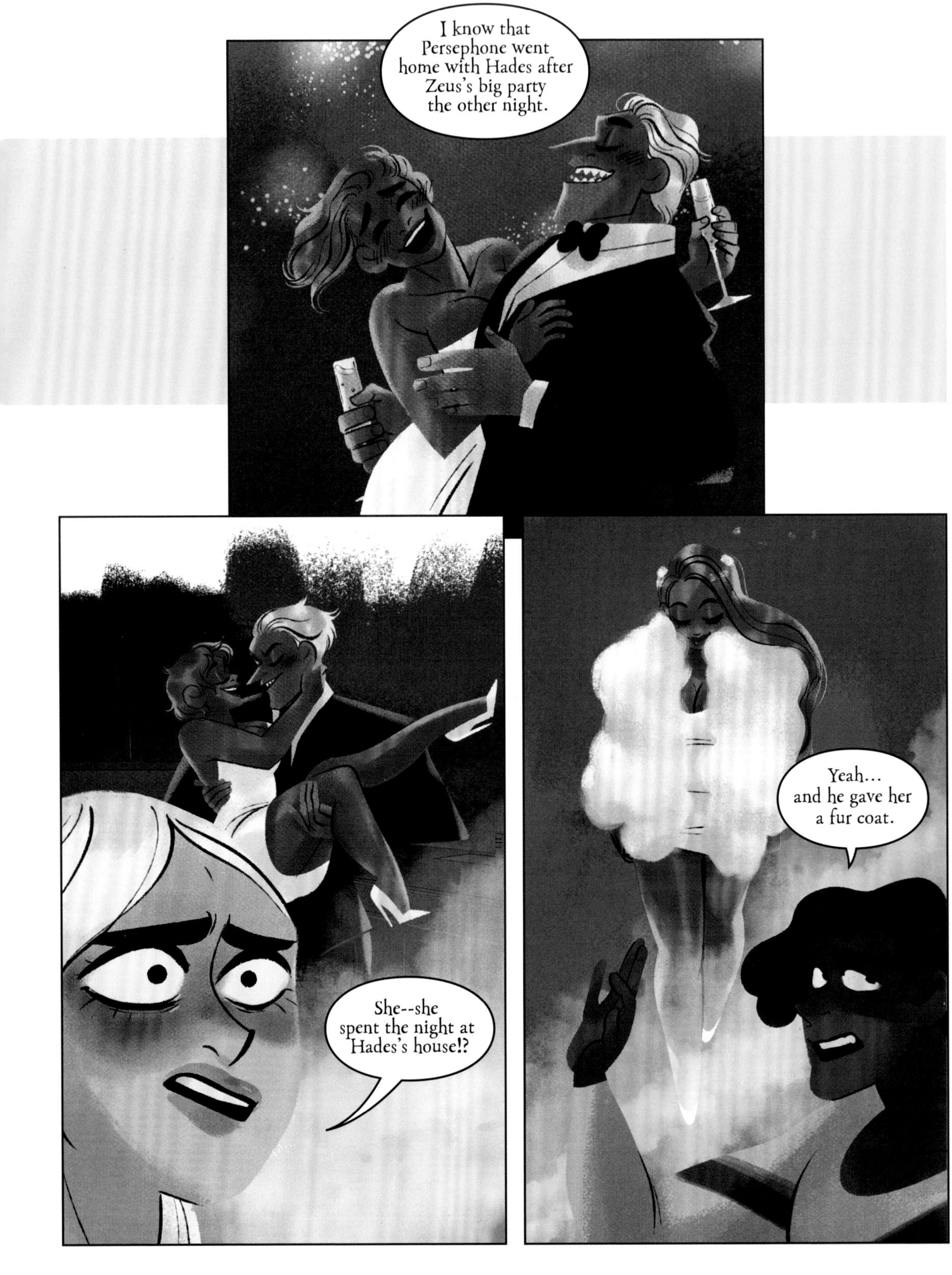
I know that Persephone went home with Hades after Zeus's big party the other night.
She--she spent the night at Hades's house!?
Yeah... and he gave her a fur coat.

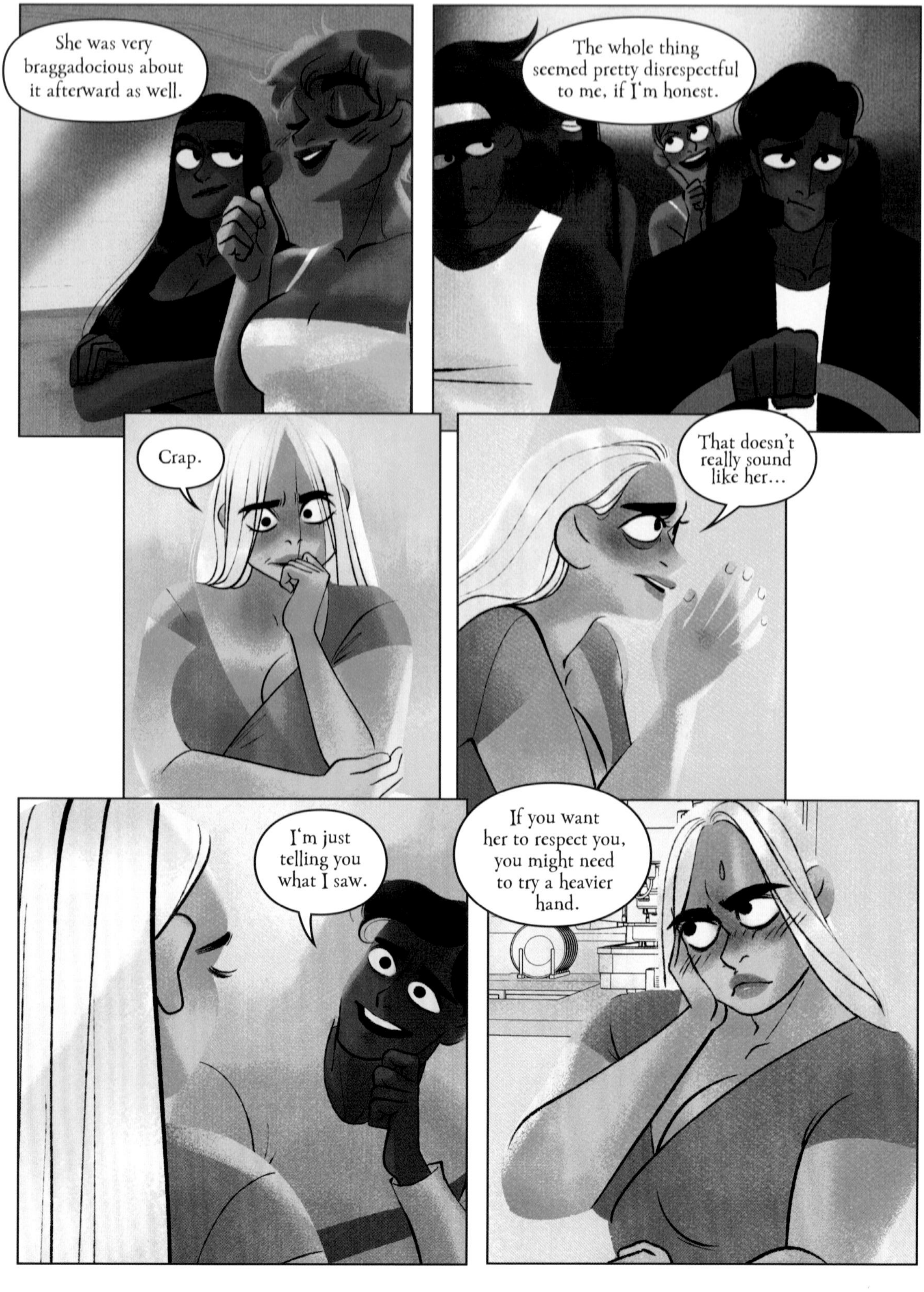
She was very braggadocious about it afterward as well.
The whole thing seemed pretty disrespectful to me, if I'm honest.
Crap.
That doesn't really sound like her…
I'm just telling you what I saw.
If you want her to respect you, you might need to try a heavier hand.

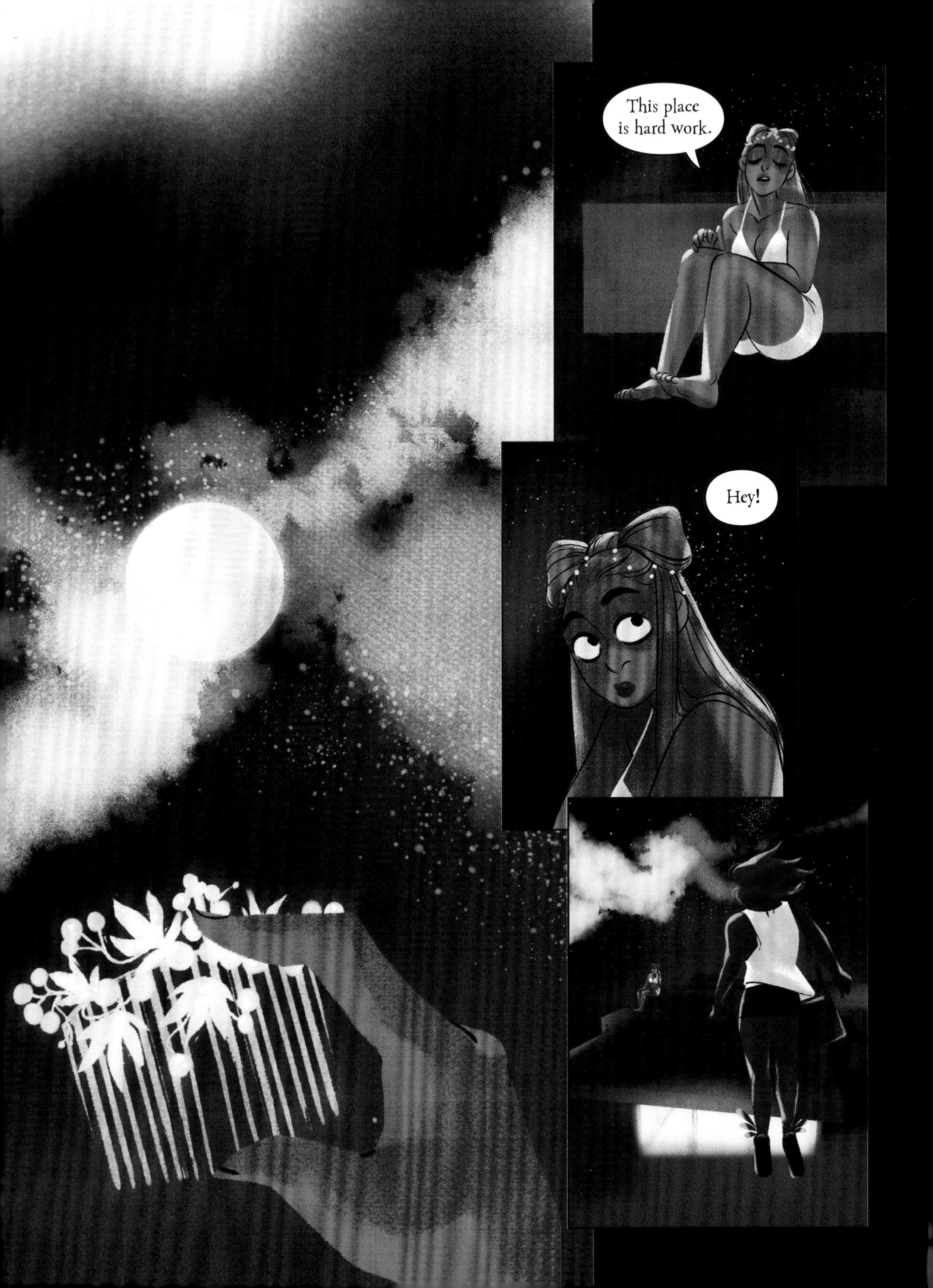
This place
is hard work.
Hey!

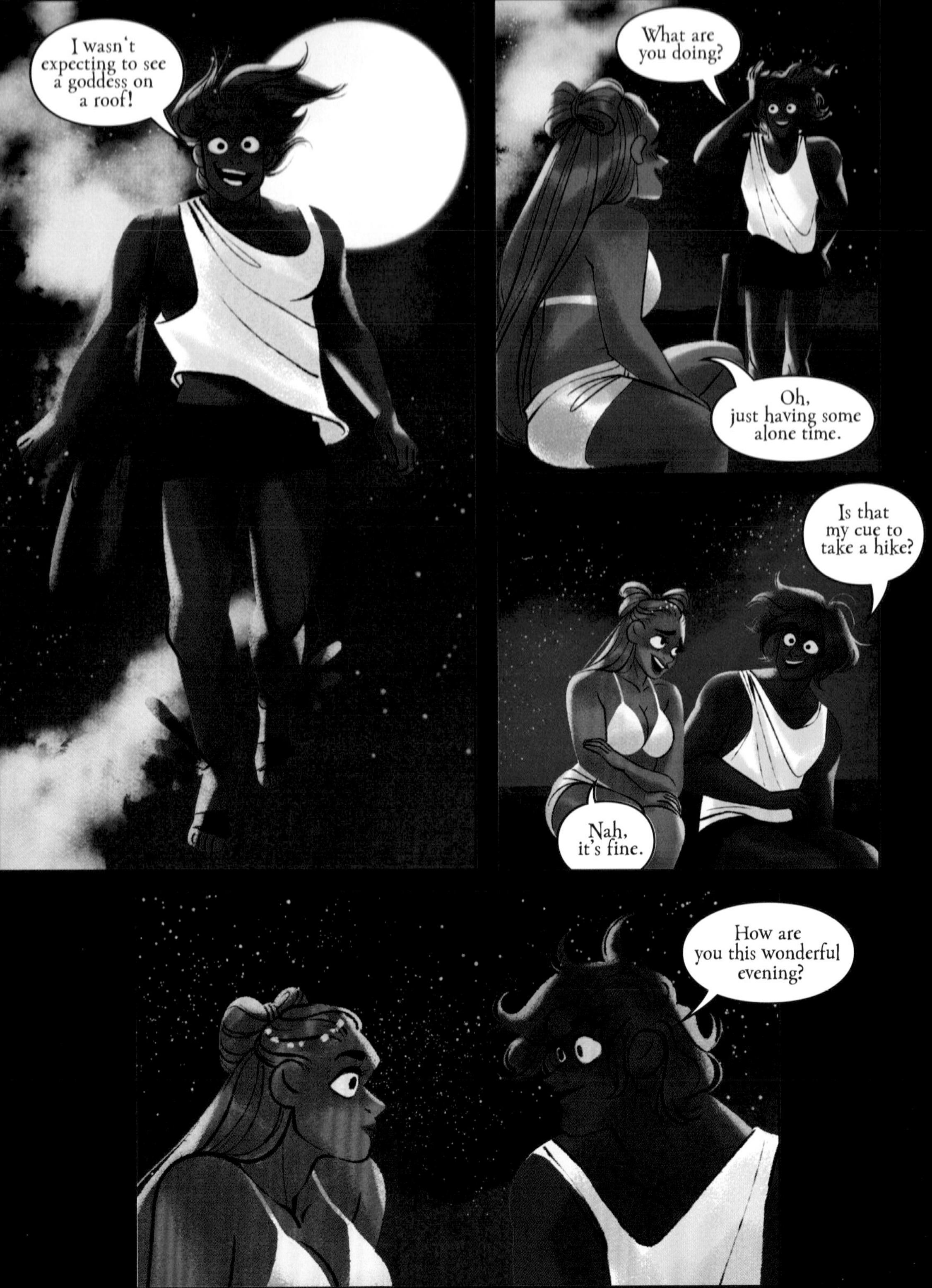
I wasn't expecting to see a goddess on a roof!
What are you doing?
Oh, just having some alone time.
Is that my cue to take a hike?
Nah, it's fine.
How are you this wonderful evening?

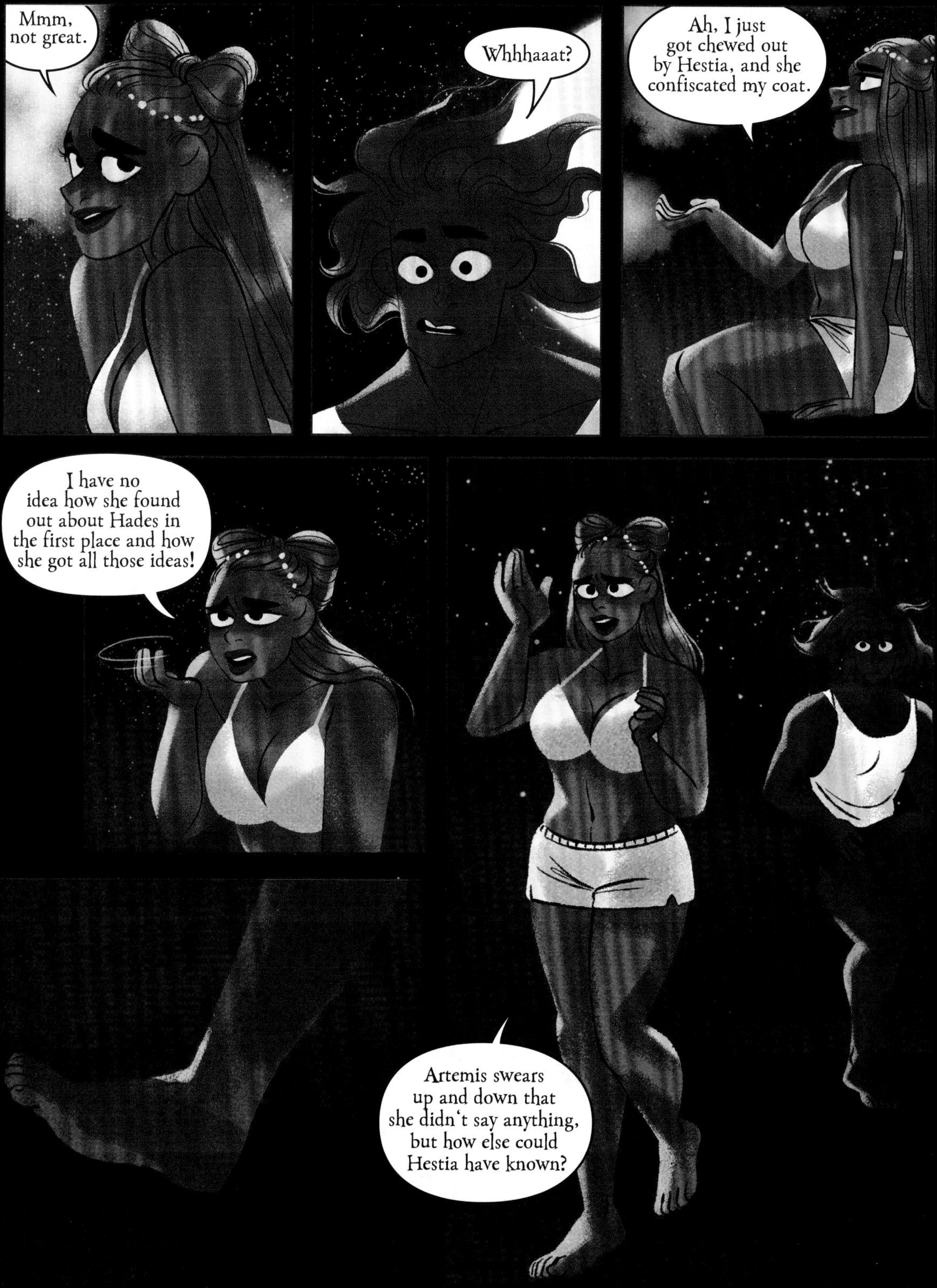
Mmm, not great.
Whhhaaat?
Ah, I just got chewed out by Hestia, and she confiscated my coat.
I have no idea how she found out about Hades in the first place and how she got all those ideas!
Artemis swears up and down that she didn't say anything, but how else could Hestia have known?

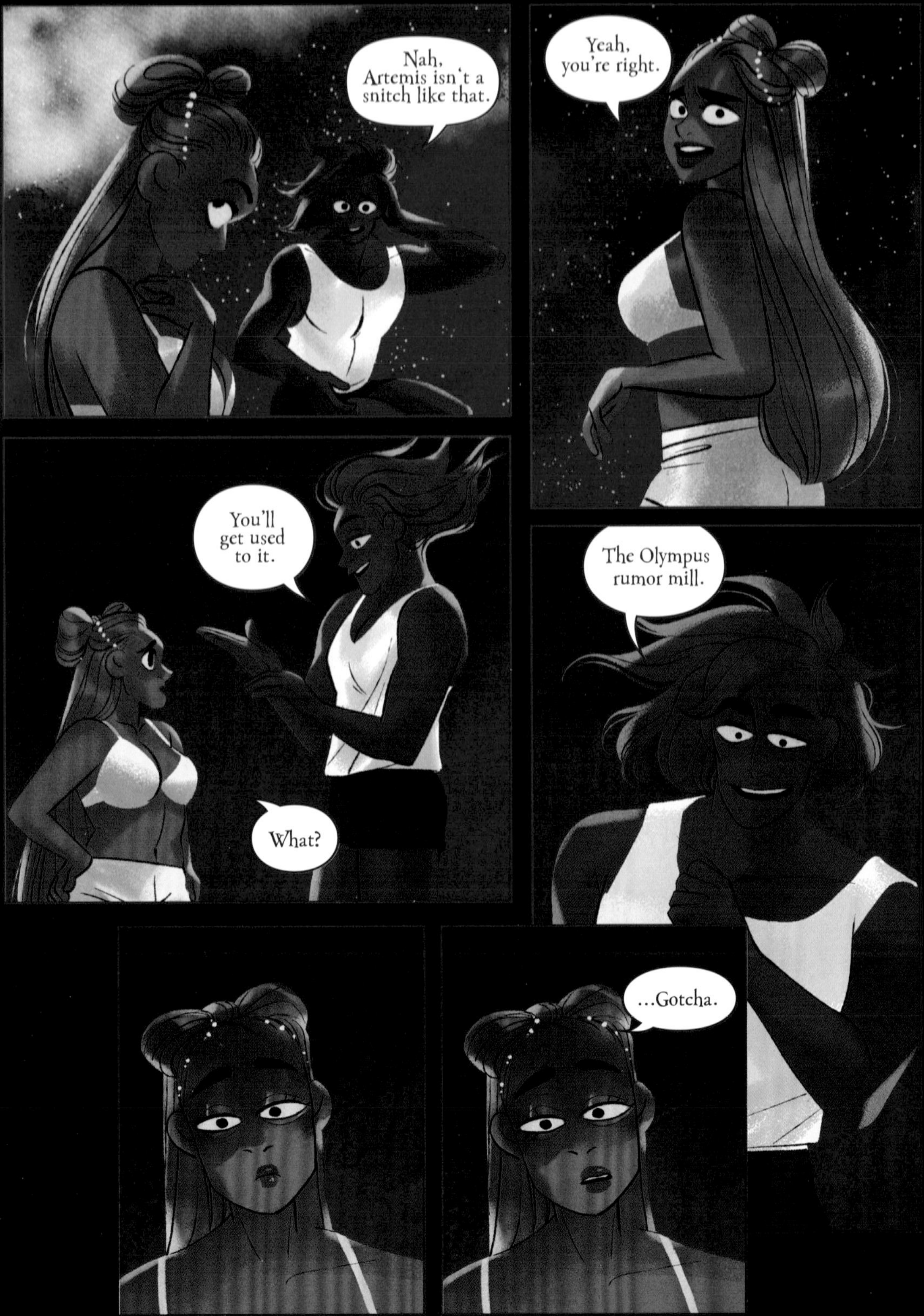
Nah, Artemis isn't a snitch like that.
Yeah, you're right.
You'll get used to it.
What?
The Olympus rumor mill.
...Gotcha.

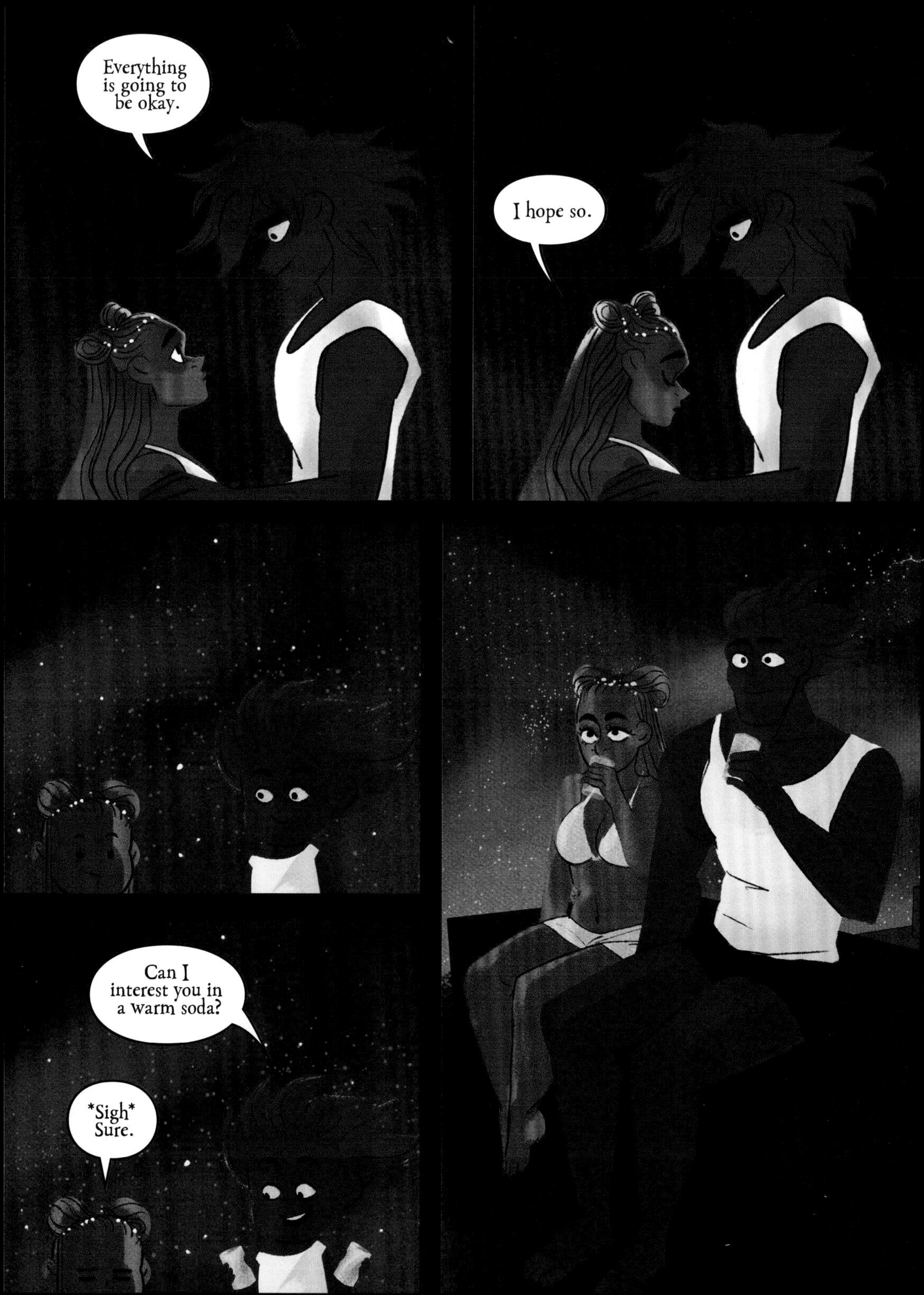
Everything is going to be okay.
I hope so.
Can I interest you in a warm soda?
Sigh Sure.

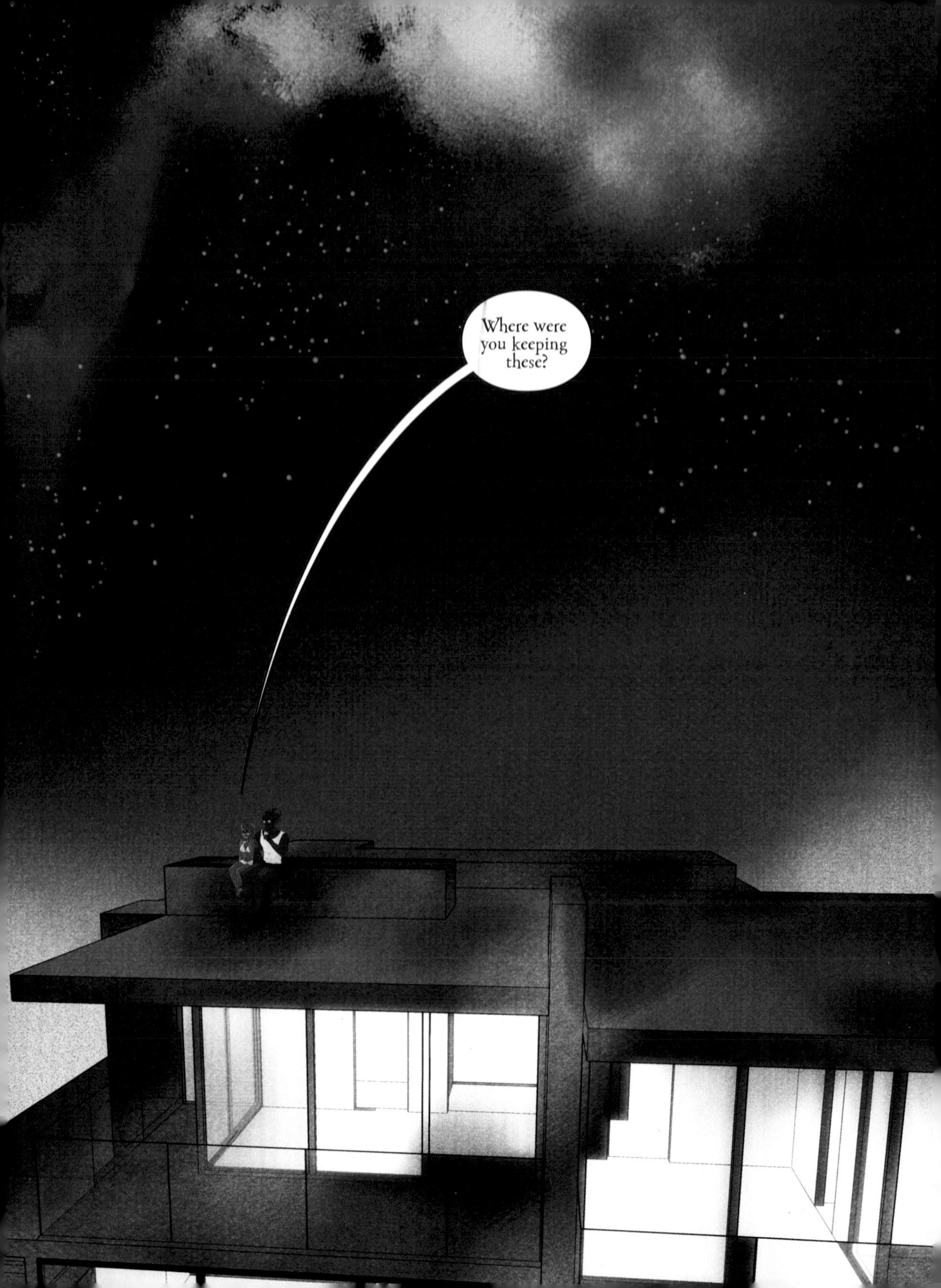
Where were you keeping these?

ABOUT THE AUTHOR

RACHEL SMYTHE is the creator of the Eisner-nominated *Lore Olympus*, published via WEBTOON.

Twitter: @used_bandaid

Instagram: @usedbandaid

Facebook.com/Usedbandaidillustration

LoreOlympusBooks.com